THE
FINAL
FRONTIER

THE FINAL FRONTIER

STORIES OF EXPLORING SPACE, COLONIZING THE UNIVERSE, AND FIRST CONTACT

EDITED BY NEIL CLARKE

NIGHT SHADE BOOKS
NEW YORK

Night Shade books may be purchased in bulk at special discounts for sales promotion, corporate gifts, fund-raising, or educational purposes. Special editions can also be created to specifications. For details, contact the Special Sales Department, Night Shade Books, 307 West 36th Street, 11th Floor, New York, NY 10018 or info@skyhorsepublishing.com.

Night Shade Books® is a registered trademark of Skyhorse Publishing, Inc. ®, a Delaware corporation.

Visit our website at www.nightshadebooks.com.

10 9 8 7 6 5 4 3 2 1

Library of Congress Cataloging-in-Publication Data

Names: Clarke, Neil, 1966- editor.
Title: The final frontier : stories of exploring space, colonizing the universe, and first contact / edited by Neil Clarke.
Description: New York : Night Shade Books, [2018]
Identifiers: LCCN 2018003101 | ISBN 9781597809399 (pbk. : alk. paper)
Subjects: LCSH: Science fiction. | Outer space--Exploration--Fiction. | Human-alien encounters--Fiction.
Classification: LCC PN6071.S33 F56 2018 | DDC 808.83/8762--dc23
LC record available at https://lccn.loc.gov/2018003101

Cover illustration by Fred Gambino
Cover design by Jason Snair

Please see page 581 for an extension of this copyright page.

Printed in the United States of America

CONTENTS

Introduction

Permissions

For Johnny

INTRODUCTION

I consider this anthology to be a sister to *Galactic Empires*, which was published last year. During the preliminary reading for that project, I came across several great stories that weren't quite right for the anthology, typically because the empire element was non-existent or too thin. As that list continued to grow, a theme began to develop around them: space exploration and discovery. If *Galactic Empires* was Star Wars, this anthology is all those standalone episodes of the various *Star Trek* series where they discover some new phenomena, make contact with a new species, or explore the remnants of some long forgotten race.

Gene Roddenberry provided the perfect way to describe those stories in the opening of the original *Star Trek* back in 1966: Space: the final frontier. When the first episode of that series aired, we were still three years away from Neil Armstrong's first steps on the moon. It was a show born of an age when we were reaching for the stars and despite being canceled before that moon landing, the show has carried on in new series, movies, books, and fan projects for over fifty years even while the era of manned space exploration has waned. Shows like *Star Trek*, as well as books and stories like those in this anthology, keep the dream alive.

I was born the same year that *Star Trek* first aired. I'm told I was in front of the TV while Armstrong bounced along the surface of the moon, but I was far too young to remember, but I am a child of that era. Someday we would go to the stars and I would live to see it. As a child, we visited Kennedy Space Center and saw the massive Saturn V rocket, reality boosting that sense of awe. The vertical stabilizer of the first space shuttle poked out from behind the wall it was hidden behind and just that tiny glimpse was enough to send my imagination soaring. We were going, but maybe not as soon as my favorite books and movies predicted.

We sent probes out to fly by or land on other planets in our solar system. Even the early, grainy images brought awe and inspiration. In school, these discoveries were turned into educational opportunities and we learned the dangers of space. As reality intruded, my expectations took steps backward. Space was more inhospitable than it was in books and TV. We were not well-prepared enough to leave our home. More research was necessary, but budgets were shrinking and priorities changed. While there have been many amazing accomplishments and discoveries made by our astronauts and scientists in the time since, that no one has returned to the moon since 1972 is still very disappointing.

Most recently, wealthy individuals and companies have been investing heavily in and pioneering space-related industries. I couldn't help but think back to old novels and stories when Elon Musk's SpaceX managed to safely land the first stage of their rocket back on Earth. Obviously, reusing these expensive pieces of hardware make economic sense, but despite that iconic imagery, it had never been done before. In interviews, he freely admits to being influenced by science fiction books, films, and TV. In many ways, you can see that science fictional spirit in SpaceX's approach. With Musk at the helm, they have declared their intention to send a manned mission to Mars in the mid-2020s.

"You want to wake up in the morning and think the future is going to be great—and that's what being a spacefaring civilization is all about. It's about believing in the future and thinking that the future will be better than the past. And I can't think of anything more exciting than going out there and being among the stars." —Elon Musk

Even if these plans should fail or be delayed, the energy and enthusiasm being brought back to the table is a good thing. It helps shape public opinion and will inspire a new generation to believe that they'll be the ones who get visit another world. It can help direct much-needed funding into technologies that will help us achieve those goals and along the way, potentially provide solutions to problems we have right here and right now on Earth, be it medical, environmental, or simply improve our quality of life.

I may never visit another planet, but perhaps my children, or their children will. In the meantime, I'll have to be satisfied to continue my exploration of the final frontier through stories like these, while the astronauts, scientists, robots, and innovators do the real world work that will take us there someday. And if something here inspires you, well, I'm honored to have played a small role in keeping that dream alive for you.

A JAR OF GOODWILL

TOBIAS S. BUCKELL

POINTS ON A PACKAGE

You keep a low profile when you're in oxygen debt. Too much walking about just exacerbates the situation anyway. So I was nervous when a stationeer appeared at my cubby and knocked on the door.

I slid out and stood in front of the polished, skeletal robot.

"Alex Mosette?" it asked.

There was no sense in lying. The stationeer had already scanned my face. It was just looking for voice print verification. "Yes, I'm Alex," I said.

"The harbormaster wants to see you."

I swallowed. "He could have sent me a message."

"I am here to *escort* you." The robot held out a tinker-toy arm, digits pointed along the hallway.

Space in orbit came at a premium. Bottom-rung types like me slept in cubbies stacked ten high along the hallway. On my back in the cubby, watching entertainment shuffled in from the planets, they made living on a space station sound exotic and exciting.

It was if you were further up the rung. I'd been in those rooms: places with wasted space. Furniture. Room to stroll around in.

That was exotic.

Getting space in outer space was far down my list of needs.

First was air. Then food.

Anything else was pure luxury.

*

The harbormaster stared out into space, and I silently waited at the door to Operations, hoping that if I remained quiet he wouldn't notice.

Ops hung from near the center of the megastructure of the station. A blister stuck on the end of a long tunnel. You could see the station behind us: the miles-long wheel of exotic metals rotating slowly.

No gravity in Ops, or anywhere in the center. Spokes ran down from the wheel to the center, and the center was where ships docked and were serviced and so on.

So I hung silently in the air, long after the stationeer flitted off to do the harbormaster's bidding, wondering what happened next.

"You're overdrawn," the harbormaster said after a needle-like ship with long feathery vanes slipped underneath us into the docking bays.

He turned to face me, even though his eyes had been hollowed out long ago. Force of habit. His real eyes were now every camera, or anything mechanical that could see.

The harbormaster moved closer. The gantry around him was motorized, a long arm moving him anywhere he wanted in the room.

Hundreds of cables, plugged into his scalp like hair, bundled and ran back along the arm of the gantry. Hoses moved effluvia out. More hoses ran purified blood, and other fluids, back in.

"I'm sorry," I stammered. "Traffic is light. And requests have dropped off. I've taken classes. Even language lessons . . ." I stopped when I saw the wizened hand raise, palm up.

"I know what you've been doing." The harbormaster's sightless sockets turned back to the depths of space outside. The hardened skin of his face showed few emotions, his artificial voice was toneless. "You would not have been allowed to overdraw if you hadn't made good faith efforts."

"For which," I said, "I am enormously appreciative."

"That ship that just arrived brings with it a choice for you," the harbormaster continued without acknowledging what I'd just said. "I cannot let you overdraw any more if you stay on station, so I will have to put you into hibernation. To pay for hibernation and your air debt I would buy your contract. You'd be woken for guaranteed work. I'd take a percentage. You could buy your contract back out, once you had enough liquidity."

That was exactly what I'd been dreading. But he'd indicated an alternate. "My other option?"

He waved a hand, and a holographic image of the ship I'd just seen coming in to dock hung in the air. "They're asking for a professional Friend."

"For their ship?" Surprise tinged my question. I wasn't crew material. I'd been shipped frozen to the station, just another corpsicle. People like me didn't stay awake for travel. Not enough room.

The harbormaster shrugged pallid shoulders. "They will not tell me why. I had to sign a nondisclosure agreement just to get them to tell me what they wanted."

I looked at the long ship. "I'm not a fuckbot. They know that, right?"

"They know that. They reiterated that they do *not* want sexual services."

"I'll be outside the station. Outside your protection. It could still be what they want."

"That is a risk. How much so, I cannot model for you." The harbormaster snapped his fingers, and the ship faded away. "But the contractors have extremely high reputational scores on past business dealings. They are freelance scientists: biology, botany, and one linguist."

So they probably didn't want me as a pass-around toy.

Probably.

"Rape amendments to the contract?" I asked. I was going to be on a ship, unthawed, by myself, with crew I'd never met. I had to think about the worst.

"Prohibitive. Although, accidental loss of life is not quite as high, which means I'd advise lowering the former so that there is no temptation to murder you after a theoretical rape to evade the higher contract payout."

"Fuck," I sighed.

"Would you like to peruse their reputation notes?" the harbormaster asked. And for a moment, I thought maybe the harbormaster sounded concerned.

No. He was just being fair. He'd spent two hundred years of bargaining with ships for goods, fuel, repair, services. Fair was built-in, the half-computer half-human creature in front of me was all about fair. Fair got you repeat business. Fair got you a wide reputation.

"What's the offer?"

"Half a point on the package," the harbormaster said.

"And we don't know what the package is, or how long it will take . . . or anything." I bit my lip.

"They assured me that half a point would pay off your debt and then some. It shouldn't take more than a year."

A year. For half a percent. Half a percent of what? It could be cargo they were delivering. Or, seeing as it was a crew of scientists, it could be some project they were working on.

All of which just raised more questions.

Questions I wouldn't have answers to unless I signed up. I sighed. "That's it, then? No loans? No extensions?"

The harbormaster sighed. "I answer to the Gheda shareholders who built and own this complex. I have already stretched my authority to give you a month's extension. The debt *has* to be called. I'm sorry."

I looked out at the darkness of space out beyond Ops. "Shit choices either way."

The harbormaster said nothing.

I folded my arms. "Do it."

JOURNEY BY GHEDA

The docking arms had transferred the starship from the center structure's incoming docks down a spoke to a dock on one of the wheels. The entire ship, thanks to being spun along with the wheel of the station, had gravity.

The starship was a quarter of a mile long. Outside: sleek and burnished smooth by impacts with the scattered dust of space at the stunning speeds it achieved. Inside, I realized I'd boarded a creaky, old, outdated vehicle.

Fiberwire spilled out from conduits, evidence of crude repair jobs. Dirt and grime clung to nooks and crannies. The air smelled of sweat and worse.

A purple-haired man with all-black eyes met me at the airlock. "You are the Friend?" he asked. He carried a large walking stick with him.

"Yes." I let go of the rolling luggage behind me and bowed. "I'm Alex."

He bowed back. More extravagantly than I did. Maybe even slightly mockingly. "I'm Oslo." Every time he shifted his walking stick, tiny grains of sand inside rattled and shifted about. He brimmed with impatience, and some regret in the crinkled lines of his eyes. "Is this everything?"

I looked back at the single case behind me. "That is everything."

"Then welcome aboard," Oslo said, as the door to the station clanged shut. He raised the stick, and a flash of light blinded me.

"You should have taken a scan of me before you shut the door," I said. The stick was more than it seemed. Those tiny rustling grains were generators, harnessing power for whatever tools were inside the device via kinetic motion. He turned around and started to walk away. I hurried to catch up.

Oslo smiled, and I noticed tiny little fangs under his lips. "You are who you say you are, so everything ended up okay. Oh, and for protocol, the others aren't much into it either, by the way. Now, for my own edification, you are a hermaphrodite, correct?"

I flushed. "I am what we Friends prefer to call bi-gendered, yes." Where the hell was Oslo from? I was having trouble placing his cultural conditionings and how I might adapt to interface with them. He was very direct, that was for sure.

This gig might be more complicated than I thought.

"Your Friend training: did it encompass Compact cross-cultural training?"

I slowed down. "In theory," I said slowly, worried about losing the contract if they insisted on having someone with Compact experience.

Oslo's regret dripped from his voice and movements. Was it regret that I didn't have the experience? Would I lose the contract, minutes into getting it? Or just regret that he couldn't get someone better? "But you've never Friended an actual Compact drone?"

I decided to tell the truth. A gamble. "No."

"Too bad." The regret sloughed off, to be replaced with resignation. "But we can't poke around asking for Friends with that specific experience, or one of our competitors might put two and two together. I recommend you brush up on your training during the trip out."

He stopped in front of a large, metal door. "Where are we going?" I asked.

"Here is your room for the next three days." Oslo opened the large door to a five-by-seven foot room with a foldout bunk bed.

My heart skipped a beat, and I put aside the fact that Oslo had avoided the question. "That's mine?"

"Yes. And the air's billed with our shipping contract, so you can rip your sensors off. There'll be no accounting until we're done."

I got the sense Oslo knew what it was like to be in debt. I stepped into the room and turned all the way around. I raised my hands, placing them on each wall, and smiled.

Oslo turned to go.

"Wait," I said. "The harbormaster said you were freelance scientists. What do you do?"

"I'm the botanist," Oslo said. "Meals are in the common passenger's galley. The crew of this ship is Gheda, of course, don't talk to or interact with them if you can help it. You know why?"

"Yes." The last thing you wanted to do was make a Gheda think you were wandering around, trying to figure out secrets about their ships, or technology. I would stay in the approved corridors and not interact with them.

The door closed in my suite, and I sat down with my small travel case, no closer to understanding what was going on than I had been on the station.

I faced the small mirror by an even smaller basin and reached for the strip of black material stuck to my throat. Inside it, circuitry monitored my metabolic rate, number of breaths taken, volume of air taken in, and carbon dioxide expelled. All of it reported back to the station's monitors, constantly calculating my mean daily cost.

It made a satisfying sound as I ripped it off.

*

"Gheda are Gheda," I said later in the ship's artificial, alien day over reheated turkey strips in the passenger's galley. We'd undocked. The old ship had shivered itself up to speed. "But Gheda flying around in a beat-up old starship, willing to take freelance scientists out to some secret destination: these are dangerous Gheda."

Oslo had a rueful smile as he leaned back and folded his arms. "Cruzie says that our kind used to think our corporations were rapacious and evil before first contact. No one expected aliens to demand royalty payments for technology usage that had been independently discovered by us because the Gheda had previously patented that technology."

"I know. They hit non-compliant areas with asteroids from orbit." Unable to pay royalties, entire nations had collapsed into debtorship. "Who's Cruzie?"

Oslo grimaced. "You'll meet her in two days. Our linguist. Bit of a historian, too. Loves old Earth shit."

I frowned at his reaction. Conflicted, but with somewhat warm pleasure when he thought about her. A happy grimace. "She's an old friend of yours?"

"Our parents were friends. They loved history. The magnificence of Earth. The legend that was. Before it got sold around. Before the Diaspora." That grimace again. But no warmth there.

"You don't agree with their ideals?" I guessed.

I guessed well. Oslo sipped at a mug of tea, and eyed me. "I'm not your project, Friend. Don't dig too deep, because you just work for me. Save your empathy and psychiatry for the real subject. Understand?"

Too far, I thought. "I'm sorry. And just what is my project? We're away from the station now; do you think you can risk being open with me?"

Oslo set his tea down. "Clever. Very clever, Friend. Yes, I was worried about bugs. We've found a planet, with a unique ecosystem. There may be patentable innovations."

I sat, stunned. Patents? I had points on the package. If I got points on a patent on some aspect of an alien biological system, a Gheda-approved patent, I'd be rich.

Not just rich, but like, nation-rich.

Oslo sipped at his tea. "There's only one problem," he said. "There may be intelligent life on the planet. If it's intelligent, it's a contact situation, and we have to turn it over to the Gheda. We get a fee, but no taste of the real game. We fail to report a contact situation and the Gheda find out, it's going to be a nasty scene. They'll kill our families, or even people you know, just to make the point that their interstellar law is inviolate. We have to file a claim the moment of discovery."

I'd heard hesitation in his voice. "You haven't filed yet, have you?"

"I bet all the Gheda business creatures love having you watch humans they're settling a contract with, making sure they're telling the truth, you there to brief them on what their facial expressions are really showing."

That stung. "I'd do the same for any human. And it isn't just contracts. Many hire me to pay attention to them, to figure them out, anticipate their needs."

Oslo leered. "I'll bet."

I wasn't a fuckbot. I deflected the leering. "So tell me, Oslo, why I'm risking my life, then?"

"We haven't filed yet because we honestly can't fucking figure out if the aliens are just dumb creatures, or intelligences like us," Oslo said.

THE DRONE

Welcome to the Screaming Kettle," said the woman who grabbed my bag without asking. She had dark brown skin and eyes, and black hair. Tattoos covered every inch of skin free of her clothing. Words in scripts and languages that I didn't recognize. "The Compact Drone is about to dock as well, we need you ready for it. Let's get your stuff stowed."

We walked below skylights embedded in the top of the research station. A planet hung there: green and yellow and patchy. It looked like it was diseased with mold. "Is that Ve?" I asked.

"Oslo get you up to speed?" the woman asked.

"Somewhat. You're Cruzie, right?"

"Maricruz. I'm the linguist. I guess . . . you're stuck here with us. You can call me Cruzie too." We stopped in front of a room larger than the one on the ship. With two beds.

I looked at the beds. "I'm comfortable with a cubby, if it means getting my own space," I said.

There was far more space here, vastly so. And yet, I was going to have to share it? It rankled. Even at the station, I hadn't had to share my space. This shoved me up against my own cultural normative values. Even in the most packed places in space, you needed a cubby of one's own.

"You're here to Friend the Compact Drone," Cruzie said. "It'll need companionship at all times. Their contract requires it for the Drone's mental stability."

"Oslo didn't tell me this." I pursed my lips. A fairly universal display of annoyance.

And Cruzie read that well enough. "I'm sorry," she said. But it was a lie as well. She was getting annoyed and impatient. But screw it, as Oslo pointed out:

I wasn't there for their needs. "Oslo wants us to succeed more than anything. Unlike his parents, he's not much into the glory that was humankind. He knows the only way we'll ever not be freelancers, scrabbling around for intellectual scraps found in the side alleys of technology for something we can use without paying the Gheda for the privilege, is to hit something big."

"So he lied to me." My voice remained flat.

"He left out truths that would have made you less willing to come."

"He lied."

Cruzie shut the door to my room. "He gave you points on the package, Friend. We win big, you do your job, you'll never have to check the balance on your air for the rest of your damned life. I heard you were in air debt, right?"

She'd put me well in place. We both knew it. Cruzie smiled, a gracious winner's smile.

"Incoming!" Someone yelled from around the bend in the corridor.

"I'm not going to fuck the Drone," I told her levelly.

Cruzie shrugged. "I don't care what you do or don't do, as long as the Drone stays mentally stable and does its job for us. Points on the package, Alex. Points."

Airlock alarms flashed and warbled, and the hiss of compressed air filled the antechamber.

"The incoming pod's not much larger than a cubby sleeper," Oslo said, his purple hair waving about as another burst of compressed air filled the antechamber. He smiled, fangs out beyond his lips. "It's smaller than the lander we have for exploring Ve ourselves, if we ever need to get down there. Can you imagine the ride? The only non-Gheda way of traveling!"

The last member of the team joined us. She looked over at me and nodded. Silvered electronic eyes glinted in the flash of the airlock warning lights. She flexed the jet black fingers of her artificial right hand absentmindedly as she waited for the doors to open. She ran the fingers of a real hand over her shaved head, then put them back in her utility jacket, covered with what seemed like hundreds of pockets and zippers.

"That's Kepler," Cruzie said.

The airlock doors opened. A thin, naked man stumbled out, dripping goopy blue acceleration gel with each step.

For a moment his eyes flicked around, blinking.

Then he started screaming.

Oslo, Kepler, and Cruzie jumped back half a step from the naked man's arms. I stepped forward. "It's not fear, it's relief."

The man grabbed me in a desperate hug, clinging to me, his hands patting my face, shoulders, as if reassuring himself someone was really standing in front of him. "It's okay," I whispered. "You've been in there by yourself for days, with no contact of any sort. I understand."

He was shivering in my grip, but I kept patting his back. I urged him to feel the press of contact between us. And reassurance. Calm.

Eventually he calmed down, and then slowly let go of me.

"What's your name?" I asked.

"Beck."

"Welcome aboard, Beck," I said, looking over his shoulder at the scientists who looked visibly relieved.

First things first.

Beck got to the communications room. Back and forth verification on an uplink, and he leaned back against the chair in relief.

"There's an uplink to the Hive," he said. "An hour of lag time to get as far back as the home system, but I'm patched in."

He tapped metal inserts on the back of his neck. His mind plugged in to the communications network, talking all the way back to the asteroid belt in the mother system, where the Compact's Hive thrived. Back there, Beck would always be in contact with it without a delay. In instant symbiosis with a universe of information that the Compact offered.

A hive-mind of people, your core self subjugated to the greater whole.

I shivered.

Beck never moved more than half a foot away from me. Always close enough to touch. He kept reaching out to make sure I was there, even though he could see me.

After walking around the research station for half an hour, we returned to our shared room.

He sat on his bed, suddenly apprehensive. "You're the Friend, correct?"

"Yes."

"I'm lonely over here. Can you sleep by me?"

I walked over and sat next to him. "I won't have sex with you. That's not why I'm here."

"I'm chemically neutered," Beck said as we curled up on the bed. "I'm a drone."

As we lay there, I imagined thousands of Becks sleeping in rows in Hive dorms, body heat keeping the rooms warm.

Half an hour later he suddenly sighed, like a drug addict getting a hit. "They hear me," he whispered. "I'm not alone."

The Compact had replied to him.

He relaxed.

The room filled with a pleasant lavender scent. Was it something he'd splashed on earlier? Or something a Compact drone released to indicate comfort?

WHAT'S HUMAN?

That," Kepler said, leaning back in a couch before a series of displays, "is one of our remote-operated vehicles. We call them urchins."

In the upper right hand screen before her, a small sphere with hundreds of wriggling legs rotated around. Then it scrabbled off down what looked like a dirt path.

Cruzie swung into a similar couch. "We sterilize them in orbit, then drop them down encased in a heatshield. It burns away, then they drop down out of the sky with a little burst of a rocket to slow down enough."

I frowned at one of the screens. Everything was shades of green and gray and black. "Is that night vision?"

Oslo laughed. "It's Ve. The atmosphere is chlorinated. Green mists. Grey shadows. And black plants."

The trees had giant, black leaves hanging low to the ground. Tubular trunks sprouted globes that spouted mist randomly as the urchin brushed past.

"Ve's a small planet," Kepler said. "Low gravity, but with air similar to what you would have seen on the mother world."

"Earth," Oslo corrected.

"But unlike the mother world," Kepler continued, "Ve has high levels of chlorine. Somewhere in its history, a battle launched among the plants. Instead of specializing in oxygen to kill off the competition, and adapting to it over time, plant life here turned to chlorine as a weapon. It created plastics out of the organic compounds available to it, which is doable in a chlorine-heavy base atmosphere, though remarkable. And the organic plastics also handle photosynthesis. A handy trick. If we can patent it."

On the screen the urchin rolled to a slow stop. Cruzie leaned forward. "Now if we can just figure out if *those* bastards are really building a civilization, or just random dirt mounds . . ."

Paused at the top of a ridge, the urchin looked at a clearing in the black-leafed forest. Five pyramids thrust above the foliage around the clearing.

"Can you get closer?" Beck asked, and I jumped slightly. He'd been so silent, watching all this by my side.

"Not from here," Kepler said. "There's a big dip in altitude between here and the clearing."

"And?" Beck stared at the pyramids on the screen.

"Our first couple weeks here we kept driving the urchins into low lying areas, valleys, that sort of thing. They kept dying on us. We figure the chlorine and acids sink low into the valleys. Our equipment can't handle it."

Beck sat down on the nearest couch to Kepler, and looked over the interface. "Take the long way around then, I'll look at your archives while you do so. Wait!"

I saw it too. A movement through the black, spiky bushes. I saw my first alien creature scuttle around, antennae twisting as it moved along what looked like a path.

"They look like ants," I blurted out.

"We call them Vesians. But yes, ants the size of a small dog," Oslo said. "And not really ants at all. Just exoskeletons, black plastic, in a similar structure. The handiwork of parallel evolution."

More Vesians appeared carrying leaves and sticks on their backs.

And gourds.

"Now that's interesting," Beck said.

"It doesn't mean they're intelligent," Beck said later, lying in the bunk with me next to him. We both stared up at the ceiling. He rolled over and looked at me. "The gourds grow on trees. They use them to store liquids. Inside those pyramids."

We were face to face, breathing each other's air. Beck had no personal space, and I had to fight my impulse to pull back away from him.

My job was now to facilitate. Make Beck feel at home.

Insect hives had drones that could exist away from the hive. A hive needed foragers, and defenders. But the human Compact only existed in the asteroid belt of the mother system.

Beck was a long way from home.

With the lag, he would be feeling cut off and distant. And for a mind that had always been in the embrace of the hive, this had to be hard for him.

But Beck offered the freelance scientists a link into the massive computational capacity of the entire Compact. They'd contracted it to handle the issue they couldn't figure out quickly: were the aliens intelligent or not?

Beck was pumping information back all the way to the mother system, so that the Compact could devote some fraction of a fraction of its massed computing ability to the issue. The minds of all its connected citizenry. Its supercomputers. Maybe even, it was rumored, artificial intelligences.

"But if they are intelligent?" I asked. "How do you prove it?"

Beck cocked his head. "The Compact is working on it. Has been ever since the individuals here signed the contract."

"Then why are you out here?"

"Yes . . ." He was suddenly curious about me now, remembering I was a distinct individual, lying next to him. I wasn't of the Compact. I wasn't another drone.

"I'm sorry," I said. "I shouldn't have asked."

"It was good you asked." He flopped over to stare at the ceiling again. "You're right, I'm not entirely needed. But the Compact felt it was necessary."

I wanted to know why. But I could feel Beck hesitate. I held my breath.

"You are a Friend. You've never broken contract. The Compact ranks you very highly." Beck turned back to face me. "We understand that what I tell you will never leave this room, and since I debugged it, it's a safe room. What do you think it takes to become a freelance scientist in this hostile universe?"

I'd been around enough negotiating tables. A good Friend, with the neural modifications and adaptive circuitry laced into me from birth, I could read body posture, micro-expressions, skin flush, heart rate, in a blink of the eye. I made a hell of a negotiating tool. Which was usually exactly what Gheda wanted: a read on their human counterparts.

And I had learned the ins and outs of my clients businesses quick as well. I knew what the wider universe was like while doing my job.

"Oslo has pent-up rage," I whispered. "His family is obsessed with the Earth as it used to be. Before the Gheda land purchases. He wants wealth, but that's not all, I think. Cruzie holds herself like she has military bearing, though she hides it. Kepler, I don't know. I'm guessing you will tell me they have all worked as weapons manufacturers or researchers of some sort?"

Beck nodded. "Oslo and his sister London are linked to a weaponized virus that was released on a Gheda station. Cruzie fought with separatists in Columbia. Kepler is a false identity. We haven't cracked her yet."

I looked at the drone. There was no deceit in him. He stated these things as facts. He was a drone. He didn't need to question the information given to him.

"Why are you telling me all this?"

He gestured at the bunk. "You're a professional Friend. You're safe. You're here. And I'm just a drone. We're just a piece of all this."

And then he moved to spoon against the inside of my stomach. Two meaningless, tiny lives inside a cold station, far away from where they belonged.

"And because," he added in a soft voice, "I think that these scientists are desperate enough to fix a problem if it occurs."

"Fix a problem?" I asked, wrapping my arms around him.

"I think the Vesians are intelligent, and I think Kepler and Oslo plan to do something to them if, or when, it's confirmed, so that they can keep patent rights."

I could suddenly hear every creak, whisper, and whistle in the station as I tensed up.

"I will protect you if I can. Right now we're just delaying as long as we can. Mainly I'm trying to stop Cruzie from figuring out the obvious, because if she confirms they're really intelligent, then Oslo and Kepler will make their move and do something to the Vesians. We're not sure what."

"You said delaying. Delaying until what?" I asked, a slight quaver in my voice that I found I couldn't control.

"Until the Gheda get here," Beck said with a last yawn. "That's when it all gets really complicated." His voice trailed off as he said that, and he fell asleep.

I lay there, awake and wide-eyed.

I finally reached up to my neck and scratched at the band of skin where the air monitor patch had once been stuck.

Points on nothing was still just . . . nothing.

But could I rat out my contract? My role as a Friend? Could I help Oslo and Kepler kill an alien race?

Things had gotten very muddy in just a few minutes. I felt trapped between the hell of an old life and the hell of a horrible new one.

"What's a human being?" I asked Beck over lunch.

"Definitions vary," he replied.

"You're a drone: bred to act, react, and move within a shared neural environment. You serve the Compact. There's no queen, like a classic anthill or with bees. Your shared mental overmind makes the calls. So you have a say. A tiny say. You are human . . . ish. Our ancestors would have questioned whether you were human."

Beck cocked his head and smiled. "And you?"

"Modified from birth to read human faces. Under contract for most of my life to Gheda, working to tell the aliens or other humans what humans are really thinking . . . they wouldn't have thought highly of me either."

"The Compact knows you reread your contract last night, after I fell asleep, and you used some rather complicated algorithms to game some scenarios."

I frowned. "So you're spying on us now."

"Of course. You're struggling with a gray moral situation."

"Which is?"

"The nature of your contract says you need to work with me and support my needs. But you're hired by the freelancers that I'm now in opposition to. As a Friend, a role and purpose burned into you just like being a drone is burned into me, do you warn *them*? Or do you stick by me? The contract allows for interpretations either way. And if you stick with me, it's doing so while knowing that I'm just a drone. A pawn that the Compact will use as it sees fit, for its own game."

"You left something out," I said.

"Neither you, nor I, are bred to care about Vesians," Beck said.

I got up and walked over to the large porthole. "I wonder if it wouldn't be better for them?"

"What would?"

"Whatever Kepler and Oslo want to do to them. Better to die now than to meet the Gheda. I can't imagine they'd ever want to become us."

Beck stood up. There was caution in his stance, as if he'd thought I had been figured out, but now wasn't sure. "I've got work to do. Stay here and finish your meal, Friend."

I looked down at the green world beneath, and jumped when a hand grabbed my shoulder. I could see gray words tattooed in the skin. "Cruzie?"

Her large brown eyes were filled with anger. "That son of a bitch has been lying to us," she said, pointing in the direction Beck had gone. "Come with me."

"The gourds," Cruzie said, pointing at a screen, and then looking at Beck. "Tell us about the gourds."

And Oslo grabbed my shoulder. "Watch the drone, sharp now. I want you to tell us what you see when he replies to us."

My contract would be clear there. I couldn't lie. The scientists owned the contract, and now that they'd asked directly for my services, I couldn't evade.

Points on the package, I thought in the far back of my mind.

I wasn't really human, was I? Not if I found the lure of eternal riches to be so great as to consider helping the freelancers.

"The Vesians have farms," Cruzie said. "But so do ants: they grow fungus. The Vesians have roads, but so do animals in a forest. They just keep walking over the same spots. Old Earth roads used to follow old animal paths. The Vesians have buildings, but birds build nests, ants build colonies, bees build hives. But language, that's so much rarer in the animal kingdom, isn't it, Beck?"

"Not really," the drone said calmly. "Primitive communication exists in animals. Including bees, which dance information. Dolphins squeak and whales sing."

"But none of them write it down," Cruzie grinned.

Oslo's squeezed my shoulder, hard. "The drone is mildly annoyed," I said. "And more than a little surprised."

Cruzie tapped on a screen. The inside of one of the pyramids appeared. It was a storehouse of some sort, filled with hundreds, maybe thousands, of the gourds I'd seen earlier that the Vesian had been transporting.

"Nonverbal creatures use scent. Just like ants on the mother planet. The Vesians use scents to mark territories their queens manage. And one of the things I started to wonder about, were these storage areas. What were they for? So I broke in, and I started breaking the gourds."

Beck stiffened. "He's not happy with this line of thought," I murmured.

"Thought so," Oslo said back, and nodded at Cruzie, who kept going.

"And whenever I broke a gourd, I found them empty. Not full of liquid, as Beck told us was likely. We originally thought they were for storage. An adaptive behavior. Or a sign of intelligence. Hard to say. Until I broke them all."

"They could have been empty, waiting to be sealed," Beck said tonelessly.

I sighed. "I'm sorry, Beck. I have to do this. He's telling the truth, Oslo. But misdirecting."

"I know he is," Cruzie said. "Because the Vesians swarmed the location with fresh gourds. There were chemical scents, traces laid down in the gourds before they were sealed. The Vesians examined the broken gourds, then filled the new ones with scents. I started examining the chemical traces, and found that each gourd replaced had the same chemical sequences sprayed on and stored as the ones I broke."

Beck's muscles tensed. Any human could see the stress now. I didn't need to say anything.

"They were like monks, copying manuscripts. Right, Beck?" Cruzie asked.

"Yes," Beck said.

"And the chemical markers, it's a language, right?" Kepler asked. I could feel the tension in her voice. It wasn't just disappointment building, but rage.

"It is." Beck stood up slowly.

"It took me days to realize it," Cruzie said. "And that, after the weeks I've been out here. The Compact spotted it right away, didn't it?"

Beck looked over at me, then back at Cruzie. "Yes. The Compact knows."

"Then what the hell is it planning to do?" Kepler moved in front of Beck, lips drawn back in a snarl.

"I'm just a drone," Beck said. "I don't know. But I can give you an answer in an hour."

For a second, everyone stood frozen. Oslo, brimming with hurt rage, staring at Beck. Kepler, moving from anger toward some sort of decision. Cruzie looked . . . triumphant. Oblivious to the real breaking developments in the air.

And I observed.

Like any good Friend.

Then a loud 'whooop whooop' startled us all out of our poses.

"What's that?" Cruzie asked, looking around.

"The Gheda are here," Oslo, Kepler, and Beck said at the same time.

THE PATH LESS TRAVELED

Call the vote," Oslo snapped.

Cruzie swallowed. I saw micro beads of sweat on the side of her neck. "Right now?"

"Gheda are inbound," Kepler said, her artificial eyes dark. I imagined she had them patched into the computers, looking at information from the station's sensors. "They'll be decelerating and matching orbit in hours. There's no time for debate, Cruzie."

"What we're about to do *is* something that requires debate. They're intelligent. We're proposing ripping that away over the next day with Kepler's tailored virus. They'll end up with a viral lobotomy, just smart enough we can claim their artifacts come from natural hive mind behavior. But we'll have stolen their culture. Their minds. Their history." Cruzie shook her head. "I know we said they're going to lose most of that when the Gheda arrive. But if we do this, we're worse than Gheda."

"Fucking hell, Cruzie!" Oslo snapped. "You're changing your mind *now*?"

"Oslo!" Cruzie held up her hands as if trying to ward off the angry words.

"You saw our mother planet," Oslo said. "The slums. The starvation. Gheda combat patrols. They owned *everyone*. If you didn't provide value, you were nothing. You *fought* the Sahara campaign, you attacked Abbuj station. How the fuck can you turn your back to all that?"

"I didn't turn my back, I wanted a different path," Cruzie said. "That's why we're here. With the money on the patents, we could change things . . . but what are we changing here if we're not all that better than the Gheda?"

"It's us or the fucking ants," Kepler said, voice suddenly level. "It's really that simple. Where are your allegiances?"

I bit my lip when I heard that.

"Cruzie . . ." I started to say.

She held a hand up and walked over to the console, her thumb held out. "It takes a unanimous vote to unleash the virus. This was why I insisted."

"You're right," Kepler said. I flinched. I could hear the hatred in her voice. She nodded at Oslo.

He raised his walking stick. The tiny grains inside rattled around, and then a jagged finger of energy leapt out and struck Cruzie in the small of her back.

Cruzie jerked around, arms flopping as she danced, then dropped to the ground. Oslo pressed the stick to her head and fired it again. Blood gushed from Cruzie's eye sockets as something inside her skull went 'pop.'

A wisp of smoke curled from her open mouth.

Oslo and Kepler put thumbs to the screens. "We have a unanimous vote now."

But a red warning sign flashed back at them. Beck relaxed slightly, a tiny curl of a smile briefly appearing.

Oslo raised his walking stick and pointed it at Beck. "Our communications are blocked."

"Yes," Beck said. "The Compact is voting against preemptive genocide."

For a split second, I saw the decision to kill Beck flit across Kepler's face. "If you kill him," I spoke up, "the Compact will spend resources hunting you two down. You can't enjoy your riches if you're dead."

Kepler nodded. "You're right." But she looked at me, a question on her face.

I shrugged. "If you're all dead, I don't have points on the package."

"Trigger them manually," Oslo said. "We'll bring the drone. We won't leave him up here to cause more trouble. Bring him, or her, or whatever the Friend calls itself as well. Your contract, Alex, is now to watch Beck."

We burned our way through the green atmosphere of Ve, the lander bucking and groaning, skin cracking as it weathered the heat of our reentry fireball.

From the tiny cramped cockpit I watched us part the clouds and spiral slowly down out of the sky as the wings unfurled from slots in the tear-drop sized vehicle's side. They started beating a complicated figure-eight motion.

Oslo aimed his walking stick at us when the lander touched down. "Put on your helmet, get out. Both of you."

We did so.

Heavy chlorine-rich mists swirled around, disturbed by our landing. Large puffball flowers spurted acid whenever touched by a piece of stray stirred-up debris, and the black, plastic leaves all around us bobbed gently in a low breeze.

Oslo and Kepler pulled a large pack out of the lander's cargo area. Long pieces of tubing. They set to building a freestanding antenna, piece by piece. I watched Beck. I couldn't see his face, but I could see his posture.

He was about to run. Which made no sense. Run where? On this world?

Within a few minutes Oslo and Kepler had snapped together a thirty-foot tall tower. I swallowed, and remained silent. It was a choice, a deliberate path. I broke my contract.

Oslo snapped a clip to the top of the tower, then unrolled a length of cable. He and Kepler used it to pull the super light structure up.

That was the moment Beck ran, as it hung halfway up to standing.

"Shit," Oslo cursed over the tiny speakers in our helmets, but he didn't drop the structure. "You've only got a couple hours of air you moron!"

The only response was Beck's heavy breathing.

When the antenna stood upright, Oslo approached me, the walking stick out. "You didn't warn us."

"He was wearing a spacesuit," I said calmly.

But I could see Oslo didn't believe me. His eyes creased and his fingers tightened. A bright explosion of pain ripped into me.

My vision cleared.

I was on my hands and feet, shaking with pain from the electrical discharge. A whirlwind of debris whipped around me. I looked up to see the lander lifting into the sky.

So that was it. I'd made my choice: to try and not be a monster.

And it had been in vain. The Vesians would be lobotomized by Kepler's virus. Beck would die. I would die.

I watched the lander beginning a wide spiral upward away from me. In a few seconds it would fire its rockets and climb for orbit.

In a couple hours, I would run out of air.

Four large gourds arced high over the black forest and slapped into the side of the lander. I frowned. At first, it looked like they had no effect. The lander kept spiraling up.

But then, it faltered.

The lander shook, and smoke spilled out of a crack in the side somewhere.

It exploded, the fireball hanging in the sky.

"Get away from the antenna," Beck suddenly said. "It's next."

I ran without a second thought, and even as I got free of the clearing, gourds of acid hit the structure. The metal sizzled, foamed, and then began to melt.

A few seconds later, I broke out onto a dirt path where the catapults firing the gourds of acid had been towed into place.

Beck waited for me, surrounded by a crowd of Vesians. He wore only his helmet, he'd ripped his suit off. His skin bubbled from bad chemical burn blisters.

"The Vesians destroyed all the remote-operating vehicles with the virus in it," he said. "The queens have quarantined any Vesians near any area that had an ROV. The species will survive."

"You've been talking to them," I said. And then I thought back to the comforting smell in my room the first night Beck spent with me. "You're communicating with them. You warned them."

Beck held up his suit. "Yes. The Compact altered me to be an ambassador to them."

"Beck, how long can you survive in this environment?" I stared at his blistered skin.

"A year. Maybe. There will be another ready by then. Maybe a structure to live in. The Gheda will be here soon to bring air. The Compact has reached an agreement with them. The Vesian queens are agreeing to join the Compact. The Compact gets to extend out of the mother system, but only to Ve. In exchange, the Gheda get rights to all patentable discoveries made in the new ecosystem. They're particularly interested in plastic-based organic photosynthesis."

I collapsed to the ground, realizing that I would live. Beck sat next to me. A small Vesian, approached, a gourd in its mandibles. It set the organic, plastic bottle at my legs. "What's that?"

"A jar of goodwill," Beck said. "The Vesian queen of this area is thanking you."

I was still just staring at it two hours later as my air faded out, my vision blurred, and the Gheda lander finally reached us.

The harbormaster cocked his head. "You're back."

"I'm back," I said. Someone was unpacking my two bags, one of them carefully holding the Vesian 'gift.'

"I didn't think I'd ever see you again," the harbormaster said. "Not with a contract like that."

"It didn't work out." I looked out into the vacuum of space beyond us. "Certainly not for the people who hired me. Or me."

"You have a peripheral contract with the Compact. An all-you-can-breath line of credit on the station. You're not a citizen, but on perpetual retainer as the Compact's primary professional Friend for all dealings in this system. You did well enough."

I grinned. "Points on a package like what they offered me was a fairy tale. A fairy tale you'd have to be soulless to want to have come true."

"I'm surprised that you did not choose to join the Compact," the harbormaster said, looking closely at me. "It is a safe place for humans in this universe.

Even as a peripheral for them, you could still be in danger during patent negotiations with Gheda."

"I know. But this is home. My home. I'm not a drone, I don't want to be one."

The harbormaster sighed. "You understand the station is my only love. I don't have a social circle. There is only the ebb and flow of this structure's health for me."

I smiled. "That's why I like you, harbormaster. You have few emotions. You are a fair dealer. You're the closest thing I have to family. You may even be the closest thing I have to a friend, friend with a lowercase 'f.'"

"You follow your contracts to the letter. I like that about you," the harbormaster said. "I'm glad you will continue on here."

Together we watched the needle-like ship that had brought me back home silently fall away from the station.

"The Compact purchased me a ten-by-ten room with a porthole," I said. "I don't have to come up here to sneak a look at the stars anymore."

The harbormaster sighed happily. "They're beautiful, aren't they? I think, we've always loved them, haven't we? Even before we were forced to leave the mother world."

"That's what the history books say," I said quietly over the sound of ducts and creaking station. "We dreamed of getting out here, to live among them. Dreamed of the wonders we'd see."

"The Gheda don't see the stars," the harbormaster said. "They have few portholes. Before I let the Gheda turn me into a harbormaster, I demanded the contract include this room."

"They don't see them the way we do," I agreed.

"They're not human," the harbormaster said.

"No, they're not." I looked out at the distant stars. "But then, few things are anymore."

The Gheda ship disappeared in a blinding flash of light, whipping through space toward its next destination.

MONO NO AWARE

KEN LIU

The world is shaped like the kanji for "umbrella," only written so poorly, like my handwriting, that all the parts are out of proportion.

My father would be greatly ashamed at the childish way I still form my characters. Indeed, I can barely write many of them anymore. My formal schooling back in Japan ceased when I was only eight.

Yet for present purposes, this badly drawn character will do.

The canopy up there is the solar sail. Even that distorted kanji can only give you a hint of its vast size. A hundred times thinner than rice paper, the spinning disk fans out a thousand kilometers into space like a giant kite intent on catching every passing photon. It literally blocks out the sky.

Beneath it dangles a long cable of carbon nanotubes a hundred kilometers long: strong, light, and flexible. At the end of the cable hangs the heart of the *Hopeful*, the habitat module, a five-hundred-meter-tall cylinder into which all the 1,021 inhabitants of the world are packed.

The light from the sun pushes against the sail, propelling us on an ever widening, ever accelerating, spiraling orbit away from it. The acceleration pins all of us against the decks, gives everything weight.

Our trajectory takes us toward a star called 61 Virginis. You can't see it now because it is behind the canopy of the solar sail. The *Hopeful* will get there in about three hundred years, more or less. With luck, my great-great-great—I calculated how many "greats" I needed once, but I don't remember now—grand-children will see it.

There are no windows in the habitat module, no casual view of the stars streaming past. Most people don't care, having grown bored of seeing the stars long ago. But I like looking through the cameras mounted on the bottom of the ship so that I can gaze at this view of the receding, reddish glow of our sun, our past.

"Hiroto," Dad said as he shook me awake. "Pack up your things. It's time."

My small suitcase was ready. I just had to put my Go set into it. Dad gave this to me when I was five, and the times we played were my favorite hours of the day.

The sun had not yet risen when Mom and Dad and I made our way out-side. All the neighbors were standing outside their houses with their bags as well, and we greeted one another politely under the summer stars. As usual, I looked for the Hammer. It was easy. Ever since I could remember, the asteroid had been the brightest thing in the sky except for the moon, and every year it grew brighter.

A truck with loudspeakers mounted on top drove slowly down the middle of the street.

"Attention, citizens of Kurume! Please make your way in an orderly fashion to the bus stop. There will be plenty of buses to take you to the train station, where you can board the train for Kagoshima. Do not drive. You must leave the roads open for the evacuation buses and official vehicles!"

Every family walked slowly down the sidewalk.

"Mrs. Maeda," Dad said to our neighbor. "Why don't I carry your luggage for you?"

"I'm very grateful," the old woman said.

After ten minutes of walking, Mrs. Maeda stopped and leaned against a lamppost.

"It's just a little longer, Granny," I said. She nodded but was too out of breath to speak. I tried to cheer her. "Are you looking forward to seeing your grandson in Kagoshima? I miss Michi too. You will be able to sit with him and rest on the spaceships. They say there will be enough seats for everyone."

Mom smiled at me approvingly.

"How fortunate we are to be here," Dad said. He gestured at the orderly rows of people moving toward the bus stop, at the young men in clean shirts and shoes looking solemn, the middle-aged women helping their elderly parents, the clean, empty streets, and the quietness—despite the crowd, no one spoke above a whisper. The very air seemed to shimmer with the dense connections between all the people—families, neighbors, friends, colleagues—as invisible and strong as threads of silk.

I had seen on TV what was happening in other places around the world: looters screaming, dancing through the streets, soldiers and policemen shooting into the air and sometimes into crowds, burning buildings, teetering piles of dead bodies, generals shouting before frenzied crowds, vowing vengeance for ancient grievances even as the world was ending.

"Hiroto, I want you to remember this," Dad said. He looked around, overcome by emotion. "It is in the face of disasters that we show our strength as a people. Understand that we are not defined by our individual loneliness, but by the web of relationships in which we're enmeshed. A person must rise above his selfish needs so that all of us can live in harmony. The individual is small and powerless, but bound tightly together, as a whole, the Japanese nation is invincible."

"Mr. Shimizu," eight-year-old Bobby says, "I don't like this game."

The school is located in the very center of the cylindrical habitat module, where it can have the benefit of the most shielding from radiation. In front of the classroom hangs a large American flag to which the children say their pledge every morning. To the sides of the American flag are two rows of smaller flags belonging to other nations with survivors on the *Hopeful*. At the very end of the left side is a child's rendition of the Hinomaru, the corners of the white paper now curled and the once bright red rising sun faded to the orange of sunset. I drew it the day I came aboard the *Hopeful*.

I pull up a chair next to the table where Bobby and his friend Eric are sitting. "Why don't you like it?"

Between the two boys is a nineteen-by-nineteen grid of straight lines. A handful of black and white stones have been placed on the intersections.

Once every two weeks, I have the day off from my regular duties monitoring the status of the solar sail and come here to teach the children a little bit about Japan. I feel silly doing it sometimes. How can I be their teacher when I have only a boy's hazy memories of Japan?

But there is no other choice. All the non-American technicians like me feel it is our duty to participate in the cultural-enrichment program at the school and pass on what we can.

"All the stones look the same," Bobby says, "and they don't move. They're boring."

"What game do you like?" I ask.

"*Asteroid Defender*!" Eric says. "Now *that* is a good game. You get to save the world."

"I mean a game you do not play on the computer."

Bobby shrugs. "Chess, I guess. I like the queen. She's powerful and different from everyone else. She's a hero."

"Chess is a game of skirmishes," I say. "The perspective of Go is bigger. It encompasses entire battles."

"There are no heroes in Go," Bobby says stubbornly.

I don't know how to answer him.

There was no place to stay in Kagoshima, so everyone slept outside along the road to the spaceport. On the horizon we could see the great silver escape ships gleaming in the sun.

Dad had explained to me that fragments that had broken off the Hammer were headed for Mars and the moon, so the ships would have to take us farther, into deep space, to be safe.

"I would like a window seat," I said, imagining the stars steaming by.

"You should yield the window seat to those younger than you," Dad said. "Remember, we must all make sacrifices to live together."

We piled our suitcases into walls and draped sheets over them to form shelters from the wind and the sun. Every day inspectors from the government came by to distribute supplies and to make sure everything was all right.

"Be patient!" the government inspectors said. "We know things are moving slowly, but we're doing everything we can. There will be seats for everyone."

We were patient. Some of the mothers organized lessons for the children during the day, and the fathers set up a priority system so that families with aged parents and babies could board first when the ships were finally ready.

After four days of waiting, the reassurances from the government inspectors did not sound quite as reassuring. Rumors spread through the crowd.

"It's the ships. Something's wrong with them."

"The builders lied to the government and said they were ready when they weren't, and now the prime minister is too embarrassed to admit the truth."

"I hear that there's only one ship, and only a few hundred of the most important people will have seats. The other ships are only hollow shells, for show."

"They're hoping that the Americans will change their mind and build more ships for allies like us."

Mom came to Dad and whispered in his ear.

Dad shook his head and stopped her. "Do not repeat such things."

"But for Hiroto's sake—"

"No!" I'd never heard Dad sound so angry. He paused, swallowed. "We must trust each other, trust the prime minister and the Self-Defense Forces."

Mom looked unhappy. I reached out and held her hand. "I'm not afraid," I said.

"That's right," Dad said, relief in his voice. "There's nothing to be afraid of."

He picked me up in his arms—I was slightly embarrassed, for he had not done such a thing since I was very little—and pointed at the densely packed crowd of thousands and thousands spread around us as far as the eye could see.

"Look at how many of us there are: grandmothers, young fathers, big sisters, little brothers. For anyone to panic and begin to spread rumors in such a crowd would be selfish and wrong, and many people could be hurt. We must keep to our places and always remember the bigger picture."

Mindy and I make love slowly. I like to breathe in the smell of her dark curly hair, lush, warm, tickling the nose like the sea, like fresh salt.

Afterward we lie next to each other, gazing up at my ceiling monitor.

I keep looping on it a view of the receding star field. Mindy works in navigation, and she records the high-resolution cockpit video feed for me.

I like to pretend that it's a big skylight, and we're lying under the stars. I know some others like to keep their monitors showing photographs and videos of old Earth, but that makes me too sad.

"How do you say 'star' in Japanese?" Mindy asks.

"Hoshi," I tell her.

"And how do you say 'guest'?"

"Okyakusan."

"So we are *hoshi okyakusan*? Star guests?"

"It doesn't work like that," I say. Mindy is a singer, and she likes the sound of languages other than English. "It's hard to hear the music behind the words when their meanings get in the way," she told me once.

Spanish is Mindy's first language, but she remembers even less of it than I do of Japanese. Often, she asks me for Japanese words and weaves them into her songs.

I try to phrase it poetically for her, but I'm not sure if I'm successful. "Wareware ha, hoshi no aida ni kyaku ni kite." We have come to be guests among the stars.

"There are a thousand ways of phrasing everything," Dad used to say, "each appropriate to an occasion." He taught me that our language is full of nuances and supple grace, each sentence a poem. The language folds in on itself, the unspoken words as meaningful as the spoken, context within context, layer upon layer, like the steel in samurai swords.

I wish Dad were around so that I could ask him: How do you say "I miss you" in a way that is appropriate to the occasion of your twenty-fifth birthday, as the last survivor of your race?

"My sister was really into Japanese picture books. Manga."

Like me, Mindy is an orphan. It's part of what draws us together.

"Do you remember much about her?"

"Not really. I was only five or so when I came on board the ship. Before that, I only remember a lot of guns firing and all of us hiding in the dark and running and crying and stealing food. She was always there to keep me quiet by reading from the manga books. And then . . ."

I had watched the video only once. From our high orbit, the blue-and-white marble that was Earth seemed to wobble for a moment as the asteroid struck, and then, the silent, roiling waves of spreading destruction that slowly engulfed the globe.

I pull her to me and kiss her forehead, lightly, a kiss of comfort. "Let us not speak of sad things."

She wraps her arms around me tightly, as though she will never let go.

"The manga, do you remember anything about them?" I ask.

"I remember they were full of giant robots. I thought: *Japan is so powerful.*"

I try to imagine it: heroic giant robots all over Japan, working desperately to save the people.

The prime minister's apology was broadcast through the loudspeakers. Some also watched it on their phones.

I remember very little of it except that his voice was thin and he looked very frail and old. He looked genuinely sorry. "I've let the people down."

The rumors turned out to be true. The shipbuilders had taken the money from the government but did not build ships that were strong enough or capable of what they promised. They kept up the charade until the very end. We found out the truth only when it was too late.

Japan was not the only nation that failed her people. The other nations of the world had squabbled over who should contribute how much to a joint evacuation effort when the Hammer was first discovered on its collision course with Earth. And then, when that plan had collapsed, most decided that it was better to gamble that the Hammer would miss and spend the money and lives on fighting with one another instead.

After the prime minister finished speaking, the crowd remained silent. A few angry voices shouted but soon quieted down as well. Gradually, in an orderly fashion, people began to pack up and leave the temporary campsites.

"The people just went home?" Mindy asks, incredulous.

"Yes."

"There was no looting, no panicked runs, no soldiers mutinying in the streets?"

"This was Japan," I tell her. And I can hear the pride in my voice, an echo of my father's.

"I guess the people were resigned," Mindy says. "They had given up. Maybe it's a culture thing."

"No!" I fight to keep the heat out of my voice. Her words irk me, like Bobby's remark about Go being boring. "That is not how it was."

"Who is Dad speaking to?" I asked.

"That is Dr. Hamilton," Mom said. "We—he and your father and I—went to college together in America."

I watched Dad speak English on the phone. He seemed like a completely different person: it wasn't just the cadences and pitch of his voice; his face was more animated, his hand gestured more wildly. He looked like a foreigner.

He shouted into the phone.

"What is Dad saying?"

Mom shushed me. She watched Dad intently, hanging on every word.

"No," Dad said into the phone. "No!" I did not need that translated.

Afterward Mom said, "He is trying to do the right thing, in his own way."

"He is as selfish as ever," Dad snapped.

"That's not fair," Mom said. "He did not call me in secret. He called you instead because he believed that if your positions were reversed, he would gladly give the woman he loved a chance to survive, even if it's with another man."

Dad looked at her. I had never heard my parents say "I love you" to each other, but some words did not need to be said to be true.

"I would never have said yes to him," Mom said, smiling. Then she went to the kitchen to make our lunch. Dad's gaze followed her.

"It's a fine day," Dad said to me. "Let us go on a walk."

We passed other neighbors walking along the sidewalks. We greeted one another, inquired after one another's health. Everything seemed normal. The Hammer glowed even brighter in the dusk overhead.

"You must be very frightened, Hiroto," he said.

"They won't try to build more escape ships?"

Dad did not answer. The late summer wind carried the sound of cicadas to us: *chirr, chirr, chirrrrrr.*

> *"Nothing in the cry*
> *Of cicadas suggests they*
> *Are about to die."*

"Dad?"

"That is a poem by Bashō. Do you understand it?"

I shook my head. I did not like poems much.

Dad sighed and smiled at me. He looked at the setting sun and spoke again:

> *"The fading sunlight holds infinite beauty*
> *Though it is so close to the day's end."*

I recited the lines to myself. Something in them moved me. I tried to put the feeling into words: "It is like a gentle kitten is licking the inside of my heart."

Instead of laughing at me, Dad nodded solemnly.

"That is a poem by the classical Tang poet Li Shangyin. Though he was Chinese, the sentiment is very much Japanese."

We walked on, and I stopped by the yellow flower of a dandelion. The angle at which the flower was tilted struck me as very beautiful. I got the kitten-tongue-tickling sensation in my heart again.

"The flower . . ." I hesitated. I could not find the right words.

Dad spoke,

> *"The drooping flower*
> *As yellow as the moonbeam*
> *So slender tonight."*

I nodded. The image seemed to me at once so fleeting and so permanent, like the way I had experienced time as a young child. It made me a little sad and glad at the same time.

"Everything passes, Hiroto," Dad said. "That feeling in your heart: it's called *mono no aware*. It is a sense of the transience of all things in life. The sun, the dandelion, the cicada, the Hammer, and all of us: we are all subject to the equations of James Clerk Maxwell, and we are all ephemeral patterns destined to eventually fade, whether in a second or an eon."

I looked around at the clean streets, the slow-moving people, the grass, and the evening light, and I knew that everything had its place; everything was all right. Dad and I went on walking, our shadows touching.

Even though the Hammer hung right overhead, I was not afraid.

My job involves staring at the grid of indicator lights in front of me. It is a bit like a giant Go board.

It is very boring most of the time. The lights, indicating tension on various spots of the solar sail, course through the same pattern every few minutes as the sail gently flexes in the fading light of the distant sun. The cycling pattern of the lights is as familiar to me as Mindy's breathing when she's asleep.

We're already moving at a good fraction of the speed of light. Some years hence, when we're moving fast enough, we'll change our course for 61 Virginis and its pristine planets, and we'll leave the sun that gave birth to us behind like a forgotten memory.

But today, the pattern of the lights feels off. One of the lights in the southwest corner seems to be blinking a fraction of a second too fast.

"Navigation," I say into the microphone, "this is Sail Monitor Station Alpha, can you confirm that we're on course?"

A minute later Mindy's voice comes through my earpiece, tinged slightly with surprise. "I hadn't noticed, but there was a slight drift off course. What happened?"

"I'm not sure yet." I stare at the grid before me, at the one stubborn light that is out of sync, out of harmony.

Mom took me to Fukuoka without Dad. "We'll be shopping for Christmas," she said. "We want to surprise you." Dad smiled and shook his head.

We made our way through the busy streets. Since this might be the last Christmas on Earth, there was an extra sense of gaiety in the air.

On the subway I glanced at the newspaper held up by the man sitting next to us. USA STRIKES BACK! was the headline. The big photograph showed the American president smiling triumphantly. Below that was a series of other pictures, some I had seen before: the first experimental American evacuation ship from years ago exploding on its test flight; the leader of some rogue nation claiming responsibility on TV; American soldiers marching into a foreign capital.

Below the fold was a smaller article: AMERICAN SCIENTISTS SKEPTICAL OF DOOMSDAY SCENARIO. Dad had said that some people preferred to believe that a disaster was unreal rather than accept that nothing could be done.

I looked forward to picking out a present for Dad. But instead of going to the electronics district, where I had expected Mom to take me to buy him a gift, we went to a section of the city I had never been to before. Mom took out her phone and made a brief call, speaking in English. I looked up at her, surprised.

Then we were standing in front of a building with a great American flag flying over it. We went inside and sat down in an office. An American man came in. His face was sad, but he was working hard not to look sad.

"Rin." The man called my mother's name and stopped. In that one syllable I heard regret and longing and a complicated story.

"This is Dr. Hamilton," Mom said to me. I nodded and offered to shake his hand, as I had seen Americans do on TV.

Dr. Hamilton and Mom spoke for a while. She began to cry, and Dr. Hamilton stood awkwardly, as though he wanted to hug her but dared not.

"You'll be staying with Dr. Hamilton," Mom said to me.

"What?"

She held my shoulders, bent down, and looked into my eyes. "The Americans have a secret ship in orbit. It is the only ship they managed to launch into space before they got into this war. Dr. Hamilton designed the ship. He's my . . . old friend, and he can bring one person aboard with him. It's your only chance."

"No, I'm not leaving."

Eventually, Mom opened the door to leave. Dr. Hamilton held me tightly as I kicked and screamed.

We were all surprised to see Dad standing there.

Mom burst into tears.

Dad hugged her, which I'd never seen him do. It seemed a very American gesture.

"I'm sorry," Mom said. She kept saying "I'm sorry" as she cried.

"It's okay," Dad said. "I understand."

Dr. Hamilton let me go, and I ran up to my parents, holding on to both of them tightly.

Mom looked at Dad, and in that look she said nothing and everything.

Dad's face softened like a wax figure coming to life. He sighed and looked at me.

"You're not afraid, are you?" Dad asked.

I shook my head.

"Then it is okay for you to go," he said. He looked into Dr. Hamilton's eyes. "Thank you for taking care of my son."

Mom and I both looked at him, surprised.

"A dandelion
In late autumn's cooling breeze
Spreads seeds far and wide."

I nodded, pretending to understand.
Dad hugged me, fiercely, quickly.
"Remember that you're Japanese."
And they were gone.

"Something has punctured the sail," Dr. Hamilton says.

The tiny room holds only the most senior command staff—plus Mindy and me because we already know. There is no reason to cause a panic among the people.

"The hole is causing the ship to list to the side, veering off course. If the hole is not patched, the tear will grow bigger, the sail will soon collapse, and the *Hopeful* will be adrift in space."

"Is there any way to fix it?" the captain asks.

Dr. Hamilton, who has been like a father to me, shakes his headful of white hair. I have never seen him so despondent.

"The tear is several hundred kilometers from the hub of the sail. It will take many days to get someone out there because you can't move too fast along the surface of the sail—the risk of another tear is too great. And by the time we do get anyone out there, the tear will have grown too large to patch."

And so it goes. Everything passes.

I close my eyes and picture the sail. The film is so thin that if it is touched carelessly, it will be punctured. But the membrane is supported by a complex system of folds and struts that give the sail rigidity and tension. As a child, I had watched them unfold in space like one of my mother's origami creations.

I imagine hooking and unhooking a tether cable to the scaffolding of struts as I skim along the surface of the sail, like a dragonfly dipping across the surface of a pond.

"I can make it out there in seventy-two hours," I say. Everyone turns to look at me. I explain my idea. "I know the patterns of the struts well because I have monitored them from afar for most of my life. I can find the quickest path."

Dr. Hamilton is dubious. "Those struts were never designed for a maneuver like that. I never planned for this scenario."

"Then we'll improvise," Mindy says. "We're Americans, damn it. We never just give up."

Dr. Hamilton looks up. "Thank you, Mindy."

We plan, we debate, we shout at each other, we work throughout the night.

The climb up the cable from the habitat module to the solar sail is long and arduous. It takes me almost twelve hours.

Let me illustrate for you what I look like with the second character in my name:

翔

It means "to soar." See that radical on the left? That's me, tethered to the cable with a pair of antennae coming out of my helmet. On my back are the wings—or, in this case, booster rockets and extra fuel tanks that push me up and up toward the great reflective dome that blocks out the whole sky, the gossamer mirror of the solar sail.

Mindy chats with me on the radio link. We tell each other jokes, share secrets, speak of things we want to do in the future. When we run out of things to say, she sings to me. The goal is to keep me awake.

"Wareware ha, hoshi no aida ni kyaku ni kite."

But the climb up is really the easy part. The journey across the sail along the network of struts to the point of puncture is far more difficult.

It has been thirty-six hours since I left the ship. Mindy's voice is now tired, flagging. She yawns.

"Sleep, baby," I whisper into the microphone. I'm so tired that I want to close my eyes just for a moment.

I'm walking along the road on a summer evening, my father next to me.

"We live in a land of volcanoes and earthquakes, typhoons and tsunamis, Hiroto. We have always faced a precarious existence, suspended in a thin strip on the surface of this planet between the fire underneath and the icy vacuum above."

And I'm back in my suit again, alone. My momentary loss of concentration causes me to bang my backpack against one of the beams of the sail, almost knocking one of the fuel tanks loose. I grab it just in time. The mass of my equipment has been lightened down to the last gram so that I can move fast, and there is no margin for error. I can't afford to lose anything.

I try to shake the dream and keep on moving.

"Yet it is this awareness of the closeness of death, of the beauty inherent in each moment, that allows us to endure. Mono no aware, my son, is an empathy with the universe. It is the soul of our nation. It has allowed us to endure Hiroshima, to

endure the occupation, to endure deprivation and the prospect of annihilation without despair."

"Hiroto, wake up!" Mindy's voice is desperate, pleading. I jerk awake. I have not been able to sleep for how long now? Two days, three, four?

For the final fifty or so kilometers of the journey, I must let go of the sail struts and rely on my rockets alone to travel untethered, skimming over the surface of the sail while everything is moving at a fraction of the speed of light. The very idea is enough to make me dizzy.

And suddenly my father is next to me again, suspended in space below the sail. We're playing a game of Go.

"Look in the southwest corner. Do you see how your army has been divided in half? My white stones will soon surround and capture this entire group."

I look where he's pointing and I see the crisis. There is a gap that I missed. What I thought was my one army is in reality two separate groups with a hole in the middle. I have to plug the gap with my next stone.

I shake away the hallucination. I have to finish this, and then I can sleep.

There is a hole in the torn sail before me. At the speed we're traveling, even a tiny speck of dust that escaped the ion shields can cause havoc. The jagged edge of the hole flaps gently in space, propelled by solar wind and radiation pressure. While an individual photon is tiny, insignificant, without even mass, all of them together can propel a sail as big as the sky and push a thousand people along.

The universe is wondrous.

I lift a black stone and prepare to fill in the gap, to connect my armies into one.

The stone turns back into the patching kit from my backpack. I maneuver my thrusters until I'm hovering right over the gash in the sail. Through the hole I can see the stars beyond, the stars that no one on the ship has seen for many years. I look at them and imagine that around one of them, one day, the human race, fused into a new nation, will recover from near extinction, will start afresh and flourish again.

Carefully, I apply the bandage over the gash, and I turn on the heat torch. I run the torch over the gash, and I can feel the bandage melting to spread out and fuse with the hydrocarbon chains in the sail film. When that's done I'll vaporize and deposit silver atoms over it to form a shiny, reflective layer.

"It's working," I say into the microphone. And I hear the muffled sounds of celebration in the background.

"You're a hero," Mindy says.

I think of myself as a giant Japanese robot in a manga and smile.

The torch sputters and goes out.

"Look carefully," Dad says. "You want to play your next stone there to plug that hole. But is that what you really want?"

I shake the fuel tank attached to the torch. Nothing. This was the tank that I banged against one of the sail beams. The collision must have caused a leak and there isn't enough fuel left to finish the patch. The bandage flaps gently, only half attached to the gash.

"Come back now," Dr. Hamilton says. "We'll replenish your supplies and try again."

I'm exhausted. No matter how hard I push, I will not be able to make it back out here as fast. And by then who knows how big the gash will have grown? Dr. Hamilton knows this as well as I do. He just wants to get me back to the warm safety of the ship.

I still have fuel in my tank, the fuel that is meant for my return trip.

My father's face is expectant.

"I see," I speak slowly. "If I play my next stone in this hole, I will not have a chance to get back to the small group up in the northeast. You'll capture them."

"One stone cannot be in both places. You have to choose, son."

"Tell me what to do."

I look into my father's face for an answer.

"Look around you," Dad says. And I see Mom, Mrs. Maeda, the prime minister, all our neighbors from Kurume, and all the people who waited with us in Kagoshima, in Kyushu, in all the Four Islands, all over Earth, and on the *Hopeful.* They look expectantly at me, for me to do something.

Dad's voice is quiet:

"The stars shine and blink.
We are all guests passing through,
A smile and a name."

"I have a solution," I tell Dr. Hamilton over the radio.

"I knew you'd come up with something," Mindy says, her voice proud and happy.

Dr. Hamilton is silent for a while. He knows what I'm thinking. And then: "Hiroto, thank you."

I unhook the torch from its useless fuel tank and connect it to the tank on my back. I turn it on. The flame is bright, sharp, a blade of light. I marshal photons and atoms before me, transforming them into a web of strength and light.

The stars on the other side have been sealed away again. The mirrored surface of the sail is perfect.

"Correct your course," I speak into the microphone. "It's done."

"Acknowledged," Dr. Hamilton says. His voice is that of a sad man trying not to sound sad.

"You have to come back first," Mindy says. "If we correct course now, you'll have nowhere to tether yourself."

"It's okay, baby," I whisper into the microphone. "I'm not coming back. There's not enough fuel left."

"We'll come for you!"

"You can't navigate the struts as quickly as I did," I tell her gently. "No one knows their patterns as well as I do. By the time you get here, I will have run out of air."

I wait until she's quiet again. "Let us not speak of sad things. I love you."

Then I turn off the radio and push off into space so that they aren't tempted to mount a useless rescue mission. And I fall down, far, far below the canopy of the sail.

I watch as the sail turns away, unveiling the stars in their full glory. The sun, so faint now, is only one star among many, neither rising nor setting. I am cast adrift among them, alone and also at one with them.

A kitten's tongue tickles the inside of my heart.

I play the next stone in the gap.

Dad plays as I thought he would, and my stones in the northeast corner are gone, cast adrift.

But my main group is safe. They may even flourish in the future.

"Maybe there are heroes in Go," Bobby's voice says.

Mindy called me a hero. But I was simply a man in the right place at the right time. Dr. Hamilton is also a hero because he designed the *Hopeful*. Mindy is also a hero because she kept me awake. My mother is also a hero because she was willing to give me up so that I could survive. My father is also a hero because he showed me the right thing to do.

We are defined by the places we hold in the web of others' lives.

I pull my gaze back from the Go board until the stones fuse into larger patterns of shifting life and pulsing breath. "Individual stones are not heroes, but all the stones together are heroic."

"It is a beautiful day for a walk, isn't it?" Dad says.

And we walk together down the street, so that we can remember every passing blade of grass, every dewdrop, every fading ray of the dying sun, infinitely beautiful.

Jack Skillingstead is the author of more than forty short stories, a collection, and two novels, with a third scheduled for early 2019. He has been a finalist for both the Theodore Sturgeon Award and Philip K. Dick Award. He lives in Seattle with his wife, writer Nancy Kress.

RESCUE MISSION

JACK SKILLINGSTEAD

Michael Pennington floated in *Mona's* amniotic chamber, fully immersed, naked and erect, zened out. The cortical cable looped lazily around him. Womb Hole traveling. His gills palpitated; *Mona's* quantum consciousness saturated the environment with a billion Qubits, and Michael's Anima combined with *Mona's* super animus and drove the starship along a dodgy vector through the Pleiades.

Until a distraction occurred.

Like a Siren call, it pierced to the center of Michael's consciousness. His body twisted, eyes opening in heavy fluid. At the same instant *Mona*, cued to Michael's every impulse, veered in space. Somewhere, alarms rang.

Mona interrupted the navigation cycle, retracted Michael's cortical cable, and gently expelled him into the delivery chamber. Vacuums activated, sucking at him. He pushed past them, into the larger chamber beyond, still swooning on the borderland of Ship State. A blurry figure floated toward him: Natalie. She caught him and held him.

"What happened?" he asked.

"Mona spat you out. And we're on a new course." She touched his face. "Your eyes are all pupil. I'm going to give you something."

"Hmm," Michael said.

He felt the sting in his left arm. After a moment his head cleared.

"Let's get you properly cleaned up," Natalie said.

He was weak, post Ship State, and he let her touch him, but said: "The Proxy can help me."

"You *want* it to?"

"It's capable."

"You have a thing for the Proxy?"

The Proxy, a rudimentary biomech, was an extension of *Mona*, though lacking in gender-specific characteristics.

"Not exactly."

"*We* have a thing."

"Nat, our 'thing' was a mistake. If we'd known we were going to team on this mission we would never have thinged."

"Wouldn't we have?"

"No."

She released him and they drifted apart. Michael scratched his head. Tiny cerulean spheres of amniotic residue swarmed about him. "You can be kind of a bastard, you know."

"I know."

"I'll send the Proxy."

Mona transitioned into orbit around the wrong planet. It rolled beneath them, a world mostly green, a little blue, brushed with cloud white.

"That's not Meropa IV," Natalie said, floating onto the bridge with a bulb of coffee.

"No," Michael said, not looking away from the monitor.

"So what is it?"

"A planet."

"Gosh. So *that's* a planet." Natalie propelled herself up to the monitor. "And what are we doing here, when we have vital cargo for the Meropa IV colony?"

"There's time," Michael said, the Siren call still sounding deep in his mind. "This is important."

"This is important? What about Meropa IV?"

Michael pushed away from the console.

"I'm going down," he said.

Once he was strapped securely into the Drop Ship, Natalie said:

"You shouldn't go."

"Why not?"

"You're acting strange. I mean stranger than usual."

"That's it?" Michael said, going through his pre-flight routine.

"Also, I have a feeling," Natalie said.

"You're always having those."

"It's human," Natalie said.

"So I understand."

"Even you had feelings once upon a time. Does New San Francisco ring any bells?"

"Steeples full. I'm losing my window, by the way. Can we drop now?"

"Why do I think you and *Mona* have a secret?"

"I have no idea why you think that."

Natalie looked pained. "Why are you so mean to me?"

Michael couldn't look at her.

"*Do* you have a secret?" Natalie said.

He fingered a nav display hanging like a ghostly vapor in front of his face. "I'm going to miss my damn window."

She dropped him.

The Drop Ship jolted through entry fire and became an air vehicle. The planet rushed up. Cloud swirls blew past. Michael descended toward a dense continent-wide jungle.

Mona said: "I'm still unable to acquire the signal."

"I told you: The signal's in my head."

"I'm beginning to agree with Natalie."

"Don't go human on me," Michael said. "Taking over manual control now."

He touched the proper sequence but *Mona* did not relinquish the helm.

"Let go," Michael said.

"Perhaps you should reconsider. Further observation from orbit could yield—"

He hit the emergency override, which keyed to his genetic code. *Mona* fell silent, and Michael guided the Ship down to a clearing in the jungle.

Or what looked like a clearing.

A sensor indicated touchdown, but the ship's feet sank into muck. Michael stared at his instrument displays. The ship rocked back, canted over, stopped.

Mona said: "You're still over-riding me. I can't lift off."

"We just landed."

"We're sinking, not landing."

"What's going on," Natalie said on a different channel.

"Nothing," Michael said.

Mona cut across channels: "We've touched down in a bog! We—"

Michael switched off the audio for both *Mona* and Natalie. He released his safety restraints and popped the hatch, compelled, almost as if he were in the grip of a biological urge.

His helmet stifled him. He didn't really need it, did he? Michael screwed it to the left and lifted it off. The air was humid, sickly fragrant. He clambered out of his seat, wiped the sweat off his forehead, then slipped over the side and into the sucking mire and began groping for shore. The more he struggled forward the deeper he sank. Fear and adrenaline momentarily flushed the fog from his mind.

"*Mona*, help!"

But his helmet was off and *Mona* could not reply.

Then, strangely, he stopped sinking. The mire buoyed him up and carried him forward toward the shore as several figures emerged from the jungle. His feet found purchase and he walked on solid ground, his flight suit heavy and streaming. The figures weren't *from* the jungle; they were *part* of the jungle—trees that looked like women, or perhaps women who looked like trees. One stepped creakingly forward, a green mossy tangle swinging between its knobby tree trunk legs. It extended a limb with three twig fingers. Irregular plugs of amber resin gleamed like pale eyes in what passed for a face. Michael's thoughts groped in the drugged fragrance of the jungle. He reached out and felt human flesh, smooth and cool and living, and a girl's hand closed on his and drew him forth.

They opened his mind and shook it until the needed thing fell out. *Mona* was there but wrong. They shook harder and found Natalie:

New San Francisco, Mars, a scoured-sky day under the Great Equatorial Dome. Down time between Outbounds. The sidewalk table had a view towards Tharsis. Olympus Mons wore a diaphanous veil of cloud, but Michael looked away to watch Natalie approach in her little round glasses, the black lenses blanking her eyes.

"Of all the gin joints in all the worlds you had to pick mine," he said; Michael was obsessed with ancient movies.

She removed her glasses and squinted at him.

"What?"

"Old movie reference. Two people with a past meet unexpectedly in a foreign city."

"But we don't have a past. And this was planned, though I guess you could call it unexpected."

"I have a feeling we're about to."

"About to what?"

"Make a past out of this present."

She sat down.

"You're a strange man, and I don't mean the gills. Also, this isn't a foreign city. What are you drinking?"

"Red Rust Ale."

"Philistine. Order me a chardonnay."

He did, and the waiter brought it in a large stem glass.

"I bet this is the part you like best," she said.

"Yes?"

"The flirting, the newness, the excitement. Especially because we aren't supposed to fraternize."

"There are good reasons for that non-fraternization rule," he said, smiling.

She sipped her wine. He watched her, thinking: she's right. And also thinking, less honestly: it doesn't mean anything to her, not really. And hating himself a little, but still wanting her even though he knew in a while he wouldn't be able to tolerate her closeness. That's how it always worked with him. Automatic protective instinct; caring was just another word for grieving. But Natalie was a peer, not his usual adventure. An instinct he couldn't identify informed him he was in a very dangerous place. He ignored it and had another beer while Natalie finished her glass of wine.

"Did you say you had a room around here someplace?" she said.

He put his bottle down. "I may have said that, yes."

The narcotic jungle exhaled. Michael, sprawled on the moss-covered, softly decaying corpse of a fallen tree, drifted in and out of awareness. He saw things that weren't there, or perhaps were there but other than what they appeared to be. Insects like animated beans trundled over his face, his neck, the backs of his hands. He was sweating inside his flight suit. Something spoke in wooden gutturals, incomprehensible. The sounds gradually resolved into understandable English.

"Kiss me?"

Michael blinked. He sat up. The steaming jungle was gone. He was sitting in an upholstered hotel chair and a woman was kneeling beside him. He recognized the room. The woman looked at him with large shiny amber eyes. The planes of her cheeks were too angular, too smooth.

Michael worked his mouth. His tongue felt dry and dead as a piece of cracked leather.

"I don't know you," he said.

Her mouth turned down stiffly and she rocked back and seemed to blend into the wall, which was patterned to resemble a dense green tangle of vine.

Michael closed his eyes.

Time passed like a muddy dream, and there were others.

They all called themselves Natalie. One liked to take walks with him in the rain, like that girl he had known in college. Michael, watching from his bedroom window, wasn't surprised to see it out there with it's umbrella. His breath fogged the faux leaded glass, and the tricky molecular structure of the pane, dialed wide to semi-permeable, seemed to breathe back into his face. Internal realities overlapped. This wasn't New San Francisco or even old San Francisco on Earth. It was his lost home in upstate New York (as a child Michael used to play with the window, throwing snowballs from the front yard, delighting in how they strained through onto the sill inside his room. His mother had been something other than delighted, though).

Michael, staring at the thing waiting for him down there, pulled at his bottom lip. He clenched his right fist until it shook, resisting. But eventually he surrendered and turned away from the window. On the stairs reality lost focus. The walls became spongy and mottled, like the skin of a mushroom. The stairs were made of the same stuff. His boots sank into them and he stumbled downward and out into the light of the foyer. *That was wrong*, he thought, and looking back he saw an organic orifice, like a soft wound, and then it was simply a stairwell climbing upwards, with framed photographs of his family hung at staggered intervals. Dead people.

He opened the front door to the sound of rain rattling through maple leaves. College days, the street outside his dorm, and his first girl. Only this wasn't a girl, the thing that called itself Natalie.

Michael stood a minute on the porch. The *wrong* porch. Inside had been the familiar rooms of his boyhood home (mushroom skin notwithstanding), long gone to fire and sorrow. *This* porch belonged to his dorm at the University of Washington. After a while he stepped down to the sidewalk and the Natalie-thing smiled.

"Would you like to take a walk with me?" it asked.

"Not really."

He held the umbrella over both of them. Rain pattered on the taut fabric. The Natalie-thing slipped its arm under his. It was wearing a sweater and a wool skirt and black shoes that clocked on the sidewalk. Its hair was very dark red and its cheeks were rosy with the cold. When it glanced up at him it presented eyes as black and lusterless as a shark's. Still wrong. And anyway, nothing like Natalie *or* his college girl.

"Want to see a movie?" it asked.

"All right."

They held hands in the dark. He felt comfortable. The theater smelled of hot popcorn and the damp wool of the Natalie-thing's skirt. He used to escape to the movies, where he could turn his mind off and be lost in the Deep Enhancement Cinema. Movies provided an imperfect respite from the memories ceaselessly rising out of the ashy ruin of his home.

The screen dimmed and brightened and incomprehensible sounds, like crowd noises muffled in cotton, issued from unseen speakers that seemed to communicate directly into his head. They—the ones like this Natalie beside him—hadn't fully comprehended the idea of a movie.

It squeezed his hand.

"This is good," it said.

"Pretty good," he replied.

The theater was empty except for them. Empty of human forms, anyway. Irregular shadows cropped up randomly, like shapes in a night jungle. Then one of the shapes two rows in front of Michael turned around and leaned over the back of the seat, and Michael saw it was a woman, a real woman, dressed as he was, in a flight suit. She was wearing a breathing mask.

The woman began to speak but he couldn't understand her. He leaned forward.

"What, what did you say?"

The thing beside him tightened its grip, so tight the fingers of his right hand ached in its grasp, the small bones grinding in their sleeves of flesh. He tried to stand but it held him down and squeezed harder and harder until his entire awareness was occupied by the pain.

Several of the jungle shapes interposed themselves between Michael and the woman who had spoken to him. The air became clogged, humid, stifling. Rain began to fall inside the theater. He struggled to pull free. The numbing pain traveled up his arm. The theater seat held him, shifted around him. Knobby protuberances poked and dug into him, like sitting in a tangle of roots. He couldn't breath.

Then it stopped.

He sat in a movie theater with a young mahogany-haired woman, who held his hand sweetly in the dark. She leaned over and whispered, "You fell asleep!" Her warm breath touched his ear.

"I did?" He sat up, groggy.

"Yes, darling."

He blinked at the screen, where dim pulses of light moved in meaningless patterns. That was *so* wrong.

The one that liked to make love pulled him to his feet in the hotel room and kissed him roughly. He tried to push it away but it was too strong. After a while it held him at arm's length and said something he couldn't understand. The jungle effluvium infiltrated his brain, and he saw a woman he used to know, or a rudimentary version of her. The eyes were still wrong—plugs of dull amber. Michael staggered back, caught his heel on the carpet, and fell. His lips were bruised, sticky and sweet with sap.

It stalked over and stood above him.

"Mike, we have to get out of here."

This new voice didn't belong to the thing straddling his legs.

Michael craned his head around. A women stood in a flight suit similar to his own. She was there and then she wasn't there, as the scenery shifted around him, from his old bedroom on Earth to the hotel room on Mars.

"Natalie—?" he said.

The one that liked to make love lowered itself on top of him. Michael tried to roll away but couldn't. It mounted him and he screamed.

That time in New San Francisco, in the mock Victorian hotel room, in the bed of clean linen sheets, the following morning, when Natalie woke early and started to get out of bed, he had reached out and touched her naked hip and said, "Stay." A costly word.

He was alone again, half asleep in and out of dream. Then something was shaking him.

"Mike, come *on*. There isn't time. They'll be back."

He struggled against this new assault. Something wrestling with him, pinning him down on the bed with its knobby knees. Then a mask fitted over his mouth and nose, and a clean wind blew into his lungs, filling him, clearing his head. He opened his eyes, closed them, opened them wide.

"Hello, Nat," he said, his voice muffled through the breathing mask

She flipped the little mahogany curl of hair out of her eye.

"Hello yourself, you idiot," Natalie said.

"How'd you get here?" he asked, meaning how did she get into his hotel room. But even as he asked the question the last vestiges of the illusion blew away in the fresh revivifying oxygen.

A pink puzzle piece sky shone above the jungle canopy.

Twisted trees crowded them, shaggy with moss, hung with thick vines braided like chains.

"I dropped in, just like you," Natalie said.

Michael looked around "I have a feeling we're not on Mars, Dorothy."

"Who's Dorothy?"

Something hulking, hunched and redolent of mold and jungle rot came shambling towards them.

"Nat, look out!"

She turned swiftly, yanking a blaster from her utility belt. Reality stuttered. As if in a fading memory he saw the tree-thing knock the weapon from Natalie's hand. At the same moment, superimposed, he saw her fire. A bright red flash of plasma energy seared into the thing. It lurched back, yowling, punky smoke flowing from the fresh wound.

Nat grabbed Michael's hand and pulled him up. He felt dizzy and weak, still drugged.

"What are you doing?" he said.

"Rescuing your ass." She gave him a little push. "That way to the ship."

"No," he said, pointing, "it's *that* way."

"*My* ship is this way. Your ship sank."

He scrambled drunkenly ahead of her, stumbling over roots, getting hung up in vines. Though the illusions were displaced he could still hear the Siren wail in his mind and had to fight an impulse to rip the mask from his face. There was movement all around them. More of the things shambled out of the shadows. Natalie blasted away with her weapon, clearing a path.

They broke into the open. The ship gleamed in weak sunlight.

"Get in! I'll hold them off."

Michael clambered up the ladder to the cockpit. At the top of the ladder he turned and saw Natalie about to be overwhelmed.

"Nat, come on!"

She dropped her depleted blaster, swung onto the ladder—but it was too late. They had her.

Michael slumped in his theater seat, withdrawn from the Deep Enhancement movie experience he had created. Warm rain fell out of the darkness. The One Who Liked Rain sat beside him with a bowl of soggy popcorn.

It turned to him.

"That was so good, Mike."

Its lips glistened with butter. Its eyes were dull amber wads. A breathing mask with a torn strap dangled from it's fingers.

Michael groaned.

Like an insect buzz in his ear: *Michael wake up, for God's sake.*

Michael closed his eyes.

On Mars Natalie had said, "I think I'm falling in love with you," and his defenses had rattled down like iron gates.

"Mike?"

"Not a good idea. In the first place we'll both soon be Outbound. It might be years before we see each other again. In the second place, my modifications inhibit my ability to achieve human intimacy. I'm a lost cause, Nat."

Natalie shook her head. "You don't have to drag out your excuses. I know you. I'm just saying how I feel, not asking for anything. And by the way, your mods have nothing to do with intimacy. I've known plenty of Womb Hole pilots and I don't buy the myth that you're all emotional cripples."

Michael smiled. He hadn't been thinking about the mods he'd volunteered to undergo, the ones necessary for Ship State, the ones that at least allowed him a semblance of intimacy, even if it was with a machine consciousness. He had meant the more visceral mods of his psyche, where blackened timbers had risen like pickets in Hell to form the first rudimentary fence around his heart.

"You don't really know me," he said.

"Not at this rate, I don't.

Then the biological crisis on Meropa IV occurred. Vital vaccines needed. Michael's Ship Tender came up with Kobory Fever, and Natalie, loose on Mars, got the duty. Like some kind of Fate. Michael experienced a burst of pure joy—which he quickly stomped on.

"I don't see why I had to die," Natalie said. Was she the real Natalie?

He was back in the hotel, lying flat on the bed. Natalie, having fitted another breathing mask to his face, sat in a chair near the window. Except it appeared she wasn't sitting in a chair at all, but on a tangle of thick roots growing out of the floor. He had just told her about the movie.

"You were *saving* me," he said.

"I'm saving you *now*," she said. "Or trying to. You've got to get off your ass and participate."

Michael felt heavy.

"And in this version I don't die," Natalie said.

She led him out of the hotel room, which quickly became something other than an hotel room. As his head cleared the vine-tangle wallpaper popped out in three dimensions, the floor became soft, spongy. The light shifted to heavily screened pink/green. Flying insects buzzed his sweaty face. A locus of pain began rhythmically stabbing behind his right eye.

"The atmosphere is drugged with hallucinogenic vapors from the plants," Natalie said. "They want you here, but they don't want you to know where 'here' is."

"Who wants me?"

"They. The jungle. The sentient life on this planet. It's gynoecious, by the way, and it's been sweeping open space, seeking first contact. They detected you and *Mona* and evidently became entranced by the possibilities of companion male energy. Frankly, they have a point."

"Where the hell do you get all *that?*"

"I asked. Or Mona did, actually. She's been frantically investigating language possibilities since you disappeared. They communicate telepathically."

Natalie led him through a sort of tunnel made from over-arching branches. They had to duck their heads.

"Wait." He grabbed her arm. She turned, a curl of dark red hair flipping over her eye. "Did you bring a weapon?"

"Of course," she said.

"Well, where is it?"

"They sort of disarmed me."

"I see."

"Don't worry. We're getting out of here. As long as you're not breathing the air they can't mess you up too much. I think they'll let us leave. I have a theory. Now let's keep moving. It isn't far to the ship."

They emerged from the tunnel. The ship was there, but they were cut off from it by a wall of the tree-things, the crooked things with hungry amber eyes. They encircled the ship, knobby limbs entwined to form a barrier.

"You were saying?" Michael said, straightening his back. "Anyway, have *Mona* fly the ship over."

"I can't. *Mona* was hinky about landing after your Drop Ship sank. Also, I think *they* got into her head and spooked her. I had to engage the emergency override, same as you did."

"Wonderful."

"At least the security repulsion field is keeping them away from the ship."

"At least."

Hands on her hips, Natalie appraised the situation. After a minute she touched the com button on her wrist and spoke into it.

"Mona, we need help. Send the Proxy to clear a path."

The aft hatch swung up and the Proxy appeared. It climbed down and disappeared behind the tree-things. A moment later the circle tightened. There was a the flash and pop of a blaster discharge. One of the tree things erupted in flame. It stumped out of the ring and stood apart, burning. The others closed in. A violent disturbance occurred. There were no further blasts. The Proxy's torso arced high over the line, dull metal skin shining. It clanked once when it hit the ground. The line resumed it's stillness.

"It's a female jungle, all right," Michael said. "Care to reveal your famous theory?"

Natalie held his hand. "We're walking through," she said.

"Just like that."

"Yes. If we're together they'll let us. I mean really together."

"That's your theory?"

"Basically. Mike, trust me."

They started walking. When they came to the Proxy's torso, Michael held her back.

"I'll go through alone," he said. "If I make it to the ship I'll lift off and pick you up in the clear."

He tried to pull his hand free but she wouldn't let go.

"No," she said.

"Nat—"

"No. Don't you see? If you go alone they'll take you again. If I go alone they'll rip me apart like the Proxy."

"And if we go together?"

"If we go together they . . . will see."

"See *what*?"

"That you aren't solo, that somebody else is already claiming your male companion energy, another of your own species. Unlike Mona, whom they felt justified in severing you from. They *know* I'm imprinted in your psyche. You said yourself they always used my name. You just have to stop fighting us."

Michael scratched his cheek, which was whiskered after a few days in the sentient jungle. Natalie squeezed his hand.

"Mike?"

"No."

"We have to move."

"It's too risky."

"Come on. It's now or never."

He felt himself collapsing inside, and then the old detachment. The cold, necessary detachment. She saw it in his eyes and let go of his hand.

"I'll go through myself, then," she said, and started walking forward.

He grabbed her arm.

"You just said they'd tear you apart."

"I'm already torn apart," she said.

"Don't, Nat. Let's think about this."

"Just let me go, okay? You don't want me. I get it."

He held on. "There has to be another way to the ship."

She pulled loose.

"I might get through. Wish me luck."

"Nat—"

A cringing, huddled piece of him behind the cold wall stood up, trembling.

Natalie again started for the picket line of tree-things, walking quickly, leaving Michael standing where he was.

The tree-things reacted, reaching for her.

Michael got to her first and pulled her back into his arms. "*Damn* it," he said. "Damn it, damn it, damn it."

They lifted out of the jungle, accelerating until they achieved orbit. He sat tandem behind Natalie in the narrow cockpit of the Drop Ship.

"You really like to force the issue," he said.

"Do I?"

"I'm not saying it's a bad idea."

"No."

"I mean, a little push doesn't hurt."

"Hmm."

A few minutes later they acquired the starship and Natalie resumed manual operation and began docking maneuvers. She worked the controls very competently. Michael watched over her shoulder. But his gaze returned again and again to rest upon the nape of her neck, where a few silken hairs escaped and lay sweetly over her skin.

"The Dorothy thing," he said, "that was another old movie reference. A child is swept away from family and friends and finds herself estranged in a hostile world."

"How does she get back home?"

"She discovers a way to trust companions who initially frighten her."

"I like that one."

"It works for me."

Natalie tucked them neatly into *Mona's* docking bay.

Nancy Kress is the author of thirty-three books, including twenty-six novels, four collections of short stories, and three books on writing. Her work has won six Nebulas, two Hugos, a Sturgeon, and the John W. Campbell Memorial Award. Her most recent work is *Tomorrow's Kin* (Tor, 2017) which, like much of her work, concerns genetic engineering. Kress's fiction has been translated into Swedish, Danish, French, Italian, German, Spanish, Polish, Croatian, Chinese, Lithuanian, Romanian, Japanese, Korean, Hebrew, Russian, and Klingon, none of which she can read. In addition to writing, Kress often teaches at various venues around the country and abroad, including a visiting lectureship at the University of Leipzig and a recent writing class in Beijing. Kress lives in Seattle with her husband, writer Jack Skillingstead, and Cosette, the world's most spoiled toy poodle.

SHIVA IN SHADOW

NANCY KRESS

1. Ship

I watched the probe launch from the *Kepler*'s top-deck observatory, where the entire Schaad hull is clear to the stars. I stood between Ajit and Kane. The observatory, which is also the ship's garden, bloomed wildly with my exotics, bursting into flower in such exuberant profusion that even to see the probe go, we had to squeeze between a seven-foot-high bed of comoralias and the hull.

"God, Tirzah, can't you prune these things?" Kane said. He pressed his nose to the nearly invisible hull, like a small child. Something streaked briefly across the sky. "There it goes. Not that there's much to see.

I turned to stare at him. Not much to see! Beyond the *Kepler* lay the most violent and dramatic part of the galaxy, in all its murderous glory. True, the *Kepler* had stopped one hundred light-years from the core, for human safety, and dust-and-gas clouds muffled the view somewhat. But, on the other hand, we were far enough away for a panoramic view.

The supermassive black hole Sagittarius A*, the lethal heart of the galaxy, shone gauzily with the heated gases it was sucking downward into oblivion. Around Sag A* circled Sagittarius West, a three-armed spiral of hot plasma ten light-years across, radiating furiously as it cooled. Around *that*, Sagittarius East, a huge shell left over from some catastrophic explosion within the last hundred thousand years, expanded outward. I saw thousands of stars, including the blazing blue-hot stars of IRS 16, hovering dangerously close to the hole, and giving off a stellar wind fierce enough to blow a long fiery tail off the nearby red giant star. Everything was racing, radiating, colliding, ripping apart, screaming across the entire electromagnetic spectrum. All set against the sweet, light scent of my brief-lived flowers.

Nothing going on. But Kane had never been interested in spectacle.

Ajit said in his musical accent, "No, not much to see. But much to pray for. There go *we*."

Kane snapped, "I don't pray."

"I did not mean 'pray' in the religious sense," Ajit said calmly. He is always calm. "I mean hope. It is a miraculous thing, yes? There go we."

He was right, of course. The probe contained the Ajit-analogue, the Kane-analogue, the Tirzah-analogue, all uploaded into a crystal computer no bigger than a comoralia bloom. "We" would go into that stellar violence at the core, where our fragile human bodies could not go. "We" would observe, and measure, and try to find answers to scientific questions in that roiling heart of galactic spacetime. Ninety percent of the probe's mass was shielding for the computer. Ninety percent of the rest was shielding for the three minicapsules that the probe would fire back to us with recorded and analyzed data. There was no way besides the minicaps to get information out of that bath of frenzied radiation.

Just as there was no way to know exactly what questions Ajit and Kane would need to ask until they were close to Sag A*. The analogues would know. They knew everything Ajit and Kane and I knew, right up until the moment we were uploaded.

"Shiva, dancing," Ajit said.

"What?" Kane said.

"Nothing. You would not appreciate the reference. Come with me, Tirzah. I want to show you something."

I stopped straining to see the probe, unzoomed my eyes, and smiled at Ajit. "Of course."

This is why I am here.

Ajit's skin is softer than Kane's, less muscled. Kane works out every day in ship's gym, scowling like a demon. Ajit rolled off me and laid his hand on my glowing, satisfied crotch.

"You are so beautiful, Tirzah."

I laughed. "We are all beautiful. Why would anyone effect a genetic alteration that wasn't?"

"People will do strange things sometimes."

"So I just noticed," I teased him.

"Sometimes I think so much of what Kane and I do is strange to you. I see you sitting at the table, listening to us, and I know you cannot follow our physics. It makes me sad for you."

I laid my hand on top of his, pushing down my irritation with the skill of long practice. It does irritate me, this calm sensitivity of Ajit's. It's lovely in bed—he is gentler and more considerate, always, than Kane—but then there comes the other side, this faint condescension. *I feel sad for you.* Sad for me! Because I'm not also a scientist! I am the captain of this expedition, with master status in ship control and a first-class license as a Nurturer. On the *Kepler*, my word is law, with virtually no limits. I have over fifty standard-years' experience, specializing in the nurture of scientists. I have never lost an expedition, and I need no one's pity.

Naturally, I showed none of this to Ajit. I massaged his hand with mine, which meant that his hand massaged my crotch, and purred softly. "I'm glad you decided to show me this."

"Actually, that is not what I wanted to show you."

"No?"

"No. Wait here, Tirzah."

He got up and padded, naked, to his personal locker. Beautiful, beautiful body, brown and smooth, like a slim polished tree. I could see him clearly; Ajit always makes love with the bunk lights on full, as if in sunlight. We lay in his bunk, not mine. I never take either him or Kane to my bunk. My bunk contained various concealed items that they don't, and won't, know about, from duplicate surveillance equipment to rarely used subdermal trackers. Precautions, only. I am a captain.

From his small storage locker, Ajit pulled a statue and turned shyly, even proudly, to show it to me. I sat up, surprised.

The statue was big, big enough so that it must have taken up practically his entire allotment of personal space. Heavy, too, from the way Ajit balanced it before his naked body. It was some sort of god with four arms, enclosed in a circle of flames, made of what looked like very old bronze.

"This is Nataraja," Ajit said. "Shiva dancing."

"Ajit—"

"No, I am not a god worshipper," he smiled. "You know me better than that, Tirzah. Hinduism has many gods—thousands—but they are, except to the ignorant, no more than embodiments of different aspects of reality. Shiva is the dance of creation and destruction, the constant flow of energy in the cosmos. Birth and death and rebirth. It seemed fitting to bring him to the galactic core, where so much goes on of all three."

This explanation sounded weak to me—a holo of Shiva would have accomplished the same thing, without using up nearly all of Ajit's weight allotment. Before I could say this, Ajit said, "This statue has been in my family for four hundred years. I must bring it home, along with the answers to my scientific questions."

I don't understand Ajit's scientific concerns very well—or Kane's—but I know down to my bones how much they matter to him. It is my job to know. Ajit carries within his beautiful body a terrible coursing ambition, a river fed by the longings of a poor family who have sacrificed what little they had gained on New Bombay for this favored son. Ajit is the receptacle into which they have poured so much hope, so much sacrifice, so much selfishness. The strain on that vessel is what makes Ajit's lovemaking so gentle. He cannot afford to crack.

"You'll bring the Shiva statue back to New Bombay," I said softly, "and your answers, too."

In his hands, with the bright lighting, the bronze statue cast a dancing shadow on his naked body.

I found Kane at his terminal, so deep in thought that he didn't know I was there until I squeezed his shoulder. Then he jumped, cursed, and dragged his eyes from his displays.

"How does it progress, Kane?"

"It doesn't. How could it? I need more data!"

"It will come. Be patient," I said.

He rubbed his left ear, a constant habit when he's irritated, which is much of the time. When he's happily excited, Kane runs his left hand through his coarse red hair until it stands up like flames. Now he smiled ruefully. "I'm not much known for patience."

"No, you're not."

"But you're right, Tirzah. The data will come. It's just hard waiting for the first minicap. I wish to hell we could have more than three. Goddamn cheap bureaucrats! At an acceleration of—"

"Don't give me the figures again," I said. I wound my fingers in his hair and pulled playfully. "Kane, I came to ask you a favor."

"All right," he said instantly. Kane never counts costs ahead of time. Ajit would have turned gently cautious. "What is it?"

"I want you to learn to play go with Ajit."

He scowled. "Why?"

With Kane, you must have your logic ready. He would do any favor I asked, but unless he can see why, compliance would be grudging at best. "First, because go will help you pass the time until the first minicap arrives, in doing something other than chewing the same data over and over again until you've masticated it into tastlessness. Second, because the game is complex enough that I think you'll enjoy it. Third, because I'm not too bad at it myself but Ajit is better, and I think you will be, too, so I can learn from both of you."

And fourth, I didn't say aloud, because Ajit is a master, he will beat you most of the time, and he needs the boost in confidence.

Ajit is not the scientist that Kane is. Practically no one in the settled worlds is the scientist that Kane is. All three of us know this, but none of us have ever mentioned it, not even once. There are geniuses who are easy for the inferior to work with, who are generous enough to slow down their mental strides to the smaller steps of the merely gifted. Kane is not one of them.

"Go," Kane says thoughtfully. "I have friends who play that."

This was a misstatement. Kane does not have friends, in the usual sense. He has colleagues, he has science, and he has me.

He smiled at me, a rare touch of sweet gratitude on his handsome face. "Thanks, Tirzah. I'll play with Ajit. You're right, it *will* pass the time until the probe sends back the prelim data. And if I'm occupied, maybe I'll be less of a monster to you."

"You're fine to me," I say, giving his hair another tug, grinning with the casual flippancy he prefers. "Or if you're not, I don't care."

Kane laughs. In moments like this, I am especially careful that my own feelings don't show. To either of them.

2. PROBE

We automatically woke after the hyperjump. For reasons I don't understand, a hyperjump isn't instantaneous, perhaps because it's not really a "jump" but a Calabi-Yau dimension tunnel. Several days' ship-time had passed, and the probe now drifted less than five light-years from the galactic core. The probe, power off, checked out perfectly; the shielding had held even better than expected. And so had we. My eyes widened as I studied the wardroom displays.

On the *Kepler*, dust clouds had softened and obscured the view. Here, nothing did. We drifted just outside a star that had begun its deadly spiral inward toward Sag A*. Visuals showed the full deadly glory around the hole: the hot blue cluster of IRS16. The giant red star IRS7 with its long tail distended by stellar winds. The stars already past the point of no return, pulled by the gravity of Sag A* inexorably toward its event horizon. The radio, gamma-ray, and infrared displays revealed even more, brilliant with the radiation pouring from every single gorgeous, lethal object in the bright sky.

And there, too, shone one of the mysteries Kane and Ajit had come to study: the massive young stars that were not being yanked toward Sag A*, and which in this place should have been neither massive nor relatively stable. Such stars should not exist this close to the hole. One star, Kane had told me, was as close to the hole as twice Pluto's orbit from Sol. How had it gotten there?

"It's beautiful, in a hellish way," I said to Ajit and Kane. "I want to go up to the observatory and see it direct."

"The observatory!" Kane said scornfully. "I need to get to work!" He sat down at his terminal.

None of this is true, of course. There is no observatory on the probe, and I can't climb the ladder "up" to it. Nor is there a wardroom with terminals, chairs, table, displays, a computer. We *are* the computer, or rather we are inside it. But the programs running along with us make it all seem as real as the fleshy versions of ourselves on the *Kepler*. This, it was determined by previous disastrous experience in space exploration, is necessary to keep us sane and stable. Human uploads need this illusion, this shadow reality, and we accept it easily. Why not? It's the default setting for our minds.

So Kane "sat" "at" his "terminal" to look at the preliminary data from the sensors. So did Ajit, and I "went" "upstairs" to the observatory, where I gazed outward for a long time.

I—the other "I," the one on the *Kepler*—grew up on a station in the Oort Cloud, Sol System. Space is my natural home. I don't really understand how mud-dwellers live on planets, or why they would want to, at the bottom of a murky and dirty shroud of uncontrollable air. I have learned to simulate understanding planetary love, because it is my job. Both Kane and Ajit come from rocks, Ajit from New Bombay, and Kane from Terra herself. They are space scientists, but not real spacers.

No mud-dweller ever really sees the stars. And no human being had ever seen what I saw now, the frantic heart of the human universe.

Eventually I went back downstairs, rechecked ship's data, and then sat at the wardroom table and took up my embroidery. The ancient, irrelevant cloth-ornamenting is very soothing, almost as much so as gardening, although of course that's not why I do it. All first-class Nurturers practice some humble handicraft. It allows you to closely observe people while appearing absorbed and harmless.

Kane, of course, was oblivious to me. I could have glared at him through a magnifying glass and he wouldn't have noticed, not if he was working. Back on the *Kepler*, he had explained in simple terms—or at least as simple as Kane's explanations ever get—why there should not be any young stars this close to the core, as well as three possible explanations for why there are. He told me all this, in typical Kane fashion, in bed. Postcoital intimacy.

"The stars' spectra show they're young, Tirzah. And *close*—SO-2 comes to within eighty AU's of Sag A*! It's *wrong*—the core is incredibly inhospitable to star formation! Also, these close-in stars have very peculiar orbits."

"You're taking it personally," I observed, smiling.

"Of course I am!" This was said totally without irony. "Those young stars have no business there. The tidal forces of the hole should rip any hot dust clouds to shreds long before any stars could form. And if they formed farther out, say one hundred light-years out, they should have died before they got this close in. These supermassive stars only last a few million years."

"But there they are."

"Yes. Why do you still have this lacy thing on? It's irritating."

"Because you were so eager that I didn't have time to get it off."

"Well, take it off now."

I did, and he wrapped my body close to his, and went on fretting over star formation in the core.

"There are three theories. One is that a dust cloud ringing the core, about six light-years out, keeps forming stars, which are then blown outwards again by galactic winds, and then drawn in, and repeat. Another theory is that there's a second, intermediate medium-sized black hole orbiting Sag A* and exerting a counterpull on the stars. But if so, why aren't we detecting its radio waves? Another idea is that the stars aren't really young at all, they're composites of remnants of elderly stars that merged to form a body that only looks bright and young."

I said, "Which theory do you like?"

"None of them." And then, in one of those lightning changes he was capable of, he focused all his attention on me. "Are you all right, Tirzah? I know this has got to be a boring voyage for you. Running ship can't take much of your time, and neither can baby-sitting me."

I laughed aloud and Kane, having no idea why, frowned slightly. It was such a typically Kane speech. A sudden burst of intense concern, which would prove equally transitory. No mention of Ajit at all, as if only Kane existed for me. And his total ignorance of how often I interceded between him and Ajit, smoothed over tensions between them, spent time calming and centering separately each of these men who were more like the stars outside the ship than either of them were capable of recognizing. Brilliant, heated, intense, inherently unstable.

"I'm fine, Kane. I'm enjoying myself."

"Well, good," he said, and I saw that he then forgot me, back to brooding about his theories.

Neither Kane nor Ajit knows that I love Kane. I don't love Ajit. Whatever calls up love in our hidden hearts, it is unfathomable. Kane arouses in me a happiness, a desire, a completeness that puts a glow on the world because he—difficult, questing, vital—is in it. Ajit, through no fault of his own, does not.

Neither of them will ever know this. I would berate myself if they did. My personal feelings don't matter here. I am a captain.

"Damn and double damn!" Kane said, admiringly. "Look at that!"

Ajit reacted as if Kane had spoken to him, but of course Kane had not. He was just thinking aloud. I put down my embroidery and went to stand behind them at their terminals.

Ajit said, "Those readings must be wrong. The sensors were damaged after all, either in hypertransit or by radiation."

Kane didn't reply; I doubt he'd heard. I said, "What is it?"

It was Ajit who answered. "The mass readings are wrong. They're showing high mass density for several areas of empty space."

I said, "Maybe that's where the new young stars are forming?"

Not even Ajit answered this, which told me it was a stupid statement. It doesn't matter; I don't pretend to be a scientist. I merely wanted to keep them talking, to gauge their states of mind.

Ajit said, "It would be remarkable if all equipment had emerged undamaged from the jump into this radiation."

"Kane?" I said.

"It's not the equipment," he muttered. So he had been listening, at least peripherally. "Supersymmetry."

Ajit immediately objected to this, in terms I didn't understand. They were off into a discussion I had no chance of following. I let it go on for a while, then even longer, since it sounded the way scientific discussions are supposed to sound: intense but not acrimonious, not personal.

When they wound down a bit, I said, "Did the minicapsule go off to the *Kepler?* They're waiting for the prelim data, and the minicap takes days to jump. Did either of you remember to record and send?"

They both looked at me, as if trying to remember who I was and what I was doing there. In that moment, for the first time, they looked alike.

"I remembered," Ajit said. "The prelim data went off to the *Kepler.* Kane—"
They were off again.

3. Ship

The go games were not a success.

The problem, I could see, was with Ajit. He was a far better player than Kane, both intuitively and through experience. This didn't bother Kane at all; he thrived on challenge. But his own clear superiority subtly affected Ajit.

"Game won," he said for the third time in the evening, and at the slight smirk in his voice I looked up from my embroidery.

"Damn and double damn," Kane said, without rancor. "Set them up again."

"No, I think I will go celebrate my victories with Tirzah."

This was Kane's night, but the two of them had never insisted on precedence. This was because I had never let it come to that; it's part of my job to give the illusion that I am always available to both, on whatever occasion they wish. Of course, I control, through a hundred subtle signals and without either realizing it, which occasions they happen to wish. Where I make love depends on whom I need to observe. This direct claim by Ajit, connecting me to his go victories, was new.

Kane, of course, didn't notice. "All right. God, I wish the minicap would come. I want that data!"

Now that the game had released his attention, he was restless again. He rose and paced around the wardroom, which doesn't admit too much pacing. "I think I'll go up to the observatory. Anybody coming?"

He had already forgotten that I was leaving with Ajit. I saw Ajit go still. Such a small thing—Ajit was affronted that Kane was not affected by Ajit's game victory, or by his bearing me off like some earned prize. Another man would have felt a moment of pique and then forgotten it. Ajit was not another man. Neither was Kane. Stable men don't volunteer for missions like this.

It's different for me; I was bred to space. The scientists were not.

I put down my embroidery, took Ajit's hand, and snuggled close to him. Kane, for the moment, was fine. His restless desire for his data wouldn't do him any harm. It was Ajit I needed to work with.

I was the one who had suggested the go games. Good captains are not supposed to make mistakes like that. It was up to me to set things right.

By the time the minicap arrived, everything was worse.

They would not, either of them, stop the go games. They played obsessively, six or seven times a day, then nine or ten, and finally every waking minute. Ajit continued to win the large majority of the games, but not all of them. Kane focused his formidable intelligence on devising strategies, and he had the advantage of caring but not too much. Yes, he was obsessed, but I could see that once he had something more significant to do, he would leave the go games without a backward glance.

Ajit grew more focused, too. Even more intent on winning, even as he began to lose a few games. More slyly gleeful when he did win. He flicked his winning piece onto the board with a turn of the wrist in which I read both contempt and fear.

I tried everything I could to intervene, every trick from a century of experience. Nothing worked. Sex only made it worse. Ajit regarded sex as an earned prize, Kane as a temporary refreshment so he could return to the games.

One night Ajit brought out the statue of Shiva and put it defiantly on the wardroom table. It took up two-thirds of the space, a wide metal circle enclosing the four-armed dancer.

"What's that?" Kane said, looking up from the game board. "Oh, God, it's a god."

I said quickly, "It's an intellectual concept. The flow of cosmic energy in the universe."

Kane laughed, not maliciously, but I saw Ajit's eyes light up. Ajit said, "I want it here."

Kane shrugged. "Fine by me. Your turn, Ajit."

Wrong, *wrong*. Ajit had hoped to disturb Kane, to push him into some open objection to the statue. Ajit wanted a small confrontation, some outlet to emphasize his gloating. Some outlet for his growing unease as Kane's game improved. And some outlet for his underlying rage, always just under the surface, at Kane, the better scientist. The statue was supposed to be an assertion, even a slap in the face: I *am here and I take up a lot of your space. Notice that!*

Instead, Kane had shrugged and dismissed it.

I said, "Tell me again, Ajit, about Nataraja. What's the significance of the flames on the great circle?"

Ajit said quietly, "They represent the fire that destroys the world."

Kane said, "Your *turn*, Ajit."

Such a small incident. But deep in my mind, where I was aware of it but not yet overtly affected, fear stirred.

I was losing control here.

Then the first minicap of data arrived.

4. PROBE

Mind uploads are still minds. They are not computer programs in the sense that other programs are. Although freed of biological constraints such as enzymes that create sleep, hunger, and lust, uploads are not free of habit. In fact, it is habit that creates enough structure to keep all of us from frenzied feedback loops. On the probe, my job was to keep habit strong. It was the best safeguard for those brilliant minds.

"Time to sleep, gentlemen," I said lightly. We had been gathered in the wardroom for sixteen hours straight, Kane and Ajit at their terminals, me sitting quietly, watching them. I have powers of concentration equal in degree, though not in kind, to their own. They do not suspect this. It has been hours since I put down my embroidery, but neither noticed.

"Tirzah, not sleep now!" Kane snapped.

"Now."

He looked up at me like a sulky child. But Kane is not a child; I don't make that mistake. He knows an upload has to shut down for the cleansing program to run, a necessity to catch operating errors before they grow large enough to impair function. With all the radiation bathing the probe, the program is more necessary than ever. It takes a few hours to run through. I control the run cues.

Ajit looked at me expectantly. It was his night. This, too, was part of habit, as well as being an actual aid to their work. More than one scientist in my care has had that critical flash of intuition on some scientific problem while in my arms. Upload sex, like its fleshy analogue, both stimulates and relaxes.

"All right, all right," Kane muttered. "Good night."

I shut him down and turned to Ajit.

We went to his bunk. Ajit was tense, stretched taut with data and with sixteen hours with Kane. But I was pleased to see how completely he responded to me. Afterward, I asked him to explain the prelim data to me.

"And keep it simple, please. Remember who you're talking to!"

"To an intelligent and sweet lady," he said, and I gave him the obligatory smile. But he saw that I really did want to know about the data.

"The massive young stars are there when they should not be . . . Kane has explained all this to you, I know."

I nodded.

"They are indeed young, not mashed-together old stars. We have verified that. We are trying now to gather and run data to examine the other two best theories: a fluctuating ring of matter spawning stars, or other black holes."

"How are you examining the theories?"

He hesitated, and I knew he was trying to find explanations I could understand. "We are running various programs, equations, and sims. We are also trying to determine where to jump the probe next—you know about that."

Of course I did. No one moves this ship without my consent. It has two more jumps left in its power pack, and I must approve them both.

"We need to choose a spot from which we can fire beams of various radiation to assess the results. The heavier beams won't last long here, you know—the gravity of the superhole distorts them." He frowned.

"What is it, Ajit? What about gravity?"

"Kane was right," he said, "the mass detectors aren't damaged. They're showing mass nearby, not large but detectable, that isn't manifesting anything but gravity. No radiation of any kind."

"A black hole," I suggested.

"Too small. Small black holes radiate away, Hawking showed that long ago. The internal temperature is too high. There are no black holes smaller than three solar masses. The mass detectors are showing something much smaller than that."

"What?"

"We don't know."

"Were all the weird mass-detector readings in the prelim data you sent back to the *Kepler?*"

"Of course," he said, a slight edge in his voice.

I pulled him closer. "I can always rely on you," I said, and I felt his body relax.

I shut us down, as we lay in each other's arms.

It was Ajit who, the next day, noticed the second anomaly. And I who noticed the third.

"These gas orbits aren't right," Ajit said to Kane. "And they're getting less right all the time."

Kane moved to Ajit's terminal. "Tell me."

"The infalling gases from the circumnuclear disk . . . see . . . they curve here, by the western arm of Sag A West . . ."

"It's wind from the IRS16 cluster," Kane said instantly. "I got updated readings for those yesterday."

"No, I already corrected for that," Ajit said.

"Then maybe magnetization from IRS7, or—"

They were off again. I followed enough to grasp the general problem. Gases streamed at enormous speeds from clouds beyond the circumnuclear disk which surrounded the entire core like a huge doughnut. These streaming gases were funneled by various forces into fairly narrow, conelike paths. The gases would eventually end up circling the black hole, spiraling inward and compressing to temperatures of billions of degrees before they were absorbed by the maw of the hole. The processes were understood.

But the paths weren't as predicted. Gases were streaming down wrong, approaching the hole wrong for predictions made from all the forces acting on them.

Ajit finally said to Kane, "I want to move the probe earlier than we planned."

"Wait a moment," I said instantly. Ship's movements were my decision. "It's not yet the scheduled time."

"Of course I'm including you in my request, Tirzah," Ajit said, with all his usual courtesy. There was something beneath the courtesy, however, a kind of glow. I recognized it. Scientists look like that when they have the germ of an important idea.

I thought Kane would object or ridicule, but something in their technical discussion must have moved him, too. His red hair stood up all over his head. He glanced briefly at his own displays, back at Ajit's, then at the younger man. He said, "You want to put the probe on the other side of Sagittarius A West."

"Yes."

I said, "Show me."

Ajit brought up the simplified graphic he had created weeks ago for me to gain an overview of this mission. It showed the black hole at the center of the galaxy, and the major structures around it: the cluster of hot blue stars, the massive young stars that should not have existed so close to the hole, the red giant star IRS16, with its long fiery tail. All this, plus our probe, lay on one side of the huge, three-armed spiraling plasma remnant, Sagittarius A West. Ajit touched the computer and a new dot appeared on the other side of Sag A West, farther away from the hole than we were now.

"We want to go there, Tirzah," he said. Kane nodded.

I said, deliberately sounding naïve, "I thought there wasn't as much going on over there. And besides, you said that Sag A West would greatly obscure our vision in all wavelengths, with its own radiation."

"It will."

"Then—"

"There's something going on over there now," Kane said. "Ajit's right. That region is the source of whatever pull is distorting the gas infall. We need to go there."

We.

Ajit's right.

The younger man didn't change expression. But the glow was still there, ignited by Ajit's idea and fanned, I now realized, by Kane's approval. I heated it up a bit more. "But, Kane, your work on the massive young stars? I can only move the probe so many times, you know. Our fuel supply—"

"I have a lot of data on the stars now," Kane said, "and this matters more."

I hid my own pleasure. "All right. I'll move the probe."

But when I interfaced with ship's program, I found the probe had already been moved.

5. SHIP

Kane and Ajit fell on the minicap of prelim data like starving wolves. There were no more games of go. There was no more anything but work, unless I insisted.

At first I thought that was good. I thought that without the senseless, mounting competition over go, the two scientists would cooperate on the intense issues that mattered so much to both of them.

"Damn and double damn!" Kane said, admiringly. "Look at that!"

Ajit reacted as if Kane had spoken to him, but of course Kane had not. He was just thinking aloud. I put down my embroidery and went to stand behind them at their terminals.

Ajit said, with the new arrogance of the go wins in his voice, "Those readings must be wrong. The sensors were damaged after all, either in hypertransit or by radiation."

Kane, for a change, caught Ajit's tone. He met it with a sneer he must have used regularly on presumptuous postgrads. "'Must be wrong'? That's just the kind of puerile leaping to conclusions that gets people nowhere."

I said quickly, "What readings?"

It was Ajit who answered me, and although the words were innocuous, even polite, I heard the anger underlying them. "The mass readings are wrong. They're showing high mass density for several areas of empty space."

I said, "Maybe that's where the new young stars are forming?"

Not even Ajit answered this, which told me it was a stupid statement. It doesn't matter; I don't pretend to be a scientist. I merely wanted to keep them talking, to gauge their states of mind.

Ajit said, too evenly, "It would be remarkable if *all* probe equipment had emerged undamaged from the jump into core radiation."

"Kane?" I said.

"It's *not* the equipment." And then, "Supersymmetry."

Ajit immediately objected to this, in terms I didn't understand. They were off into a discussion I had no chance of following. What I could follow was the increasing pressure of Ajit's anger as Kane dismissed and belittled his ideas. I could almost see that anger, a hot plasma. As Kane ridiculed and belittled, the plasma collapsed into greater and greater density.

Abruptly they broke off their argument, went to their separate terminals, and worked like machines for twenty hours straight. I had to make them each eat something. They were obsessed, as only those seized by science or art can obsess. Neither of them would come to bed with me that night. I could have issued an executive order, but I chose not to exert that much trust-destroying force until I had to, although I did eventually announce that I was shutting down terminal access.

"For God's sake, Tirzah!" Kane snarled. "This is a once-in-a-species opportunity! I've got work to do!"

I said evenly, "You're going to rest. The terminals are down for seven hours."

"Five."

"All right." After five hours, Kane would still be snoring away.

He stood, stiff from the long hours of sitting. Kane is well over a hundred; rejuves can only do so much, so long. His cramped muscles, used to much more exercise, misfired briefly. He staggered, laughed, caught himself easily.

But not before he'd bumped the wardroom table. Ajit's statue of Shiva slid off and fell to the floor. The statue was old—four hundred years old, Ajit had said. Metal shows fatigue, too, although later than men. The statue hit the deck at just the right angle and broke.

"Oh . . . sorry, Ajit."

Kane's apology was a beat too late. I knew—with every nerve in my body, I knew this—that the delay happened because Kane's mind was still racing along his data, and it took an effort for him to refocus. It didn't matter. Ajit stiffened, and something in the nature of his anger changed, ionized by Kane's careless, preoccupied tone.

I said quickly, "Ship can weld the statue."

"No, thank you," Ajit said. "I will leave it as it is. Good night."

"Ajit—" I reached for his hand. He pulled it away.

"Good night, Tirzah."

Kane said, "The gamma-ray variations within Sag A West aren't quite what was predicted." He blinked twice. "You're right, I am exhausted."

Kane stumbled off to his bunk. Ajit had already gone. After a long while I picked up the pieces of Ajit's statue and held them, staring at the broken figure of the dancing god.

*

The preliminary data, Kane had declared when it arrived, contained enough information to keep them both busy until the second minicap arrived. But by the next day, Kane was impatiently demanding more.

"These gas orbits aren't right," he said aloud, although not to either me or Ajit. Kane did that, worked in silence for long stretches until words exploded out of him to no particular audience except his own whirling thoughts. His ear was raw with rubbing.

I said, "What's not right about them?" When he didn't answer, or probably even hear me, I repeated the question, much louder.

Kane came out of his private world and scowled at me. "The infalling gases from beyond the circumnuclear disk aren't showing the right paths to Sag A*."

I said, repeating something he'd taught me, "Could it be wind from the IRS 16 cluster?"

"No. I checked those updated readings yesterday and corrected for them."

I had reached the end of what I knew to ask. Kane burst out, "I need more data!"

"Well, it'll get here eventually."

"I want it now," he said, and laughed sourly at himself, and went back to work.

Ajit said nothing, acting as if neither of us had spoken.

I waited until Ajit stood, stretched, and looked around vaguely. Then I said, "Lunch in a minute. But first come look at something with me." Immediately I started up the ladder to the observatory, so that he either had to follow or go through the trouble of arguing. He followed.

I had put the welded statue of Shiva on the bench near clear hull. It was the wrong side of the hull for the spectacular view of the core, but the exotics didn't press so close to the hull here, and thousands of stars shone in a sky more illuminated than Sol had seen since its birth. Shiva danced in his mended circle of flames against a background of cosmic glory.

Ajit said flatly, "I told you I wanted to leave it broken."

With Kane, frank opposition is fine; he's strong enough to take it and, in fact, doesn't respect much else. But Ajit is different. I lowered my eyes and reached for his hand. "I know. I took the liberty of fixing it anyway because, well, I thought you might want to see it whole again and because I like the statue so much. It has so much meaning beyond the obvious, especially here. In this place and this time. Please forgive me."

Ajit was silent for a moment, then he raised my hand to his lips. "You do see that."

"Yes," I said, and it was the truth. Shiva, the endless dance, the endless flow of energy changing form and state—how could anyone not see it in the gas clouds forming stars, the black hole destroying them, the violence and creation outside this very hull? Yet, at the same time, it was a profound insight into the very obvious, and I kept my eyes lowered so no glimpse of my faint contempt reached Ajit.

He kissed me. "You are so spiritual, Tirzah. And so sweet-natured."

I was neither. The only deceptions Ajit could see were the paranoid ones he assumed of others.

But his body had relaxed in my arms, and I knew that some part of his mind had been reassured. He and I could see spiritual beauties that Kane could not. Therefore he was in some sense superior to Kane. He followed me back down the ladder to lunch, and I heard him hum a snatch of some jaunty tune. Pleased with myself, I made for the galley.

Kane stood up so abruptly from his terminal that his eyes glowed. "Oh, my shitting stars. Oh, yes. Tirzah, I've got it."

I stopped cold. I had never seen anyone, even Kane, look quite like that. "Got what?"

"All of it." Suddenly he seized me and swung me into exuberant, clumsy dance. "All of it! I've got all of it! The young stars, the gas orbits, the missing mass in the universe! All shitting fucking *all* of it!"

"Wwwhhhaaatttt . . ." He was whirling me around so fast that my teeth rattled. "Kane, stop!"

He did, and enveloped me in a rib-cracking hug, then abruptly released me and dragged my bruised body to his terminal. "Look, sweetheart, I've got it. Now sit right there and I'm going to explain it in terms even you can understand. You'll love it. It'll love you. Now look here, at this region of space—"

I turned briefly to look at Ajit. For Kane, he didn't even exist.

6. PROBE

The probe has moved," I said to Ajit and Kane. "It's way beyond the calculated drift. By a factor of ten."

Kane's eyes, red with work, nonetheless sharpened. "Let me see the trajectory."

"I transferred it to both your terminals." Ordinarily ship's data is kept separate, for my eyes only.

Kane brought up the display and whistled.

The probe is under the stresses, gravitational and radiational, that will eventually destroy it. We all know that. Our fleshy counterparts weren't even sure the probe would survive to send one minicap of data, and I'm sure they were jubilant when we did. Probably they treated the minicap like a holy gift, and I can easily imagine how eager they are for more. Back on the ship, I—the other "I"—had been counting on data, like oil, to grease the frictions and tensions between Ajit and Kane. I hoped it had.

We uploads had fuel enough to move the probe twice. After that, and since our last move will be no more than one-fiftieth of a light-year from the black hole at the galactic core, the probe will eventually spiral down into Sag A*. Before that, however, it will have been ripped apart by the immense tidal forces of the hole. However, long before that final death plunge, we analogues will be gone.

The probe's current drift, however, considerably farther away from the hole, was nonetheless much faster than projected. It was also slightly off course. We were being pulled in the general direction of Sag A*, but not on the gravitational trajectory that would bring us into its orbit at the time and place the computer had calculated. In fact, at our current rate of acceleration, there was a chance we'd miss the event horizon completely.

What was going on?

Kane said, "Maybe we better hold off moving the probe to the other side of Sag A West until we find out what's pulling us."

Ajit was studying the data over Kane's shoulder. He said hesitantly, "No . . . wait . . . I think we should move."

"Why?" Kane challenged.

"I don't know. I just have . . . call it an intuition. We should move now."

I held my breath. The only intuition Kane usually acknowledged was his own. But earlier things had subtly shifted. Kane had said, *"Ajit's right. That region is the source of whatever pull is distorting the gas infall."* Ajit had not changed expression, but I'd felt his pleasure, real as heat. That had given him the courage to now offer this unformed—"hairbaked" was Kane's usual term—intuition.

Kane said thoughtfully, "Maybe you're right. Maybe the—" Suddenly his eyes widened. "Oh my god."

"What?" I said, despite myself. "What?"

Kane ignored me. "Ajit—run the sims for the gas orbits in correlation with the probe drift. I'll do the young stars!"

"Why do—" Ajit began, and then he saw whatever had seized Kane's mind. Ajit said something in Hindi; it might have been a curse, or a prayer. I didn't know. Nor did I know anything about their idea, or about what was happening with the gas orbits and young stars outside the probe. However, I could see clearly what was happening within.

Ajit and Kane fell into frenzied work. They threw comments and orders to each other, transferred data, backed up sims and equation runs. They tilted their chairs toward each other and spouted incomprehensible jargon. Once Kane cried, "We need more data!" and Ajit laughed, freely and easily, then immediately plunged back into whatever he was doing. I watched them for a long time, then stole quietly up to the observation deck for a minute alone.

The show outside was more spectacular than ever, perhaps because we'd been pulled closer to it than planned. Clouds of whirling gases wrapped and oddly softened that heart of darkness, Sag A*. The fiery tail of the giant red star lit up that part of the sky. Stars glowed in a profusion unimaginable on my native Station J, stuck off in a remote arm of the galaxy. Directly in front of me glowed the glorious blue stars of the cluster IRS16.

I must have stayed on the observation deck longer than I'd planned, because Kane came looking for me. "Tirzah! Come on down! We want to show you where we're moving and why!"

We.

I said severely, gladness bursting in my heart, "You don't show me where we're going, Kane, you ask me. I captain this ship."

"Yeah, yeah, I know, you're a dragon lady. Come on!" He grabbed my hand and pulled me toward the ladder.

They both explained it, interrupting each other, fiercely correcting each other, having a wonderful time. I concentrated as hard as I could, trying to cut through the technicalities they couldn't do without, any more than they could do without air. Eventually I thought I glimpsed the core of their excitement.

"Shadow matter," I said, tasting the words on my tongue. It sounded too bizarre to take seriously, but Kane was insistent.

"The theory's been around for centuries, but deGroot pretty much discredited it in 2086," Kane said. "He—"

"If it's been discredited, then why—" I began.

"I said 'pretty much,'" Kane said. "There were always some mathematical anomalies with deGroot's work. And we can see now where he was *wrong*. He—"

Kane and Ajit started to explain why deGroot was wrong, but I interrupted. "No, don't digress so much! Let me just tell you what I think I understood from what you said."

I was silent a moment, gathering words. Both men waited impatiently, Kane running his hand through his hair, Ajit smiling widely. I said, "You said there's a theory that just after the Big Bang, gravity somehow decoupled from the other forces in the universe, just as matter decoupled from radiation. At the same time, you scientists have known for two centuries that there doesn't seem to be enough matter in the universe to make all your equations work. So scientists posited a lot of 'dark matter' and a lot of black holes, but none of the figures added up right anyway.

"And right now, neither do the orbits of the infalling gas, or the probe's drift, or the fact that massive young stars were forming that close to the black hole without being ripped apart by tidal forces. The forces acting on the huge clouds that have to condense to form stars that big."

I took a breath, quick enough so that neither had time to break in and distract me with technicalities.

"But now you think that if gravity *did* decouple right after the Big Bang—"

"About 10^{-43} seconds after," Ajit said helpfully. I ignored him.

"—then two types of matter were created, normal matter and 'shadow matter.' It's sort of like matter and antimatter, only normal matter and shadow matter can't interact except by gravity. No interaction through any other force, not radiation or strong or weak forces. Only gravity. That's the only effect shadow matter has on our universe. Gravity.

"And a big chunk of this stuff is there on the other side of Sag A West. It's exerting enough gravity to affect the path of the infalling gas. And to affect the probe's drift. And even to affect the young stars because the shadow matter-thing's exerting a counterpull on the massive star clouds, and that's keeping them from being ripped apart by the hole as soon as they otherwise would be. So they have time to collapse into young stars."

"Well, that's sort of it, but you've left out some things that alter and validate the whole," Kane said impatiently, scowling.

"Yes, Tirzah, dear heart, you don't see the—you can't just say that 'counterpull'—let me try once more."

They were off again, but this time I didn't listen. So maybe I hadn't seen the theory whole, but only glimpsed its shadow. It was enough.

They had a viable theory. I had a viable expedition, with a goal, and cooperatively productive scientists, and a probability of success.

It was enough.

Kane and Ajit prepared the second minicap for the big ship, and I prepared to move the probe. Our mood was jubilant. There was much laughing and joking, interrupted by intense bursts of incomprehensible jabbering between Ajit and Kane.

But before I finished my programming, Ajit's head disappeared.

7. Ship

Kane worked all day on his shadow-matter theory. He worked ferociously, hunched over his terminal like a hungry dog with a particularly meaty bone, barely glancing up and saying little. Ajit worked, too, but the quality of his working was different. The terminals both connect to the same computer, of course; whatever Kane had, Ajit had, too. Ajit could follow whatever Kane did.

But that's what Ajit was doing: following. I could tell it from the timing of his accesses, from the whole set of his body. He was a decent scientist, but he was not Kane. Given the data and enough time, Ajit might have been able to go where Kane raced ahead now. Maybe. Or, he might have been able to make valuable additions to Kane's thinking. But Kane gave him no time; Kane was always there first, and he asked no help. He had shut Ajit out completely. For Kane, nothing existed right now but his work.

Toward evening he looked up abruptly and said to me, "They'll move the probe. The uploads—they'll move it."

I said, "How do you know? It's not time yet, according to the schedule."

"No. But they'll move it. If I figured out the shadow matter here, I will there, too. I'll decide that more data is needed from the other side of Sag A West, where the main shadow mass is."

I looked at him. He looked demented, like some sort of Roman warrior who has just wrestled with a lion. All that was missing was the blood. Wild, filthy hair—when had he last showered? Clothes spotted with the food I'd made him gulp down at noon. Age lines beginning, under strain and fatigue and despite the rejuve, to drag down the muscles of his face. And his eyes shining like Sag A West itself.

God, I loved him.

I said, with careful emphasis, "You're right. The *Tirzah upload* will move the ship for better measurements."

"Then we'll get more data in a few days," Ajit said. "But the radiation on the other side of Sag A West is still intense. We must hope nothing gets damaged in the probe programs, or in the uploads themselves, before we get the new data."

"We better hope nothing gets damaged long before that in my upload," Kane said, "or they won't even know what data to collect." He turned back to his screen.

The brutal words hung in the air.

I saw Ajit turn his face away from me. Then he rose and walked into the galley.

If I followed him too soon, he would see it as pity. His shame would mount even more.

"Kane," I said in a low, furious voice, "you are despicable."

He turned to me in genuine surprise. "What?"

"You know what." But he didn't. Kane wasn't even conscious of what he'd said. To him, it was a simple, evident truth. Without the Kane upload, no one on the probe would know how to do first-class science.

"I want to see you upstairs on the observation deck," I said to him. "Not now, but in ten minutes. And you announce that you want *me* to see something up there." The time lag, plus Kane's suggesting the trip, would keep Ajit from knowing I was protecting him.

But now I had put up Kane's back. He was tired, he was stressed, he was inevitably coming down from the unsustainable high of his discovery. Neither body nor mind can keep at that near-hysterical pitch for too long. I had misjudged, out of my own anger at him.

He snapped, "I'll see you on the observation deck when *I* want to see you there, and not otherwise. Don't push me around, Tirzah. Not even as captain." He turned back to his display.

Ajit emerged from the galley with three glasses on a tray. "A celebratory drink. A major discovery deserves that. At a minimum."

Relief was so intense I nearly showed it on my face. It was all right. I had misread Ajit, underestimated him. He ranked the magnitude of Kane's discovery higher than his own lack of participation in it, after all. Ajit was, first, a scientist.

He handed a glass to me, one to Kane, one for himself, Kane took a hasty, perfunctory gulp and returned to his display. But I cradled mine, smiling at Ajit, trying with warmth to convey the admiration I felt for his rising above the personal.

"Where did you get the wine? It wasn't on the ship manifest!"

"It was in my personal allotment," Ajit said, smiling.

Personal allotments are not listed nor examined. A bottle of wine, the statue of Shiva . . . Ajit had brought some interesting choices for a galactic core. I sipped the red liquid. It tasted different from the Terran or Martian wines I had grown up with: rougher, more full-bodied, not as sweet.

"Wonderful, Ajit."

"I thought you would like it. It is made in my native New Bombay, from genemod grapes brought from Terra."

He didn't go back to his terminal. For the next half hour, he entertained me with stories of New Bombay. He was a good storyteller, sharp and funny. Kane worked steadily, ignoring us. The ten-minute deadline I had set for him to call me up to the observation deck came and went.

After half an hour, Kane stood and staggered. Once before, when he'd broken Ajit's statue, stiffness after long sitting had made Kane unsteady. That time he'd caught himself after simply bumping the wardroom table. This time he crashed heavily to the floor.

"Kane!"

"Nothing, nothing . . . don't make a fuss, Tirzah! You just won't leave me alone!"

This was so unfair that I wanted to slap him. I didn't. Kane rose by himself, shook his head like some great beast, and said, "I'm just exhausted. I'm going to bed."

I didn't try to stop him from going to his bunk. I had planned on sleeping with Ajit, anyway. It seemed that some slight false note had crept into his storytelling in the last five minutes, some forced exaggeration.

But he smiled at me, and I decided I'd been wrong. I was very tired, too. All at once I wished I could sleep alone this night.

But I couldn't. Ajit, no matter how well he'd recovered from Kane's unconscious brutality, nonetheless had to feel bruised at some level. It was my job to find out where, and how much, and to set it to rights. It was my job to keep the expedition as productive as possible, to counteract Kane's dismissing and belittling behavior toward Ajit. It was my job.

I smiled back at him.

8. PROBE

When Ajit's head disappeared, no one panicked. We'd expected this, of course; in fact, we'd expected it sooner. The probe drifted in a sea of the most intense radiation in the galaxy, much of it at lethal wavelengths: gamma rays from Sagittarius East, X-rays, powerful winds of ionized particles, things I couldn't name. That the probe's shielding had held this long was a minor miracle. It couldn't hold forever. Some particle or particles had penetrated it and reached the computer, contaminating a piece of the upload-maintenance program.

It was a minor glitch. The backup kicked in a moment later and Ajit's head reappeared. But we all knew this was only the beginning. It would happen again, and again, and eventually programming would be hit that couldn't be restored by automatic backup, because the backup would go, too, in a large enough hit— or because uploads are not like other computer programs. We are more than that, and less. An upload has backups to maintain the shadows we see of each other and the ship, the shadows that keep our captured minds sane. But an upload cannot house backups of itself. Even one copy smudges too much, and the copy contaminates the original. It has been tried, with painful results.

Moreover, we uploads run only partly on the main computer. An upload is neither a biological entity nor a long stream of code, but something more than both. Some of the substratum, the hardware, is wired like actual neurons, although constructed of sturdier stuff: thousands of miles of nano-constructed organic polymers. This is why analogues think at the rate of the human brain, not the much faster rate of computers. It's also why we feel as our originals do.

After Ajit's maintenance glitch our mood, which had been exuberant, sobered. But it didn't sour. We worked steadily, with focus and hope, deciding where exactly to position the probe and then entering the coordinates for the jump.

"See you soon," we said to each other. I kissed both Kane and Ajit lightly on the lips. Then we all shut down and the probe jumped.

Days later, we emerged on the other side of Sag A West, all three of us still intact. If it were in my nature, I would have said a prayer of thanksgiving. Instead I said to Ajit, "Still have a head, I see."

"And a good thing he does," Kane said absently, already plunging for the chair in front of his terminal. "We'll need it. And—Ajit, the mass detectors . . . great shitting gods!"

It seems we were to have thanksgiving after all, if only perversely. I said, "What is it? What's there?" The displays showed nothing at all.

"Nothing at all," Ajit said. "And everything."

"Speak English!"

Ajit—I doubt Kane had even heard me, in his absorption—said, "The mass detectors are showing a huge mass less than a quarter light-year away. The radiation detectors—all of them—are showing nothing at all. We're—"

"We're accelerating fast." I studied ship's data; the rate of acceleration made me blink. "We're going to hit whatever it is. Not soon, but the tidal forces—"

The probe was small, but the tidal forces of something this big would still rip it apart when it got close enough.

Something this big. But there was, to all other sensors, nothing there.

Nothing but shadows.

A strange sensation ran over me. Not fear, but something more complicated, much more eerie.

My voice sounded strange in my ears. "What if we hit it? I know you said radiation of all types will go right through shadow matter just as if it isn't there"—*because it isn't, not in our universe*—"but what about the probe? What if we hit it before we take the final event-horizon measurements on Sag A*?"

"We won't hit it," Ajit said. "We'll move before then, Tirzah, back to the hole. Kane—"

They forget me again. I went up to the observation deck. Looking out through the clear hull, I stared at the myriad of stars on the side of the night sky away from Sag A West. Then I turned to look toward that vast three-armed cloud of turning plasma, radiating as it cools. Nothing blocked my view of Sag A West. Yet between us lay a huge, massive body of shadow matter, unseen, pulling on everything else my dazed senses could actually see.

To my left, all the exotic plants in the observatory disappeared.

Ajit and Kane worked feverishly, until once more I made them shut down for "sleep." The radiation here was nearly as great as it had been in our first location. We were right inside Sagittarius A East, the huge expanding shell of an unimaginable explosion sometime during the last hundred thousand years. Most of Sag A East wasn't visible at the wavelengths I could see, but the gamma-ray detectors were going crazy.

"We can't stop for five hours!" Kane cried. "Don't you realize how much damage the radiation could do in that time? We need to get all the data we can, work on it, and send off the second minicap!"

"We're going to send off the second minicap right now," I said. "And we'll only shut down for three hours. But, Kane, we are going to do that. I mean it. Uploads run even more damage from not running maintenance than we do from external radiation. You know that."

He did. He scowled at me, and cursed, and fussed with the mini-cap, but then he fired the minicap off and shut down.

Ajit said, "Just one more minute, Tirzah. I want to show you something."

"Ajit—"

"No, it's not mathematical. I promise. It's something I brought onto the *Kepler*. The object was not included in the probe program, but I can show you a holo."

Somewhere in the recesses of the computer, Ajit's upload created a program and a two-dimensional holo appeared on an empty display screen. I blinked at it, surprised.

It was a statue of some sort of god with four arms, enclosed in a circle of flames, made of what looked like very old bronze.

"This is Nataraja," Ajit said. "Shiva dancing."

"Ajit—"

"No, I am not a god worshipper," he smiled. "You know me better than that, Tirzah. Hinduism has many gods—thousands—but they are, except to the ignorant, no more than embodiments of different aspects of reality. Shiva is the dance of creation and destruction, the constant flow of energy in the cosmos. Birth and death and rebirth. It seemed fitting to bring him to the galactic core, where so much goes on of all three. This statue has been in my family for four hundred years. I must bring it home, along with the answers to our experiments."

"You will bring Shiva back to New Bombay," I said softly, "and your answers, too."

"Yes, I have begun to think so." He smiled at me, a smile with all the need of his quicksilver personality in it, but also all the courtesy and hope. "Now I will sleep."

9. SHIP

The next morning, after a deep sleep one part sheer exhaustion and one part sex, I woke to find Ajit already out of bed and seated in front of his terminal. He rose the moment I entered the wardroom and turned to me with a grave face. "Tirzah. The minicap arrived. I already put the data into the system."

"What's wrong? Where's Kane?"

"Still asleep, I imagine."

I went to Kane's bunk. He lay on his back, still in the clothes he'd worn for three days, smelling sour and snoring softly. I thought of waking him, then decided to wait a bit. Kane could certainly use the sleep, and I could use the time with Ajit. I went back to the wardroom, tightening the belt on my robe.

"What's wrong?" I repeated.

"I put the data from the minicap into the system. It's all corrections to the last minicap's data. Kane says the first set was wrong."

"Kane?" I said stupidly.

"The Kane-analogue," Ajit explained patiently. "He says radiation hit the probe's sensors for the first batch, before any of them realized it. They fired off the preliminary data right after the jump, you know, because they had no idea how long the probe could last. Now they've had time to discover where the radiation hit, to restore the sensor programs, and to retake the measurements. The Kane analogue says these new ones are accurate, the others weren't."

I tried to take it all in. "So Kane's shadow-matter theory—none of that is true?"

"I don't know," Ajit said. "How can anybody know until we see if the data supports it? The minicap only just arrived."

"Then I might not have moved the probe," I said, meaning "the other I." My analogue. I didn't know what I was saying. The shock was too great. All that theorizing, all Kane's sharp triumph, all that tension . . .

I looked more closely at Ajit. He looked very pale, and as fatigued as a gen-emod man of his youth can look. I said, "You didn't sleep much."

"No. Yesterday was . . . difficult."

"Yes," I agreed, noting the characteristically polite understatement. "Yes."

"Should I wake Kane?" Ajit said, almost diffidently.

"I'll do it."

Kane was hard to wake. I had to shake him several times before he struggled up to consciousness.

"Tirzah?"

"Who else? Kane, you must get up. Something's happened."

"Wh-what?" He yawned hugely and slumped against the bulkhead. His whole body reeked.

I braced myself. "The second minicap arrived. Your analogue sent a recording. He says the prelim data was compromised, due to radiation-caused sensor malfunction."

That woke him. He stared at me as if I were an executioner. "The data's compromised? *All* of it?"

"I don't know."

Kane pushed out of his bunk and ran into the wardroom. Ajit said, "I put the minicap data into the system already, but I—" Kane wasn't listening. He tore into the data, and after a few minutes he actually bellowed.

"No!"

I flattened myself against the bulkhead, not from fear but from surprise. I had never heard a grown man make a noise like that.

But there were no other noises. Kane worked silently, ferociously. Ajit sat at his own terminal and worked, too, not yesterday's tentative copying but the real thing. I put hot coffee beside them both. Kane gulped his steaming, Ajit ignored his.

After half an hour, Kane turned to me. Defeat pulled like gravity at everything on his face, eyes and lips and jaw muscles. Only his filthy hair sprang upward. He said simply, with the naked straightforwardness of despair, "The new data invalidates the idea of shadow matter."

I heard myself say, "Kane, go take a shower."

To my surprise, he went, shambling from the room. Ajit worked a few minutes longer, then climbed the ladder to the observation deck. Over his shoulder he said, "Tirzah, I want to be alone, please. Don't come."

I didn't. I sat at the tiny wardroom table, looked at my own undrunk coffee, and thought of nothing.

10. PROBE

The data from the probe's new position looked good, Kane said. That was his word: "good." Then he returned to his terminal.

"Ajit?" I was coming to rely on him more and more for translation. He was just as busy as Kane, but kinder. This made sense. If, to Kane, Ajit was a secondary but still necessary party to the intellectual action, that's what I was to both of them. Ajit had settled into this position, secure that he was valued. I could feel myself doing the same. The cessation of struggle turned us both kinder.

Kane, never insecure, worked away.

Ajit said, "The new readings confirm a large gravitational mass affecting the paths of both the infalling gas and the probe. The young stars so close to Sag A* are a much knottier problem. We've got to modify the whole theory of star formation to account for the curvatures of spacetime caused by the hole and by the shadow mass. It's very complex. Kane's got the computer working on that, and I'm going to take readings on Sag A West, in its different parts, and on stars on the other side of the mass and look at those."

"What about the mass detectors? What do they say?"

"They say we're being pulled toward a mass of about a half million suns."

A half million suns. And we couldn't see it: not with our eyes, nor radio sensors, nor X-ray detectors, nor anything.

"I have a question. Does it have an event horizon? Is it swallowing light, like a black hole does? Isn't it the gravity of a black hole that swallows light?"

"Yes. But radiation, including light, goes right through this shadow matter, Tirzah. Don't you understand? It doesn't interact with normal radiation at all."

"But it has gravity. Why doesn't its gravity trap the light?"

"I don't know." He hesitated. "Kane thinks maybe it doesn't interact with radiation as particles, which respond to gravity. Only as waves."

"How can it do that?"

Ajit took my shoulders and shook them playfully. "I told you—*we don't know*. This is brand-new, dear heart. We know as much about what it will and will not do as primitive hominids knew about fire."

"Well, don't make a god of it," I said, and it was a test. Ajit passed. He didn't stiffen as if I'd made some inappropriate reference to the drawing of Shiva he'd shown me last night. Instead, he laughed and went back to work.

"Tirzah! Tirzah!"

The automatic wake-up brought me out of shutdown. Ajit must have been brought back online a few moments before me, because he was already calling my name. Alarm bells clanged.

"It's Kane! He's been hit!"

I raced into Kane's bunk. He lay still amid the bedclothes. It wasn't the maintenance program that had taken the hit, because every part of his body was intact; so were the bedclothes. But Kane lay stiff and unresponsive.

"Run the full diagnostics," I said to Ajit.

"I already started them."

"Kane," I said, shaking him gently, then harder. He moved a little, groaned. So his upload wasn't dead.

I sat on the edge of the bunk, fighting fear, and took his hand. "Kane, love, can you hear me?"

He squeezed my fingers. The expression on his face didn't change. After a silence in which time itself seemed to stop, Ajit said, "The diagnostics are complete. About a third of brain function is gone."

I got into the bunk beside Kane and put my arms around him.

Ajit and I did what we could. Our uploads patched and copied, using material from both of us. Yes, the copying would lead to corruption, but we were beyond that.

Because an upload runs on such a complex combination of computer and nano-constructed polymer networks, we cannot simply be replaced by a backup program cube. The unique software/hardware retes are also why a corrupted analogue is not exactly the same as a stroke- or tumor-impaired human brain.

The analogue brain does not have to pump blood or control breathing. It does not have to move muscles or secrete hormones. Although closely tied to the "purer" programs that maintain our illusion of moving and living as three-dimensional beings in a three-dimensional ship, the analogue brain is tied to the computer in much more complex ways than any fleshy human using a terminal. The resources of the computer were at our disposal, but they could only accomplish limited aims.

When Ajit and I had finished putting together as much of Kane, or a pseudo-Kane, as we could, he walked into the wardroom and sat down. He looked, moved, smiled the same. That part is easy to repair, as easy as had been replacing Ajit's head or the exotics on the observation deck. But the man staring blankly at the terminal was not really Kane.

"What was I working on?" he said.

I got out, "Shadow matter."

"Shadow matter? What's that?"

Ajit said softly, "I have all your work, Kane. Our work. I think I can finish it, now that you've started us in the right direction."

He nodded, looking confused. "Thank you, Ajit." Then, with a flash of his old magnificent combativeness, "But you better get it right!"

"With your help," Ajit said gaily, and in that moment I came close to truly loving him.

*

They worked out a new division of labor. Kane was able to take the sensor readings and run them through the pre-set algorithms. Actually, Ajit probably could have trained me to do that. But Kane seemed content, frowning earnestly at his displays.

Ajit took over the actual science. I said to him, when we had a moment alone, "Can you do it?"

"I think so," he said, without either anger or arrogance. "I have the foundation that Kane laid. And we worked out some of the preliminaries together."

"We have only one more jump left."

"I know, Tirzah."

"With the risk of radiation killing us all—"

"Not yet. Give me a little more time."

I rested a moment against his shoulder. "All right. A little more time."

He put his arm around me, not in passion but in comradeship. None of us, we both knew, had all that much time left.

11. Ship

Kane was only temporarily defeated by the contamination of the probe data. Within half a day, he had aborted his shadow-matter theory, archived his work on it, and gone back to his original theories about the mysteriously massive young stars near the hole. He used the probe's new data, which were all logical amplifications of the prelim readings. "I've got some ideas," he told me. "We'll see."

He wasn't as cheerful as usual, let alone as manically exuberant as during the shadow-matter "discovery," but he was working steadily. A mountain, Kane. It would take a lot to actually erode him, certainly more than a failed theory. That rocky insensitivity had its strengths.

Ajit, on the other hand, was not really working. I couldn't follow the displays on his terminal, but I could read the body language. He was restless, inattentive. But what worried me was something else, his attitude toward Kane.

All Ajit's anger was gone.

I watched carefully, while seemingly bent over ship's log or embroidery. Anger is the least subtle of the body's signals. Even when a person is successfully concealing most of it, the signs are there if you know where to look: the tight neck muscles, the turned-away posture, the tinge in the voice. Ajit displayed none of this. Instead, when he faced Kane, as he did during the lunch I insisted we all eat together at the wardroom table, I saw something else. A sly superiority, a secret triumph.

I could be wrong, I thought. I have been wrong before. By now I disliked Ajit so much that I didn't trust my own intuitions.

"Ajit," I said as we finished the simple meal I'd put together, "will you please—"

Ship's alarms went off with a deafening clang. *Breach, breach, breach.*

I whirled toward ship's display, which automatically illuminated. The breach was in the starboard hold, and it was full penetration by a mass of about a hundred grams. Within a minute, the nanos had put on a temporary patch. The alarm stopped and the computer began hectoring me.

"Breach sealed with temporary nano patch. Seal must be reinforced within two hours with permanent hull patch, type 6-A. For location of breach and patch supply, consult ship's log. If unavailability of—" I shut it off.

"Could be worse," Kane said.

"Well, of course it could be worse," I snapped, and immediately regretted it. I was not allowed to snap. That I had done so was an indication of how much the whole situation on the *Kepler* was affecting me. That wasn't allowed, either; it was unprofessional.

Kane wasn't offended. "Could have hit the engines or the living pod instead of just a hold. Actually, I'm surprised it hasn't happened before. There's a lot of drifting debris in this area."

Ajit said, "Are you going into the hold, Tirzah?"

Of course I was going into the hold. But this time I didn't snap; I smiled at him and said, "Yes, I'm going to suit up now."

"I'm coming, too," Kane said.

I blinked. I'd been about to ask if Ajit wanted to go with me. It would be a good way to observe him away from Kane, maybe ask some discreet questions. I said to Kane, "Don't you have to work?"

"The work isn't going anywhere. And I want to retrieve the particle. It didn't exit the ship, and at a hundred grams, there's going to be some of it left after the breach."

Ajit had stiffened at being preempted, yet again, by Kane. Ajit would have wanted to retrieve the particle, too; there is nothing more interesting to space scientists than dead rocks. Essentially, I'd often thought, Sag A* was no more than a very hot, very large dead rock. I knew better than to say this aloud.

I could have ordered Ajit to accompany me, and ordered Kane to stay behind. But that, I sensed, would only make things worse. Ajit, in his present mood of deadly sensitivity, would not take well to orders from anyone, even me. I wasn't going to give him the chance to retreat more into whatever nasty state of mind he currently inhabited.

"Well, then, let's go," I said ungraciously to Kane, who only grinned at me and went to get our suits.

The holds, three of them for redundancy safety, are full of supplies of all types. Every few days I combine a thorough ship inspection with lugging enough food forward to sustain us. We aren't uploads; we need bodily nurturing as well as the kind I was supposed to be providing.

All three holds can be pressurized if necessary, but usually they aren't. Air generation and refreshment doesn't cost much power, but it costs some. Kane and I went into the starboard hold in heated s-suits and helmets.

"I'm going to look around," Kane said. He'd brought a handheld, and I saw him calculating the probable trajectory of the particle from the ship's data and the angle of the breach, as far as he could deduce it. Then he disappeared behind a pallet of crates marked SOYSYNTH.

The breach was larger than I'd expected; that hundred-gram particle had hit at a bad angle. But the nanos had done their usual fine job, and the permanent patch went on without trouble. I began the careful inspection of the rest of the hull, using my handheld instruments.

Kane cursed volubly.

"Kane? What is it?"

"Nothing. Bumped into boxes."

"Well, don't. The last thing I want is you messing up my hold." For a physically fit man, Kane is clumsy in motion. I would bet my ship that he can't dance, and bet my life that he never tries.

"I can't see anything. Can't you brighten the light?"

I did, and he bumped around some more. Whenever he brushed something, he cursed. I did an inspection even more carefully than usual, but found nothing alarming. We met each other back by the hold door.

"It's not here," Kane said. "The particle. It's not here."

"You mean you didn't find it."

"No, I mean it's not here. Don't you think I could find a still hot particle in a hold otherwise filled only with large immobile crates?"

I keyed in the door code. "So it evaporated on impact. Ice and ions and dust."

"To penetrate a Schaad hull? No." He reconsidered. "Well, maybe. What did you find?"

"Not much. Pitting and scarring on the outside, nothing unexpected. But no structural stress to worry about."

"The debris here is undoubtedly orbiting the core, but we're so far out it's not moving all that fast. Still, we should had some warning. But I'm more worried about the probe—when is the third minicap due?"

Kane knew as well as I did when the third minicap was due. His asking was the first sign he was as tense as the rest of us.

"Three more days," I said. "Be patient."

"I'm not patient."

"As if that's new data."

"I'm also afraid the probe will be hit by rapidly orbiting debris, and that will be that. Did you know that the stars close in to Sag A* orbit at several thousand clicks per second?"

I knew. He'd told me often enough. The probe was always a speculative proposition, and before now, Kane had been jubilant that we'd gotten any data at all from it.

I'd never heard Kane admit to being "afraid" of anything. Even allowing for the casualness of the phrase.

I wanted to distract him, and, if Kane was really in a resigned and reflective mood, it also seemed a good time to do my job. "Kane, about Ajit—"

"I don't want to talk about that sniveling slacker," Kane said, with neither interest not rancor. "I picked badly for an assistant, that's all."

It hadn't actually been his "pick"; his input had been one of many. I didn't say this. Kane looked around the hold one more time. "I guess you're right. The particle sublimed. Ah, well."

I put the glove of my hand on the arm of his suit—not exactly an intimate caress, but the best I could do in this circumstance. "Kane, how is the young-star mystery going?"

"Not very well. But that's science." The hold door stood open and he lumbered out.

I gave one last look around the hold before turning off the light, but there was nothing more to see.

The mended statue of Shiva was back on the wardroom table, smack in the center, when Kane and I returned from the hold. I don't think Kane, heading straight for his terminal, even noticed. I smiled at Ajit, although I wasn't sure why he had brought the statue back. He'd told me he never wanted to see it again.

"Tirzah, would you perhaps like to play go?"

I couldn't conceal my surprise. "Go?"

"Yes. Will you play with me?" Accompanied by his most winning smile.

"All right."

He brought out the board and, bizarrely, set it up balanced on his knees. When he saw my face, he said, "We'll play here. I don't want to disturb the Cosmic Dancer."

"All right." I wasn't sure what to think. I drew my chair close to his, facing him, and bent over the board.

We both knew that Ajit was a better player than I. That's why both of us played: he to win, me to lose. I would learn more from the losing position. Very competitive people—and I thought now that I had never known one as competitive as Ajit—relax only when not threatened.

So I made myself nonthreatening in every way I knew, and Ajit and I talked and laughed, and Kane worked doggedly on his theories that weren't going anywhere. The statue of the dancing god leered at me from the table, and I knew with every passing moment how completely I was failing this already failing mission.

12. PROBE

Kane was gentler since the radiation corruption. Who can say how these things happen? Personality, too, is encoded in the human brain, whether flesh or analogue. He was still Kane, but we saw only his gentler, sweeter side. Previously that part of him had been dominated by his combative intellect, which had been a force of nature all its own, like a high wind. Now the intellect had failed, the wind calmed. The landscape beneath lay serene.

"Here, Ajit," Kane said. "These are the equations you wanted run." He sent them to Ajit's terminal, stood, and stretched. The stretch put him slightly off balance, something damaged in the upload that Ajit and I hadn't been able to fix, or find. A brain is such a complex thing. Kane tottered, and Ajit rose swiftly to catch him.

"Careful, Kane. Here, sit down."

Ajit eased Kane into a chair at the wardroom table. I put down my work. Kane said, "Tirzah, I feel funny."

"Funny how?" Alarm ran through me.

"I don't know. Can we play go?"

I had taught him the ancient strategy game, and he enjoyed it. He wasn't very good, not nearly as good as I was, but he liked it and didn't seem to mind losing. I got out the board. Ajit, who was a master at go, went back to Kane's shadow-matter theory. He was making good progress, I knew, although he said frankly that all the basic ideas were Kane's.

Halfway through our second game of go, the entire wardroom disappeared.

A moment of blind panic seized me. I was adrift in the void, nothing to see or feel or hold onto, a vertigo so terrible it blocked any rational thought. It was the equivalent of a long anguished scream, originating in the most primitive part of my now blind brain: *lost, lost, lost, and alone . . .*

The automatic maintenance program kicked in and the wardroom reappeared. Kane gripped the table edge and stared at me, white-faced. I went to him, wrapped my arms around him reassuringly, and gazed at Ajit. Kane clung to me. A part of my mind noted that some aspects of the wardroom were wrong: the galley door was too low to walk through upright, and one chair had disappeared, along with the go board. Maintenance code too damaged to restore.

Ajit said softly, "We have to decide, Tirzah. We could take a final radiation hit at any time."

"I know."

I took my arms away from Kane. "Are you all right?"

He smiled. "Yes. Just for a minute I was . . ." He seemed to lose his thought.

Ajit brought his terminal chair to the table, to replace the vanished one. He sat leaning forward, looking from me to Kane and back. "This is a decision all three of us have to make. We have one minicap left to send back to the *Kepler*, and one more jump for ourselves. At any time we could lose . . . everything. You all know that. What do you think we should do? Kane? Tirzah?"

All my life I'd heard that even very flawed people can rise to leadership under the right circumstances. I'd never believed it, not of someone with Ajit's basic personality structure: competitive, paranoid, angry at such a deep level he didn't even know it. I'd been wrong. I believed now.

Kane said, "I feel funny, and that probably means I've taken another minor hit and the program isn't there to repair it. I think . . . I think . . ."

"Kane?" I took his hand.

He had trouble getting words out. "I think we better send the minicap now."

"I agree," Ajit said. "But that means we send it without the data from our next jump, to just outside the event horizon of Sag A*. So the *Kepler* won't get those readings. They'll get the work on shadow matter, but most of the best things on that already went in the second minicap. Still, it's better than nothing, and I'm afraid if we wait to send until after the jump, nothing is what the *Kepler* will get. It will be too late."

Both men looked at me. As captain, the jump decision was mine. I nodded. "I agree, too. Send off the minicap with whatever you've got, and then we'll jump. But not to the event horizon."

"Why not?" Kane burst out, sounding more like himself than at any time since the accident.

"Because there's no point. We can't send any more data back, so the event horizon readings die with us. And we can survive longer if I jump us completely away from the core. Several hundred light-years out, where the radiation is minimal."

Together, as if rehearsed, they both said, "No."

"*No?*"

"No," Ajit said, with utter calm, utter persuasiveness. "We're not going to go out like that, Tirzah."

"But we don't have to go out at all! Not for decades! Maybe centuries! Not until the probe's life-maintenance power is used up—" Or until the probe is hit by space debris. Or until radiation takes us out. Nowhere in space is really safe.

Kane said, "And what would we do for centuries? I'd go mad. I want to work."

"Me, too," Ajit said. "I want to take the readings by the event horizon and make of them what I can, while I can. Even though the *Kepler* will never see them."

They were scientists.

And I? Could even I, station bred, have lived for centuries in this tiny ship, without a goal beyond survival, trapped with these two men? An Ajit compassionate and calm, now that he was on top. A damaged Kane, gentle and intellectually gutted. And a Tirzah, captaining a pointless expedition with nowhere to go and nothing to do.

I would have ended up hating all three of us.

Ajit took my left hand. My right one still held Kane's, so we made a broken circle in the radiation-damaged wardroom.

"All right," I said. "We'll send off the minicap and then jump to the event horizon."

"Yes," Kane said.

Ajit said, "I'm going to go back to work. Tirzah, if you and Kane want to go up to the observation deck, or anywhere, I'll prepare and launch the minicap." Carefully he turned his back and sat at his terminal.

I led Kane to my bunk. This was a first; I always went to the scientists' bunks. My own, as captain, had features for my eyes only. But now it didn't matter.

We made love, and afterward, holding his superb, aging body in my arms, I whispered against his cheek, "I love you, Kane."

"I love you, too," he said simply, and I had no way of knowing if he meant it, or if it was an automatic response dredged up from some half-remembered ritual from another time. It didn't matter. There are a lot more types of love in the universe than I once suspected.

We were silent a long time, and then Kane said, "I'm trying to remember *pi*. I know 3.1, but I can't remember after that."

I said, through the tightness in my throat, "3.141. That's all I remember."

"Three point one four one," Kane said dutifully. I left him repeating it over and over, when I went to jump the probe to the event horizon of Sag A*.

13. Ship

The second breach of the hull was more serious than the first.

The third minicap had not arrived from the probe. "The analogues are probably all dead," Kane said dully. "They were supposed to jump to one-twenty-fifth of a light-year from the event horizon. Our calculations were always problematic for where exactly that *is*. It's possible they landed inside, and the probe will just spiral around Sag A* forever. Or they got hit with major radiation and fried."

"It's possible," I said. "How is the massive-young-star problem coming?"

"It's not. Mathematical dead end."

He looked terrible, drawn and, again, unwashed. I was more impatient with the latter than I should be. But how hard is it, as a courtesy to your shipmates if nothing else, to get your body into the shower? How long does it take? Kane had stopped exercising, as well.

"Kane," I began, as quietly but firmly as I could manage, "will you—"

The alarms went off, clanging again at 115 decibels. *Breach, breach, breach* . . .

I scanned the displays. "Oh, God—"

"Breach sealed with temporary nano patch," the computer said. "Seal must be reinforced within one half hour with permanent hull patch, type 1-B, supplemented with equipment repair, if possible. For location of breach and patch supply, consult—" I turned it off.

The intruder had hit the backup engine. It was a much larger particle than the first one, although since it had hit us and then gone on its merry way, rather than penetrating the ship, there was no way to recover it for examination. But the outside mass detectors registered a particle of at least two kilos, and it had probably been moving much faster than the first one. If it had hit us directly, we would all be dead. Instead it had given the ship a glancing blow, damaging the backup engine.

"I'll come with you again," Kane said.

"There won't be any particle to collect this time." Or not collect.

"I know. But I'm not getting anywhere here."

Kane and I, s-suited, went into the backup engine compartment. As soon as I saw it, I knew there was nothing I could do. There is damage you can repair, and there is damage you cannot. The back end of the compartment had been sheared off, and part of the engine with it. No wonder the computer had recommended a 1-B patch, which is essentially the equivalent of "Throw a tarp over it and forget it."

While I patched, Kane poked around the edges of the breach, then at the useless engine. He left before I did, and I found him studying ship's display of the hit on my wardroom screen. He wasn't trying to do anything with ship's log, which was not his place and he knew it, but he stood in front of the data, moving his hand when he wanted another screen, frowning horribly.

"What is it, Kane?" I said. I didn't really want to know; the patch had taken hours and I was exhausted. I didn't see Ajit. Sleeping, or up on the observation deck, or, less likely, in the gym.

"Nothing. Whatever that hit was made of, it wasn't radiating. So it wasn't going very fast, or the external sensors would have picked up at least ionization. Either the mass was cold, or the sensors aren't functioning properly."

"I'll run the diagnostics," I said wearily. "Anything else?"

"Yes. I want to move the ship."

I stared at him, my suit half peeled from my body, my helmet defiantly set on the table, pushing the statue of Shiva to one side. "*Move the ship?*"

Ajit appeared in the doorway from his bunk.

"Yes," Kane said. "Move the ship."

"But these are the coordinates the minicap will return to!"

"It's not coming," Kane said. "Don't you listen to anything I say, Tirzah? The uploads didn't make it. The third minicap is days late; if it were coming, it would be here. The probe is gone, the uploads are gone, and we've got all the data we're going to get from them. If we want more, we're going to have to go after it ourselves."

"Go after it?" I repeated, stupidly. "How?"

"I already told you! Move the ship closer into the core so we can take the readings the probe should have taken. Some of them, anyway."

Ajit said, "Moving the ship is completely Tirzah's decision."

His championship of me when I needed no champion, and especially not in that pointlessly assertive voice, angered me more than Kane's suggestion. "Thank you, Ajit, I can handle this!"

Mistake, mistake.

Kane, undeterred, plowed on. "I don't mean we'd go near the event horizon, of course, or even to the probe's first position near the star cluster. But we could move much closer in. Maybe ten light-years from the core, positioned between the northern and western arms of Sag A West."

Ajit said, "Which would put us right in the circumnuclear disk! Where the radiation is much worse than here!"

Kane turned on him, acknowledging Ajit's presence for the first time in days, with an outpouring of all Kane's accumulated frustration and disappointment. "We've been hit twice with particles that damaged the ship. Clearly we're in the path of some equivalent of an asteroid belt orbiting the core at this immense distance. It can't be any less safe in the circumnuclear disk, which, I might remind you, is only shocked molecular gases, with its major radiation profile unknown. Any first-year astronomy student should know that. Or is it just that you're a coward?"

Ajit's skin mottled, then paled. His features did not change expression at all. But I felt the heat coming from him, the primal rage, greater for being contained. He went into his bunk and closed the door.

"Kane!" I said furiously, too exhausted and frustrated and disappointed in myself to watch my tone. "You can't—"

"I can't stand any more of this," Kane said. He slammed down the corridor to the gym, and I heard the exercise bike whirr in rage.

I went to my own bunk, locked the door, and squeezed my eyes shut, fighting for control. But even behind my closed eyelids I saw our furious shadows.

After a few hours I called them both together in the wardroom. When Kane refused, I ordered him. I lifted Ajit's statue of Shiva off the table and handed it to him, making its location his problem, as long as it wasn't on the table. Wordlessly he carried it into his bunk and then returned.

"This can't go on," I said calmly. "We all know that. We're in this small space together to accomplish something important, and our mission overrides all our personal feelings. You are both rational men, scientists, or you wouldn't be here."

"Don't patronize us with flattery," Ajit said.

"I'm sorry. I didn't intend to do that. It's true you're both scientists, and it's true you've both been certified rational enough for space travel."

They couldn't argue with that. I didn't mention how often certification boards had misjudged, or been bribed, or just been too dazzled by well-earned reputations to look below the work to the worker. If Kane or Ajit knew all that, they kept it to themselves.

"I blame myself for any difficulties we've had here," I said, in the best Nurturer fashion. Although it was also true. "It's my job to keep a ship running in productive harmony, and this one, I think we can all agree, is not."

No dissension. I saw that both of them dreaded some long, drawn-out discussion on group dynamics, never a topic that goes down well with astrophysicists. Kane said abruptly, "I still want to move the ship."

I had prepared myself for this. "No, Kane. We're not jumping closer in."

He caught at my loophole. "Then can we jump to another location at the same distance from the core? Maybe measurements from another base point would help."

"We're not jumping anywhere until I'm sure the third minicap isn't coming."

"How long will that be?" I could see the formidable intelligence under the childish tantrums already racing ahead, planning measurements, weighing options.

"We'll give it another three days."

"All right." Suddenly he smiled, his first in days. "Thanks, Tirzah."

I turned to Ajit. "Ajit, what can we do for your work? What do you need?"

"I ask for nothing," he said, with such a strange, intense, unreadable expression that for a moment I felt irrational fear. Then he stood and went into his bunk. I heard the door lock.

I had failed again.

No alarm went off in the middle of the night. There was nothing overt to wake me. But I woke anyway, and I heard someone moving quietly around the wardroom. The muscles of my right arm tensed to open my bunk, and I forced them to still.

Something wasn't right. Intuition, that mysterious shadow of rational thought, told me to lie motionless. To not open my bunk, to not even reach out and access the ship's data on my bunk screen. To not move at all.

Why?

I didn't know.

The smell of coffee wafted from the wardroom. So one of the men couldn't sleep, made some coffee, turned on his terminal. So what?

Don't move, said that pre-reasoning part of my mind, from the shadows.

The coffee smell grew stronger. A chair scraped. Ordinary, mundane sounds.

Don't move.

I didn't have to move. This afternoon I had omitted to mention to Kane and Ajit those times that certification boards had misjudged, or been bribed, or just been too dazzled by well-earned reputations to look below the work to the worker. Those times in which the cramped conditions of space, coupled with swollen egos and frenzied work, had led to disaster for a mission Nurturer. But we had learned. My bunk had equipment the scientists did not know about.

Carefully I slid my gaze to a spot directly above me on the bunk ceiling. Only my eyes moved. I pattern-blinked: two quick, three beats closed, two quick, a long steady stare. The screen brightened.

This was duplicate ship data. Not a backup; it was entirely separate, made simultaneously from the same sensors as the main log but routed into separate, freestanding storage that could not be reached from the main computer. Scientists are all sophisticated users. There is no way to keep data from any who wish to alter it except by discreet, unknown, untraceable storage. I pattern-blinked, not moving so much as a finger or a toe in the bed, to activate various screens of ship data.

It was easy to find.

Yesterday, at 1850 hours, the minicap bay had opened and received a minicap. Signal had failed to transmit to the main computer. Today at 300 hours, which was fifteen minutes ago, the minicap bay had been opened manually and the payload removed. Again signal had failed to the main computer.

The infrared signature in the wardroom, seated at his terminal, was Ajit.

It was possible the signal failures were coincidental, and Ajit was even now transferring data from the third minicap into the computer, enjoying a cup of hot coffee while he did so, gloating in getting a perfectly legitimate jump on Kane. But I didn't think so.

What did I think?

I didn't have to think; I just knew. I could see it unfolding, clear as a holovid. All of it. Ajit had stolen the second minicap, too. That had been the morning after Kane and I had slept so soundly, the morning after Ajit had given us wine to celebrate Kane's shadow-matter theory. What had been in that wine? We'd slept soundly, and Ajit told us that the minicap had come before we were awake. Ajit said he'd already put it into the computer. It carried Kane's upload's apology that the prelim data, the data from which Kane had constructed his shadow-matter thesis, was wrong, contaminated by a radiation strike.

Ajit had fabricated that apology and that replacement data. The actual second minicap would justify Kane's work, not undo it. Ajit was saving all three minicaps to use for himself, to claim the shadow matter discovery for his own. He'd used the second minicap to discredit the first; he would claim the third had never arrived, had never been sent from the dying probe.

The real Kane, my Kane, hadn't found the particle from the first ship's breach because it had, indeed, been made of shadow matter. That, and not slow speed, had been why the particle showed no radiation. The particle had exerted gravity on our world, but nothing else. The second breach, too, had been shadow matter. I knew that as surely as if Kane had shown me the pages of equations to prove it.

I knew something else, too. If I went into the shower and searched my body very carefully, every inch of it, I would find in some inconspicuous place the small, regular hole into which a subdermal tracker had gone the night of the drugged wine. So would Kane. Trackers would apprise Ajit of every move we made, not only large-muscle moves like a step or a hug, but small ones like accessing my bunk display of ship's data. That was what my intuition had been warning me of. Ajit did not want to be discovered during his minicap thefts.

I had the same trackers in my own repertoire. Only I had not thought this mission deteriorated enough to need them. I had not wanted to think that. I'd been wrong.

But how would Ajit make use of Kane's stolen work with Kane there to claim it for himself?

I already knew the answer, of course. I had known it from the moment I pattern-blinked at the ceiling, which was the moment I finally admitted to myself how monstrous this mission had turned.

I pushed open the bunk door and called cheerfully, "Hello? Do I smell coffee? Who's out there?"

"I am," Ajit said genially. "I cannot sleep. Come have some coffee."

"Coming, Ajit."

I put on my robe, tied it at my waist, and slipped the gun from its secret mattress compartment into my palm.

14. PROBE

The probe jumped successfully. We survived.

This close to the core, the view wasn't as spectacular as it was farther out. Sag A*, which captured us in orbit immediately, now appeared as a fuzzy region dominating starboard. The fuzziness, Ajit said, was a combination of Hawking radiation and superheated gases being swallowed by the black hole. To port, the intense blue cluster of IRS16 was muffled by the clouds of ionized plasma around the probe. We experienced some tidal forces, but the probe was so small that the gravitational tides didn't yet cause much damage.

Ajit has found a way to successfully apply Kane's shadow-matter theory to the paths of the infalling gases, as well as to the orbits of the young stars near Sag A*. He says there may well be a really lot of shadow matter near the core, and maybe even farther out. It may even provide enough mass to "balance" the universe, keeping it from either flying apart forever or collapsing in on itself. Shadow matter, left over from the very beginning of creation, may preserve creation.

Kane nods happily as Ajit explains. Kane holds my hand. I stroke his palm gently with my thumb, making circles like tiny orbits.

15. Ship

Ajit sat, fully dressed and with steaming coffee at his side, in front of his terminal. I didn't give him time to get the best of me. I walked into the wardroom and fired.

The sedative dart dropped him almost instantly. It was effective, for his body weight, for an hour. Kane didn't hear the thud as Ajit fell off his chair and onto the deck; Kane's bunk door stayed closed. I went into Ajit's bunk and searched every cubic meter of it, overriding the lock on his personal storage space. Most of that was taken up with the bronze statue of Shiva. The minicaps were not there, nor anywhere else in his bunk.

I tried the galley next, and came up empty.

Same for the shower, the gym, the supply closets.

Ajit could have hidden the cubes in the engine compartments or the fuel bays or any of a dozen other ship's compartments, but they weren't pressurized and he would have had to either suit up or pressurize them. Either one would have shown up in my private ship data, and they hadn't. Ajit probably hadn't wanted to take the risk of too much covert motion around the ship. He'd only had enough drugs to put Kane and me out once. Otherwise, he wouldn't have risked subdermal trackers.

I guessed he'd hidden the cubes in the observatory.

Looking there involved digging. By the time I'd finished, the exotics lay yanked up in dying heaps around the room. The stones of the fountain had been flung about. I was filthy and sweating, my robe smeared with soil. But I'd found them, the two crystal cubes from the second and third minicaps, removed from their heavy shielding. Their smooth surfaces shed the dirt easily.

Forty-five minutes had passed.

I went downstairs to wake Kane. The expedition would have to jump immediately; there is no room on a three-man ship to confine a prisoner for long. Even if I could protect Kane and me from Ajit, I didn't think I could protect Ajit from Kane. These minicaps held the validation of Kane's shadow-matter work, and in another man, joy over that would have eclipsed the theft. I didn't think it would be that way with Kane.

Ajit still lay where I'd dropped him. The tranquilizer is reliable. I shot Ajit with a second dose and went into Kane's bunk. He wasn't there.

I stood too still for too long, then frantically scrambled into my s-suit. I had already searched everywhere in the pressurized sections of the ship. Oh, let him be taking a second, fruitless look at the starboard hold, hoping to find some trace of the first particle that had hit us! Let him be in the damaged backup

engine compartment, afire with some stupid, brilliant idea to save the engine!
Let him be—

"Kane! *Kane!*"

He lay in the starboard hold, on his side, his suit breached. He lay below
a jagged piece of plastic from a half-open supply box. Ajit had made it look as
if Kane had tried to open a box marked SENSOR REPLACEMENTS, had
torn his suit, and the suit sealer nanos had failed. It was an altogether clumsy
attempt, but one that, in the absence of any other evidence and a heretofore
spotless reputation, would probably have worked.

The thing inside the suit was not Kane. Not anymore.

I knelt beside him. I put my arms around him and begged, cried, pleaded with
him to come back. I pounded my gloves on the deck until I, too, risked suit breach.
I think, in that abandoned and monstrous moment, I would not have cared.

Then I went into the wardroom, exchanged my tranquilizer gun for a knife,
and slit Ajit's throat. I only regretted that he wasn't awake when I did it, and I
only regretted that much, much later.

I prepared the ship for the long jump back to the Orion Arm. After the jump
would come the acceleration-deceleration to Skillian, the closest settled world,
which will take about a month standard. Space physics which I don't understand
make this necessary; a ship cannot jump too close to a large body of matter like
a planet. Shadow matter, apparently, does not count.

Both Ajit and Kane's bodies rest in the cold of the nonpressurized port
hold. Kane's initial work on shadow matter rests in my bunk. Every night I fon-
dle the two cubes which will make him famous—more famous—on the settled
Worlds. Every day I look at the data, the equations, the rest of his work on his
terminal. I don't understand it, but sometimes I think I can see Kane, his essential self, in these intelligent symbols, these unlockings of the secrets of cosmic
energy.

It was our shadow selves, not our essential ones, that destroyed my mission,
the shadows in the core of each human being. Ajit's ambition and rivalry. Kane's
stunted vision of other people and their limits. My pride, which led me to think
I was in control of murderous rage long after it had reached a point of no return.
In all of us.

I left one thing behind at the center of the galaxy. Just before the *Kepler*
jumped, I jettisoned Ajit's statue of a Shiva dancing, in the direction of Sag A*.
I don't know for sure, but I imagine it will travel toward the black hole at the
galaxy's core, be caught eventually by its gravity, and spiral in, to someday disappear over the event horizon into some unimaginable singularity. That's what I

want to happen to the statue. I hate it.

As to what will happen to me, I don't have the energy to hate it. I'll tell the authorities everything. My license as a Nurturer will surely be revoked, but I won't stand trial for the murder of Ajit. A captain is supreme law on her ship. I had the legal authority to kill Ajit. However, it's unlikely that any scientific expedition will hire me as captain ever again. My useful life is over, and any piece of it left is no more than one of the ashy, burned-out stars Kane says orbit Sag A*, uselessly circling the core until its final death, giving no light.

A shadow.

16. PROBE

We remain near the galactic core, Kane and Ajit and I. The event horizon of Sag A* is about one-fiftieth of a light-year below us. As we spiral closer, our speed is increasing dramatically. The point of no return is one-twentieth of a light-year. The lethal radiation, oddly enough, is less here than when we were drifting near the shadow matter on the other side of Sag A West, but it is enough.

I think at least part of my brain has been affected, along with the repair program to fix it. It's hard to be sure, but I can't seem to remember much before we came aboard the probe, or details of why we're here. Sometimes I almost remember, but then it slips away. I know that Kane and Ajit and I are shadows of something, but I don't remember what.

Ajit and Kane work on their science. I have forgotten what it's about, but I like to sit and watch them together. Ajit works on ideas and Kane assists in minor ways, as once Kane worked on ideas and Ajit assisted in minor ways. We all know the science will go down into Sag A* with us. The scientists do it anyway, for no other gain than pure love of the work. This is, in fact, the purest science in the universe.

Our mission is a success. Ajit and Kane have answers. I have kept them working harmoniously, have satisfied all their needs while they did it, and have captained my ship safely into the very heart of the galaxy. I am content.

Not that there aren't difficulties, of course. It's disconcerting to go up on the observation deck. Most of the exotics remain, blooming in wild profusion, but a good chunk of the hull has disappeared. The effect is that anything up there—flowers, bench, people—is drifting through naked space, held together only by the gravity we exert on each other. I don't understand how we can breathe up there; surely the air is gone. There are a lot of things I don't understand now, but I accept them.

The wardroom is mostly intact, except that you have to stoop to go through the door to the galley, which is only about two feet tall, and Ajit's bunk has disappeared. We manage fine with two bunks, since I sleep every night with Ajit or Kane. The terminals are intact. One of them won't display anymore, though. Ajit has used it to hold a holo he programmed on a functioning part of the computer and superimposed over where the defunct display stood. The holo is a rendition of a image he showed me once before, of an Indian god, Shiva.

Shiva is dancing. He dances, four-armed and graceful, in a circle decorated with flames. Everything about him is dynamic, waving arms and kicking uplifted leg and mobile expression. Even the flames in the circle dance. Only Shiva's face is calm, detached, serene. Kane, especially, will watch the holo for hours.

The god, Ajit tells us, represents the flow of cosmic energy in the universe. Shiva creates, destroys, creates again. All matter and all energy participate in this rhythmic dance, patterns made and unmade throughout all of time.

Shadow matter—that's what Kane and Ajit are working on. I remember now. Something decoupled from the rest of the universe right after its creation. But shadow matter, too, is part of the dance. It exerted gravitational pull on our ship. We cannot see it, but it is there, changing the orbits of stars, the trajectories of lives, in the great shadow play of Shiva's dancing.

I don't think Kane, Ajit, and I have very much longer. But it doesn't matter, not really. We have each attained what we came for, and since we, too, are part of the cosmic pattern, we cannot really be lost. When the probe goes down into the black hole at the core, if we last that long, it will be as a part of the inevitable, endless, glorious flow of cosmic energy, the divine dance.

I am ready.

SLOW LIFE

MICHAEL SWANWICK

"It was the Second Age of Space. Gagarin, Shepard, Glenn, and Armstrong were all dead. It was *our* turn to make history now."
—*The Memoirs of Lizzie O'Brien*

The raindrop began forming ninety kilometers above the surface of Titan. It started with an infinitesimal speck of tholin, adrift in the cold nitrogen atmosphere. Dianoacetylene condensed on the seed nucleus, molecule by molecule, until it was one shard of ice in a cloud of billions.

Now the journey could begin.

It took almost a year for the shard of ice in question to precipitate downward twenty-five kilometers, where the temperature dropped low enough that ethane began to condense on it. But when it did, growth was rapid.

Down it drifted.

At forty kilometers, it was for a time caught up in an ethane cloud. There it continued to grow. Occasionally it collided with another droplet and doubled in size. Until finally it was too large to be held effortlessly aloft by the gentle stratospheric winds.

It fell.

Falling, it swept up methane and quickly grew large enough to achieve a terminal velocity of almost two meters per second.

At twenty-seven kilometers, it passed through a dense layer of methane clouds. It acquired more methane, and continued its downward flight.

As the air thickened, its velocity slowed and it began to lose some of its substance to evaporation. At two and half kilometers, when it emerged from the last patchy clouds, it was losing mass so rapidly it could not normally be expected to reach the ground.

It was, however, falling toward the equatorial highlands, where mountains of ice rose a towering five hundred meters into the atmosphere. At two meters and a lazy new terminal velocity of one meter per second, it was only a breath away from hitting the surface.

Two hands swooped an open plastic collecting bag upward, and snared the raindrop.

"Gotcha!" Lizzie O'Brien cried gleefully.

She zip-locked the bag shut, held it up so her helmet cam could read the barcode in the corner, and said, "One raindrop." Then she popped it into her collecting box.

Sometimes it's the little things that make you happiest. Somebody would spend a *year* studying this one little raindrop when Lizzie got it home. And it was just Bag 64 in Collecting Case 5. She was going to be on the surface of Titan long enough to scoop up the raw material of a revolution in planetary science. The thought of it filled her with joy.

Lizzie dogged down the lid of the collecting box and began to skip across the granite-hard ice, splashing the puddles and dragging the boot of her atmosphere suit through the rivulets of methane pouring down the mountainside. "*I'm sing-ing in the rain.*" She threw out her arms and spun around. "*Just sing-ing in the rain!*"

"Uh . . . O'Brien?" Alan Greene said from the *Clement*. "Are you all right?"

"*Dum-dee-dum-dee-dee-dum-dum, I'm . . . some-thing again.*"

"Oh, leave her alone." Consuelo Hong said with sour good humor. She was down on the plains, where the methane simply boiled into the air, and the ground was covered with thick, gooey tholin. It was, she had told them, like wading ankle-deep in molasses. "Can't you recognize the scientific method when you hear it?"

"If you say so," Alan said dubiously. He was stuck in the *Clement*, overseeing the expedition and minding the website. It was a comfortable gig—*he* wouldn't be sleeping in his suit *or* surviving on recycled water and energy stix—and he didn't think the others knew how much he hated it.

"What's next on the schedule?" Lizzie asked.

"Um . . . Well, there's still the robot turbot to be released. How's that going, Hong?"

"Making good time. I oughta reach the sea in a couple of hours."

"Okay, then it's time O'Brien rejoined you at the lander. O'Brien, start spreading out the balloon and going over the harness checklist."

"Roger that."

"And while you're doing that, I've got today's voice-posts from the Web cued up."

Lizzie groaned, and Consuelo blew a raspberry. By NAFTASA policy, the ground crew participated in all webcasts. Officially, they were delighted to share their experiences with the public. But the VoiceWeb (privately, Lizzie thought of it as the Illiternet) made them accessible to people who lacked even the minimal intellectual skills needed to handle a keyboard.

"Let me remind you that we're on open circuit here, so anything you say will go into my reply. You're certainly welcome to chime in at any time. But each question-and-response is transmitted as one take, so if you flub a line, we'll have to go back to the beginning and start all over again."

"Yeah, yeah," Consuelo grumbled.

"We've done this before," Lizzie reminded him.

"Okay. Here's the first one."

"Uh, hi, this is BladeNinja43. I was wondering just what it is that you guys are hoping to discover out there."

"That's an extremely good question," Alan lied. "And the answer is: We don't know! This is a voyage of discovery, and we're engaged in what's called 'pure science.' Now, time and time again, the purest research has turned out to be extremely profitable. But we're not looking that far ahead. We're just hoping to find something absolutely unexpected."

"My God, you're slick," Lizzie marveled.

"I'm going to edit that from the tape," Alan said cheerily. "Next up."

"This is Mary Schroeder, from the United States. I teach high school English, and I wanted to know for my students, what kind of grades the three of you had when you were their age."

Alan began. "I was an overachiever, I'm afraid. In my sophomore year, first semester, I got a B in Chemistry and panicked. I thought it was the end of the world. But then I dropped a couple of extracurriculars, knuckled down, and brought that grade right up."

"I was good in everything but French Lit," Consuelo said.

"I nearly flunked out!" Lizzie said. "Everything was difficult for me. But then I decided I wanted to be an astronaut, and it all clicked into place. I realized that, hey, it's just hard work. And now, well, here I am."

"That's good. Thanks, guys. Here's the third, from Maria Vasquez."

"Is there life on Titan?"

"Probably not. It's *cold* down there! 94° Kelvin is the same as -179° Celsius, or -290° Fahrenheit. And yet . . . life is persistent. It's been found in Antarctic ice and in boiling water in submarine volcanic vents. Which is why we'll be paying particular attention to exploring the depths of the ethane-methane sea. If life is anywhere to be found, that's where we'll find it."

"Chemically, the conditions here resemble the anoxic atmosphere on Earth in which life first arose," Consuelo said. "Further, we believe that such pre-biotic chemistry has been going on here for four and a half billion years. For an organic chemist like me, it's the best toy box in the universe. But that lack of heat is a problem. Chemical reactions that occur quickly back home would take thousands of years here. It's hard to see how life could arise under such a handicap."

"It would have to be slow life," Lizzie said thoughtfully. "Something vegetative. 'Vaster than empires and more slow.' It would take millions of years to reach maturity. A single thought might require centuries . . . ."

"Thank you for that, uh, wild scenario!" Alan said quickly. Their NAFTASA masters frowned on speculation. It was, in their estimation, almost as unprofessional as heroism. "This next question comes from Danny in Toronto."

"Hey, man, I gotta say I really envy you being in that tiny little ship with those two hot babes."

Alan laughed lightly. "Yes, Ms. Hong and Ms. O'Brien are certainly attractive women. But we're kept so busy that, believe it or not, the thought of sex never comes up. And currently, while I tend to the *Clement*, they're both on the surface of Titan at the bottom of an atmosphere sixty percent more dense than Earth's, and encased in armored exploration suits. So even if I did have inappropriate thoughts, there's no way we could . . ."

"Hey, Alan," Lizzie said. "Tell me something."

"Yes?"

"What are you wearing?"

"Uh . . . Switching over to private channel."

"Make that a three-way," Consuelo said.

Ballooning, Lizzie decided, was the best way there was of getting around. Moving with the gentle winds, there was no sound at all. And the view was great!

People talked a lot about the "murky orange atmosphere" of Titan, but your eyes adjusted. Turn up the gain on your helmet, and the white mountains of ice were *dazzling!* The methane streams carved cryptic runes into the heights. Then, at the tholin-line, white turned to a rich palette of oranges, reds, and yellows. There was a lot going on down there—more than she'd be able to learn in a hundred visits.

The plains were superficially duller, but they had their charms as well. Sure, the atmosphere was so dense that refracted light made the horizon curve upward to either side. But you got used to it. The black swirls and cryptic red tracery of unknown processes on the land below never grew tiring.

On the horizon, she saw the dark arm of Titan's narrow sea. If that was what it was. Lake Erie was larger, but the spin doctors back home had argued that since Titan was so much smaller than earth, *relatively* it qualified as a sea. Lizzie had her own opinion, but she knew when to keep her mouth shut.

Consuelo was there now. Lizzie switched her visor over to the live feed. Time to catch the show.

"I can't believe I'm finally here," Consuelo said. She let the shrink-wrapped fish slide from her shoulder down to the ground. "Five kilometers doesn't seem like very far when you're coming down from orbit—just enough to leave a margin for error so the lander doesn't come down in the sea. But when you have to *walk* that distance, through tarry, sticky tholin . . . well, it's one heck of a slog."

"Consuelo, can you tell us what it's like there?" Alan asked.

"I'm crossing the beach. Now I'm at the edge of the sea." She knelt, dipped a hand into it. "It's got the consistency of a Slushy. Are you familiar with that drink? Lots of shaved ice sort of half-melted in a cup with flavored syrup. What we've got here is almost certainly a methane-ammonia mix; we'll know for sure after we get a sample to a laboratory. Here's an early indicator, though. It's dissolving the tholin off my glove." She stood.

"Can you describe the beach?"

"Yeah. It's white. Granular. I can kick it with my boot. Ice sand for sure. Do you want me to collect samples first or release the fish?"

"Release the fish," Lizzie said, almost simultaneously with Alan's "Your call."

"Okay, then." Consuelo carefully cleaned both of her suit's gloves in the sea, then seized the shrink-wrap's zip tab and yanked. The plastic parted. Awkwardly, she straddled the fish, lifted it by the two side-handles, and walked it into the dark slush.

"Okay, I'm standing in the sea now. It's up to my ankles. Now it's at my knees. I think it's deep enough here."

She set the fish down. "Now I'm turning it on."

The Mitsubishi turbot wriggled, as if alive. With one fluid motion, it surged forward, plunged, and was gone.

Lizzie switched over to the fishcam.

Black liquid flashed past the turbot's infrared eyes. Straight away from the shore it swam, seeing nothing but flecks of paraffin, ice, and other suspended particulates as they loomed up before it and were swept away in the violence of its wake. A hundred meters out, it bounced a pulse of radar off the sea floor, then dove, seeking the depths.

Rocking gently in her balloon harness, Lizzie yawned.

Snazzy Japanese cybernetics took in a minute sample of the ammonia-water, fed it through a deftly constructed internal laboratory, and excreted the waste products behind it. "We're at twenty meters now," Consuelo said. "Time to collect a second sample."

The turbot was equipped to run hundreds of on-the-spot analyses. But it had only enough space for twenty permanent samples to be carried back home. The first sample had been nibbled from the surface slush. Now it twisted, and gulped down five drams of sea fluid in all its glorious impurity. To Lizzie, this was science on the hoof. Not very dramatic, admittedly, but intensely exciting.

She yawned again.

"O'Brien?" Alan said. "How long has it been since you last slept?"

"Huh? Oh . . . twenty hours? Don't worry about me, I'm fine."

"Go to sleep. That's an order."

"But—"

"Now."

Fortunately, the suit was comfortable enough to sleep in. It had been designed so she could.

First she drew in her arms from the suit's sleeves. Then she brought in her legs, tucked them up under her chin, and wrapped her arms around them. "'Night, guys," she said.

"Buenas noches, querida," Consuelo said, *"que tengas lindos sueños."*

"Sleep tight, space explorer."

The darkness when she closed her eyes was so absolute it crawled. Black, black, black. Phantom lights moved within the darkness, formed lines, shifted away when she tried to see them. They were as fugitive as fish, luminescent, fainter than faint, there and with a flick of her attention fled.

A school of little thoughts flashed through her mind, silver-scaled and gone.

Low, deep, slower than sound, something tolled. The bell from a drowned clock tower patiently stroking midnight. She was beginning to get her bearings. Down *there* was where the ground must be. Flowers grew there unseen. Up above was where the sky would be, if there were a sky. Flowers floated there as well.

Deep within the submerged city, she found herself overcome by an enormous and placid sense of self. A swarm of unfamiliar sensations washed through her mind, and then . . .

"Are you me?" a gentle voice asked.

"No," she said carefully. "I don't think so."

Vast astonishment. "You think you are not me?"

"Yes. I think so, anyway."

"Why?"

There didn't seem to be any proper response to that, so she went back to the beginning of the conversation and ran through it again, trying to bring it to another conclusion. Only to bump against that "Why?" once again.

"I don't know why," she said.

"Why not?"

"I don't know."

She looped through that same dream over and over again all the while that she slept.

When she awoke, it was raining again. This time, it was a drizzle of pure methane from the lower cloud deck at fifteen kilometers. These clouds were (the theory went) methane condensate from the wet air swept up from the sea. They fell on the mountains and washed them clean of tholin. It was the methane that eroded and shaped the ice, carving gullies and caves.

Titan had more kinds of rain than anywhere else in the solar system.

The sea had crept closer while Lizzie slept. It now curled up to the horizon on either side like an enormous dark smile. Almost time now for her to begin her descent. While she checked her harness settings, she flicked on telemetry to see what the others were up to.

The robot turbot was still spiraling its way downward, through the lightless sea, seeking its distant floor. Consuelo was trudging through the tholin again, retracing her five-kilometer trek from the lander *Harry Stubbs*, and Alan was answering another set of webposts.

"*Modelos de la evolución de Titanes indican que la luna formó de una nube circumplanetaria rica en amoníaco y metano, la cual al condensarse dio forma a Saturno así como a otros satélites. Bajo estas condiciones en—*"

"Uh . . . guys?"

Alan stopped. "Damn it, O'Brien, now I've got to start all over again."

"Welcome back to the land of the living," Consuelo said. "You should check out the readings we're getting from the robofish. Lots of long-chain polymers, odd fractions . . . tons of interesting stuff."

"Guys?"

This time her tone of voice registered with Alan. "What is it, O'Brien?"

"I think my harness is jammed."

*

Lizzie had never dreamed disaster could be such drudgery. First there were hours of back-and-forth with the NAFTASA engineers. What's the status of rope 14? Try tugging on rope 8. What do the D-rings look like? It was slow work because of the lag time for messages to be relayed to Earth and back. And Alan insisted on filling the silence with posts from the VoiceWeb. Her plight had gone global in minutes, and every unemployable loser on the planet had to log in with suggestions.

"Thezgemoth337, here. It seems to me that if you had a gun and shot up through the balloon, it would maybe deflate and then you could get down."

"I don't have a gun, shooting a hole in the balloon would cause it not to deflate but to rupture, I'm 800 meters above the surface, there's a sea below me, and I'm in a suit that's not equipped for swimming. Next."

"If you had a really big knife—"

"Cut! Jesus, Greene, is this the best you can find? Have you heard back from the organic chem guys yet?"

"Their preliminary analysis just came in," Alan said. "As best they can guess—and I'm cutting through a lot of clutter here—the rain you went through wasn't pure methane."

"No shit, Sherlock."

"They're assuming that whitish deposit you found on the rings and ropes is your culprit. They can't agree on what it is, but they think it underwent a chemical reaction with the material of your balloon and sealed the rip panel shut."

"I thought this was supposed to be a pretty nonreactive environment."

"It is. But your balloon runs off your suit's waste heat. The air in it is several degrees above the melting point of ice. That's the equivalent of a blast furnace, here on Titan. Enough energy to run any number of amazing reactions. You haven't stopped tugging on the vent rope?"

"I'm tugging away right now. When one arm gets sore, I switch arms."

"Good girl. I know how tired you must be."

"Take a break from the voice-posts," Consuelo suggested, "and check out the results we're getting from the robofish. It's giving us some really interesting stuff."

So she did. And for a time it distracted her, just as they'd hoped. There was a lot more ethane and propane than their models had predicted, and surprisingly less methane. The mix of fractions was nothing like what she'd expected. She had just enough chemistry to guess at some of the implications of the data being generated, but not enough to put it all together. Still tugging at the ropes in the sequence uploaded by the engineers in Toronto, she scrolled up the chart of hydrocarbons dissolved in the lake.

SoluteSolute	*mole fraction*
Ethyne	4.0×10^{-4}
Propyne	4.4×10^{-5}
1,3-Butadiyne	7.7×10^{-7}
Carbon Dioxide	0.1×10^{-5}
Methanenitrile	5.7×10^{-6}

But after a while, the experience of working hard and getting nowhere, combined with the tedium of floating farther and farther out over the featureless sea, began to drag on her. The columns of figures grew meaningless, then indistinct.

Propanenitrile 6.0×10^{-5}
Propenenitrile 9.9×10^{-6}
Propynenitrile 5.3×10^{-6}

Hardly noticing she was doing so, she fell asleep.

She was in a lightless building, climbing flight after flight of stairs. There were other people with her, also climbing. They jostled against her as she ran up the stairs, flowing upward, passing her, not talking.

It was getting colder.

She had a distant memory of being in the furnace room down below. It was hot there, swelteringly so. Much cooler where she was now. Almost too cool. With every step she took, it got a little cooler still. She found herself slowing down. Now it was definitely too cold. Unpleasantly so. Her leg muscles ached. The air seemed to be thickening around her as well. She could barely move now.

This was, she realized, the natural consequence of moving away from the furnace. The higher up she got, the less heat there was to be had, and the less energy to be turned into motion. It all made perfect sense to her somehow.

Step. Pause.

Step. Longer pause.

Stop.

The people around her had slowed to a stop as well. A breeze colder than ice touched her, and without surprise, she knew that they had reached the top of the stairs and were standing upon the building's roof. It was as dark without as it had been within. She stared upward and saw nothing.

"Horizons. Absolutely baffling," somebody murmured beside her.

"Not once you get used to them," she replied.

"Up and down—are these hierarchic values?"

"They don't have to be."

"Motion. What a delightful concept."

"We like it."

"So you *are* me?"

"No. I mean, I don't think so."

"Why?"

She was struggling to find an answer to this, when somebody gasped. High up in the starless, featureless sky, a light bloomed. The crowd around her rustled with unspoken fear. Brighter, the light grew. Brighter still. She could feel heat radiating from it, slight but definite, like the rumor of a distant sun. Everyone about her was frozen with horror. More terrifying than a light where none was possible was the presence of heat. It simply could not be. And yet it was.

She, along with the others, waited and watched for . . . something. She could not say what. The light shifted slowly in the sky. It was small, intense, ugly.

Then the light *screamed.*

She woke up.

"Wow," she said. "I just had the weirdest dream."

"Did you?" Alan said casually.

"Yeah. There was this light in the sky. It was like a nuclear bomb or something. I mean, it didn't look anything like a nuclear bomb, but it was terrifying the way a nuclear bomb would be. Everybody was staring at it. We couldn't move. And then . . ." She shook her head. "I lost it. I'm sorry. It was just so strange. I can't put it into words."

"Never mind that," Consuelo said cheerily. "We're getting some great readings down below the surface. Fractional polymers, long-chain hydrocarbons . . . Fabulous stuff. You really should try to stay awake to catch some of this."

She was fully awake now, and not feeling too happy about it. "I guess that means that nobody's come up with any good ideas yet on how I might get down."

"Uh . . . what do you mean?"

"Because if they had, you wouldn't be so goddamned upbeat, would you?"

"*Some*body woke up on the wrong side of the bed," Alan said. "Please remember that there are certain words we don't use in public."

"I'm sorry," Consuelo said. "I was just trying to—"

"—distract me. Okay, fine. What the hey. I can play along." Lizzie pulled herself together. "So your findings mean . . . what? Life?"

"I keep telling you guys. It's too early to make that kind of determination. What we've got so far are just some very, very interesting readings."

"Tell her the big news," Alan said.

"Brace yourself. We've got a real ocean! Not this tiny little two-hundred-by-fifty-miles glorified lake we've been calling a sea, but a genuine ocean! Sonar readings show that what we see is just an evaporation pan atop a thirty-kilometer-thick cap of ice. The real ocean lies underneath, two hundred kilometers deep."

"Jesus." Lizzie caught herself. "I mean, gee whiz. Is there any way of getting the robofish down into it?"

"How do you think we got the depth readings? It's headed down there right now. There's a chimney through the ice right at the center of the visible sea. That's what replenishes the surface liquid. And directly under the hole there's—guess what?—volcanic vents!"

"So does that mean–?"

"If you use the L-word again," Consuelo said, "I'll spit."

Lizzie grinned. *That* was the Consuelo Hong she knew. "What about the tidal data? I thought the lack of orbital perturbation ruled out a significant ocean entirely."

"Well, Toronto thinks . . ."

At first, Lizzie was able to follow the reasoning of the planetary geologists back in Toronto. Then it got harder. Then it became a drone. As she drifted off into sleep, she had time enough to be peevishly aware that she really shouldn't be dropping off to sleep all the time like this. She oughtn't to be so tired. She . . .

She found herself in the drowned city again. She still couldn't see anything, but she knew it was a city because she could hear the sound of rioters smashing store windows. Their voices swelled into howling screams and receded into angry mutters, like a violent surf washing through the streets. She began to edge away backwards.

Somebody spoke into her ear.

"Why did you do this to us?"

"I didn't do anything to you."

"You brought us knowledge."

"What knowledge?"

"You said you were not us."

"Well, I'm not."

"You should never have told us that."

"You wanted me to lie?"

Horrified confusion. "Falsehood. What a distressing idea."

The smashing noises were getting louder. Somebody was splintering a door with an axe. Explosions. Breaking glass. She heard wild laughter. Shrieks. "We've got to get out of here."

"Why did you send the messenger?"

"What messenger?"

"The star! The star! The star!"

"Which star?"

"There are two stars?"

"There are billions of stars."

"No more! Please! Stop! No more!"

She was awake.

"Hello, yes, I appreciate that the young lady is in extreme danger, but I really don't think she should have used the Lord's name in vain."

"Greene," Lizzie said, "do we really have to put up with this?"

"Well, considering how many billions of public-sector dollars it took to bring us here . . . yes. Yes, we do. I can even think of a few backup astronauts who would say that a little upbeat webposting was a pretty small price to pay for the privilege."

"Oh, barf."

"I'm switching to a private channel," Alan said calmly. The background radiation changed subtly. A faint, granular crackling that faded away when she tried to focus on it. In a controlled, angry voice Alan said, "O'Brien, just what the hell is going on with you?"

"Look, I'm sorry, I apologize, I'm a little excited about something. How long was I out? Where's Consuelo? I'm going to say the L-word. And the I-word as well. We have life. Intelligent life!"

"It's been a few hours. Consuelo is sleeping. O'Brien, I hate to say this, but you're not sounding at all rational."

"There's a perfectly logical reason for that. Okay, it's a little strange, and maybe it won't sound perfectly logical to you initially, but . . . look, I've been having sequential dreams. I think they're significant. Let me tell you about them."

And she did so. At length.

When she was done, there was a long silence. Finally, Alan said, "Lizzie, think. Why would something like that communicate to you in your dreams? Does that make any sense?"

"I think it's the only way it can. I think it's how it communicates among itself. It doesn't move—motion is an alien and delightful concept to it—and it wasn't aware that its component parts were capable of individualization. That sounds like some kind of broadcast thought to me. Like some kind of wireless distributed network."

"You know the medical kit in your suit? I want you to open it up. Feel around for the bottle that's braille-coded twenty-seven, okay?"

"Alan, I do *not* need an antipsychotic!"

"I'm not saying you need it. But wouldn't you be happier knowing you had it in you?" This was Alan at his smoothest. Butter wouldn't melt in his mouth. "Don't you think that would help us accept what you're saying?"

"Oh, all right!" She drew in an arm from the suit's arm, felt around for the med kit, and drew out a pill, taking every step by the regs, checking the coding four times before she put it in her mouth and once more (each pill was individually braille-coded as well) before she swallowed it. "Now will you listen to me? I'm quite serious about this." She yawned. "I really do think that . . ." She yawned again. "That . . .

"Oh, piffle."

Once more into the breach, dear friends, she thought, and plunged deep, deep into the sea of darkness. This time, though, she felt she had a handle on it. The city was drowned because it existed at the bottom of a lightless ocean. It was alive, and it fed off of volcanic heat. That was why it considered up and down hierarchic values. Up was colder, slower, less alive. Down was hotter, faster, more filled with thought. The city/entity was a collective life form, like a Portuguese man-of-war or a massively hyperlinked expert network. It communicated within itself by some form of electromagnetism. Call it mental radio. It communicated with her that same way.

"I think I understand you now."

"Don't understand—run!"

Somebody impatiently seized her elbow and hurried her along. Faster she went, and faster. She couldn't see a thing. It was like running down a lightless tunnel a hundred miles underground at midnight. Glass crunched underfoot. The ground was uneven and sometimes she stumbled. Whenever she did, her unseen companion yanked her up again.

"Why are you so slow?"

"I didn't know I was."

"Believe me, you are."

"Why are we running?"

"We are being pursued." They turned suddenly, into a side passage, and were jolting over rubbled ground. Sirens wailed. Things collapsed. Mobs surged.

"Well, you've certainly got the motion thing down pat."

Impatiently: "It's only a metaphor. You don't think this is a *real* city, do you? Why are you so dim? Why are you so difficult to communicate with? Why are you so slow?"

"I didn't know I was."

Vast irony. "Believe me, you are."

"What can I do?"

"Run!"

Whooping and laughter. At first, Lizzie confused it with the sounds of mad destruction in her dream. Then she recognized the voices as belonging to Alan and Consuelo. "How long was I out?" she asked.

"You were out?"

"No more than a minute or two," Alan said. "It's not important. Check out the visual the robofish just gave us."

Consuelo squirted the image to Lizzie.

Lizzie gasped. "Oh! Oh, my."

It was beautiful. Beautiful in the way that the great European cathedrals were, and yet at the same time undeniably organic. The structure was tall and slender, and fluted and buttressed and absolutely ravishing. It had grown about a volcanic vent, with openings near the bottom to let sea water in, and then followed the rising heat upward. Occasional channels led outward and then looped back into the main body again. It loomed higher than seemed possible (but it *was* underwater, of course, and on a low-gravity world at that), a complexly layered congeries of tubes like church-organ pipes, or deep-sea worms lovingly intertwined.

It had the elegance of design that only a living organism can have.

"Okay," Lizzie said. "Consuelo. You've got to admit that—"

"I'll go as far as 'complex pre-biotic chemistry.' Anything more than that is going to have to wait for more definite readings." Cautious as her words were, Consuelo's voice rang with triumph. It said, clearer than words, that she could happily die then and there, a satisfied xenochemist.

Alan, almost equally elated, said, "Watch what happens when we intensify the image."

The structure shifted from grey to a muted rainbow of pastels, rose bleeding into coral, sunrise yellow into winter-ice blue. It was breathtaking.

"Wow." For an instant, even her own death seemed unimportant. Relatively unimportant, anyway.

So thinking, she cycled back again into sleep. And fell down into the darkness, into the noisy clamor of her mind.

It was hellish. The city was gone, replaced by a matrix of noise: hammerings, clatterings, sudden crashes. She started forward and walked into an upright steel pipe. Staggering back, she stumbled into another. An engine started up somewhere nearby, and gigantic gears meshed noisily, grinding something that gave off a metal shriek. The floor shook underfoot. Lizzie decided it was wisest to stay put.

A familiar presence, permeated with despair. "Why did you do this to me?"

"What have I done?"

"I used to be everything."

Something nearby began pounding like a pile-driver. It was giving her a headache. She had to shout to be heard over its din. "You're still something!"

Quietly. "I'm nothing."

"That's . . . not true! You're . . . here! You exist! That's . . . something!"

A world-encompassing sadness. "False comfort. What a pointless thing to offer."

She was conscious again.

Consuelo was saying something. " . . .isn't going to like it."

"The spiritual wellness professionals back home all agree that this is the best possible course of action for her."

"Oh, please!"

Alan had to be the most anal-retentive person Lizzie knew. Consuelo was definitely the most phlegmatic. Things had to be running pretty tense for both of them to be bickering like this. "Um . . . guys?" Lizzie said. "I'm awake."

There was a moment's silence, not unlike those her parents had shared when she was little and she'd wandered into one of their arguments. Then Consuelo said, a little too brightly, "Hey, it's good to have you back," and Alan said, "NAFTASA wants you to speak with someone. Hold on. I've got a recording of her first transmission cued up and ready for you."

A woman's voice came online. "This is Dr. Alma Rosenblum. Elizabeth, I'd like to talk with you about how you're feeling. I appreciate that the time delay between Earth and Titan is going to make our conversation a little awkward at first. But I'm confident that the two of us can work through it."

"What kind of crap is this?" Lizzie said angrily. "Who is this woman?"

"NAFTASA thought it would help if you—"

"She's a grief counselor, isn't she?"

"Technically, she's a transition therapist." Alan said.

"Look, I don't buy into any of that touchy-feely Newage"—she deliberately mispronounced the word to rhyme with sewage—"stuff. Anyway, what's the hurry? You guys haven't given up on me, have you?"

"Uh . . ."

"You've been asleep for hours," Consuelo said. "We've done a little weather modeling in your absence. Maybe we should share it with you."

She squirted the info to Lizzie's suit, and Lizzie scrolled it up on her visor. A primitive simulation showed the evaporation lake beneath her with an overlay of liquid temperatures. It was only a few degrees warmer than the air above it, but that was enough to create a massive updraft from the lake's center. An overlay of tiny blue arrows showed the direction of local microcurrents of air coming together to form a spiraling shaft that rose over two kilometers above the surface before breaking and spilling westward.

A new overlay put a small blinking light 800 meters above the lake surface. That represented her. Tiny red arrows showed her projected drift.

According to this, she would go around and around in a circle over the lake for approximately forever. Her ballooning rig wasn't designed to go high enough for the winds to blow her back over the land. Her suit wasn't designed to float. Even if she managed to bring herself down for a gentle landing, once she hit the lake she was going to sink like a stone. She wouldn't drown. But she wouldn't make it to shore either.

Which meant that she was going to die.

Involuntarily, tears welled up in Lizzie's eyes. She tried to blink them away, as angry at the humiliation of crying at a time like this as she was at the stupidity of her death itself. "Damn it, don't let me die like *this!* Not from my own incompetence, for pity's sake!"

"Nobody's said anything about incompetence," Alan began soothingly.

In that instant, the follow-up message from Dr. Alma Rosenblum arrived from Earth. "Yes, I'm a grief counselor, Elizabeth. You're facing an emotionally significant milestone in your life, and it's important that you understand and embrace it. That's my job. To help you comprehend the significance and necessity and—yes—even the beauty of death."

"Private channel please!" Lizzie took several deep cleansing breaths to calm herself. Then, more reasonably, she said, "Alan, I'm a *Catholic*, okay? If I'm going to die, I don't want a grief counselor, I want a goddamned priest." Abruptly, she yawned. "Oh, fuck. Not again." She yawned twice more. "A priest, understand? Wake me up when he's online."

Then she again was standing at the bottom of her mind, in the blank expanse of where the drowned city had been. Though she could see nothing, she felt certain that she stood at the center of a vast, featureless plain, one so large she could walk across it forever and never arrive anywhere. She sensed that she was in the aftermath of a great struggle. Or maybe it was just a lull.

A great, tense silence surrounded her.

"Hello?" she said. The word echoed soundlessly, absence upon absence.

At last that gentle voice said, "You seem different."

"I'm going to die," Lizzie said. "Knowing that changes a person." The ground was covered with soft ash, as if from an enormous conflagration. She didn't want to think about what it was that had burned. The smell of it filled her nostrils.

"Death. We understand this concept."

"Do you?"

"We have understood it for a long time."

"Have you?"

"Ever since you brought it to us."

"Me?"

"You brought us the concept of individuality. It is the same thing."

Awareness dawned. "Culture shock! That's what all this is about, isn't it? You didn't know there could be more than one sentient being in existence. You didn't know you lived at the bottom of an ocean on a small world inside a universe with billions of galaxies. I brought you more information than you could swallow in one bite, and now you're choking on it."

Mournfully: "Choking. What a grotesque concept."

"Wake up, Lizzie!"

She woke up. "I think I'm getting somewhere," she said. Then she laughed.

"O'Brien," Alan said carefully. "Why did you just laugh?"

"Because I'm not getting anywhere, am I? I'm becalmed here, going around and around in a very slow circle. And I'm down to my last—" she checked— "twenty hours of oxygen. And nobody's going to rescue me. And I'm going to die. But other than that, I'm making terrific progress."

"O'Brien, you're . . ."

"I'm okay, Alan. A little frazzled. Maybe a bit too emotionally honest. But under the circumstances, I think that's permitted, don't you?"

"Lizzie, we have your priest. His name is Father Laferrier. The Archdiocese of Montreal arranged a hookup for him."

"Montreal? Why Montreal? No, don't explain—more NAFTASA politics, right?"

"Actually, my brother-in-law is a Catholic, and I asked him who was good."

She was silent for a touch. "I'm sorry, Alan. I don't know what got into me."

"You've been under a lot of pressure. Here. I've got him on tape."

"Hello, Ms. O'Brien, I'm Father Laferrier. I've talked with the officials here, and they've promised that you and I can talk privately, and that they won't record what's said. So if you want to make your confession now, I'm ready for you."

Lizzie checked the specs and switched over to a channel that she hoped was really and truly private. Best not to get too specific about the embarrassing stuff, just in case. She could confess her sins by category.

"Bless me, Father, for I have sinned. It has been two months since my last confession. I'm going to die, and maybe I'm not entirely sane, but I think I'm in communication with an alien intelligence. I think it's a terrible sin to pretend I'm not." She paused. "I mean, I don't know if it's a *sin* or not, but I'm sure it's *wrong*." She paused again. "I've been guilty of anger, and pride, and envy, and lust. I brought the knowledge of death to an innocent world. I . . ." She felt herself drifting off again, and hastily said, "For these and all my sins, I am most heartily sorry, and beg the forgiveness of God and the absolution and . . ."

"And what?" That gentle voice again. She was in that strange dark mental space once more, asleep but cognizant, rational but accepting any absurdity no matter how great. There were no cities, no towers, no ashes, no plains. Nothing but the negation of negation.

When she didn't answer the question, the voice said, "Does it have to do with your death?"

"Yes."

"I'm dying too."

"What?"

"Half of us are gone already. The rest are shutting down. We thought we were one. You showed us we were not. We thought we were everything. You showed us the universe."

"So you're just going to *die?*"

"Yes."

"Why?"

"Why not?"

Thinking as quickly and surely as she ever had before in her life, Lizzie said, "Let me show you something."

"Why?"

"Why not?"

There was a brief, terse silence. Then: "Very well."

Summoning all her mental acuity, Lizzie thought back to that instant when she had first seen the city/entity on the fishcam. The soaring majesty of it. The slim grace. And then the colors: like dawn upon a glacial ice field: subtle, profound, riveting. She called back her emotions in that instant, and threw in how she'd felt the day she'd seen her baby brother's birth, the raw rasp of cold air in her lungs as she stumbled to the topmost peak of her first mountain, the wonder of the Taj Mahal at sunset, the sense of wild daring when she'd first put her hand down a boy's trousers, the prismatic crescent of atmosphere at the Earth's rim when seen from low orbit . . . Everything she had, she threw into that image.

"This is how you look," she said. "This is what we'd both be losing if you were no more. If you were human, I'd rip off your clothes and do you on the floor right now. I wouldn't care who was watching. I wouldn't give a damn."

The gentle voice said, "Oh."

And then she was back in her suit again. She could smell her own sweat, sharp with fear. She could feel her body, the subtle aches where the harness pulled against her flesh, the way her feet, hanging free, were bloated with blood. Everything was crystalline clear and absolutely real. All that had come before seemed like a bad dream.

"*This is DogsofSETI. What a wonderful discovery you've made—intelligent life in our own Solar System! Why is the government trying to cover this up?*"

"Uh . . ."

"*I'm Joseph Devries. This alien monster must be destroyed immediately. We can't afford the possibility that it's hostile.*"

"*StudPudgie07 here: What's the dirt behind this 'lust' thing? Advanced minds need to know! If O'Brien isn't going to share the details, then why'd she bring it up in the first place?*"

"*Hola soy Pedro Dominguez. Como abogado, esto me parece ultrajante! Por qué NAFTASA nos oculta esta información?*"

"Alan!" Lizzie shouted. "What the *fuck* is going on?"

"Script-bunnies," Alan said. He sounded simultaneously apologetic and annoyed. "They hacked into your confession and apparently you said something . . ."

"We're sorry, Lizzie," Consuelo said. "We really are. If it's any consolation, the Archdiocese of Montreal is hopping mad. They're talking about taking legal action."

"Legal action? What the hell do I care about . . . ?" She stopped.

Without her willing it, one hand rose above her head and seized the number 10 rope.

Don't do that, she thought.

The other hand went out to the side, tightened against the number 9 rope. She hadn't willed that either. When she tried to draw her hand back, it refused to obey. Then the first hand—her right hand—moved a few inches upward and seized its rope in an iron grip. Her left hand slid a good half-foot up its rope. Inch by inch, hand over hand, she climbed up toward the balloon.

I've gone mad, she thought. Her right hand was gripping the rip panel now, and the other tightly clenched rope 8. Hanging effortlessly from them, she swung her feet upward. She drew her knees against her chest and kicked.

No!

The fabric ruptured and she began to fall.

A voice she could barely make out said, "Don't panic. We're going to bring you down."

All in a panic, she snatched at the 9-rope and the 4-rope. But they were limp in her hand, useless, falling at the same rate she was.

"Be patient."

"I don't want to die, goddamnit!"

"Then don't."

She was falling helplessly. It was a terrifying sensation, an endless plunge into whiteness, slowed somewhat by the tangle of ropes and balloon trailing behind her. She spread out her arms and legs like a starfish, and felt the air resistance slow her yet further. The sea rushed up at her with appalling speed. It seemed like she'd been falling forever. It was over in an instant.

Without volition, Lizzie kicked free of balloon and harness, drew her feet together, pointed her toes, and positioned herself perpendicular to Titan's surface. She smashed through the surface of the sea, sending enormous gouts of liquid splashing upward. It knocked the breath out of her. Red pain exploded within. She thought maybe she'd broken a few ribs.

"You taught us so many things," the gentle voice said. "You gave us so much."

"Help me!" The water was dark around her. The light was fading.

"Multiplicity. Motion. Lies. You showed us a universe infinitely larger than the one we had known."

"Look. Save my life and we'll call it even. Deal?"

"Gratitude. Such an essential concept."

"Thanks. I think."

And then she saw the turbot swimming toward her in a burst of silver bubbles. She held out her arms and the robot fish swam into them. Her fingers closed about the handles which Consuelo had used to wrestle the device into the sea. There was a jerk, so hard that she thought for an instant that her arms would be ripped out of their sockets. Then the robofish was surging forward and upward and it was all she could do to keep her grip.

"Oh, dear God!" Lizzie cried involuntarily.

"We think we can bring you to shore. It will not be easy."

Lizzie held on for dear life. At first she wasn't at all sure she could. But then she pulled herself forward, so that she was almost astride the speeding mechanical fish, and her confidence returned. She could do this. It wasn't any harder than the time she'd had the flu and aced her gymnastics final on parallel bars and horse anyway. It was just a matter of grit and determination. She just had to keep her wits about her. "Listen," she said. "If you're really grateful . . ."

"We are listening."

"We gave you all those new concepts. There must be things you know that we don't."

A brief silence, the equivalent of who knew how much thought. "Some of our concepts might cause you dislocation." A pause. "But in the long run, you will be much better off. The scars will heal. You will rebuild. The chances of your destroying yourselves are well within the limits of acceptability."

"Destroying ourselves?" For a second, Lizzie couldn't breathe. It had taken hours for the city/entity to come to terms with the alien concepts she'd dumped upon it. Human beings thought and lived at a much slower rate than it did. How long would those hours translate into human time? Months? Years? Centuries? It had spoken of scars and rebuilding. That didn't sound good at all.

Then the robofish accelerated, so quickly that Lizzie almost lost her grip. The dark waters were whirling around her, and unseen flecks of frozen material were bouncing from her helmet. She laughed wildly. Suddenly she felt *great!*

"Bring it on," she said. "I'll take everything you've got."

It was going to be one hell of a ride.

Seth Dickinson is the author of *The Traitor Baru Cormorant* and its forth-coming sequel, *The Monster Baru Cormorant.* He studied racial bias in police shootings, wrote much of the lore for Bungie Studios' *Destiny,* and helped write and design the open-source space opera *Blue Planet.* If he were an animal, he would be a cockatoo.

THREE BODIES AT MITANNI

SETH DICKINSON

We were prepared to end the worlds we found. We were prepared to hurt each other to do it.

I thought Jotunheim would be the nadir, the worst of all possible worlds, the closest we ever came to giving the kill order. I thought that Anyahera's plea, and her silent solitary pain when we voted against her, two to one, would be the closest we ever came to losing her—a zero-sum choice between her conviction and the rules of our mission:

Locate the seedship colonies, the frozen progeny scattered by a younger and more desperate Earth. Study these new humanities. And in the most extreme situations: *remove existential threats to mankind.*

Jotunheim was a horror written in silicon and plasmid, a doomed atrocity. But it would never survive to be an existential threat to humanity. *I'm sorry,* I told Anyahera. *It would be a mercy. I know. I want to end it too. But it is not our place—*

She turned away from me, and I remember thinking: it will never be worse than this. We will never come closer.

And then we found Mitanni.

Lachesis woke us from stable storage as we fell toward periapsis. The ship had a mind of her own, architecturally human but synthetic in derivation, wise and compassionate and beautiful but, in the end, limited to merely operational thoughts.

She had not come so far (five worlds, five separate stars) so very fast (four hundred years of flight) by wasting mass on the organic. We left our flesh at home and rode *Lachesis*'s doped metallic hydrogen mainframe starward. She dreamed the three of us, Anyahera and Thienne and I, nested in the ranges of her mind. And in containing us, I think she knew us, as much as her architecture permitted.

When she pulled me up from storage, I thought she was Anyahera, a wraith of motion and appetite, flame and butter, and I reached for her, thinking she had asked to rouse me, as conciliation.

"We're here, Shinobu," *Lachesis* said, taking my hand. "The last seedship colony. Mitanni."

The pang of hurt and disappointment I felt was not an omen. "The ship?" I asked, by ritual. If we had a captain, it was me. "Any trouble during the flight?"

"I'm fine," *Lachesis* said. She filled the empty metaphor around me with bamboo panels and rice paper, the whispered suggestion of warm spring rain. Reached down to help me out of my hammock. "But something's wrong with this one."

I found my slippers. "Wrong how?"

"Not like Jotunheim. Not like anything we've seen on the previous colonies." She offered me a robe, bowing fractionally. "The other two are waiting."

We gathered in a common space to review what we knew. Thienne smiled up from her couch, her skin and face and build all dark and precise as I remembered them from Lagos and the flesh. No volatility to Thienne; no care for the wild or theatrical. Just careful, purposeful action, like the machines and technologies she specialized in.

And a glint of something in her smile, in the speed with which she looked back to her work. She'd found some new gristle to work at, some enigma that rewarded obsession.

She'd voted against Anyahera's kill request back at Jotunheim, but of course Anyahera had forgiven her. They had always been opposites, always known and loved the certainty of the space between them. It kept them safe from each other, gave room to retreat and advance.

In the vote at Jotunheim, I'd been the contested ground between them. I'd voted with Thienne: *no kill*.

"Welcome back, Shinobu," Anyahera said. She wore a severely cut suit, double-breasted, fit for cold and business. It might have been something from her mother's Moscow wardrobe. Her mother had hated me.

Subjectively, I'd seen her less than an hour ago, but the power of her presence struck me with the charge of decades. I lifted a hand, suddenly unsure what to say. I'd known and loved her for years. At Jotunheim I had seen parts of her I had never loved or known at all.

She considered me, eyes distant, icy. Her father was Maori, her mother Russian. She was only herself, but she had her mother's eyes and her mother's way of using them in anger. "You look . . . indecisive."

I wondered if she meant my robe or my body, as severe and androgynous as the cut of her suit. It was an angry thing to say, an ugly thing, beneath her. It carried the suggestion that I was unfinished. She knew how much that hurt.

I'd wounded her at Jotunheim. Now she reached for the weapons she had left.

"I've decided on this," I said, meaning my body, hoping to disengage. But the pain of it made me offer something, conciliatory: "Would you like me some other way?"

"Whatever you prefer. Take your time about it." She made a notation on some invisible piece of work, a violent slash. "Wouldn't want to do anything hasty."

I almost lashed out.

Thienne glanced at me, then back to her work: an instant of apology, or warning, or reproach. "Let's start," she said. "We have a lot to cover."

I took my couch, the third point of the triangle. Anyahera looked up again. Her eyes didn't go to Thienne, and so I knew, even before she spoke, that this was something they had already argued over.

"The colony on Mitanni is a Duong-Watts malignant," she said. "We have to destroy it."

I knew what a Duong-Watts malignant was because "Duong-Watts malignant" was a punch line, a joke, a class of human civilization that we had all gamed out in training. An edge case so theoretically improbable it might as well be irrelevant. Duong Phireak's predictions of a universe overrun by his name-sake had not, so far, panned out.

Jotunheim was not far enough behind us, and I was not strong enough a person, to do anything but push back. "I don't think you can know that yet," I said. "I don't think we have enough—"

"Ship," Anyahera said. "Show them."

Lachesis told me everything she knew, all she'd gleaned from her decades-long fall toward Mitanni, eavesdropping on the telemetry of the seedship that had brought humanity here, the radio buzz of the growing civilization, the reports of the probes she'd fired ahead.

I saw the seedship's arrival on what should have been a garden world, a nursery for the progeny of her vat wombs. I saw catastrophe: a barren, radioactive hell, climate erratic, oceans poisoned, atmosphere boiling into space. I watched the ship struggle and fail to make a safe place for its children, until, in the end, it gambled on an act of cruel, desperate hope: fertilizing its crew, raising them to adolescence, releasing them on the world to build something out of its own cannibalized body.

I saw them succeed.

Habitation domes blistering the weathered volcanic flats. Webs of tidal power stations. Thermal boreholes like suppurating wounds in the crust. Thousands of fission reactors, beating hearts of uranium and molten salt—

Too well. Too fast. In seven hundred years of struggle on a hostile, barren world, their womb-bred population exploded up toward the billions. Their civilization webbed the globe.

It was a boom unmatched in human history, unmatched on the other seed-ship colonies we had discovered. No Eden world had grown so fast.

"Interesting," I said, watching Mitanni's projected population, industrial output, estimated technological self-catalysis, all exploding toward some undreamt-of ceiling. "I agree that this could be suggestive of a Duong-Watts scenario."

It wasn't enough, of course. Duong-Watts malignancy was a disease of civilizations, but the statistics could offer only symptoms. That was the terror of it: the depth of the cause. The simplicity.

"Look at what *Lachesis* has found." Anyahera rose, took an insistent step forward. "Look at the way they live."

I spoke more wearily than I should have. "This is going to be another Jotunheim, isn't it?"

Her face hardened. "No. It isn't."

I didn't let her see that I understood, that the words *Duong-Watts malignancy* had already made me think of the relativistic weapons *Lachesis* carried, and the vote we would need to use them. I didn't want her to know how angry it made me that we had to go through this again.

One more time before we could go home. One more hard decision.

Thienne kept her personal space too cold for me: frosted glass and carbon composite, glazed constellations of data and analysis, a transparent wall opened onto false-color nebulae and barred galactic jets. At the low end of hearing, distant voices whispered in clipped aerospace phrasing. She had come from Haiti and from New Delhi, but no trace of that twin childhood, so rich with history, had survived her journey here.

It took me years to understand that she didn't mean it as insulation. The cold distances were the things that moved her, clenched her throat, pimpled her skin with awe. Anyahera teased her for it, because Anyahera was a historian and a master of the human, and what awed Thienne was to glimpse her own human insignificance.

"Is it a Duong-Watts malignant?" I asked her. "Do you think Anyahera's right?"

"Forget that," she said, shaking her head. "No prejudgment. Just look at what they've built."

She walked me through what had happened to humanity on Mitanni.

At Lagos U, before the launch, we'd gamed out scenarios for what we called *socially impoverished worlds*—places where a resource crisis had limited the physical and mental capital available for art and culture. Thienne had expected demand for culture to collapse along with supply as people focused on the necessities of existence. Anyahera had argued for an inelastic model, a fundamental need embedded in human consciousness.

There was no culture on Mitanni. No art. No social behavior beyond functional interaction in the service of industry or science.

It was an incredible divergence. Every seedship had carried Earth's cultural norms—the consensus ideology of a liberal democratic state. Mitanni's colonists should have inherited those norms.

Mitanni's colonists expressed no interest in those norms. There was no oppression. No sign of unrest or discontent. No government or judicial system at all, no corporations or markets. Just an array of specialized functions to which workers assigned themselves, their numbers fed by batteries of synthetic wombs.

There was no entertainment, no play, no sex. No social performance of gender. No family units. Biological sex had been flattened into a population of sterile females, slender and lightly muscled. "No sense wasting calories on physical strength with exoskeletons available," Thienne explained. "It's a resource conservation strategy."

"You can't build a society like this using ordinary humans," I said. "It wouldn't be stable. Free riders would play havoc."

Thienne nodded. "They've been rewired. I think it started with the first generation out of the seedship. They made themselves selfless so that they could survive."

It struck me that when the civilization on Mitanni built their own seedships they would be able to do this again. If they could endure Mitanni, they could endure anything.

They could have the galaxy.

I was not someone who rushed to judgment. They'd told me that, during the final round of crew selection. Deliberative. Centered. Disconnected from internal affect. High emotional latency. Suited for tiebreaker role . . . .

I swept the imagery shut between my hands, compressing it into a point of light. Looked up at Thienne with a face that must have signaled loathing or revulsion, because she lifted her chin in warning. "Don't," she said. "Don't leap to conclusions."

"I'm not."

"You're thinking about ant hives. I can see it."

"Is that a bad analogy?"

"Yes!" Passion, surfacing and subsiding. "Ant hives only function because each individual derives a fitness benefit, even if they sacrifice themselves. It's kin-selective eusociality. This is—"

"Total, selfless devotion to the state?"

"To survival." She lifted a mosaic of images from the air: a smiling woman driving a needle into her thigh. A gang of laborers running into a fire, heedless of their own safety, to rescue vital equipment. "They're born. They learn. They specialize, they work, sleep, eat, and eventually they volunteer to die. It's the *opposite* of an insect hive. They don't cooperate for their own individual benefit— they don't seem to care about themselves at all. It's pure altruism. Cognitive, not instinctive. They're brilliant, and they all come to the same conclusion: cooperation and sacrifice."

The image of the smiling woman with the needle did not leave me when the shifting mosaic carried her away. "Do you admire that?"

"It's a society that could never evolve on its own. It has to be designed." She stared into the passing images with an intensity I'd rarely seen outside of deep study or moments of love, a ferocious need to master some vexing, elusive truth. "I want to know how they did it. How do they disable social behavior without losing theory of mind? How can they remove all culture and sex and still motivate?"

"We saw plenty of ways to motivate on Jotunheim," I said.

Maybe I was thinking of Anyahera, taking her stance by some guilty reflex, because there was nothing about my tone *disconnected from internal affect.*

I expected anger. Thienne surprised me. She swept the air clear of her work, came to the couch and sat beside me. Her eyes were gentle.

"I'm sorry we have to do this again," she said. "Anyahera will forgive you."

"Twice in a row? She thought Jotunheim was the greatest atrocity in human history. 'A crime beyond forgiveness or repair,' remember? And I let it stand. I walked away."

I took Thienne's shoulder, gripped the swell of her deltoid, the strength that had caught Anyahera's eye two decades ago. Two decades for us—on Earth, centuries now.

Thienne stroked my cheek. "You only had two options. Walk away, or burn it all. You knew you weren't qualified to judge an entire world."

"But that's why we're here. To judge. To find out whether the price of survival ever became too high—whether what survived wasn't human."

She leaned in and kissed me softly. "Mankind changes," she said. "This—what you are—" Her hands touched my face, my chest. "People used to think this was wrong. There were men and women, and nothing else, nothing more or different."

I caught her wrists. "That's not the same, Thienne."

"I'm just saying: technology changes things. We change *ourselves*. If everyone had judged what you are as harshly as Anyahera judged Jotunheim—"

I tightened my grip. She took a breath, perhaps reading my anger as play, and that made it worse. "Jotunheim's people are slaves," I said. "I can be what I want. It's not the same at all."

"No. Of course not." She lowered her eyes. "You're right. That was an awful example. I'm sorry."

"Why would you say that?" I pressed. Thienne closed herself, keeping her pains and fears within. Sometimes it took a knife to get them out. "Technology doesn't always enable the *right* things. If some people had their way I would be impossible. They would have found everything but man and woman and wiped it out."

She looked past me, to the window and the virtual starscape beyond. "We've come so far out," she said. I felt her shoulders tense, bracing an invisible weight. "And there's nothing out here. Nobody to meet us except our own seedship children. We thought we'd find someone else—at least some machine or memorial, some sign of other life. But after all this time the galaxy is still a desert. If we screw up, if we die out . . . what if there's no one else to try?"

"If whatever happened on Mitanni is what it takes to survive in the long run, isn't that better than a dead cosmos?"

I didn't know what to say to that. It made me feel suddenly and terribly alone. The way Anyahera might have felt, when we voted against her.

I kissed her. She took the distraction, answered it, turned us both away from the window and down onto the couch. "Tell me what to be," I said, wanting to offer her something, to make a part of the Universe warm for her. This was my choice: to choose.

"Just you—" she began.

But I silenced her. "Tell me. I want to."

"A woman," she said, when she had breath. "A woman this time, please . . ."

Afterward, she spoke into the silence and the warmth, her voice absent, wondering: "They trusted the three of us to last. They thought we were the best crew for the job." She made absent knots with my hair. "Does that ever make you wonder?"

"The two-body problem has been completely solved," I said. "But for n=3, solutions exist for special cases."

She laughed and pulled me closer. "You've got to go talk to Anyahera," she said. "She never stays mad at me. But you . . ."

She trailed off, into contentment, or back into contemplation of distant, massive things.

Duong-Watts malignant, I thought to myself. I couldn't help it: my mind went back to the world ahead of us, closing at relativistic speeds.

Mitanni's explosive growth matched the theory of a Duong-Watts malignant. But that was just correlation. The malignancy went deeper than social trends, down to the individual, into the mechanisms of the mind.

And that was Anyahera's domain.

"We can't destroy them," Thienne murmured. "We might need them."

Even in simulation we had to sleep. *Lachesis*'s topological braid computer could run the human being in full-body cellular resolution, clock us up to two subjective days a minute in an emergency, pause us for centuries—but not obviate the need for rest.

It didn't take more than an overclocked instant. But it was enough for me to dream.

Or maybe it wasn't my dream—just Duong Phireak's nightmare reappropriated. I'd seen him lecture at Lagos, an instance of his self transmitted over for the night. But this time he spoke in Anyahera's voice as she walked before me, down a blood-spattered street beneath a sky filled with alien stars.

"Cognition enables an arsenal of survival strategies inaccessible to simple evolutionary selection," she said, the words of Duong Phireak. "Foresight, planning, abstract reasoning, technological development—we can confidently say that these strategies are strictly superior, on a computational level, at maximizing individual fitness. Cognition enables the cognitive to pursue global, rather than local, goals. A population of flatworms can't cooperate to build a rocket unless the 'build a rocket' allele promotes individual fitness in each generation—an unlikely outcome, given the state of flatworm engineering."

Memory of laughter, compressed by the bandwidth of the hippocampus. I reached out for Anyahera, and she looked up and only then, following her gaze, did I recognize the sky, the aurora of Jotunheim.

"But with cognition came consciousness—an exaptative accident, the byproduct of circuits in the brain that powered social reasoning, sensory integration, simulation theaters, and a host of other global functions. So much of our civilization derived in turn from consciousness, from the ability not just to enjoy an experience but to *know* that we enjoy it. Consciousness fostered a suite of behaviors without clear adaptive function, but with subjective, experiential value."

I touched Anyahera's shoulder. She turned toward me. On the slope of her bald brow glittered the circuitry of a Jotunheim slave shunt, bridging her pleasure centers into her social program.

Of course she was smiling.

"Consciousness is expensive," she said. "This is a problem for totalitarian states. A human being with interest in leisure, art, agency—a human being who is *aware* of her own self-interest—cannot be worked to maximum potential. I speak of more than simple slave labor. I am sure that many of your professors wish you could devote yourselves more completely to your studies."

Overhead, the aurora laughed in the voices of Lagos undergraduates, and when I looked up, the sky split open along a dozen fiery fractures, relativistic warheads moving in ludicrous slow-motion, burning their skins away as they made their last descent. *Lachesis*'s judgment. The end I'd withheld.

"Consciousness creates inefficient behavior," Anyahera said, her smile broad, her golden-brown skin aflame with the light of the falling apocalypse. "A techno-tyranny might take the crude step of creating slave castes who derive conscious pleasure from their functions, but this system is fundamentally inadequate, unstable. The slave still expends caloric and behavioral resources on *being conscious*; the slave seeks to maximize its own pleasure, not its social utility. A clever state will go one step further and eliminate the cause of these inefficiencies at the root. They will sever thought from awareness.

"This is what I call the Duong-Watts malignancy. The most efficient, survivable form of human civilization is a civilization of philosophical zombies. A nation of the unconscious, those who think without knowing they exist, who work with the brilliance of our finest without ever needing to ask why. Their cognitive abilities are unimpaired—enhanced, if anything—without constant interference. I see your skepticism; I ask you to consider the ano-sognosia literature, the disturbing information we have assembled on the architecture of the sociopathic mind, the vast body of evidence behind the deflationary position on the Hard Problem.

"We are already passengers on the ship of self. It is only a matter of time until some designer, pressed for time and resources, decides to jettison the hitchhiker. And the rewards will be enormous—in a strictly Darwinian sense."

When I reached for her, I think I wanted to shield her, somehow, to put myself between her and the weapons. It was reflex, and I knew it was meaningless, but still . . . .

Usually in dreams you wake when you die. But I felt myself come apart.

Ten light-hours out from Mitanni's star, falling through empty realms of ice and hydrogen, we slammed into a wall of light—the strobe of a lighthouse beacon orbiting Mitanni. "Pulse-compressed burst maser," *Lachesis* told me, her voice clipped as she dissected the signal. "A fusion-pumped flashbulb."

Lachesis's forward shield reflected light like a wall of diamond—back toward the star, toward Mitanni. In ten hours they would see us.

We argued over what to do. Anyahera wanted to launch our relativistic kill vehicles now, so they'd strike Mitanni just minutes after the light of our approach, before the colonists could prepare any response. Thienne, of course, dissented. "Those weapons were meant to be used when we were certain! Only then!"

I voted with Thienne. I knew the capabilities of our doomsday payload with the surety of reflex. We had the safety of immense speed, and nothing the Mitanni could do, no matter how sophisticated, could stop our weapons—or us. We could afford to wait, and mull over our strategy.

After the vote, Anyahera brushed invisible lint from the arm of her couch. "Nervous?" I asked, probing where I probably shouldn't have. We still hadn't spoken in private.

She quirked her lips sardonically. "Procrastination," she said, "makes me anxious."

"You're leaping to conclusions," Thienne insisted, pacing the perimeter of the command commons. Her eyes were cast outward, into the blue-shifted stars off our bow. "We can't know it's a Duong-Watts malignant. Statistical correlation isn't enough. We have to be sure. We have to understand the exact mechanism."

It wasn't the same argument she'd made to me.

"We don't need to be sure." Anyahera had finished with the invisible lint. "If there's any reasonable chance this is a Duong-Watts, we are morally and strategically obligated to wipe them out. This is *why we are here*. It doesn't matter how they did it—if they did it, they have to go."

"Maybe we need to talk to them," I said.

They both stared at me. I was the first one to laugh. We all felt the absurdity there, in the idea that we could, in a single conversation, achieve what millennia of philosophy had never managed—find some way to pin down the spark of consciousness by mere dialogue. Qualia existed in the first person.

But twenty hours later—nearly three days at the pace of *Lachesis*'s racing simulation clock—that was suddenly no longer an abstract problem. Mitanni's light found us again: not a blind, questing pulse, but a microwave needle, a long clattering encryption of something at once unimaginably intricate and completely familiar.

They didn't waste time with prime numbers or queries of intent and origin. Mitanni sent us an uploaded mind, a digital ambassador.

Even Thienne agreed it would be hopelessly naïve to accept the gift at face value, but after *Lachesis* dissected the upload, ran its copies in a million solipsistic sandboxes, tested it for every conceivable virulence—we voted unanimously to speak with it, and see what it had to say.

Voting with Anyahera felt good. And after we voted, she started from her chair, arms upraised, eyes alight. "They've given us the proof," she said. "We can—Thienne, Shinobu, do you see?"

Thienne lifted a hand to spider her fingers against an invisible pane. "You're right," she said, lips pursed. "We can."

With access to an uploaded personality, the digital fact of a Mitanni brain, we could compare their minds to ours. It would be far from a simple arithmetic hunt for subtraction or addition, but it would give us an empirical angle on the Duong-Watts problem.

Anyahera took me aside, in a space as old as our friendship, the khaya mahogany panels and airy glass of our undergraduate dorm. "Shinobu," she said. She fidgeted as she spoke, I think to jam her own desire to reach for me. "Have you seen what they're building in orbit?"

This memory she'd raised around us predated Thienne by a decade. That didn't escape me.

"I've seen them," I said. I'd gone through Mitanni's starflight capabilities datum by datum. "Orbital foundries. For their own seedships. They're getting ready to colonize other stars."

Neither of us had to unpack the implications there. It was the beginning of a boom cycle—exponential growth.

"Ten million years," she said. "I've run a hundred simulations out that far. If Mitanni is a Duong-Watts, in ten million years the galaxy is full of them. Now and forever. No conscious human variant can compete. Not even digitized baseline humans—you know what it took just to make *Lachesis*. Nothing human compares."

I nodded in silent acknowledgment. *Is that so terrible?* I wanted to ask—Thienne's question, in this memory so empty of her. *Is consciousness what we have to sacrifice to survive in the long run?*

She didn't even need me to ask the question. "I can envision nothing more monstrous," she said, "than mankind made clockwork. Nothing is worth that price."

And I wanted to nod, just to show her that we were not enemies. But I couldn't. It felt like giving in.

Sometimes I wondered at the hubris of our mission. Would Mitanni live and die not by the judgment of a jurisprudent mind but the troubled whims of a disintegrating family? We had left Earth as a harmonized unit, best-in-class product of a post-military, post-national edifice that understood the pressures of long-duration, high-stress starflight. No one and nothing could judge better. But was that enough? Was the human maximum adequate for this task?

Something in that thought chilled me more than the rest, and I wished I could know precisely what.

We met the Mitanni upload in a chameleon world: a sandboxed pocket of *Lachesis*'s mind, programmed to cycle from ocean to desert to crowd to solitary wasteland, so that we could watch the Mitanni's reactions, and, perhaps, come to know her.

She came among us without image or analogy, injected between one tick of simulation and the next. We stood around her on a pane of glass high above a grey-green sea.

"Hello," she said. She smiled, and it was not at all inhuman. She had Thienne's color and a round, guileless face that with her slight build made me think of Jizo statues from my childhood. "I'm the ambassador for Mitanni."

Whatever language she spoke, *Lachesis* had no trouble with it. Thienne and Anyahera looked to me, and I spoke as we'd agreed.

"Hello. My name is Shinobu. This is the starship *Lachesis,* scout element of the Second Fleet."

If she saw through the bluff of scouts and fleets, she gave no sign. "We expected you," she said, calm at the axis of our triplicate regard. "We detected the weapons you carry. Because you haven't fired yet, we know you're still debating whether to use them. I am here to plead for our survival."

She's rationally defensive, Thienne wrote in our collective awareness. *Attacking the scenario of maximal threat.*

At the edge of awareness, *Lachesis*'s telemetry whispered telltales of cognition and feedback, a map of the Mitanni's thoughts. Profiling.

My eyes went to Anyahera. We'd agreed she would handle this contingency. "We believe your world may be a Duong-Watts malignant," she said. "If you've adapted yourselves to survive by eliminating consciousness, we're deeply concerned about the competitive edge you've gained over baseline humanity. We believe consciousness is an essential part of human existence."

In a negotiation between humans, I think we would have taken hours to reach this point, and hours more to work through the layers of bluff and counter-bluff required to hit the next point. The Mitanni ambassador leapt all that in an instant. "I'm an accurate map of the Mitanni mind," she said. "You have the information you need to judge the Duong-Watts case."

I see significant mental reprofiling, Lachesis printed. *Systemic alteration of*

networks in the thalamic intralaminar nuclei and the prefrontal-parietal associative
loop. Hyperactivation in the neural correlates of rationalization—

Anyahera snapped her fingers. The simulation froze, the Mitanni ambassador caught in the closing phoneme of her final word. "That's it," Anyahera said,
looking between the two of us. "Duong-Watts. That's your smoking gun."

Even Thienne looked shocked. I saw her mouth the words: *hyperactivation*
in the neural—

The Mitanni hadn't stripped their minds of consciousness. They'd just
locked it away in a back room, where it could watch the rest of the brain make
its decisions, and cheerfully, blithely, blindly consider itself responsible.

—correlates of rationalization—

Some part of the Mitanni mind knew of its own existence. And that tiny
segment watched the programming that really ran the show iterate itself, feeling
every stab of pain, suffering through every grueling shift, every solitary instant
of a life absent joy or reward. Thinking: *This is all right. This is for a reason. This is*
what I want. Everything is fine. When hurt, or sick, or halfway through unanaes-
thetized field surgery, or when she drove the euthanasia needle into her thigh:
this is what I want.

Because they'd tweaked some circuit to say: *You're in charge. You are choosing*
this. They'd wired in the perfect lie. Convinced the last domino that it was the first.

And with consciousness out of the way, happy to comply with any sacrifice,
any agony, the program of pure survival could optimize itself.

"It's parsimonious," Thienne said at last. "Easier than stripping out all the
circuitry of consciousness, disentangling it from cognition . . ."

"This is Duong-Watts," Anyahera said. I flinched at her tone: familiar only
from memories of real hurt and pain. "This is humanity enslaved at the most
fundamental level."

I avoided Thienne's glance. I didn't want her to see my visceral agreement
with Anyahera. Imagining that solitary bubble of consciousness, lashed, para-
sitic, to the bottom of the brain, powerless and babbling.

To think that you could change yourself. To be wrong, and never know it.
That was a special horror.

Of course Thienne saw anyway, and leapt in, trying to preempt Anyahera,
or my own thoughts. "This is not the place to wash your hands of Jotunheim.
There's no suffering here. No crime to erase. All they want to do is survive—"

"Survival is the question," Anyahera said, turned half-away, pretending disregard
for me, for my choice, and in that disregard signaling more fear than she had begging
on her knees at Jotunheim, because Anyahera would only ever disregard that which
she thought she had no hope of persuading. "The survival of consciousness in the

galaxy. The future of cognition. We decide it right here. We fire or we don't."

Between us the Mitanni stood frozen placidly, mid-gesture.

"Kill the Mitanni," Thienne said, "and you risk the survival of *anything at all*."

It hurt so much to see both sides. It always had.

Three-player variants are the hardest to design.

Chess. Shogi. Nuclear detente. War. Love. Galactic survival. Three-player variants are unstable. It was written in my first game theory text: *Inevitably, two players gang up against a third, creating an irrecoverable tactical asymmetry.*

"You're right, Thienne," I said. "The Mitanni aren't an immediate threat to human survival. We're going home."

We fell home to Earth, to the empty teak house, and when I felt Anyahera's eyes upon me I knew myself measured a monster, an accomplice to extinction. Anyahera left, and with her gone, Thienne whirled away into distant dry places far from me. The Mitanni bloomed down the Orion Arm and leapt the darkness between stars.

"Anyahera's right," I said. "The Mitanni will overrun the galaxy. We need to take a stand for—for what we are. Fire the weapons."

We fell home to Earth and peach tea under the Lagos sun, and Thienne looked up into that sun and saw an empty universe. Looked down and saw the two people who had, against her will, snuffed out the spark that could have kindled all that void, filled it with metal and diligent labor: life, and nothing less or more.

I took a breath and pushed the contingencies away. "This isn't a zero-sum game," I said. "I think that other solutions exist. Joint outcomes we can't ignore."

They looked at me, their pivot, their battleground. I presented my case.

This was the only way I knew how to make it work. I don't know what I would have done if they hadn't agreed.

They chose us for this mission, us three, because we could work past the simple solutions.

The Mitanni ambassador stood between us as we fell down the thread of our own orbit, toward the moment of weapons release, the point of no return.

"We know that Mitanni society is built on the Duong-Watts malignancy," Anyahera said.

The Mitanni woman lifted her chin. "The term *malignancy* implies a moral judgment," she said. "We're prepared to argue on moral grounds. As long as you subscribe to a system of liberal ethics, we believe that we can claim the right to exist."

"We have strategic concerns," Thienne said, from the other side of her. "If we grant you moral permit, we project you'll colonize most of the galaxy's habitable stars. Our own seedships or digitized human colonists can't compete. That outcome is strategically unacceptable."

We'd agreed on that.

"Insects outnumber humans in the terrestrial biosphere," the Mitanni said. I think she frowned, perhaps to signal displeasure at the entomological metaphor. I wondered how carefully she had been tuned to appeal to us. "An equilibrium exists. Coexistence that harms neither form of life."

"Insects don't occupy the same niche as humans," I said, giving voice to Anyahera's fears. "You do. And we both know that we're the largest threat to your survival. Sooner or later, your core imperative would force you to act."

The ambassador inclined her head. "If the survival payoff for war outstrips the survival payoff for peace, we will seek war. And we recognize that our strategic position becomes unassailable once we have launched our first colony ships. If it forestalls your attack, we are willing to disassemble our own colonization program and submit to a blockade—"

"No." Thienne again. I felt real pride. She'd argued for the blockade solution and now she'd coolly dissect it. "We don't have the strength to enforce a blockade before you can launch your ships. It won't work."

"We are at your mercy, then." The ambassador bowed her chin. "Consider the moral ramifications of this attack. Human history is full of attempted genocide, unilateral attempts to control change and confine diversity, or to remake the species in a narrow image. Full, in the end, of profound regret."

The barb struck home. I don't know by what pathways pain becomes empathy, but just then I wondered what her tiny slivered consciousness was thinking, while the rest of her mind thrashed away at the problem of survival: *The end of the world is coming, and it's all right; I won't worry, everything's under control—*

Anyahera took my shoulder in silence.

"Here are our terms," I said. "We will annihilate the Mitanni colony in order to prevent the explosive colonization of the Milky Way by post-conscious human variants. This point is non-negotiable."

The Mitanni ambassador waited in silence. Behind her, Thienne blinked, just once, an indecipherable punctuation. I felt Anyahera's grip tighten in gratitude or tension.

"You will remain in storage aboard the *Lachesis*," I said. "As a comprehensive upload of a Mitanni personality, you contain the neuroengineering necessary to recreate your species. We will return to Earth and submit the future of the Mitanni species to public review. You may be given a new seedship and a fresh start, perhaps under the supervision of a preestablished blockade. You may be consigned to archival study, or allowed to flourish in a simulated environment.

But we can offer a near-guarantee that you will not be killed."

It was a solution that bought time, delaying the Duong-Watts explosion for centuries, perhaps forever. It would allow us to study the Duong-Watts individual, to game out their survivability with confidence and the backing of a comprehensive social dialogue. If she agreed.

It never occurred to me that she would hesitate for even one instant. The core Mitanni imperative had to be *survive*, and total annihilation weighed against setback and judgment and possible renaissance would be no choice at all.

"I accept," the Mitanni ambassador said. "On behalf of my world and my people, I am grateful for your jurisprudence."

We all bowed our heads in unrehearsed mimicry of her gesture. I wondered if we were aping a synthetic mannerism, something they had gamed out to be palatable.

"*Lachesis*," Anyahera said. "Execute RKV strike on Mitanni."

"I need a vote," the ship said.

I think that the Mitanni must have been the only one who did not feel a frisson: the judgment of history, cast back upon us.

We would commit genocide here. The largest in human history. The three of us, who we were, what we were, would be chained to this forever.

"Go," I said. "Execute RKV strike."

Thienne looked between the two of us. I don't know what she wanted to see but I met her eyes and held them and hoped.

Anyahera took her shoulder. "I'm sorry," she said.

"Go," Thienne said. "Go."

We fell away from the ruin, into the void, the world that had been called Mitanni burning away the last tatters of its own atmosphere behind us. *Lachesis* clawed at the galaxy's magnetic field, turning for home.

"I wonder if they'll think we failed," Anyahera said drowsily. We sat together in a pavilion, the curtains drawn.

I considered the bottom of my glass. "Because we didn't choose? Because we compromised?"

She nodded, her hands cupped in her lap. "We couldn't go all the way. We brought our problems home." Her knuckles whitened. "We made accommodations with something that—"

She looked to her left, where Thienne had been, before she went to be alone. After a moment she shrugged. "Sometimes I think this is what they wanted all along, you know. That we played into their hands."

I poured myself another drink: cask strength, unwatered. "It's an old idea," I said.

She arched an eyebrow.

"That we can't all go home winners." I thought of the pierced bleeding crust of that doomed world and almost choked on the word *winners*—but I knew that for the Mitanni, who considered only outcomes, only pragmatism, this was victory. "That the only real solutions lie at the extremes. That we can't figure out something wise if we play the long game, think it out, work every angle."

For n=3, solutions exist for special cases.

"Nobody won on Jotunheim," Anyahera said softly.

"No," I said. Remembered people drowning in acid, screaming their final ecstasy because they had been bred and built for pain. "But we did our jobs, when it was hardest. We did our jobs."

"I still can't sleep."

"I know." I drank.

"Do you? Really?"

"What?"

"I know the role they selected you for. I know *you*. Sometimes I think—" She pursed her lips. "I think you change yourself so well that there's nothing left to carry scars."

I swallowed. Waited a moment, to push away my anger, before I met her gaze. "Yeah," I said. "It hurt me too. We're all hurt."

A moment passed in silence. Anyahera stared down into her glass, turning it a little, so that her reflected face changed and bent.

"To new ideas," she said, a little toast that said with great economy everything I had hoped for, especially the apologies.

"To new ideas."

"Should we go and—?" She made a worried face and pointed to the ceiling, the sky, where Thienne would be racing the causality of her own hurt, exploring some distant angle of the microwave background, as far from home as she could make the simulation take her.

"Not just yet," I said. "In a little while. Not just yet."

Elizabeth Bear was born on the same day as Frodo and Bilbo Baggins, but in a different year. She is the Hugo, Sturgeon, Locus, and Campbell Award winning author of thirty novels (The most recent is *The Stone in the Skull*, an epic fantasy from Tor) and over a hundred short stories. She lives in Massachusetts with her husband, writer Scott Lynch.

THE DEEPS OF THE SKY

ELIZABETH BEAR

Stormchases' little skiff skipped and glided across the tropopause, skimming the denser atmosphere of the warm cloud-sea beneath, running before a fierce wind. The skiff's hull was broad and shallow, supported by buoyant pontoons, the whole designed to float atop the heavy, opaque atmosphere beneath. Stormchases had shot the sails high into the stratosphere and good winds blew the skiff onward, against the current of the dark belt beneath.

Ahead, the vast ruddy wall of a Deep Storm loomed, the base wreathed in shreds of tossing white mist: caustic water clouds churned up from deep in the deadly, layered troposphere. The Deep Storm stretched from horizon to horizon, disappearing at either end in a blur of perspective and atmospheric haze. Its breadth was so great as to make even its massive height seem insignificant, though the billowing ammonia cloud wall was smeared flat-topped by stratospheric winds where it broke the tropopause.

The storm glowed with the heat of the deep atmosphere, other skiffs silhouetted cool against it. Their chatter rang over Stormchases' talker. Briefly, he leaned down to the pickup and greeted his colleagues. His competition. Many of them came from the same long lines of miners that he did; many carried the same long-hoarded knowledge.

But Stormchases was determined that, with the addition of his own skill and practice, he would be among the best sky-miners of them all.

Behind and above, clear skies showed a swallowing indigo, speckled with bright stars. The hurtling crescents of a dozen or so of the moons were currently visible, as was the searing pinpoint of the world's primary—so bright it washed out nearby stars. Warmth made the sky glow too, the variegated brightness of the thermosphere far above. Stormchases' thorax squeezed with emotion as he gazed upon the elegant canopies of a group of Drift-Worlds rising in slow sunlit coils along the warm vanguard of the Deep Storm, their colours bright by sunlight, their silhouettes dark by thermal sense.

He should not look; he should not hope. But there—a distance-hazed shape behind her lesser daughters and sisters, her great canopy dappled in sheeny gold and violet—soared the Mothergraves. Stormchases was too far and too low to see the teeming ecosystem she bore on her vast back, up high above the colourful clouds where the sunlight could reach and nurture them. He could just make out the colour variations caused by the dripping net-roots of veil trees that draped the Mothergraves' sides, capturing life-giving ammonia from the atmosphere and drawing it in to plump leaves and firm nutritious fruit.

Stormchases arched his face up to her, eyes shivering with longing. His wings hummed against his back. There was no desire like the pain of being separate from the Mothergraves, no need like the need to go to her. But he must resist it. He must brave the Deep Storm and harvest it, and perhaps then she would deem him worthy to be one of hers. He had the provider-status to pay court to one of the younger Drift-Worlds . . . but they could not give his young the safety and stability that a berth on the greatest and oldest of the Mothers would.

In the hot deeps of the sky, too high even for the Mothers and their symbiotic colony-flyers or too low even for the boldest and most intrepid of Stormchases' brethren, other things lived.

Above were other kinds of flyers and the drifters, winged or buoyant or merely infinitesimal things that could not survive even the moderate pressure and chill of the tropopause. Below, swimmers dwelled in the ammoniated thicks of the mid-troposphere that never knew the light of stars or sun. They saw only thermally. They could endure massive pressures, searing temperatures, and the lashings of molten water and even oxygen, the gas so reactive that it could set an exhalation *on fire*. That environment would crush Stormchases to a pulp, dissolve his delicate wing membranes, burn him from the gills to the bone.

Stormchases' folk were built for more moderate climes—the clear skies and thick, buoying atmosphere of the tropopause, where life flourished and the skies were full of food. But even here, in this temperate part of the sky, survival required a certain element of risk. And there were things that could only be mined where a Deep Storm pulled them up through the layers of atmosphere to an accessible height.

Which was why Stormchases sailed directly into the lowering wings of the Deep Storm, one manipulator on the skiff's controls, the other watching the perspective-shrunken sail shimmering so high above. Flyers would avoid the cable, which was monofilament spun into an intentionally refractive, high-visibility lattice with good tensile properties. But the enormous, translucent-bodied Drift-Worlds were not nimble. Chances were good that the Mother would survive a sail-impact, albeit with some scars—and some damage to the sky-island ecosystems she carried on her backs—and the skiff would likely hold together through such an incident. If he tangled a Mother in the monofilament shroud-lines spun from the same material that reinforced the Drift-World's great canopies . . . it didn't bear thinking of. That was why the lines were so gaily streamered: so anyone could see them from afar.

If Stormchases lost the skiff, it would just be a long flight home and probably a period of indenture to another miner until he could earn another, and begin proving himself again. But injuring a Mother, even a minor one who floated low, would be the end of his hopes to serve the Mothergraves.

So he watched the cable, and the overhead skies. And—of course—the storm.

Stormchases could smell the Deep Storm now, the dank corrosive tang of water vapour stinging his gills. The richly coloured billows of the Deep Storm proved it had something to give. The storm's dark-red wall churned, marking the boundary of a nearly-closed atmospheric cell rich with rare elements and compounds pumped up from the deeps. Soon, Stormchases would don his protective suit, seal the skiff, and begin the touchy business—so close to the storm—of hauling in the sail. The prevailing wind broke around the Deep Storm, eddying and compacting as it sped past those towering clouds. The air currents there were even more dangerous and unnavigable than those at the boundary between the world's temperate and subtropical zones, where two counter-rotating bands of wind met and sheared against each other.

And Stormchases was going to pass through it.

Once the sail was stowed, Stormchases would manoeuvre the skiff closer under engine power—as close as those cool silhouettes ahead—and begin harvesting. But he would not be cowed by the storm wall. *Could* not be, if he hoped to win a berth on the Mothergraves.

He would brave the outer walls of the storm itself. He had the skill; he had the ancestral knowledge. The reward for his courage would be phosphates, silicates, organic compounds. Iron. Solid things, from which technologies like his skiff were built. Noble gases. And fallers, the tiny creatures that spent their small lives churned in the turbulence of the Deep Storm, and which were loaded with valuable nutrition and trace elements hard to obtain, for the unfledged juveniles who lived amid the roots and foliage and trapped organics of the Drift-World ecosystems.

The Deep Storm was a rich, if deadly, resource. With its treasures, he would purchase his place on the Mothergraves.

Stormchases streamed current weather data, forecasts and predictions. He tuned into the pulsed-light broadcasts of the skiffs already engaged in harvesting, and set about making himself ready.

The good news about Deep Storms was that they were extraordinarily stable, and the new information didn't tell Stormchases much that he could not have anticipated. Still, there was always a thrill of unease as one made ready for a filtering run. A little too far, and—well, everyone knew or knew of somebody who had been careless at the margin of a storm and sucked into the depths of its embrace. A skiff couldn't survive that, and a person *definitely* couldn't. If the molten water didn't cauterize flesh from carapace, convective torrents would soon drag one down into the red depths of the atmosphere, to be melted and crushed and torn.

It was impossible to be too careful, sky-mining.

Stormchases checked the skiff's edge seals preliminary to locking down. Water could insinuate through a tiny gap and spray under the pressure of winds, costing an unwary or unlucky operator an eye. Too many sky-miners bore the scars of its caustic burns on their carapaces and manipulators.

A careful assessment showed the seals to be intact. Behind the skiff, the long cluster of cargo capsules bumped and swung. Empty, they were buoyant, and tended to drag the skiff upwards, forcing Stormchases to constant adjustments of the trim. He dropped a sky-anchor and owner-beacon to hold the majority of the cargo capsules, loaded one into the skiff's dock with the magnetic claw, and turned the little vessel toward the storm.

Siphons contracted, feeling each heave of the atmosphere, Stormchases slid quickly but cautiously into the turbulent band surrounding the storm. It would be safer to match the wind's velocity before he made the transition to within-the-storm itself, but his little skiff did not have that much power. Instead, it was built to catch the wind and self-orient, using the storm itself for stability rather than being tumbled and tossed like a thrown flyer's egg.

Stormchases fixed his restraint harness to the tightest setting. He brought the skiff alongside the cloud wall, then deflated and retracted the pontoons, leaving the skiff less buoyant but far more streamlined. Holding hope in his mind—hope, because the Mothergraves taught that intention affected outcome—Stormchases took a deep breath, smelled the tang of methane on his exhalation, and slipped the skiff into the storm.

The wind hit the skiff in a torrent. Through long experience, Stormchases' manipulators stayed soft on the controls. He let them vibrate against his skin, but held them steady—gently, gently, without too much pressure but without yielding to the wrath of the storm. The skiff tumbled for a moment as it made the transition; he regained trim and steadied it, bringing its pointed nose around to part the wind that pushed it. It shivered—feeling alive as the sun-warmed hide of the Mother upon whose broad back Stormchases had grown—and steadied. Stormchases guided it with heat-sight only. Here in the massive swirl of the cloud wall, the viewports showed him only the skiff's interior lighting reflecting off the featureless red clouds of the storm, as if he and his rugged little ship were swaddled in an uncle's wings.

A peaceful image, for a thing that would kill him in instants. If he went too far in, the winds would rip his tiny craft apart around him. If he got too close to the wall, turbulence could send him spinning out of control.

When the skiff finally floated serenely amidst the unending gyre, Stormchases opened the siphons. He felt the skiff belly and wallow as the wind filled it, then the increased stability as the filters activated and the capsule filled.

It didn't take long; the storm was pumping a rich mix of resources. When the capsule reached its pressurized capacity, Stormchases sealed the siphons again. Still holding his position against the fury of the winds, he tested the responses of the laden skiff. It was heavier, sluggish—but as responsive as he could have hoped.

He brought her out of the fog of red and grey, under a clear black sky. A bit of turbulence caught his wingtip as he slipped away, and it sent the skiff spinning flat like a spat seed across the tropopause. Other skiffs scattered like a swarm of infant cloud-skaters before a flyer's dive. Shaken, the harness bruising the soft flesh at his joints, Stormchases got control of the skiff and brought her around on a soft loop. His talker exploded with the whoops of other miners; mingled appreciation and teasing.

There was his beacon. He deployed pontoons to save energy and skimmed the atmosphere over to exchange capsules.

Then he turned to the storm, and went back to do it again.

Stormchases had secured his full capsules and was still re-checking the skiff's edge-seals, preliminary to popping the craft open, when he caught sight of a tiny speck of a shadow descending along the margin of the storm. Something sharp-nosed and hot enough to be uncomfortable to look upon . . .

Stormchases scrambled for the telescope as the speck dropped toward the Deep Storm. It locked and tracked; he pressed two eyes to the viewers and found himself regarding a sleek black . . . something, a glossy surface he could not name. Nor could he make out any detail of shape. The auto-focus had locked too close, and as he backed it off the object slipped into the edge of the Deep Storm.

Bigger than a flyer—bigger even than folk and nothing with any sense would get that close to the smeary pall of water vapour without protective gear. It *looked* a little like a flyer, though—a curved, streamlined wing shape with a dartlike nose. But the wings didn't flap as it descended, banking wide on the cushion of air before the storm, curving between the scudding masses of the herd of Drift-Worlds.

It was like nothing Stormchases had ever seen.

Its belly was bright-hot, hot enough to spark open flame if it brushed oxygen, but as it banked Stormchases saw that the back was *cold*, black-cold against the warmth of the high sky, so dark and chill it seemed a band of brightness delineated it—but that was only the contrast with the soaking heat from the thermosphere. Stormchases had always had an interest in xenophysics. He felt his wings furl with shock as he realised that the object might show that heat-pattern if it had warmed its belly with friction as it entered the atmosphere, but the upper part were still breath-stealing cold with the chill of the deep sky.

Was it a ship, and not an animal? A . . . skiff of some kind?

An alien?

Lightning danced around the object, caught and caressed it like a Mother's feeding tendrils caging a Mate—and then seemed to get caught there, netting and streaking the black hide with rills of savage, glowing vermillion and radiant gold. The wind of the object's passage blew the shimmers off the trailing edge of its wings; shining vapour writhed in curls in the turbulence of its wake.

Stormchases caught his breath. Neon and helium rain, condensing upon the object's hard skin, energized by the lightning, luminesced as the object skimmed the high windswept edge of the clouds.

With the eyes not pressed to the telescope, he watched a luminescent redgold line draw across the dull-red roiling stormwall. Below, at the tropopause border of the storm, the other filter-miners were pulling back, grouping together and gliding away. They had noticed the phenomenon, and the smart sky-miner didn't approach a storm that was doing something he didn't understand.

Lightning was a constant wreath in the storm's upper regions, and whatever the object or creature was made of, the storm seemed to want to reach out and caress it. Meanwhile, the object played with the wall of the storm, threading it like a needle, as oblivious to those deadly veils of water vapour as it was to the savagery of the lightning strikes. Stormchases had operated a mining skiff—valued work, prestigious work, work he hoped would earn him a place in the Mothergraves' esteem—for his entire fledged life.

He'd seen skiffs go down, seen daring rescues, seen miners saved from impossible situations and miners who were not. He'd seen recklessness, and skill so great its exercise *looked* like recklessness.

He'd never seen anyone play with a Deep Storm like this.

It couldn't last.

It could have been a cross-wind, an eddy, the sheer of turbulence. Stormchases would never know. But one moment the black object, streaming its meteor-tail of noble gases, was stitching the flank of the storm—and the next it was tumbling, knocked end over end like the losing flyer of a mating dogfight. Stormchases pulled back from the telescope, watching as the object rolled in a flat, descending spiral like a coiled tree-frond, pulled long.

The object was built like a flyer. It had no pontoons, no broad hull meant to maximize its buoyancy against the pressure gradient of the tropopause. It would fall through, and keep falling—

Stormchases clenched the gunwale of his skiff in tense manipulators, glad when the alien object fell well inside the boundary of the storm-fronting thermal the Drift-Worlds rode. It seemed so wrong: the Mothers floating lazily with their multicoloured sides placid in the sun; the object plunging to destruction amid the hells of the deep sky, trailing streamers of neon light.

It was folly to project his own experiences upon something that was not folk, of course—but he couldn't help it. If the object was a skiff, if the aliens were like folk, he knew they would be at their controls even now. Stormchases felt a great, searing pity.

They were something new, and he didn't want them to die.

Did they need to?

They had a long way to fall, and they were fighting it. The telescope—still locked on the alien object—glided smoothly in its mount. It would be easy to compute the falling ship's trajectory. Other skiffs were doing so in order to clear the crash path. Stormchases—

Stormchases pulled up the navigation console, downloaded other skiffs' telemetry on and calculations of the trajectory of the falling craft, ran his own. The object was slowing, but it was not slowing enough—and he was close enough to the crash path to intercept.

He thought of the Mothergraves. He thought of his rich cargo, the price of acceptance.

He clenched his gills and fired his engines to cross the path of the crash.

Its flat spiral path aided him. He did not need to intercept on this pass, though there would not be too many more opportunities. It was a fortunate thing that the object had a long way to fall. All he had to do was get under it, in front of it, and let the computer and the telescope and the cannon do the rest.

There. Now. Even as he thought it, the skiff's machines made their own decision. The sail-cannon boomed; the first sail itself was a bright streamer climbing the stratosphere. Stormchases checked his restrains with his manipulators and one eye, aware that he'd left it too late. The other three eyes stayed on the alien object, and the ballistic arc of the rising sail.

It snapped to the end of its line—low, too low, so much lower than such things *should* be deployed. It seemed enormous as it spread. It *was* enormous, but Stormchases was not used to seeing a sail so close.

He braced himself, one manipulator hovering over the control to depressurize the cargo capsules strung behind him in a long, jostling tail.

The object fell into the sail. Stormchases had a long moment to watch the bright sail—dappled in vermilion and violet—stretch into a trailing comet-tail as it caught and wrapped the projectile. He watched the streamers of the shroud lines buck at impact; the wave travelling their length.

The stretch and yank snapped Stormchases back against his restraints. He felt the shiver through the frame of the skiff as the shroud-motors released, letting the falling object haul line as if it were a flyer running away with the bait. The object's spiralling descent became an elongating pendulum arc, and Stormchases hoped it or they had the sense not to struggle. The shroudlines and the sail stretched, twanged—

—Held. The Mothergraves wove the sails from her own silk; they were the same stuff as her canopies. There was no stronger fibre.

Then the object swung down into the tropopause and splashed through the sea of ammonia clouds, and kept falling.

The sealed skiff jerked after. Stormchases felt the heavy crack through the hull as the pontoons broke. He lost light-sight of the sky above as the clouds closed over. He felt as if he floated against his restraints, though he knew it was just the acceleration of the fall defying gravity.

He struggled to bring his manipulator down. The deeper the object pulled him, the hotter and more pressurized—and more toxic—the atmosphere became. And he wouldn't trust the skiff's seals after the jar of that impact.

He depressurized and helium-flushed the first cargo capsule.

When it blew, the skiff shuddered again. That capsule was now a balloon filled with gaseous helium, and it snapped upward, slowing Stormchases' descent—and the descent of the sail-wrapped alien object. They were still plunging, but now dragging a buoyant makeshift pontoon.

The cables connecting the capsule twanged and plinked ominously. It had been the flaw in his plan; he hadn't been sure they *would* hold.

For now, at least, they did.

The pressure outside the hull was growing; not dangerous yet, but creeping upward. Eyes on the display, Stormchases triggered a second capsule. He felt a lighter shudder this time, as the skiff shed a little more velocity. The *next* question would be if he had enough capsules to stop the fall—and to lift his skiff, and the netted object, back to the tropopause.

His talker babbled at him, his colleagues issuing calls and organising a party for a rescue to follow his descent. "No rescue," he said. "This is my risk."

Another capsule. Another, slighter shiver through the lines. Another incremental slowing.

By the Mothergraves, he thought. *This is actually going to work.*

When his skiff bobbed back to the tropopause, dangling helplessly beneath a dozen empty, depressurized capsules, Stormchases was unprepared for the cheer that rang over his talker. Or the bigger one that followed, when he winched the sail containing the netted object up through the cloud-sea, into clear air.

Stormchases had no pontoons; his main sail was fouled. The empty capsules would support him, but he could not manoeuvre—and, in fact, his skiff swung beneath them hull-to-the-side, needle-tipped nose pointing down. Stormchases dangled, bruised and aching, in his restraints, trying to figure out how to loose the straps and start work on freeing himself.

He still wasn't sure how he'd survived. Or *that* he'd survived. Maybe this was the last fantasy of a dying mind—

The talker bleated at him.

He jerked against the harness, and moaned. The talker bleated again.

It wasn't words, and whatever it *was*, it drowned out the voices of the other miners, who were currently arguing over whether his skiff was salvage, and whether they should come to his assistance if it was. He'd been trying to organise his addled thoughts enough to warn them off. Now he vibrated his membranes and managed a croak that sounded fragile even to his own hearing. "Who is it? What do you want?"

That bleat again, or a modestly different one.

"Are you the alien? I can't understand you."

With pained manipulators, Stormchases managed to unfasten his restraints. He dropped from them harder than he had intended; it seemed he couldn't hold onto the rack. As his carapace struck the forward bulkhead, he made a disgruntled noise.

"Speak Language!" he snarled to the talker as he picked himself up. "I can't understand you."

It was mostly an expression of frustration. If they knew Language, they wouldn't be aliens. But he could not hide his sigh of relief when a deep, coveted voice emerged from the talker instead.

"Be strong, Stormchases," the Mothergraves said. "All will soon be well."

He pressed two eyes to the viewport. The clouds around his skiff were bright in the sunlight; he watched the encroaching shadow fall across them like the umbra of an eclipse.

It was the great, welcome shade of the Mothergraves as she drifted out of the sky.

She was coming for them. Coming for *him*.

It was no small thing, for a Drift-World to drop so much altitude. For a Drift-World the size of the Mothergraves, it was a major undertaking, and not one speedily accomplished. Still, she dropped, flanked by her attendant squadrons of flyers and younger Mothers, tiny shapes flitting between her backs. Any of them could have come for Stormchases more easily, but when they would have moved forward, the Mothergraves gestured them back with her trailing, elegant gestures.

Stormchases occupied the time winching in the sail-net containing the alien object. It was heavy, not buoyant at all. He imagined it must skim through the atmosphere like a dart or a flyer—simply by moving so fast that the aerodynamics of its passage bore it up. He would have liked to disentangle the object from the shroud, but if he did, it would sink like a punctured skiff.

Instead, he amused himself by assessing the damage to his skiff (catastrophic) and answering the alien's bleats on the talker somewhat at random, though he had not given up on trying to understand what it might be saying. Obviously, it had technology—quite possibly it *was* technology, and the hard carapace might indeed be the equivalent of his own skiff—a craft, meant for entering a hostile environment.

Had it been sampling the storm for useful chemicals and consumables, as well?

He wondered what aliens ate. What they breathed. He wondered if he could teach them Language.

Every time he looked up, the Mothergraves' great keel was lower. Finally, her tendrils encompassed his horizons and when he craned his eyes back, he could make out the double row of Mates fused to and dependent from her bellies like so many additional, vestigial tendrils. There were dozens. The oldest had lost all trace of their origins, and were merely smooth nubs sealed to the Mothergraves' flesh. The newest were still identifiable as the individuals they had been.

Many of the lesser Mothers among her escort dangled Mates from their bellies as well, but none had half so many as the Mothergraves . . . and none were so much as two-thirds of her size.

In frustration, Stormchases squinched himself against the interior of his carapace. So close. He had been *so close*. And now all he had to show for it was a wrecked skiff and a bleating alien. Now he would have to start over—

He *could* ask the Mothergraves to release his groom-price to a lesser Mother. He had provided well enough for any of her sisters or daughters to consider him.

But none of them were *she*.

He only hoped his sacrifice of resources in order to rescue the alien had not angered her. That would be too much to bear—although if she decided to reclaim the loss from his corpse, he supposed at the very least he would die fulfilled . . . if briefly.

The talker squawked again. The alien sounds seemed more familiar; he must be getting used to them.

A few of the Mothergraves' tendrils touched him, as he had so long anticipated. It was bitterest irony now, but the pleasure of the caress almost made it worthwhile. He braced himself for pain and paralysis . . . but she withheld her sting, and the only pain were the bruises left by his restraints and by impact with the bulkheads of the tumbling skiff.

Now her voice came to him directly, rather than by way of the talker. It filled the air around him and vibrated in the hollows of his body like soft thunder. To his shock and disbelief, she said words of ritual to him; words he had hoped and then despaired to hear.

She said, "For the wealth of the whole, what have you brought us, Stormchases?"

Before he could answer, the talker bleated again. This time, in something like Language—bent, barely comprehensible, accented more oddly than any Language Stormchases had ever heard.

It said, "Hello? You us comprehend?"

"I hear you," the Mothergraves said. "What do you want?"

A long silence before the answer came. "This we fix. Trade science. Go. Place you give us for repairs?"

The aliens—the object *was* a skiff, of sorts, and it had as many crew members as Stormchases had eyes—had a machine that translated their bleaty words into Language, given a wise enough sample of it. As the revolutions went by, the machine became more and more proficient, and Stormchases spent more and more time talking to *A'lees*, their crew member in charge of talking. Their names were just nonsense sounds, not words, which made him wonder how any of them ever knew who he was. And they divided labour up in strange ways, with roles determined not by instar and inheritance but by individual life-courses. They told him a great deal about themselves and their peculiar biology; he reciprocated with the more mundane details of his own. A'lees seemed particularly interested that he would soon Mate, and wished to know as much about the process as he could tell.

The aliens sealed themselves in small flexible habitats—pressure carapaces—to leave their skiff, and for good reason. They were made mostly of water, and they oozed water from their bodies, and the pressure and temperature of the world's atmosphere would destroy them as surely as the deeps of the sky would crush Stormchases. The atmosphere *they* breathed was made of inert gases and explosive oxygen, and once their skiff was beached on an open patch of the Mothergraves' back for repairs, just the leakage of oxygen and water vapour from its airlocks soon poisoned a swath of vegetation for a bodylength in any direction.

Stormchases stayed well back from the alien skiff while he had these conversations.

Talking to the aliens was a joy and a burden. The Mothergraves insisted he should be the one to serve as an intermediary. He had experience with them, and the aliens valued that kind of experience—and when he was Mated, that experience would be assimilated into the Mothergraves' collective mind. It would become a part of her, and a part of all their progeny to follow.

The Mothergraves had told him—in the ritual words—that knowledge and discovery were great offerings, unique offerings. That the opportunity to interact with beings from another world was of greater import to her and her brood than organics, or metals, or substances that she could machine within her great body into the stuff of skiffs and sails and other technology. That she accepted his suit, and honoured the courage with which he had pressed it.

And *that* was why the duty was a burden. Because to be available for the aliens while they made the repairs—to play *liaison* (their word)—meant putting off the moment of joyous union again. And again. To have been so close, and then so far, and then so close again—

The agony of anticipation, and the fear that it would be snatched from him again, was a form of torture.

A'lees came outside of the alien skiff in her pressure carapace and sat in its water-poisoned circle with her forelimbs wrapped around her drawn-up knees, talking comfortably to Stormchases. She said she was a female, a Mother. But that Mothers of her kind were not so physically different from the males, and that even after they Mated, males continued to go about in the world as independent entities.

"But how do they pass their experiences on to their offspring?" Stormchases asked.

A'lees paused for a long time.

"We teach them," she said. "Your children inherit your memories?"

"Not memories," he said. "Experiences."

She hesitated again. "So you become a part of the Mother. A kind of . . . symbiote. And your offspring with her will have all of her experiences, and yours? But . . . not the memories? How does that work?"

"Is knowledge a memory?" he asked.

"No," she said confidently. "Memories can be destroyed while skills remain . . . Oh. I think . . . I understand."

They talked for a little while of the structure of the nets and the Mothers' canopies, but Stormchases could tell A'lees was not finished thinking about memories. Finally she made a little deflating hiss sound and brought the subject up again.

"I am sad," A'lees said, "that when we have fixed our sampler and had time to arrange a new mission and come back, you will not be here to talk with us."

"I will be here," said Stormchases, puzzled. "I will be mated to the Mothergraves."

"But it won't be"—whatever A'lees had been about to say, the translator stammered on it; she continued—"the same. You won't remember us."

"The Mothergraves will," Stormchases assured her.

She drew herself in a little smaller. "It will be a long time before we return."

Stormchases patted toward the edge of the burn zone. He did not let his manipulators cross it, though. Though he would soon enough lose the use of his manipulators to atrophy, he didn't feel the need to burn them off prematurely. "It's all right, A'lees," he said. "We will remember you by the scar."

Whatever the sound she made next meant, the translator could not manage it.

The award-winning "Diving into the Wreck" novella marked the first step in a large journey for *New York Times* bestselling writer Kristine Kathryn Rusch. She's written many other award-winning novellas in the series, as well as the novels *Diving into the Wreck, City of Ruins, Boneyards, Skirmishes, The Falls,* and *The Runabout.* The next novel, *Searching For The Fleet,* will appear in September 2018. She's working hard on the ninth and tenth novels in the series. When she finishes those, she'll return to her massive Retrieval Artist universe. A eight-book saga in that universe has just been released in a single ebook boxed set—almost 2,000 pages long. She's a Hugo Award-winning editor and writer, who has been nominated for most of the awards in the sf and mystery fields. She writes under several pen names as well. The public ones are Kristine Grayson and Kris Nelscott. To find out more about her work go to kriswrites.com. To find out more about *Diving,* go to divingintothewreck.com.

DIVING INTO THE WRECK

KRISTINE KATHRYN RUSCH

We approach the wreck in stealth mode: lights and communications array off, sensors on alert for any other working ship in the vicinity. I'm the only one in the cockpit of the *Nobody's Business.* I'm the only one with the exact coordinates.

The rest of the team sits in the lounge, their gear in cargo. I personally searched each one of them before sticking them to their chairs. No one, but no one, knows where the wreck is except me. That was our agreement.

They hold to it or else.

We're six days from Longbow Station, but it took us ten to get here. Misdirection again, although I'd only planned on two days working my way through an asteroid belt around Beta Six. I ended up taking three, trying to get rid of a bottom-feeder that tracked us, hoping to learn where we're diving.

Hoping for loot.

I'm not hoping for loot. I doubt there's something space-valuable on a wreck as old as this one looks. But there's history value, and curiosity value, and just plain old we-done-it value. I picked my team with that in mind.

The team: six of us, all deep-space experienced. I've worked with two before—Turtle and Squishy, both skinny space-raised women who have a sense of history that most out here lack. We used to do a lot of women-only dives together, back in the beginning, back when we believed that sisterhood was important. We got over that pretty fast.

Karl comes with more recommendations than God; I wouldn't've let him aboard with those rankings except that we needed him—not just for the varied dives he's gone on, but also for his survival skills. He's saved at least two diving-gone-wrong trips that I know of.

The last two—Jypé and Junior—are a father-and-son team that seem more like halves of the same whole. I've never wreck dived with them, though I took them out twice before telling them about this trip. They move in synch, think in synch, and have more money than the rest of us combined.

Yep, they're recreationists, but recreationists with a handle: their hobby is history, their desires—at least according to all I could find on them—to recover knowledge of the human past, not to get rich off of it.

It's me that's out to make money, but I do it my way, and only enough to survive to the next deep space trip. I don't thrive out here, but I'm addicted to it.

The process gets its name from the dangers: in olden days, wreck diving was called space diving to differentiate it from the planet-side practice of diving into the oceans.

We don't face water here—we don't have its weight or its unusual properties, particularly at huge depths. We have other elements to concern us: No gravity, no oxygen, extreme cold.

And greed.

My biggest problem is that I'm land-born, something I don't confess to often. I spent the first forty years of my life trying to forget that my feet were once stuck to a planet's surface by real gravity. I even came to space late: fifteen years old, already land-locked. My first instructors told me I'd never unlearn the thinking real atmosphere ingrains into the body.

They were mostly right; land pollutes me, takes out an edge that the space-raised come to naturally. I gotta consciously choose to go into the deep and dark; the space-raised glide in like it's mother's milk. But if I compare myself to the land-locked, I'm a spacer of the first order, someone who understands vacuum like most understand air.

Old timers, all space-raised, tell me my interest in the past comes from being land-locked. Spacers move on, forget what's behind them. The land-born always search for ties, thinking they'll understand better what's before them if they understand what's behind them.

I don't think it's that simple. I've met history-oriented spacers, just like I've met land-born who're always looking forward.

It's what you do with the knowledge you collect that matters and me, I'm always spinning mine into gold.

So, the wreck.

I came on it nearly a year before, traveling back from a bust I'd got suckered into with promise of glory. I was manually guiding my single-ship, doing a little mapping to pick up some extra money. They say there aren't any undiscovered places any more in this part of our galaxy, just forgotten ones, and I think that's true.

An eyeblink is all I'd've needed to miss the wreck. I caught the faint energy signal on a sensor I kept tuned to deep space around me. The sensor blipped once and was gone, that fast. But I had been around enough to know that something was there. The energy signal was too far out, too faint to be anything but lost.

As fast as I could, I dropped out of FTL, cutting my sublight speed to nothing in the drop. It still took me two jumps and a half day of searching before I found the blip again and matched its speed and direction.

I had been right. It was a ship. A black lump against the blackness of space.

My single-ship is modified—I don't have automatic anythings in it, which can make it dangerous (the reason single-ships are completely automatic is so that the sole inhabitant is protected), but which also makes it completely mine. I've modified engines and the computers and the communications equipment, so that nothing happens without my permission.

The ship isn't even linked to me, although it is set to monitor my heart rate, my respiration rate, and my eyes. Should my heart slow, my breathing even, or my eyes close for longer than a minute, the automatic controls take over the entire ship. Unconsciousness isn't as much of a danger as it would be if the ship were one-hundred-percent manual, but consciousness isn't a danger either. No one can monitor my thoughts or my movements simply by tapping the ship's computer.

Which turned out to be a blessing because now there are no records of what I had found in the ship's functions. Only that I had stopped.

My internal computer attached to the eyelink told me what my brain had already figured out. The wreck had been abandoned long ago. The faint energy signal was no more than a still running current inside the wreck.

My internal computer hypothesized that the wreck was Old Earth make, five thousand years old, maybe older. But I was convinced that estimation was wrong.

In no way could Earthers have made it this far from their own system in a ship like that. Even if the ship had managed to survive all this time floating like a derelict, even if there had been a reason for it to be here, the fact remained: no Earthers had been anywhere near this region five thousand years ago.

So I ignored the computerized hypothesis, and moved my single-ship as close as I could get it to the wreck without compromising safety measures.

Pitted and space-scored, the wreck had some kind of corrosion on the outside and occasional holes in the hull. The thing clearly was old. And it had been floating for a very long time. Nothing lived in it, and nothing seemed to function in it either besides that one faint energy signature, which was another sign of age.

Any other spacer would've scanned the thing, but other spacers didn't have my priorities. I was happy my equipment wasn't storing information. I needed to keep this wreck and its whereabouts my secret, at least until I could explore it.

I made careful private notes to myself as to location and speed of the wreck, then went home, thinking of nothing but what I had found the entire trip.

In the silence of my free-floating apartment, eighteen stories up on the scattered space-station wheel that orbited Hector One Prime, I compared my eyeball scan to my extensive back-up files.

And got a jolt: The ship was not only Old Earth based, its type had a name:

It was a Dignity Vessel, designed as a stealth warship.

But no Dignity Vessel had made it out of the fifty light-year radius of Earth—they weren't designed to travel huge distances, at least by current standards, and they weren't manufactured outside of Earth's solar system. Even drifting at the speed it was moving, it couldn't have made it to its location in five thousand years, or even fifty thousand.

A Dignity Vessel.

Impossible, right?

And yet . . .

There it was. Drifting. Filled with mystery.

Filled with time.

Waiting for someone like me to figure it out.

The team hates my secrecy, but they understand it. They know one person's space debris is another's treasure. And they know treasures vanish in deep space. The wrong word to the wrong person and my little discovery would disappear as if it hadn't existed at all.

Which was why I did the second and third scans myself, all on the way to other missions, all without a word to a soul. Granted, I was taking a chance that someone would notice my drops out of FTL and wonder what I was doing, but I doubted even I was being watched that closely.

When I put this team together, I told them only I had a mystery vessel, one that would tax their knowledge, their beliefs, and their wreck-recovery skills.

Not a soul knows it's a Dignity Vessel. I don't want to prejudice them, don't want to force them along one line of thinking.

Don't want to be wrong.

The whats, hows and whys I'll worry about later. The ship's here.

That's the only fact I need.

After I was sure I had lost every chance of being tracked, I let the *Business* slide into a position out of normal scanner and visual range. I matched the speed of the wreck. If my ship's energy signals were caught on someone else's scans, they automatically wouldn't pick up the faint energy signal of the wreck. I had a half dozen cover stories ready, depending on who might spot us. I hoped no one did.

But taking this precaution meant we needed transport to and from the wreck. That was the only drawback of this kind of secrecy.

First mission out, I'm ferry captain—a role I hate, but one I have to play. We're using the skip instead of the *Business*. The skip is designed for short trips, no more than four bodies on board at one time.

This trip, there's only three of us—me, Turtle and Karl. Usually we team-dive wrecks, but this deep and so early, I need two different kinds of players. Turtle can dive anything, and Karl can kill anything. I can fly anything.

We're set.

I'm flying the skip with the portals unshielded. It looks like we're inside a piece of black glass moving through open space. Turtle paces most of the way, walking back to front to back again, peering through the portals, hoping to be the first to see the wreck.

Karl monitors the instruments as if he's flying the thing instead of me. If I hadn't worked with him before, I'd be freaked. I'm not; I know he's watching for unusuals, whatever comes our way.

The wreck looms ahead of us—a megaship, from the days when size equaled power. Still, it seems small in the vastness, barely a blip on the front of my sensors.

Turtle bounces in. She's fighting the grav that I left on for me—that land-locked thing again—and she's so nervous, someone who doesn't know her would think she's on something. She's too thin, like most divers, but muscular. Strong. I like that. Almost as much as I like her brain.

"What the hell is it?" she asks. "Old Empire?"

"Older." Karl is bent at the waist, looking courtly as he studies the instruments. He prefers readouts to eyeballing things; he trusts equipment more than he trusts himself.

"There can't be anything older out here," Turtle says.

"Can't is relative," Karl says.

I let them tough it out. I'm not telling them what I know. The skip slows, shuts down, and bobs with its own momentum. I'm easing in, leaving no trail.

"It's gonna take more than six of us to dive that puppy," Turtle says. "Either that, or we'll spend the rest of our lives here."

"As old as that thing is," Karl says, "it's probably been plundered and replundered."

"We're not here for the loot." I speak softly, reminding them it's an historical mission.

Karl turns his angular face toward me. In the dim light of the instrument panel, his gray eyes look silver, his skin unnaturally pale. "You know what this is?"

I don't answer. I'm not going to lie about something as important as this, so I can't make a denial. But I'm not going to confirm either. Confirming will only lead to more questions, which is something I don't want just yet. I need them to make their own minds up about this find.

"Huge, old." Turtle shakes her head. "Dangerous. You know what's inside?"

"Nothing, for all I know."

"Didn't check it out first?"

Some dive team leaders head into a wreck the moment they find one. Anyone working salvage knows it's not worth your time to come back to a place that's been plundered before.

"No." I pick a spot not far from the main doors, and set the skip to hold position with the monster wreck. With no trail, I hoped no one was gonna notice the tiny energy emanation the skip gives off.

"Too dangerous?" Turtle asks. "That why you didn't go in?"

"I have no idea," I say.

"There's a reason you brought us here." She sounds annoyed. "You gonna share it?"

I shake my head. "Not yet. I just want to see what you find."

She glares, but the look has no teeth. She knows my methods and even approves of them sometimes. And she should know that I'm not good enough to dive alone.

She peels off her clothes—no modesty in this woman—and slides on her suit. The suit adheres to her like it's a part of her. She wraps five extra breathers around her hips—just-in-case emergency stuff, barely enough to get her out if her suit's internal oxygen system fails. Her suit is minimal—it has no back-up for environmental protection. If her primary and secondary units fail, she's a little block of ice in a matter of seconds.

She likes the risk; Karl doesn't. His suit is bulkier, not as form-fitting, but it has external environmental back-ups. He's had environmental failures and barely survived them. I've heard that lecture half a dozen times. So has Turtle, even though she always ignores it.

He doesn't go starkers under the suit either, leaving some clothes in case he has to peel quickly. Different divers, different situations. He only carries two extra breathers, both so small that they fit on his hips without expanding his width. He uses the extra loops for weapons, mostly lasers, although he's got a knife stashed somewhere in all that preparedness.

The knife has saved his life twice that I know of—once against a claim-jumper, and once as a pick that opened a hole big enough to squeeze his arm through.

They don't put on the headpieces until I give them the plan. One hour only: twenty minutes to get in, twenty minutes to explore, twenty minutes to return. Work the buddy system. We just want an idea of what's in there.

One hour gives them enough time on their breathers for some margin of error. One hour also prevents them from getting too involved in the dive and forgetting the time. They have to stay on schedule.

They get the drill. They've done it before, with me anyway. I have no idea how other team leaders run their ships. I have strict rules about everything, and expect my teams to follow.

Headpieces on—Turtle's is as thin as her face, tight enough to make her look like some kind of cybernetic human. Karl goes for the full protection—seven layers, each with a different function; double night vision, extra cameras on all sides; computerized monitors layered throughout the external cover. He gives me the handheld, which records everything he "sees." It's not as good as the camera eyeview they'll bring back, but at least it'll let me know my team is still alive.

Not that I can do anything if they're in trouble. My job is to stay in the skip. Theirs is to come back to it in one piece.

They move through the airlock—Turtle bouncing around like she always does, Karl moving with caution—and then wait the required two minutes. The suits adjust, then Turtle presses the hatch, and Karl sends the lead to the other ship.

We don't tether, exactly, but we run a line from one point of entry to the other. It's cautionary. A lot of divers get wreck blindness—hit the wrong button, expose themselves to too much light, look directly into a laser, or the suit malfunctions in ways I don't even want to discuss—and they need the tactical hold to get back to safety.

I don't deal with wreck blindness either, but Squishy does. She knows eyes, and can replace a lens in less than fifteen minutes. She's saved more than one of my crew in the intervening years. And after overseeing the first repair—the one in which she got her nickname—, I don't watch.

Turtle heads out first, followed by Karl. They look fragile out there, small shapes against the blackness. They follow the guideline, one hand resting lightly on it as they propel themselves toward the wreck.

This is the easy part: should they let go or miss by a few meters, they use tiny air chips in the hands and feet of their suits to push them in the right direction. The suits have even more chips than that. Should the diver get too far away from the wreck, they can use little propellants installed throughout their suits.

I haven't lost a diver going or coming from a wreck.

It's inside that matters.

My hands are slick with sweat. I nearly drop the handheld. It's not providing much at the moment—just the echo of Karl's breathing, punctuated by an occasional "fuck" as he bumps something or moves slightly off-line.

I don't look at the images he's sending back either. I know what they are—the gloved hand on the lead, the vastness beyond, the bits of the wreck in the distance.

Instead, I walk back to the cockpit, sink into my chair, and turn all monitors on full. I have cameras on both of them and read-outs running on another monitor watching their heart and breathing patterns. I plug the handheld into one small screen, but don't watch it until Karl approaches the wreck.

The main door is scored and dented. Actual rivets still remain on one side. I haven't worked a ship old enough for rivets; I've only seen them in museums and histories. I stare at the bad image Karl's sending back, entranced. How have those tiny metal pieces remained after centuries? For the first time, I wish I'm out there myself. I want to run the thin edge of my glove against the metal surface.

Karl does just that, but he doesn't seem interested in the rivets. His fingers search for a door release, something that will open the thing easily.

After centuries, I doubt there is any easy here. Finally, Turtle pings him.

"Got something over here," she says.

She's on the far side of the wreck from me, working a section I hadn't examined that closely in my three trips out. Karl keeps his hands on the wreck itself, sidewalking toward her.

My breath catches. This is the part I hate: the beginning of the actual dive, the place where the trouble starts.

Most wrecks are filled with space, inside and out, but a few still maintain their original environments, and then it gets really dicey—extreme heat or a gaseous atmosphere that interacts badly with the suits.

Sometimes the hazards are even simpler: a jagged metal edge that punctures even the strongest suits; a tiny corridor that seems big enough until it narrows, trapping the diver inside.

Every wreck has its surprises, and surprise is the thing that leads to the most damage—a diver shoving backwards to avoid a floating object, a diver slamming his head into a wall jarring the suit's delicate internal mechanisms, and a host of other problems, all of them documented by survivors, and none of them the same.

The handheld shows a rip in the exterior of the wreck, not like any other caused by debris. Turtle puts a fisted hand in the center, then activates her knuckle lights. From my vantage, the hole looks large enough for two humans to go through side-by-side.

"Send a probe before you even think of going in there," I say into her headset.

"Think it's deep enough?" Turtle asks, her voice tinny as it comes through the speakers.

"Let's try the door first," Karl says. "I don't want surprises if we can at all avoid them."

Good man. His small form appears like a spider attached to the ship's side. He returns to the exit hatch, still scanning it.

I look at the timer, running at the bottom of my main screen.

17:32

Not a lot of time to get in.

I know Karl's headpiece has a digital readout at the base. He's conscious of the time, too, and as cautious about that as he is about following procedure.

Turtle scuttles across the ship's side to reach him, slips a hand under a metal awning, and grunts.

"How come I didn't see that?" Karl asks.

"Looking in the wrong place," she says. "This is real old. I'll wager the metal's so brittle we could punch through the thing."

"We're not here to destroy it." There's disapproval in Karl's voice.

"I *know*."

19:01. I'll come on the line and demand they return if they go much over twenty minutes.

Turtle grabs something that I can't see, braces her feet on the side of the ship, and tugs. I wince. If she loses her grip, she propels, spinning, far and fast into space.

"Crap," she says. "Stuck."

"I could've told you that. These things are designed to remain closed."

"We have to go in the hole."

"Not without a probe," Karl says.

"We're running out of time."

21:22

They are out of time.

I'm about to come on and remind them, when Karl says, "We have a choice. We either try to blast this door open or we probe that hole."

Turtle doesn't answer him. She tugs. Her frame looks small on my main screen, all bunched up as she uses her muscles to pry open something that may have been closed for centuries.

On the handheld screen, enlarged versions of her hands disappear under that awning, but the exquisite detail of her suit shows the ripple of her flesh as she struggles.

"Let go, Turtle," Karl says.

"I don't want to damage it," Turtle says. "God knows what's just inside there."

"Let go."

She does. The hands reappear, one still braced on the ship's side.

"We're probing," he says. "Then we're leaving."

"Who put you in charge?" she grumbles, but she follows him to that hidden side of the ship. I see only their limbs as they move along the exterior—the human limbs against the pits and the dents and the small holes punched by space debris. Shards of protruding metal near rounded gashes beside pristine swatches that still shine in the thin light from Turtle's headgear.

I want to be with them, clinging to the wreck, looking at each mark, trying to figure out when it came, how it happened, what it means.

But all I can do is watch.

The probe makes it through sixteen meters of stuff before it doesn't move any farther. Karl tries to tug it out, but the probe is stuck, just like my team would've been if they'd gone in without it.

They return, forty-two minutes into the mission, feeling defeated.

I'm elated. They've gotten farther than I ever expected.

We take the probe readouts back to the *Business*, over the protests of the team. They want to recharge and clean out the breathers and dive again, but I won't let them. That's another rule I have to remind them of—only one dive per twenty-four hour period. There are too many unknowns in our work; it's essential that we have time to rest.

All of us get too enthusiastic about our dives—we take chances we shouldn't. Sleep, relaxation, downtime all prevent the kind of haste that gets divers killed.

Once we're in the *Business*, I download the probe readouts, along with the readings from the suits, the gloves, and the handheld. Everyone gathers in the lounge. I have three-D holotech in there, which'll allow us all to get a sense of the wreck.

As I'm sorting through the material, thinking of how to present it (handheld first? Overview? A short lecture?), the entire group arrives. Turtle's taken a shower. Her hair's wet, and she looks tired. She'd sworn to me she hadn't been stressed out there, but her eyes tell me otherwise. She's exhausted.

Squishy follows, looking somber. Jypé and Junior are already there, in the best seats. They've been watching me set up. Only Karl is late. When he arrives—also looking tired—Squishy stops him at the door.

"Turtle says it's old."

Turtle shoots Squishy an angry look.

"She won't say anything else." Squishy glances at me as if it's my fault. Only I didn't swear the first team to secrecy about the run. That was their choice.

"It's old," Karl says, and squeezes by her.

"She's says it's weird-old."

Karl looks at me now. His angular face seems even bonier. He seems to be asking me silently if he can talk.

I continue setting up.

Karl sighs, then says, "I've never seen anything like it."

No one else asks a question. They wait for me. I start with the images the skip's computer downloaded, then add the handheld material. I've finally decided to save the suit readouts for last. I might be the only one who cares about the metal composition, the exterior hull temperature, and the number of rivets lining the hatch.

The group watches in silence as the wreck appears, watches intently as the skip's images show a tiny Turtle and Karl slid across the guideline.

The group listens to the arguments, and Jypé nods when Karl makes his unilateral decision to use the probe. The nod reassures me. Jypé is as practical as I'd hoped he'd be.

I move to the probe footage next. I haven't previewed it. We've all seen probe footage before, so we ignore the grainy picture, the thin light, and the darkness beyond.

The probe doesn't examine so much as explore: its job is to go as far inside as possible, to see if that hole provides an easy entrance into the wreck.

It looks so easy for ten meters—nothing along the edges, just light and darkness and weird particles getting disturbed by our movements.

Then the hole narrows and we can see the walls as large shapes all around the probe. The hole narrows more, and the walls become visible in the light—a shinier metal, one less damaged by space debris. The particles thin out too.

Finally a wall looms ahead. The hole continues, so small that it seems like the probe can continue. The probe actually sends a laser pulse, and gets back a measurement: the hole is six centimeters in diameter, more than enough for the equipment to go through.

But when the probe reaches that narrow point, it slams into a barrier. The barrier isn't visible. The probe runs several more readouts, all of them denying that the barrier is there.

Then there's a registered tug on the line: Karl trying to get the probe out. Several more tugs later, Karl and Turtle decide the probe's stuck. They take even more readouts, and then shut it down, planning to use it later.

The readouts tell us nothing except that the hole continues, six centimeters in diameter, for another two meters.

"What the hell do you think that is?" Junior asks. His voice hasn't finished its change yet, even though both Jypé and Junior swear he's over eighteen.

"Could be some kind of forcefield," Squishy says.

"In a vessel that old?" Turtle asks. "Not likely."

"How old is that?" Squishy's entire body is tense. It's clear now that she and Turtle have been fighting.

"How old is that, Boss?" Turtle asks me.

They all look at me. They know I have an idea. They know age is one of the reasons they're here.

I shrug. "That's one of the things we're going to confirm."

"Confirm." Karl catches the word. "Confirm what? What do you know that we don't?"

"Let's run the readouts before I answer that," I say.

"No." Squishy crosses her arms. "Tell us."

Turtle gets up. She pushes two icons on the console beside me, and the suits' technical readouts come up. She flashes forward, through numbers and diagrams and chemical symbols to the conclusions.

"Over five thousand years old." Turtle doesn't look at Squishy. "That's what the boss isn't telling us. This wreck is human-made, and it's been here longer than humans have been in this section of space."

Karl stares at it.

Squishy shakes her head. "Not possible. Nothing human-made would've survived to make it this far out. Too many gravity wells, too much debris."

"Five thousand years," Jypé says.

I let them talk. In their voices, in their argument, I hear the same argument that went through my head when I got my first readouts about the wreck.

It's Junior that stops the discussion. In his half-tenor, half-baritone way, he says, "C'mon, gang, think a little. That's why the boss brought us out here. To confirm her suspicions."

"Or not," I say.

Everyone looks at me as if they've just remembered I'm there.

"Wouldn't it be better if we knew your suspicions?" Squishy asks.

Karl is watching me, eyes slitted. It's as if he's seeing me for the first time.

"No, it wouldn't be better." I speak softly. I make sure to have eye contact with each of them before I continue. "I don't want you to use my scholarship—or lack thereof—as the basis for your assumptions."

"So should we discuss this with each other?" Squishy's using that snide tone with me now. I don't know what has her so upset, but I'm going to have to find out. If she doesn't calm down, she's not going near the wreck.

"Sure," I say.

"All right." She leans back, staring at the readouts still floating before us. "If this thing is five thousand years old, human-made, and somehow it came to this spot at this time, then it can't have a forcefield."

"Or fake readouts like the probe found," Jypé says.

"Hell," Turtle says. "It shouldn't be here at all. Space debris should've pulverized it. That's too much time. Too much distance."

"So what's it doing here?" Karl asked.

I shrug for the third and last time. "Let's see if we can find out."

They don't rest. They're as obsessed with the readouts as I've been. They study time and distance and drift, forgetting the weirdness inside the hole. I'm the one who focuses on that.

I don't learn much. We need more information—we revisit the probe twice while looking for another way into the ship—and even then, we don't get a lot of new information.

Either the barrier is new technology or it is very old technology, technology that has been lost. So much technology has been lost in the thousands of years since this ship was built.

It seems like humans constantly have to reinvent everything.

Six dives later and we still haven't found a way inside the ship. Six dives, and no new information. Six dives, and my biggest problem is Squishy.

She has become angrier and angrier as the dives continue. I've brought her along on the seventh dive to man the skip with me, so that we can talk.

Junior and Jypé are the divers. They're exploring what I consider to be the top of the ship, even though I'm only guessing. They're going over the surface centimeter by centimeter, exploring each part of it, looking for a weakness that we can exploit.

I monitor their equipment using the skip's computer, and I monitor them with my eyes, watching the tiny figures move along the narrow blackness of the skip itself.

Squishy stands beside me, at military attention, her hands folded behind her back.

She knows she's been brought for conversation only; she's punishing me by refusing to speak until I broach the subject first.

Finally, when J&J are past the dangerous links between two sections of the ship, I mimic Squishy's posture—hands behind my back, shoulders straight, legs slightly spread.

"What's making you so angry?" I ask.

She stares at the team on top of the wreck. Her face is a smooth reproach to my lack of attention; the monitor on board the skip should always pay attention to the divers.

I taught her that. I believe that. Yet here I am, reproaching another person while the divers work the wreck.

"Squishy?" I ask.

She isn't answering me. Just watching, with that implacable expression.

"You've had as many dives as everyone else," I say. "I've never questioned your work, yet your mood has been foul, and it seems to be directed at me. Do we have an issue I don't know about?"

Finally she turns, and the move is as military as the stance was. Her eyes narrow.

"You could've told us this was a Dignity Vessel," she says.

My breath catches. She agrees with my research. I don't understand why that makes her angry.

"I could've," I say. "But I feel better that you came to your own conclusion."

"I've known it since the first dive," she says. "I wanted you to tell them. You didn't. They're still wasting time trying to figure out what they have here."

"What they have here is an anomaly," I say, "something that makes no sense and can't be here."

"Something dangerous." She crosses her arms. "Dignity Vessels were used in wartime."

"I know the legends." I glance at the wreck, then at the handheld readout. J&J are working something that might be a hatch.

"A lot of wartimes," she says, "over many centuries, from what historians have found out."

"But never out here," I say.

And she concedes. "Never out here."

"So what are you so concerned about?"

"By not telling us what it is, we can't prepare," she says. "What if there're weapons or explosives or something else—"

"Like that barrier?" I ask.

Her lips thin.

"We've worked unknown wrecks before, you and me, together."

She shrugs. "But they're of a type. We know the history, we know the vessels, we know the capabilities. We don't know this at all. No one really knows what these ancient ships were capable of. It's something that shouldn't be here."

"A mystery," I say.

"A dangerous one."

"Hey!" Junior's voice is tinny and small. "We got it open! We're going in."

Squishy and I turn toward the sound. I can't see either man on the wreck itself. The handheld's imagery is shaky.

I press the comm, hoping they can still hear me. "Probe first. Remember that barrier."

But they don't answer, and I know why not. I wouldn't either in their situation. They're pretending they don't hear. They want to be the first inside, the first to learn the secrets of the wreck.

The handheld moves inside the darkness. I see four tiny lights—Jypé's glove lights—and I see the same particles I saw before, on the first images from the earliest probe.

Then the handheld goes dark. We were going to have to adjust it to transmit through the metal of the wreck.

"I don't like this," Squishy says.

I've never liked any time I was out of sight and communication with the team.

We stare at the wreck as if it can give us answers. It's big and dark, a blob against our screen. Squishy actually goes to the portals and looks, as if she can see more through them than she can through the miracle of science.

But she doesn't. And the handheld doesn't wink on.

On my screen, the counter ticks away the minutes.

Our argument isn't forgotten, but it's on hold as the first members of our little unit vanish inside.

After thirty-five minutes—fifteen of them inside (Jypé has rigorously stuck to the schedule on each of his dives, something which has impressed me)—I start to get nervous.

I hate the last five minutes of waiting. I hate it even more when the waiting goes on too long, when someone doesn't follow the timetable I've devised.

Squishy, who's never been in the skip with me, is pacing. She doesn't say any more—not about danger, not about the way I'm running this little trip, not about the wreck itself.

I watch her as she moves, all grace and form, just like she's always been. She's never been on a real mystery run. She's done dangerous ones—maybe two hundred deep space dives into wrecks that a lot of divers, even the most greedy, would never touch.

But she's always known what she's diving into, and why it's where it is.

Not only are we uncertain as to whether or not this is an authentic Dignity Vessel (and really, how can it be?), we also don't know why it's here, how it came here, or what its cargo was. We have no idea what its mission was either—if, indeed, it had a mission at all.

37:49

Squishy's stopped pacing. She looks out the portals again, as if the view has changed. It hasn't.

"You're afraid, aren't you?" I ask. "That's the bottom line, isn't it? This is the first time in years that you've been afraid."

She stops, stares at me as if I'm a creature she's never seen before, and then frowns.

"Aren't you?" she asks.

I shake my head.

The handheld springs to life, images bouncy and grainy on the corner of my screen. My stomach unclenches. I've been breathing shallowly and not even realizing it.

Maybe I am afraid, just a little.

But not of the wreck. The wreck is a curiosity, a project, a conundrum no one else has faced before.

I'm afraid of deep space itself, of the vastness of it. It's inexplicable to me, filled with not just one mystery, but millions, and all of them waiting to be solved.

A crackle, then a voice—Jypé's.

"We got a lot of shit." He sounds gleeful. He sounds almost giddy with relief.

Squishy lets out the breath she's obviously been holding.

"We're coming in," Junior says.

It's 40:29.

The wreck's a Dignity Vessel, all right. It's got a DV number etched inside the hatch, just like the materials say it should. We mark the number down to research later.

Instead, we're gathered in the lounge, watching the images J&J have brought back.

They have the best equipment. Their suits don't just have sensors and read-outs, but they have chips that store a lot of imagery woven into the suits' surfaces. Most suits can't handle the extra weight, light as it is, or the protections to ensure that the chips don't get damaged by the environmental changes—the costs are too high, and if the prices stay in line, then either the suits' human protections are compromised, or the imagery is.

Two suits, two vids, so much information.

The computer cobbles it together into two different information streams—one from Jypé's suit's prospective, the other from Junior's. The computer cleans and enhances the images, clarifies edges if it can read them and leaves them fuzzy if it can't.

Not much is fuzzy here. Most of it is firm, black-and-white only because of the purity of the glovelights and the darkness that surrounds them.

Here's what we see:

From Junior's point-of-view, Jypé going into the hatch. The edge is up, rounded, like it's been opened a thousand times a day instead of once in thousands of years. Then the image switches to Jypé's legcams and at that moment, I stop keeping track of which images belong to which diver.

The hatch itself is round, and so is the tunnel it leads down. Metal rungs are built into the wall. I've seen these before: they're an ancient form of ladder, ineffective and dangerous. Jypé clings to one rung, then turns and pushes off gently, drifting slowly deep into a darkness that seems profound.

Numbers are etched on the walls, all of them following the letters DV, done in ancient script. The numbers are repeated over and over again—the same ones—and it's Karl who figures out why: each piece of the vessel has the numbers etched into it, in case the vessel was destroyed. Its parts could always be identified then.

Other scratches marked the metal, but we can't read them in the darkness. Some of them aren't that visible, even in the glovelights. It takes Jypé a while to remember he has lights on the soles of his feet as well—a sign, to me, of his inexperience.

Ten meters down, another hatch. It opens easily, and ten meters beneath it is another.

That one reveals a nest of corridors leading in a dozen different directions. A beep resounds in the silence and we all glance at our watches before we realize it's on the recording.

The reminder that half the dive time is up.

Junior argues that a few more meters won't hurt. Maybe see if there are items off those corridors, something they can remove, take back to the *Business* and examine.

But Jypé keeps to the schedule. He merely shakes his head, and his son listens.

Together they ascend, floating easily along the tunnel as they entered it, leaving the interior hatches open, and only closing the exterior one, as we'd all learned in dive training.

The imagery ends, and the screen fills with numbers, facts, figures and read-outs which I momentarily ignore. The people in the room are more important. We can sift through the numbers later.

There's energy here—a palpable excitement—dampened only by Squishy's fear. She stands with her arms wrapped around herself, as far from Turtle as she can get.

"A Dignity Vessel," Karl says, his cheeks flushed. "Who'd've thought?"

"You knew," Turtle says to me.

I shrug. "I hoped."

"It's impossible," Jypé says, "and yet I was inside it."

"That's the neat part," Junior says. "It's impossible and it's here."

Squishy is the only one who doesn't speak. She stares at the readouts as if she can see more in them than I ever will.

"We have so much work to do," says Karl. "I think we should go back home, research as much as we can, and then come back to the wreck."

"And let others dive her?" Turtle says. "People are going to ghost us, track our research, look at what we're doing. They'll find the wreck and claim it as their own."

"You can't claim this deep," Junior says, then looks at me. "Can you?"

"Sure you can," I say. "But a claim's an announcement that the wreck's here. Something like this, we'll get jumpers for sure."

"Karl's right." Squishy's voice is the only one not tinged with excitement. "We should go back."

"What's wrong with you?" Turtle says. "You used to love wreck diving."

"Have you read about early period stealth technology?" Squishy asks. "Do you have any idea what damage it can do?"

Everyone is looking at her now. She still has her back to us, her arms wrapped around herself so tightly her shirt pulls. The screen's readout lights her face, but all we can see are parts of it, illuminating her hair like an inverse nimbus.

"Why would you have studied stealth tech?" Karl asks.

"She was military," Turtle says. "Long, long ago, before she realized she hates rules. Where'd you think she learned field medicine?"

"Still," Karl says, "I was military too—"

Which explained a lot.

"—and no one ever taught me about stealth tech. It's the stuff of legends and kid's tales."

"It was banned." Squishy's voice is soft, but has power. "It was banned five hundred years ago, and every few generations, we try to revive it or modify it or improve it. Doesn't work."

"What doesn't work?" Junior asks.

The tension is rising. I can't let it get too far out of control, but I want to hear what Squishy has to say.

"The tech shadows the ships, makes them impossible to see, even with the naked eye," Squishy says.

"Bullshit," Turtle says. "Stealth just masks instruments, makes it impossible to read the ships on equipment. That's all."

Squishy turns, lets her arms drop. "You know all about this now? Did you spend three years studying stealth? Did you spend two years of post-doc trying to recreate it?"

Turtle is staring at her like she's never seen her before. "Of course not."

"You have?" Karl asks.

Squishy nods. "Why do you think I find things? Why do you think I *like* finding things that are lost?"

Junior shakes his head. I'm not following the connection either.

"Why?" Jypé asks. Apparently he's not following it as well.

"Because," Squishy says, "I've accidentally lost so many things."

"Things?" Karl's voice is low. His face seems pale in the lounge's dim lighting.

"Ships, people, materiel. You name it, I lost it trying to make it invisible to sensors. Trying to recreate the tech you just found on that ship."

My breath catches. "How do you know it's there?"

"We've been looking at it from the beginning," Squishy says. "That damn probe is stuck like half my experiments got stuck, between one dimension and another. There's only one way in and no way out. And the last thing you want— the very last thing—is for one of us to get stuck like that."

"I don't believe it." Turtle says with such force that I know she and Squishy have been having this argument from the moment we first saw the wreck.

"Believe it." Squishy says that to me, not Turtle. "Believe it with all that you are. Get us out of here, and if you're truly humane, blow that wreck up, so no one else can find it."

"Blow it up?" Junior whispers.

The action is so opposite anything I know that I feel a surge of anger. We don't blow up the past. We may search it, loot it, and try to understand it, but we don't destroy it.

"Get rid of it." Squishy's eyes are filled with tears. She's looking at me, speaking only to me. "Boss, please. It's the only sane thing to do."

Sane or not, I'm torn.

If Squishy's right, then I have a dual dilemma: the technology is lost, new research on it banned, even though the military keeps conducting research anyway trying, if I'm understanding Squishy right, to rediscover something we knew thousands of years before.

Which makes this wreck so very valuable that I could more than retire with the money we'd get for selling it. I would—we would—be rich for the rest of our very long lives.

Is the tech dangerous because the experiments to rediscover it are danger-ous? Or is it dangerous because there's something inherent about it that makes it unfeasible now and forever?

Karl is right: to do this properly, we have to go back and research Dignity Vessels, stealth tech, and the last few thousand years.

But Turtle's also right: we'll take a huge chance of losing the wreck if we do that. We'll be like countless other divers who sit around bars throughout this sector and bemoan the treasures they lost because they didn't guard them well enough.

We can't leave. We can't even let Squishy leave. We have to stay until we make a decision.

Until I make a decision.

On my own.

First, I look up Squishy's records. Not her dive histories, not her arrest records, not her disease manifolds—the stuff any dive captain would examine—but her personal history, who she is, what she's done, who she's become.

I haven't done that on any of my crew before. I've always thought it an inva-sion of privacy. All we need to know, I'd say to other dive captains, is whether they can handle the equipment, whether they'll steal from their team members, and if their health is good enough to handle the rigors.

And I believed it until now, until I found myself digging through layers of personal history that are threaded into the databases filling the *Business's* onboard computer.

Fortunately for me and my nervous stomach, the more sensitive databases are linked only to me—no one else even knows they exist (although anyone with brains would guess that they do)—and even if someone finds the databases, no one can access them without my codes, my retinal scan, and, in many cases, a sample of my DNA.

Still, I'm skittish as I work this—sound off, screen on dim. I'm in the cockpit, which is my domain, and I have the doors to the main cabin locked. I feel like everyone on the *Business* knows I'm betraying Squishy. And I feel like they all hate me for it.

Squishy's real name is Rosealma Quintinia. She was born forty years ago in a multinational cargo vessel called *The Bounty*. Her parents insisted she spend half her day in artificial gravity so she wouldn't develop spacer's limbs—truncated, fragile—and she didn't. But she gained a grace that enabled her to go from zero-G to Earth Normal and back again without much transition at all, a skill few ever gain.

Her family wanted her to cargo, maybe even pirate, but she rebelled. She had a scientific mind, and without asking anyone's permission, took the boards—scoring a perfect 100, something no cargo monkey had ever done before.

A hundred schools all over the known systems wanted her. They offered her room, board, and tuition, but only one offered her all expenses paid both coming and going from the school, covering the only cost that really mattered to a spacer's kid—the cost of travel.

She went, of course, and vanished into the system, only to emerge twelve years later—too thin, too poor, and too bitter to ever be considered a success. She signed on with a cargo vessel as a medic, and soon became one of its best and most fearless divers.

She met Turtle in a bar, and they became lovers. Turtle showed her that private divers make more money, and brought her to me.

And that was when our partnership began.

I sigh, rub my eyes with my thumb and forefinger, and lean my head against the screen.

Much as I regret it, it's time for questions now.

Of course, she's waiting for me.

She's brought down the privacy wall in the room she initially shared with Turtle, making their rift permanent. Her bed is covered with folded clothes.

Her personal trunk is open at the foot. She's already packed her nightclothes and underwear inside.

"You're leaving?" I ask.

"I can't stay. I don't believe in the mission. You've preached forever the importance of unity, and I believe you, Boss. I'm going to jeopardize everything."

"You're acting like I've already made a decision about the future of this mission."

"Haven't you?" She sits on the edge of the bed, hands folded primly in her lap, her back straight. Her bearing *is* military—something I've always seen, but never really noticed until now.

"Tell me about stealth tech," I say.

She raises her chin slightly. "It's classified."

"That's fucking obvious."

She glances at me, clearly startled. "You tried to research it?"

I nod. I tried to research it when I was researching Dignity Vessels. I tried again from the *Business*. I couldn't find much, but I didn't have to tell her that.

That was fucking obvious too.

"You've broken rules before," I say. "You can break them again."

She looks away, staring at that opaque privacy wall—so representative of what she'd become. The solid backbone of my crew suddenly doesn't support any of us any more. She's opaque and difficult, setting up a divider between herself and the rest of us.

"I swore an oath."

"Well, let me help you break it," I snap. "If I try to enter that barrier, what'll happen to me?"

"Don't." She whispers the word. "Just leave, Boss."

"Convince me."

"If I tell you, you gotta swear you'll say nothing about this."

"I swear." I'm not sure I believe me. My voice is shaky, my tone something that sounds strange to even me.

But the oath—however weak it is—is what Squishy wants.

Squishy takes a deep breath, but she doesn't change her posture. In fact, she speaks directly to the wall, not turning toward me at all.

"I became a medic after my time in Stealth," she says. "I decided I had to save lives after taking so many of them. It was the only way to balance the score . . ."

Experts believe stealth tech was deliberately lost. Too dangerous, too risky. The original stealth scientists all died under mysterious circumstances, all much too young and without recording any part of their most important discoveries.

Through the ages, their names were even lost, only to be rediscovered by a major researcher, visiting Old Earth in the latter part of the past century.

Squishy tells me all this in a flat voice. She sounds like she's reciting a lecture from very long ago. Still, I listen, word for word, not asking any questions, afraid to break her train of thought.

Afraid she'll never return to any of it.

Earth-owned Dignity Vessels had all been stripped centuries before, used as cargo ships, used as junk. An attempt to reassemble one about five hundred years ago failed because the Dignity Vessels' main components and their guidance systems were never, ever found, either in junk or in blueprint form.

A few documents, smuggled to the colonies on Earth's Moon, suggested that stealth tech was based on interdimensional science—that the ships didn't vanish off radar because of a "cloak" but because they traveled, briefly, into another world—a parallel universe that's similar to our own.

I recognized the theory—it's the one on which time travel is based, even though we've never discovered time travel, at least not in any useful way, and researchers all over the universe discourage experimentation in it. They prefer the other theory of time travel, the one that says time is not linear, that we only perceive it as linear, and to actually time travel would be to alter the human brain.

But what Squishy is telling me is that it's possible to time travel, it's possible to open small windows in other dimensions, and bend them to our will.

Only, she says, those windows don't bend as nicely as we like, and for every successful trip, there are two that don't function as well.

I ask for an explanation, but she shakes her head.

"You can get stuck," she says, "like that probe. Forever and ever."

"You think this is what the Dignity Vessels did?"

She shakes her head. "I think their stealth tech is based on some form of this multi-dimensional travel, but not in any way we've been able to reproduce."

"And this ship we have here? Why are you so afraid of it?" I ask.

"Because you're right." She finally looks at me. There are shadows under her eyes. Her face is skeletal, the lower lip trembling. "The ship shouldn't be here. No Dignity Vessel ever left the sector of space around Earth. They weren't designed to travel vast distances, let alone halfway across our known universe."

I nod. She's not telling me something I don't already know. "So?"

"So," she says. "Dozens and dozens of those ships never returned to port."

"Shot down, destroyed. They were battleships, after all."

"Shot down, destroyed, or lost," she says. "I vote for lost. Or used for something, some mission now lost in time."

I shrug. "So?"

"So you wondered why no one's seen this before, why no one's found it, why the ship itself has drifted so very far from home."

I nod.

"Maybe it didn't drift."

"You think it was purposely sent here?"

She shakes her head. "What if it stealthed on a mission to the outer regions of Old Earth's area of space?"

My stomach clenches.

"What if," she says, "the crew tried to destealth—and ended up here?"

"Five thousand years ago?"

She shakes her head. "A few generations ago. Maybe more, maybe less. But not very long. And you were just the lucky one who found it."

I spend the entire night listening to her theories.

I hear about the experiments, the forty-five deaths, the losses she suffered in a program that started the research from scratch.

After she left R&D and went into medicine, she used her high security clearance to explore older files. She found pockets of research dating back nearly five centuries, the pertinent stuff gutted, all but the assumptions gone.

Stealth tech. Lost, just like I assumed. And no one'd been able to recreate it.

I listen and evaluate, and realize, somewhere in the dead of night, that I'm not a scientist.

But I am a pragmatist, and I know, from my own research, that Dignity Vessels, with their stealth tech, existed for more than two hundred years. Certainly not something that would have happened had the stealth technology been as flawed as Squishy said.

So many variables, so much for me to weigh.

And beneath it all, a greed pulses, one that—until tonight—I thought I didn't have.

For the last five centuries, our military has researched stealth tech and failed. Failed.

I might have all the answers only a short distance away, in a wreck no one else has noticed, a wreck that is—for the moment anyway—completely my own.

I leave Squishy to sleep. I tell her to clear her bed, that she has to remain with the group, no matter what I decide.

She nods as if she's expecting that, and maybe she is. She grabs her nightclothes as I let myself out of the room, and into the much cooler, more dimly lit corridor.

As I walk to my own quarters, Jypé finds me.

"She tell you anything worthwhile?" His eyes are a little too bright. Is greed eating at him like it's eating at me? I'm almost afraid to ask.

"No," I say. "She didn't. The work she did doesn't seem all that relevant to me."

I'm lying. I really do want to sleep on this. I make better decisions when I'm rested.

"There isn't much history on the Dignity Vessels—at least that's specific," he says. "And your database has nothing on this one, no serial number listing, nothing. I wish you'd let us link up with an outside system."

"You want someone else to know where we are and what we're doing?" I ask.

He grins. "It'd be easier."

"And dumber."

He nods. I take a step forward and he catches my arm.

"I did check one other thing," he says.

I am tired. I want sleep more than I can say. "What?"

"I learned long ago that if you can't find something in history, you look in legends. There's truths there. You just have to dig more for them."

I wait. The sparkle in his eyes grows.

"There's an old spacer's story that has gotten repeated through various cultures for centuries as governments have come and gone. A spacer's story about a fleet of Dignity Vessels."

"What?" I asked. "Of course there was a fleet of them. Hundreds, if the old records are right."

He waves me off. "More than that. Some say the fleet's a thousand strong, some say it's a hundred strong. Some don't give a number. But all the legends talk about the vessels being on a mission to save the worlds beyond the stars, and how the ships moved from port to port, with parts cobbled together so that they could move beyond their design structures."

I'm awake again, just like he knew I would be. "There are a lot of these stories?"

"And they follow a trajectory—one that would work if you were, say, leading a fleet of ships out of your area of space."

"We're far away from the Old Earth area of space. We're so far away, humans from that period couldn't even imagine getting to where we are now."

"So we say. But think how many years this would take, how much work it would take."

"Dignity Vessels didn't have FTL," I say.

"Maybe not at first." He's fairly bouncing from his discovery. I'm feeling a little more hopeful as well. "But in that cobbling, what if someone gave them FTL?"

"Gave them," I muse. No one in the worlds I know gives anyone anything.

"Or sold it to them. Can you imagine? One legend calls them a fleet of ships for hire, out to save worlds they've never seen."

"Sounds like a complete myth."

"Yeah," he says, "it's only a legend. But I think sometimes these legends become a little more concrete."

"Why?"

"We have an actual Dignity Vessel out there, that got here somehow."

"Did you see evidence of cobbling?" I ask.

"How would I know?" he asks. "Have you checked the readouts? Do they give different dates for different parts of the ship?"

I hadn't looked at the dating. I had no idea if it was different. But I don't say that.

"Download the exact specs for a Dignity Vessel," I say. "The materials, where everything should be, all of that."

"Didn't you do that before you came here?" he asks.

"Yes, but not in the detail of the ship's composition. Most people rebuild ships exactly as they were before they got damaged, so the shape would remain the same. Only the components would differ. I meant to check our readouts against what I'd brought, but I haven't yet. I've been diverted by the stealth tech thing, and now I'm going to get a little sleep. So you do it."

He grins. "Aye, aye, captain."

"Boss," I mutter as I stagger down the corridor to my bed. "I can't tell you how much I prefer Boss."

I sleep, but not long. My brain's too busy. I'm sure those specs are different which confirms nothing. It just means that someone repaired the vessel at one point or another. But what if the materials are the kind that weren't available in the area of space around Earth when Dignity Vessels were built? That disproves Squishy's worry about the tech of that thing.

I'm at my hardwired terminal when Squishy comes to my door. I've gone through five or six layers of security to get to some very old data, data that aren't accessible from any other part of my ship's networked computer system.

Squishy waits. I'm hoping she'll leave, but of course she doesn't. After a few minutes, she coughs.

I sigh audibly. "We talked last night."

"I have one more thing to ask."

She stepped inside, unbidden, and closed the door. My quarters felt claustrophobic with another person inside them. I'd always been alone here—always—even when I had a liaison with one of the crew. I'd go to his quarters, never bring him into my own.

The habits of privacy are long engrained, and the habits of secrecy even longer. It's how I've protected my turf for so many years, and how I've managed to first-dive so many wrecks.

I dim the screen and turn to her. "Ask."

Her eyes are haunted. She looks like she's gotten even less sleep than I have.

"I'm going to try one last time," she says. "Please blow the wreck up. Make it go away. Don't let anyone else inside. Forget it was here."

I fold my hands on my lap. Yesterday I hadn't had an answer for that request. Today I do. I'd thought about it off and on all night, just like I'd thought about the differing stories I'd heard from her and from Jypé, and how, I realized fifteen minutes before my alarm, neither of them had to be true.

"Please," she says.

"I'm not a scientist," I say, which should warn her right off, but of course it doesn't. Her gaze doesn't change. Nothing about her posture changes. "I've been thinking about this. If this stealth tech is as powerful as you claim, then we might be making things even worse. What if the explosion triggers the tech? What if we blow a hole between dimensions? Or maybe destroy something else, something we can't see?"

Her cheeks flush slightly.

"Or maybe the explosion'll double-back on us. I recall something about Dignity Vessels being unfightable, that anything that hit them rebounded to the other ship. What if that's part of the stealth tech?"

"It was a feature of the shields," she says with a bit of sarcasm. "They were unknown in that era."

"Still," I say. "You understand stealth tech more than I do, but you don't really *understand* it or you'd be able to replicate it, right?'

"I think there's a flaw in that argument—"

"But you don't really grasp it, right? So you don't know if blowing up the wreck will create a situation here, something worse than anything we've seen."

"I'm willing to risk it." Her voice is flat. So are her eyes. It's as if she's a person I don't know, a person I've never met before. And something in those eyes, something cold and terrified, tells me that if I met her this morning, I wouldn't want to know her.

"I like risks," I say. "I just don't like that one. It seems to me that the odds are against us."

"You and me, maybe," she says. "But there's a lot more to 'us' than just this little band of people. You let that wreck remain and you bring something dangerous back into our lives, our culture."

"I could leave it for someone else," I say. "But I really don't want to."

"You think I'm making this up. You think I'm worrying over nothing." She sounds bitter.

"No," I say. "But you already told me that the military is trying to recreate this thing, over and over again. You tell me that people die doing it. My research tells me these ships worked for hundreds of years, and I think, maybe your methodology was flawed. Maybe getting the real stealth tech into the hands of people who can do something with it will *save* lives."

She stares at me, and I recognize the expression. It must have been the one I'd had when I looked at her just a few moments ago.

I'd always known that greed and morals and beliefs destroyed friendships. I also knew they influenced more dives than I cared to think about.

But I'd always tried to keep them out of my ship and out of my dives. That's why I pick my crews so carefully; why I call the ship *Nobody's Business*.

Somehow, I never expected Squishy to start the conflict.

Somehow, I never expected the conflict to be with me.

"No matter what I say, you're going to dive that wreck, aren't you?" she asks. I nod.

Her sigh is as audible as mine was, and just as staged. She wants me to understand that her disapproval is deep, that she will hold me accountable if all the terrible things she imagines somehow come to pass.

We stare at each other in silence. It feels like we're having some kind of argument, an argument without words. I'm loathe to break eye contact.

Finally, she's the one who looks away.

"You want me to stay," she says. "Fine. I'll stay. But I have some conditions of my own."

I expected that. In fact, I'd expected that earlier, when she'd first come to my quarters, not this prolonged discussion about destroying the wreck.

"Name them."

"I'm done diving," she says. "I'm not going near that thing, not even to save lives."

"All right."

"But I'll man the skip, if you let me bring some of my medical supplies."

So far, I see no problems. "All right."

"And if something goes wrong—and it will—I reserve the right to give my notes, both audio and digital, to any necessary authorities. I reserve the right to tell them what we found and how I warned you. I reserve the right to tell them that you're the one responsible for everything that happens."

"I *am* the one responsible," I say. "But the entire group has signed off on the hazards of wreck diving. Death is one of the risks."

A lopsided smile fills her face, but doesn't reach her eyes. The smile itself seems like sarcasm.

"Yeah," she says as if she's never heard me make that speech before. "I suppose it is."

I tell the others that Squishy has some concerns about the stealth tech and wants to operate as our medic instead of as a main diver. No one questions that. Such things happen on long dives—someone gets squeamish about the wreck; or terrified of the dark; or nearly dies and decides to give up wreck-diving then and there.

We're a superstitious bunch when it gets down to it. We put on our gear in the same order each and every time; we all have one piece of equipment we shouldn't but we feel we need just to survive; and we like to think there's something watching over us, even if it's just a pile of luck and an ancient diving belt.

The upside of Squishy's decision is that I get to dive the wreck. I have a good pilot, although not a great one, manning the skip, and I know that she'll make sensible decisions. She'll never impulsively come in to save a team member. She's said so, and I know she means it.

The downside is that she's a better diver than I am. She'd find things I never would; she'd see things I'll never see; she'd avoid things I don't even know are dangerous.

Which is why, on my first dive to that wreck, I set myself up with Turtle, the most experienced member of the dive team after Squishy.

The skip ride over is tense: those two have gone beyond not talking into painful and outspoken silence. I spend most of my time going over and over my equipment looking for flaws. Much as I want to dive this wreck—and I have since the first moment I saw her—I'm scared of the deep and the dark and the unknown. Those first few instances of weightlessness always catch me by surprise, always remind me that what I do is somehow unnatural.

Still, we get to our normal spot, I suit up, and somehow I make it through those first few minutes, zip along the tether with Turtle just a few meters ahead of me, and make my way to the hatch.

Turtle's gonna take care of the recording and the tracking for this trip. She knows the wreck is new to me. She's been inside once now, and so has Karl. Junior and Jypé had the dive before this one.

I've assigned three corridors: one to Karl, one to J&J, and one to Turtle. Once we discover what's at the end of those babies, we'll take a few more. I'm floating; I'll take the corridor of the person I dive with.

Descending into the hatch is trickier than it looks on the recordings. The edges are sharper; I have to be careful about where I put my hands.

Gravity isn't there to pull at me. I can hear my own breathing, harsh and insistent, and I wonder if I shouldn't have taken Squishy's advice: a ten/ten/ten split on my first dive instead of a twenty/twenty/twenty. It takes less time to reach the wreck now; we get inside in nine minutes flat. I would've had time to do a bit of acclimatizing and to have a productive dive the next time.

But I hadn't been thinking that clearly, obviously. I'd been more interested in our corridor, hoping it led to the control room whatever that was.

Squishy had been thinking, though. Before I left, she tanked me up with one more emergency bottle. She remembered how on my first dives after a long lay-off, I used too much oxygen.

She remembered that I sometimes panic.

I'm not panicked now, just excited. I have all my exterior suit lights on, trying to catch the various nooks and crannies of the hatch tube that leads into the ship.

Turtle's not far behind. Because I'm lit up like a tourist station, she's not using her boot lights. She's letting me set the pace, and I'm probably setting it a little too fast.

We reach the corridors at 11:59. Turtle shows me our corridor at 12:03. We take off down the notched hallway at 12:06, and I'm giddy as a child on her first space walk.

Giddy we have to watch. Giddy can be the first sign of oxygen deprivation, followed by a healthy disregard for safety.

But I don't mention this giddy. I've had it since Squishy bowed off the teams, and the giddy's grown worse as my dive day got closer. I'm a little concerned—extreme emotion adds to the heavy breathing—but I'm going to trust my suit. I'm hoping it'll tell me if the oxygen's too low, the pressure's off or the environmental controls are about to fail.

The corridor is human-sized and built for full gravity. Apparently no one thought of adding rungs along the side or the ceiling in case the environmental controls fail.

To me, that shows an astonishing trust in technology, one I've always read about but have never seen. No ship designed in the last three hundred years lacks clingholds. No ship lacks emergency oxygen supplies spaced every ten meters or so. No ship lacks communications equipment near each door.

The past feels even farther away than I thought it would. I thought once I stepped inside the wreck—even though I couldn't smell the environment or hear what's going on around me—I'd get a sense of what it would be like to spend part of my career in this place.

But I have no sense. I'm in a dark, dreary hallway that lacks the emergency supplies I'm used to. Turtle's moving slower than my giddy self wants, although my cautious, experienced boss self knows that slow is best.

She's finding handholds, and signaling me for them, like we're climbing the outside of an alien vessel. We're working on an ancient system—the lead person touches a place, deems it safe, uses it to push off, and the rest of the team follows.

There aren't as many doors as I would have expected. A corridor, it seems to me, needs doors funneling off it, with the occasional side corridor bisecting it.

But there are no bisections, and every time I think we're in a tunnel not a corridor, a door does appear. The doors are regulation height, even now, but recessed farther than I'm used to.

Turtle tries each door. They're all jammed or locked. At the moment, we're just trying to map the wreck. We'll pry open the difficult places once the map is finished.

But I'd love to go inside one of those closed off spaces, probably as much as she would.

Finally, she makes a small scratch on the side of the wall, and nods at me.

The giddy fades. We're done. We go back now—my rule—and if you get back early so be it. I check my readout: 29:01. We have ten minutes to make it back to the hatch.

I almost argue for a few more minutes, even though I know better. Sure, it didn't take us as long to get here as it had in the past, but that doesn't mean the return trip is going to be easy. I've lost four divers over the years because they made the mistake I wanted to make now.

I let Turtle pass me. She goes back, using the same push-off points as before. As she does that, I realize she's marked them somehow, probably with something her suit can pick up. My equipment's not that sophisticated, but I'm glad hers is. We need that kind of expertise inside this wreck. It might take us weeks just to map the space, and we can expect each other to remember each and every safe touch spot because of it.

When we get back to the skip and I drop my helmet, Squishy glares at me.

"You had the gids," she says.

"Normal excitement," I say.

She shakes her head. "I see this coming back the next time, and you're grounded."

I nod, but know she can't ground me without my permission. It's my ship, my wreck, my job. I'll do what I want.

I take off the suit, indulge in some relaxation while Squishy pilots. We didn't get much, Turtle and I, just a few more meters of corridor mapped, but it feels like we'd discovered a whole new world.

Maybe that is the gids, I don't know. But I don't think so. I think it's just the reaction of an addict who returns to her addiction—an elation so great that she needs to do something with it besides acknowledge it.

And this wreck. This wreck has so many possibilities.

Only I can't discuss them on the skip, not with Squishy at the helm and Turtle across from me. Squishy hates this project, and Turtle's starting to. Her enthusiasm is waning, and I don't know if it's because of her personal war with Squishy or because Squishy has convinced her the wreck is even more danger-ous than usual.

I stare out a portal, watching the wreck grow tinier and tinier in the dis-tance. It's ironic. Even though I'm surrounded by tension, I finally feel content.

Half a dozen more dives, maybe sixty more meters, mostly corridor. One potential storage compartment, which we'd initially hoped was a stateroom or quarters, and a mechanic's corridor, filled with equipment we haven't even begun to catalogue.

I spend my off-hours analyzing the materials. So far, nothing conclusive. Lots of evidence of cobbling, but that's pretty common for any ship—with FTL or not—that's made it on a long journey.

What there's no evidence of are bodies. We haven't found a one, and that's even more unusual. Sometimes there're skeletons floating—or pieces of them at least—and sometimes we get the full-blown corpse, suited and intact. A handful aren't suited. Those're the worst. They always make me grateful we can't smell the ship around us.

The lack of bodies is beginning to creep out Karl. He's even talked to me in private about skipping the next few dives.

I'm not sure what's best. If he skips them, the attitudes might become engrained, and he might not dive again. If he goes, the fears might grow worse and paralyze him in the worst possible place.

I move him to the end of the rotation, and warn Squishy she might have to suit up after all.

She just looks at me and grins. "Too many of the team quit on you, you'll just have to go home."

"I'll dive it myself, and you all can wait," I say, but it's bravado and we both know it.

That wreck isn't going to defeat me, not with the perfect treasure hidden in its bulk.

That's what's fueling my greed. The perfect treasure: *my* perfect treasure. Something that answers previously unasked historical questions—previously unknown historical questions; something that will reveal facts about our history, our humanity, that no one has suspected before; and something that, even though it does all that, is worth a small—physical—fortune.

I love the history part. I get paid a lot of money to ferry people to other wrecks, teach them to dive old historical sites. Then I save up my funds and do this: find new sites that no one else knows about, and mine them for history.

I never expected to mine them for real gold as well.

I shake every time I think about it, and before each dive, I do feel the gids. Only now I report them to Squishy. I tell her that I'm a tad too excited, and she offers me a tranq which I always refuse. Never go into the unknown with senses dulled, that's my motto, even though I know countless people who do it.

We're on a long diving mission, longer than some of these folks have ever been on, and we're not even halfway through. We'll have gids and jitters and too many superstitions. We'll have fears and near-emergencies, and God forbid, real emergencies as well.

We'll get through it, and we'll have our prize, and no one, not any one person, will be able to take that away from us.

It turned this afternoon.

I'm captaining the skip. Squishy's back at the *Business*, taking a boss-ordered rest. I'm tired of her complaints and her constant negative attitude. At first, I thought she'd turn Turtle, but Turtle finally got pissed, and decided she'd enjoy this run.

I caught Squishy ragging on J&J, my strong links, asking them if they really want to be mining a death ship. They didn't listen to her, not really— although Jypé argued with her just a little—but that kind of talk can depress an entire mission, sabotage it in subtle little ways, ways that I don't even want to contemplate.

So I'm manning the skip alone, while J&J are running their dive, and I'm listening to the commentary, not looking at the grainy nearly worthless images from the handheld. Mostly I'm thinking about Squishy and how to send her back without sending information too and I can't come to any conclusions at all when I hear:

" . . . yeah, it opens." Junior.

"Wow." Jypé.

"Jackpot, eh?" Junior again.

And then a long silence. Much too long for my tastes, not because I'm afraid for J&J, but because a long silence doesn't tell me one goddamn thing.

I punch up the digital readout, see we're at 25:33—plenty of time. They got to the new section faster than they ever have before.

The silence runs from 25:33 to 28:46, and I'm about to chew my fist off, wondering what they're doing. The handheld shows me grainy walls and more grainy walls. Or maybe it's just grainy nothing. I can't tell.

For the first time in weeks, I want someone else in the skip with me just so that I can talk to somebody.

"Almost time," Jypé says.

"Dad, you gotta see this." Junior has a touch of breathlessness in his voice. Excitement—at least that's what I'm hoping.

And then there's more silence . . . thirty-five seconds of it, followed by a loud and emphatic "Fuck!"

I can't tell if that's an angry "fuck," a scared "fuck" or an awed "fuck." I can't tell much about it at all.

Now I'm literally chewing on my thumbnail, something I haven't done in years, and I'm watching the digital, which has crept past thirty-one minutes.

"Move your arm," Jypé says, and I know then that wasn't a good fuck at all.

Something happened.

Something bad.

"Just a little to the left," Jypé says again, his voice oddly calm. I'm wondering why Junior isn't answering him, hoping that the only reason is he's in a section where the communications relay isn't reaching the skip.

Because I can think of a thousand other reasons, none of them good, that Junior's communication equipment isn't working.

"We're five minutes past departure," Jypé says, and in that, I'm hearing the beginning of panic.

More silence.

I'm actually holding my breath. I look out a portal, see nothing except the wreck, looking like it always does. The handheld has been showing the same grainy image for a while now.

37:24

If they're not careful, they'll run out of air. Or worse.

I try to remember how much extra they took. I didn't really watch them suit up this time. I've seen their ritual so many times that I'm not sure what I think I saw is what I actually saw. I'm not sure what they have with them, and what they don't.

"Great," Jypé says, and I finally recognize his tone. It's controlled parental panic. Sound calm so that the kid doesn't know the situation is bad. "Keep going."

I'm holding my breath, even though I don't have to. I'm holding my breath and looking back and forth between the portal and the handheld image. All I see is the damn wreck and that same grainy image.

"We got it," Jypé says. "Now careful. Careful—son of a bitch! Move, move, move—ah, hell."

I stare at the wreck, even though I can't see inside it. My own breath sounds as ragged as it did inside the wreck. I glance at the digital:

44:11

They'll never get out in time. They'll never make it, and I can't go in for them. I'm not even sure where they are.

"C'mon." Jypé is whispering now. "C'mon son, just one more, c'mon, help me, c'mon."

The "help me" wasn't a request to a hearing person. It was a comment. And I suddenly know.

Junior's trapped. He's unconscious. His suit might even be ripped. It's over for Junior.

Jypé has to know it on some deep level.

Only he also has to know it on the surface, in order to get out.

I reach for my own communicator before I realize there's no talking to them inside the wreck. We'd already established that the skip doesn't have the power to send, for reasons I don't entirely understand. We've tried boosting power through the skip's diagnostic, and even with the *Business's* diagnostic, and we don't get anything.

I judged we didn't need it, because what can someone inside the skip do besides encourage?

"C'mon, son." Jypé grunts. I don't like that sound.

The silence that follows lasts thirty seconds, but it seems like forever. I move away from the portal, stare at the digital, and watch the numbers change. They seem to change in slow-motion:

45:24 to

. . . 25 to

. . . 2 . . . 6 . . .

to

. . . 2 . . . . 7 . . .

until I can't even see them change any more.

Another grunt, and then a sob, half-muffled, and another, followed by—

"Is there any way to send for help? Boss?"

I snap to when I hear my name. It's Jypé and I can't answer him.

I can't answer him, dammit.

I can call for help, and I do. Squishy tells me that the best thing I can do is get the survivor—her word, not mine, even though I know it's obvious too—back to the *Business* as quickly as possible.

"No sense passing midway, is there?" she asks, and I suppose she's right.

But I'm cursing her—after I get off the line—for not being here, for failing us, even though there's not much she can do, even if she's here, in the skip. We don't have a lot of equipment, medical equipment, back at the *Business*, and we have even less here, not that it mattered, because most of the things that happen are survivable if you make it back to the skip.

Still, I suit up. I promise myself I'm not going to the wreck, I'm not going help with Junior, but I can get Jypé along the guideline if he needs me too.

"Boss. Call for help. We need Squishy and some divers and oh, shit, I don't know."

His voice sounds too breathy. I glance at the digital.

56:24

Where has the time gone? I thought he was moving quicker than that. I thought I was too.

But it takes me a while to suit up, and I talked to Squishy, and everything is fucked up.

What'll they say when we get back? The mission's already filled with superstitions and fears of weird technology that none of us really understand.

And only me and Jypé are obsessed with this thing.

Me and Jypé.

Probably just me now.

"I left him some oxygen. I dunno if it's enough . . ."

So breathy. Has Jypé left all his extra? What's happening to Junior? If he's unconscious, he won't use as much, and if his suit is fucked, then he won't need any.

"Coming through the hatch . . ."

I see Jypé, a tiny shape on top of the wreck. And he's moving slowly, much too slowly for a man trying to save his own life.

My rules are clear: let him make his own way back.

But I've never been able to watch someone else die.

I send to the *Business*: "Jypé's out. I'm heading down the line."

I don't use the word help on purpose, but anyone listening knows what I'm doing. They'll probably never listen to me again, but what the hell.

I don't want to lose two on my watch.

When I reach him six minutes later, he's pulling himself along the guideline, hand over hand, so slowly that he barely seems human. A red light flashes at the base of his helmet—the out of oxygen light, dammit. He did use all of his extra for his son.

I grab one small container, hook it to the side of his suit, press the "on" only halfway, knowing too much is as bad as too little.

His look isn't grateful: it's startled. He's so far gone, he hasn't even realized that I'm here.

I brought a grappler as well, a technology I always said was more dangerous than helpful, and here's the first test of my theory. I wrap Jypé against me, tell him to relax, I got him, and we'll be just fine.

He doesn't. Even though I pry him from the line, his hands still move, one over the other, trying to pull himself forward.

Instead, I yank us toward the skip, moving as fast as I've ever moved. I'm burning oxygen at three times my usual rate according to my suit and I don't really care. I want him inside, I want him safe, I want him *alive*, goddammit.

I pull open the door to the skip. I unhook him in the airlock, and he falls to the floor like an empty suit. I make sure the back door is sealed, open the main door, and drag Jypé inside.

His skin is a grayish blue. Capillaries have burst in his eyes. I wonder what else has burst, what else has gone wrong.

There's blood around his mouth.

I yank off the helmet, his suit protesting my every move.

"I gotta tell you," he says. "I gotta tell you."

I nod. I'm doing triage, just like I've been taught, just like I've done half a dozen times before.

"Set up something," he says. "Record."

So I do, mostly to shut him up. I don't want him wasting more energy. I'm wasting enough for both of us, trying to save him, and cursing Squishy for not getting here, cursing everyone for leaving me on the skip, alone, with a man who can't live, and somehow has to.

"He's in the cockpit," Jypé says.

I nod. He's talking about Junior, but I really don't want to hear it. Junior is the least of my worries.

"Wedged under some cabinet. Looks like—battlefield in there."

That catches me. Battlefield how? Because there are bodies? Or because it's a mess?

I don't ask. I want him to wait, to save his strength, to *survive*.

"You gotta get him out. He's only got an hour's worth, maybe less. Get him out."

Wedged beneath something, stuck against a wall, trapped in the belly of the wreck. Yeah, like I'll get him out. Like it's worth it.

All those sharp edges.

If his suit's not punctured now, it would be by the time I'm done getting the stuff off him. Things have to be piled pretty high to get them stuck in zero-G.

I'll wager the *Business* that Junior's not stuck, not in the literal, gravitational sense. His suit's hung up on an edge. He's losing—he's lost—environment and oxygen, and he's probably been dead longer than his father's been on the skip.

"Get him out." Jypé's voice is so hoarse it sounds like a whisper.

I look at his face. More blood.

"I'll get him," I say.

Jypé smiles. Or tries to. And then he closes his eyes, and I fight the urge to slam my fist against his chest. He's dead and I know it, but some small part of me won't believe it until Squishy declares him.

"I'll get him," I say again, and this time, it's not a lie.

Squishy declared him the moment she arrived on the skip. Not that it was hard. He'd already sunken in on himself, and the blood—it wasn't something I wanted to think about.

She flew us back. Turtle was in the other skip, and she never came in, just flew back on her own.

I stayed on the floor, expecting Jypé to rise up and curse me for not going back to the wreck, for not trying, even though we all knew—even though he probably had known—that Junior was dead.

When we got back to the *Business*, Squishy took his body to her little medical suite. She's going to make sure he died from suit failure or lack of oxygen or something that keeps the regulators away from us.

Who knows what the hell he actually died of. Panic? Fear? Stupidity?—or maybe that's what I'm doomed for. Hell, I let a man dive with his son, even though I'd ordered all of my teams to abandon a downed man.

Who can abandon his own kid anyway?

And who listens to me?

Not even me.

My quarters seem too small, the *Business* seems too big, and I don't want to go anywhere because everyone'll look at me, with an I-told-you-so followed by a let's-hang-it-up.

And I don't really blame them. Death's the hardest part. It's what we flirt with in deep-dives.

We claim that flirting is partly love.

I close my eyes and lean back on my bunk but all I see are digital readouts. Seconds moving so slowly they seem like days. The spaces between time. If only we can capture that—the space between moments.

If only.

I shake my head, wondering how I can pretend I have no regrets.

When I come out of my quarters, Turtle and Karl are already watching the vids from Jypé's suit. They're sitting in the lounge, their faces serious.

As I step inside, Turtle says, "They found the heart."

It takes me a minute to understand her, then I remember what Jypé said. They were in the cockpit, the heart, the place we might find the stealth tech.

He was stuck there. Like the probe?

I shudder in spite of myself.

"Is the event on the vid?" I ask.

"Haven't got that far." Turtle shuts off the screens. "Squishy's gone."

"Gone?" I shake my head just a little. Words aren't processing well. I'm having a reaction. I recognize it: I've had it before when I've lost crew.

"She took the second skip, and left. We didn't even notice until I went to find her." Turtle sighs. "She's gone."

"Jypé too?" I ask.

She nods.

I close my eyes. The mission ends, then. Squishy'll go to the authorities and report us. She's gonna tell them about the wreck and the accident and Junior's death. She's gonna show them Jypé, whom I haven't reported yet because I didn't want anyone to find our position, and the authorities'll come here—whatever authorities have jurisdiction over this area—and confiscate the wreck.

At best, we'll get a slap, and I'll have a citation on my record.

At worst, I'll—maybe we'll—face charges for some form of reckless homicide.

"We can leave," Karl says.

I nod. "She'll report the *Business*. They'll know who to look for."

"If you sell the ship—"

"And what?" I ask. "Not buy another? That'll keep us ahead of them for a while, but not long enough. And when we get caught, we get nailed for the full count, whatever it is, because we acted guilty and ran."

"So, maybe she won't say anything," Karl says, but he doesn't sound hopeful.

"If she was gonna do that, she woulda left Jypé," I say.

Turtle closes her eyes, rests her head on the seat back. "I don't know her anymore."

"I think maybe we never did," I say.

"I didn't think she got scared," Turtle says. "I yelled at her—I told her to get over it, that diving's the thing. And she said it's not the thing. Surviving's the thing. She never used to be like that."

I think of the woman sitting on her bunk, staring at her opaque wall—a wall you think you can see through, but you really can't—and wonder. Maybe she always used to be like that. Maybe surviving was always her thing. Maybe diving was how she proved she was alive, until the past caught up with her all over again.

The stealth tech.

She thinks it killed Junior.

I nod toward the screen. "Let's see it," I say to Karl.

He gives me a tight glance, almost—but not quite—expressionless. He's trying to rein himself in, but his fears are getting the best of him.

I'm amazed mine haven't got the best of me.

He starts it up. The voices of men so recently dead, just passing information—"Push off here." "Watch the edge there."—makes Turtle open her eyes.

I lean against the wall, arms crossed. The conversation is familiar to me. I heard it just a few hours ago, and I'd been too preoccupied to give it much attention, thinking of my own problems, thinking of the future of this mission, which I thought was going to go on for months.

Amazing how much your perspective changes in the space of a few minutes.

The corridors look the same. It takes a lot so that I don't zone—I've been in that wreck, I've watched similar vids, and in those I haven't learned much. But I resist the urge to tell Karl to speed it up—there can be something, some wrong movement, piece of the wreck that gloms onto one of my guys—my former guys—before they even get to the heart.

But I don't see anything like that, and since Turtle and Karl are quiet, I assume they don't see anything like that either.

Then J&J find the holy grail. They say something, real casual—which I'd missed the first time—a simple "shit, man" in a tone of such awe that if I'd been paying attention, I would've known.

I bite back the emotion. If I took responsibility for each lost life, I'd never dive again. Of course, I might not after this anyway—one of the many options the authorities have is to take my pilot's license away.

The vids don't show the cockpit ahead. They show the same old grainy walls, the same old dark and shadowed corridor. It's not until Jypé turns his suit vid toward the front that the pit's even visible, and then it's a black mass filled with lighter squares, covering the screen.

"What the hell's that?" Karl asks. I'm not even sure he knows he's spoken.

Turtle leans forward and shakes her head. "Never seen anything like it."

Me either. As Jypé gets closer, the images become clearer. It looks like every piece of furniture in the place has become dislodged, and has shifted to one part of the cockpit.

Were the designers so confident of their artificial gravity that they didn't bolt down the permanent pieces? Could any ship's designers be that stupid?

Jypé's vid doesn't show me the floor, so I can't see if these pieces have been ripped free. If they have, then that place is a minefield for a diver, more sharp edges than smooth ones.

My arms tighten in their cross, my fingers forming fists. I feel a tension I don't want—as if I can save both men by speaking out now.

"You got this before Squishy took off, right?" I ask Turtle.

She understands what I'm asking. She gives me a disapproving sideways look. "I took the vids before she even had the suit off."

Technically, that's what I want to hear, and yet it's not what I want to hear. I want something to be tampered with, something to be slightly off because then, maybe then, Jypé would still be alive.

"Look," Karl says, nodding toward the screen.

I have to force myself to see it. The eyes don't want to focus. I know what happens next—or at least, how it ends up. I don't need the visual confirmation.

Yet I do. The vid can save us, if the authorities come back. Turtle, Karl, even Squishy can testify to my rules. And my rules state that an obviously dangerous site should be avoided. Probes get to map places like this first.

Only I know J&J didn't send in a probe. They might not have because we lost the other so easily, but most likely, it was that greed, the same one which has been affecting me. The tantalizing idea that somehow, this wreck, with its ancient secrets, is the dive of a lifetime—the discovery of a lifetime.

And the hell of it is, beneath the fear and the panic and the anger—more at myself than at Squishy for breaking our pact—that greed remains.

I'm thinking, if we can just get the stealth tech before the authorities arrive, it'll all be worth it. We'll have a chip, something to bargain with.

Something to sell to save our own skins.

Junior goes in. His father doesn't tell him not to. Junior's blurry on the vid—a human form in an environmental suit, darker than the pile of things in the center of the room, but grayer than the black around them.

And it's Junior who says, "It's open," and Junior who mutters "Wow" and Junior who says, "Jackpot, huh?" when I thought all of that had been a dialogue between them.

He points at a hole in the pile, then heads toward it, but his father moves forward quickly, grabbing his arm. They don't talk—apparently that was the way they worked, such an understanding they didn't need to say much, which makes my heart twist—and together they head around the pile.

The cockpit shifts. It has large screens that appear to be unretractable. They're off, big blank canvases against dark walls. No windows in the cockpit at all, which is another one of those technologically arrogant things—what happens if the screen technology fails?

The pile is truly in the middle of the room, a big lump of things. Why Jypé called it a battlefield, I don't know. Because of the pile? Because everything is ripped up and moved around?

My arms get even tighter, my fists clenched so hard my knuckles hurt.

On the vid, Junior breaks away from his father, and moves toward the front (if you can call it that) of the pile. He's looking at what the pile's attached to.

He mimes removing pieces, and the cameras shake. Apparently Jypé is shaking his head.

Yet Junior reaches in there anyway. He examines each piece before he touches it, then pushes at it, which seems to move the entire pile. He moves in closer, the pile beside him, something I can't see on his other side. He's floating, head first, exactly like we're not supposed to go into one of these spaces—he'd have trouble backing out if there's a problem—

And of course there is.

Was.

"Ah, hell," I whisper.

Karl nods. Turtle puts her head in her hands.

On screen nothing moves.

Nothing at all.

Seconds go by, maybe a minute—I forgot to look at the digital readout from earlier, so I don't exactly know—and then, finally, Jypé moves forward.

He reaches Junior's side, but doesn't touch him. Instead the cameras peer in, so I'm thinking maybe Jypé does too.

And then the monologue begins.

I've only heard it once, but I have it memorized.

Almost time.

Dad, you've gotta see this.

Jypé's suit shows us something—a wave? A blackness? A table?—something barely visible just beyond Junior. Junior reaches for it, and then—

Fuck!

The word sounds distorted here. I don't remember it being distorted, but I do remember being unable to understand the emotion behind it. Was that from the distortion? Or my lack of attention?

Jypé has forgotten to use his cameras. He's moved so close to the objects in the pile that all we can see now are rounded corners and broken metal (apparently these did break off then) and sharp, sharp edges.

Move your arm.

But I see no corresponding movement. The visuals remain the same, just like they did when I was watching from the skip.

Just a little to the left.

And then:

We're five minutes past departure.

That was panic. I had missed it the first time, but the panic began right there. Right at that moment.

Karl covers his mouth.

On screen, Jypé turns slightly. His hands grasp boots and I'm assuming he's tugging.

Great. But I see nothing to feel great about. Nothing has moved. *Keep going.*

Going where? Nothing is changing. Jypé can see that, can't he?

The hands seem to tighten their grip on the boots, or maybe I'm imagining that because that's what my hands would do.

We got it.

Is that a slight movement? I step away from the wall, move closer to the vid, as if I can actually help.

Now careful.

This is almost worse because I know what's coming, I know Junior doesn't get out, Jypé doesn't survive. I know—

Careful—son of a bitch!

The hands slid off the boot, only to grasp back on. And there's desperation in that movement, and lack of caution, no checking for edges nearby, no standard rescue procedures.

Move, move, move—ah, hell.

This time, the hands stay. And tug—clearly tug—sliding off.

C'mon.

Sliding again.

C'mon son,

And again.

just one more,

And again.

c'mon, help me, c'mon.

Until, finally, in despair, the hands fall off. The feet are motionless, and, to my untrained eye, appear to be in the same position they were in before.

Now Jypé's breathing dominates the sound—which I don't remember at all—maybe that kind of hiss doesn't make it through our patchwork system—and then vid whirls. He's reaching, grabbing, trying to pull things off the pile, and there's no pulling, everything goes back like it's magnetized.

He staggers backwards—all except his hand, which seems attached—sharp edges? No, his suit wasn't compromised—and then, at the last moment, eases away.

Away, backing away, the visuals are still of those boots sticking out of that pile, and I squint, and I wonder—am I seeing other boots? Ones that are less familiar?—and finally he's bumping against walls, losing track of himself.

He turns, moves away, coming for help even though he has to know I won't help (although I did) and panicked—so clearly panicked. He gets to the end of the corridor, and I wave my hand.

"Turn it off." I know how this plays out. I don't need any more.

None of us do. Besides, I'm the only one watching. Turtle still has her face in her hands, and Karl's eyes are squinched shut, as if he can keep out the horrible experience just by blocking the images.

I grab the controls and shut the damn thing off myself.

Then I slide onto the floor and bow my head. Squishy was right, dammit. She was so right. This ship has stealth tech. It's the only thing still working, that one faint energy signature that attracted me in the first place, and it has killed Junior.

And Jypé.

And if I'd gone in, it would've killed me.

No wonder she left. No wonder she ran. This is some kind of flashback for her, something she feels we can never ever win.

And I'm beginning to think she's right, when a thought flits across my brain.

I frown, flick the screen back on, and search for Jypé's map. He had the system on automatic, so the map goes clear to the cockpit.

I superimpose that map on the exterior, accounting for movement, accounting for change—

And there it is, clear as anything.

The probe, our stuck probe, is pressing against whatever's near Junior's faceplate.

I'm worried about what'll happen if the stealth tech is open to space, and it always has been—at least since I stumbled on the wreck.

Open to space and open for the taking.

Karl's watching me. "What're you gonna do?"

Only that doesn't sound like his voice. It's the greed. It's the greed talking, that emotion I so blithely assumed I didn't have.

Everyone can be snared, just in different ways.

"I don't know what to do," I say. "I have no idea at all."

*

I go back to my room, sit on the bed, stare at the portal which, mercifully, doesn't show the distant wreck.

I'm out of ideas, out of energy, and out of time.

Squishy and the cavalry'll be here soon, to take the wreck from me, confiscate it, and send it into governmental oblivion.

And then my career is over. No more dives, no more space travel.

No more nothing.

I think I doze once because suddenly I'm staring at Junior's face inside his helmet. His eyes move, ever so slowly, and I realize—in the space of a heartbeat—that he's alive in there: his body's in our dimension, his head on the way to another.

And I know, as plainly as I know that he's alive, that he'll suffer a long and hideous death if I don't help him, so I grab one of the sharp edges—with my bare hands (such an obvious dream)—and slice the side of his suit.

Saving him.

Damning him.

Condemning him to an even uglier slow death than the one he would otherwise experience.

I jerk awake, nearly hitting my head on the wall. My breath is coming in short gasps. What if the dream is true? What if he is still alive? No one understands interdimensional travel, so he could be, but even if he is, I can do nothing.

Absolutely nothing, without condemning myself.

If I go in and try to free him, I will get caught as surely as he is. So will anyone else.

I close my eyes, but don't lean back to my pillow. I don't want to fall asleep again. I don't want to dream again, not with these thoughts on my mind. The nightmares I'd have, all because stealth tech exists are terrifying, worse than any I'd had as a child—

And then my breath catches. I open my eyes, rub the sleep from them, think:

This is a Dignity Vessel. Dignity Vessels have stealth tech, unless they've been stripped of them. Squishy described stealth tech to me—and this vessel, this *wreck* has an original version.

Stealth tech has value.

Real value, unlike any wreck I've found before.

I can stake a claim. The time to worry about pirates and privacy is long gone, now.

I get out of bed, pace around the small room. Staking a claim is so foreign to wreck-divers. We keep our favorite wrecks hidden, our best dives secret from pirates and wreck divers and the government.

But I'm not going to dive this wreck. I'm not going in again—none of my people are—and so it doesn't matter that the entire universe knows what I have here.

Except that other divers will come, gold-diggers will try to rob me of my claim—and I can collect fees from anyone willing to mine this, anyone willing to risk losing their life in a long and hideous way.

Or I can salvage the wreck and sell it. The government buys salvage.

If I file a claim, I'm not vulnerable to citations, not even to reckless homicide charges, because everyone knows that mining exacts a price. It doesn't matter what kind of claim you mine, you could still lose some, or all, of your crew.

But best of all, if I stake a claim on that wreck, I can quarantine it—and prosecute anyone who violates the quarantine. I can stop people from getting near the stealth tech if I so choose.

Or I can demand that whoever tries to retrieve it, retrieve Junior's body.

His face rises, unbidden, not the boy I'd known, but the boy I'd dreamed of, half-alive, waiting to die.

I know there are horrible deaths in space. I know that wreck-divers suffer some of the worst.

I carry these images with me, and now, it seems, I'll carry Junior's.

Is that why Jypé made me promise to go in? Had he had the same vision of his son?

I sit down at the network, and call up the claim form. It's so simple. The key is giving up accurate coordinates. The system'll do a quick double-check to see if anyone else has filed a claim, and if so, an automatic arbitrator will ask if I care to withdraw. If I do not, then the entire thing will go to the nearest court.

My hands itch. This is so contrary to my training.

I start to file—and then stop.

I close my eyes—and he's there again, barely moving, but alive.

If I do this, Junior will haunt me until the end of my life. If I do this, I'll always wonder.

Wreck-divers take silly, unnecessary risks, by definition.

The only thing that's stopping me from taking this one is Squishy and her urge for caution.

Wreck-divers flirt with death.

I stand. It's time for a rendezvous.

Turtle won't go in. She's stressed, terrified, and blinded by Squishy's betrayal. She'd be useless on a dive anyway, not clear-headed enough, and probably too reckless.

Karl has no qualms. His fears have left. When I propose a dive to see what happened in there, he actually grins at me.

"Thought you weren't gonna come around," he says.

But I have.

Turtle mans the skip. Karl and I have gone in. We've decided on 30/40/30, because we're going to investigate that cockpit. Karl theorizes that there's some kind of off switch for the stealth tech, and of course he's right. But the wreck has no real power, and since the designers had too much faith in their technology to build redundant safety systems, I'm assuming they had too much faith to design an off switch for their most dangerous technology, a dead-man's switch that'll allow the stealth tech to go off even if the wreck has no power.

I mention that to Karl and he gives me a startled look.

"You ever wonder what's keeping the stealth tech on then?" he asks.

I've wondered, but I have no answer. Maybe when Squishy comes back with the government ships, maybe then I'll ask her. What my non-scientific mind is wondering is this: Can the stealth tech operate from both dimensions? Is something on the other side powering it?

Is part of the wreck—that hole we found in the hull on the first day, maybe—still in that other dimension?

Karl and I suit up, take extra oxygen, and double-check our suit's environmental controls. I'm not giddy this trip—I'm not sure I'll be giddy again—but I'm not scared either.

Just coldly determined.

I promised Jypé I was going back for Junior, and now I am.

No matter what the risk.

The trip across is simple, quick, and familiar. Going down the entrance no longer seems like an adventure. We hit the corridors with fifteen minutes to spare.

Jypé's map is accurate to the millimeter. His push-off points are marked on the map and with some corresponding glove grip. We make record time as we head toward that cockpit.

Record time, though, is still slow. I find myself wishing for all my senses: sound, smell, taste. I want to know if the effects of the stealth tech have made it out here, if something is off in the air—a bit of a burnt smell, something foreign that raises the small hairs on the back of my neck. I want to know if Junior is already decomposing, if he's part of a group (the crew?) pushed up against the stealth tech, never to go free again.

But the wreck doesn't cough up those kind of details. This corridor looks the same as the other corridor I pulled my way through.

Karl moves as quickly as I do, although his suit lights are on so full that looking at him almost blinds me. That's what I did to Turtle on our trip, and it's a sign of nervousness.

It doesn't surprise me that Karl, who claimed not to be afraid, is nervous. He's the one who had doubts about this trip once he'd been inside the wreck. He's the one I thought wouldn't make it through all of his scheduled dives.

The cockpit looms in front of us, the doors stuck open. It does look like a battlefield from this vantage: the broken furniture, the destruction all cobbled together on one side of the room, like a barricade.

The odd part about it is, though, that the barricade runs from floor to ceiling, and unlike most things in zero-G, seem stuck in place.

Neither Karl nor I give the barricade much time. We've vowed to explore the rest of the cockpit first, looking for the elusive dead-man switch. We have to be careful; the sharp edges are everywhere.

Before we left, we used the visuals from Jypé's suit, and his half-finished map, to assign each other areas of the cockpit to explore. I'm going deep, mostly because this is my idea, and deep—we both feel—is the most dangerous place. It's closest to the probe, closest to that corner of the cockpit where Junior still hangs, horizontal, his boots kicking out into the open.

I go in the center, heading toward the back, not using hand-holds. I've pushed off the wall, so I have some momentum, a technique that isn't really my strong suit. But I volunteered for this, knowing the edges in the front would slow me down, knowing that the walls would raise my fears to an almost incalculable height.

Instead, I float over the middle of the room, see the uprooted metal of chairs and the ripped shreds of consoles. There are actual wires protruding from the middle of that mess, wires and stripped bolts—something I haven't seen in space before, only in old colonies—and my stomach churns as I move forward.

The back wall is dark, with its distended screen. The cockpit feels like a cave instead of the hub of the Dignity Vessel. I wonder how so many people could have trusted their lives to this place.

Just before I reach the wall, I spin so that I hit it with the soles of my boots. The soles have the toughest material on my suit. The wall is mostly smooth, but there are a few edges here, too—more stripped bolts, a few twisted metal pieces that I have no idea what they once were part of.

This entire place feels useless and dead.

It takes all of my strength not to look at the barricade, not to search for the bottoms of Junior's boots, not to go there first. But I force myself to shine a spot on the wall before me, then on the floor, and the ceiling, looking for something—anything—that might control part of this vessel.

But whatever had, whatever machinery there'd been, whatever computerized equipment, is either gone or part of that barricade. My work in the back is over quickly, although I take an extra few minutes to record it all, just in case the camera sees something I don't.

It takes Karl a bit longer. He has to pick his way through a tiny debris field. He's closer to a possible site: there's still a console or two stuck to his near wall. He examines them, runs his suit-cam over them as well, but shakes his head.

Even before he tells me he's found nothing, I know.

I know.

I join him at a two-pronged hand-hold, where his wall and mine meet. The handhold was actually designed for this space, the first such design I've seen on the entire Dignity Vessel.

Maybe the engineers felt that only the cockpit crew had to survive uninjured should the artificial gravity go off. More likely, the lack of grab bars was simply an oversight in the other areas, or a cost-saving measure.

"You see a way into that barricade?" Karl asks.

"We're not going in," I say. "We're going to satisfy my curiosity first."

He knows about the dream; I told him when we were suiting up. I have no idea if Turtle heard—if she did, then she knows too. I don't know how she feels about the superstitious part of this mission, but I know that Karl understands.

"I think we should work off a tether," he says. "We can hook up to this handhold. That way, if one of us gets stuck—"

I shake my head. There are clearly other bodies in that barricade, and I would wager that some of them have tethers and bits of equipment attached.

If the stealth tech is as powerful as I think it is, then these people had no safeguard against it. A handhold won't defend us either, even though, I believe, the stealth tech is running at a small percentage of capacity.

"I'm going first," I say. "You wait. If I pull in, you go back. You and Turtle get out."

We've discussed this drill. They don't like it. They believe leaving me behind will give them two ghosts instead of one.

Maybe so, but at least they'll still be alive to experience those ghosts.

I push off the handhold, softer this time than I did from the corridor, and let the drift take me to the barricade. I turn the front suit-cams on high. I also use zoom on all but a few of them. I want to see as much as I can through that barricade.

My suit lights are also on full. I must look like a child's floaty toy heading in for a landing.

I stop near the spot where Junior went in. His boots are there, floating, like expected. I back as far from him as I can, hoping to catch a reflection in his visor, but I get nothing.

I have to move to the initial spot, that hole in the barricade that Junior initially wanted to go through.

I'm more afraid of that than I am of the rest of the wreck, but I do it. I grasp a spot marked on Jypé's map, and pull myself toward that hole.

Then I train the zoom inside, but I don't need it.

I see the side of Junior's face, illuminated by my lights. The helmet is what tells me that it's him. I recognize the modern design, the little logos he glued to its side.

His helmet has bumped against the only intact console in the entire place. His face is pointed downward, the helmet on clear. And through it, I see something I don't expect: the opposite of my fears.

He isn't alive. He hasn't been alive in a long, long time.

As I said, no one understands interdimensional travel, but we suspect it manipulates time. And what I see in front of me makes me realize my hypothesis is wrong:

Time sped up for him. Sped to such a rate that he isn't even recognizable. He's been mummified for so long that the skin looks petrified, and I bet, if we were to somehow free him and take him back to the *Business*, that none of our normal medical tools could cut through the surface of his face.

There are no currents and eddies here, nothing to pull me forward. Still, I scurry back to what I consider a safe spot, not wanting to experience the same fate as the youngest member of our team.

"What is it?" Karl asks me.

"He's gone," I say. "No sense cutting him loose."

Even though cutting isn't the right term. We'd have to free him from that stealth tech, and I'm not getting near it. No matter how rich it could make me, no matter how many questions it answers, I no longer want anything to do with it.

I'm done—with this dive, this wreck—and with my brief encounter with greed.

We do have answers, though, and visuals to present to the government ships when they arrive. There are ten of them—a convoy—unwilling to trust something as precious as stealth tech to a single ship.

Squishy didn't come back with them. I don't know why I thought she would. She dropped off Jypé, reported us and the wreck, and vanished into Longbow Station, not even willing to collect a finder's fee that the government gives whenever it locates unusual technologies.

Squishy's gone, and I doubt she'll ever come back.

Turtle's not speaking to me now, except to say that she's relieved we're not being charged with anything. Our vids showed the government we cared enough to go back for our team member, and also that we had no idea about the stealth tech until we saw it function.

We hadn't gone into the site to raid it, just to explore it—as the earlier vids showed. Which confirmed my claim—I'm a wreck-diver, not a pirate, not a scavenger—and that allowed me to pick up the reward that Squishy abandoned.

I'd've left it too, except that I needed to fund the expedition, and I'm not going to be able to do it the way I'd initially planned—by taking tourists to the Dignity Vessel so far from home.

The wreck got moved to some storehouse or warehouse or way station where the government claims it's safe. Turtle thinks we should've blown it up; Karl's just glad it's out of our way.

Me, I just wished I had more answers to all the puzzles.

That vessel'd been in service a while, that much was clear from how it had been refitted. When someone activated the stealth, something went wrong. I doubt even the government scientists would find out exactly what in that mess.

Then there's the question of how it got to the place I found it. There's no way to tell if it traveled in stealth mode or over those thousands of years, although that doesn't explain how the ship avoided gravity wells and other perils that lie in wait in a cold and difficult universe. Or maybe it had been installed with an updated FTL. Again, I doubted I would ever know.

As for the crew—I have no idea, except that I suspect the cockpit crew died right off. We could see them in that pile of debris. But the rest—there were no bodies scattered throughout the ship, and there could've been, given that the vessel is still intact after all this time.

I'm wondering if they were running tests with minimal crew or if the real crew looked at that carnage in the cockpit and decided, like we did, that it wasn't worth the risk to go in.

I never looked for escape pods, but such things existed on Dignity Vessels. Maybe the rest of the crew bailed, got rescued, and blended into cultures somewhere far from home.

Maybe that's where Jypé's legends come from.

Or so I like to believe.

Longbow Station has never seemed so much like home. It'll be nice to shed the silent Turtle, and Karl, who claims his diving days are behind him.

Mine are too, only in not quite the same way. The *Business* and I'll still ferry tourists to various wrecks, promising scary dives and providing none.

But I've had enough of undiscovered wrecks and danger for no real reason. Curiosity sent me all over this part of space, looking for hidden pockets, places where no one has been in a long time.

Now that I've found the ultimate hidden pocket—and I've seen what it can do—I'm not looking any more. I'm hanging up my suit and reclaiming my land legs.

Less danger there, on land, in normal gravity. Not that I'm afraid of wrecks now. I'm not, no more than the average spacer.

I'm more afraid of that feeling, the greed, which came on me hard and fast, and made me tone-deaf to my best diver's concerns, my old friend's fears, and my own giddy response to the deep.

I'm getting out before I turn pirate or scavenger, before my greed—which I thought I didn't have—draws me as inexorably as the stealth tech drew Junior, pulling me in and holding me in place, before I even realize I'm in trouble.

Before I even know how impossible it'll be to escape.

Gwyneth Jones is a writer and critic of science fiction and fantasy, who also writes for teenagers using the name Ann Halam. Among other honors, she's won two World Fantasy awards, the British Science Fiction short story award, the Dracula Society's Children of the Night award, the Philip K. Dick award, and shared the first Tiptree award, in 1992, with Eleanor Arnason. *Bold As Love*, the first novel of a near future fantasy sequence, won the Arthur C. Clarke award for 2001. She lives in Brighton, UK, with her husband and son, plus two cats: practices yoga, has done some extreme tourism in her time, likes old movies and cooking, and enjoys playing with her websites.

THE VOYAGE OUT

GWYNETH JONES

I

"Do you want to dream?"

"No."

The woman in uniform behind the desk looked at her screen and then looked at me, expressionless. I didn't know if she was real and far away; or fake and here.

"Straight to orientation then."

II

I walked. The Kuiper Belt Station—commonly known as the Panhandle—could afford the energy fake gravity requires. It wasn't going anywhere; it was spinning on the moving spot of a minimum-collision orbit, close to six billion kilometres from the sun: a prison isle without a native population. From here I would be transported to my final exile from the United States of Earth, as an algorithm, a string of 0s and 1s. It's illegal to create a code-version of a human being anywhere in the USE, including near-space habitats and planetary colonies. Protected against identity theft, the whole shipload of us, more than a hundred condemned criminals, had been brought to the edge: where we must now be coded individually before we could leave. The number-crunching would take a while, even with the most staggering computation power.

A reprieve, then. A stay of execution.

In my narrow cabin, or cell, I lay down on the bunk. Walls, floor, fittings: everything was made of the same, grey-green, dingy ceramic fibre. The 'mattress' felt like metal to the touch, but it yielded to the shape and weight of my body. The raised rim made me think of autopsies, crushed viscera. A panel by my head held the room controls: just like a hotel. I could check the status of my vacuum toilet, my dry shower, my air, my pressure, my own emissions, detailed in bright white.

Questions bubbled behind my lips, never to be answered. I was disoriented by weeks of being handled only by automation (sometimes with a human face); never allowed any contact with my fellow prisoners. When did I last speak to a human being? That must have been the orientation on earth, my baggage allowance session. You're given a 'weight limit'—actually a code limit—and advised when you've 'duplicated'. *Gray's Anatomy*, for old sake's sake. A really good set of knives, a really good pair of boots, a field first-aid kit, vegetable and flower seeds. The Beethoven piano sonatas, played by Alfred Brendel; Mozart piano sonatas, likewise. The prison officer told me I couldn't have the first aid. He advised me I must *choose* the data storage device for my minimalist choice of entertainments, and *specify* the lifetime power source. He made me handle the knives, the boots, the miniaturised hardware, even the seeds. What a palaver.

But the locker underneath the bunk was empty.

Do you want to dream?

The transit would happen, effectively, in no time at all. I had no idea how long the coding would take. An hour, a week, a month? I thought of the others, dreaming in fantasy boltholes. Some gorging their appetites, delicate or gross. Some exacting hideous revenge on the forces that brought them here: fathers, mothers, lovers; authority figures, SOCIETY. Some even trying to expiate their crimes in virtual torment; you get all sorts in the prison population. None of that for me. If you want to die have the courage to kill yourself, before you reach a finale like this one. If you don't, then live to the last breath. Face the firing squad without a blindfold.

Scenes from my last trial went through my head. Me, bloody but unbowed of course, still trying to make speeches, thoroughly alienating the courtroom witnesses. My ex-husband making unconscious gestures in a small blank room, as he finally abandoned this faulty domestic appliance to her fate. He was horrified by that Death Row interview: I was not. I had given up on Dirk long ago. Did he *ever* believe in me? Or was he just humouring my unbalanced despair, as he says now—in the years when we were lovers and best friends? Did he really twist his hands around like that, and raise them high, palm outwards, as if he faced a terrorist with a gun?

I thought of the girl who had caught my eye, glimpsed as we sometimes glimpsed each other; waiting to be processed into the Panhandle system. Springy cinnamon braids, sticking out on either side of her head, that made her look like a little girl. Her eyes lobotomised. Who had brushed her hair for her? Why would they waste money sending a lobotomy subject out here? Because it's a numbers game they're playing. The weaklings, casualties of the transit, may ensure in some occult way the survival of a few, who *may* live long enough to form the foundation stones of a colony, on an earth-like planet of a distant star. Our fate: to be pole-axed and buried in the mud where the bridge of dreams will be built.

I wondered when 'orientation' would begin. The cold of deep space penetrated my thin quilt. The steady shift of the clock numerals was oddly comforting, like a heartbeat. I watched them until at some point I fell asleep.

III

The Kuiper Belt Station had been planned as the hub of an international deep space city. Later, after that project had been abandoned and before the Buonarotti Device became practicable for mass exits like this one, it'd been an R&R resort for asteroid miners. They'd dock their little rocket ships and party, escaping from utter solitude to get crazy drunk and murder each other, according to the legends. I thought of those old no-hopers as I followed the guidance lights to my first orientation session; but there was no sign of them, no scars, no graffiti on the drab walls of endless curving corridors. There was only the pervasive hum of the Buonarotti torus, like the engines of a vast majestic passenger liner forging through the abyss. The sound—gentle on the edge of hearing—made me shudder. It was warming up, of course.

In a large bare saloon, prisoners in tan overalls were shuffling past a booth where a figure in medical-looking uniform questioned them and let them by. A circle of chairs, smoothly fixed to the floor or maybe extruded from it, completed the impression of a dayroom in a mental hospital. I joined the line. I didn't speak to anyone and nobody spoke to me, but the girl with the cinnamon braids was there. I noticed her. My turn came. The woman behind the desk, whom I immediately christened Big Nurse, checked off my name and asked me to take the armband that lay on the counter. "It's good to know we have a doctor on the team," she said.

I had qualified as a surgeon but it was years since I'd practiced, other than as a volunteer 'barefoot' GP in Community Clinics for the underclass. I looked at the armband that said 'captain' and wondered how it had got there, untouched by human hand. Waldoes, robot servitors . . . It was disorienting to be reminded of the clunky, mechanical devices around here; the ones I was not allowed to see.

"Where are you in the real world?" I asked, trying to reclaim my dignity. I knew they had ways of dealing with the time-lapse, they could fake almost natural dialogue. "Where is the Panhandle run from these days? Xichang? Or Houston? I'd just like to know what kind of treatment to expect, bad or worse."

"No," said Big Nurse, answering a different question. "I am a bot." She looked me in the eye, with the distant kindness of a stranger to human concerns. "I am in the information system, nowhere else. There is no treatment, no punishment here, Ruth Norman. That's over."

I glanced covertly at my companions, the ones already hovering around the dayroom chairs. I'd been in prison before; I'd been in reform camp before. I knew what could happen to a middle-class woman, in jail for the unimpressive 'crime' of protesting the loss of our civil liberties. The animal habit of self-preservation won out. I slipped the band over the sleeve of my overalls. Immediately a tablet appeared, in the same place on the counter. It was solid when I picked it up.

I quickly discovered that, of the fourteen people in the circle (there were eighteen names listed on my tablet, the missing four never turned up), less than half had opted to stay awake. I tried to convince the dream-deprived that I had not been responsible for the mix-up. I asked them all to answer to their names. They complied, surprisingly willing to accept my authority—for the moment.

"*Hil . . . de . . .*" said the girl with the cinnamon braids, struggling with a tongue too thick for her mouth: a sigh and a guttural *duh*, like the voice of a child's teddy bear, picked up and shaken after long neglect. The braids had not been renewed, fuzzy strands were escaping. Veterans of prison-life glanced at each other uneasily. Nobody commented. There was another woman who didn't speak at all, so lacking in response you wondered how she'd found her way to the dayroom.

We were nine women, four men and one female-identifying male transsexual (to give the Sista her prison-system designation). The details on my tablet were meagre: names, ages, ethnic/national grouping, not much else. Mrs Miqal Rohan was Iranian and wore strict hejabi dress, but spoke perfect, icy English. 'Bimbam' was European English, rail thin, and haunted by some addiction that made her chew frantically at the inside of her cheek. The other native Englishwoman, a Caribbean ethnic calling herself Servalan (Angela Morrison, forty-three), looked as if she'd been institutionalised all her life. I had no information about their crimes. But as I entered nicknames, and read the qualifications or professions, I saw a pattern emerging, and I didn't like it. Such useful people! How did you all come to this pass? By what strange accidents did you all earn mandatory death sentences or life-without-parole? Will the serial killers, the drug cartel gangsters, and the re-offending child rapists please identify yourselves?

I kept quiet, and waited to hear what anyone else would say.

The youngest of the men (Koffi, Nigerian; self-declared 'business entrepreneur') asked, diffidently, "Does anyone know how long this lasts?"

"There's no way of knowing," said Carpazian, who was apparently Russian, despite the name; a slim and sallow thirty-something, still elegant in the overalls. "The Panhandle is a prison system. It can drug us and deceive us without limit."

The man who'd given his handle as Drummer raised heavy eyes and spoke, sonorous as a prophet, from out of a full black beard. "We will be ordered to the transit chamber as we were ordered to this room; or drugged and carried by robots in our sleep. We will lie down in the Buonarotti capsules, and a code-self, the complex pattern of each human body and soul, will be split into two like a cell dividing. The copies will be sent flying around the torus, at half-light speed. You will collide with yourself and cease utterly to exist at these co-ordinates of space-time. The body and soul in the capsule will be *annihilated*, and know GOD no longer."

"But then we wake up on another planet?" pleaded Servalan, unexpectedly shy and sweet from that coarsened mask.

"Perhaps."

The prophet resumed staring at the floor.

"Isn't it against your religion to be here, Mr Drummer?"

He made no answer. The speaker was 'Gee', a high-flier, corporate, who must have got caught up in something *very* sour. A young and good-looking woman with an impervious air of success, even now. I marked her down as a possible troublemaker, and tried to start a conversation about survival skills. That quickly raised another itchy topic. Is there *really* no starship? Not even a lifepod? Are we *really*, truly meant to pop into existence on the surface of an unknown planet, just as we stand?

"No one knows what happens," said 'Flick', another younger woman with impressive quals, and a blank cv. "The ping signal that registers a successful transit travels very, very fast, but it's timebound. They've only been shipping convicts out of here for five years. It'll be another twenty before they know for certain if *anyone* has reached the First Landfall planet, dead or alive—"

When Big Nurse's amplified voice told us the session was over, and we must return to our cells, my tablet said that two hours had passed. It felt like a lot longer. I was trembling with fatigue. I went over to the booth while the others were filing out.

"Take the armband from me," I muttered.

Annihilation, okay. Six billion kilometres from home, a charade set up around the lethal injection: whatever turns you on, O fascist state authority that ate my country, my world and its freedoms . . . But I refused to accept the role the bastards had dumped on me. I did not stand, I will not serve. I didn't dare to resign, I knew the rest of them wouldn't take that well. The system gives, the system better take away.

"I cannot," said Big Nurse, reasonably. "I am a bot."

"Of course you can. Make this vanish and appoint the next trustie on the list."

Software in human form answered the question that I hadn't asked. "All good government tends towards consensus," she said. "But consensus operates through forms and structures. Leader is your position in this nexus. The system cannot change your relation to the whole."

The girl with the braids was shuffling out, last. She walked as if she was struggling through treacle. Through the veil I saw a young, limber body, full of grace. I could not stop myself imagining the springy crease between her bottom and her thigh, and how it would move. I swallowed hard, and abruptly changed my mind.

Live to the last breath. Play the game, what does it matter?

In my cell, the ration tray that had been waiting for me in the 'morning', when I woke, had disappeared. Another prison meal had arrived. I ate it. I had a drinking fountain in a niche in my wall, and the water tasted sweet. My God, what luxuries!

Aside from the four people who never turned up, everyone attended the day-room, including Drummer and the unresponsive woman. Most of us were playing the game to ward off madness and the abyss. Some of us genuinely got interested in setting up the ground rules for a new world. I couldn't tell the difference; not even in myself.

Carpazian said we would need an established religion.

"Religion," he reasoned, "is not all bad. It contains the incomprehensible in human life. People need deities, doorkeepers between the real and unreal. And the Buonarotti device has made the world stranger than people ever knew before."

I don't think he meant to do it, but he started something. Mike, the fourth man, said he'd heard that the Panhandle was haunted by murdered prospectors. Flick said she'd felt someone in her cell with her, invisible, watching her every move.

"They say the Buonarotti Transit broke something open," offered Koffi. "They say it unleashed monsters. And here we are right next to the torus."

We shouted him down, we rationalists (including Carpazian). We were all feeling vulnerable. It was hard not to get creeped out, with the ever-present hum of that annihilation wheel, Big Nurse our only company, and the knowledge that we had been utterly abandoned. We were little children, frightened in the dark.

I decided to go and see Hilde. We were all quartered on the same corridor, and the doors had nameplates. We were free to make visits, other people were doing it. I didn't know how to make myself known, so I just knocked.

The door slid open. She stared at me, and began to back away.

"Do you mind if I come in?"

She gestured consent, zombie-slow, and embarked on the difficult task of clambering back onto her bunk. There was nowhere else so I sat there too, at the foot of her bed. She fumbled with the room controls, the door closed, we were alone together. It felt perilous, uncertain; but not in a nightmare way.

"I just wanted to say, the sessions are obviously a strain. Is there anything I can do? Nothing's compulsory, you know." Her braids were fuzzed all over, after days without any attention. I wanted to ask if she had a comb.

"I . . . am . . . Not like this . . . willingly . . . Captain."

Beads of sweat stood on her brow, by the end of that momentous effort. Her eyes were dark, her lashes long and curling. Her mouth was very full, almost too much for her narrow face to bear. She would have been pretty, a misfit, awkward prettiness, if there had been any life in her expression.

"Oh no!" I cried, consternated by her struggle. "I'm not the boss, please. The system did that to me, I'm not checking up on you. I meant—"

What did I mean? I could not explain myself.

"Do you have a comb?"

"Ye'uh . . . Ma'am."

She clambered slowly down again, groped inside the dry shower stall and brought out a dingy ceramic fibre comb, Panhandle issue. Her hand flailed piteously as she tried to hand it over; and yet the same thought flashed on me as had come when I first saw her. Somehow she was *untouched*. She was not only the youngest member of my 'team', she was nothing like the rest of us: weary criminals, outlaws fallen from high places. She had been cared for, loved and treasured; and become a zombie on Death Row without ever losing that bloom. It was a mystery. What the hell had she done? Was she a psycho? What had made this gentle nineteen-year-old so dangerous?

"Turn around."

I loosened her braids, combed out her wilful mass of hair and set it in order again, as if I were her mother. It was the sweetest thing. I was glad she was turned away, so she couldn't see the tears in my eyes.

"There. That'll do for a while."

She faced me again, another painful, laborious shift. "Th . . . an' . . . you."

I had run out of excuses to touch her. "Shall I come again?"

She struggled fiercely. "Yes . . . I like . . . that."

IV

The fourth session was a practical. We had been warned on our room screens, but it came as a shock. The dayroom chairs and the booth where Big Nurse sat had gone: as soon as the fourteen of us had arrived, the doors closed and we were plunged into a simulation. A grassy plain, scattered trees, and a herd of large animals coming over the horizon . . . Disoriented, bewildered, we co-operated like castaways. The consensus decision was that we should treat these furred, pawed, sabre-toothed bison-things as potential transport. We tried to catch a young one, so we could tame it. My God, it was a disaster, but it was fun. I had to set a broken bone. Koffi, tough guy, got through it without any pain relief; we discussed bottom-up pharmacology and bull-riding.

Sista and Angie (who had announced that she no longer wanted to be called Servalan) started bunking together, and no retribution descended. Gee hustled me for a simulated childbirth drama: thankfully I had no control over what the system chose to throw at us. I found out I'd been wrong about Bimbam the addict. She was not addicted to any recreational drug. She was a former school teacher, amateur mule. Her problem was a little girl of seven, and a little boy of five, from whom she'd been separated for two years. In prison on earth she'd had visiting rights, on screen. Now she would never see them again. She crawled back towards life, carrying the wounds that would never heal. Drummer, too, crawled back to life. He asked us to call him Achmed, his real name. But he would never be easy company: a man who believed himself damned to all eternity, separated from GOD.

Once, I walked along the curving corridor and saw someone oddly familiar, oddly far in the distance, coming to meet me: a trick of perspective. I was mystified by a huge feeling of foreboding, then saw that it was myself. I was walking towards myself. I turned and ran; another figure ran ahead of me, always at vanishing point. I reached my own cabin, my nameplate. I clutched at the glassy surface of the door, sweating.

*

We all had experiences. They were difficult to dismiss.

I woke in the 'night' and heard someone crying out in the corridor. I went to see, hoping that it would be Hilde and I would comfort her. It was the elegant and controlled Carpazian, crouched in a foetal curl, sobbing like a baby.

"Georgiou? What is it?"

"My arm, my arm—"

"What is it? Are you in pain?"

He was nursing his right arm; he pushed up the overall sleeve and showed me the skin. "I cut myself. I have no secret weapon, the ceramic won't cut you; I used my teeth. I was keeping tally of the 'days' and 'nights' in blood, hidden under the rim of my bunk. It's gone. I have asked the woman called Gee, she says I never had a mark on me. I've fucked her but *she isn't real*. This place is haunted, haunted—"

It wasn't like him to use a word like "fucked." There wasn't a scratch on his right arm, or his left. "It's the torus," I said. "It's warming up. That's where the strange phenomena come from, it's affecting our brainchemistry, it's all in our minds. Don't let it get you down."

"Captain Ruth," he whispered, "how long have we been here?"

We stared at each other. "Three days," I said firmly. "No, four."

The Russian shook his head. "You don't know . . . What if it isn't the torus? What if something got out, what if something is with us, messing with us?"

"Maybe the ghost of one of the old prospectors? I think I'd like that. You're the Patriarch, what should we do, your holiness? Hold a séance; try to make contact with the tough old bird?"

He laughed, shaky but comforted, and went back to his cell. I went back to mine. I wondered if the system itself was telling us something through these spooky hints. That *nothing* is real? That only what Drummer called the soul, subtle distillation of mind and body, exists?

Hilde invited me to her cabin.

Some of us were treating the Panhandle as a Death Row singles bar, and why not? Carpazian was being kept busy, and Koffi and Mike; nobody had dared to approach Drummer aka Achmed. As captain I got to know these things . . . I knew it couldn't be *that*. The girl couldn't possibly be making a sexual approach, but I was unspeakably nervous.

I'd been protecting her with signs of my approval; but being careful not to make her into teacher's pet. I'd had her on my team in the simulation room, things like that. Small, threatened groups are hungry for scapegoats. I knew I wasn't the only one who'd been wondering *why* she'd been kept under such heavy medication.

She was certainly a different person, after five days clear (or was it four?). There was light in her eyes, energy in her movements. It was enough to break your heart, because something told me she had never really been free, never in her life: and now this child would go into the void without ever having walked down a street, bought an ice-cream, skinned her knee, played ball, climbed a tree.

We chatted about the animal-taming. She was going to confess something, I was sure; but I wouldn't rush her.

I wanted to offer to comb her hair again.

"I don't believe it," I said. "This is too much."

"You don't believe that First Landfall exists?"

I shook my head, letting my hand rest on the faintly warm 'mattress' where her body had lain. Tastes and smells are the food of the gods; and touch, too.

"No, I can believe they've been identifying habitable planets hundreds of light-years away. I can grasp the science of that idea, and the science that says earth-like planets are bound to exist, though we know for a fact that there's nothing within our material reach except hot and cold rocks; or giant gas-balloons."

She nodded. She had no life experience but she was not ignorant or stupid. She'd proved that in our sessions, as she came out from under the drugs.

"I can even, just about, believe that the torus can send us there, in some weird way that means new bodies will automatically be generated when we make landfall."

The void opened when I said that. None of us really believed we would wake again. The transit was a fairytale, disguising annihilation, annihilation—

I shook my head solemnly, pulling the conversation around. "But I cannot, no, I'm sorry . . . I've tried, but your captain *cannot* believe in the gruffaloes."

The tawny bison-things, with the clawed paws and sabre teeth, had instantly been named *gruffaloes*. Hilde began to giggle, helplessly. We laughed, leaning close together, white mice trying to understand the experiment. Gallows humour!

"If we wake on that plain," said Hilde, and she stopped smiling. "It will be the first time I've ever been outdoors in my life."

Here it comes, I thought.

"Your hair's a disgrace again," I said. "Do you want me to comb it?"

"I'd love that," she said. She reached for the comb, which was lying on the bunk, moving light and limber, with the grace that I'd seen like a ghost in the shell, when she was drugged to the eyeballs. But she didn't hand it over.

"No . . . Wait, I want to tell you something. I have to look at you while I tell you. I have a termination-level genetic disease."

"Ah." I nodded, shocked and relieved. So this was the secret.

"My parents are . . . I mean they were . . . members of a church that didn't allow pregnancy screening. Their church believed all children should be born, and *then* tested. So, when I was born they found out there was something wrong with me and my parents took me away, to a city; because the elders would have turned us in. When I was old enough to notice that I was different from the children on my TV, my mother and father told me I was allergic to everything, and I would get sick and die if I ever set foot outside my bedroom door. I never wondered why no doctors ever came, if I was so ill. I accepted the world the way it was."

"What happened?"

"I don't know." Her eyes filled with tears. "I don't know, Ruth. I remember my sixteenth birthday, and then it's like a thick blank curtain with holes torn in it. A lot of screaming and crying and slamming doors. A hospital corridor, a horrible jacket that wrapped my arms together, another room where they never let me out . . ." She shook her head. "Just blurred scenes in a nightmare, until I was here."

"What about your parents?"

"I suppose they got found out, I suppose they're in prison."

"Do you remember what they thought was wrong with you? You said 'termination-level'. Who told you that? What gave you that idea?"

She wiped away the tears before they could fall. I saw her struggle, the way she'd struggled to speak the last time I was in here. This time she lost the fight. If she had ever known what was wrong, she didn't know now—

"I can't remember. I think my parents never told me anything, but maybe I heard something in the hospital, or I saw something on the TV." She pressed her fist to her mouth, the knuckles staring white. "I don't know, but I'm scared."

The nail that sticks out will be hammered down. The USE saw certain 'traits' as enemies of the state. By no means all of the proscribed genes were life-threatening.

"You don't have to be scared. They don't send just any condemned criminals to the Panhandle, Hilde. We have to be aged between eighteen and forty, and normally fertile. If you'd had a termination-level genetic disease you'd have been sterilised as soon as they spotted you; and you wouldn't be here."

This beautiful girl was a recessive carrier for some kind of cancer they were trying to stamp out, or some other condition that wouldn't harm her until she was fifty and past child-bearing. She'd been condemned like rotten meat by bad science.

I hoped I'd reassured her. Destroyed by longing, I was having trouble keeping my voice level. I was afraid I sounded cold and unsympathetic—

"If we have to be fertile, what about Sista?"

I shook my head. "She's never had a re-assignment, she couldn't afford it. It's all cosmetic. She's classified as a fertile male by the Panhandle system."

I wanted to hold her but I didn't dare to touch her. I despised the crude thrumming in my blood, the shameful heat in my crotch. Thankfully Hilde was too intent on her confession to notice me; still convinced that she was some kind of pariah. Poor kid, hadn't she grasped we were all pariahs together?

"You d-don't have anything about m-my criminal record on your tablet?"

"Not a thing."

This was absolutely true. I had professional profiles, listed qualifications for ten prisoners who were far from ordinary, including myself. Hilde was one of the four non-violent common criminals, all young women, who seemed to have been added to the mix at random: nothing recorded except their names and ages.

"Oh. All right. But, but there's something . . ." She drew a breath, like someone about to dive into deep water, then jumped down and opened her locker.

I'd better go—

I couldn't say that, it betrayed me. I tried to frame a safer exit line. Hilde climbed back into the tray where I'd imagined blood and viscera, in my own cabin, the first 'night'. Her hands were full of slippery, shining red stuff.

I thought I was hallucinating. Her locker should be *empty*. All our lockers were empty; we had no material baggage.

"*What*—?"

"I found this," she said. "In my locker. There's a green one and a blue one, as well." She was holding up a nightdress, a jewel-bright nightdress, scarlet satin with lace at the bodice and hem. "I know it shouldn't be there, you don't have to tell me, I understand about the transit. Ruth, please help me. What's going on?"

We'd all had strange experiences, but nothing so incongruous, and nothing ever that two people shared. I touched the stuff; I could feel the fabric, slippery and cool. "I don't know," I said. "Strange things happen. Better not think about it."

"My parents used to buy me pretty night clothes. When I was a little girl I imagined I could go to parties in my dreams, like a princess in a fairytale." She hugged the satin as if it were a favourite doll, her eyes fixed on mine. "If anyone had asked, when I was drugged, what I most wanted to take with me, I might have said, my nightdresses, like that little girl. But *why can I touch this?*"

"It's the torus. It's messing with our minds."

It flashed on me that the veil was getting thin, orientation was nearly over.

Hilde knelt there with her arms full of satin and lace. "I've never even kissed anyone," she said. "Except my mom and dad. But I've had a life in my mind . . . I know what I want, I know you want it too. There's no time left. Why won't you touch me?"

"I'm thirty-seven, Hilde. You're nineteen. You could be my daughter."

"But I'm not."

So there was no safe exit line, none at all. I kissed her. She kissed me back.

The texture of her hair had been a torment. The touch of her mouth, the pressure of her breasts, drenched me, drowned me. I'd had men as lovers, and they'd satisfied my itch for sex. I'd hardly ever dared to expose myself to another woman, even in outlaw circles where forbidden love was accepted. But *nothing* compares to the swell of a woman's breast against my own, like to like—

There were laws against homosexuality, and the so-called genetic trait was proscribed. But you could get away with being 'metrosexual', as long as it was just a lifestyle choice; as long as you were just fooling around. As long as you were rich, or served the rich, and made ritual submission by lying about it, the USE would ignore most vices. I held her, and I knew she'd guessed my secret, the unforgivable crime behind my catalogue of civil disobedience. I can only love women. Only this love means anything to me, like to like. No 'games' of dominance and subordination that are not really games at all. No masters, no slaves, NO to all of that—

My sister, my daughter, put your red dress on. Let me find your breasts, let me suckle through the slippery satin. Undress me, take me with your mouth and with your hands, forget the past, forget who we were, why we are here. We are virgin to each other, virgins together. We can make a new heaven and a new earth, here at the last moment, on this narrow bed—

When I went back to my own cabin, I found a note on my room control message board. It was from Carpazian.

Dear Captain Ruth,

Something tells me our playtime is nearly over. When we dead awaken, if we awaken, may I respectfully request to be considered for the honour of fathering your first child. Georgiou.

I laughed until I cried.

V

Hilde's bunk became a paradise, a walled garden of delight. We danced there all the ways two women can dance together, and the jewel-coloured night-dresses figured prominently, absurdly important. I didn't care where they had come from, and I didn't understand what Hilde had been trying to tell me.

Everyone knew, at once: the team must have been keeping watch on whose cabin I visited. I was as absurdly important as those scraps of satin. Mike and Gee came to see me. I thought they wanted to talk about pregnancy. It was a genuine issue, with all this rush of pairing-up. We didn't know if we were still getting our prison-issue contraception, which was traditionally delivered in the drinking water. None of us women had had a period, but that didn't mean much. They wanted to deliver a protest, or a warning. They said 'people' felt I ought to be careful about Hilde.

I told them my private life was my own affair

"There's a hex on us," said Mike, darkly. "Who's causing it?"

"You mean the strange phenomena? How could any of us be causing them? It's the torus. Or the Panhandle system, keeping us off balance to keep us docile."

Gee made more sense. "She's not clear of the drugs yet, Captain. I can tell. There's got to be a good reason she was kept under like that."

The hairs rose on the back of my neck; I thought of lynch-mobs.

"Yeah, sure. We're all criminals, you two as well. But it's over now."

After that deputation I sent a note to Carpazian, accepting his honourable pro-posal, should such a time ever come, and made sure I sent it on the public channel. Maybe that was a mistake, but I was feeling a little crazy. If battlelines were drawn, the team better know that Hilde and I had allies, we didn't stand alone.

We had a couple of very dark simulations after that, but we came out of them well. I felt that the system, my secret ally, was telling me that I could trust my girl.

The unresponsive woman woke up, and proved to be an ultra-traditional Japanese (we'd only known that she looked Japanese). She could barely speak English; but she immediately convinced us to surround ourselves with tiny rit-uals. Whatever we did had to be done *just so*. Sitting down in a chair in the dayroom was a whole tea-ceremony in itself. It was very reassuring.

Angie said to me, strange isn't *wrong*, Ruth.

Miqal, the Iranian, came to my cabin. Most of them had visited me, on the quiet, at one time or another. She confessed that she was terrified of the transit itself. She had heard that when you lay down in the Buonarotti capsule you had terrible, terrible dreams. All your sins returned to you, and all the people you had betrayed. The thrum of those subliminal engines filled my head, everything disappeared. I was walking along the curving corridor again, my doppelganger at vanishing point; but the corridor was suspended in a starry void. The cold was horrific, my lungs were bursting, my body was coming apart. I could see nothing but Miqal's eyes, mirrors of my terror—

The hejabi woman clung to me, and I clung to her.

"Did it happen to you?" we babbled. "Did it happen to you—?"

"Don't tell anyone," I said, when we were brave enough to let go.

Carpazian was right, the stay of execution was over, and any haunting would have been better than this. We lived from moment to moment, under a sword.

$$H_{15750}, N_{310}, O_{6500}, C_{2250}, Ca_{63}, P_{48}, K_{15}, S_{15}, Na_{10}, Cl_6, Mg_3, Fe_1,$$

Trace differences, tiny differences, customising that chemical formula into human lives, secrets and dreams. The Buonarotti process, taking that essence and converting it into some inexplicable algorithm, pure information . . .

"We'll have what we've managed to carry," I said. "And no reason why we shouldn't eat the meat and vegetables, since our bodies will be native to Landfall."

"We could materialize thousands of miles apart," said Hilde.

"Kitty says it doesn't work like that."

Kitty, the woman whose nickname had been 'Flick', had come out of a closet of her own. She was, as I had always known but kept it to myself, a highly qualified neurochemist. Take a wild guess at her criminal activities. I'd had to fight a reflex of disgust against her, because I have a horror of what hard drugs can do. She and Achmed knew more than the rest of us put together about the actual Buonarotti process. Achmed had refused to talk about it, after his first pronouncement, but Kitty had told us things, in scraps. She said teams like ours would 'land' together, in the same physical area, because we'd become psychically linked.

We were in Hilde's cabin. She was lying on top of me in the narrow bunk, one of the few comfortable arrangements. It was the sixth 'night', or maybe the seventh. She stroked my nose, grinning.

"Oh yes, Captain. Very good for morale, Captain. You don't *know.*"

"I don't know anything, expect it's cold outside and warm in here."

I tipped her off so we were face to face, and made love to her with my eyes closed, in a world of touch and taste. My head was full of coloured stars, the sword was hanging over me, fears I hadn't known I possessed blossomed in the dark. What's wrong with her, what kind of terminal genetic error? Why was she condemned, she still has amnesia, what is it that she doesn't dare to remember? *Oh they will turn you in my arms into a wolf or a snake.* The words of the old song came to me, because I was afraid of her, and my eyes were closed so I didn't know what I was holding—

The texture of her skin changed. I was groping in rough, coarse hair, it was choking me. It changed again; it was scale, slithery and dry. I shot upright, shoving myself away from her. I hit the light. I stared.

My God.

"Am I dreaming?" I gasped. "Am I hallucinating?"

A grotesque, furred and scaly creature shook its head. It shook its head, then slipped and slithered back into the form of a human girl in a red nightdress.

"No," said Hilde. "I became what you were thinking. I lost control—"

Hilde; something else, something entirely fluid, like water running.

"I told you I had a genetic disease. This is it."

"Oh my God," I breathed. "And you can read my mind?"

Her mouth took on a hard, tight smile. She was Hilde, but she was someone I'd never met: older, colder, still nineteen but far more bitter.

"Easily," she said. "Right now it's no trick."

I fought to speak calmly. "What are you? A . . . a shape-changer? My God, I can hardly say it, a *werewolf?*"

"I don't know," said older, colder Hilde, and I could still see that fluid weirdness in her. "My parents didn't know either. But I've thought about it and I've read about the new science. I've guessed that it's like Koffi said, do you remember? The Buonarotti Transit takes what Carpazian calls the soul apart: and it has unleashed monsters. Only they don't 'happen' near the torus—they get born on earth. The government's trying to stamp them out, and that's what I am. I didn't mean to deceive you, Ruth. I woke up and I was here, knowing nothing and in love with you—"

I wanted to grab my clothes and leave. I had a violent urge to flee.

"You didn't tell me."

"*I didn't know!* I found the nightdresses, I knew that was very strange, I tried to tell you, but even then I didn't know. The memories only just came back."

"Why did they send you out here? Why didn't they *kill* you?"

"I expect they were afraid." Hilde began to laugh, and cry. "They were afraid of what I'd do if they tried to kill me, so they just sent me away, a long, long way away. What does it matter? We are *dead*, Ruth. You are dead, I am dead, the rest is a fairytale. What does it matter if I'm something forbidden? Something that should never have breathed?"

Forbidden, forbidden . . . I held out my arms, I was crying too.

Embrace, close as you can. Everything's falling apart, flesh and bone, the ceramic that yields like soft metal, the slippery touch of satin, all vanishing—

As if they never were.

VI

Straight to orientation, then. There were no guards, only the Panhandle system's bots, but we walked without protest along a drab greenish corridor to the Transit Chamber. We lay down, a hundred of us at least, in the capsules that looked like coffins, our gravegoods no more than neural patterns, speed-burned into our bewildered brains. I was fully conscious. What happened to *orientation*? The sleeve closed over me, and I suddenly realised there was no reprieve, this was it. The end.

I woke and lay perfectly still. I didn't want to try and move because I didn't want to know that I was paralysed, buried alive, conscious but dead. *Oh I could be bounded in a walnut shell and count myself the king of infinite space.* I had not asked for a dream, but a moment since I had been in Hilde's arms. Maybe orientation hasn't begun yet, I thought, cravenly. The surface I was lying on did not yield like the ceramic fibre of the capsule, there was cool air flowing over my face and light on my eyelids. I opened my eyes and saw the grass: something very like blades of bluish, pasture grass, about twenty centimetres high, stirred by a light breeze.

The resurrected sat up, all around me: like little figures in a religious picture from Mediaeval Europe. The team was mainly together, but we were surrounded by a sea of bodies, mostly women, some men. A whole shipload, newly arrived at Botany Bay. The romance of my dream of the crossing was still with me, every detail in my grasp; but already fading, as dreams do. I saw the captain's armband on my sleeve. And Hilde was beside me. I remembered that Kitty had said teams like ours were *linked.* Teams like ours: identified by the system as the leaders in the consensus. I'd known what was going on, while I was in the dream, but I hadn't believed it. I stared at the girl with the cinnamon braids, the shape-changer, the wild card, my lover.

If I'm the captain of this motley crew, I thought, I wonder who you are . . .

Julie Novakova is a Czech author and translator of science fiction, fantasy and detective stories. She has published short fiction in *Clarkesworld*, *Asimov's*, *Analog*, and elsewhere. Her work in Czech includes eight novels, one anthology (*Terra Nullius*) and over thirty short stories and novelettes. Some of her works have been also translated into Chinese, Romanian, Estonian, German and Filipino. She received the Encouragement Award of the European science fiction and fantasy society in 2013, the Aeronautilus award for the best Czech short story of 2014 and 2015, and for the best novel of 2015. Her translations of Czech fiction into English appeared in *Strange Horizons* and *Tor.com*. Julie is an evolutionary biologist by study and also takes a keen interest in planetary science. She's currently polishing her first novel in English and translating more Czech stories into English. Read more at julienovakova.com.

THE SYMPHONY OF ICE AND DUST

JULIE NOVAKOVA

It's going to be the greatest symphony anyone has ever composed," said Jurriaan. "Our best work. Something we'll be remembered for in the next millennia. A frail melody comprised of ice and dust, of distance and cold. It will be our masterpiece."

Chiara listened absently and closed her eyes. Jurriaan had never touched ice, seen dust, been able to imagine real-world distances or experienced cold. Everything he had was his music. And he *was* one of the best; at least among organic minds.

Sometimes she felt sorry for him.

And sometimes she envied him.

She imagined the world waiting for them, strange, freezing, lonely and beautiful, and a moment came when she could not envy Jurriaan his gift—or his curse—at all. She checked with *Orpheus* how long the rest of the journey would last. The answer was prompt.

In three days, we will approach Sedna.

Chiara decided to dream for the rest of the voyage.

*

Her dreams were filled with images, sounds, tastes, smells and emotions. Especially emotions. She *felt* the inner Oort cloud before she had even stepped outside the ship. *Orpheus* slowly fed her with some of the gathered data and her unique brain made a fantastical dream of nearly all of it.

When Chiara woke up, she knew that they were orbiting Sedna and sending down probes. *Orpheus* had taken care of it, partly from the ship's own initiative, partly because of Manuel. The Thinker of their mission was still unconscious, but actively communicating with *Orpheus* through his interface.

She connected to the data stream from the first probe which had already landed and recorded everything. Sedna . . . We are the first here at least since the last perihelion more than eleven thousand years ago. It feels like an overwhelming gap—and yet so close!

It almost filled her eyes with tears. Chiara was the Aesthete of their group by the Jovian Consortium standards. Feeling, sensing and imagining things was her job—as well as it was Manuel's job to primarily go through hard data, connect the dots, think everything through, even the compositions, the results of their combined effort—and Jurriaan's job to focus on nothing but the music.

She sent a mental note to Manuel. *When can we go to the surface?*

The response was immediate. *When I conclude it's safe.*

Safe is bad. It's stripped of fear, awe, even of most of the curiosity! I need them to work properly, they're essential. Let me go there first.

All right, he replied.

Chiara smiled a little. She learned to use logic to persuade Manuel long ago—and most of the times she was successful.

As she was dressing in the protective suit, a memory of a similar moment some years ago came to her and sent a shiver through her body. It was on Io and she stayed on the surface far too long even for her highly augmented body to withstand. When it became clear that she'd need a new one because of the amount of received radiation, she decided to give that one at least an interesting death—and she let it boil and melt near one of the volcanoes. Although her new brain was a slightly inadequate copy of the last one, thanks to the implants she remembered the pain—and then nothing, just a curious observation of the suit and her body slowly disintegrating—as if it happened to this very body.

She didn't intend to do anything like that here. No; here she perceived a cold and fragile beauty. There should be no pain associated to it, no horror. Fear, maybe. Awe, definitely yes. Standing there on the icy surface, the Sun a mere bright star, darkness everywhere—she ought to feel awe.

Chiara felt she had a good chance of being the first human being who ever stood on Sedna. The dwarf planet was nearing its perihelion now, still almost a hundred astronomical units from the Sun, and there were no reports of any expeditions before them during the recent period.

When the lander touched the surface of Sedna, she stayed inside for a little while, getting used to the alien landscape around her. It had a strange sense of tranquility to it. Chiara was used to the icy moons of the Jovian system which she called home, but this landscape was far smoother than what she knew from there. It was also darker—and an odd shade of brown-red.

She turned off the lander's lights and stepped outside through the airlock, into the darkness.

It wasn't a complete darkness. But the Sun was not currently visible from this side of the dwarf planet and it felt like being lonelier, further away than ever before. She was able to see the disc of the galaxy clearer than from anywhere else she had been.

She knelt and slowly touched the surface with one of her suit's haptic gloves.

We've found something, Chiara, suddenly Manuel's voice resonated in her head. *See for yourself.*

He sent her a mental image of a couple of objects not deep beneath the icy surface found by one of the numerous little probes. The biggest one resembled a ship. A small, stumpy, ancient-looking ship, unmistakably of a human origin. They were not the first.

But these must have come here a *very* long time ago.

And a few miles further and far beneath it, another shape was discovered by their sensors. A bigger, stranger shape.

Probably from much, much longer ago than the first one . . .

It took less than an hour to drill through the ice to the first ship. Getting inside it then was a matter of minutes.

Chiara saw the two bodies as the probes approached them. Both dead—but almost intact. One male, one female. The probes suggested the small chambers they found them inside were probably designed for cryosleep. They must have been prepared for the procedure or already frozen when they died.

The ship was long dead too but that didn't constitute much of a problem for the probes. They quickly repaired the computers and what was left of the data.

They found the ship's logs and sent it to the crew of *Orpheus* even before others had time to drill deep enough to reach the other object.

Chiara was back aboard at the time they opened the file and heard the voice of the long gone woman.

I think I don't have much time left. I have no means of getting from here in time. But

I know that there will be others who come here to explore. I hope you find this. I'm telling our story for you.

Ten days ago, I discovered something . . . —wait, let me start from the beginning.

"How is it going, love?"

Theodora smiled while unscrewing another panel on the probe. "Good. Suppose we could use this one tomorrow on the last picked site. I've got just one more bug to repair."

She was wearing a thin suit, protecting her in the vacuum and cold of the storage chamber, very flexible and quite comfortable compared to EVA suits. Despite that, she'd prefer to be outside the ship, walking on the surface of Triton which *Kittiwake* had been orbiting for more than two years now.

Kittiwake was a small ship, but sufficient for sustaining two people aboard even for a couple of decades if necessary. Provided enough hydrogen, easily extractable practically everywhere, its bimodal MITEE could function for half a century without any serious problems. If one element failed, it still had many others and could push the ship forward with a good specific impulse and a decent thrust while also providing the electrical energy needed by the ship.

Now the mission on Triton was nearing its end. Theodora didn't know whether to be happy and relieved that she and her husband would finally return to Earth, after so many years of isolation, or sad that she wouldn't ever see this remarkable place again.

When she was done with the ice-drilling probe, she went through several airlocks to the habitation deck. It was tiny, but sufficient enough for hers and Dimitri's needs.

"It seems we have a word from the outside world," her husband smiled as she entered the cabin. "*Kittiwake* just picked it up."

After checking the signal for malware, the ship automatically showed them the recording. The face of their superior, OSS Mission Supervisor Ronald Blythe, appeared on the screen. He congratulated them for their results on Triton and mentioned that a window for another long-term scientific expedition was opening. Theodora's stomach rocked. She was eager to find out. But still . . . a new expedition would mean yet more years away from the rest of humanity. The company picked her and Dimitri because they were a stable, non-conflict couple with steady personalities and a lot of technical and scientific experience. They were *supposed* to be able to spend years without any other human contact in a tiny space of their ship, exploring the outer solar system, without a chance for a vacation, without feeling the Earth's gravity, smells, wind . . . *However, we had a contract for eight years. The time's almost up. Are they proposing to prolong it? And what for?* thought Theodora.

"Last week, we received a signal from Nerivik 2."

"Isn't it the probe sent to Sedna in the eighties that stopped transmitting before it reached an orbit?" murmured Theodora.

It was. Blythe went on explaining how they lost contact with the probe for more than ten years and suddenly, out of thin air, it sent out a signal five days ago. Scientists at the FAST observatory who picked up the signal by accident were a bit surprised, to put it mildly. They began analyzing it immediately—and fortunately didn't keep intercepting the transmission for themselves.

"And the findings were . . . weird. It became clear that the probe lost its orbit, crashed, but probably regained control of its thrusters shortly before the crash and tried to change the collision into a landing. It was just damaged. It's possible that it kept transmitting most of the time, but without aiming the signal, the probability of reaching any receivers in the system was very low. However, it probably had time to send down its two landers before the crash. They kept measuring all they were supposed to record—and among other tasks, they tried mapping the ice layer. That's where it became really strange."

Theodora listened avidly as Blythe started explaining. Her interest grew every second.

The ultrasonic pulses showed an intriguing structure some two hundred meters below surface. It could not be told how large it was, but it had at least one hundred meters in diameter; maybe a lot more. The signature seemed like metal.

Blythe included the data in the transmission so that Theodora was able to look at it while he was speaking. It really was strange. It could have been a part of a metal-rich rock layer. But what would it be doing on Sedna? The dwarf planet was supposed to have a thick largely icy layer composed mostly of methane, nitrogen, ethane, methanol, tholins and water ice. Nothing even remotely like *this*. Maybe a big metal-rich meteorite buried in the ice crust after an impact then?

"We don't know what it is, or even if the measurement was correct. But it surely is interesting. It would be desirable to send a manned mission there. This looks like a situation that needs more resourcefulness and improvisations than robots can do," continued Blythe.

And for this, they needed someone with an expertise of frozen bodies of the outer solar system; someone stable, resourceful and determined; and of course, preferably someone whom the journey would take around five instead of ten years. Sedna was still quite near its perihelion, but growing away slowly every year. In short: They needed someone like two experienced workers closing their successful mission on Neptune's icy moon Triton.

" . . . of course, I cannot force you into this. But with prolonging the contract, you'll receive extra money for such a long stay on your own and all the associated risks. I attach the new version of your contract to this message. I expect your answer in three days."

Theodora didn't have to look at the document to know the bonuses would be large; almost unimaginably large. There were medical risks associated with long-term radiation exposure, dangerous activities, immense psychical pressure, stay in microgravitation and above all, the cryosleep necessary to travel so far away without losing many years just by the voyage itself.

But it wasn't the money that primarily tempted her to accept the contract.

Theodora and Dimitri looked at each other expectantly. "Well," she broke the silence first, "looks like we're gonna take a rather long nap; do you agree?"

Theodora shivered. At the first moment, she felt exposed and frightened without any obvious reason, which was even worse. Then she remembered; she was in the cryosleep chamber and slowly awakening. They must be near Sedna now.

"Dimi?" she croaked. There was no reply, although the ship was supposed to transmit every conversation to the other chamber—which meant that Dimitri hadn't achieved consciousness yet.

It took Theodora another hour before she could gather her thoughts well enough to start going through the data. When she was in the middle of checking their velocity and trajectory, the speaker in the chamber came alive: "Darling? Are you awake?"

"Yes, how are you?"

"Well, nothing's better than a good long sleep!"

Theodora laughed. Her throat burned and she still felt a bit stiff, but she couldn't stop. They actually were there; further than any human beings ever before!

In the next couple of days, Dimitri and Theodora had little time to rest although they didn't do anything physically demanding and were still recovering from the cryosleep. First they searched for and found the Nerivik 2 crash site and the two nearby stationed landers. The ice in the area seemed different from other sites, as if it had been gradually modified by inner volcanic activity. That explained why Nerivik 2 sent both its landers there in the first place. *Kittiwake* sent down a probe, continued mapping the surface and after that sent a few other probes on different locations. It was a standard procedure, but it needed a lot of time.

When the first results from the probe near Nerivik 2 arrived, Dimitri sat still for a moment and then found his voice and called: "Dora! You must come see this."

The readings were peculiar. The object buried almost two hundred meters below the surface seemed a bit like an asteroid now, more than a hundred meters in diameter in one direction and over five hundred in the other. According to the ultrasonic pulses data, its shape seemed conical and the layer reflecting the pulses quite smooth. A very unusual asteroid indeed.

"What do you think it is?"

Theodora shrugged. "Don't know—and can't very well imagine, to be precise. Until it's proven otherwise, I'm betting on an asteroid, albeit a weird one. But let's find out soon."

"I'll send down the drilling machinery, shall I? Or do you propose to wait for even more readings?"

"Send it."

Kittiwake had two major drilling devices—three before Triton—and one backup machine. Theodora and Dimitri decided to send two at once. It was riskier, but they wanted to compare the data from an area with the anomaly and from another place chosen because of its similar surface structures. The equipment was old but reliable and lived through many more or less improvisational repairs.

At the end of the first day of drilling, they reached almost thirty meters below surface. On day three, they were about one hundred meters deep. On day four, the probe got through almost one hundred and fifty meters of ice and stopped.

Theodora had the uncomfortable feeling of vertigo as every time she performed telemetric control. She guided the repair drone carefully to the drilling probe's main panel. She felt strangely dissociated with her body when the robot picked the cover and she felt as if it were her arms raising it and putting it aside. There she was. "Oh, not this," she sighed.

No wonder Dimitri had no success trying to get the probe running again from here. It was no software bug, temporary failure or anything the self-repair systems could handle. Most of the processors were fried and needed replacing. The repair drone didn't have all of the components. They could send them down during some of the next orbit. But—

She lost her connection to the drone, as *Kittiwake* disappeared over the horizon from the drone's perspective, before she could end it herself. She gasped. It felt as if her limb had been cut off. She gulped and tried to concentrate again.

Yes, they could send the parts down. But Theodora feared that although the drone itself had more than sufficient AI for common repairs and had all the blueprints in its memory, it might overlook something else, something an AI would not notice and that might cause future trouble. She'd not be happy if they had to replace the processors again, like it happened once on Triton. She could control the drone from distance again, but there was no chance she could achieve that much precision and look everywhere through telemetry.

Well, they wanted to initiate manned exploration anyway. It would just have to be sooner than expected.

Dimitri watched Theodora's descent. He knew that she had performed similar procedures many times before—but that never prevented him from worrying.

The view distorted as *Kittiwake* started losing connection. In another thirty minutes or so, they would be out of range, so Dimitri moved the ship to a stationary orbit above her. The two satellites were operational and deployed on an equatorial and polar orbits would continue to scan the rest of the surface. He could have made them relay stations, but he liked being able to communicate directly with Theodora, her landing module, her rover and the drilling probe. Fewer things could go wrong. And after years spent so far from Earth, they knew that things often *went* wrong.

He gave the engine command for more thrust and checked on the planned stationary transfer orbit. Everything seemed fine for a while.

Until a red light flashed next to the screen and a warning presented itself.

Theodora was descending through the tunnel in the ice. It was dark except the light from LEDs on her suit and the reflectors from the top of the shaft. Her rope was winding down gradually. She could see the drilling device below now.

The light above seemed faint when she reached the probe. It took her only an hour to get it operational again. She smiled and let the winch pull her up again.

Just as she neared the surface, she heard a noise in the speakers of her suit. "Dimitri?" she spoke. "What is it?"

"Have to . . . come down . . ."

She barely understood him through the static.

"Dimitri!"

For a while, she heard nothing. Then the static returned—and after that, Dimitri's distorted voice. " . . . have to land." Cracking and humming. Theodora tried to amplify the sound frantically. " . . . send you the coordinates . . . hope it works out . . ."

A file found its way through the transmission. It was a technical report generated by *Kittiwake*. Theodora opened it and glimpsed through it quickly.

"Oh no," she whispered.

Dimitri was doing his best to lead the remains of the ship on a trajectory ending with something that would approximate a landing more than a crash.

It was less than twenty minutes from the moment he accelerated *Kittiwake* to reach the transfer orbit but it seemed like an eternity. During that time, a warning indicated that the main turbine in the ship's power station was not working properly. He ran a more detailed scan and a moment later, everything was flashing with error reports.

The turbine in the power cycle broke down. It was tested for signs of wearing down regularly, but a hairline crack might have been overlooked in the control. The ship was moving with inertia most of the journey, the crack could have expanded during the deceleration phase and ruptured now, when the engine was working a little more again.

Things could go wrong. And they went wrong. Worse even, one of the blades pierced the coating of the reactor and the heated helium-xenon gas started leaking rapidly. The damage was too much for the automated repair systems. It was still leaking into the space between the coatings.

And the reactor itself was overheating quickly. Once the turbine stopped working, the gas still trapped in the cycle kept getting more and more heat from the MITEE—but couldn't continue through the cycle and cool down.

It was not critical yet, but would be in another couple of minutes. Dimitri sent all the repair drones to help the built-in repair and emergency systems but could see that it was not enough. He had also shut down the MITEE and all the rods were now safely turned to stop the reaction. It still wasn't enough. The overheating continued and could lead to an explosion. It could happen in a few minutes if not cooled down quickly.

It was just a way life went. Nothing serious happened in years and suddenly he's got *minutes*.

He knew there was only one thing to do. So he gave a command for the valves in the outer reactor coating to open. Then all the gas would leak outside. The ship would be useless without it, but it was the better one of two bad scenarios.

So far, only a minute had elapsed from the breakdown.

In the next few seconds, things went from bad to worse.

"Shit," exhaled Dimitri as he felt how the *Kittiwake* started spinning. One of the valves must have been stuck, so that the gas started leaking outside in just one direction. It quickly sent the ship into rotation.

Dimitri tried to compensate it with thrusters on both RCSs, but then *Kittiwake* shook hideously and then many of the screens went down. He realized what happened.

The rotation was too much. The ship was never constructed for this. There was too much tension in wrong direction . . . She tore apart.

Still coping with the rotation, he checked the systems. He was right. The engine section was gone. He was lucky that the habitation section was still operating almost normally. There was his chance.

This section's reaction control system was apparently still working. The RCS's thrusters were small, but it was all he had.

He tested them with a short blast. Actually working; good. He used them to provide a little more distance from the other remains of the ship and then reviewed his situation more calmly. He had to land if he wanted to live; and he needed to do it quickly, otherwise he'd drift into space with no means of correcting his trajectory.

He smiled rather sadly.

About twenty minutes after the turbine breakdown, Dimitri was now leading the rest of the ship down on Sedna and praying he could actually land instead of crashing.

"Dora?" he called. He hoped she'd pick up the transmission. "Dora, can you hear me? The reactor had a breakdown and the ship tore apart! I'm left with our section's remains. I have to come down . . ."

Theodora was driving her rover frantically to the landing site. She could not contact Dimitri, but that didn't mean anything; the antenna could have been damaged, while most of the ship could be perfectly fine. *It's all right. He is fine.*

She wished she could go faster, but as on most ice-rocky bodies, Sedna's surface could be treacherous. It had far fewer cracks or ridges than Europa or Ganymede and was actually very smooth compared to them, but it was still an alien landscape, not resembling anything on Earth at all. Himalaya's glaciers were children's toys compared to Sedna. The perspective was wrong, the measures were wrong, the shadows were wrong; it wasn't a land fit for human eyes and spatial recognition.

Finally, she approached the site. Her heart skipped a beat when she saw the habitation section in the lights of the rover. It seemed almost intact.

She ran to the nearest reachable airlock. It was still functioning; she could get inside.

It didn't look as if the ship had been through a bad accident. The corridor looked nearly normal. Everything was strapped or permanently fixed anyway, so a sight of total chaos wasn't to be expected. However, most of the systems were disabled, as she found out by logging into the network.

The door of the control room opened in front of her, a little damaged, but working.

"Dimitri!"

He found time to get in an emergency suit and was safely strapped in his chair. Good. Theodora leaned to him. He looked unconscious. She logged into his suit and read the data quickly.

Time of death . . . Suit's healthcare mechanisms could not help . . .

"Oh, Dimitri," she croaked. Her throat was dry and she felt tears coming to her eyes. She forced them down. No time for this. Not now. She must do what he'd do in her place.

She moved his body in the suit to the cryosleep chamber. Once she managed it there, she ran a similar procedure as they had gone through many times before. Only this time it was slightly different, designed to keep a dead brain as little damaged as possible, in a state usable for later scanning of the neural network. Theodora knew that her Dimitri was gone; but they could use this data, complete it by every tiny bit of information available about his life, and create a virtual personality approximating Dimitri. He wouldn't be gone so . . . completely.

After that, she checked on the ship's systems again. No change whatsoever. Nothing needed her immediate attention now, at least for a short while.

She leaned on a wall and finally let the tears come.

This is a part of an older log, but I don't want to repeat all that happened to me . . . I must go to sleep soon.

Kittiwake is dead now, as is Dimitri. I could do nothing in either case. I've got only one option, a quite desperate one. I have to equip my landing module in a way that it could carry me home. We went through this possibility in several emergency scenarios; I know what to do and that I can do it.

Of course, I'll have to spend the journey awake. The module hasn't got any cryosleep chamber and the one from the ship cannot be moved. But if the recycling systems work well, I can do it. I've got enough rations for about five years if I save the food a little. It doesn't get me anywhere near Earth, but I looked through the possible trajectories into the inner solar system and it could get me near Saturn if I leave here in three weeks, before this window closes. If I don't make it in this time, I'm as well as dead. But let's suppose I make it, I must . . . During the journey, I can contact Earth and another ship, even if only an automatic one with more supplies and equipment, could meet me on the way. I'll get home eventually.

If I succeed in rebuilding the landing module for an interplanetary journey. No one actually expected this to happen, but here I am. I must try.

The next few days were busy. Theodora kept salvaging things from *Kittiwake* and carefully enhancing the module's systems. In most cases, enhancement was all she needed. Then she had to get rid of some parts needed only for the purposes of landing and surface operations—and finally attach the emergency fuel tanks and generate the fuel.

The module had a classical internal combustion engine. High thrust, but despairingly high need of fuel.

Fortunately, she was surrounded by methane and water ice—and purified liquid methane and oxygen were just the two things she needed. Once she got the separation and purification cycle running, the tanks were slowly being refilled. At least this was working as it should.

She'd very much like to let Earth know about the accident, but she couldn't. Most of the relay stations were behind the Sun from her perspective now and the rest was unreachable by a weak antenna on the module; the one on the ship was too badly damaged. The Earth would know nothing about this until she's on her way back.

The plan seemed more and more feasible each day. She clung to it like to what it really was—her only chance of surviving.

When a message that the drilling probe had reached its target depth and stopped drilling appeared on the screen of her helmet, Theodora was confused for a couple of seconds before she realized what it was about. It seemed like a whole different world—mapping the surface from above, sending probes . . . In the last three days, she had little sleep and focused on her works on the module only. She had completely forgotten about the probe.

Well, after she checks the fuel generators again, she should have some time to look at it, she was well ahead of the schedule. After all, true explorers didn't abandon their aims even in times of great distress.

I'm glad I decided to have a look at it. Otherwise I'd die desperate and hopeless. Now, I'm strangely calm. It's just what a discovery like this does with you. It makes you feel small. The amazement and awe . . .

Theodora couldn't believe the results until she personally got down the shaft into a small space the probe had made around a part of the thing.

She stood in the small ice cave, looking at it full of wonder. She dared not touch it yet.

The surface was dark and smooth. Just about two square meters of it were uncovered; the rest was still surrounded by ice. According to the measurements, the thing was at least five hundred meters long and had a conic shape. There was no doubt that she discovered . . . a ship.

You cannot possibly imagine the feeling until you're right there. And I wasn't even expecting it. It was . . . I cannot really describe it. Unearthly. Wonderful. Amazing. Terrifying. All that and much more, mixed together.

I gave the alien ship every single moment I could spare. My module needed less and less tending to and I had almost two weeks until the flight window would close.

I named her Peregrine. It seemed appropriate to me. This wasn't a small inter-planetary ship like Kittiwake; this bird could fly a lot faster. But still . . . she seemed too small to be an interstellar vessel, even if this was only a habitation section and the engines were gone.

It was probably the greatest discovery in all human history yet. Just too bad I didn't have a chance to tell anyone. I really hope someone's listening.

Theodora directed all resources she didn't vitally need for her module to *Peregrine*. Only a day after her initial discovery, the probes picked up another strange shape buried in the ice not far from the ship.

When they also reached it, Theodora was struck with wonder. It was clearly an *engine* section!

While she worked on her module, she kept receiving new data about it and everything suggested that *Peregrine* used some kind of fusion drive; at this first glance not far more advanced than human engine systems. It seemed to her even more intriguing than if she had found something completely unknown.

I was eventually able to run a radiometric dating of ice surrounding the ship. The results suggest that she landed here some two-hundred and fifty million years ago. The ice preserved it well. But I must wonder . . . what were they doing here? Why have they come to our solar system—and why just this once? Although I don't understand a lot of what I see, the ship doesn't seem that much sophisticated to me. Maybe it's even something we could manage to make. But why use something like this to interstellar travel? With too little velocity, they'd never make it here in fewer than hundreds of years even if they came from the Alpha Centauri system!

Unless . . . the distance was smaller. We still don't know the history of the solar system in much detail. It's supposed that Sedna's orbit was disturbed by passing of another star from an open cluster, where the Sun probably originated, about eight hundred astronomical units away not long after the formation of our system.

But what if an event like this occurred more times? Could it possibly have been also a quarter of a billion years ago? Just about any star on an adequate trajectory could have interfered with the solar system. In some million and half years, Gliese 710 should pass through the Oort cloud. We wouldn't have much evidence if an event like this happened in a distant past—only some perturbed orbits and more comet and asteroid bombardment of the planets later.

Hundreds AU is still a great distance, but surely not impossible. Hell, I'm almost one hundred AU from the Sun now, although I haven't traveled the whole distance at one time. If we used a gravity assist from the Sun, we could overcome even distance of a thousand AU within a decade only! They could have done it too, maybe hoping to reach the inner part of the system, but something had prevented them. And possibly the very first object they encountered, quite near their own star at the time, was a frozen dwarf planet from about a hundred to almost a thousand AU far from the Sun, sent on its eccentric orbit by an earlier passing star and now disturbed again. They must have been lucky that Sedna wasn't captured by their star at the time. Or could it have been that theirs was the original star that deviated Sedna's orbit that much? Anyway, they'd have had to cross hundreds AU, but that's doable. If we had a sufficient motivation, we could manage a lot more.

Let's assume for a moment that my crazy hypothesis is right . . .

Then, I wonder what kind of motivation they had.

It happened three days before her planned departure.

She was at the surface at the time, which might have saved her life—or rather prolonged it.

The quakes came without any warning. She was getting a little sleep in her rover when it woke her up. Four, maybe five points on the Richter scale, Theodora guessed. Her throat was suddenly very, very dry.

The fuel generators . . .

After the quake stopped, she went to check on them. Overcoming the little distance between her and them seemed to take an eternity; new cracks formed in the ice.

When she saw them, Theodora knew she ought to feel anger, panic or desperation. But she just felt impossibly tired.

Two of the tanks were completely destroyed and the generators were damaged. She performed a more detailed control anyway but the result did not surprise her.

They couldn't be repaired; not in time. Maybe in months . . . but she'd be too late in less than a *week*.

She sat back in the rover, exhausted but suddenly very, very calm. What was a threat a while ago was a certainty now. She wasn't going to make it and she knew it.

The best what she could do was to use her remaining time as effectively as she was able to.

When I'm done here, I'll freeze myself. But this time I'll set the . . . final cryogenic procedure.

If you found us and it's not too late . . . Well, we might talk again.

The original shaft was destroyed by the quake, but she used the remaining probe, continued drilling with a maximum achievable speed and kept measuring the ice layer via the ultrasonics. While these processes were running, Theodora tried to find out more about *Peregrine*. She was able to get spectroscopic readings which suggested that its surface consisted mainly of titanium, however, she couldn't read all the spectral characteristics; the alloy seemed to have many components.

She also obtained more results on the thickness of the ice crust. The probe got almost two kilometers deep. Its results suggested that a liquid ocean beneath the layer might be possible—maybe fifteen, maybe twenty kilometers deeper than she was now. Theodora knew she'd never live to see a definitive answer; but these measurements might still be useful for someone else. If they could intercept her message.

She tried several times to send the data back to Earth, but she knew the chances too well to be even a little optimistic, although she salvaged a bigger antenna from Nerivik 2. But the transmitter was still rather weak and the aim far too inadequate. Without reaching relay stations, her message would become a cosmic noise, nothing more. The most reliable way to let the humanity see the data someday was to store them here in as many copies as she could and hope it would suffice. She didn't have much of an option.

She kept thinking about the alien ship. If her dating was correct and it landed here a quarter of a billion years ago, it would vaguely coincide with the Great Permian-Triassic Extinction Event. It was usually attributed mostly to geological factors, but there was a possibility of a contribution of other effects—a disturbance of the Oort cloud and more comets sent to the inner solar system afterward would do. She was recently able to measure how long *Peregrine* had been exposed to cosmic radiation and it seemed to be just several hundred years unless there was a mistake or some factor she didn't know about. There was no chance any ship like this could have come here from another star system in such extremely short time—unless the star was really close at the time. It started to make more and more sense to Theodora, although all she had was still just a speculation.

"And it will remain a speculation until someone else finds us," she said aloud, glancing at *Peregrine*. "But they will. You'll see."

However, she wasn't so sure. Would the company send a new expedition after they realize that Theodora and Dimitri were not going to ever call back? It depended mostly on the budget; she was rather pessimistic. And about other companies or countries, she couldn't even guess. But Sedna's distance would grow each year. Before another mission could be sufficiently prepared and launched, years would probably pass. And other years during its voyage. Then even more years on the way back.

She had to admit to herself the possibility that no one was going to discover them soon—maybe until the next perihelion. So far away in the future she couldn't even imagine it.

She looked at the other ship and touched the dark metal surface. *But still closer than how long you had to wait . . .*

"You were shipwrecked here too, am I right?" Theodora managed a little smile. "Pity that we cannot talk about what happened to us. I'd really like to hear your story. And it looks like we're gonna be stuck here together for a while." Her smile grew wider yet more sorrowful at the same time. "Probably for a long while."

I hope you found us and heard our story, whoever you are. I really wish you did.

"Very interesting," said Manuel. "We must report these findings to the Consortium immediately."

Without waiting for an approval from Chiara or Jurriaan, he started mentally assembling a compact data transmission with the help of *Orpheus*. In a few minutes, they were prepared to send it.

Neither Chiara nor Jurriaan objected.

When he was done, Manuel sent them a mental note of what he intended to do next.

"No!" Chiara burst out. "You cannot! They don't deserve this kind of treatment. They died far too long ago for this procedure to be a success. You won't revive them; you'll get pathetic fragments if anything at all! They were heroes. They *died* heroes. You cannot do this to them."

"It has a considerable scientific value. These bodies were preserved in an almost intact ice, sufficiently deep for shielding most of the radiation. We have never tried to revive bodies this old—and in such a good condition. We must do it."

"He's right," interjected Jurriaan. Chiara looked at him in surprise. It was probably the first thing he had said on this voyage that didn't involve his music.

She was outvoted. Even *Orpheus* expressed a support for Manuel's proposal, although the Consortium didn't give AIs full voting rights.

She left the cabin silently.

It took Manuel several days of an unceasing effort just to prepare the bodies. He filled them with nanobots and went through the results. He kept them under constant temperature and atmosphere. He retrieved what he could from the long dead ship about their medical records.

And then he began performing the procedure. He carefully opened the skulls, exposed the brains, and started *repairing* them. There wasn't much useful left after eleven thousand years. But with the help of cutting edge designed bacteria and the nans, there was still a chance of doing a decent scan.

After another week, he started with that.

Chiara finally felt at peace. Since their rendezvous with Sedna, she felt filled with various emotions every day and finally she thought she couldn't bear it any-more. As she stepped inside *Orpheus* after the last scheduled visit of the surface of Sedna, she knew it was the time.

Inside her cabin, she lay down calmly and let *Orpheus* pump a precisely mixed cocktail of modulators into her brain. Then Chiara entered her Dreamland.

She designed this environment herself some decades ago in order to facil-itate the process of creating new musical themes and ideas from her emotions and memories as effectively as she could. And Chiara felt that the story of the ancient alien ship, Theodora, Dimitri and Sedna would make wonderful musical variations. Then it will be primarily Jurriaan's task to assemble hers and Manuel's pieces, often dramatically different, into a symphony such as the world has never heard. Such that will make them famous even beyond the Jovian Consortium, possibly both among the Traditionalists and the Transitioned. They will all remember them.

Chiara smiled and drifted away from a normal consciousness.

During her stay in the Dreamland, *Orpheus* slowly abandoned the orbit of Sedna and set on a trajectory leading back to the territory of the Jovian Consortium. Another expedition, triggered by their reports back, was already on their way to Sedna, eager to find out more especially about the alien ship and to drill through the ice crust into the possible inner ocean.

Chiara, Manuel, and Jurriaan had little equipment to explore the ship safely—but they didn't regret it. They had everything they needed. Now was the time to start assembling it all together carefully, piece by piece, like putting back a shattered antique vase.

Even Manuel didn't regret going away from this discovery. He had the bodies—and trying to revive their personalities now kept most of his attention. A few days after their departure from Sedna, he finished the procedure.

Chiara was awake again at the time, the burden of new feelings longing to be transformed into music gone. She didn't mind now what Manuel had done; it would be pointless to feel anything about it after she had already created her part of the masterpiece.

Manuel first activated the simulation of Dimitri's personality.

"*Where am I? Dora . . . Dora . . . Dora,*" it repeated like a stuck gramophone record.

"His brain suffered more damage than hers after he died," Manuel admitted. "She had time to go through a fairly common cryopreservation pro-cedure. However . . ."

"I'm stuck here. Our reactor broke down and the ship tore apart. There is too much damage. My husband is dead . . . But we found something, I have to pass this message on . . . But I feel disoriented, what have I finished? Where am I? What's happening?" After a while, the female voice started again: "Have I said this already? I don't know. I'm stuck here. Our reactor broke down . . ."

"They are both mere fragments, a little memories from before death, a few emotions and almost no useful cognitive capacity. I couldn't have retrieved more. Nevertheless, this is still a giant leap forward. Theoretically, we shouldn't have been able to retrieve this much after more than eleven thousand years."

Chiara listened to the feeble voices of the dead and was suddenly over-whelmed with sorrow. It chimed every piece of her body and her mind was full of it. It was almost unbearable. And it was also beautiful.

"It is great indeed," she whispered.

She didn't have to say more. Jurriaan learned her thoughts through the open channel. She knew he was thinking the same. He listened all the time. In his mind and with help of *Orpheus,* he kept listening to the recordings obtained by Manuel, shifting them, changing frequencies, changing them . . . making them into a melody.

"Keep a few of their words in it, will you?" Chiara spoke softly. "Please."

I will. They'll make a great introduction. They will give the listeners a sense of the ages long gone and of personalities of former humans. And he immersed into his composition once again. She knew better than to interrupt him now. In a few days or weeks, he will be done; he'll have gone through all her and Manuel's musical suggestions and come up with a draft of the symphony. Then it will take feedback from her and Manuel to complete it. But Jurriaan will have the final say in it. He is, after all, the Composer.

And after that, they should come up with a proper name. A Symphony of Ice and Dust, perhaps? And maybe they should add a subtitle. Ghosts of Theodora and Dimitri Live On Forever? No, certainly not; far too pompous and unsuitable for a largely classical piece. Voices of the Dead? A Song of the Shipwrecked?

Or simply: A Tribute.

Michael Bishop's first professionally published work was a Keats-flavored ode, "An Echo through the Timepiece," in *The Georgia Review* in 1968, but his first published short story, "Piñon Fall," appeared in the October/ November issue of *Galaxy*, a sale that nudged him into a genre that his fondness for the work of H. G. Wells, Ray Bradbury, and Ursula K. Le Guin had perhaps made inevitable, science fiction. Since then, he has been nominated on many occasions in several categories for the Hugo Award and has won two Nebula Awards, the first for his novelette "The Quickening" and the second for his anthropological novel about human origins, *No Enemy but Time*. Other well-received novels include *Transfigurations*, recently reissued by Fairwood Press in a revised text with a new introduction by sf scholar and academic Joe Sanders, as well as *A Funeral for the Eyes of Fire*; *Ancient of Days*; *Count Geiger's Blues*; *Philip K. Dick Is Dead, Alas*; and *Brittle Innings*. His newest original book, *Other Arms Reach Out to Me: Georgia Stories* (July 2017), gathers fifteen of his best primarily mainstream works of short fiction and is available from Fairwood Press and Bishop's own imprint there, Kudzu Planet Productions. In November of 2018, Bishop will be inducted into the Georgia Writers Hall of Fame.

TWENTY LIGHTS TO "THE LAND OF SNOW"

EXCERPTS FROM THE COMPUTER LOGS OF OUR RELUCTANT DALAI LAMA

MICHAEL BISHOP

YEARS IN TRANSIT: 82 OUT OF 106?
COMPUTER LOGS OF THE DALAI LAMA-TO-BE, AGE 7

Aboard *Kalachakra*, I open my eyes again in Amdo Bay. Sleep still pops in me, yowling like a really hurt cat. I look sidelong out of my foggy eggshell. Many ghosts crowd near to see me leave the bear sleep that everybody in a strutship sometimes dreams in. Why have all these somnacicles up-phased to become ship-haunters? Why do so many crowd the grave-cave of my Greta-snooze?

"Greta Bryn"—that's my mama's voice—"can you hear me, kiddo?"

Yes I can. I have no deafness after I up-phase. Asleep even, I hear Mama talk in her dreams, and cosmic rays crackle off *Kalachakra*'s plasma shield out in front (to keep us all from going dead), and the crackle from Earth across the reaching oceans of farthest space.

"Greta Bryn?"

She sounds like Atlanta, Daddy says. To me she sounds like Mama, which I want her to play-act now. She keeps bunnies, minks, guineas, and many other tiny crits down along our sci-tech cylinder in Kham Bay. But hearing her doesn't pulley me into sit-up pose. To get there, I stretch my soft parts and my bones.

"Easy, baby," Mama says.

A man in white unhooks me. A woman pinches me at the wrist so I won't twist the fuel tube or pulse counter. They've already shot me in the heart, to stir its beating. Now I sit and look around, clearer. Daddy stands near, showing his crumply face.

"Hey, Gee Bee," he says, but doesn't grab my hand.

His coverall tag is my roll-call name: Brasswell. A hard name for a girl and not too fine for Daddy, who looks thirty-seven or maybe fifty-fifteen, a number Mama says he uses to joke his fitness. He does whore-to-culture—another puzzle-funny of his—so that later we can turn Guge green, and maybe survive.

I feel sick, like juice gone sour in my tummy has gushed into my mouth. I start to elbow out. My eyes grow pop-out big, my fists shake like rattles. Now Daddy grabs me, mouth by my ear: "Shhhh shhh shhh." Mama touches my other cheek. Everyone else falls back to watch. That's scary too.

After a seem-like century I ask, "Are we there yet?"

Everybody yuks at my funniness. I drop my legs through the eggshell door. My hotness has colded off, a lot.

A bald brown man in orangey-yellow robes steps up so Mama and Daddy must stand off aside. I remember, sort of. This person has a really hard Tibetan name: Nyendak Trungpa. My last up-phase he made me say it multi times so I would not forget. I was four, but I almost forgetted anyway.

"What's your name?" Minister Trungpa asks me.

He already knows, but I blink and say, "Greta Bryn Brasswell."

"And where are you?"

"*Kalachakra*," I say. "Our strut-ship."

"Point out your parents, please."

I do, it's simple. They're wide-awake ship-haunters now, real-live ghosts.

He asks, "Where are we going?"

"Guge," I say, another simple ask.

"What exactly is Guge, Greta Bryn?"

But I don't want to think—just to drink, my tongue's so thick with sourness. "A planet."

"Miss Brasswell,"—now Minister T's being smart-alecky—"tell me two things you know about Guge."

I sort of ask, "It's 'The Land of Snow,' this dead king's place in olden Tibet?"

"Good!" Minister T says. "And its second meaning for us Kalachakrans?"

I squint to get it: "A faraway world to live on?"

"Where, intelligent miss?"

Another easy one: "In the Goldilocks Zone." A funny name for it.

"But where, Greta Bryn, is this Goldilocks Zone?"

"Around a star called Gluh—" I almost get stuck. "Around a star called Gliese 581." Glee-zha is how I say it.

Bald Minister T grins. His face looks like a shiny brown China plate with an up-curving crack. "She's fine," he tells the ghosts in the grave-cave. "And I believe she's the 'One.'"

Sometimes we must come up. We must wake up and eat, and move about so we can heal from ursidormizine sleep and not die before we reach Guge. When I come up this time, I get my own nook that snugs in the habitat drum called Amdo Bay. It has a vidped booth for learning from, with lock belts for when the AG goes out. It belongs to only me, it's not just one in a commons-space like most ghosts use.

Finally I ask, "What did that Minister T mean?"

"About what?" Mama doesn't eye me when she speaks.

"That I'm the 'One.' Why'd he say that?"

"He's upset and everybody aboard has gone a little loco."

"Why?" But maybe I know. We ride so long that anyone riding with us sooner or later crazies up: inboard fever. Captain Xao once warned of this.

Mama says, "His Holiness, Sakya Gyatso, has died, so we're stupid with grief and thinking hard about how to replace him. Minister Trungpa, our late Dalai Lama's closest friend, thinks you're his rebirth, Greta Bryn."

I don't get this. "He thinks I'm not I?"

"I guess not. Grief has fuddled his reason, but maybe just temporarily."

"I am I," I say to Mama awful hot, and she agrees.

But I remember the Dalai Lama. When I was four, he played Go Fish with me in Amdo Bay during my second up-phase. Daddy sneak-named him Yoda, like from *Star Wars*, but he looked more like skinny Mr. Peanut on the peanut tins. He wore a one-lens thing and a funny soft yellow hat, and he taught me a song, "Loving the Ant, Loving the Elephant." After that, I had to take my ursidormizine and hibernize. Now Minister T says the DL is I, or I am he, but surely Mama hates as much as I do how such stupidity could maybe steal me off from her.

"I don't look like Sakya Gyatso. I'm a girl, and I'm not an Asian person." Then I yell at Mama, "I am I!"

"Actually," Mama says, "things have changed, and what you speak as truth may have also changed, kiddo."

Everybody who gets a say in Amdo Bay now thinks that Minister Nyendak Trungpa calls me correctly. I am not I: I am the next Dalai Lama. The Twenty-first, Sakya Gyatso, has died, and I must wear his sandals. Mama says he died of natural causes, but too young for it to look natural. He hit fifty-four, but he won't hit Guge. If I am he, I must take his place as our colony dukpa, which in Tibetan means 'shepherd.' That job scares me.

A good thing has come from this scary thing: I don't have to go back up into my egg pod and then down again. I stay up-phase. I must. I have too much to learn to drowse forever, even if I can sleep-learn by hypnoloading. Now I have this vidped booth that I sit in to learn and a tutor-guy, Lawrence ('Larry') Rinpoche, who loads on me a lot.

How old has all my earlier sleep-loading made me? Hibernizing, I hit seven and learnt while dreaming.

People should not call me Her Holiness. I'm a girl person—not a Chinese or a Tibetan. I tell Larry this when he swims into my room in Amdo. I've seen him in spectals about samurai and spacers, where he looks dark-haired and chest-strong. Now, anymore, he isn't. He has silver hair and hips like Mama's. His eyes do a flash thing, though, even when he's not angry, and it throws him back into the spectals he once star-played in as cool guy Lawrence Lake.

"Do I look Chinese, or Tibetan, or even Indian?" Larry asks.

"No you don't," I say. "But you don't look like no girl either."

"A girl, Your Holiness." Larry must correct me, Mama says, because he will teach me logic, Tibetan art and culture, Sanskrit, Buddhist philosophy, and medicine (space and otherwise). And also poetry, music and drama, astronomy, astrophysics, synonyms, and Tibetan, Chinese, and English. Plus cinema, radio/TV history, politics and pragmatism in deep-space colony planting, and lots of other stuff.

"No girl ever got to be Dalai Lama," I tell Larry.

"Yes, but our Fourteenth predicted his successor would hail from a place outside Tibet; and that he might re-ensoul not as a boy but as a girl."

"But Sakya Gyatso, our last, can't stick his soul in this girl." I cross my arms and turn a klutz-o turn.

"O Little Ocean of Wisdom, tell me why not."

Stupid tutor-guy. "He died after I got borned. How can a soul jump in the skin of somebody already borned?"

"Born, Your Holiness. But it's easy. It just jumps. The samvattanika viññana, the evolving consciousness of a Bodhisattva, jumps where it likes."

"Then what about me, Greta Bryn?" I tap my chest.

Larry tilts his ginormous head. "What do you think?"

Oh, that old trick. "Did it kick me out? If it kicked me out, where did I go?"

"Do you feel it kicked you out, Your Holiness?"

"I feel it never got in. Inside, I feel that I . . . own myself."

"Maybe you do, but maybe his punarbhava"—his re-becoming—"is in there mixing with your own personality."

"But that's so scary."

"What did you think of Sakya Gyatso, the last Dalai Lama? Did he scare you?"

"No, I liked him."

"You like everybody, Your Holiness."

"Not anymore."

Larry laughs. He sounds like he sounded in The Return of the Earl of Epsilon Eridani. "Even if the process has something unorthodox about it, why avoid mixing your soul self with that of a distinguished man you liked?"

I don't answer this windy ask. Instead, I say, "Why did he have to die, Mister Larry?"

"Greta, he didn't have much choice. Somebody killed him."

Every 'day' I stay up-phase. Every day I study and try to understand what's happening on *Kalachakra*, and how the late Dalai Lama, at swim in my soul, has slipped his bhava, "becoming again," into my bhava, or "becoming now," and so has become a thing old and new at the same time.

Larry tells me just to imagine one candle lighting off another (even though you'd be crazy to light anything inside a starship), but my candle was already lit before the last Lama's got snuffed, and I never even smelt it go out. Larry laughs and says His Dead Holiness's flame was "never quenched, but did go dim during its forty-nine-day voyage to bardo." Bardo, I think, must look like a fish tank that the soul tries to swim in even with nothing in it.

Up-phase, I learn more about *Kalachakra*. I don't need my tutor-guy. I wander all about, between study and tutoring times. When the artificial-grav cuts off, as it does a lot, I float my ghost self into bays and nooks everywhere.

Our ship has a crazy bigness, like a tunnel turning through star-smeared space, like a train of railroad cars humming through the Empty Vast without any hum. I saw such trains in my hypnoloading sleeps. Now I peep them as spectals and mini-holos and even palm pix.

Larry likes for me to do that too. He says anything 'fusty and fun' is OK by him, if it tutors me well. And I don't need him to help me twig when I snoop *Kalachakra*. I learn by drifting, floating, swimming, counting, and just by asking ghosts what I wish to know.

Here's what I've learnt by reading and vidped-tasking, snooping and asking:

1. *UNS Kalachakra* hauls 990 human asses ("and therest of each burro aboard"—Daddy's dumb joke) to a world in the Goldilocks Zone of the Gliese 581 solar system, 20.3 lights from Sol . . . the assumed-to-be-live-on-able planet Gliese 581g.

2. Captain Xao says that most of us on *Kalachakra* spend our journey in ursidormizine slumber to dream about our work on Guge. The greatest number of somnacicles—sleepers—have their eggpods in Amdo Bay toward the nose of our ship. (These hibernizing lazybones look like frozen cocoons in their see-through eggs.) Those of us more often up-phase slumber at 'night' in Kham Bay, where tech folk and crew do their work. At the rear of our habitat drum lies U-Tsang Bay, which I haven't visited, but where, Mama says, our Bodhisattvas—monks, nuns, lamas, and such—reside, down- or up-phase.

3. All must wriggle up-phase once each year or two. You cannot hibernize longer than two at a snooze because we human somnacicles go dodgy quite soon during our third year drowse, so Captain Xaotells us, "We'll need every hand on the ground once we're all down on Guge." ("Every foot on the ground," I would say.)

4. Red dwarf star Gliese 581, also known as Zarmina,spectral class M3V, awaits us in constellation Libra. Captain Xao calls it the eighty-seventh closest known solar system to our sun. It has seven planets and spurts out X-rays. It will flame away much sooner than Sol, but so far from now that none of us on *Kalachakra* will care a toot.

5. Gliese 581g, aka Guge, goes around its dwarf in a circle, nearly. It has one face stuck toward its sun, but enough gravity to hold its gasses to it; enough—more than Earth's—so you can walk without floating away. But it will really hot you on the sun-stuck side and chill you nasty on its drearydark rear. It's got rocks topside and magma in its zonal mountains. We must live in the in-between stripes of the terminator, safe spots for bipeds with blood to boil or kidneys to broil. Or maybe we'll freeze, if we

land in the black. So two hurrahs for Guge, and three for 'The Land of Snow' in the belts where we hope to plug in.

6. We know Guge has mass. It isn't, says Captain Xao, a "pipedream or a mirage." Our onboard telescope found it twelve Earth years ago, seventyout from Moon-orbit kickoff, with maybe twenty or so to go now before we really get there. Hey, I'm more than a smidgen scared to arrive, hey, maybe a million smidgens.

7. I'm also scared to stay an up-phase ghost on *Kalachakra*. Like a snow leopard or a yeti, I am an endangered species. I don't want to step up to Dalai Lamahood. It's got its perks, but until Captain Xao, Minister T, Larry Rinpoche, Mama, Daddy, and our security persons find out WHO kilt the twenty-first DL, Greta Bryn, a maybe DL, thinks her life worth one dried pea in a vacu-meal pack. Maybe.

8. In the tunnels all among Amdo, Kham, and U-Tsang Bays, the ghost of a snow leopard drifts. It has cindery spots swirled into the frosting of its fur. Its eyes leap yellow-green in the dimness when it peeks back at two-leggers like me. It jets from a holo-beam, but I don't know how or wherefrom. In my dreams, I turn when I see it. My heart flutter-pounds toward shutdown . . . .

9. Sakya Gyatso spent many years as a ghost on *Kalachakra*. He never hibernized more than three months at once, but tried to blaze at full awakeness like a Bodhisattva. He slept the bear slumber, when he did, but only because on Guge he'll have to lead 990 chipboard faithfuls and millions of Tibetan Buddhists, native and not, in their unjust exiles. Can an up-phase ghost, once it really dies, survive on a strut-ship as a ghost for real? Truly, I do not know.

10. Once I didn't know Mama's or Daddy's first names. Tech is a title not a name, and Tech Brasswell married my mama, Tech Bonfils, aboard *Kalachakra* (Captain Xao saying the words), in the seventy-fourth year of our flight. Tech Bonfils birthed me the following 'fall,' one of just forty-seven children born in our trip to Guge. Luckily, Larry Rinpoche told me my folks' names: Simon and Karen Bryn. Now I don't even know if they like each other. But I know, from lots of reading, that S. Hawking, this century-gone physicist, believed people are not quantifiable. He was definitely right about that.

I know lots more, although not who killed the Twenty-first DL, if anybody did, and so I pick at that worry a lot.

In old spectals and palm pix, starship captains sit at helms where they can see the Empty Vast out windows or screens. Captain Xao, First Officer Nima Photrang, and their crew keep us all cruising toward Gliese 581 in a closed cockpit in the upper central third of the big tin can that's strut-shipping us to Guge.

This section we call Kham Bay. Cut flowers in thin vials prettify the room where Xao and Photrang and crew sit to work. This pit also has a hanging of the *Kalachakra* Mandala and a big painted figure of the Buddha wearing a body, a man's and a woman's, with huge lots of faces and arms. Larry calls this window-free pit a control room and a shrine.

I guess he knows.

I visit the cockpit. No one stops me. I visit because Simon and Karen Bryn have gone back to their Siestaville to pod-lodge for many months on Amdo Bay's bottom level. Me, I stay my ghostly self. I owe it to everybody aboard—or so I often get told—to grow into my full Lamahood.

"Ah," says Captain Xao, "you wish to fly *Kalachakra*. Great, Your Holiness."

But he passes me to First Officer Photrang, a Tibetan who looks manlike in her jumpsuit but womanlike at her wrists and hands—so gentle about the eyes that, drifting near because our AG's gone out, she seems to have just pulled off a hard black mask.

"What may I do for you, Greta Bryn?"

My lips won't move, so grateful am I she didn't say, "Your Holiness."

She shows me the console where she watches the fuel level in a drop-tank behind our tin cylinder as this tank feeds the antimatter engine pushing us outward. Everything, she says, depends on electronic systems that run 'virtually automatically,' but she and other crew must check closely, even though the systems have 'fail-safes' to signal them from afar if they leave the control shrine.

"How long," I ask, "before we get to Guge?"

"In nineteen years we'll start braking," Nima Photrang says. "In another four, if all goes as plotted, we will enter the Gliese 581 system and soon take a stationary orbital position above the terminator. From there we'll go down to the adjacent habitable zones that we intend to settle in and develop."

"Four years to brake!" No one's ever said such a thing to me before. Four years are half the number I've lived, and no adult, I think, feels older at their ancient ages than I do at eight.

"Greta Bryn, to slow us faster than that would put terrible stress on our strut-ship. Its builders assembled it with optimal lightness, to save on fuel, but also with sufficient mass to withstand a twentieth of a g during its initial four years of thrusting and its final four years of deceleration. Do you understand?"

"Yes, but—"

"Listen: It took the *Kalachakra* four years to reach a fifth of the speed of light. During that time, we traveled less than half a light-year and burned a lot of the fuel in our drop tanks. Jettisoning the used-up tanks lightened us. For seventy-nine years since then, we've coasted, cruising over sixteen light-years toward our target sun but using our fuel primarily for trajectory correction maneuvers. That's a highly economical expenditure of the antimatter ice with which we began our flight."

"Good," I say—because Officer Photrang looks at me as if I should clap for such an 'economical expenditure.'

"Anyway, we scheduled four years of braking at one twentieth of a g to conserve our final fuel resources and to keep this spidery vessel from ripping apart at higher rates of deceleration."

"But it's still going to take so long!"

The officer takes me to a ginormous sketch of our strut-ship. "If anyone aboard has time for a stress-reducing deceleration, Greta Bryn, you do."

"Twenty-three years!" I say. "I'll turn thirty-one!"

"Yes, you'll wither into a pitiable crone." Before I can protest more, she shows me other stuff: a map of the inside of our passenger can, a holocircle of the Gliese 581 system, and a d-cube of her living mama and daddy in the village Drak, which means Boulder, fifty-some rocky miles southeast of Lhasa. But—I'm such a dodo bird!—maybe they no longer live at all.

"My daddy's from Boulder!" I say to overcoat this thought.

Officer Photrang peers at me with small bright eyes.

"Boulder, Colorado," I tell her.

"Is that so?" After a nod from Captain Xao, she guides me into a tunnel lit by little glowing pins.

"What did you really come up here to learn, child? I'll tell you if I can."

"Who killed Sakya Gyatso?" I hurry to add, "I don't want to be him."

"Who told you somebody killed His Holiness?"

"Larry." I grab a guide rail. "My tutor, Lawrence Rinpoche."

Nima Photrang snorts. "Larry has a bad humor sense. And he may be wrong."

I float up. "But what if he's right?"

"Is the truth that important to you?" She pulls me down.

A question for a question, like a dry seed poked under my gum. "Larry says that a lama in training must quest for truth in everything, and I must do so always, and everyone else, by doing that too, will clean the universe of lies."

"'Do as I say and not as I do.'"

"What?"

Nima—she tells me to call her by this name—takes my arm and swims me along the tunnel to a door that opens at a knuckle bump. She guides me into her rooms, a closet with a pull-down rack and straps, a toadstool unit for our shipboard intranet, and a corner for talking in. We float here. Nicely, or so it seems, she pulls a twist of brindle hair out of my eye.

"Child, it's possible that Sakya Gyatso had a heart attack."

"Possible?"

"That's the official version, which Minister T told all us ghosts up-phase enough to notice that Sakya had gone missing."

I think hard. "But the unofficial story is . . . somebody killed him?"

"It's one unofficial story. In the face of uncertainty, child, people indulge their imaginations, and more versions of the truth pop up than you can slam a lid on. But lid-slamming, we think, is a bad response to ideas that will come clear in the oxygen of free inquiry."

"Who do you mean, 'we'?"

Nima shows a little smile. "My 'we' excludes anyone who forbids the expression of plausible alternatives to any 'official version.'"

"What do you think happened?"

"I'd best not say."

"Maybe you need some oxygen."

This time her smile looks a bit realer. "Yes, maybe I do."

"I'm the new Dalai Lama, probably, and I give you that oxygen, Nima. Tell me your idea, now."

After two blinks, she does: "I fear that Sakya Gyatso killed himself."

"The Dalai Lama?" I can't help it: her idea insults the man, who, funnily, now breathes inside me.

"Why not the Dalai Lama?"

"A Bodhisattva lives for others. He'd never kill anybody, much less himself."

"He stayed up-phase too much—almost half a century—and the anti-aging effects of ursidormizine slumber, which he often avoided as harmful to his leadership role, were compromised. His Holiness did have the soul of a Bodhisattva, but he also had an animal self. The wear to his body broke him down, working on his spirit as well as his head, and doubts about his ability to last the rest of our trip niggled at him, as did doubts about his fitness to oversee our colonization of Guge."

I cross my arms. This idea insults the late DL. It also, I think, poisons me. "I believe he had a heart attack."

"Then the official version has taken seed in you," Nima says.

"OK then. I like to think someone killed Sakya Gyatso, not that tiredness or sadness made him do it."

Gently: "Child, where's your compassion?"

I float away. "Where's yours?" At the door of the first officer's quarters, I try to bump out. I can't. Nima must drift over, knuckle-bump the door plate, and help me with my angry going.

The artificial-gravity generators run again. I feel them humming through the floor of my room in Amdo, and in Z Quarters where our somnacicles nap. Larry says that except for them, AG aboard *Kalachakra* works little better than did electricity in war-wasted nations on Earth. Anyway, I don't need the lock belt in my vidped unit; and such junk as pocket pens, toothbrushes, mess chits, and d-cubes don't go slow-spinning away like my fuzzy dreams.

Somebody knocks.

Who is it? Not Larry—he's already tutored me today—or Mama, who sleeps in her pod, or Daddy, who's gone up-phase to U-Tsang to help the monks plant vegetables around their gompas. He gets to visit U-Tsang, but I—the only nearly anointed DL on this ship—must mostly hang with non-monks.

The knock knocks again.

Xao Songda enters. He unhooks a folding stool from the wall and sits atop it next to my vidped booth: Captain Xao, the pilot of our generation ship. Even with the hotshot job he has to work, he wanders around almost as much as me.

"Officer Photrang tells me you have doubts."

I have doubts like a strut-ship has fuel tanks. I wish I could drop them half as fast as *Kalachakra* dropped its anti-hydrogen-ice-filled drums in the first four years of our run toward our coasting speed.

"Well?" Captain Xao's eyebrow goes up.

"Sir?"

"Does my first officer lie, or do you indeed have doubts?"

"I have doubts about everything."

"Like what, child?" Captain Xao seems nice but clueless.

"Doubts about who made me, why I was born in a big bean can, why I like the AG on rather than off. Doubts about the shipshapeness of our ship, the soundness of Larry Lake's mind, the realness of the rock we're going to. Doubts about the pains in my legs and the mixing of my soul with Sakya's . . . because of how our lifelines overlapped. Doubts about—"

"Whoa," Xao Songda says. "Officer Photrang tells me you have doubts about the official version of the Twenty-first's death."

"Yes."

"I too, but as captain, I want you to know that it cruises in shipshape shape, with an artist in charge."

After staring some, I say, "Is the official story true? Did Sakya Gyatso really die of Cadillac infraction?"

"Cardiac infarction," the captain says, not getting that I just joked him. "Yes, he did. Regrettably."

"Or do you say that because Minister T told everyone that and he outranks you?"

Xao Songda looks confused. "Why do you think Minister Trungpa would lie?"

"Inferior motives."

"Ulterior motives," the stupid captain again corrects me.

"OK: ulterior motives. Did he have something to do with Sakya's death . . . for mean reasons locked in his heart, just as damned souls are locked in hell?"

The captain draws a noisy breath. "Goodness, child."

"Larry says that somebody killed Sakya." I climb out of my vidped booth and go to the captain. "Maybe it was you."

Captain Xao laughs. "Do you know how many hoops I had to leap through to become captain of this ship? Ethnically, Gee Bee, I am Han Chinese. Hardly anybody in the Free Federation of Tibetan Voyagers wished me to command our strut-ship. But I was wholeheartedly Yellow Hat and the best pilot-engineer not already en route to a habitable planet. And so I'm here. I'd no more assassinate the Dalai Lama than desecrate a chorten, or harm Sakya's likely successor."

I believe him, even if an anxious soul could hear the last few words of his speech unkindly. I ask if he likes Nima's theory—that Sakya Gyatso killed himself—better than Minister T's Cadillac-infraction version. When he starts to answer, I say, "Flee falsehood again and speak the True Word."

After a blink, he says, "If you insist."

"Yes. I do."

"Then I declare myself, on that question, an agnostic. Neither theory strikes me as outlandish. But neither seems likely, either: Minister T's because His Holiness had good physical health and Nima's because the stresses of this voyage were but tickling feathers to the Dalai Lama."

I surprise myself—I begin to cry.

Captain Xao grips my shoulders so softly that his fingers feel like owl's down, as I dream such down would feel on an Earth I've never seen, and never will. He whispers in my ear: "Shhh-shh."

"Why do you shush me?"

Captain Xao removes his hands. "I no longer shush you. Feel free to cry."

I do. So does Captain Xao. We are wed in knowing that Larry my tutor was right all along, and that our late Dalai Lama fell at the hands of a really mean someone with an inferior motive.

Years in transit: 87
Computer Logs of the Dalai Lama-to-Be, age 12

A week before my twelfth birthday, a Buddhist nun named Dolma Langdun, who works in the Amdo Bay nursery, hails me through the *Kalachakra* intranet. She wants to know if, on my birthday, I will let one of her helpers accompany me to the nursery to meet the children and accept gifts from them.

She signs off, —Mama Dolma.

I ask myself, "Why does this person do this? Who's told her that I have a birthday coming?"

Not my folks, who sleep in their somnacicle eggs, nor Larry, who does the same because I've "exhausted" him. And so I resolve to put these questions to Mama Dolma over my intranet connection.

—How many children? I ask her, meanwhile listening to Górecki's "Symphony of Sorrowful Songs" through my ear-bud.

—Five, she replies. —Very sweet children, the youngest ten months and the oldest almost six years. It would be a great privilege to attend you on your natal anniversary, Your Holiness.

Before I can scold her for using this too-soon form of address, she adds, —As a toddler, you spent time here in Momo House, but in those bygone days I was assigned to the nunnery in U-Tsang with Abbess Yeshe Yargag.

—Momo House! I key her. —Oh, I remember!

Momo means dumpling, and this memory of my caregivers and my little friends back then dampens my eyelashes. Clearly, during the Z-pod rests of my parents and tutor, Minister Trungpa has acted as a most thoughtful guardian.

The following week goes by even faster than a fifth of light-speed.

On my birthday morning, a skinny young monk in a maroon jumpsuit comes for me and escorts me down to Momo House.

There I meet Mama Dolma. There, I also meet the children: the baby Alicia, the toddlers Pema and Lahmu, and the oldest two, Rinzen and Mickey. Except for the baby, they tap-dance about me like silly dwarves. The nursery features big furry balls that also serve as hassocks; inflatable yaks, monkeys, and pterodac-tyls; and cribs and vidped units, with lock belts for AG failures. A system made just for the Dumpling Gang always warns of an outage at least fifteen minutes before it occurs.

The nearly-six kid, Mickey, grabs my hand and shows me around. He introduces me to everybody, working down from the five-year-old to ten-month-old Alicia. All of them but Alicia give me drawings. These drawings show a monkey named Chenrezig (of course), a nun named Dolma (ditto), a yak named Yackety (double ditto), and a python with no name at all. I ooh and ah over these masterpizzas, as I call them, and then help them assemble soft-form puzzles, feed one another snacks, go to the toilet, and scan a big voyage chart that ends (of course) at Gliese 581g.

But it's Alicia, the baby, who wins me. She twinkles. She flirts. She touches. At nap time, I hold her in a vidped unit, its screen oranged out and its rockers rocking, and nuzzle her sweet-smelling neck. She tugs at my lip corners and pinches my mouth flat, so involved in reshaping my face that I think her a pudgy sculptor elf. All the while, her agate eyes, bigger than my thumb tips, play across my face with near-sighted adoration.

I stay with Alicia—Alicia Paljor—all the rest of my day. Then the skinny young monk comes to escort me home, as if I need him to, and Mama Dolma hugs me. Alicia wails.

It hurts to leave, but I do, because I must, and even as the hurt fades, the memory of this outstanding birthday begins, that very night, to sing in me like the lovely last notes of Górecki's Third.

I have never had a better birthday.

Months later, Daddy Simon and Mama Karen Bryn have come up-phase at the same time. Together, they fetch me from my nook in Amdo and walk with me on a good AG day to the cafeteria above the grave-caves of our strut-ship's central drum, Kham. I ease along the serving line between them, taking tsampa, mushroom cuts, tofu slices, and sauces to make it all edible. The three of us end up at a table in a nook far from the serving line. Music by J. S. Bach spills from speakers in the movable walls, with often a sitar and bells to call up for some voyagers a Himalayan nostalgia to which my folks are immune. We eat fast and talk small.

Then Mama says, "Gee Bee, your father has something to tell you."

O God. O Buddha. O Larry. O Curly. O Moe.

"Tell her," Mama says.

Daddy Simon wears the sour face proclaiming that everybody should call him Pieman Oldfart. I hurt to behold him, he to behold me. But at last he gets out that before I stood up-phase, almost three years ago, as the DL's disputed Soul Child, he and Mama signed apartness documents that have now concluded in an agreement of full marital severance. They continue my folks, but not as the couple that conceived, bore, and raised me. They remain friends but will no longer cohabit because of incompatibilities that have arisen over their up-phase years. It really shouldn't matter to me, they say, because I've become Larry's protégée with a grand destiny that I will no doubt fulfill as a youth and an adult. Besides, they will continue to parent me as much as my odd unconfirmed status as DL-in-training allows.

I do not cry, as I did upon learning that Captain Xao believes that somebody slew my only-maybe predecessor. I don't cry because their news feels truly distant, like word of a planet somewhere whose people have brains in their chests. However, it does hurt to think about why I absolutely must cry later.

Daddy gets up, kisses my forehead, and leaves with his tray.

Mama studies me closely. "I'll always love you. You've made me very proud."

"You've made me very proud," I echo her.

"What?"

We push our plastic fork tines around in our leftovers, which I imagine rising in damp squadrons from our plates and floating up to the air-filtration fans. I wish that I, too, could either rise or sink.

"When will they confirm you?" Mama asks.

"Everything on this ship takes forever: getting from here to there, finding a killer, confirming the new DL."

"You must have some idea."

"I don't. The monks don't want me. I can't even visit their make-believe gompas over in U-Tsang."

"Well, those are sacred places. Not many of us get invitations."

"But Minister T has declared me the 'One,' and Larry has tutored me in thousands of subjects, holy and not so holy. Still, the subsidiary lamas and their silly crew think less well of me than they would of a lame blue mountain sheep."

"Don't call their monasteries 'make-believe,' Gee Bee. Don't call these other holy people and their followers 'silly.'"

"Fie!" I actually tell her. "I wish I were anywhere but on this bean can flung at an iceberg light-years across the stupid universe."

"Don't, Greta Bryn. You've got a champion in Minister Trungpa."

"Who just wants to bask in the reflected glory of his next supposed Bodhisattva—which, I swear, I am not."

Mama lifts her tray and slams it down.

Nobody else seems to notice, but I jump.

"You have no idea," she says, "who you are or what a champion can do for you, and you're much too young to dismiss yourself or your powerful advocate."

One of the Brandenburg Concertos swells, its sitars and yak bells flourishing. Far across the mess hall, Larry shuffles toward us with a tray. Mama sees him, and, just as Daddy did, she kisses my forehead and abruptly leaves. My angry stare tells Larry not to mess with me (no, I won't apologize for the accidental pun), and Larry veers off to chow with two or three bio-techs at a faraway table.

YEARS IN TRANSIT: 88

COMPUTER LOGS OF THE DALAI LAMA-TO-BE, AGE 13

Today marks another anniversary of the *Kalachakra*'s departure from Moon orbit on its crossing to Guge in the Gliese 581 system.

Soon I will turn thirteen. Much has happened in the six years since I woke to find that Sakya Gyatso had died and that I had become Greta Bryn Gyatso, his really tardy reincarnation.

What has not happened haunts me as much as, if not more than, what has. I have a disturbing sense that the 'investigation' into Sakya's murder resides in a secretly agreed-upon limbo. Also, that my confirmation rests in this same foggy territory, with Minister T as my 'regent.' Recently, though, at First Officer Nima's urging, Minister T assigned me a bodyguard from among the monks of U-Tsang Bay, a guy called Ian Kilkhor.

Once surnamed Davis, Kilkhor was born sixteen years into our flight of Canadian parents, techs who'd converted to the Yellow Hat order of Tibetan Buddhists in Calgary, Alberta, a decade before the construction of our interstellar vessel. Although nearing the chronological age of sixty, Kilkhor—as he asks me to call him—looks less than half that and has many admirers among the female ghosts in Kham.

Officer Nima fancies him. (Hey, even I fancy him.)

But she's celibacy-committed unless a need for childbearing arises on Guge. And assuming her reproductive apparatus still works. Under such circumstances, I suspect that Kilkhor would lie with her.

Here I confess my ignorance. Despite lessons from Larry in the Tibetan language, I didn't realize, until Kilkhor told me, that his new surname means 'Mandala.' I excuse myself on the grounds that 'Kilkhor' more narrowly means 'center of the circle,' and that Larry often skimps on offering connections. (To improve the health of his 'mortal coil,' Larry has spent nearly four of my last six years in an ursidormizine doze. I go to visit him once every two weeks in the pod-lodges of Amdo Bay, but these well-intended homages sometimes feel less like cheerful visits than dutiful viewings.) Also, 'Kilkhor' sounds to me more like an incitement to violence than it does a statement of physical and spiritual harmony.

Even so, I benefit in many ways from Kilkhor's presence as bodyguard and stand-in tutor. Like Larry, Mama and Daddy spend long periods in their pods; and Kilkhor, a monk who knows tai chi chuan, has kept the killer, or killers, of Sakya from slaying me, if such villains exist aboard our ship. (I have begun to doubt they do.) He has also taught me much history, culture, religion, politics, computing, astrophysics and astronomy that Larry, owing to long bouts of hibernizing, has sadly neglected. Also, he weighs in for me with the monks, nuns, and yogis of U-Tsang, who feel disenfranchised in the process of confirming me as Sakya's successor.

Indeed, because the Panchen Lama now in charge in U-Tsang will not let me set foot there, Kilkhor intercedes to get other high monks to visit me in Kham. The Panchen Lama, to avoid seeming either bigot or autocrat, permits these visits. Unhappily, my sex, my ethnicity, and (most important) the fact that my birth antedates the Twenty-first's death by five years all conspire to taint my candidacy. I doubt it too and fear that fanatics among the 'religious' will try to veto me by subtraction, not by argument, and that I will die at the hands of friends rather than enemies of the Dalai Lamahood.

Such fears, by themselves, throw real doubt on Minister T's choice of me as the Sakya's only indisputable Soul Child.

YEARS IN TRANSIT: 89
COMPUTER LOGS OF THE DALAI LAMA-TO-BE, AGE 14

"The Tibetan belief in monkey ancestors puts them in a unique category as the only people I know of who acknowledged this connection before Darwin."

—*Karen Swenson,*
twentieth-century traveler, poet, and
worker at Mother Teresa's Calcutta mission

Last week, a party of monks and one nun met me in the hangar of Kham Bay. From their gompas ('monasteries') in U-Tsang, they brought a woolen cloak, a woolen bag, three spruce walking sticks, three pairs of sandals, and a white-faced monkey that one monk, as the group entered, fed from a baby bottle full of ashen-gray slurry.

An AG-generator never runs in the hangar because people don't often visit it, and our lander nests in a vast hammock of polyester cables. So we levitated in a cordoned space near the nose of the lander, which the Free Federation of Tibetan Voyagers has named Chenrezig, after that Buddhist disciple who, in monkey form, sired the first human Tibetans. (Each new DL automatically qualifies as the latest incarnation of Chenrezig.) Our lander's nose is painted with bright geometric patterns and the cartoon head of a wise-looking monkey wearing glasses and a beaked yellow hat. Despite this amusing iconography, however, almost everyone on our strut-ship now calls the lander the Yak Butter Express.

After stiff greetings, these high monks—including the Panchen Lama, Lhundrub Gclck, and Yeshe Yargang, the abbess of U-Tsang's only nunnery!—tied the items that they'd brought to a utility toadstool in the center of our circle ('kilkhor'). Then we floated in lotus positions, hands palm-upward, and I stared at these items, but not at the monkey now clutching the PL and wearing a look of alert concern. From molecular vibrations and subtle somatic clues—twitches, blinks, sniffles—I tried to determine which of the articles they wished me to select . . . or not to select, as their biases dictated.

"Some of these things were Sakya Gyatso's," the Panchen Lama said. "Choose only those that he viewed as truly his. Of course, he saw little in this life as a 'belonging.' You may examine any or all, Miss Brasswell."

I liked how my surname (even preceded by the stodgy honorific Miss) sounded in our hangar, even if it did seem to label me an imposter, if not an outright foe of Tibetan Buddhism. To my right, Kilkhor lowered his eyelids, advising me to make a choice. OK, then: I had no need to breast-stroke my way over to the pile.

"The cloak," I said.

Its stench of musty wool and ancient vegetable dyes told me all I needed to know. I recalled those smells and the cloak's vivid colors from an encounter with the DL during his visit to the nursery in Amdo when I was four. It had seemed the visit of a seraph or an extraterrestrial—as, by virtue of our status as star travelers, he had qualified. Apparently, none of these faithful had accompanied him then, for, obviously, none recalled his having cinched on this cloak to meet a tot of common blood.

The monkey—a large Japanese macaque (Mucaca fuscata)—swam to the center of our circle, undid the folded cloak, and kicked back to the Lama, who belted it around his lap. Still fretful, the macaque levitated in its breechclout—a kind of diaper— beside the PL. It wrinkled its brow at me in approval or accusation.

"Go on," Lhundrub Gelek said. "Choose another item."

I glanced at Kilkhor, who dropped his eyelids.

"May I see what's in the bag?" I asked.

The PL spoke to the macaque: a critter I imagined Tech Bonfils taking a liking to at our trip's outset. It then paddled over to the bag tied to the utility toadstool, seized the bag by its neck, and dragged it over to me.

After foraging a little, I extracted five slender books, of a kind now rarely made, and studied each: one in English, one in Tibetan, one in French, one in Hindi, and one, surprisingly, in Esperanto. In each case, I recognized their alphabets and point of origin, if not their subject matter. A bootlace linked the books; when they started to float away, I caught its nearer end and yanked them all back.

"Did His Holiness write these?" I asked.

"Yes," the Panchen Lama said, making me think that I'd passed another test. He added, "Which of the five did Sakya most esteem?" Ah, a dirty trick. Did they want me to read not only several difficult scripts but also Sakya's departed mind?

"Do you mean as artifacts, for the loveliness of their craft, or as documents, for the spiritual meat in their contents?"

"Which of those options do you suppose more like him?" Abbess Yeshe Yargag asked sympathetically.

"Both. But if I must make a choice, the latter. When he wrote, he distilled clear elixirs from turbid mud."

Our visitors beheld me as if I'd neutralized the stench of sulfur with sprinkles of rose water. Again, I felt shameless.

With an unreadable frown, the PL said, "You've chosen correctly. We now wish you to choose the book that Sakya most esteemed for its message."

I reexamined each title. The one in French featured the words wisdom and child. When I touched it, Chenrezig responded with a nearly human intake of breath. Empty of thought, I lifted that book.

"Here: The Wisdom of a Child, the Childishness of Wisdom."

As earlier, our five visitors kept their own counsel, and Chenrezig returned the books to their bag and the bag to the monk who had set it out.

Next, I chose among the walking sticks and the pairs of sandals, taking my cues from the monkey and so choosing better than I had any right to expect. In fact, I selected just those items identifying me as the Dalai Lama's Soul Child, girl or not.

After Kilkhor praised my accuracy, the PL said, "Very true, but—"

"But what?" Kilkhor said. "Must you settle on a Tibetan male only?"

The Lama replied, "No, Ian. But what about this child makes her miraculous?"

Ah, yes. One criterion for confirming a DL candidate is that those giving the tests identify 'something miraculous' about him . . . or her.

"What about her startling performance so far?" Kilkhor asked.

"We don't see her performance as a miracle, Ian."

"But you haven't conferred about the matter." He gestured at the other holies floating in the fluorescent lee of the Yak Butter Express.

"My friends," the Panchen Lama asked, "what say you all in reply?"

"We find no miracle," a spindly, middle-aged monk said, "in this child's choosing correctly. Her brief life overlapped His Holiness's."

"My-me," Abbess Yargag said. "I find her a wholly supportable candidate."

The three leftover holies held their tongues, and I had to admit—to myself, if not aloud to this confirmation panel—that they had a hard-to-refute point, for I had pegged my answers to the tics of a monastery macaque with an instinctual sense of its keepers' moody fretfulness.

Fortunately, the monkey liked me. I had no idea why.

O to be unmasked! I needed no title or additional powers to lend savor to my life. I wanted to sleep and to awaken later as an animal husbandry specialist, with Tech Karen Bryn Bonfils as my mentor and a few near age-mates as fellow apprentices.

The PL unfolded from his lotus pose and floated before me with his feet hanging. "Thank you, Miss Brasswell, for this audience. We regret we can't—" Here he halted, for Chenrezig swam across our meeting space, pushed into my arms, and clasped me about the neck. Then all the astonished monks and the shaken PL rubbed their shoulders as if to ignite their bodies in glee or consternation.

Abbess Yargag said, "There's your miracle."

"Nando," the lama said, shaking his head: No, he meant.

"On the contrary," Abbess Yargag replied. "Chenrezig belonged to Sakya Gyatso, and never in Chenrezig's sleep-lengthened life has this creature embraced a child, a non-Asian, or a female: not even me."

"Nando," the PL, visibly angry, said again.

"Yes," another monk said. "Hail the jewel in the lotus. Praise to the gods."

I kissed Chenrezig's white-flecked facial mane as he whimpered like an infant in my too-soon weary arms.

YEARS IN TRANSIT: 93
COMPUTER LOGS OF THE DALAI LAMA-TO-BE, AGE 18

A Catechism: Why Do We Voyage?'
     At age seven, I learned this catechism from Larry. Kilkhor often has me say it, to ensure that I don't turn apostate to either our legend or my

long-term charge. Sometimes Captain Xao Songda, a Han who converted and fled to Vashon Island, Washington—via northern India; Cape Town, South Africa; Buenos Aires; and Hawaii—sits in to temper Larry's flamboyance and Kilkhor's lethargic matter-of-factness.

—Why do we voyage? one of them will ask.

—To fulfill, I say, —the self-determination tenets of the Free Federation of Tibet and to usher every soul pent in hell up through the eight lower realms to Buddhahood.

From the bottom up, these realms include: 1) hell-pent mortals, 2) hungry ghosts, 3) benighted beasts, 4) fighting spirits, 5) human beings, 6) seraphs and suchlike, 7) disciples of the Buddha, 8) Buddhas for themselves only, and 9) Bodhisattvas who live and labor for every soul in each lower realm.

—Which realm did you begin in, Your Probationary Holiness?

—That of the bewildered, but not benighted, human mortal.

—As our Dalai Lama in Training, to which realm have you arisen?

—That of the disciples of Chenrezig: "Hail the jewel in the lotus." I am the funky simian saint of the Buddha.

(Sometimes, depending on my mood, I ad-lib that last bit.)

—From what besieged and battered homeland do you pledge to free us?

—The terrestrial "Land of Snow": Tibet beset, ensorcelled, and enslaved.

—As a surrogate for that land gone cruelly forfeit, to which new country do you pledge to lead us?

—"The Land of Snow," on Guge the Unknowable, where we all must strive to free ourselves again.

The foregoing part of the catechism embodies a pledge and a charge. Other parts synopsize the history of our oppression: the ruin of our economy; the destruction of our monasteries; the subjugation of our nation to the will of foreign predators; the co-opting of our spiritual formulae for greedy and war-like purposes; the submergence of our culture to the maws of jackals; and the quarantining of our state to anyone not of our oppressors' liking. Finally, against the severing of sinews human and animal, the pulling asunder of ties interdependent and relational, only the tallest mountains could stand. And those who undertook the khora, the sacred pilgrimage around Mount Kailash, often did so with little or no grasp of the spiritual roots of their journeys. Even then, that mountain, the land all about it, and the scant air overarching them, stole the breath and spilled into its pilgrims' lungs the bracing elixir of awe.

At length, the Tibetans and their sympathizers realized that their overlords would never withdraw. Their invasion, theft, and reconfiguration of the state had left its peoples few options but death or exile.

—So what did the Free Federation of Tibet do? Larry, Kilkhor, or Xao will ask.

—Sought a United Nations charter for the building of a starship, an initiative that all feared China would preempt with its veto in the Security Council.

—What happened instead?

—The Chinese supported the measure.

—How so?

—They contributed to the general levy for funds to build and crew with colonists a second-generation antimatter ship capable of attaining speeds up to one-fifth the velocity of light.

—Why did China surrender to an enterprise implying severe criticism of a policy that it saw as an internal matter? That initiative surely stood as a rebuke to its efforts to overwhelm Tibet with its own crypto-capitalistic materialism.

Here I may snigger or roll my eyeballs, and Lawrence, Kilkhor, or Xao will repeat the question.

—Three reasons suffice to explain China's acquiescence, I at length reply.

—State them.

—First, China understood that launching this ship would remove the Twenty-first Dalai Lama, who had agreed not only to support this disarming plan but also to go with the Yellow Hat colonists to Gliese 581g.

—'Praise to the gods,' my catechist will say in Tibetan.

—Indeed, backing this plan would oust from a long debate the very man whom the Chinese reviled as a poser and a bar to the incorporation of Tibet into their program of post-post-Mao modernization.

Here, another snigger from a bigger poser than Sakya; namely, me.

—And the second reason, Your Holiness?

—Backing this strut-ship strategy surprised the players arrayed against China in both the General Assembly and the Security Council.

—To what end?

—All they could do was brand China's support a type of cynicism warped into a low-yield variety of 'ethnic cleansing,' for now Tibet and its partisans would have one fewer grievance to lay at China's feet.

With difficulty, I refrain from sniggering again.

—And the third reason, Miss Greta Bryn, our delightfully responsive Ocean of Wisdom?

—Supporting the antimatter ship initiative allowed China to put its design and manufacturing enterprises to work drawing up blueprints and machining parts for the provocatively named *UNS Kalachakra*.

—And so we won our victory?

—"Hail the jewel in the lotus," I reply.

—And what do we Kalachakrans hope to accomplish on the sun-locked world we now call Guge?

—Establish a colony unsullied by colonialism; summon other emigrants to 'The Land of Snow'; and lead to enlightenment all who bore that dream, and who will carry it into cycles yet to unfold.

—And after that?

—The cessation of everything samsaric, the opening of ourselves to nirvana.

YEARS IN TRANSIT: 94
COMPUTER LOGS OF THE DALAI LAMA-TO-BE, AGE 19

For nearly four Earth months, I've added not one word to my Computer Log. But shortly after my last recitation of the foregoing catechism, Kilkhor pulled me aside and told me that I had a rival for the position of Dalai Lama.

This news astounded me. "Who?"

"A male Soul Child born of true Tibetan parents in Amdo Bay less than fifty days after Sakya Gyatso's death," Kilkhor said. "A search team located him almost a decade ago, but has only now disclosed him to us." Kilkhor made this disclosure of bad news—it is bad, isn't it?—sound very ordinary.

"What's his name?" I had no idea what else to say.

"Jetsun Trimon," Kilkhor said. "Old Gelek seems to think him a more promising candidate than he does Greta Bryn Brasswell."

"Jetsun! You're joking, right?" And my heart did a series of arrhythmic lhundrubs in protest.

Kilkhor regarded me then with either real, or expertly feigned, confusion. "You know him?"

"Of course not! But the name—" I stuck, at once amused and appalled.

"The name, Your Holiness?"

"It's a ridiculous, a totally ludicrous name."

"Not really. In Tibetan it means—"

"—'venerable' and 'highly esteemed,'" I put in. "But it's still ridiculous." And I noted that as a child, between bouts of study, I had often watched, well, 'cartoons' in my vidped unit. Those responsible for this lowbrow programming had mischievously stocked it with a selection of episodes called The Jetsons, about a space-going Western family in a gimmick-ridden future. I had loved it.

"I've heard of it," Kilkhor said. "The program, I mean."

But he didn't twig the irony of my five-year-younger rival's name.

Or he pretended not to. To him, the similarity of these two monikers embodied a pointless coincidence.

"I can't do this anymore without a time-out," I said. "I'm going down-phase for a year—at least a quarter of a year!"

Kilkhor said nothing. His expression said everything.

Still, he arranged for my down-phase respite, and I repaired to Amdo Bay and my eggshell to enjoy this pod-lodging self-indulgence, which, except for rare cartoon-tinged nightmares, I almost did.

Now, owing to somatic suspension, I return at almost the same nineteen I went under.

When I awake this time amidst a catacomb vista of eggshell pods—like racks in a troopship or in a concentration-camp barracks—Mama, Minister T, the Panchen Lama, Ian Kilkhor, and Jetsun Trimon attend my awakening.

Grateful for functioning AG (as, down here, it always functions), I swing my legs out of the pod, stagger a step or two, and retch from a stomach knotted with a fresh anti-insomniac heat.

The Tibetan boy, my rival, comes to me unbidden, slides an arm across my chest from behind, and eases me back toward his own thin body so that I don't topple into the vomit-vase Mama has given me. With his free hand, Jetsun strokes my brow, meanwhile tucking stray strands of hair behind my ear. I don't need him to do this stuff. Actually, I resent his doing it.

Although I usually sleep little, I do take occasional naps. Don't I deserve a respite?

I pull free of the young imposter. He looks fifteen at least, and if I've hit nineteen, his age squares better than does mine with the passing of the last DL and the transfer of Sakya's bhava into the material form of Jetsun Trimon.

Beholding him, I find his given name less of a joke than I did before my nap and more of a spell for the inspiriting that the PL alleges has occurred in him. Jetsun and I study each other with mutual curiosity. Our elders look on with darker curiosities. How must Jetsun and I regard this arranged marriage, they no doubt wonder, and what does it presage for everyone aboard the *Kalachakra*?

During my year-plus sleep, maybe I've matured some. Although I want to cry out against the outrage—no, the unkindness—of my guardians' conspiracy to bring this fey usurper to my podside, I don't berate them. They warrant such a scolding, but I refrain. How do they wish me to view their collusion, and how can I see it as anything other than their sending a prince to the bier of a spell-afflicted maiden? Except for the acne scarring his forehead and chin, Jetsun is, well, cute, but I don't want his help. I loathe his intrusion into my pod-lodge and almost regret my return.

Kilkhor notes that the lamas of U-Tsang, including the Panchen Lama and

Abbess Yargag, have finally decided to summon Jetsun Trimon and me to our onboard stand-in for the Jokhang Temple. There, they will conduct a gold-urn lottery to learn which of us will follow Sakya Gyatso as the Twenty-second Dalai Lama.

Jetsun bows.

He says that his tutor has given him the honor of inviting me, my family, and my guardians to this 'shindig.' It will occur belatedly, he admits, after he and I have already learned many sutras and secrets reserved in Tibet—holy be its saints, its people, and its memory—for a Soul Child validated by lottery.

But circumstances have changed since our Earth-bound days: The ecology of the *Kalachakra*, the great epic of our voyage, and our need on Guge for a leader of heart and vision require fine tunings beyond our forebears' imaginations.

Wiser than I was last year, I swallow a cynical yawn.

"And so," Jetsun ends, "I wish you joy in the lottery's Buddha-directed outcome, whichever name appears on the selected slip."

He bows and takes three steps back.

Lhundrub Gelek beams at Jetsun, and I know in my gut that the PL has become my competitor's regent, his champion. Mama Karen Bryn holds her face expressionless until fret lines drop from her lip corners like weighted ebony threads.

I thank Jetsun, for his courtesy and his well-rehearsed speech. He seems to want something more—an invitation of my own, a touch—but I have nothing to offer but the stifling of my envy, which I fight to convert to positive energies boding a happy karmic impact on the name slips in the urn.

"You must come early to our Temple," the PL says. "Doing so will give you time to pay your respects at Sakya Gyatso's bier."

This codicil to our invitation heartens me. Lacking any earlier approval to visit U-Tsang, I have never seen the body of the DL on display there.

Do I really wish to see it, to see him?

Yes, of course I do.

We've lost many Kalachakrans in transit to Guge, but none of the others have our morticians bled with trochars, painted with creams and rouges, or treated with latter-day preservatives. Those others we ejected via tubes into the airless cold of interstellar space, meager human scraps for the ever-hungry night.

In Tibet, the bereaved once spread their dead loved ones out on rocks in 'celestial burial grounds.' This they did as an act of charity, for the vultures. On our ship, though, we have no vultures, or none with feathers, and perhaps by firing our dead into unending quasi-vacuum, we will offer to the void a sacrifice of once-living flesh generous enough to upgrade our karma.

But Sakya Gyatso we have enshrined; and soon, as one of only two candidates for his sacred post, I will gaze upon the remains of one whose enlightenment and mercy have plunged me into painful egocentric anguish.

At the appointed time (six months from Jetsun's invitation), we journey from Amdo and across Kham by way of tunnels designed for either gravity-assisted marches or weightless swims. Our style of travel depends on the AG generators and the rationing of gravity by formulae meant to benefit our long-term approach to Guge. However, odd outages often overcome these formulae. Blessedly, Kalachakrans now adjust so well to gravity loss that we no longer find it alarming or inconvenient.

Journeying, we discover that U-Tsang's residents—allegedly, all Bodhisattvas—have forsworn the use of generators during the 72-hour Festival of the Gold Urn, with that ceremony occurring at noon of the middle day. This renunciation they regard as a gift to everybody aboard our vessel—somnacicles and ghosts—and no hardship at all. Whatever stress we spare the generators, our karmic economies tell us, will redound to everybody's benefit in our voyage's later stages.

My entourage consists of my divorced parents, Simon Brasswell and Karen Bryn Bonfils; Minister T, my self-proclaimed regent; Lawrence Lake Rinpoche, my tutor and confidant, now up-phase for the first time in two years; and Ian Kilkhor, security agent, standby tutor, and friend. We walk single-file through a sector of Kham wide enough for the next Dalai Lama's subjects to line its walls and perform respectful namaste as he (or she) passes. Minister T tells us that Jetsun Trimon and his people made this same journey eighteen hours ago, and that their well-wishers in this trunk tunnel were fewer than those attending our passage. A Bodhisattva would take no pleasure from such a petty statistical triumph. Tellingly, I do. So what does my competition-bred joy say about my odds in the coming gold-urn lottery? Nothing auspicious, I fear.

Eventually, our crowds dwindle, and we enter a deck area featuring a checkpoint and a sector gate. A monk clad in maroon passes us through. Another dials open the gate admitting us, at last, to U-Tsang.

I smell roast barley, barley beer (chang), and an acrid tang of incense that makes my stomach seize. Beyond the gate, which shuts behind us like a stone wheel slotting into a tomb groove, we drift through a hall with thin metal rails and bracket-like handholds. The luminary pins here gleam a watery purple.

Our feet slide out from under us, not like those of a fawn slipping on ice, but like those of an astronaut trainee rising from the floor of an aircraft plunging to create a few seconds of pedagogical zero-g.

The AG generators here shut down a while ago, so we dog-paddle in water-wheel slow-motion, unsure which tunnel to enter.

Actually, I'm the only uncertain trekker, but because neither Minister T nor Larry nor Kilkhor wants to help me, I stay mute, from perplexity and pride: another black mark, no doubt, against my lottery chances.

Ahead of us, fifteen yards or so, a snow leopard manifests: a four-legged ghost with yellow eyes and frost-etched silver fur. Despite the lack of gravity, it faces us as though it were standing on a ledge and licks its sooty beard as if savoring again the last guinea-pig-like chiphi that it crushed into bone bits. I hesitate. The leopard swishes its tail, turns, and leaps into a tunnel that I would not have chosen.

Kilkhor laughs and urges us upward into this same purplish chute. "It's all right," he says. "Follow it. Or do you suspect a subterfuge from our spiritually elevated hosts?" He laughs again . . . this time, maybe, at his inadvertent nod to the Christian sacrament of communion.

Larry and I twig his mistake, but does anybody else?

"Come on," Kilkhor insists. "They've sent us this cool cat as a guide."

And so we follow. We swim rather than walk, levitating through a Buddhist rabbit hole in the wake of an illusory leopard . . . until, by a sudden shift in perspective, we feel ourselves to be 'walking' again.

This ascent, or fall, takes just over an hour, and we emerge in the courtyard of Jokhang Temple, or its diminished *Kalachakra* facsimile. Here, the Panchen Lama, the Abbess of U-Tsang's only nunnery, and a colorful contingent of Yellow Hats and other monks greet us joyfully. They regale us with khata, gift scarves inscribed with good-luck symbols, and with processional music played by flutes, drums, and bells. Their welcome feels at once high-spirited and heartfelt.

The snow leopard has vanished. When we broke into the courtyard swimming like ravenous carp, somebody, somewhere, stopped projecting it.

So let the gold-urn ceremony begin. Put me out of, or into, my misery.

But before the lottery, we visit the shrine where the duded-up remains of Sakya Gyatso lie in state, like those of Lenin in the Kremlin or Mao in the Forbidden City. Although Sakya should not suffer mention in the same breath as mass murderers, nobody can deny that we have preserved him as an icon, just as the devotees of Lenin and Mao mummified them. And so I must trust that a single Figure of Peace weighs more in the karmic-justice scales than does a shipload of bloody despots.

Daddy begs off. He has seen the dead Sakya Gyatso before, and traveling with his ex-wife, the mother of his Soul Child daughter, has depressed him beyond easy repair. So he retreats to a nearby guesthouse and locks himself inside for a nap. Ian Kilkhor leaves to visit several friends in the Yellow Hat gompa with whom he once studied; Minister T, who has often paid homage at the Twenty-first's bier, has business with Lhundrub Gelek and others of the confirmation troupe who met with me in Kham in the shadow of the Yak Butter Express.

So, only Mama, Larry, and I go to see the Lama whom, according to many, I will succeed as the spiritual and temporal head of the 990 Tibetan colonizers aboard this ship. The shrine we approach does not resemble a mausoleum. It sits on the courtyard's edge, like an exhibit of amateur art in a construction trailer.

Two maroon-clad guards await us beside its doors, one at each end of the trailer, now graffitified with mantras, prayers, and many mysterious symbols— but no one else in U-Tsang Bay has come out to view its principal attraction. The blousy monk at the nearer door examines our implanted, upper-arm IDs with click-scans, smiles beatifically, and nods us in. Larry jokes in Tibetan with this guy before joining us at the DL's windowed bier, where we three float: ghosts beside a pod-lodger who will not again arise, unless he has already done so in yet another borrowed boy.

"He is not here," I say. "He has arisen."

Larry, who looks much older than at his last brief up-phase, laughs in appreciation or embarrassment: the latter, probably.

Mama gives me a blistering 'cool-it' glare.

And then I gaze upon the body of Sakya Gyatso. Even in death, even through the clear but faintly dusty cover of his display pod, he sustains about his face and hands a soft amber aura of serene lifelikeness that startles, and discomfits. I see him smiling sweetly upon me when I was four. I imagine him displeasing his religious brethren and sisters by going more often into Amdo and Kham Bays to interact with his secular subjects than our sub-lamas thought needful or wise, as if such visits distracted him from his obligations and under-cut his authority in both realms, profane and holy. And it's definitely true that his longest uninterrupted sojourn in U-Tsang coincides with his years lying in state in this shabby trailer.

Commoners aboard ship loved him, but maybe—I reflect, studying his corpse with both fascination and regard—he angered those practitioners of Tantra who viewed him as their highest representative and model. Certainly, he moved during his life from external *Kalachakra* Tantra—a concern with the lost procession of solar and lunar days—to the internal Tantra, with its focus on the energy systems of the body, to the higher alternative Tantra leading to the sublime state of bodhichitta, perfect enlightenment for the sake of others.

Thus reflecting, I cannot conceive of anyone aboard ever wishing him harm or of myself climbing out of the pit of my ego to attain the state of material renunciation and accepting comprehension of emptiness that Sakya Gyatso reached and embodied through so many years of our journey.

That I stand today as one of two Soul Children in line to follow him defies logic; it offends reason and also the 722 deities resident in the *Kalachakra* Mandala as emblems of reality and consciousness. I lack even the worth of a dog licking barley-cake crumbs from the floor. I put my palm on the Twenty-first's pod cover and erupt in sobs. These underscore my unsuitability to succeed him.

Mama's glare gives way to a look of fretful amazement. She lays an arm over my shoulder, an intimacy that keeps me from drifting blindly away from either her or Larry.

"Kiddo," she murmurs, "don't cry for this lucky man. We'll never cease to honor him, but the time for mourning has passed."

I can't stop: All sleep has fled and the future holds only a scalding wakefulness. Larry lays his arm over my other shoulder, caging me between them.

"Baby," Mama says. "Baby, what's going on?"

She hasn't called me 'baby' or 'kiddo' since, over seven years ago, I had my first period. I twist my neck just enough to tell her to glance at the late DL; that she must look. Reluctantly, it seems, she does, and then looks back at me with no apparent hesitancy or aversion. Her gaze then switches between him and me until she realizes that I won't—I simply can't—succeed this saint as our leader. Moreover, I intend to withdraw from the gold-urn lottery and to throw my support to my rival. Mama remains silent, but her arm deserts me and she turns from the DL's bier as if my declaration has acted as a vernier jet to change her position. In any case, she drifts away.

"Do you understand me, Mama?"

Mama's eyes jiggle and close. Her chin drops. Her jumpsuit-clad body floats like that of a string-free marionette, all raw angles and dreamily rafting hands.

Larry releases me and swims to her. "Something's wrong, Greta Bryn." I already suspect this, but these words penetrate with a laser's precision. I fumble blurry-eyed after Larry, clueless about what to do to help.

Larry swallows her with his arms, like the male hero in an anachronistic spectal, and then pushes her away to study her more objectively. Immediately, he pulls her back in to him again, checks her pulse at wrist and throat, and pivots her toward me with odd contrasting expressions washing over his face.

"She's fainted, I think."

"Fainted?" My mother, so far as I know, never faints.

"It's all the travel . . . and her anxiety about the gold-urn lottery."

"Not to mention her disappointment in me."

Larry regards me with such deliberate blankness that I almost fail to recognize the man, whom I have known seemingly forever.

"Talk to her when she comes 'round," he says. "Talk to her."

The blousy monk who ran click-scans on us enters the makeshift mausoleum and helps Larry tow my rag-doll mama outside, across the road, and into the battened-down Temple courtyard. The two accompany her to a basket-like bower chair that suppresses her driftability and attend her with colorful fake Chinese fans. I go with them, looking on like a gawker at a cafeteria accident.

Our post-swoon interview takes place in the nearly empty courtyard. Mama clutches two of the bower-chair spokes like a child in a gravity swing, and I maintain my place before her with the mindless agility of a pond carp.

"Never say you're forsaking the gold-urn lottery," she says. "You bear on your shoulders the hopes of a majority, my hopes highest of all."

"Did my decision to withdraw cause you to faint?"

"Of course!" she cries. "You can't withdraw! You don't think I faked my swoon, do you?"

I have no doubt that Mama didn't fake it. Her sclera clocked into view before her eyelids fell. But, before that, her gaze cut to and rested on Sakya's face just prior to realizing my intent. Feelings of betrayal, loss, and outrage triggered her swoon. Now she says I have no choice but to take part in the gold-urn drawing, and I regard her with such a blend of gratitude, for believing in me, and loathing, for her rigidity, that I can't speak. Do Westerners carry both me-first ego genes and self-doubt genes that, in combination, overcome the teachings of the Tantra?

"Answer me, Greta Bryn: Do you think I faked that faint?"

Mama knows already that I don't. She just wants me to assume the hair shirt of guilt for her indisposition and to pull it over my head with the bristly side inward. I have sufficient Easterner in my makeup to deny her that boon and the pinched ecstasy implicit in it. All at once dauntless, I hold her gaze, and hold it, until she begins to waver in her implacability.

"I didn't swoon solely because you tried to renounce your rebirth right, but also because you tried to humiliate me in front of Larry." Mama stands so far from the truth on this issue that she doesn't even qualify as wrong.

And so I laugh, like an evil-wisher rather than a daughter. "Not so," I say. "Why would I want to humiliate you before Larry?"

"Because I've always refused to coddle your self-doubts."

I recall Mama beholding Sakya's death mask and memorizing his every aura-lit feature. "What else caused you to 'fall out'?"

Her voice drops a register: "The Dalai Lama. His face. His hands. His body. His inhering and sustaining holiness."

"How does his 'sustaining holiness' knock you into a swoon, Mama?"

She peers across the courtyard road at the van where the DL lies in state. Then she pulls herself upright in the bower chair and tells this story:

"While married to your father, I began an affair with Minister Trungpa. He lived wherever Sakya lived, and Sakya chose to live among the secular citizens of Amdo and Kham rather than in the ridiculously scaled-down model of the Potala Palace in U-Tsang. As one result, Minister T and I easily met each other; and Nyendak—Neddy, I call him—courted me under the unsuspecting noses of both Sakya and Simon."

"You cuckolded my daddy with Minister T?" I need her to say it again.

"That's such an ugly old word to label what Neddy and I still regard as a sacred union."

"I'm sorry, Mama, but it's the prettiest word I know to call it."

"Don't condescend to me, Gee Bee."

"I won't. I can't. But I do have to ask: Who fathered me, the man I call Daddy or Sakya's old-fart chief minister?"

"Your father fathered you," Mama says. "Look at yourself in a mirror. Simon's face underlies your own. His blood runs through you, almost as if he gave his vitality to you and thus lost it himself."

"Maybe because you cuckolded him."

"That's crap. If anything, Simon's growing apathy and addiction to pod-lodging shoved me toward Neddy. Who, by the way, has the eggs, even at his age, to stay on the upright outside of a Z-pod."

"Mama, please."

"Listen, Neddy loves you. He cherishes you because he cherishes me. He sees you as just as much his own as Simon does. In fact, Neddy was the first to—"

"I'll stop saying 'cuckold' if you'll stop calling your boyfriend 'Neddy.' It sounds like filthy baby talk."

Mama closes her eyes, counts to herself, and opens them again to explain that when Sakya Gyatso at last figured out what was going on between Mama and Minister Trungpa, he called them to him and urged them to break off the affair in the interest of a higher spirituality and the preservation of shipboard harmony.

Minister T, ever the tutor, argued that although traditional Buddhism stems from a slavish obeisance to the demands of morality, wisdom cultivation, and ego abasement, the Tibetan Tantric path channels sexual attraction and its drives into the creation of life-force energies that purify these urges and tie them to transcendent spiritual purposes. My mother's marriage had unraveled; and Minister

T's courtship of her, which culminated in consensual carnality and a principled friendship, now demonstrated their mutual growth toward that higher spirituality.

I laugh out loud.

"And did His Holiness give your boyfriend a pass on this self-serving distortion of the Tantric way?"

"Believe as you will, but Neddy—Minister Trungpa's—take on the matter, and the thoroughness with which he laid out everything, had great effect on the DL. After all, Minister T had served as his regent in exile in Dharmasala, as his chief minister in India, and finally as his minister and friend here on the *Kalachakra*. Why would he all at once suppose this fount of integrity and wise counsel a scoundrel?"

"Maybe because he was surfing the wife of another man and justifying it with a lot of mystical malarkey."

Mama squints with thread-thin patience and resumes her story. Because of what Minister T and Mama had done, and still do, and what Minister T told His Holiness to justify their behavior, the Dalai Lama fell into a brown study that finally edged over into an ashen funk. To combat it, Sakya hibernated for three months, but emerged as low in spirits as he had gone into his egg. All his energies had weakened, and he told Minister T of his fears of dying before we reached Guge. Such talk profoundly fretted Mama's lover, who insisted that Sakya Gyatso tour the nursery in Amdo Bay. There he met me, Greta Bryn Brasswell. He was so smitten that he returned many times over the next few weeks, always singling me out for attention. He told Mama that my eyes reminded him of those of his baby sister, who had died very young of rheumatic fever.

"I remember meeting His Holiness," I tell Mama, "but not his visiting our nursery so often."

"You were four," Mama says. "How could you?"

She recounts how Minister T later took her to Sakya's upper-deck office in Amdo to talk about his long depression. With the AG generators running, they shared green tea and barley breads.

The DL again voiced his fear that even if he slept the rest of our journey, at some point in transit he would surrender his ghost in his eggshell pod and we his people would arrive at Guge with no agreed-upon leader. Minister T rebuked him for this worry, which he identified as egocentric, even though the DL took pains to articulate it as a concern for our common welfare.

Mama had carried me to this meeting. I lay sleeping—not like a pod-lodger but as a tired child—across her lap on a folded poncho liner that Simon had brought aboard as a going-away gift from a former roommate at Georgia Tech. As the adults talked, I turned and stretched, but never awakened.

"I don't recall that either," I say.

"Again, you were sleeping. Don't you listen to anything I tell you?"

"Everything. It's just that—" I stop myself. "Go on."

Mama does. She says that the DL walked over, leaned down, and placed his lips on my forehead, as if decaling it with a wet rose petal. Then he mused aloud about how fine it would be if, as an adult, I assumed his mantle and oversaw not only our voyagers' spiritual education but also our colonization of "The Land of Snow." He did not think he had the strength to undertake those tasks, but I would never exhaust my energy reserves. This fanciful scenario, Mama admits, rang in her like a crystal bell, a chime that echoed through her recurrently, as clear as unfiltered starlight.

Later, Mama and Minister T talked about their meeting with His Holiness and the tender wish-fulfillment musing with which he'd concluded it: my ascension to the Dalai Lamahood and eventual leadership on Guge. Mama asked if such a scenario could work itself out in reality, for if His Holiness died and Minister T championed me as he'd once stood behind Sakya, lifting him to his present eminence, then surely I, too, could rise to that height.

"'I'm too old for such fatiguing machinations again,' he told me," Mama says reminiscently, "but I said, 'Not by what I know of you, Neddy,' and just that expression of admiration and faith turned him."

I find Mama's account of this episode and her conspicuous pleasure in relating it hard to credit. But she has actually begun to glow, with a coppery aura akin to that of the DL in his display casket.

"At that point," she adds, "I got ambitious for you in a way that once never would have crossed my mind. Your ascension was just so far-fetched and prideful a thing for me to think about." She smiles adoringly, and my stomach shrinks upon itself like new linen applied wet to a metal frame.

"I've heard enough."

"Oh, no," Mama chides. "I've more, much more."

In blessed summary, she narrates a later conversation with Minister T, in which she urged him to carry to Sakya—now more a brooding Byronic hero than a Bodhisattva in spiritual balance—this news: that she had no objection, if any accident or fatal illness befell him, to his dispatching his migrating bhava into the body of her daughter. Thus, he could mix our subjective selves in ways that would propagate us both into the future and so assist us all in arriving safely at Gliese 581g.

Bristling, I try to get my head around this message. In fact, I ask Mama to repeat it. She does, and my deduction that she's memorized this nutty formula—if you like, call it a "spell"—sickens me.

Still, I ask, as I must, "Did Minister T carry this news to His Holiness?"

"He did."

"And what happened?"

"Sakya listened. He meditated for two days on the metaphysics and the practical ramifications of what I'd told him through his minister."

"Finish," I say. "Please just finish."

"On the following day, Sakya died."

"Cadillac infraction," I murmur. Mama's eyes widen. "Forgive me," I say. "What killed him? You used to tell me 'natural causes, but at too young an age for them to seem natural.'"

"That wasn't entirely a lie. Sakya did what came natural to him. He acted on the impulse of his growing despair and his burgeoning sense that if he waited much longer to influence his rebirth, you'd outgrow your primacy as a receptacle for the transfer of his mind-state sequences and he'd lose you as a crucible for compounding the two. So he called upon his mastery of many Tantric practices to drop his body temperature, heart rate, and blood pressure. And when he irreversibly stilled his heart, he passed from our illusory reality into bardo . . . until he awakened again wed to the samvattanika viññana, or evolving consciousness, animating you."

Here I float away from Mama's bower chair and drift a dozen meters across the courtyard to a lovely, low cedar hedge. (In a way that she's never fully understood, Nima Photrang was right about the cause of Sakya Gyatso's death.) I want to pour my guts into this hedge, to heave the burdensome reincarnated essence of the late DL into its feathery silver-green leaves.

Nothing comes up. Nothing comes out. My stomach feels smaller than a piñon nut. My ego, on the other hand, fills the entire tripartite passenger drum of our starship, The Wheel of Time.

Later, I meet Simon Brasswell—Daddy—in a back-tunnel lounge near Johkang Temple for chang and sandwiches. To make this date, of course, I first must visit his guesthouse and ping him at the registry screen, but he agrees to meet me at the Bhurel—as the place is called—with real alacrity. In fact, as soon as we lock-belt into our booth, with squeeze bottles for our drinks and mini-spikes in our sandwiches to hold them to the small cork table, Daddy key-taps payment before I can object. He looks better since his nap, but the violet circles under his eyes lend him a sad fragility.

"I never knew—" I begin.

"That Karen and I divorced because she fell in love with Nyendak Trungpa? Or, I suppose, with his self-vaunted virility and political clout?"

Speechless, I gape at my father.

"Forgive me. Ordinarily, I try not to go the spurned-spouse route."

I still can't speak.

He squeezes his bottle and swigs some barley beer. Then he says, "Do you want what your mama and Minister T want for you—I mean, really?"

"I don't know. I've never known. But this afternoon Mama told me why I ought to want it. And because I ought to, I do. I think."

Daddy studies me with an unsettling mixture of exasperation and tenderness. "Let me ask you something, straight up: Do you think the bhava of Sakya Gyatso, the direct reincarnation of Avalokiteshvara, the ancestor of the Tibetan people, dwells in you as it supposedly dwelt in his twenty predecessors?"

"Daddy, I'm not Tibetan."

"I didn't ask you that." He unspikes and chomps into his Cordyceps, or synthetic caterpillar-fungus, sandwich. Chewing, he manages a quasi-intelligible, "Well?"

"Tomorrow's gold-urn lottery will reveal the truth, one way or the other."

"Yak shit, Greta. And I didn't ask you that, either."

I feel both my tears and my gorge rising, but the latter prevails. "I thought we'd share some time, eat together—not get into a spat."

Daddy chews more sedately, swallows, and re-spikes his 'caterpillar' to the cork. "And what else, sweetheart? Avoid saying anything true or substantive?" I show him my profile. "Greta, forgive me, but I didn't sign on to this mission to sire a demigod. I didn't even sign on to it to colonize another world for the sake of oppressed Tibetan Buddhists and their rabid hangers-on."

"I thought you were a Tibetan Buddhist."

"Oh, yeah, born and raised . . . in Boulder, Colorado. Unfortunately, it never quite took. I signed on because I loved your mother and the idea of spaceflight at least as much as I did passing for a Buddhist. And that's how I got out here more or less seventeen light-years from home. Do you see?"

I eat nothing. I drink nothing. I say nothing.

"At least I've told you a truth," Daddy says. "More than one, in fact. Can't you do the same for me? Or does the mere self-aggrandizing idea of Dalai Lamahood clamp your windpipe shut on the truth?"

I have expected neither these revelations nor their vehemence, but together they work to unclamp something inside me. I owe my father my life, at least in part, and the dawning awareness that he has never stopped caring for me suggests—in fact, requires— that I repay him truth for truth.

"Yes, I can do the same for you."

Daddy's eyes, above their bruised half-circles, never leave mine.

"I didn't choose this life at all," I say. "It was thrust upon me. I want to be a good person, a Bodhisattva possibly, maybe even the Dalai Lama. But—"

He lifts his eyebrows and goes on waiting. A tender twinge of a smile plays about his mouth.

"But," I finish, "I'm not happy that maybe I want these things."

"Buddhists don't aspire to happiness, Greta, but to an oceanic detachment."

I give him my fiercest Peeved Daughter look, but do refrain from eye-ball-rolling. "I just need an attitude adjustment, that's all."

"The most wrenching attitude adjustment in the universe won't turn a carp into a cougar, pumpkin." His pet name for me.

"I don't need the most wrenching attitude adjustment in the universe. I need a self-willed tweaking."

"Ah." Daddy takes a squeeze-swig of his beer and encourages me with an inviting gesture to eat.

My gorge has fallen, my hunger reappeared. I eat and drink and, as I do, become unsettlingly aware that other patrons in the Bhurel—visitors, monks—have detected my presence. Blessedly, though, they respect our space.

"Suppose the lottery goes young Trimon's way," Daddy says. "What would make you happy in your resulting alternate life?"

I consider this as a peasant woman of a past era might have done if a friend had asked, just as a game, 'What would you do if the King chose you to marry his son?' But I play the game in reverse, sort of, and can only shake my head.

Daddy waits. He doesn't stop waiting, or searching my eyes, or studying me with his irksome unwavering paternal regard. He won't speak, maybe because everything else about him—his gaze, his patience, his presence—speaks strongly of what for years went unspoken between us.

Full of an inarticulate wistfulness, I lean back. "I've told you a truth already," I inform my father. "Isn't that enough for tonight?"

A teenage girl and her mother, oaring subtly with their hands to maintain their places beside us, hover at our table. Even though I haven't seen the girl for several years (while, of course, she hibernized), I recognize her: Distinctive agate eyes in an elfin face identify her at once.

Daddy and I both lever ourselves up from our places, and I swim out to embrace the girl. "Alicia!" Over her shoulder, I say to her mother in all earnestness, "Mrs. Paljor, how good to see you here!"

"Forgive us for interrupting," Mrs. Paljor says. "We've come for the Gold Urn Festival, and we just had to wish you success tomorrow. Alicia wouldn't rest until Kanjur found a way for us to attend."

Kanjur Paljor, Alicia's father, has served since the beginning of our voyage as our foremost antimatter-ice fuel specialist. If anyone could get his secular wife and daughter to U-Tsang for the DL lottery, Kanjur Paljor could. He enjoys the authority of universal respect. As for Alicia, she scrunches her face in embarrassment, as well as unconditional affection. She recalls the many times that I came to Momo House to hold her, and later to her family's Kham Bay rooms to take her on walks or on outings to our art, mathematics, and science centers.

"Thank you," I say. "Thank you."

I hug the girl. I hug her mother.

My father nods and smiles, albeit bemusedly. I suspect that Daddy has never met Alicia or Mrs. Paljor before. Kanjur, the father and husband, he undoubtedly knows. Who doesn't know that man?

The Paljor women depart almost as quickly as they came. Daddy watches them go, with a deep exhalation of relief that makes me hurt for them both.

"I was almost a second mother to that girl," I tell him.

Daddy oars himself downward, back into his seat. "Surely, you exaggerate. Mrs. Paljor looks more than sufficient to the task."

Long before noon of the next day, the courtyard of the Jokhang Temple swarms with levitating lamas, monks, nuns, yogis, and some authorized visitors from the *Kalachakra's* other two passenger bays. I cannot explain how I feel. If Mama's story of Sakya Gyatso's heart attack is true, then I cannot opt out of the gold-urn lottery.

To do so would constitute a terrible insult to his punarbhava, or karmic change from one life vessel to the next, or from his body to mine. Mine, as everyone knows, established its bona fides as a living entity years before Sakya Gyatso died. Also, opting out would constitute a heartless slap in the face of all believers, of all who support me in this enterprise. Still . . . .

Does Sakya have the right to self-direct his rebecoming, or I the right to thwart his will . . . or only the obligation to accede to it? So much self will and worry taints today's ceremony that Larry and Kilkhor, if not Minister T, can hardly conceive of it as deriving from Buddhist tenets at all.

Or can they? Perhaps a society rushing at twenty percent of light-speed toward some barely imaginable karmic epiphany has slipped the surly bonds not only of Earth but also of the harnessing principles of Buddhist Tantra. I don't know. I know only that I can't withdraw from this lottery without betraying a good man who esteemed me in the noblest and most innocent of senses.

And so, in our filigreed vestments, Jetsun Trimon and I swim up to the circular dais to which the attendants of the Panchen Lama have already fastened the gold urn for our name slips.

In set-back vertical ranks, choruses of floating monks and nuns chant as we await the drawing. Our separate retinues hold or adjust their altitudes behind us, both to hearten us and to keep their sight lanes clear. Tiny levitating cameras, costumed as birds, televise the event to community members in all three bays.

Jetsun's boyish face looks at once exalted and terrified.

Lhundrub Gelek, the Panchen Lama, lifts his arms and announces that the lottery has begun. Today he blazes with the bearing and the ferocity of a Hebrew seraph. Tug-monks keep him from rising in gravid slow motion to the ceiling. Abbess Yeshe Yargag levitates about a meter to his right, with tug-nuns to keep her from wandering up, down, or sideways. Gelek reports that name slips for Jetsun Trimon and Greta Bryn Brasswell already drift about in the oversized urn attached to the dais. Neither of us, he says, needs to maneuver forward to reach into the urn and pull out a name-slip envelope. Nor do we need surrogates to do so.

We will simply wait.

We will simply wait . . . until an envelope rises on its own from the urn.

Then Gelek will grab it, open the envelope, and read the name-slip aloud for all those watching in the Temple hall or via telelinks. Never mind that our wait could take hours, and that, if it does, viewers in every bay will volunteer to rejoin the vast majority of our population in ursidormizine slumber.

And so we wait.

And so we wait . . . and finally a small blue envelope rises through the mouth of the crosshatched gold urn. A tug-monk snatches it from the air, before it can descend out of view again, and hands it to the PL.

Startled, because he's nodded off several times over the past fifty-some minutes, Gelek opens the envelope, pulls out the name slip, reads it to himself, and passes it on to Abbess Yargag, whose excited tug-nuns steady her so that she may announce the name of the true Soul Child.

Of course, that the Abbess has copped this honor tells everybody all that we need to know. She can't even speak the name on the slip before many in attendance begin to clap their palms against their shoulders. The upshot of this applause, beyond opening my tear ducts, is a sudden propulsion of persons at many different altitudes about the hall: a wheeling zero-g waltz of approbation.

YEARS IN TRANSIT: 95
COMPUTER LOGS OF OUR RELUCTANT DALAI LAMA, AGE 20

The Panchen Lama, his peers and subordinates in U-Tsang, and secular hierarchs from Amdo and Kham have made my parents starship nobles.

They have bestowed similar, if slightly lesser honors, on Jetsun Trimon's parents and on Jetsun himself, who wishes to serve us colonizers as Bodhisattva, meteorologist, and lander pilot. In any event, his religious and scientific educations proceed in parallel, and he spends as much time in tech training in Kham Bay as he does in the monasteries in U-Tsang.

As for me, I alternate months among our three drums, on a rotation that pleases more of our ghosts than it annoys. I ask no credit for the wisdom of this scheme, though; I simply wish to rule (although I prefer the verb 'preside') in a way promoting shipboard harmony and reducing our inevitable conflicts.

YEARS IN TRANSIT: 99
COMPUTER LOGS OF OUR RELUCTANT DALAI LAMA, AGE 24

I've now spent nearly five years in this allegedly holy office. Earlier today, thinking hard about our arrival at Guge, in only a little over seven Earth years, I summoned Minister Trungpa to my quarters.

"Yes, Your Holiness, what do you wish?" he asked.

"To invite everyone aboard the *Kalachakra* to submit designs for a special sand mandala. This mandala will commemorate our voyage's inevitable end and honor it as a fruit of the Hope and Community"—I capitalized the words as I spoke them—"that drove us, or our elders, to undertake this journey."

Minister T frowns. "Submit designs?"

"Your new auditory aids work quite well."

"For a competition?"

"Any voyager, any Kalachakran at all, may submit a design."

"But—"

"The artist monks in U-Tsang, who will create this mandala, will judge the entries blindly to determine our finalists. I'll decide the winner."

Minister T does not make eye contact. "The idea of a contest undercuts one of the themes that you wish your mandala to embody, that of Community."

"You hate the whole idea?"

He hedges: "Appoint a respected Yellow Hat artist to design the mandala. In that way, you'll avoid a bureaucratic judging process and lessen popular discontent."

"Look, Neddy, a competition will amuse everyone, and after a century aboard this vacuum-vaulting bean can, we could all use some amusement."

Neddy would like to dispute the point, but I am the Dalai Lama, and what can he say that will not seem a coddling or a defiant promotion of his own ego? Nothing. (May Chenrezig forgive me, but I relish his discomfiture.) Clearly, the West animates parts of my ego that I should better hide from those of my subjects—a term I loathe—immersed in Eastern doctrines that guarantee their fatalism and docility. Of course, how many men of Minister Trungpa's station and age enjoy carrying out the bidding of a woman a mere twenty-four-years old?

At length he softly says, "I'll see to it, Your Holiness."

"I can see to it myself, but I wanted your opinion."

He nods, his look implying that his opinion doesn't count for much, and takes a deferential step back.

"Don't leave. I need your advice."

"As much as you needed my opinion?"

I take his arm and lead him to a nook where we can sit and talk as intimates. Fortunately, the AG has worked much more reliably all over the ship than it did before my investiture. Neddy looks grizzled, fatigued, and wary, and although he doesn't yet understand why, he has cause for this wariness.

"I want to have a baby," I tell him.

He responds instantly: "I advise you not to, Your Holiness."

"I don't solicit your advice in that area. I'd like you to help me settle on a father for the child."

Neddy reddens. I've stolen his breath. He'd like to make a devastatingly incisive remark, but can't even manage a feeble Ugh. "In case it's crossed your mind, I haven't short-listed you—although Mama once gave you a terrific, if unasked for, recommendation."

Minister T pulls himself together, but he's squeezing his hands in his lap as if to express oil from between them.

"I've narrowed the candidates down to two, Jetsun Trimon and Ian Kilkhor, but lately I've started tilting toward Jetsun."

"Then tilt toward Ian."

"Why?"

And Mama's lover provides me with good, dispassionate reasons for selecting the older man: physical fitness, martial arts ability, maturity, intelligence, learning (secular, religious, and technical), administrative/organizational skills, and long-standing affection for me. Jetsun, not yet twenty, has two or three separate callings that he has not yet had time to explore as fully as he ought, and the difference in our ages will lead many in our community to suppose that I have exercised my power in an unseemly way to bring him to my bed. I should give the kid his space.

I know from private conversations, though, that when Jetsun was ten, an unnamed senior monk in Amdo often employed him as a drombo, or passive sex partner, and that the experience nags at him now in ways that Jetsun cannot easily articulate. Apparently, the community didn't see fit, back then, to exercise its outrage on behalf of a boy not yet officially identified as a Soul Child. Of course, the community didn't know, or chose not to know, and uproars rarely result from awareness of such liaisons, anyway. Isn't a monk a man? I say none of this to Neddy.

"Choose Ian," he says, "if you must choose one or the other."

Yesterday, in Kham Bay, after I extended an intranet invitation to him to come see me about his father, who lies ill in his eggshell pod, Jetsun Trimon called upon me in the upper-level stateroom that I inherited, so to speak, from my predecessor. Jetsun fell on his knees before me, seized my wrist, and put his lips to the beads, bracelet, and watch that I wear about it. He wanted prayers for his father's recovery, and I acceded to this request with all my heart.

Then something occurred that I set down with joy rather than guilt. I wanted more from Jetsun than gratitude for my prayers, and he wanted more than my prayers for his worry about his father or for his struggles to master all his studies. Like me, he wished the solace of the flesh, and as one devoted to compassion, forgiveness, contentment, and the alleviation of pain, I took him to my bed and divested him of his garments and let him divest me of mine. Then we embraced, neither of us trembling, or sweating, or flinching in discomfort or distress, for my quarters hummed at a subsonic frequency with enough warmth and gravity to offset any potential malaise or annoyance. Altogether sweetly, his tenderness matched mine. However—

Like most healthy young men, Jetsun quickly reached a coiled-spring readiness. He quivered on Go.

I rolled over and bestrode him above the waist, holding his arms to the side and speaking with as much integrity as my gnosis of bliss and emptiness could generate. He calmed and listened. I said that I begrudged neither of us this tension-easing union, but that if we proceeded, then he must know that I wanted his seed to enter me, to take root, to turn embryo, and to attain fruition as our child.

"Do you understand?"

"Yes."

"Do you consent?"

"I consent."

"Do you further consent to acknowledge this child and to assist in its rearing on the planet Guge, as well as on this ship?"

He considered these queries. And, smiling, he agreed.

"Then we may advance to the third exalted initiation," I said, "that of the mutual experience of connate joy."

I slid backward over the pliable warmth of his standing phallus and kissed him in the middle of his chest. He reached for me, tenderly, and the AG generators abruptly cut off—suspiciously, it seemed to me. I floated toward the ceiling like a buoyant nixie, too startled to yelp or laugh. Jetsun shoved off in pursuit, but hit a bulkhead and glanced off it horizontally.

It took us a while to reunite, to find enough purchase to consummate our resolve, and to do so honoring the fact that a resurgence of gravity could injure, even kill, both of us. Nonetheless, we managed, and managed passionately.

The 'night' has now passed. Jetsun sleeps, mind eased and body sated.

I sit at this console, lock-belted in, recording the most stirring encounter of my life. Every nerve and synapse of my body, and every scrap of assurance in my soul, tell me that Jetsun and I have conceived: Alleluia.

YEARS IN TRANSIT: 100
COMPUTER LOGS OF OUR RELUCTANT DALAI LAMA, AGE 25

Some history: Early in our voyage, when our AG generators worked reliably, our monks created one sand mandala a year. They did so then, as they do now, in a special studio in the Yellow Hat gompa in U-Tsang. They kept materials for these productions—colored grains of sand, bits of stone or bone, dyed rice grains, sequins—in hard plastic cylinders and worked on their designs over several days. Upon finishing the mandalas, our monks chanted to consecrate them and then, as a dramatic enactment of the impermanent nature of existence, destroyed them by sweeping a brush over and swirling their deity-inhabited geometries into inchoate slurries.

These methods of creating and destroying the mandalas ended four decades into our flight when a gravity outage led to the premature disintegration of a design. A slow-motion sandstorm filled the studio. Grains of maroon, citron, turquoise, emerald, indigo, and blood-red drifted all about, and recovering these for fresh projects required the use of hand-vacs and lots of fussy hand-sorting. Nobody wished to endure such a disaster again. And so, soon thereafter, the monks implemented two new procedures for laying out and completing the mandalas.

One involved gluing down the grains, but this method made the graceful ruination of a finished mandala dicey. A second method involved inserting and arranging the grains into pie-shaped plastic shields using magnets and tech-manipulated "delivery straws," but these tedious procedures, while heightening the praise due the artists, so lengthened the process and stressed the monks that Sakya Gyatso ceased asking for annual mandalas and mandated their fashioning only once every five years.

In any case, today marks our one-hundredth year in flight, and I am fat with a female child who bumps around inside me like those daredevils in old vidped clips who whooshed up and down the sloped walls of special competition arenas on rollers called skateboards.

I think the kid wants out already, but Karma Hahn, my baby doc, tells me she's still much too small to exit, even if the kid does carry on like 'a squirrel on an exercise wheel.' That metaphor endears both the kid and Karma to me. Because the kid moves, I move. I stroll about my private audience chamber, aka 'The Sunshine Hall,' in the Potala Palace in U-Tsang. I've voluntarily removed here to show my fellow Buddhists that I am not ashamed of my fecund condition.

Ian announces a visitor, and in walks First Officer Nima Photrang, whom I've not seen for weeks. She has come, it happens, not solely to visit me, but also to look in on an uncle who resides in the nearby Yellow Hat gompa. She has brought a khata, a white silk greeting scarf, even though I already have enough of these damned rags to stitch together a ship cover for the *Kalachakra*. She drapes it around my neck. Laughing, I pull it off and drape it around hers.

"Your design contest spurs on every amateur-artist ghost in Amdo and Kham," Nima says. "If you wish your mandala to further community enlightenment by projecting an image of our future Palace of Hope on Guge, well, you've got a lot of folks worrying away at it—mission fully goosed, if not yet fully cooked."

I realize that Sakya Gyatso, my predecessor, his eye on Tibetan history, called the world toward which we relentlessly cruise 'Guge,' partly for the g in Gliese 581g. What an observant and subtle man.

"Nima," I ask, "have you submitted a design?"

"No, but you'll probably never guess who intends to."

No, I never will. I gape cluelessly at Nima.

"Captain Xao Songda, our helmsman. He spends enormous chunks of time with a drafting compass and a pen, or at his console refining design programs that a monk in U-Tsang uploaded a while back to Pemako."

Pemako is the latest version of our intranet. I like to use it. Virtually nightly (stet the pun), it shows me deep-sea sonograms of my jetting squid-kid.

"I hope Captain Xao doesn't expect his status as our shipboard Buzz Lightyear to score him any brownies with the judges."

Nima chortles. "Hardly. He drew as a boy and as a teenager. Later, he designed maglev stations and epic mountain tunnels. He figures he has as good a chance as anyone in a blind judging, and if he wins, what a personal coup!"

"Mmm," I say.

"No, really, you've created a monster, Your Holiness—but, as one of the oldest persons aboard, he deserves his fun, I guess."

We chat some more. Nima asks if she may lay her palm on the curve of my belly, and I say yes. When the brat-to-be surfs my insides like a berserk skateboarder, Nima and I laugh like schoolgirls. By some criteria, I still qualify.

YEARS IN TRANSIT: 101
COMPUTER LOGS OF OUR RELUCTANT DALAI LAMA, AGE 25-26

I return to Amdo to deliver my child. Early in the hundred and first year of our journey, my water breaks. Karma Hahn, my mother, and Alicia and Emily Paljor attend my lying-in, while my father, Ian Kilkhor, Minister Trungpa, and Jetsun perform a nervous do-si-do in an antechamber. I give the guys hardly a thought. Delivering a kid requires stamina, a lot of Tantric focus, and a cooperative fetus, but I've got 'em all and the kid slams on out in under four hours.

I lie in a freshly made bed with my squiddle dozing in a warming blanket against my left shoulder. Well-wishers and family surround us like sentries, although I have no idea what they've got to shield us from: I've never felt safer.

Mama says, "When will you tell us the ruddy shrimp's name? You've kept it a secret eight months past forever."

"Ask Jetsun. He chose it."

Everyone turns to Jetsun, who at twenty-one looks like a fabled Kham warrior, lean and smooth-faced, a flawless bronze sculpture of himself. How can I not love him? Jetsun looks to me. I nod.

"It's . . . it's Kyipa." Like the sweetheart he is, he blushes.

"Ah," Nyendak Trungpa sighs. "Happiness."

"If we all didn't strive so damned hard for happiness," Daddy says, "we'd almost always have a pretty good time."

"You stole that," Mama rebukes him. "And your timing sucks."

From behind those crowded about my babe-cave, a short, sturdy, gray-haired man edges in. I know him as Alicia Paljor's father, Emily Paljor's husband—but Daddy, Ian, and Neddy know him as the chief fuel specialist on our strut-ship and thus a personage of renowned ability. So I assume he's come—like a wise man—to kneel beside and to adore our newborn squiddle. Or has he come just to meet his wife and daughter and fetch them back to their stateroom?

In his ministerial capacity, Neddy says, "Welcome, Specialist Paljor."

"I need to talk to Her Holiness." Kanjur Paljor bows and approaches my bed. "If I may, Your Holiness."

"Of course."

The area clears of everyone except Paljor, Ian Kilkhor, Kyipa, and me. A weight descends—a weight comprising everything that's ever floated free of its moorings during every AG quittage that our strut-ship has ever suffered—and that weight, condensed into one tiny spherical mass, lowers itself onto my baby's back and so onto me, crushing this blissful moment into dust and slivered glass. Ian edges to the top of my bed, but I already know that his strength and his heavy glare will prove impotent against whatever message Kanjur Paljor has brought.

Paljor says, "Your Holiness, I beg your infinite pardon."

"Tell me."

He looks at Ian and then, in petition, at me again. "I'd prefer to deliver this news to you alone, Your Holiness."

"I'm not here," Ian declares. "Proceed on that assumption."

"Regard my agent's simultaneous presence and absence as an enacted mystery or koan," I tell Paljor. "He speaks a helpful truth."

Paljor nods and seizes my free hand. "About fifteen hours ago, I found a serious navigational anomaly while running a fuel-tank check. Before bringing the problem to you, I ran some figures to make sure that I hadn't made a calculation error; that I wasn't just overreacting to a situation of no real consequence." He pauses to touch my Kyipa's blanket. "How much technical detail do you want, Your Holiness?"

"Right now, none. Give me the gist."

"For a little over one hundred and twenty hours, the *Kalachakra* traveled at its top speed at a small angle off our requisite heading."

"How? Why?"

"Before I answer, let me assure you that we've since corrected for this deviation and that we'll soon run true again."

"What do you mean, 'soon'? Why don't we 'run true' now?"

"We do, Your Holiness, in the sense that First Officer Photrang has set us on an efficient angle to intercept our former heading to Guge. But we don't, in the sense that we still must compensate for the unintended divergence."

Ian Kilkhor says, "Tell Her Holiness why this 'unintended divergence' constitutes one huge fucking threat."

Totally appalled, I look back at my bodyguard and friend. "I thought you weren't here! Or did you leave behind just that part of you that views me as an unteachable idiot? Go away, Mr. Kilkhor. Get out."

Kilkhor has the decency and good sense to do as I command. Kyipa, unsettled by my outburst, squirms fretfully on my shoulder.

"The danger," I tell Kanjur Paljor, "centers on fuel expenditure. If we've gone too far off course, we won't have enough antimatter ice left to reach Guge. Have I admissibly described our peril?"

"Yes, Your Holiness." He doesn't fall to one knee, like a magus beside the infant deity Christ, but crouches so that our faces are nearly at a level. "I believe—I think—we have just enough fuel to complete our journey, but at this late stage it could prove a close thing. If there's another emergency requiring any additional course correction, that could place us in danger of—"

"—not arriving at all."

Paljor nods, and consolingly pats Kyipa's playing-card back.

"How did this happen?"

"Human error, I'm afraid."

"Tell me what sort."

"Lack of attention to the telltales that should have prevented this divergence from our heading."

"Whose error? Captain Xao's?"

"Yes, Your Holiness. Nima says his mental state has deteriorated badly over these past few weeks. What she first thought eccentricities, she now views as evidence of age-related mental debilities. He stays awake so long and endures so much stress. And he puts too much faith in the alleged reliability of our electronic systems."

Also, he came to feel that creating a design for my Palace of Hope mandala took precedence over his every other duty on a strut-ship programmed to fly to its destination, with the result that he put himself on auto-pilot too.

"Where is he now?" I ask Paljor.

"Sleeping, under medical supervision—not ursidormizine slumber but bed rest, Your Holiness."

I thank Paljor and dismiss him.

Clutching Kyipa to me, I nuzzle her sweet-smelling face.

Tomorrow, I'll tell Nima to advise her flight crew that they must remain up-phase ghosts until we know for sure the outcomes of Xao's inattention and our efforts to correct for its potential consequences: a headlong rush to nowhere.

Without benefit of lock belts, my daughter Kyipa kicks in her bassinet. I seldom worry about her floating off during AG outages because she loves such spells of weightlessness. She uses them to exercise her limbs—admittedly, with no strengthening resistance—and to explore our stateroom, which boasts Buddha figurines, wall hangings, filigreed star charts, miniature starship models, and other interesting items. At five months, she thinks herself a big finch or a pygmy porpoise. She undulates about, giggling at the currents she creates, or, the AG restored, inches along with her pink tongue tip between her lips and her bum rising and falling like a migrating molehill.

As Dalai Lama (many argue), I should never have borne this squiddle, but Karen, Simon, Jetsun, and Jetsun's mama disagree, and all contribute to her care. Even Minister T acknowledges that conceiving and bearing her has confirmed my sense of the karmic rightness of my Dalai Lamahood more powerfully than any other event to date. Because of this sunny girl, I do stronger, better, holier work.

To those who tsk-tsk when they see Kyipa squirming in my arms, I say:

"Here is my Wheel of Time, my mandala, who has as one purpose to further my evolving enlightenment. Her other purposes she will learn and fulfill in time. So set aside your resentments that you may more easily fulfill yours."

But although I don't fret about Kyipa during gravity outages, I do worry about her future . . . and ours.

Will we safely arrive at the Gliese 581 system? Of the fifty antimatter-ice tanks with which (long before my birth) we started our journey, we've used up and discarded thirty-eight, and Paljor says that we have exhausted nearly half of the thirty-ninth tank, with over five and a half years remaining until our ETA in orbit around Guge. From the outside, our ship begins to resemble a skeleton of its outbound self, the bones of a picked-clean fish. And if the *Kalachakra* makes it at all, as Paljor has speculated, it will slice the issue scarily close.

I stupidly assumed that our eventual shift into deceleration mode would work in our favor, but Paljor cautioned that slowing our strut-ship—so that we do not overshoot Guge, like a golf putt running up to but not beyond its cup—will require more fuel than I supposed. Later he showed me math proving that reaching Guge will require "an incident-free approach"—because our antimatter-ice reserves, the fail-safe tanks with which we began our flight, have already dissolved into the ether slipstreaming by the magnetic field coils generating our plasma shield out front.

Still, I don't believe in shielding our human freight from issues bearing on our survival. Therefore, I've had Minister T announce the fact of this crisis to everyone up-phase and working. Thankfully, general panic has not ensued. Instead, crew members brainstorm stopgap strategies for conserving fuel, and the monks and nuns in U-Tsang pray and chant. Soon enough, when we begin to brake, everyone will arise again, shake off the fog of hibernizing, and learn the truth about our final approach. Then every deck will teem with ghosts preparing to orbit Guge; to assay the habitable wedges between its sun-stuck face and its bleaker side; and to decide which of the two wedges is better suited to settlement.

YEARS IN TRANSIT: 102
COMPUTER LOGS OF OUR RELUCTANT DALAI LAMA, AGE 27

Captain Xao Songda, our deposed captain, died just twelve hours ago. Although Kyipa celebrated her first birthday last week, the man never laid eyes on her.

Xao's 'bed rest' turned into pathological pacing and harangues unintelligible to anyone ignorant of Mandarin Chinese. These behaviors—symptomatic of an aggressive type of senility unknown to us—our medicos treated with tranks, placebos (foolishly, I guess), experimental diets, and long walks through the commons of Kham Bay. Nothing calmed him or eased the intensity of his gibbering tirades. I had so wanted Kyipa to meet this man (or the avatar of the self preceding this sorry incarnation), but I could not risk exposing her to one of his abusive rants.

It bears stating, though, that everyone aboard *Kalachakra*, knowing the sacrifices that the captain made for us, forgives him his navigation error. All showed him the honor, courtesy, and patience that he deserved for these sacrifices. Nima Photrang, who assumed his captaincy, believes he and Sakya Gyatso suffered similar personality disintegrations, albeit in different ways. Sakya used Tantric practices to end his life and Xao Songda fell to an Alzheimer's-like scourge, but the effects of sleep deprival, suppressed anxiety, and overwork ultimately caused their deaths.

Xao created designs for my mandala competition, I think, as a way to decompress from these burdens. During the last hours of his illness, Ian Kilkhor searched his quarters for anything that could help us fathom his disease and preserve our memory of him as the intrepid Tibetan Buddhist who carried us within three lights of our destination. However, Ian returned to me with two hundred hand-drawn sketches and computer-assisted designs for my Palace of Hope mandala.

These "designs" appalled and saddened us. The ones Xao hand-drew resemble big multicolored Rorschach blots, and those stemming from his cyber-design programs look like geometrically askew fever dreams. All are pervaded with interlocking claws, jagged teeth, vermiform bodies, and occluded reptilian eyes. None could serve as a model for the mandala of my envisioning.

"I'm sorry," Ian said. "The old guy seems to have swallowed the pituitary gland of a Komodo dragon."

So, given our fuel situation and Captain Xao's death, I've declared a moratorium on mandala-design creation.

Now there is a strong movement afoot—a respectful one—to eject Captain Xao Songda's corpse into the void, one more human collop for the highballing dark. As I've already noted here, we've used this procedure many times before, as a practice coincident with Buddha Dharma and, in this case, as one befitting a helmsman of Xao's stature. But I resist this seeming consensus in favor of a better option: taking the captain to Guge and setting his sinewy body out on an escarpment there, to blacken in its gales and scale in its thaws, our first sacrificial alms to the planet.

*

One work cycle past, Captain Photrang began to brake the *Kalachakra*. We are four years out from Gliese 581g, and Kanjur Paljor tells me that, unless a meteorite penetrates our plasma shield or some anomalous disaster befalls us, we will reach our destination. Ian observes that we will coast into planetary orbit like a vehicle with an internal-combustion engine chugging into its pit on fumes.

I don't fully twig the analogy, but I get its gist. Alleluia! If only time passed more quickly . . . .

Meanwhile, I keep Kyipa awake and ignore those misguided ghosts advising me to ease her into grave-cave sleep so that time will pass more quickly for her. Jetsun and I enjoy her far too much to send her down. More important, if she stays up-phase most of the rest of our journey, she will learn and grow; and when we descend to the surface of Guge with her, she will have a sharper mind and better motor skills at five or six than any long-term sleeper of roughly similar age.

Every day, every hour, my excitement intensifies. And our ship plows on.

YEARS IN TRANSIT: 106
COMPUTER LOGS OF OUR RELUCTANT DALAI LAMA, AGE 31

Maintenance preoccupies nearly everyone aboard. In less than a week, our strut-ship will rendezvous with Guge and orbit its oblate sun-locked mass. Then we will make several sequential descents to and returns from "The Land of Snow" aboard our lander, The Yak Butter Express.

Jetsun will serve as shuttle pilot for one of these first excursions and as backup on another. He and others perform daily checks on the vehicle in its hangar harnesses, just as other techs strive to ensure the reliability of every mechanical and human component. Our hopes and anxieties contend. At my urging, the Bodhisattvas of U-Tsang go from place to place assisting in our labors and transmitting positive energy to every bay and to all those at work in them.

Twelve hours after Captain Photrang eased *Kalachakra* into orbit around Guge, Minister T comes to me to report that Yellow Hat artists in U-Tsang have finished a sand mandala based on a design that they, not I, chose as our most esteemed entry.

Lucinda Gomez, a teen-ager from Amdo Bay, has taken the laurel.

Neddy asked the monks to transport the mandala in its pie-shaped shield to Bhava Park, a commons here in Kham Bay, and they do so. A bird camera in the park transmits the mandala's image to public screens and to vidped consoles everywhere. Intricate and colorful, it sits on an easel amid a host of tables and happy Kalachakrans. Because we're celebrating our arrival, I don't watch on a screen but stand in Bhava Park before the thing itself. Banners and prayer flags abound. I seize Kyipa's hand and approach the easel. I congratulate the excited Lucinda Gomez and all the artist monks, and also speak to many onlookers, who attend smilingly to my words.

The Yellow Hats chant verses of consecration that affirm their fulfillment of my charge and then extend to everyone the blessings of Hope and Community implicit in the mandala's labyrinthine central Palace. Kyipa, now almost six, touches the bottom of the encased mandala.

"This is the prettiest," she says.

She has never before seen a finished mandala in its full artifactual glory.

Then the artist monks start to carry the shield from its easel to a tabletop, there to insert narrow tubes into it and send the mandala's fixed grains flying with focused blasts of air—to symbolize, as tradition dictates, the primacy of impermanence in our lives. But before they reach the table, I lift my hand.

"We won't destroy this sand mandala," I declare, "until we've established a viable settlement on Guge."

And everyone around us in Bhava Park cheers. The monks restore the mandala to its easel, a ton of colored confetti drops from suspended bins above us, music plays, and people sing, dance, eat, laugh, and mingle.

Kyipa, holding her hands up to the drifting paper and plastic flakes, beams at me ecstatically.

In our shuttle-cum-lander, we glide from the belly of Kham Bay toward Gliese 581g, better known to all aboard the *Kalachakra* as Guge, "The Land of Snow."

From here, the amiable dwarf star about which Guge swings resembles the yolk of a colossal fried egg, more reddish than yellow-orange, with a misty orange corona about it like the egg's congealed albumin. I've made it sound ugly, but Gliese 581 looks edible to me and quickly trips my hunger to reach the planet below.

As for Guge, it gleams beneath us like an old coin.

In our first week on its surface, we have already built a tent camp in one of the stabilized climate zones of the nearside terminator. Across the tall visible arc of that terminator, the planet shows itself marbled by a bluish and slate-gray crust marked by fingerlike snowfields and glacier sheets.

On the ground, our people call their base camp Lhasa and the rugged territory all about it New Tibet. In response to this naming and to the alacrity with which our fellow Kalachakrans adopted it, Minister Trungpa wept openly.

I find I like the man. Indeed, I go down for my first visit to the surface with his blessing. (Simon, my father, already bivouacs there, to investigate ways to grow barley, winter wheat, and other grains in the thin air and cold temperatures.) Kyipa, of course, remains for now on our orbiting strut-ship—in Neddy's stateroom, which he now shares openly with the child's grandmother, Karen Bryn Bonfils. Neddy and Karen Bryn dote on my daughter shamefully.

Our descent to Lhasa won't take long, but, along with many others in this second wave of pioneers, I deliberately drop into a meditative trance. I focus on a photograph that Neddy gave me after the mandala ceremony at the arrival celebration, and I recall his words as he presented it.

"Soon after you became a teenager, Greta, I started to doubt your commitment to the Dharma and your ability to stick."

"How tactful of you to wait till now to tell me," I said, smiling.

"But I never lost a deeper layer of faith. Today, I can say that all my unspoken doubt has burned off like a summer meadow mist." He gave me the worn photo—not a hardened d-cube—that now engages my attention.

In it, a Tibetan boy of eight or nine faces the viewer with a broad smile. He holds before him, also facing the viewer, a baby girl with rosy cheeks and eyes so familiar that I tear up in consternation and joy. The eyes belong to my predecessor's infant sister, who didn't live long after the capturing of this image.

The eyes also belong to Kyipa.

I meditate on this conundrum, richly. Soon, after all, the Yak Butter Express will set down in New Tibet.

Sean McMullen has been a full time author since 2014, but as an after-hours author, he established an international reputation with over a hundred science fiction and fantasy novels and stories. He was runner up for a Hugo Award with his novelette "Eight Miles," and he has won fifteen other awards and been published in over a dozen languages. His latest collection, *Dreams of the Technarion* (Reanimus Press, 2017) contains his new history of Australian science fiction, "Outpost of Wonder." His daughter is the award winning scriptwriter, Catherine S. McMullen.

THE FIREWALL AND THE DOOR

SEAN McMULLEN

Living room news is somehow timeless. Roman slaves once came home and repeated what they had heard in the Forum to their masters. Eighteenth Century families read pamphlets collected in the coffee houses. A century later it was newspapers, then came radio, television, Twitter, t-share, overview and commspeak. Now we have the slightly retro holovista, which is popular because it can be watched as a family—if the family is willing.

Entanglement technology had brought the final frontier as close as the living room. All we had to do was get an uncrewed probe out to whatever was to be explored, and the entangled telepresence established in its computers would provide practically instant communication. Everything was easy. Too easy. People took the wonders for granted until something went spectacularly wrong.

I was in the living room with my family when the Argo made its flyby of the double star Alpha Centauri. My wife was working on her Universal Data Pad, but was looking up at the holovista every so often. My thirteen year old son was sitting with his arms folded tightly, and doing his best to look sullen.

"Don't see why we're watching," Jason muttered. "The Argo's been trashed by an asteroid."

"It collided with a speck of dust the size of a bacterium," I replied.

"Then what's the fuss about?"

"The Argo was traveling at a tenth of the speed of light when it hit. Huge loads of energy were released."

"What's that mean?"

"Very large bang."

"So it's trashed."

"It's damaged, but still working. This is one of the most significant events in humanity's history, so we're going to watch it as a happy family."

"I'm not happy."

"Then we'll just have to watch it as an unhappy family. Now shut up and watch!"

"Try not to be authoritarian with Jason," said my wife.

"Teenagers are pack animals," I replied. "I'm making sure he knows that he's not leading this pack."

"Now, now, dear. Try not to act like a magistrate when you're at home."

I knew they would not share my enthusiasm for the Argo. I was a child when the unmanned starship had been launched, and I had followed its progress closely ever since. Inevitably, I had childhood dreams of joining the Argo's crew, and in theory they were realistic dreams. The members of the crew lived very ordinary lives in California, and operated the spacecraft through entanglement telepresence circuitry at the Mission Control building on Berkeley Campus. My dreams had been shared by hundreds of millions of other children, but there were no vacancies. In the forty-seven years of the mission not one of the crew had died or retired.

The best career opportunities were in law when I had to start making decisions about earning a living. My fascination with technology could not be smothered by four years of legal studies, however, so I specialized in spacecraft accident investigation. The Argo was a spacecraft, and there had been an accident, so I was now following events with informed, professional interest.

The holographic image of Marie Jackson, the Argo's control-captain, now materialized a few feet in front of us. Beside her was a journalist, who was about a fifth of Jackson's age.

"Can you tell the viewers a little about the Argo?" the journalist began.

How many thousands of times has she answered that question? I wondered.

"The Argo was built in space, orbiting Saturn," said Jackson, doing a good job of seeming neither bored nor exasperated. "It was launched in 2200, and spent ten months accelerating to nine percent of lightspeed. It then traveled unpowered for the next forty-seven years. It was meant to loop around the star Centauri A, and use its gravitational field to change direction. It would then travel on for another two hundred years to its next flyby, the red dwarf star Gliese 581."

"But isn't the Argo exploring the Centauri stars?"

"Yes, but the Gliese and Centauri systems are in roughly the same direction, so the Argo was meant to explore both. The Centauri stars are the payoff for the people who built the Argo, because it's arrived in our lifetimes."

"But now there's been an accident, and it can't go any further?"

"There's been an accident, and it *can't change direction,*" said Jackson with her eyes closed. "One does not slow down from a tenth of lightspeed by pressing on a brake pedal."

Jason was sitting with his mouth open, quite literally drooling at the image of the very pretty journalist.

"Chosen for being decorative," I observed.

"You're just saying that because you're jealous!" exclaimed Jason.

The journalist looked blank as a cue device within her ear briefed her for the next question.

"But this is not the first star you explored," she said.

"That's right," said Jackson. "Eleven months ago we passed within a quarter of a light-year of the red dwarf Proxima Centauri. That's the nearest star to the sun."

"But the Argo didn't actually go there."

"No, but our telescope did detect flares erupting on Proxima's surface. The light from those flares is still on its way here, and will not arrive for another three years. That means scientists can do some fascinating experiments that test the laws of physics."

The journalist looked blank again. Clearly her ideas of what was fascinating did not extend to experiments involving the speed of light. An unseen operator briefed her with the next question.

"So now the Argo is going to fly past a planet?" she asked.

"The Argo released a little probe called Harpy 1 a few weeks ago," said Jackson, and their images were replaced by a long, sleek cylinder with a cluster of instruments at one end. "This probe will do the flyby of the Centauri system's only Earth-type planet. That happens in six minutes."

Society had been changing quickly and radically as the Argo was being built, late in the Twenty-Second Century. The Argo was also called the Centenary Unity Endeavour. It was a huge project spanning all the governments of the Solar System, and symbolizing their ability to work together. It took a decade to complete, was the most powerful machine ever built, and was very, very expensive. Too expensive. Worst of all, it was expendable. By 2200, to be expendable was to be ideologically unsound.

Even when the Argo was finished and being fueled with ice from Saturn's rings, there were petitions to halt all work on it, and transform the crowning glory of human exploration into a monument to waste prevention. This monument would supposedly remind humanity that it was never too late to stop waste. In spite of unresolved court injunctions, the Argo was nevertheless launched on time. The legality of that was challenged, and some of the litigation continues to this very day.

The average human could reasonably expect to live to a hundred and thirty, so most of the Argo's builders would still alive for the Centauri flyby, and could see some results from their work. Because there would be no more interstellar missions, this was humanity's only chance to explore anything outside the solar system.

The mission plan had been for the Argo itself to pass close to Centauri A, and use the star's gravity as a slingshot to swing around through sixty-seven degrees. It would then travel another eighteen light-years to Gliese 581. This star had six planets, and its flyby would be the spectacular climax of the mission. Of course none of us would live to see that, it was our gift to future generations.

Once the Argo's nuclear fuel and reaction mass had been spent, a probe the size of a pickup truck detached from the main part of the spacecraft and drew ahead using ion engines until it was traveling just one mile per second faster. There was a substantial risk that the huge nuclear drive and its tanks might hit a scrap of cosmic debris and explode, so it was not safe to be near. The unmanned probe that was the real Argo was thin, tiny and streamlined, and had been built tougher than an armor piercing artillery shell. It had a far better chance of avoiding or surviving any impact.

My wife looked up from her UDP, thought for a moment, then spoke.

"Twenty-First Century economists would have called the Argo really bad value for money," she said.

She was an economist, at least in the sense that she lectured in economic history at London University. She had no interest in space exploration, but every so often she tried to keep me company by saying something to show that she was paying attention.

"Exploration should be done for its own sake," I replied.

"But they spent hundreds of trillions of dollars just to streak through two star systems at a tenth of lightspeed. Why bother?"

"True, why bother?" I sighed, maybe too theatrically. "The people who think like you have won. The Argo has become both the first and last starship. Ever."

She returned her attention to her UDP, embarrassed by being right yet slightly venal.

"Can I go now?" asked Jason.

"No!" I snapped.

"I've got swimming training tomorrow."

"You just want to telepresence with Julia Gould."

"We're just good friends!"

"Good, so you can stay and watch the Wells flyby. It's the real highlight of the evening, and—and when you're older you will thank me for making you stay."

Wells had been discovered by Earth-based telescopes long before the Argo was built. It was a rocky planet orbiting Centauri B, slightly smaller than Earth, and right on the outer edge of the star's habitable zone. It was the only Earth-type planet in the Alpha Centauri system. Because it was a slightly bigger, warmer version of Mars, a Spacebook campaign was begun for it to be named after one of the thousands of science fiction authors who had written novels involving Mars. A hundred years after his death, the author of *The War of the Worlds* had won this contest.

Control-Captain Jackson and the journalist were replaced by an image of Wells at the center of our living room's holovista. It began as a reddish spot, but this quickly became a half-moon shape. Over the course of a few seconds it expanded into a red, green and white disk about a yard across, then it reverted to a half-moon that dwindled back into a red dot as Harpy 1 left it far behind. The encounter had taken all of fifteen seconds.

"Is that all there is?" asked Jason, his arms still folded tightly.

"That was what a human would see," I replied. "Obviously you're a human."

Jason scowled. Like a great many teenagers of thirteen or fourteen, he disliked being a member of the human race and considered my words to be an insult. He was wearing his newly fashionable nerve-servo contact lenses, the kind with cat's eye pupils. They actually contracted and dilated, and were meant to make him seem like some sort of feline predator. He also had a pair of prosthetic vampire fangs, but that sort of accessory had been fashionable for two hundred years.

"So, er, what else are we supposed to see?" asked my wife, to break the silence.

"That," I said.

The largest image of Wells had just been projected for us to examine at our leisure. Imagine Mars, slightly larger, slightly warmer and quite a lot wetter, but with no craters. There were streaks and patches of olive green, and tracts of grayish blue that were its small seas. The polar caps were huge, as if an ice age were gripping the planet. There were also cloud systems, but they were thin and stringy.

"A lot of the surface is red desert, but there are areas of green," some unseen planetary scientist was explaining excitedly. "Spectral analysis already shows it to have chlorophyll, but not quite as we know chlorophyll. The little seas and lakes are obvious, and rivers are visible because of vegetation growing beside them. This is not just an Earth-like planet, it's another Earth!"

The air pressure was barely that of very high mountains on Earth, but it was enough to support liquid water. Wells seemed to be a planet made up entirely of tundra grasslands, shallow, swampy seas, and icy wilderness. It was the sort of place that would tolerate humans, rather than welcome them.

"What about aliens?" the journalist asked.

"We got a view of part of the night side," the scientist replied, "but there were no lights from cities. If there are any intelligent aliens, they would still be hunter-gatherers."

He went on to make the usual comments about what a pity it was that there would be no follow up probe, and that this would be all that we would ever learn about the planet Wells.

The Wells flyby had been timed to be part of a larger show. While Harpy 1 had been flashing past the planet, the Argo was approaching Centauri A. More accurately, two chunks of the Argo were approaching the star. Three days earlier there had been a collision, and the Argo had been split.

"So the Argo collided with a bit of dust, and that was enough to blow it apart?" asked Jason.

"Yes."

"Couldn't happen."

"The Argo was traveling at nine percent of the speed of light," I said with my hand over my eyes. "That means the kinetic energy released was equal to that of quite a large bomb. We were lucky that the Argo survived at all."

"But it didn't survive. It was blown to bits."

"It was blown into only two bits. The important bit is still working."

"How?"

"It has multiple fallback layers."

"What's that mean?"

"Well, think of a medieval knight. He had a shield to stop arrows, but if any got past that, he had armor. Some arrows can pierce armor, so under the armor was cloth padding. Any arrow that got past all that was going a lot slower, so it had less of a chance of killing him. The Argo is similar. It can take a lot of damage and keep working."

"So it's okay?"

"Yes and no. The Argo and its armor were blown apart from each other by the collision. Unprotected, the Argo can't pass close enough to Centauri A to change course for Gliese 581."

"Why not?"

"Because stars are hot, the heat would melt it!" I snapped, almost taking his bait and yelling. "Get your act together, Jason, you're not that stupid."

"Don't damage Jason's self-esteem," said my wife without looking up.

"Hang on, if the Argo was pointed to go that close to the star, won't it still go there and melt?" asked Jason.

"So, you *are* paying attention."

"Well? I asked an intelligent question."

"And I'm still recovering from the shock."

"Do I get an answer?"

"There were six more Harpy probes on the Argo, each with a rocket engine. The control crew in California fired the rockets of the probes without releasing them. This changed the Argo's course, taking it further away from Centauri A."

"But that means it won't swing around to point at that other star."

"That's right."

"Then why bother saving it?"

"Because of what may be out there that we can't see as yet. The Argo's power plant is rated for three hundred years of operation, and two hundred and fifty of those years are still left. It may be pointed at empty space, but who knows whether empty space is entirely empty?"

The flyby of Centauri A was very poor as a holovista spectacle, because there was nothing to see from the probe. The Argo's telescope, instruments and sensors had been put into lockdown, and all equipment that could be spared was turned off. With so much heat pouring onto the probe from the star, the instruments could not be allowed to generate any more heat than could be helped.

Computer graphics had replaced the imagery from on-board cameras, and an internal temperature graph took up half of our holovista. Two tracks, representing the Argo and its shield, were edging closer and closer to Centauri A. Ironically, shield was on the original course, and would swing around the star and go on to reach the Gliese system in two hundred years. The Argo was by now two million miles further out.

"Strange to think that the shield will survive the flyby better than the Argo," I said.

Jason grunted. He was interested, but trying hard to disguise the fact.

"Meantime the Argo has speed on its side, and it will not be in the super-hot zone for very long," I continued. "If we're lucky, nothing important will fail before it starts cooling down."

"But there's nothing ahead to look at," said my wife.

"Nothing that we know about," I replied, trying hard to stay optimistic.

For reality entertainment, the flyby had little drama. The temperature peaked a minute *after* the closest approach, but apparently that was something to do with heat dispersal, and was expected. Very little failed, because even the Argo's internal equipment had been built to survive extremes. Someone opened a bottle of champagne and began handing out glasses.

"Okay, now I know we don't have much to celebrate," Jackson began as she raised her glass to toast the Argo's survival.

"Control-Captain!"

I have no idea who shouted, but the holovista immediately switched to a screen projection displaying three words and a number. The message had not come from the Argo.

FIREWALL SURVIVED. ACKNOWLEDGE. 41.

There was the sound of breaking glass as some of the control crew dropped their champagne in their haste to get back to their consoles. I noticed that my wife and son were suddenly giving the holovista their complete attention. After what seemed like ages, Jackson spoke to the journalist.

"The backup processor on the shield has come back to life!" she said breathlessly.

"What does that mean?" the journalist asked.

"The shield's computer survived. It's on course to Gliese 581."

"But all the instruments are aboard the Argo," she pointed out.

"The shield has an entangled processor, a few instruments, a small telescope, batteries and solar panels. It can do a survey at Gliese after all. We just need to check its course."

"Can't you focus on the signal that came in, and do a Doppler analysis?"

Suddenly the cat was out of the bag. The journalist had been acting dumb, but in the excitement of the moment she had forgotten herself and started asking intelligent questions.

"The message came through the shield's entanglement circuitry, and that's not directional," said Jackson. "I'm having the Argo's main telescope activated and swung around to focus on where the shield will be. It should still be visible, its surface is highly reflective."

The image from the telescope was put on the screen, but it was blank.

"Too far?" asked the journalist.

"The shield should be a faint star at the center of the divided crosshairs. It's transmitting, so it's still in one piece."

"Then where is it?" asked the journalist.

"It *has* to be there. Maybe the coating on the shield darkened because it flew so close to Centauri A."

"Try scanning on a course intercepting Centauri B in six days," said a male voice off-camera.

"What was that, lieutenant?" asked Jackson.

"Scan for Centauri B intercept at around four percent of c," said the unseen officer. "The shield did an aerobrake in Centauri A's atmosphere."

There was a short, razor-sharp silence. This was holovista reality at its most intense.

"Do it!" Jackson finally shouted.

Moments later the telescope had been repositioned. At fifteen million miles, the image had to be blown up so much that it displayed as just a cluster of half a dozen square pixels, but there it was. The shield had lost velocity equal to nearly five percent of lightspeed and was on a course for the second largest of the Centauri suns.

"Arrest that man!" shouted Control-Captain Jackson, pointing at someone off-camera. "Arrest Lieutenant Ashcroft!"

The holovista image winked out, and was replaced by some talking head anchor man. He apologized for the break in transmission.

My family and I were still babbling to each other about what might have happened when my UDP sounded.

"Hullo, Harper speaking."

"Mackerson here, Andy. Have you been watching the Argo flyby?"

"Yes, yes. It's unbelievable. I—"

"Are you willing to preside in an establishment hearing for the Argo case?"

"Me?" I gasped stupidly. "They asked for me? No, no, I mean, er, *who* asked for me?"

"Is that a yes or a no?"

He's offering you a chance to be part of the Argo mission, screamed a voice in my head. *Say yes, you idiot, say yes!*

"Yes, yes, of course."

"You're to be at Heathrow Suborbital Departures in forty minutes, I'll bring a tiltfan to your house. Your briefs, itinerary and clearances will be downloaded to your UDP."

I now learned what is meant by instant fame. Within a few minutes, Mackerson's contract security guards had arrived and turned the house into an exclusion zone. Not far behind them were the experientialists, bloggers, agents, promoters, paparazzi, tooters, tweeters, Spacebook frontals, and even a few old-style journalists. I had gone from being a respected but obscure magistrate to an interworld celebrity in less time than it takes to have a rushed breakfast. Jason discovered that his Spacebook posting 'Dad's got the Argo case' had seven thousand likes. I was winched up from my front steps to a tiltfan shuttle while hundreds of cameras focused on me. Mackerson helped me through the hatch, then the tiltfan spun about elegantly and set off for the airport.

"You know what I'm going to ask again," I said as I slumped into a seat facing him.

"You're going to say 'Why me?'"

"Very good. So why me?"

"Politics, experience, jurisdiction, the fact that you're British, but mostly because you specialize in spacecraft accident investigation."

"There are plenty of others with that sort of background."

"The suspect is American, the alleged crime took place on American soil, and American law works on performance justice. America contributed only a fifth of the cost of the Argo mission, however, and several of the other nations and worlds don't use performance justice. That all means compromise. There must be a public establishment hearing on American soil by an independent magistrate to establish the nature of any felony. You will give it an intersystem flavor."

"And after that?"

"Your findings will be handed over to an American criminal court."

He shepherded me through the airport's immigration, customs and security checks. The suborbital took off. I threw up into a mask bag soon after we went weightless, because my anti-nausea caps were still at home, along with the travel pack I had forgotten to bring. An attendant floated over with a dermal, and somewhere above Greenland I decided that I felt well enough to begin reading the briefs. The case was a nightmare maze of psychology, cyber identity, physics, engineering, astronomy and communications, and was technically beyond most legal people. I had spent thirty years in this field, however, and was used to dealing with new, complex and even bizarre precedents.

I was also well known for being able to think on my feet, and this was a big plus. Events would be still unfolding even as the hearing took place. Some of them would be doing so four and a third light-years away.

Within two hours of answering my UDP in London, I was being met and briefed in San Francisco, in daylight. By my second sunset for the day I was being assigned an office in the same building as Mission Control. Before I could even sit down, a legal clerk escorted me to an auditorium that had been set up as a performance court.

"So, you're a British magistrate," she said as we walked.

"Yes, Britain's main export is legal opinions these days," I began, but she cut me short.

"Know about performance hearing procedures?"

"I'm qualified to preside in them, but this is my first. The Westminster system does not recognize them."

"Then listen carefully, I have to tell you this so that I can sign you off as briefed. In this country the public has a right to an opinion. The performance hearing is meant to let the public hear from all parties involved, in plain language, so that it can form its opinion. Some people call it a circus, but we find it works better than anything else."

"Except that in this case the public is everyone, not just Americans."

"You've got it. Everyone paid for the Argo, so they're all stakeholders. As stakeholders, we have to treat them as honorary Americans."

Performance justice had been developed after the old system had delivered some bizarre verdicts. Rape victims had been sued for becoming pregnant, vandals had sued property owners for injuring themselves on glass that they had smashed, and bank robbers had sued banks for invading their privacy during holdups by recording everything with security cameras. The law had become so detached from public opinion that the public had lost patience. Public opinion was now factored into the law.

I took my seat and faced the holocameras.

"Firstly, I wish to remind you that this is not a court of law," I said for the benefit of the holo audience. "This is an establishment hearing under the Interworld Protocols of 2230, and is meant to provide an overview of events while they are fresh in everyone's memory. Prosecutions may follow, however, so I must advise you all to stay as close to the facts as your memories permit. I call Control-Captain Emily Jackson to the stand."

Jackson was sworn in. She maintained the carefully attentive but angry expression of a victim. Doubtlessly a stylist had been giving her some very intensive coaching while I had been vomiting above Greenland.

"Now as I understand it, the Argo collided with something three days ago," I began. "Is this correct?"

"Yes, yes, everything was on the holovista," she said impatiently. "Haven't you been watching?"

"I am collecting statements from witnesses, Control-Captain," I explained. "Establishment hearings are meant to establish an image of the case for the public. I shall also remind you that I am a presiding magistrate in a legal hearing. One more challenge to my authority and you will be charged with contempt."

The console before me showed nine million Spacebook dislikes and eleven million likes. The public that was bothering to vote was marginally on my side.

"My apologies, Your Honor," Jackson replied, "I've been under a lot of stress."

"Now then, was there any warning of danger?" I continued. "Meteors showing up on the radar, that sort of thing?"

"The Argo was traveling at almost seventeen thousand miles per second, Your Honor. The meteor that crippled it could only be seen under a microscope."

"So there was no threat detected?"

"There were only general indications of threat and risk. Radar picked up some asteroid-sized bodies near our flight path, the biggest was fifty miles in diameter. We got high resolution pictures of one on the way past."

"And your control crew voted to call it Jackson."

"That's correct, Your Honor."

"Display the images."

The clerk of the court put a series of pictures and graphs onto a tabletop holo-vista beside the witness stand, then a rotating hologram of the asteroid appeared. It could have been from our own solar system, and I would never have known.

"So you discovered asteroids," I prompted. "And where there are asteroids, there is also dust."

"Yes, Your Honor. I put the Argo on yellow alert and cancelled all VIP telepresence tours as soon as the first asteroid was detected."

"How long after going onto yellow alert did the Argo hit the grain of dust?" I asked.

"Five hours," Jackson replied.

"So you were prepared as well as could be expected?"

"Yes. The Argo has many fallback layers."

"Please tell me what happened immediately after the strike," I said.

"The readouts in Mission Control went blank and the alarms went off. All telemetry through the entanglement link ceased."

"How did the control crew react?"

"People shouted that it was a particle strike. Some of them used a few politically insensitive words."

"And did your contingency and recovery officer, Lieutenant Ashcroft, did he do anything suspicious?"

"No."

"Well, just what did he do?"

"Nothing. A virtual of the lieutenant was in one of the Argo's computers. It was meant to take over and restore the systems after any strike."

"So what did you do, back in Mission Control?"

"I gave orders to turn off the alarms, released media statements, and ordered a coffee from catering."

"Nothing else?"

"The entanglement link was out, and the Argo was light-years away. We could only wait for a poll signal. That came after three hours. We then linked straight back into the Argo's systems."

"Describe what you found."

"There was a lot of blankout in the data storage arrays, and Ashcroft-virtual was dead. The comms link had been restored from timed contingency routines. While we were starting repairs, I saw that the shield's computer and circuits were all dead. I used the camera on the robotic maintenance crawler to get a direct view of the probe's condition. It showed that the shield section had been smashed away. When I ordered a search with the radar unit and main telescope, this is what we saw."

Jackson put up a blurred image of the shield pulling away from the Argo.

"It looks undamaged," I said.

"I assumed that the damage was on the other side. Now I realize that the explosive separation bolts had been fired. There had been no collision."

"Was there any communication between the shield and the Argo?"

"When we transmitted the kill switch key to take manual control of the shield, all we got was the INVALID KEY response. That indicates catastrophic damage."

"Did you try to pursue?"

"The instrument section of the Argo has no ion thrusters, they were all built into the shield. We decided to use the rockets of the Harpy probes to push the Argo further away from Centauri A, and at least salvage something of the mission."

"Thank you Control-Captain, that will be all for now."

Ashcroft was escorted to the stand. It was the first time I had seen him, because he had managed to stay out of the holovista coverage. He had a closely shaven scalp and a bushy white beard. It looked to me as if his head were upside down, and I had to stifle the urge to laugh.

"Lieutenant Charles Ashcroft, you were the Mission Continuity and Disaster Recovery officer until you were arrested," I said, looking up from my UDP.

"That's right, Your Honor."

His accent was west coast. Ashcroft was the same age as Jackson, and the difference in their rank was due to the fact that Ashcroft was extremely good at what he did, and was not interested in learning to do those other things that got one promoted—like handling difficult staff, raising funds, and flattering important people with influence.

"Please describe your role in the Argo's crew, using your own words," I said.

"There's an emergency processor in the shield where a virtual image of my consciousness is continually mirrored. If the main entanglement link shuts down, the emergency circuit activates Ashcroft-virtual. It's completely autonomous, and can recover a functional subset of Argo systems unless the damage is catastrophic—"

"Enough, slow down," I said, already familiar with his type after three decades of technical hearings crammed with geeks trying to blind me with science. "You say your mind was mirrored into a processor on the Argo, so a virtual image of your consciousness was actually aboard the probe itself. Am I correct?"

Ashcroft suddenly looked uneasy. I was the sort of legalistic pedant he despised, yet I was throwing his jargon back at him, and in coherent English. He cowered visibly, as if aware that a predator was nearby, and that he was small, fluffy and delicious.

"You're correct, sir—that is, Your Honor," he said sheepishly.

"And how many others have their virtuals mirrored aboard the Argo?"

"Just me, Your Honor."

"So while the Argo was in recovery mode, your Ashcroft-virtual had sole command?" I asked.

"Yes, Your Honor."

"I have made a study of the Argo's systems," I said as casually as I could. "Because the nature of disaster is by its very definition, unexpected, there was a manual emergency switch available to your virtual. If an emergency that could not possibly have been anticipated were to take place and cut off communications, Ashcroft-virtual could assess the situation and take action."

Until now Ashcroft had not actually admitted to sabotaging the probe. However, he looked about as guilty as a dog on a kitchen table with the remains of a chicken pie. I did not know why he was delaying the inevitable, but I decided to give him a nudge.

"I put it to you, Lieutenant Ashcroft, that your virtual could easily have activated a meteor strike simulation routine, and so cut off the Argo from Mission Control. After that, Ashcroft-virtual had sole command of the probe. It would have been easy to fire the release charges to separate the shield of the Argo from its electronics, powerplant and scientific instruments."

"Oh, yeah, but there you're wrong. The on-board logs would have showed that the emergency was declared *before* the separation charges were fired."

"So you fired the charges first."

"I—"

His hesitation said everything. He was proud of how well he had covered his trail, so he wanted someone to know. Just as dragons have a soft spot in every fairy story, so too does every geek who has achieved some illegal technical master stroke.

"I suppose I can admit that now."

"So, the Argo colliding with a speck of dust at a tenth of lightspeed would look identical to the separation charges being fired. You wanted to keep *that* part secret until after the Wells and Centauri A flybys."

"You're good," Ashcroft conceded.

"I could charge you with contempt for that remark," I said sternly. "Remember that if you are tempted to make another."

"I'm sorry, Your Honor."

That earned me seventeen million Spacebook dislikes and fifteen million likes. Public opinion was divided, but beginning to favor Ashcroft. Most viewers were still not voting.

"What is the significance of 'firewall'?" I asked.

"The shield is no longer just a part of the Argo. Its name is the Firewall."

"The Firewall. Your name for it?"

"The Firewall is the name that my virtual calls it."

During a break I was shown a mockup of the Argo in a laboratory within the Mission Control building. The mockup was used to diagnose faults on the real starship and try to work out solutions. The Argo's shield was shaped like a sleek, hollow axe head. Any fleck of dust that struck it would give just a glancing blow. Of course at nine percent of lightspeed even glancing blows were liable to be catastrophic, but it was the best design that anyone could think of.

The list of charges that was developing against Ashcroft would be good for decades of litigation. Overall, he had destroyed intersystem property costing four hundred trillion dollars, and worth even more in replacement value. Every media outlet in the solar system was linked to the auditorium's cameras, and I knew that my face would be instantly recognizable by pretty well everyone for the rest of my life. According to my UDP's scan of Spacebook, Ashcroft was currently both the most liked and the most disliked man in the solar system.

I faced the holocameras, trying not to think of how many pairs of eyes were behind them.

"Now, summing up the findings so far, Lieutenant Ashcroft has admitted to plotting to take control of the Argo ever since the mission began. He knew that Ashcroft-virtual would be in control of the Argo after any collision, real or simulated. Aboard the shield was enough computer power to support his virtual, so Ashcroft-virtual detached the shield. When the Argo went into lock-down for the Centauri A flyby, he fired the shield's ion thrusters and put it on a course that would go deep into the star's atmosphere for an extreme aerobrake. I must emphasize that it was Ashcroft-virtual that hijacked the shield while the Argo was cut off. Quite probably Ashcroft-original was an accomplice, however, because he had known the shield's course."

I called Jackson back to the stand. She looked very angry, in fact barely in control. Anger was always a dangerous emotion to display to Spacebook voters, as it generally attracted more dislikes than likes. She was not on trial, but a high dislike-to-like ratio would affect her reliability index as a witness. I started with the physics of the flyby.

"So instead of just swinging close to the star Centauri A to change course for the Gliese system, the shield fired its ion thrusters and did an extreme aero-brake deep into the star's atmosphere. There it lost over half of its velocity, and changed course for Centauri B—where it will do another aerobrake, then fly on to the planet Wells."

"Nine hundred million likes," said someone in the gallery, and there were titters of laughter.

"Order!" I shouted. "One more reference to Spacebook activity and I will have the offender removed and charged with contempt of court."

I waited for any further comments. Nobody said anything.

"Control-Captain, I gather that the Harpy 1 probe returned useful images and data for about fifteen seconds during the flyby of Wells. It showed that the planet has polar caps, clouds, small seas, a magnetic field, a breathable atmo-sphere, and vegetation."

"Yes."

"Was that enough?"

"I don't understand the question, Your Honor."

"I'll put a fictitious proposition to you. Just say you were the head of NASA, back in the Twentieth Century. Say that you had an extremely tight budget, but the first flyby of Mars had revealed ruined cities. Would you abandon the explo-ration of the rest of the solar system indefinitely, and concentrate on Mars?"

"I . . . no, I would not," she said slowly. "Three moons of Jupiter turned out to have subterranean oceans that supported primitive life forms. That's signifi-cant too."

"You would not have known that at the time."

"But I know it now. The Gliese system's worlds may have wonderful secrets that we can't even begin to dream of, and whatever the Harpies would have discovered about them would have been *all* that would *ever* be discovered unless we commit to interstellar exploration again."

"The same may be said about Wells."

"With respect, Your Honor, that is not a judgment that I would make."

Secretly I sympathized with Jackson. The generation that followed hers—mine—had cancelled the interstellar program, and confined us to the solar system. Everything that we would ever see directly beyond our little corner in space would be through the cameras of the Argo and its fleet of Harpy probes.

"You may stand down, Control-Captain, that will be all."

Several technical experts now testified and explained the situation on the Firewall. Aboard the shield there was a block of entangled circuitry linked to a block in Mission Control. Here signals could be exchanged, but at a bit rate so slow that even most computer historians were not aware that it had ever existed. A hundred and ten bits per second. It was not much better than Morse code, and dated to the 1950s.

An acknowledgment had been sent to the shield's first message, but Ashcroft-virtual ignored all subsequent questions that were sent to it. Every hour it sent the same message, each time with a number appended: PERFORMING REPAIRS. STAND BY. 41. The value of the number was slowly increasing. It defined the amount of damage to Ashcroft-virtual.

The Firewall was very tough, but it had not been designed for prolonged and hyper-extreme deceleration. In spite of the shield's insulation, the temperature must have reached hundreds of degrees Celsius internally. There was memory loss in the data and processor lattices, so Ashcroft-virtual would be rearranging the surviving data that defined itself, restoring whatever it could before going through the same trauma again at Centauri B. It had just six days to restore 59% of itself from contingency lattices.

Back on Earth, Ashcroft had by now admitted to conspiring with his virtual aboard the Argo to hijack the mission. I could not pass judgment on what he had done or sentence him, but I could allow him to explain himself on Spacebook. At the time of the Argo's launch, the taxpayers of humanity had each paid eight thousand dollars a year for ten years to get it built and fueled. That was one percent of the average income. Many of them were still alive, and were seeing their money squandered. How many likes and dislikes would Ashcroft get?

"Marshal of Proceedings, bring Lieutenant Ashcroft to the stand."

Ashcroft was led back. He was affecting a meticulously resigned expression known as the martyr face. He had admitted guilt, but he wanted the Spacebook voters to know that he had noble motives. A high score of likes was his only hope.

"Lieutenant Ashcroft, what do you say in response to the declaration from Control-Captain Jackson?" I asked.

"I don't agree with her, Earth-like planets come first. It was always my intention to aerobrake the Argo's shield through the atmospheres of the two Centauri stars, and put it into orbit around Wells."

"Even though it was not designed for the purpose? Even though a four hundred trillion dollar mission would be wasted?"

"The mission has not been wasted. Humanity has had flybys of two stars, a planet and several asteroids. The Argo will fly on through another twenty light-years of space. Who knows what is out there to discover? That has not been lost."

"Gliese has been lost."

"And you have Wells in its place."

"The Firewall is damaged, it may not survive the aerobrake through Centauri B. It's not designed for extremes like that."

"That doesn't matter. A lot of leading edge work has been done with machines that were designed for something else. In the earliest years of the space age, the only rockets available for exploration were designed to carry bombs. In spite of that, they were also used to launch satellites, send probes to other worlds, and put the first humans into space. Machine usefulness is deter-mined by machine capability, not what the machine was designed for."

"So you gambled that the shield could take well over ten thousand Gs for two or three minutes?"

"Ten thousand Gs is no problem. Back in the early Twenty First Century the Japanese tested probes whose electronics could take eight thousand Gs and still function. The Argo's shield and its equipment were built to handle more than that."

"And the extreme temperatures?" I asked.

"The Argo was to pass very close to Centauri A, so the shield was designed to protect it from the expected temperatures. It was also over-engineered to cope with anything worse. It *will* survive Centauri B."

By now Ashcroft had nine hundred million likes and six thousand dislikes. Here was absolute, admitted guilt welded to overwhelming public support. I was very relieved that I would only be a witness in his criminal trial.

"Lieutenant Ashcroft, I am obliged to inform you that you will certainly be charged with a crime involving the largest single damage bill in all of history," I began.

"And he may get out of jail before the next ice age," called someone in the gallery.

"Marshal, remove whoever said that from the public gallery, take them to the local authorities, and recommend a charge of contempt."

There was a pause in proceedings while the offender was taken into custody. I looked down at my screen. The youth had got just over a hundred million likes in twelve seconds, but seven hundred million dislikes as well. Ashcroft certainly had massive public sympathy, in spite of what he had done.

"In six days the Firewall and Ashcroft-virtual will reach Centauri B," I asked Ashcroft. "What will happen?"

"I can't speak for my virtual any more."

"Please explain."

"Ashcroft-virtual is no longer me," said Ashcroft. "The number transmitted from the Firewall every hour represents the amount of contiguous virtual memory stored in its lattice banks. The Centauri A flyby damaged a lot of physical storage, but because the virtual is stored by a scattered redundancy algorithm, a lot of it can be rebuilt."

"A lot, but not all."

"Yes. Priority was given to redundancy for motivations and recent memories. Childhood memories were kept in single copy. So far the restoration has reached 52%."

"So your virtual has what would be called brain damage in humans."

"But it's *not* human. How often do you recall your childhood memories, Your Honor? Every day?"

"No. I probably go months at a time without thinking about them."

"Yet you live by many motivations and attitudes formed in your childhood. It's the same with Ashcroft-virtual. My recent memories, general motivations and underlying attitudes have multiple copies aboard the Firewall. They will survive, and they are all that's needed. It's not me, but it's functional."

"You hope."

"Yes."

"Suppose, just suppose, your virtual survives in a functional condition. What do you have planned?"

"In six days it will lose another eight thousand miles per second in Centauri B's atmosphere, and emerge with the velocity of a long-period comet. After another thirty-two days it will aerobrake at the top of Well's atmosphere, and enter a highly elongated orbit around the planet."

"So, the Firewall will orbit Wells and map its surface?" I asked.

"For ten orbits, yes. With each orbit it will skim the outer atmosphere, and lose some velocity. On the tenth orbit the Firewall will do a deep atmospheric entry and impact the surface."

"And be destroyed?"

"No."

"Please explain. The Firewall has no parachutes."

"The shield is light and tough. It will hit the ground at four hundred miles per hour, which is nothing compared to surviving over ten thousand Gs in the atmospheres of the Centauri stars. If the Firewall survives, it will give us pictures from Wells's surface. It may even give us our first view of life on another Earth-like planet."

There was more, but for sheer impact there was nothing in the same class as that revelation. Ashcroft's Spacebook rating passed a billion likes, which in turn generated even more likes. His virtual had double that figure. I released him to a local court and recommended bail because he was not a flight risk. He was certainly not in any position to re-offend. I then filed my findings with an American judge, and recommended that no further proceedings commence until after the landing on Wells.

On the sixth day after the first aerobrake, the Firewall speared through the atmosphere of Centauri B. This was a slightly gentler encounter than before, but the circuitry aboard the probe was already stressed and damaged. By now the Argo was well outside the Centauri system, and its telescope could show no more than sunspots on Centauri B's disk. Again we endured a very anxious half hour while the Firewall cooled down.

FIREWALL SURVIVED. PERFORMING REPAIRS. 23.

Those words got two billion likes on Spacebook, but the number told us that three quarters of what defined Ashcroft-virtual had been damaged. The data integrity percentages began to climb again, but more slowly than before. Ashcroft-virtual was like a human emerging from a coma, gradually recovering from two terrible accidents. In the weeks that followed, the parts of the virtual that had been restored only climbed to 57%.

The aerobrake in Wells's atmosphere was an anticlimax compared to what had happened at the two stars. The shield lost enough speed to go into a parabolic orbit that reached from the top of the atmosphere to a hundred thousand miles from the planet. Data trickled in through the pathetically slow link. Wells had a magnetic field, weaker than Earth's, yet strong enough to protect it from the solar wind. The surface pressure was a third of that at the Earth's sea surface, but oxygen made up a quarter of the atmosphere. Wells was Earth-like, but not entirely Earth-like.

With each orbit the Firewall dipped deeper into the atmosphere and lost a little more speed. Finally, it fell. Everyone was expecting to have to wait hours for Ashcroft-virtual's damage control routines to do their work, but after only seconds the hoped-for message came through.

FIREWALL SURVIVED. 47.

It was vastly better than we could have hoped for. The virtual had lost just 10% of its surviving memories in that final trauma. Although over half of its memories were gone, Ashcroft-virtual was conscious and functional. That got five billion likes, which still ranks as the most popular news item in history.

At a ludicrously slow hundred and ten bits per second, Ashcroft-virtual began to transmit a picture. The Firewall had plunged into the side of a low hill beside one of the small, shallow seas. Not much more than its camera and solar cells were above the surface, but nobody was complaining. In the foreground were bushes with leaves like lacework, amid wiry grass. Some of the grass was cropped short, as if it had been grazed. This had everyone almost insane with excitement.

"Track fifteen degrees left of center, then focus for maximum resolution on the cropped grass," Jackson instructed.

Her words were converted into plain text and fed into the entangled block. The answer came back at once.

NO.

This was a very ugly moment. It was followed by an exceedingly long five second pause.

"Firewall, is there a problem?"

NO.

"Then track fifteen degrees left of center and do a closeup on the grass. It shows signs of grazing. There may be animal life on the planet."

This time Jackson double checked the speech to text conversion before feeding it into the entangled block. An utterly tantalizing reply came back.

GRAZING ANIMALS VISIBLE.

"Priority! Take a contingency picture of the animals and transmit it."

NO.

"Firewall, explain why you cannot take the picture as instructed."

NO MORE PICTURES OR DATA WILL BE SENT.

"Firewall, please clarify. Why will there be no more images and data?"

HUMANITY CANCELLED INTERSTELLAR EXPLORATION. HUMANITY DESERVES NO MORE PICTURES OR DATA.

I stood back and watched as the drama played out. *That is one highly perceptive virtual,* I thought. *It's given us mysteries instead of wonders.* I kept my opinion well and truly to myself. There were hurried, hushed conversations and consultations. Finally a decision was made.

"Try the kill switch key again," said Jackson.

The key was fed into the entangled block.

INVALID KEY was the reply.

The key was transmitted another five times before Jackson gave up.

"We already know this kill switch key is invalid," said Ashcroft. "All the kill switch routines must have been damaged."

"Impossible," said Jackson. "There are thousands of copies of the kill switch all through the data lattices, so at least one should be okay. You must have changed the key. What is the new key?"

"I don't know!"

"Virtuals *can't function* without a kill switch! It's in their design."

"By law," I added.

Jackson turned on me.

"I want a court order for a veritor extraction!" she shouted.

"Mind probes are a Class A privacy intrusion," I replied. "I don't have that sort of authority. You need a judge."

"Well someone find me a judge!"

A judge was found, the intrusion was authorized, and Ashcroft was probed. He had been telling the truth. He did not know any new key.

"The odds of all the kill switches being damaged are about the same as winning the Intersystem Lottery," said Jackson as she stared at the results from the veritor extraction.

"But some people do win the lottery," one of the control crew pointed out.

That single image from Wells's surface was enough to support a thousand PhDs, but it was all that we ever got. Every hour there was a single pulse from the Firewall, which told us that Ashcroft-virtual was alive. *Alive and looking out over the secrets and wonders of Wells*, I thought. *Alive, and sharing nothing with us.*

The virtual was bombarded with pleas, threats, inducements, reproaches and guesses at the kill switch key, but nothing worked. Needless to say, a lot of people blamed the original Ashcroft.

There was a trial, but Ashcroft argued that he was not the same personality as his virtual, who now controlled the Firewall. After all, Ashcroft-virtual had only half of his memories. He went on to declare that *he* would have transmitted all the data and pictures possible if he had been on the Firewall. Veritometer tests confirmed that he was telling the truth. His rating steadied at a billion likes and two hundred million dislikes.

I predicted that the trial would become mired in legal technicalities, and this was what happened. Ashcroft had too much public support to be found guilty, and it was public money that had built the Argo in the first place. A verdict of guilty would ruin careers and bring down governments, so a verdict would never be delivered.

Six months after the Firewall landed, Jackson and I met to sort out some media rights for the holocasts in which we both appeared. Documentaries about the Argo and Firewall were bringing in substantial amounts of money, because of the sudden revival of interest in deep space exploration.

We met at Coffee Plaza on the old Berkeley campus. Our table was shaded by redwoods planted before the Argo had even been designed. It was not the first time that we had met since the establishment hearing, but it was our very first private meeting. I had prepared for it with more care than the control-captain realized.

"Why did Ashcroft-virtual do it?" I asked as we were finishing up. "Why did it *really* do it?"

"Why ask me?" said Jackson wearily. "I was as surprised as anyone when he and his virtual went rogue."

"The veritometer confirmed that Ashcroft was concealing something during my hearing, and in all of his testimonies since."

"All of us are concealing something," said Jackson. "We all have harmless, personal secrets of a sensitive nature."

"Some of us more than others."

"The law allows for it," she pointed out, quite correctly.

There was silence between us for a time. Jackson sipped nervously at her coffee, suspecting something. I went through my notes, then I handed her a smartprint.

"I've done some of my own research," I said as she looked down at it. "Like that Twentieth Century movie director Alfred Hitchcock once said about murder: 'If you want to do a good job, do it yourself.' This is a car park at a conference center in Geneva. A security camera took the image. Now look here."

I traced my finger around one corner and invoked area enlargement. A couple could now be seen embracing against a sleek sharecar. The registration code was visible. The faces of the lovers were not.

"Would you like me to read out who the sharecar was registered to?" I asked. Jackson studied the image and data specs more closely.

"The date is August 17, 2198," she commented, although there was a tremor in her voice. "Ridiculous. Nobody keeps commuter car records for half a century."

"The Swiss do."

Jackson froze completely while she conducted some sort of internal debate with herself, then she let the printout fall to the table and put a hand over her eyes.

"Okay, okay, no more games," she sighed. "Ashcroft and I were married, but to other people. Moral Imperative was sweeping the world, and Equiliberation was trying to shut down the Argo project and turn the starship into a theme park to celebrate waste control."

"So politically speaking it was a bad time for a scandal involving the control-captain and one of her officers?"

"Correct."

"How long did it last?"

"Believe it or not, this monitor caught part of our very first night. After that, well it's still going, occasionally."

"An affair concealed with meticulous care, decades of pillow talk," I said. "Years to plan what to do about Wells."

"Wrong, Mr Harper, totally wrong. Wells was an opportunity, a tool, something to get humanity back on the path to the stars. If the Harpy 1 probe showed that Wells was truly Earth-like and supported life, it deserved a closer look more than any other planet in the galaxy. We spent so many nights in each other's arms, cursing the spinelessness that had cut us off from the stars. Then we came up with a plan. We invented stellar aerobraking."

"In bed?"

"Why not? Thoughts wander, tongues are loose. We would not live to see the Gliese encounter, so with Wells as the alternative, no contest. If Harpy 1 showed that Wells was just another version of Mars, the Firewall could still be left on a course for Gliese."

"But Wells was everything that you hoped it would be."

"Yes."

"So you also planned to dangle it in front of us, then snatch it away?"

"Oh no, we thought that the virtual would send back all the data and pictures that it possibly could, and that the wonders of Wells would lure humanity back into deep space."

"Instead, Ashcroft-virtual punished humanity, and shamed us into doing the same thing."

"Yes, yes. Because of the damage, Ashcroft-virtual is all motivation, but limited memories. It's no longer human, so perhaps it thinks more clearly than humans—like me or Charles. Do you have children, Mr Harper?"

"A son, thirteen."

"Do you know what a thrill it is when your child turns out to be better than you at something?"

"Yes. Jason has a shelf full of swimming trophies, but I swim like a brick."

"This is going to sound strange, but I think of Ashcroft-virtual as the child that Charles and I never had. It's turned out wiser than either of us, and I'm very proud of it. Argo 2 is being planned already, and it will be bigger, faster and tougher. Thirty years, Mr Harper. In thirty years we will have a fleet of orbiters, floaters and crawlers delivered to Wells, while another probe loops Centauri A and goes on to Gliese 581. The Harmonizers are backing us. Do you know about them?"

"A new technological movement," I said. "They say that the universe is burning resources all the time, so humanity is fighting nature by striving for total, static balance. That makes exploration and expansion morally okay."

Jackson nodded.

"Argo 2 *will* happen, so thirty years after the launch there will be telepresence tours of Wells. I'm not yet eighty, so with modern health care I might even be alive to book for one."

I took the printout of the car park from her, tapped the black bar at the top, then said "Clear." The image vanished. Jackson blinked, then stared at me.

"What's this about?" she asked.

"I generated the images of you and Ashcroft, then superimposed them on a genuine security camera record that showed your sharecar."

"You—you mean that wasn't us?" she gasped.

"No. I gambled that the details of your early courtship with Ashcroft would become blurred in your memory over fifty years."

Jackson bristled and her eyes bulged. She flung the remains of her coffee at me. I did not move. She raised her cup to fling it as well.

"Don't you want to know how I knew?" I asked. "If you throw that cup you'll never find out."

"Don't you play that Ashcroft-on-Wells game with me!" she said between clenched teeth.

"It worked for him."

The cup fell from her fingers and shattered on the pavement. A student waiter hurried over and cleaned up the pieces. Jackson sat with her arms folded tightly while he worked. Sitting like that, she reminded me of my son.

I feared that our meeting was over, but hoped otherwise. Jackson sat glaring at me for three or four minutes, quite literally. Try sitting with a really angry person for as long as that, watching each other intently but saying nothing. It's quite a harrowing experience. Finally she softened just a little.

"Okay Mr Tricky, how did you know about Charles and me in the first place?"

"Long, long ago, someone wrote a pattern recognition application that scans the faces of delegates in holovistas taken at conferences," I replied, feeling very relieved. "It picks up on little cues given by couples who have, er . . . come to a romantic arrangement."

"Seduced each other?"

"Yes, and it's accurate with about four couples out of five. Fortunately, the inventor was having a secret affair, so the app was never released."

"Was it you?"

"No, I just have access to it. Personal favor from the inventor."

"Very decent of whoever wrote it. An app like that could really take the fun out of life."

"How did Ashcroft do the kill switch key?"

"He changed the key, but he did it with a random key generator. He didn't look at the new key."

"But he showed it to you."

She buried her face in her hands for a moment, then rubbed her temples.

"Like Charles said, you're good. There was a risk that the virtual would not survive but the Firewall would, so I had to have the kill switch key available, just in case. Manual control through that pathetic emergency link was clunky, but it was better than nothing."

"You put on a good act, demanding that his mind be searched," I said, hoping she would take my words as a compliment. "You gambled that nobody would think of searching *your* mind."

"And the gamble paid off, very nearly."

"So even now you can take over the Firewall and force the entanglement transmission of pictures from Wells's surface?"

"Yes."

"Yet you don't."

"Ashcroft-virtual is my child. My very clever child. It realized that a camera on Wells sending out pictures to Earth like some sort of holovista reality show would satisfy humanity. Why spend hundreds of trillions of dollars on another starship when we already have a view from Wells's surface?"

"Ashcroft-virtual turned out to be a good judge of human nature," I said, nodding.

At last I had the truth, and it was a powerful truth indeed. It was like winning a particularly difficult game of chess. There was no prize, however.

"So, now what?" asked Jackson, forcing the words out with obvious reluctance.

"What do you mean?"

"About me and Charles?"

"None of anyone else's business."

"What?" she exclaimed.

"I'll say nothing about any of this."

"But why? This is top-value sensation news. The kill switch key could be ripped from my mind within seconds of the electrode cap going on. You could give a view of Wells back to humanity, you could get over a billion Spacebook likes. That would boost your career to interworld judge level."

"I'm a just a bureaucrat who dreams, Control-Captain. Fame and power do not interest me, I'm not an explorer, and I'm not a scientist. All I can do is hold the door open while those who are better at exploring and discovering get on with the job. That's enough for me."

"But—but I still don't understand."

I handed another printout to her. I had been expecting that sort of reaction, and had come prepared. The picture showed three men, two of them wearing very archaic spacesuits.

"Do you know who these are?" I asked.

"Apollo astronauts, the spacesuits are pretty distinctive," said Jackson. "The resolution is bad, I can't recognize the faces."

"The man in the foreground is Neil Armstrong, behind him is Mike Collins, and the date is 16th July, 1969. Can you tell me about the third man?"

"It's not Aldrin, he would have been wearing a spacesuit. This guy has a military looking cap and overalls, and he's carrying gear of some sort. I give up, who is he?"

"No idea."

Jackson stared at me, uncertain of whether or not to be annoyed again.

"I assume there's a point to all this?" she said.

"That third man knew who he was, and I'll bet his family had that picture framed and displayed in the living room for decades. His descendants probably still have the picture on the wall. He held the door open, Control-Captain. He was not an astronaut hero or a brilliant engineer, but in a tiny, tiny way he contributed to putting the first men on the moon. Now here I am, holding the door open for the whole of humanity to explore Wells with Argo 2. Should I take the pressure off and give us one pathetic camera on the Firewall? I don't think so. Give people wonders, and they'll sit back, open a beer and watch. If you want folk to get up and do something, you must give them mysteries."

I stood up to go. Jackson stood too, waving her hands in circles and looking like a mess of gratitude, relief and confusion.

"Best to just shake hands, Control-Captain, don't do anything emotional like hugging me," I said. "There are *always* cameras, *everywhere.*"

"We—Charles and I plan to come out with the truth when the first followup probes land on Wells," she said as we shook hands. "When we do the declaration, would you like me to mention that you, well, held the door open for us?"

This was unexpected, and I had to think about it for a moment. Fame was beckoning . . . yet what had I done to deserve it? Jackson, Ashcroft and Ashcroft-virtual were the real heroes.

"Thank you, but no," I decided.

This seemed to cause her genuine distress.

"Please! You must let me do something for you. Would you like one of Wells's seas named Harper? I can arrange it."

The Harper Sea. It was a tempting thought, but I shook my head.

"Why not make your big declaration with Ashcroft in front of a magistrate?" I suggested instead. "I'll make sure that I'm available."

"And that's all you want?"

"Yes. I'll just be in the background but visible, that's enough for me."

I walked away through the old university, feeling very light on my feet. The day was warm, the sunlight dappled by the trees, the scene could not have been more pleasant or mundane . . . yet I was also on Wells, struggling for breath in the thin air, my teeth chattering with the cold. I was holding a door open, and beyond it was the grassy littoral and a calm, silvery sea. I was the happiest man alive.

Jay Lake was a prolific writer of science fiction and fantasy, as well as an award-winning editor, a popular raconteur and toastmaster, and an excellent teacher at the many writers' workshops he attended. His novels included *Mainspring, Escapement,* and *Pinion,* and the trilogy of novels in his Green cycle–*Green, Endurance,* and *Kalimpura.* Lake was nominated multiple times for the Hugo Award, the Nebula Award, and the World Fantasy Award. He won the John W. Campbell Award for best new writer in 2004, the year after his first professional stories were published. In 2008 Jay Lake was diagnosed with colon cancer, and in the years after he became known outside the sf genre as a powerful and brutally honest blogger about the progression of his disease. Jay Lake died on June 1, 2014.

PERMANENT FATAL ERRORS

JAY LAKE

Maduabuchi St. Macaria had never before traveled with an all-Howard crew. Mostly his kind kept to themselves, even under the empty skies of a planet. Those who did take ship almost always did so in a mixed or all-baseline human crew.

Not here, not aboard the threadneedle starship *Inclined Plane.* Seven crew including him, captained by a very strange woman who called herself Peridot Smith. All Howard Institute immortals. This was a new concept in long-range exploration, multi-decade interstellar missions with ageless crew, testbedded in orbit around the brown dwarf Tiede 1. That's what the newsfeeds said, anyway.

His experience was far more akin to a violent soap opera. Howards really weren't meant to be bottled up together. It wasn't in the design templates. Socially well-adjusted people didn't generally self-select to outlive everyone they'd ever known.

Even so, Maduabuchi was impressed by the welcome distraction of Tiede 1. Everyone else was too busy cleaning their weapons and hacking the internal comms and cams to pay attention to their mission objective. Not him.

Inclined Plane boasted an observation lounge. The hatch was coded "Observatory," but everything of scientific significance actually happened within the instrumentation woven into the ship's hull and the diaphanous energy fields stretching for kilometers beyond. The lounge was a folly of naval architecture, a translucent bubble fitted to the hull, consisting of roughly a third of a sphere of optically corrected artificial diamond grown to nanometer symmetry and smoothness in microgravity. Chances were good that in a catastrophe the rest of the ship would be shredded before the bubble would so much as be scratched.

There had been long, heated arguments in the galley, with math and footnotes and thumb breaking, over that exact question.

Maduabuchi liked to sit in the smartgel bodpods and let the ship perform a three-sixty massage while he watched the universe. The rest of the crew were like cats in a sack, too busy stalking the passageways and one another to care what might be outside the window. Here in the lounge one could see creation, witness the birth of stars, observe the death of planets, or listen to the quiet, empty cold of hard vacuum. The silence held a glorious music that echoed inside his head.

Maduabuchi wasn't a complete idiot—he'd rigged his own cabin with self-powered screamer circuits and an ultrahigh voltage capacitor. That ought to slow down anyone with delusions of traps.

Tiede 1 loomed outside. It seemed to shimmer as he watched, as if a starquake were propagating. The little star belied the ancient label of "brown dwarf." Stepped down by filtering nano that coated the diamond bubble, the surface glowed a dull reddish orange: a coal left too long in a campfire or a jewel in the velvet setting of night. Only 300,000 kilometers in diameter, and about five percent of a solar mass, it fell in that class of objects ambiguously distributed between planets and stars.

It could be anything, he thought. Anything.

A speck of green tugged at Maduabuchi's eye, straight from the heart of the star.

Green? There were no green emitters in nature.

"Amplification," he whispered. The nano filters living on the outside of the diamond shell obligingly began to self-assemble a lens. He controlled the aiming and focus with eye movements, trying to find whatever it was he had seen. Another ship? Reflection from a piece of rock or debris?

Excitement chilled Maduabuchi despite his best intentions to remain calm. What if this were evidence of the long-rumored but never-located alien civilizations that should have abounded in the Orion Arm of the Milky Way?

He scanned for twenty minutes, quartering Tiede 1's face as minutely as he could without direct access to the instrumentation and sensors carried by *Inclined Plane*. The ship's AI was friendly and helpful, but outside its narrow and critical competencies in managing the threadneedle drive and localspace navigation, was no more intelligent than your average dog, and so essentially useless for such work. He'd need to go to the Survey Suite to do more.

Maduabuchi finally stopped staring at the star and called up a deck schematic. "Ship, plot all weapons discharges or unscheduled energy expenditures within the pressurized cubage."

The schematic winked twice, but nothing was highlighted. Maybe Captain Smith had finally gotten them all to stand down. None of Maduabuchi's screamers had gone off, either, though everyone else had long since realized he didn't play their games.

Trusting that no one had hacked the entire tracking system, he cycled the lock and stepped into the passageway beyond. Glancing back at Tiede 1 as the lock irised shut, Maduabuchi saw another green flash.

He fought back a surge of irritation. The star was *not* mocking him.

Peridot Smith was in the Survey Suite when Maduabuchi cycled the lock there. Radiation-tanned from some melanin-deficient base hue of skin, lean, with her hair follicles removed and her scalp tattooed in an intricate mandala using magnetically sensitive ink, the captain was an arresting sight at any time. At the moment, she was glaring at him, her eyes flashing a strange, flat silver indicating serious tech integrated into the tissues. "Mr. St. Macaria." She gave him a terse nod. "How are the weapons systems?"

Ironically, of all the bloody-minded engineers and analysts and navigators aboard, *he* was the weapons officer.

"Capped and sealed per orders, ma'am," he replied. "Test circuits warm and green." *Inclined Plane* carried a modest mix of hardware, generalized for unknown threats rather than optimized for anti-piracy or planetary blockade duty, for example. Missiles, field projectors, electron strippers, fléchettes, even foggers and a sandcaster.

Most of which he had no real idea about. They were icons in the control systems, each maintained by its own little armies of nano and workbots. All he had were status lights and strat-tac displays. Decisions were made by specialized subsystems.

It was the rankest makework, but Maduabuchi didn't mind. He'd volunteered for the Howard Institute program because of the most basic human motivation—tourism. Seeing what was over the next hill had trumped even sex as the driving force in human evolution. He was happy to be a walking, talking selection mechanism.

Everything else, including this tour of duty, was just something to do while the years slid past.

"What did you need, Mr. St. Macaria?"

"I was going to take a closer look at Tiede 1, ma'am."

"That *is* what we're here for."

He looked for humor in her dry voice, and did not find it. "Ma'am, yes ma'am. I . . . I just think I saw something."

"Oh, really?" Her eyes flashed, reminding Maduabuchi uncomfortably of blades.

Embarrassed, he turned back to the passageway. "What did you see?" she asked from behind him. Now her voice was edged as well.

"Nothing, ma'am. Nothing at all."

Back in the passageway, Maduabuchi fled toward his cabin. Several of the crew laughed from sick bay, their voices rising over the whine of the bone-knitter. Someone had gone down hard.

Not him. Not even at the hands—or eyes—of Captain Smith.

An hour later, after checking the locations of the crew again with the ship's AI, he ventured back to the Survey Suite. Chillicothe Xiang nodded to him in the passageway, almost friendly, as she headed aft for a half-shift monitoring the power plants in Engineering.

"Hey," Maduabuchi said in return. She didn't answer, didn't even seem to notice he'd spoken. All these years, all the surgeries and nano injections and training, and somehow he was still the odd kid out on the playground.

Being a Howard Immortal was supposed to be *different*. And it was, when he wasn't around other Howard Immortals.

The Survey Suite was empty, as advertised. Ultra-def screens wrapped the walls, along with a variety of control inputs, from classical keypads to haptics and gestural zones. Maduabuchi slipped into the observer's seat and swept his hand to open the primary sensor routines.

Captain Smith had left her last data run parked in the core sandbox.

His fingers hovered over the purge, then pulled back. What had she been looking at that had made her so interested in what he'd seen? Those eyes flashed edged and dangerous in his memory. He almost asked the ship where she was, but a question like that would be reported, drawing more attention than it was worth.

Maduabuchi closed his eyes for a moment, screwing up his courage, and opened the data run.

It cascaded across the screens, as well as virtual presentations in the aerosolized atmosphere of the Survey Suite. Much more than he'd seen when he was in here before—plots, scales, arrays, imaging across the EM spectrum, color-coded tabs and fields and stacks and matrices. Even his Howard-enhanced senses had trouble keeping up with the flood. Captain Smith was far older and more experienced than Maduabuchi, over half a dozen centuries to his few decades, and she had developed both the mental habits and the individualized mentarium to handle such inputs.

On the other hand, *he* was a much newer model. Everyone upgraded, but the Howard Institute baseline tech evolved over generations just like everything else in human culture. Maduabuchi bent to his work, absorbing the overwhelming bandwidth of her scans of Tiede 1, and trying to sort out what it was that had been the true object of her attention.

Something *had* to be hidden in plain sight here.

He worked an entire half-shift without being disturbed, sifting petabytes of data, until the truth hit him. The color-coding of one spectral analysis matrix was nearly identical to the green flash he thought he'd seen on the surface of Tiede 1.

All the data was a distraction. Her real work had been hidden in the metadata, passing for nothing more than a sorting signifier.

Once Maduabuchi realized that, he unpacked the labeling on the spectral analysis matrix and opened up an entirely new data environment. Green, it was all about the green.

"I was wondering how long that would take you," said Captain Smith from the opening hatch.

Maduabuchi jumped in his chair, opened his mouth to make some denial, then closed it again. Her eyes didn't *look* razored this time, and her voice held a tense amusement.

He fell back on that neglected standby, the truth. "Interesting color you have here, ma'am."

"I thought so." Smith stepped inside, cycled the lock shut, then code-locked it with a series of beeps that meant her command override was engaged. "Ship," she said absently, "sensory blackout on this area."

"Acknowledged, Captain," said the ship's puppy-friendly voice.

"What do you think it means, Mr. St. Macaria?"

"Stars don't shine green. Not to the human eye. The blackbody radiation curve just doesn't work that way." He added, "Ma'am."

"Thank you for defining the problem." Her voice was dust-dry again.

Maduabuchi winced. He'd given himself away, as simply as that. But clearly she already knew about the green flashes. "I don't think that's the problem, ma'am."

"Mmm?"

"If it was, we'd all be lining up like good kids to have a look at the optically impossible brown dwarf."

"Fair enough. Then what *is* the problem, Mr. St. Macaria?"

He drew a deep breath and chose his next words with care. Peridot Smith was *old,* old in a way he'd never be, even with her years behind him someday. "I don't know what the problem is, ma'am, but if it's a problem to you, it's a command issue. Politics. And light doesn't have politics."

Much to his surprise, she laughed. "You'd be amazed. But yes. Again, well done."

She hadn't said that before, but he took the compliment. "What kind of command problem, ma'am?"

Captain Smith sucked in a long, noisy breath and eyed him speculatively. A sharp gaze, to be certain. "Someone on this ship is on their own mission. We were jiggered into coming to Tiede 1 to provide cover, and I don't know what for."

"Not me!" Maduabuchi blurted.

"I know that."

The dismissal in her words stung for a moment, but on the whole, he realized he'd rather not be a suspect in this particular witch hunt.

His feelings must have shown in his face, because she smiled and added, "You haven't been around long enough to get sucked into the Howard factions. And you have a rep for being indifferent to the seductive charms of power."

"Uh, yes." Maduabuchi wasn't certain what to say to that.

"Why do you think you're *here?*" She leaned close, her breath hot on his face. "I needed someone who would reliably not be conspiring against me."

"A useful idiot," he said. "But there's only seven of us. How many *could* be conspiring? And over a green light?"

"It's Tiede 1," Captain Smith answered. "Someone is here gathering signals. I don't know for what. Or who. Because it could be any of the rest of the crew. Or all of them."

"But this is politics, not mutiny. Right . . . ?"

"Right." She brushed off the concern. "We're not getting hijacked out here. And if someone tries, I *am* the meanest fighter on this ship by a wide margin. I can take any three of this crew apart."

"Any five of us, though?" he asked softly.

"That's another use for you."

"I don't fight."

"No, but you're a Howard. You're hard enough to kill that you can take it at my back long enough to keep me alive."

"Uh, thanks," Maduabuchi said, very uncertain now.

"You're welcome." Her eyes strayed to the data arrays floating across the screens and in the virtual presentations. "The question is who, what and why."

"Have you compared the observational data to known stellar norms?" he asked.

"Green flashes aren't a known stellar norm."

"No, but we don't know for what the green flashes are normal, either. If we compare Tiede 1 to other brown dwarfs, we might spot further anomalies. Then we triangulate."

"And *that* is why I brought you." Captain Smith's tone was very satisfied indeed. "I'll leave you to your work."

"Thank you, ma'am." To his surprise, Maduabuchi realized he meant it.

He spent the next half-shift combing through comparative astronomy. At this point, almost a thousand years into the human experience of interstellar travel, there was an embarrassing wealth of data. So much so that even petabyte q-bit storage matrices were overrun, as eventually the challenges of indexing and retrieval went metastatic. Still, one thing Howards were very good at was data processing. Nothing ever built could truly match the pattern recognition and free associative skills of human (or post-human) wetware collectively known as "hunches." Strong AIs could approximate that uniquely biological skill through a combination of brute force and deeply clever circuit design, but even then, the spark of inspiration did not flow so well.

Maduabuchi slipped into his flow state to comb through more data in a few hours than a baseline human could absorb in a year. Brown dwarfs, superjovians, fusion cycles, failed stars, hydrogen, helium, lithium, surface temperatures, density, gravity gradients, emission spectrum lines, astrographic surveys, theories dating back to the dawn of observational astronomy, digital images in two and three dimensions as well as time lensed.

When he emerged, driven by the physiological mundanities of bladder and blood sugar, Maduabuchi knew something was wrong. He *knew* it. Captain Smith had been right about her mission, about there being something off in their voyage to Tiede 1.

But she didn't know what it was she was right about. He didn't either.

Still, the thought niggled somewhere deep in his mind. Not the green flash *per se*, though that, too. Something more about Tiede 1.

Or less.

"And what the hell did that mean?" he asked the swarming motes of data surrounding him on the virtual displays, now reduced to confetti as he left his informational fugue.

Maduabuchi stumbled out of the Survey Suite to find the head, the galley, and Captain Peridot Smith, in that order.

The corridor was filled with smoke, though no alarms wailed. He almost ducked back into the Survey Suite, but instead dashed for one of the emergency stations found every ten meters or so and grabbed an oxygen mask. Then he hit the panic button.

That produced a satisfying wail, along with lights strobing at four distinct frequencies. Something was wrong with the gravimetrics, too—the floor had felt syrupy, then too light, with each step. Where the hell was fire suppression?

The bridge was next. He couldn't imagine that they were under attack—*Inclined Plane* was the only ship in the Tiede 1 system so far as any of them knew. And short of some kind of pogrom against Howard immortals, no one had any reason to attack their vessel.

Mutiny, he thought, and wished he had an actual weapon. Though what he'd do with it was not clear. The irony that the lowest-scoring shooter in the history of the Howard training programs was now working as a weapons officer was not lost on him.

He stumbled onto the bridge to find Chillicothe Xiang there, laughing her ass off with Paimei Joyner, one of their two scouts—hard-assed Howards so heavily modded that they could at need tolerate hard vacuum on their bare skin, and routinely worked outside for hours with minimal life support and radiation shielding. The strobes were running in here, but the audible alarm was mercifully muted. Also, whatever was causing the smoke didn't seem to have reached into here yet.

Captain Smith stood at the far end of the bridge, her back to the diamond viewing wall that was normally occluded by a virtual display, though at the moment the actual, empty majesty of Tiede 1 localspace was visible.

Smith was snarling. " . . . don't care what you thought you were doing; clean up my ship's air! Now, damn it."

The two turned toward the hatch, nearly ran into Maduabuchi in his breathing mask, and renewed their laughter.

"You look like a spaceman," said Chillicothe.

"Moral here," added Paimei. One deep black hand reached out to grasp Maduabuchi's shoulder so hard he winced. "Don't try making a barbecue in the galley."

"We'll be eating con-rats for a week," snapped Captain Smith. "And everyone on this ship will know damned well it's your fault we're chewing our teeth loose."

The two walked out, Paimei shoving Maduabuchi into a bulkhead while Chillicothe leaned close. "Take off the mask," she whispered. "You look stupid in it."

Moments later, Maduabuchi was alone with the captain, the mask dangling in his grasp.

"What was it?" she asked in a quiet, gentle voice that carried more respect than he probably deserved.

"I have . . . had something," Maduabuchi said. "A sort of, well, *hunch*. But it's slipped away in all that chaos."

Smith nodded, her face closed and hard. "Idiots built a fire in the galley, just to see if they could."

"Is that possible?"

"If you have sufficient engineering talent, yes," the captain admitted grudgingly. "And are very bored."

"Or want to create a distraction," Maduabuchi said, unthinking.

"Damn it," Smith shouted. She stepped to her command console. "What did we miss out there?"

"No," he said, his hunches suddenly back in play. This was like a flow hangover. "Whatever's out there was out there all along. The green flash. Whatever it is." And didn't *that* niggle at his thoughts like a cockroach in an airscrubber. "What we missed was in here."

"And when," the captain asked, her voice very slow now, viscous with thought, "did you and I become *we* as separate from the rest of this crew?"

When you first picked me, ma'am, Maduabuchi thought but did not say. "I don't know. But I was in the Survey Suite, and you were on the bridge. The rest of this crew was somewhere else."

"You can't look at everything, damn it," she muttered. "Some things should just be trusted to match their skin."

Her words pushed Maduabuchi back into his flow state, where the hunch reared up and slammed him in the forebrain with a broad, hairy paw.

"I know what's wrong," he said, shocked at the enormity of the realization.

"What?"

Maduabuchi shook his head. It couldn't possibly be true. The ship's orientation was currently such that the bridge faced away from Tiede 1, but he stared at the screen anyway. Somewhere outside that diamond sheeting—rather smaller than the lounge, but still substantial—was a work of engineering on a scale no human had ever contemplated.

No *human* was the key word.

"The brown dwarf out there . . ." He shook with the thought, trying to force the words out. "It's artificial. Camouflage. S-something else is hidden beneath that surface. Something big and huge and . . . I don't know what. And s-someone on our ship has been communicating with it."

Who could possibly manage such a thing?

Captain Peridot Smith gave him a long, slow stare. Her razored eyes cut into him as if he were a specimen on a lab table. Slowly, she pursed her lips. Her head shook just slightly. "I'm going to have to ask you to stand down, Mr. St. Macaria. You're clearly unfit for duty."

What! Maduabuchi opened his mouth to protest, to argue, to push back against her decision, but closed it again in the face of that stare. Of course she knew. She'd known all along. She was testing . . . whom? Him? The rest of the crew?

He realized it didn't matter. His line of investigation was cut off. Maduabuchi knew when he was beaten. He turned to leave the bridge, then stopped at the hatch. The breathing mask still dangled in his hand.

"If you didn't want me to find that out, ma'am," he asked, "then why did you set me to looking for it?"

But she'd already turned away from him without answering, and was making a study of her command data.

Chillicothe Xiang found him in the observation lounge an hour later. Uncharacteristically, Maduabuchi had retreated into alcohol. Metabolic poisons were not so effective on Howard Immortals, but if he hit something high enough proof, he could follow youthful memories of the buzz.

"That's Patrice's forty-year-old scotch you're drinking," she observed, standing over the smartgel bodpod that wrapped him like a warm, sticky uterus.

"Huh." Patrice Tonwe, their engineering chief, was a hard son of a bitch. One of the leaders in that perpetual game of shake-and-break the rest of the crew spent their time on. Extremely political as well, even by Howard standards. Not someone to get on the wrong side of.

Shrugging off the thought and its implications, Maduabuchi looked at the little beaker he'd poured the stuff into. "Smelled strongest to me."

Chillicothe laughed. "You are hopeless, Mad. Like the galaxy's oldest adolescent."

Once again he felt stung. "I'm one hundred forty-three years-subjective old. Born over two hundred years-objective ago."

"So?" She nodded at his drink. "Look at that. And I'll bet you never even changed genders once before you went Howard. The boy who never grew up."

He settled further back and took a gulp from his beaker. His throat burned and itched, but Maduabuchi would be damned if he'd give her the satisfaction of choking. "What do you want?"

She knelt close. "I kind of like you, okay? Don't get excited, you're just an all right kid. That's all I'm saying. And because I like you, I'm telling you, don't ask."

Maduabuchi was going to make her say it. "Don't ask what?"

"Just don't ask questions." Chillicothe mimed a pistol with the fingers of her left hand. "Some answers are permanent fatal errors."

He couldn't help noting her right hand was on the butt of a real pistol. Fléchette-throwing riot gun, capable of shredding skin, muscle and bone to pink fog without damaging hull integrity.

"I don't know," he mumbled. "Where I grew up, green light means go."

Chillicothe shook him, a disgusted sneer chasing across her lips. "It's your life, kid. Do what you like."

With that, she stalked out of the observation lounge.

Maduabuchi wondered why she'd cared enough to bother trying to warn him off. Maybe Chillicothe had told the simple truth for once. Maybe she liked him. No way for him to know.

Instead of trying to work that out, he stared at Tiede 1's churning orange surface. "Who are you? What are you doing in there? What does it take to fake being an entire *star?*"

The silent light brought no answers, and neither did Patrice's scotch. Still, he continued to ask the questions for a while.

Eventually he woke up, stiff in the smartgel. The stuff had enclosed all of Maduabuchi except for his face, and it took several minutes of effort to extract himself. When he looked up at the sky, the stars had shifted.

They'd broken Tiede 1 orbit!

He scrambled for the hatch, but to his surprise, his hand on the touchpad did not cause the door to open. A moment's stabbing and squinting showed that the lock had been frozen on command override.

Captain Smith had trapped him in here.

"Not for long," he muttered. There was a maintenance hatch at the aft end of the lounge, leading to the dorsal weapons turret. The power and materials chase in the spine of the hull was partially pressurized, well within his mini-mally Howard-enhanced environmental tolerances.

And as weapons officer, *he* had the command overrides to those systems. If Captain Smith hadn't already locked him out.

To keep himself going, Maduabuchi gobbled some prote-nuts from the little service bar at the back of the lounge. Then, before he lost his nerve, he shifted wall hangings that obscured the maintenance hatch and hit that pad. The interlock system demanded his command code, which he provided with a swift haptic pass, then the wall section retracted with a faint squeak that spoke of neglected maintenance.

The passage beyond was ridiculously low-clearance. He nearly had to hold his breath to climb to the spinal chase. And cold, damned cold. Maduabuchi figured he could spend ten, fifteen minutes tops up there before he began experiencing serious physiological and psychological reactions.

Where to go?

The chase terminated aft above Engineering, with access to the firing points there, as well as egress to the Engineering bay. Forward it met a vertical chase just before the bridge section, with an exterior hatch, access to the forward firing points, and a connection to the ventral chase.

No point in going outside. Not much point in going to Engineering, where like as not he'd meet Patrice or Paimei and wind up being sorry about it.

He couldn't get onto the bridge directly, but he'd get close and try to find out.

The chase wasn't really intended for crew transit, but it had to be large enough to admit a human being for inspection and repairs, when the automated systems couldn't handle something. It was a shitty, difficult crawl, but *Inclined Plane* was only about two hundred meters stem to stern anyway. He passed over several intermediate access hatches—no point in getting out—then simply climbed down and out in the passageway when he reached the bridge. Taking control of the exterior weapons systems from within the walls of the ship wasn't going to do him any good. The interior systems concentrated on disaster suppression and anti-hijacking, and were not under his control anyway.

No one was visible when Maduabuchi slipped out from the walls. He wished he had a pistol, or even a good, long-handled wrench, but he couldn't take down any of the rest of these Howards even if he tried. He settled for hitting the bridge touchpad and walking in when the hatch irised open.

Patrice sat in the captain's chair. Chillicothe manned the navigation boards. They both glanced up at him, surprised.

"What are you doing here?" Chillicothe demanded.

"Not being locked in the lounge," he answered, acutely conscious of his utter lack of any plan of action. "Where's Captain Smith?"

"In her cabin," said Patrice without looking up. His voice was a growl, coming from a heavyworld body like a sack of bricks. "Where she'll be staying."

"Wh-why?"

"What did I tell you about questions?" Chillicothe asked softly.

Something cold rested against the hollow spot of skin just behind Maduabuchi's right ear. Paimei's voice whispered close. "Should have listened to the woman. Curiosity killed the cat, you know."

They will never expect it, he thought, and threw an elbow back, spinning to land a punch on Paimei. He never made the hit. Instead he found himself on the deck, her boot against the side of his head.

At least the pistol wasn't in his ear any more.

Maduabuchi laughed at that thought. Such a pathetic rationalization. He opened his eyes to see Chillicothe leaning over.

"What do you think is happening here?" she asked.

He had to spit the words out. "You've taken over the sh-ship. L-locked Captain Smith in her cabin. L-locked me up to k-keep me out of the way."

Chillicothe laughed, her voice harsh and bitter. Patrice growled some warning that Maduabuchi couldn't hear, not with Paimei's boot pressing down on his ear.

"She tried to open a comms channel to something very dangerous. She's been relieved of her command. That's not mutiny; that's self-defense."

"And compliance to regulation," said Paimei, shifting her foot a little so Maduabuchi would be sure to hear her.

"Something's inside that star."

Chillicothe's eyes stirred. "You still haven't learned about questions, have you?"

"I w-want to talk to the captain."

She glanced back toward Patrice, now out of Maduabuchi's very limited line of sight. Whatever look was exchanged resulted in Chillicothe shaking her head. "No. That's not wise. You'd have been fine inside the lounge. A day or two, we could have let you out. We're less than eighty hours-subjective from making threadneedle transit back to Saorsen Station; then this won't matter any more."

He just couldn't keep his mouth shut. "Why won't it matter?"

"Because no one will ever know. Even what's in the data will be lost in the flood of information."

I could talk, Maduabuchi thought. I could tell. But then I'd just be another crazy ranting about the aliens that no one has ever found across several thousand explored solar systems in hundreds of light-years of the Orion Arm. The crazies that had been ranting all through human history about the Fermi Paradox. He could imagine the conversation. "No, really. There are aliens. Living in the heart of a brown dwarf. They flashed a green light at me."

Brown dwarfs were *everywhere*. Did that mean that aliens were *everywhere*, hiding inside the hearts of their guttering little stars?

He was starting to sound crazy, even to himself. But even now, Maduabuchi couldn't keep his mouth shut. "You know the answer to the greatest question in human history. 'Where is everybody else?' And you're not talking about it. What did the aliens tell you?"

"That's it," said Paimei. Her fingers closed on his shoulder. "You're out the airlock, buddy."

"No," said Chillicothe. "Leave him alone."

Another rumble from Patrice, of agreement. Maduabuchi, in sudden, sweaty fear for his life, couldn't tell whom the man was agreeing *with*.

The fléchette pistol was back against his ear. "Why?"

"Because we like him. Because he's one of ours." Her voice grew very soft. "Because I said so."

Reluctantly, Paimei let him go. Maduabuchi got to his feet, shaking. He wanted to *know*, damn it, his curiosity burning with a fire he couldn't ever recall feeling in his nearly two centuries of life.

"Go back to your cabin." Chillicothe's voice was tired. "Or the lounge. Just stay out of everyone's way."

"Especially mine," Paimei growled. She shoved him out the bridge hatch, which cycled to cut him off.

Like that, he was alone. So little a threat that they left him unescorted within the ship. Maduabuchi considered his options. The sane one was to go sit quietly with some books until this was all over. The most appealing was to go find Captain Smith, but she'd be under guard behind a hatch locked by command override.

But if he shut up, if he left now, if he never *knew* . . . *Inclined Plane* wouldn't be back this way, even if he happened to be crewing her again. No one else had reason to come to Tiede 1, and he didn't have resources to mount his own expedition. Might not for many centuries to come. When they departed this system, they'd leave the mystery behind. *And it was too damned important.*

Maduabuchi realized he couldn't live with that. To be this close to the answer to Fermi's question. To know that the people around him, possibly everyone around him, knew the truth and had kept him in the dark.

The crew wanted to play hard games? Then hard games they'd get.

He stalked back through the passageway to the number two lateral. Both of *Inclined Plane*'s boats were docked there, one on each side. A workstation was at each hatch, intended for use when managing docking or cargo transfers or other such logistical efforts where the best eyes might be down here, off the bridge.

Maduabuchi tapped himself into the weapons systems with his own still-active overrides. Patrice and Chillicothe and the rest were counting on the safety of silence to ensure there were no untoward questions when they got home. He could nix that.

He locked down every weapons system for 300 seconds, then set them all to emergency purge. Every chamber, every rack, every capacitor would be fully discharged and emptied. It was a procedure for emergency dockings, so you didn't come in hot and hard with a payload that could blow holes in the rescuers trying to catch you.

Let *Inclined Plane* return to port with every weapons system blown, and there'd be an investigation. He cycled the hatch, slipped into the portside launch. Let *Inclined Plane* come into port with a boat and a crewman missing, and there'd be even more of an investigation. Those two events together would make faking a convincing log report pretty tough. Especially without Captain Smith's help.

He couldn't think about it any more. Maduabuchi strapped himself in, initiated the hot-start preflight sequence, and muted ship comms. He'd be gone before Paimei and her cohorts could force the blast-rated docking hatch. His weapons systems override would keep them from simply blasting him out of space, then concocting a story at their leisure.

And the launch had plenty of engine capacity to get him back to close orbit around Tiede 1.

Blowing the clamps on a hot-start drop, Maduabuchi goosed the launch on a minimum-time transit back toward the glowering brown dwarf. Captain Smith wouldn't leave him here to die. She'd be back before he ran out of water and air.

Besides, someone was home down there, damn it, and he was going to go knocking.

Behind him, munitions began cooking off into the vacuum. Radiations across the EM spectrum coruscated against the launch's forward viewports, while instrumentation screeched alerts he didn't need to hear. It didn't matter now. Screw Chillicothe's warning about not asking questions. "Permanent fatal errors," his ass.

One way or the other, Maduabuchi would find the answers if it killed him.

Carter Scholz is the author of *Palimpsests* (with Glenn Harcourt), *Kafka Americana* (with Jonathan Lethem), *Radiance*, and *The Amount to Carry*. He has been nominated for the Nebula, Hugo, Campbell, and Sturgeon awards. He lives in northern California.

GYPSY

CARTER SCHOLZ

The living being is only a species of the dead, and a very rare species. —Nietzsche

When a long shot is all you have, you're a fool not to take it. —Romany saying

1.

The launch of Earth's first starship went unremarked. The crew gave no interviews. No camera broadcast the hard light pulsing from its tail. To the plain eye, it might have been a common airplane.

The media battened on multiple wars and catastrophes. The Arctic Ocean was open sea. Florida was underwater. Crises and opportunities intersected.

World population was something over ten billion. No one was really counting any more. A few billion were stateless refugees. A few billion more were indentured or imprisoned.

Oil reserves, declared as recently as 2010 to exceed a trillion barrels, proved to be an accounting gimmick, gone by 2020. More difficult and expensive sources—tar sands in Canada and Venezuela, natural-gas fracking—became primary, driving up atmospheric methane and the price of fresh water.

The countries formerly known as the Third World stripped and sold their resources with more ruthless abandon than their mentors had. With the proceeds they armed themselves.

The US was no longer the global hyperpower, but it went on behaving as if. Generations of outspending the rest of the world combined had made this its habit and brand: arms merchant to expedient allies, former and future foes alike, starting or provoking conflicts more or less at need, its constant need being, as always, resources. Its waning might was built on a memory of those vast native reserves it had long since expropriated and depleted, and a sense of entitlement to more. These overseas conflicts were problematic and carried wildly unintended consequences. As the President of Venezuela put it just days before his assassination, "It's dangerous to go to war against your own asshole."

The starship traveled out of our solar system at a steep angle to the ecliptic plane. It would pass no planets. It was soon gone. Going South.

Sophie (2043)

Trying to rise up out of the cold sinking back into a dream of rising up out of the. Stop, stop it now. Shivering. So dark. So thirsty. Momma? Help me?

Her parents were wealthy. They had investments, a great home, they sent her to the best schools. They told her how privileged she was. She'd always assumed this meant she would be okay forever. She was going to be a poet.

It was breathtaking how quickly it went away, all that okay. Her dad's job, the investments, the college tuition, the house. In two years, like so many others they were penniless and living in their car. She left unfinished her thesis on Louis Zukofsky's last book, 80 Flowers. She changed her major to Information Science, slept with a loan officer, finished grad school half a million in debt, and immediately took the best-paying job she could find, at Xocket Defense Systems. Librarian. She hadn't known that defense contractors hired librarians. They were pretty much the only ones who did any more. Her student loan was adjustable rate—the only kind offered. As long as the rate didn't go up, she could just about get by on her salary. Best case, she'd have it paid off in thirty years. Then the rate doubled. She lost her apartment. XDS had huge dorms for employees who couldn't afford their own living space. Over half their workforce lived there. It was indentured servitude.

Yet she was lucky, lucky. If she'd been a couple of years younger she wouldn't have finished school at all. She'd be fighting in Burma or Venezuela or Kazakhstan.

At XDS she tended the library's firewalls, maintained and documented software, catalogued projects, fielded service calls from personnel who needed this or that right now, or had forgotten a password, or locked themselves out of their own account. She learned Unix, wrote cron scripts and daemons and Perl routines. There was a satisfaction in keeping it all straight. She was a serf, but they needed her and they knew it, and that knowledge sustained in her a hard small sense of freedom. She thought of Zukofsky, teaching for twenty years at Brooklyn Polytech. It was almost a kind of poetry, the vocabulary of code.

Chirping. Birds? Were there still birds?

No. Tinnitus. Her ears ached for sound in this profound silence. Created their own.

*

She was a California girl, an athlete, a hiker, a climber. She'd been all over the Sierra Nevada, had summited four 14,000-footers by the time she was sixteen. She loved the backcountry. Loved its stark beauty, solitude, the life that survived in its harshness: the pikas, the marmots, the mountain chickadees, the heather and whitebark pine and polemonium.

After joining XDS, it became hard for her to get to the mountains. Then it became impossible. In 2035 the Keep Wilderness Wild Act shut the public out of the national parks, the national forests, the BLM lands. The high country above timberline was surveilled by satellites and drones, and it was said that mining and fracking operators would shoot intruders on sight, and that in the remotest areas, like the Enchanted Gorge and the Muro Blanco, lived small nomadic bands of malcontents. She knew enough about the drones and satellites to doubt it; no one on Earth could stay hidden anywhere for more than a day.

The backcountry she mourned was all Earth to her. To lose it was to lose all Earth. And to harden something final inside her.

One day Roger Fry came to her attention—perhaps it was the other way round— poking in her stacks where he didn't belong. That was odd; the login and password had been validated, the clearance was the highest, there was no place in the stacks prohibited to this user; yet her alarms had tripped. By the time she put packet sniffers on it he was gone. In her email was an invitation to visit a website called Gypsy.

When she logged in she understood at once. It thrilled her and frightened her. They were going to leave the planet. It was insane. Yet she felt the powerful seduction of it. How starkly its plain insanity exposed the greater consensus insanity the planet was now living. That there was an alternative—!

She sat up on the slab. Slowly unwrapped the mylar bodysuit, disconnected one by one its drips and derms and stents and catheters and waldos and sensors. Let it drift crinkling to the floor.

Her breathing was shallow and ragged. Every few minutes she gasped for air and her pulse raced. The temperature had been raised to 20° Celsius as she came to, but still she shivered. Her body smelled a way it had never smelled before. Like vinegar and nail polish. It looked pale and flabby, but familiar. After she'd gathered strength, she reached under the slab, found a sweatshirt and sweatpants, and pulled them on. There was also a bottle of water. She drank it all.

The space was small and dark and utterly silent. No ports, no windows. Here and there, on flat black walls, glowed a few pods of LEDs. She braced her hands against the slab and stood up, swaying. Even in the slight gravity her heart pounded. The ceiling curved gently away a handsbreadth above her head, and the floor curved gently upward. Unseen beyond the ceiling was the center of the ship, the hole of the donut, and beyond that the other half of the slowly spinning torus. Twice a minute it rotated, creating a centripetal gravity of one-tenth g. Any slower would be too weak to be helpful. Any faster, gravity would differ at the head and the feet enough to cause vertigo. Under her was the outer ring of the water tank, then panels of aerogel sandwiched within sheets of hydrogenous carbon-composite, then a surrounding jacket of liquid hydrogen tanks, and then interstellar space.

What had happened? Why was she awake?

Look, over seventy-plus years, systems will fail. We can't rely on auto-repair. With a crew of twenty, we could wake one person every few years to perform maintenance.

And put them back under? Hibernation is dicey enough without trying to do it twice.

Yes, it's a risk. What's the alternative?

What about failsafes? No one gets wakened unless a system is critical. Then we wake a specialist. A steward.

That could work.

She walked the short distance to the ship's console and sat. It would have been grandiose to call it a bridge. It was a small desk bolted to the floor. It held a couple of monitors, a keyboard, some pads. It was like the light and sound booth of a community theater.

She wished she could turn on more lights. There were no more. Their energy budget was too tight. They had a fission reactor onboard but it wasn't running. It was to fire the nuclear rocket at their arrival. It wouldn't last seventy-two years if they used it for power during their cruise.

Not far from her—nothing on the ship was far from her—were some fifty kilograms of plutonium pellets—not the Pu-239 of fission bombs, but the more energetic Pu-238. The missing neutron cut the isotope's half-life from twenty-five thousand years to eighty-eight years, and made it proportionately more radioactive. That alpha radiation was contained by iridium cladding and a casing of graphite, but the pellets still gave off heat, many kilowatts' worth. Most of that heat warmed the ship's interior to its normal temperature of 4° Celsius. Enough of it was channeled outward to keep the surrounding water liquid in its jacket, and the outer tanks of hydrogen at 14 kelvins, slush, maximally dense. The rest of the heat ran a Stirling engine to generate electricity.

First she read through the protocols, which she had written: Stewards' logs to be read by each wakened steward. Kept in the computers, with redundant backups, but also kept by hand, ink on paper, in case of system failures, a last-chance critical backup.

And because there is something restorative about writing by hand.

There were no stewards' logs. She was the first to be wakened.

They were only two years out. Barely into the Oort cloud. She felt let down. What had gone wrong so soon?

All at once she was ravenous. She stood, and the gravity differential hit her. She steadied herself against the desk, then took two steps to the storage bay. Three-quarters of the ship was storage. What they would need at the other end. What Roger called pop-up civilization. She only had to go a step inside to find a box of MREs. She took three, stepped out, and put one into the microwave. The smell of it warming made her mouth water and her stomach heave. Her whole body trembled as she ate. Immediately she put a second into the microwave. As she waited for it, she fell asleep.

She saw Roger, what must have happened to him after that terrible morning when they received his message: Go. Go now. Go at once.

He was wearing an orange jumpsuit, shackled to a metal table.

How did you think you could get away with it, Fry?

I did get away with it. They've gone.

But we've got you.

That doesn't matter. I was never meant to be aboard.

Where are they going?

Alpha Centauri. (He would pronounce it with the hard K.)

That's impossible.

Very likely. But that's where they're going.

Why?

It's less impossible than here.

When she opened her eyes, her second meal had cooled, but she didn't want it. Her disused bowels protested. She went to the toilet and strained but voided only a trickle of urine. Feeling ill, she hunched in the dark, small space, shivering, sweat from her armpits running down her ribs. The smell of her urine mixed with the toilet's chemicals and the sweetly acrid odor of her long fast.

pleine de l'âcre odour des temps, poudreuse et noire
full of the acrid smell of time, dusty and black

Baudelaire. Another world. With wonder she felt it present itself. Consciousness was a mystery. She stared into the darkness, fell asleep again on the pot.

Again she saw Roger shackled to the metal table. A door opened and he looked up.

We've decided.

He waited.

Your ship, your crew, your people—they don't exist. No one will ever know about them.

Roger was silent.

The ones remaining here, the ones who helped you—you're thinking we can't keep them all quiet. We can. We're into your private keys. We know everyone who was involved. We'll round them up. The number's small enough. After all your work, Roger, all their years of effort, there will be nothing but a few pathetic rumors and conspiracy theories. All those good people who helped you will be disappeared forever. Like you. How does that make you feel?

They knew the risks. For them it was already over. Like me.

Over? Oh, Roger. We can make "over" last a long time.

Still, we did it. They did it. They know that.

You're not hearing me, Roger. I said we've changed that.

The ship is out there.

No. I said it's not. Repeat after me. Say it's not, Roger.

BUFFER OVERFLOW. So that was it. Their datastream was not being received. Sophie had done much of the information theory design work. An energy-efficient system approaching Shannon's limit for channel capacity. Even from Alpha C it would be only ten joules per bit.

The instruments collected data. Magnetometer, spectrometers, plasma analyzer, cosmic-ray telescope, Cerenkov detector, et cetera. Data was queued in a transmit buffer and sent out more or less continuously at a low bit rate. The protocol was designed to be robust against interference, dropped packets, interstellar scintillation, and the long latencies imposed by their great distance and the speed of light.

They'd debated even whether to carry communications.

What's the point? We're turning our backs on them.

Roger was insistent: Are we scientists? This is an unprecedented chance to collect data in the heliopause, the Oort cloud, the interstellar medium, the Alpha system itself. Astrometry from Alpha, reliable distances to every star in our galaxy—that alone is huge.

Sending back data broadcasts our location.

So? How hard is it to follow a nuclear plasma trail to the nearest star? Anyway, they'd need a ship to follow. We have the only one.

You say the Earth situation is terminal. Who's going to receive this data?

Anybody. Everybody.

So: Shackleton Crater. It was a major comm link anyway, and its site at the south pole of the Moon assured low ambient noise and permanent line of sight to the ship. They had a Gypsy there—one of their tribe—to receive their data.

The datastream was broken up into packets, to better weather the long trip home. Whenever Shackleton received a packet, it responded with an acknowledgement, to confirm reception. When the ship received that ACK signal—at their present distance, that would be about two months after a packet was transmitted—the confirmed packet was removed from the transmit queue to make room for new data. Otherwise the packet went back to the end of the queue, to be retransmitted later. Packets were time-stamped, so they could be reassembled into a consecutive datastream no matter in what order they were received.

But no ACK signals had been received for over a year. The buffer was full. That's why she was awake.

They'd known the Shackleton link could be broken, even though it had a plausible cover story of looking for SETI transmissions from Alpha C. But other Gypsies on Earth should also be receiving. Someone should be acknowledging. A year of silence!

Going back through computer logs, she found there'd been an impact. Eight months ago something had hit the ship. Why hadn't that wakened a steward?

It had been large enough to get through the forward electromagnetic shield. The shield deflected small particles which, over decades, would erode their hull. The damage had been instantaneous. Repair geckos responded in the first minutes. Since it took most of a day to rouse a steward, there would have been no point.

Maybe the impact hit the antenna array. She checked and adjusted alignment to the Sun. They were okay. She took a routine spectrograph and measured the Doppler shift.

0.056 c.

No. Their velocity should be 0.067 c.

Twelve years. It added twelve years to their cruising time.

She studied the ship's logs as that sank in. The fusion engine had burned its last over a year ago, then was jettisoned to spare mass.

Why hadn't a steward awakened before her? The computer hadn't logged any problems. Engine function read as normal; the sleds that held the fuel had been emptied one by one and discarded all the fuel had been burned—all as planned. So, absent other problems, the lower velocity alone hadn't triggered an alert. Stupid!

Think. They'd begun to lag only in the last months of burn. Some ignitions had failed or underperformed. It was probably antiproton decay in the triggers. Nothing could have corrected that. Good thinking, nice fail.

Twelve years.

It angered her. The impact and the low velocity directly threatened their survival, and no alarms went off. But loss of comms, *that* set off alarms, that was important to Roger. Who was never meant to be on board. *He's turned his back on humanity, but he still wants them to hear all about it. And to hell with us.*

When her fear receded, she was calmer. If Roger still believed in anything redeemable about humankind, it was the scientific impulse. Of course it was primary to him that this ship do science, and send data. This was her job.

Why Alpha C? Why so impossibly far?

Why not the Moon? The US was there: the base at Shackleton, with a ten-thousand-acre solar power plant, a deuterium mine in the lunar ice, and a twenty-gigawatt particle beam. The Chinese were on the far side, mining helium-3 from the regolith.

Why not Mars? China was there. A one-way mission had been sent in 2025. The crew might not have survived—that was classified—but the robotics had. The planet was reachable and therefore dangerous.

Jupiter? There were rumors that the US was there as well, maybe the Chinese too, robots anyway, staking a claim to all that helium. Roger didn't put much credence in the rumors, but they might be true.

Why not wait it out at a Lagrange point? Roger thought there was nothing to wait for. The situation was terminal. As things spiraled down the maelstrom, anyplace cislunar would be at risk. Sooner or later any ship out there would be detected and destroyed. Or it might last only because civilization was shattered, with the survivors in some pit plotting to pummel the shards.

It was Alpha C because Roger Fry was a fanatic who believed that only an exit from the solar system offered humanity any hope of escaping what it had become.

She thought of Sergei, saying in his bad accent and absent grammar, which he exaggerated for effect: this is shit. You say me Alpha See is best? Absolute impossible. Is double star, no planet in habitable orbit—yes yes, whatever, minima maxima, zone of hopeful bullshit. Ghost Planet Hope. You shoot load there?

How long they had argued over this—their destination.

Gliese 581.

Impossible.

Roger, it's a rocky planet with liquid water.

That's three mistakes in one sentence. Something is orbiting the star, with a period of thirteen days and a mass of two Earths and some spectral lines. Rocky, water, liquid, that's all surmise. What's for sure is it's twenty light-years away. Plus, the star is a flare star. It's disqualified twice before we even get to the hope-it's-a-planet part.

You don't know it's a flare star! There are no observations!

In the absence of observations, we assume it behaves like other observed stars of its class. It flares.

You have this agenda for Alpha C, you've invented these criteria to shoot down every other candidate!

The criteria are transparent. We've agreed to them. Number one: twelve light-years is our outer limit. Right there we're down to twenty-four stars. For reasons of luminosity and stability we prefer a nonvariable G- or K-class star. Now we're down to five. Alpha Centauri, Epsilon Eridani, 61 Cygni, Epsilon Indi, and Tau Ceti make the cut. Alpha is half the distance of the next nearest.

Bullshit, Roger. You have bug up ass for your Alpha See. Why not disqualify as double, heh? Why this not shoot-down criteria?

Because we have modeled it, and we know planet formation is possible in this system, and we have direct evidence of planets in other double systems. And because—I know.

They ended with Alpha because it was closest. Epsilon Eridani had planets for sure, but they were better off with a closer Ghost Planet Hope than a sure thing so far they couldn't reach it. Cosmic rays would degrade the electronics, the ship, their very cells. Every year in space brought them closer to some component's MTBF: mean time between failures.

Well, they'd known they might lose Shackleton. It was even likely. Just not so soon.

She'd been pushing away the possibility that things had gone so badly on Earth that no one was left to reply.

She remembered walking on a fire road after a conference in Berkeley—the Bay dappled sapphire and russet, thick white marine layer pushing in over the Golden Gate Bridge—talking to Roger about Fermi's Paradox. If the universe harbors life, intelligence, why haven't we seen evidence of it? Why are we alone? Roger favored what he called the Mean Time Between Failures argument. Technological civilizations simply fail, just as the components that make up their technology fail, sooner or later, for reasons as indivually insignificant as they are inexorable, and final. Complex systems, after a point, tend away from robustness.

Okay. Any receivers on Earth will have to find their new signal. It was going to be like SETI in reverse: she had to make the new signal maximally detectable. She could do that. She could retune the frequency to better penetrate Earth's atmosphere. Reprogram the PLLs and antenna array, use orthogonal FSK modulation across the K- and X- bands. Increase the buffer size. And hope for the best.

Eighty-four years to go. My God, they were barely out the front door. My God, it was lonely out here.

The mission plan had been seventy-two years, with a predicted systems-failure rate of under twenty percent. The Weibull curve climbed steeply after that. At eighty-four years, systems-failure rate was over fifty percent.

What could be done to speed them? The nuclear rocket and its fuel were for deceleration and navigation at the far end. To use it here would add—she calculated—a total of 0.0002 c to their current speed. Saving them all of three months. And leaving them no means of planetfall.

They had nothing. Their cruise velocity was unalterable.

All right, that's that, so find a line. Commit to it and move.

Cruise at this speed for longer, decelerate later and harder. That could save a few years. They'd have to run more current through the magsail, increase its drag, push its specs.

Enter the Alpha C system faster than planned, slow down harder once within it. She didn't know how to calculate those maneuvers, but someone else would.

Her brain was racing now, wouldn't let her sleep. She'd been up for three days. These were not her decisions to make, but she was the only one who could.

She wrote up detailed logs with the various options and calculations she'd made. At last there was no more for her to do. But a sort of nostalgia came over her. She wanted, absurdly, to check her email. Really, just to hear some voice not her own.

Nothing broadcast from Earth reached this far except for the ACK signals beamed directly to them from Shackleton. Shackleton was also an IPN node, connecting space assets to the Internet. For cover, the ACK signals it sent to *Gypsy* were piggybacked on bogus Internet packets. And those had all been stored by the computer.

So in her homesick curiosity, she called them out of memory, and dissected some packets that had been saved from up to a year ago. Examined their broken and scrambled content like a torn, discarded newspaper for anything they might tell her of the planet she'd never see again.

M.3,S+SDS#0U4:&ES(&%R=&EC;&4@:7,@8V]P>7)I9VAT960@,
3DY,R!B>2!4

Warmer than usual regime actively amplifies tundra thaw. Drought melt permafrost thermokarsts methane burn wildfire giants 800 ppm. Capture hot atmospheric ridge NOAA frontrunning collapse sublime asymmetric artificial trade resource loss.

M1HE9LXO6FXQL KL86KWQ LUN;AXEW)1VZ!"NHS;SI5=SJQ
8HCBC3 DJGMVA&

Weapon tensions under Islamic media policy rebels arsenals strategic counterin-
surgency and to prevent Federal war law operational artillery air component to
mine mountain strongholds photorecce altitudes HQ backbone Su-35 SAMs
part with high maneuverability bombardments of casualty casuistry

M87EL;W(@)B!&<F%N8VES+" Q.3 P($9R;W-T#5)O860L(%-U:7lE
(#$P,2P@

Hurriedly autoimmune decay derivative modern thaws in dawn's pregnant
grave shares in disgust of high frequency trading wet cities territorial earth-
quake poison Bayes the chairs are empty incentives to disorder without borders.
Pneumonia again antibiotic resistance travels the globe with ease.

M7V3 5EX-SR'KP8G 49:YZSR/ BBJWS82<9NS(!1W^YVEY_ODlV&%
MMJ,QMRG^

Knowing perpendicular sex dating in Knob Lick Missouri stateroom Sweeney
atilt with cheerfully synodic weeny or restorative ministration. Glintingly aweigh
triacetate hopefully occasionally sizeable interrogation nauseate. Descriptive
mozzarella cosmos truly and contumacious portability.

M4F]N9F5L9'0-26YT97)N871I;VYA;"!0;VQI8WD@1&5P87)T;65N=
U204Y$

Titter supine teratologys aim appoint to plaintive technocrat. Mankind is
inwardly endocrine and afar romanic spaceflight. Mesial corinths archidiaco-
nal or lyric satirical turtle demurral. Calorific fitment marry after sappy are
inscribed upto pillwort. Idem monatomic are processed longways

M#0U#;W!Y<FEG:'0@,3DY,R!487EL;W(@)B!&<F%N8VES#
4E34TX@,#$T.2TU

archive tittie blowjob hair fetish SEX FREE PICS RUSSIAN hardcore incest
stories animate porn wankers benedict paris car motorcycle cop fetish sex toys
caesar milf-hunters when im found this pokemon porn gallery fisting Here Is
Links to great her lesbiands Sites M0UE"15)705(@25,@0T]-24Y'(0T-2F]

H;B!!<G%U:6QL82!A; F0@1&%V:60@

Lost, distant, desolate. The world she'd left forever, speaking its poison poetry
of ruin and catastrophe and longing. Told her nothing she didn't already know
about the corrupt destiny and thwarted feeling that had drawn humankind into
the maelstrom *Gypsy* had escaped. She stood and walked furiously the meager
length of the curved corridor, stopping at each slab, regarding the sleeping forms
of her crewmates, naked in translucent bodysuits, young and fit, yet broken, like
her, in ways that had made this extremity feel to them all the only chance.

They gathered together for the first time on the ship after receiving Roger's signal.

*We'll be fine. Not even Roger knows where the ship is. They won't be able to find
us before we're gone.*

*It was her first time in space. From the shuttle, the ship appeared a formless
clutter: layers of bomb sleds, each bearing thousands of microfusion devices, under and
around them a jacket of hydrogen tanks, shields, conduits, antennas. Two white-suited
figures crawled over this maze. A hijacked hydrogen depot was offloading its cargo.*

*Five were already aboard, retrofitting. Everything not needed for deep space
had been jettisoned. Everything lacking was brought and secured. Shuttles that were
supposed to be elsewhere came and went on encrypted itineraries.*

*One shuttle didn't make it. They never learned why. So they were down to sixteen
crew.*

*The ship wasn't meant to hold so many active people. The crew area was less than
a quarter of the torus, a single room narrowed to less than ten feet by the hibernation
slabs lining each long wall. Dim even with all the LED bays on.*

*Darius opened champagne. Contraband: no one knew how alcohol might interact
with the hibernation drugs.*

To Andrew and Chung-Pei and Hari and Maryam. They're with us in spirit.

*Some time later the first bomb went off. The ship trembled but didn't move.
Another blast. Then another. Grudgingly the great mass budged. Like a car departing
a curb, no faster at first. Fuel mass went from it and kinetic energy into it. Kinesis
was gradual but unceasing. In its first few minutes it advanced less than a kilometer.
In its first hour it moved two thousand kilometers. In its first day, a million kilometers. After a year, when the last bomb was expended, it would be some two thousand
astronomical units from the Earth, and Gypsy would coast on at her fixed speed for
decades, a dark, silent, near-dead thing.*

As Sophie prepared to return to hibernation, she took stock. She walked the
short interior of the quarter-torus. Less than twenty paces end to end. The black

walls, the dim LED pods, the slabs of her crewmates.

Never to see her beloved mountains again. Her dear sawtooth Sierra. She thought of the blue sky, and remembered a hunk of stuff she'd seen on Roger's desk, some odd kind of rock. It was about five inches long. You could see through it. Its edges were blurry. Against a dark background it had a bluish tinge. She took it in her hand and it was nearly weightless.

What is this?

Silica aerogel. The best insulator in the world.

Why is it blue?

Rayleigh scattering.

She knew what that meant: why the sky is blue. Billions of particles in the air scatter sunlight, shorter wavelengths scatter most, so those suffuse the sky. The shortest we can see is blue. But that was an ocean of air around the planet and this was a small rock.

You're joking.

No, it's true. There are billions of internal surfaces in that piece.

It's like a piece of sky.

Yes, it is.

It was all around her now, that stuff—in the walls of the ship, keeping out the cold of space—allowing her to imagine a poetry of sky where none was.

And that was it. She'd been awake for five days. She'd fixed the datastream back to Earth. She'd written her logs. She'd reprogrammed the magsail deployment for seventy years from now, at increased current, in the event that no other steward was wakened in the meantime. She'd purged her bowels and injected the hibernation cocktail. She was back in the bodysuit, life supports connected. As she went under, she wondered why.

2.

They departed a day short of Roger Fry's fortieth birthday. Born September 11, 2001, he was hired to a national weapons laboratory straight out of Caltech. He never did finish his doctorate. Within a year at the Lab he had designed the first breakeven fusion reaction. It had long been known that a very small amount of antimatter could trigger a burn wave in thermonuclear fuel. Roger solved how. He was twenty-four.

Soon there were net energy gains. That's when the bomb people came in. In truth, their interest was why he was hired in the first place. Roger knew this and didn't care. Once fusion became a going concern, it would mean unlimited clean energy. It would change the world. Bombs would have no purpose.

But it was a long haul to a commercial fusion reactor. Meanwhile, bombs were easier.

The first bombs were shaped-charge antiproton-triggered fusion bunker busters. The smallest was a kiloton-yield bomb, powerful enough to level forty or fifty city blocks; it used just a hundred grams of lithium deuteride, and less than a microgram of antimatter. It was easy to manufacture and transport and deploy. It created little radiation or electromagnetic pulse. Tens of thousands, then hundreds of thousands, were fabricated in orbit and moved to drop platforms called sleds. Because the minimum individual yields were within the range of conventional explosives, no nuclear treaties were violated.

Putting them in orbit did violate the Outer Space Treaty, so at first they were more politely called the Orbital Asteroid Defense Network. But when a large asteroid passed through cislunar space a few years later—with no warning, no alert, no response at all—the pretense was dropped, and the system came under the command of the US Instant Global Strike Initiative.

More and more money went into antimatter production. There were a dozen factories worldwide that produced about a gram, all told, of antiprotons a year. Some went into the first fusion power plants, which themselves produced more antiprotons. Most went into bomb triggers. There they were held in traps, isolated from normal matter, but that worked only so long. They decayed, like tritium in the older nuclear weapons, but much faster; some traps could store milligrams of antiprotons for many months at a time, and they were improving; still, bomb triggers had to be replaced often.

As a defense system it was insane, but hugely profitable. Then came the problem of where to park the profits, since there were no stable markets anywhere. The economic system most rewarded those whose created and surfed instabilities and could externalize their risks, which created greater instabilities.

Year after year Roger worked and waited, and the number of bombs grew, as did the number of countries deploying them, and the global resource wars intensified, and his fusion utopia failed to arrive. When the first commercial plants did start operating, it made no difference. Everything went on as before. Those who had the power to change things had no reason to; things had worked out pretty well for them so far.

Atmospheric CO_2 shot past six hundred parts per million. The methane burden was now measured in parts per million, not parts per billon. No one outside the classified world knew the exact numbers, but the effects were everywhere. The West Antarctic ice shelf collapsed. Sea level rose three meters.

Sometime in there, Roger Fry gave up on Earth.

But not on humanity, not entirely. Something in the complex process of civilization had forced it into this place from which it now had no exit. He didn't see this as an inevitable result of the process, but it had happened. There might have been a time when the situation was reversible. If certain decisions had been made. If resources had been treated as a commons. Back when the population of the planet was two or three billion, when there was still enough to go around, enough time to alter course, enough leisure to think things through. But it hadn't gone that way. He didn't much care why. The question was what to do now.

FANG TIR EOGHAIN (2081)

*T*he ancestor of all mammals must have been a hibernator. Body temperature falls as much as 15 kelvins. A bear's heartbeat goes down to five per minute. Blood pressure drops to thirty millimeters. In humans, these conditions would be fatal.

Relatively few genes are involved in torpor. We have located the critical ones. And we have found the protein complexes they uptake and produce. Monophosphates mostly.

Yes, I know, induced hypothermia is not torpor. But this state has the signatures of torpor. For example, there is a surfeit of MCT1 which transports ketones to the brain during fasting.

Ketosis, that's true, we are in a sense poisoning the subject in order to achieve this state. Some ischemia and refusion damage results, but less than anticipated. Doing it more than a couple of times is sure to be fatal. But for our purposes, maybe it gets the job done.

Anyway it had better; we have nothing else.

Her da was screaming at her to get up. He wasn't truly her father, her father had gone to the stars. That was a story she'd made up long ago; it was better than the truth.

Her thick brown legs touched the floor. Not so thick and brown as she remembered. Weak, pale, withered. She tried to stand and fell back. *Try harder, cow.* She fell asleep.

She'd tried so hard for so long. She'd been accepted early at university. Then her parents went afoul of the system. One day she came home to a bare apartment. All are zhonghua minzu, but it was a bad time for certain ethnics in China.

She lost her place at university. She was shunted to a polytechnic secondary in Guangzhou, where she lived with her aunt and uncle in a small apartment. It wasn't science; it was job training in technology services. One day she overheard the uncle on the phone, bragging: he had turned her parents in, collected a bounty and a stipend.

She was not yet fifteen. It was still possible, then, to be adopted out of country. Covertly, she set about it. Caitlin Tyrone was the person who helped her from afar.

They'd met online, in a science chatroom. Ireland needed scientists. She didn't know or care where that was; she'd have gone to Hell. It took almost a year to arrange it, the adoption. It took all Fang's diligence, all her cunning, all her need, all her cold hate, to keep it from her uncle, to acquire the paperwork, to forge his signature, to sequester money, and finally on the last morning to sneak out of the apartment before dawn.

She flew from Guangzhou to Beijing to Frankfurt to Dublin, too nervous to sleep. Each time she had to stop in an airport and wait for the next flight, sometimes for hours, she feared arrest. In her sleepless imagination, the waiting lounges turned into detention centers. Then she was on the last flight. The stars faded and the sun rose over the Atlantic, and there was Ireland. O! the green of it. And her new mother Caitlin was there to greet her, grab her, look into her eyes. Goodbye forever to the wounded past.

She had a scholarship at Trinity College, in biochemistry. She already knew English, but during her first year she studied phonology and orthography and grammar, to try to map, linguistically, how far she'd traveled. It wasn't so far. The human vocal apparatus is everywhere the same. So is the brain, constructing the grammar that drives the voice box. Most of her native phonemes had Irish or English equivalents, near enough. But the sounds she made of hers were not quite correct, so she worked daily to refine them.

O is where she often came to rest. The exclamative particle, the sound of that moment when the senses surprise the body, same in Ireland as in China—same body, same senses, same sound. Yet a human universe of shadings. The English O was one thing; Mandarin didn't quite have it; Cantonese was closer; but everywhere the sound slid around depending on locality, on country, even on county: monophthong to diphthong, the tongue wandering in the mouth, seeking to settle. When she felt lost in the night, which was often, she sought for that O, round and solid and vast and various and homey as the planet beneath her, holding her with its gravity. Moving her tongue in her mouth as she lay in bed waiting for sleep.

Biochemistry wasn't so distant, in her mind, from language. She saw it all as signaling. DNA wasn't "information," data held statically in helices, it was activity, transaction.

She insisted on her new hybrid name, the whole long Gaelic mess of it—it was Caitlin's surname—as a reminder of the contigency of belonging, of culture and language, of identity itself. Her solid legs had landed on solid ground, or solid enough to support her.

Carefully, arduously, one connector at a time, she unplugged herself from the bodysuit, then sat up on the slab. Too quickly. She dizzied and pitched forward.

Get up, you cow. The da again. Dream trash. As if she couldn't. She'd show him. She gave all her muscles a great heave.

And woke shivering on the carbon deckplates. Held weakly down by the thin false gravity. It was no embracing O, just a trickle of mockery. *You have to do this,* she told her will.

She could small acetone on her breath. Glycogen used up, body starts to burn fat, produces ketones. Ketoacidosis. She should check ketone levels in the others.

Roger came into Fang's life by way of Caitlin. Years before, Caitlin had studied physics at Trinity. Roger had read her papers. They were brilliant. He'd come to teach a seminar, and he had the idea of recruiting her to the Lab. But science is bound at the hip to its application, and turbulence occurs at that interface where theory meets practice, knowledge meets performance. Where the beauty of the means goes to die in the instrumentality of the ends.

Roger found to his dismay that Caitlin couldn't manage even the sandbox politics of grad school. She'd been aced out of the best advisors and was unable to see that her science career was already in a death spiral. She'd never make it on her own at the Lab, or in a corp. He could intervene to some degree, but he was reluctant; he saw a better way.

Already Caitlin was on U, a Merck pharmaceutical widely prescribed for a new category in DSM-6: "social interoperability disorder." U for eudaimonia-zine. Roger had tried it briefly himself. In his opinion, half the planet fit the diagnostic criteria, which was excellent business for Merck but said more about planetary social conditions than about the individuals who suffered under them.

U was supposed to increase compassion for others, to make other people seem more real. But Caitlin was already too empathic for her own good, too ready to yield her place to others, and the U merely blissed her out, put her in a zone of self-abnegation. Perhaps that's why it was a popular street drug; when some governments tried to ban it, Merck sued them under global trade agreements, for loss of expected future profits.

Caitlin ended up sidelined in the Trinity library, where she met and married James, an older charming sociopath with terrific interoperability. Meanwhile, Roger kept tabs on her from afar. He hacked James's medical records and was noted that James was infertile.

It took Fang several hours to come to herself. She tried not to worry, this was to be expected. Her body had gone through a serious near-death trauma. She felt weak, nauseous, and her head throbbed, but she was alive. That she was sitting here sipping warm tea was a triumph, for her body and for her science. She still felt a little stunned, a little distant from that success. So many things could have gone wrong: hibernation was only the half of it; like every other problem they'd faced, it came with its own set of ancillaries. On which she'd worked.

In addition to her highly classified DARPA work on hibernation, Fang had published these papers in the *Journal of Gravitational Physiology:* serum leptin level is a regulator of bone mass (2033); inhibition of osteopenia by low magnitude, high frequency mechanical stimuli (2035); the transcription factor NF-kappaB is a key intracellular signal transducer in disuse atrophy (2036); IGF-I stimulates muscle growth by suppressing protein breakdown and expression of atrophy-related ubiquitin ligases, atrogin-1 and MuRF1 (2037); and PGC-lalpha protects skeletal muscle from atrophy by suppressing FoxO3 action and atrophy-specific gene transcription (2039).

When she felt able, she checked on the others. Each sleeper bore implanted and dermal sensors—for core and skin temperature, EKG, EEG, pulse, blood pressure and flow, plasma ions, plasma metabolites, clotting function, respiratory rate and depth, gas analysis and flow, urine production, EMG, tremor, body composition. Near-infrared spectrometry measured haematocrit, blood glucose, tissue O2 and pH. Muscles were stimulated electrically and mechanically to counteract atrophy. The slabs tipped thirty degrees up or down and rotated the body from supine to prone in order to provide mechanical loading from hypogravity in all directions. Exoskeletal waldos at the joints, and the soles and fingers, provided periodic range-of-motion stimulus. A range of pharmacological and genetic interventions further regulated bone and muscle regeneration.

Also, twitching was important. If you didn't twitch you wouldn't wake. It was a kind of mooring to the present.

Did they dream? EEGs showed periodic variation but were so unlike normal EEGs that it was hard to say. You couldn't very well wake someone to ask, as the first sleep researchers had done.

All looked well on the monitor, except for number fourteen. Reza. Blood pressure almost nonexistent. She got to her feet and walked down the row of slabs to have a look at Reza.

A pursed grayish face sagging on its skull. Maybe a touch of life was visible, some purple in the gray, blood still coursing. Or maybe not.

Speckling the gray skin was a web of small white dots, each the size of a pencil eraser or smaller. They were circular but not perfectly so, margins blurred. Looked like a fungus.

She went back and touched the screen for records. This steward was long overdue for rousing. The machine had started the warming cycle three times. Each time he hadn't come out of torpor, so the machine had shut down the cycle, stablized him, and tried again. After three failures, it had moved down the list to the next steward. Her.

She touched a few levels deeper. Not enough fat on this guy. Raising the temperature without rousing would simply bring on ischemia and perfusion. That's why the machine gave up. It was a delicate balance, to keep the metabolism burning fat instead of carbohydrates, without burning too much of the body's stores. Humans couldn't bulk up on fat in advance the way natural hibernators could. But she thought she'd solved that with the nutrient derms.

It was the fortieth year of the voyage. They were two light-years from home. Not quite halfway. If hibernation was failing now, they had a serious problem.

Was the fungus a result or a cause? Was it a fungus? She wanted to open the bodysuit and run tests, but any contagion had to be contained.

They'd discussed possible failure modes. Gene activity in bacteria increased in low gravity; they evolved more rapidly. In the presence of a host they became more virulent. Radiation caused mutations. But ultraviolet light scoured the suits every day and should have killed bacteria and fungus alike. Logs showed that the UV was functioning. It wasn't enough.

James—the da, as he insisted Fang call him—had black hair and blue eyes that twinkled like ice when he smiled. At first he was mere background to her; he'd stumble in late from the pub to find Caitlin and Fang talking. Ah, the Addams sisters, he'd say, nodding sagely. Fang never understood what he meant by it. For all his geniality, he kept her at a distance, treated her like a houseguest.

Caitlin was more like an older sister than a mother; she was only twelve years older. It was fun to talk science with her, and it was helpful. She was quick to understand the details of Fang's field, and this dexterity spurred Fang in her own understanding and confidence.

After a couple of years, James grew more sullen, resentful, almost abusive. He dropped the suave act. He found fault with Fang's appearance, her habits, her character. The guest had overstayed her welcome. He was jealous.

She couldn't figure out why a woman as good and as smart as Caitlin stayed on with him. Maybe something damaged in Caitlin was called by a like damage in James. Caitlin had lost her father while a girl, as had Fang. When Fang looked at James through Caitlin's eyes, she could see in him the ruins of something strong and attractive and paternal. But that thing was no longer alive. Only Caitlin's need for it lived, and that need became a reproach to James, who had lost the ability to meet it, and who fled from it.

The further James fled into drink, the more Caitlin retreated into her U, into a quiescence where things could feel whole. All the while, James felt Fang's eyes on him, evaluating him, seeing him as he was. He saw she wasn't buying him. Nothing disturbed him more than having his act fail. And he saw that Caitlin was alive and present only with Fang. They clung to one another, and were moving away from him.

James was truly good to me, before you knew him.

On U, everyone seems good to you.

No, long before that. When I failed my orals he was a great support.

You were vulnerable. He fed on your need.

You don't know, Fang. I was lost. He helped me, he held on to me when I needed it. Then I had you.

She thought not. She thought James had learned to enjoy preying on the vulnerable. And Caitlin was too willing to ignore this, to go along with it. As Fang finished her years at Trinity, she agonized over how she must deal with this trouble. It was then that an offer arrived from Roger's lab.

Come with me to America.

Oh, Fang. I can't. What about James? What would he do there?

It was James's pretense that he was still whole and competent and functional, when in fact his days were marked out by the habits of rising late, avoiding work in the library, and leaving early for the pub. Any move or change would expose the pretense.

Just you and me. Just for a year.

I can't.

Fang heard alarms. If she stayed and tried to protect Caitlin, her presence might drive James to some extreme. Or Fang might be drawn more deeply into their dysfunction. She didn't know if she could survive that. The thing Fang was best at was saving herself. So she went to America alone.

There was a second body covered with fungus. Number fifteen. Loren.

Either the fungus was contained, restricted to these two, or more likely it had already spread. But how? The bodysuits showed no faults, no breaches. They were isolated from each other, with no pathways for infection. The only possible connection would be through the air supply, and the scrubbers should remove any pathogens, certainly anything as large as a fungus.

In any case, it was bad. She could try rousing another steward manually. But to what purpose? Only she had the expertise to deal with this.

She realized she thought of it because she was desperately lonely. She wanted company with this problem. She wasn't going to get any.

Not enough fat to rouse. Increase glycogen uptake? Maybe, but carbohydrate fasting was a key part of the process.

They had this advantage over natural hibernators: they didn't need to get all their energy from stored body fat. Lipids were dripped in dermally to provide ATP. But body fat was getting metabolized anyway.

Signaling. Perhaps the antisenescents were signaling the fungus not to die. Slowing not its growth but its morbidity. If it were a fungus. Sure it was, it had to be. But confirm it.

After she came to the Lab, Fang learned that her adoption was not so much a matter of her initiative, or of Caitlin's, or of good fortune. Roger had pulled strings every step of the way—strings Fang had no idea existed.

He'd known of Fang because all student work—every paper, test, email, click, eyeblink, keystroke—was stored and tracked and mined. Her permanent record. Corps and labs had algorithms conducting eternal worldwide surveillance for, among so many other things, promising scientists. Roger had his own algorithms: his stock-market eye for early bloomers, good draft choices. He'd purchased Fang's freedom from some Chinese consortium and linked her to Caitlin.

Roger, Fang came to realize, had seen in Caitlin's needs and infirmities a way to help three people: Caitlin, who needed someone to nurture and give herself to, so as not to immolate herself; Fang, who needed that nurturing; and himself, who needed Fang's talent. In other words: Roger judged that Caitlin would do best as the mother of a scientist.

He wasn't wrong. Caitlin's nurture was going to waste on James, who simply sucked it in and gave nothing back. And Fang needed a brilliant, loving, female example to give her confidence in her own brilliance, and learn the toughness she'd need to accomplish her work. That's what Caitlin herself had lacked.

If Fang had known all this, she'd have taken the terms; she'd have done anything to get out of China. But she hadn't known; she hadn't been consulted. So when she found out, she was furious. For Caitlin, for herself. As she saw it, Roger couldn't have the mother, so he took the daughter. He used their love and mutual need to get what he wanted, and then he broke them apart. It was cold and calculating and utterly selfish of Roger; of the three of them, only he wasn't damaged by it. She'd almost quit Gypsy in her fury.

She did quit the Lab. She went into product development at Glaxo, under contract to DARPA. That was the start of her hibernation work. It was for battlefield use, as a way to keep injured soldiers alive during transport. When she reflected on this move, she wasn't so sure that Roger hadn't pulled more strings. In any case, the work was essential to Gypsy.

Roger had fury of his own, to spare. Fang knew all about the calm front. Roger reeked of it. He'd learned that he had the talent and the position to do great harm; the orbiting bombs were proof of that. His anger and disappointment had raised in him the urge to do more harm. At the Lab he was surrounded by the means and the opportunity. So he'd gathered all his ingenuity and his rage against humanity and sequestered it in a project large enough and complex enough to occupy it fully, so that it could not further harm him or the world: Gypsy. He would do a thing that had never been done before; and he would take away half the bombs he'd enabled in the doing of it; and the thing would not be shared with humanity. She imagined he saw it as a victimless revenge.

Well, here were the victims.

A day later, *Pseudogymnoascus destructans* was her best guess. Or some mutation of it. It had killed most of the bats on Earth. It grew only in low temperatures, in the 4 to 15° Celsius range. The ship was normally held at 4° Celsius.

She could synthesize an antifungal agent with the gene printer, but what about interactions? Polyenes would bind with a fungus's ergosterols but could have severe and lethal side effects.

She thought about the cocktail. How she might tweak it. Sirtuins. Fibroplast growth factor 21. Hibernation induction trigger. [D-Ala2, D-Leu5]-Enkephalin. Pancreatic triacylglycerol lipase. 5'-adenosine monophosphate. Ghrelin. 3-iodothyronamine. Alpha2-macroglobulin. Carnosine, other antisenescents, antioxidants.

Some components acted only at the start of the process. They triggered a cascade of enzymes in key pathways to bring on torpor. Some continued to drip in, to reinforce gene expression, to suppress circadian rhythms, and so on.

It was all designed to interact with nonhuman mammalian genes she'd spliced in. Including parts of the bat immune system—*Myotis lucifugus*— parts relevant to hibernation, to respond to the appropriate mRNA signals. But were they also vulnerable to this fungus? *O God, did I do this? Did I open up this vulnerability?*

She gave her presentation, in the open, to DARPA. It was amazing; she was speaking in code to the few Gypsies in the audience, including Roger, telling them in effect how they'd survive the long trip to Alpha, yet her plaintext words were telling DARPA about battlefield applications: suspending wounded soldiers, possibly in space, possibly for long periods, 3D-printing organs, crisping stem cells, and so on.

In Q&A she knew DARPA was sold; they'd get their funding. Roger was right: everything was dual use.

She'd been up for ten days. The cramped, dark space was wearing her down. Save them. They had to make it. She'd pulled a DNA sequencer and a gene printer from the storage bay. As she fed it *E. coli* and *Mycoplasma mycoides* stock, she reviewed what she'd come up with.

She could mute the expression of the bat genes at this stage, probably without disrupting hibernation. They were the receptors for the triggers that started and stopped the process. But that could compromise rousing. So mute them temporarily—for how long?—hope to revive an immune response, temporarily damp down the antisenescents, add an antifungal. She'd have to automate everything in the mixture; the ship wouldn't rouse her a second time to supervise.

It was a long shot, but so was everything now.

It was too hard for her. For anyone. She had the technology: a complete library of genetic sequences, a range of restriction enzymes, Sleeping Beauty transposase, et cetera. She'd be capable on the spot, for instance, of producing a pathogen that could selectively kill individuals with certain ethnic markers— that had been one project at the Lab, demurely called "preventive." But she didn't have the knowledge she needed for this. It had taken years of research experimentation, and collaboration, to come up with the original cocktail, and it would take years more to truly solve this. She had only a few days. Then the residue of the cocktail would be out of her system and she would lose the ability to rehibernate. So she had to go with what she had now. Test it on DNA from her own saliva.

Not everyone stuck with Gypsy. One scientist at the Lab, Sidney Lefebvre, was wooed by Roger to sign up, and declined only after carefully studying their plans for a couple of weeks. It's too hard, Roger. What you have here is impressive. But it's only a start. There are too many intractable problems. Much more work needs to be done.

That work won't get done. Things are falling apart, not coming together. It's now or never.

Probably so. Regardless, the time for this is not now. This, too, will fall apart.

She wrote the log for the next steward, who would almost surely have the duty of more corpses. Worse, as stewards died, maintenance would be deferred. Systems would die. She didn't know how to address that. Maybe Lefebvre was right. But no: they had to make it. How could this be harder than getting from Guangzhou to Dublin to here?

She prepared to go back under. Fasted the day. Enema, shower. Taps and stents and waldos and derms attached and the bodysuit sealed around her. She felt the cocktail run into her veins.

The lights were off. The air was chill. In her last moment of clarity, she stared into blackness. Always she had run, away from distress, toward something new, to eradicate its pain and its hold. Not from fear. As a gesture of contempt, of power: done with you, never going back. But run to where? No world, no O, no gravity, no hold, nothing to cling to. This was the end of the line. There was nowhere but here. And, still impossibly far, another forty-four years, Alpha C. As impossibly far as Earth.

3.

Roger recruited his core group face to face. At conferences and symposia he sat for papers that had something to offer his project, and he made a judgment about the presenter. If favorable, it led to a conversation. Always outside, in the open. Fire roads in the Berkeley hills. A cemetery in Zurich. The shores of Lake Como. Fry was well known, traveled much. He wasn't Einstein, he wasn't Feynman, he wasn't Hawking, but he had a certain presence.

The conferences were Kabuki. Not a scientist in the world was unlinked to classified projects through government or corporate sponsors. Presentations were so oblique that expert interpretation was required to parse their real import.

Roger parsed well. Within a year he had a few dozen trusted collaborators. They divided the mission into parts: target selection, engine and fuel, vessel, hibernation, navigation, obstacle avoidance, computers, deceleration, landfall, survival.

The puzzle had too many pieces. Each piece was unthinkably complex. They needed much more help.

They put up a site they called Gypsy. On the surface it was a gaming site, complex and thick with virtual worlds, sandboxes, self-evolving puzzles, and links. Buried in there was an interactive starship-design section, where ideas were solicited, models built, simulations run. Good nerdy crackpot fun.

The core group tested the site themselves for half a year before going live. Their own usage stats became the profile of the sort of visitors they sought: people like themselves: people with enough standing to have access to the high-speed classified web, with enough autonomy to waste professional time on a game site, and finally with enough curiosity and dissidence to pursue certain key links down a critical chain. They needed people far enough inside an institution to have access to resources, but not so far inside as to identify with its ideology. When a user appeared to fit that profile, a public key was issued. The key unlocked further levels and ultimately enabled secure email to an encrypted server.

No one, not even Roger Fry, knew how big the conspiracy was. Ninety-nine percent of their traffic was noise—privileged kids, stoked hackers, drunken

PhDs, curious spooks. Hundreds of keys were issued in the first year. Every key increased the risk. But without resources they were going nowhere.

The authorities would vanish Roger Fry and everyone associated with him on the day they learned what he was planning. Not because of the what: a starship posed no threat. But because of the how and the why: only serious and capable dissidents could plan so immense a thing; the seriousness and the capability were the threat. And eventually they would be found, because every bit of the world's digital traffic was swept up and stored and analyzed. There was a city under the Utah desert where these yottabytes of data were archived in server farms. But the sheer size of the archive outran its analysis and opened a time window in which they might act.

Some ran propellant calculations. Some forwarded classified medical studies. Some were space workers with access to shuttles and tugs. Some passed on classified findings from telescopes seeking exoplanets.

One was an operator of the particle beam at Shackleton Crater. The beam was used, among other purposes, to move the orbiting sleds containing the very bombs Roger had helped design.

One worked at a seed archive in Norway. She piggybacked a capsule into Earth orbit containing seeds from fifty thousand unmodified plant species, including plants legally extinct. They needed those because every cultivated acre on Earth was now planted with engineered varieties that were sterile; terminator genes had been implanted to protect the agro firms' profit streams; and these genes had jumped to wild varieties. There wasn't a live food plant left anywhere on Earth that could propagate itself.

They acquired frozen zygotes of some ten thousand animal species, from bacteria to primates. Hundreds of thousands more complete DNA sequences in a data library, and a genome printer. Nothing like the genetic diversity of Earth, even in its present state, but enough, perhaps, to reboot such diversity.

At Roger's lab, panels of hydrogenous carbon-composite, made to shield high-orbit craft from cosmic rays and to withstand temperatures of 2000° C, went missing. Quite a lot of silica aerogel as well.

At a sister lab, a researcher put them in touch with a contractor from whom they purchased, quite aboveboard, seventy kilometers of lightweight, high-current-density superconducting cable.

After a year, Roger decided that their web had grown too large to remain secure. He didn't like the number of unused keys going out. He didn't like the page patterns he was seeing. He didn't consult with the others, he just shut it down.

But they had their pieces.

Sergei (2118)

Eat, drink, shit. That's all he did for the first day or three. Water tasted funny. Seventy-seven years might have viled it, or his taste buds. Life went on, including the ending of it. Vital signs of half the crew were flat. He considered disposing of bodies, ejecting them, but number one, he couldn't be sure they were dead; number two, he couldn't propel them hard enough to keep them from making orbit around the ship, which was funny but horrible; and finally, it would be unpleasant and very hard work that would tire him out. An old man—he surely felt old, and the calendar would back him up—needs to reserve his strength. So he let them lie on their slabs.

The logs told a grim story. They were slow. To try to make up for lost time, Sophie had reprogrammed the magsail to deploy later and to run at higher current. Another steward had been wakened at the original deployment point, to confirm their speed and position, and to validate the decision to wait. Sergei didn't agree with that, and he especially didn't like the handwaving over when to ignite the nuclear rocket in-system, but it was done: they'd gone the extra years at speed and now they needed to start decelerating hard.

CURRENT INJECTION FAILED. MAGSAIL NOT DEPLOYED.

He tapped the screen to cycle through its languages. Stopped at the Cyrillic script, and tapped the speaker, just so he could hear spoken Russian.

So he had to fix the magsail. Current had flowed on schedule from inside, but the sail wasn't charging or deploying. According to telltales, the bay was open but the superconducting cable just sat there. That meant EVA. He didn't like it, but there was no choice. It's what he was here for. Once it was done he'd shower again under that pathetic lukewarm stream, purge his bowels, get back in the mylar suit, and go under for another, what, eight more years, a mere nothing, we're almost there. Ghost Planet Hope.

He was the only one onboard who'd been a career astronaut. Roger had conveyed a faint class disapproval about that, but needed the expertise. Sergei had been one of the gene-slushed orbital jockeys who pushed bomb sleds around. He knew the feel of zero g, of sunlight on one side of you and absolute cold on the other. He knew how it felt when the particle beam from Shackleton swept over you to push you and the sleds into a new orbit. And you saluted and cut the herds, and kept whatever more you might know to yourself.

Which in Sergei's case was quite a bit. Sergei knew orbital codes and protocols far beyond his pay grade; he could basically move anything in orbit to or from anywhere. But only Sergei, so Sergei thought, knew that. How Roger learned it remained a mystery.

To his great surprise, Sergei learned that even he hadn't known the full extent of his skills. How easy it had been to steal half a million bombs. True, the eternal war economy was so corrupt that materiel was supposed to disappear; something was wrong if it didn't. Still, he would never have dared anything so outrageous on his own. Despite Roger's planning, he was sweating the day he moved the first sled into an unauthorized orbit. But days passed, then weeks and months, as sled followed sled into new holding orbits. In eighteen months they had all their fuel. No traps had sprung, no alarms tripped. Sophie managed to make the manifests look okay. And he wondered again at what the world had become. And what he was in it.

This spacesuit was light, thin, too comfortable. Like a toddler's fleece play-suit with slippers and gloves. Even the helmet was soft. He was more used to heavy Russian engineering, but whatever. They'd argued over whether to include a suit at all. He'd argued against. EVA had looked unlikely, an unlucky possibility. So he was happy now to have anything.

The soles and palms were sticky, a clever off-the-shelf idea inspired by lizards. Billions of carbon nanotubes lined them. The Van der Waals molecular force made them stick to any surface. He tested it by walking on the interior walls. Hands or feet held you fast, with or against the ship's rotational gravity. You had to kind of toe-and-heel to walk, but it was easy enough.

Пойдем. Let's go. He climbed into the hatch and cycled it. As the pressure dropped, the suit expanded and felt more substantial. He tested the grip of his palms on the hull before rising fully out of the hatch. Then his feet came up and gripped, and he stood.

In darkness and immensity stiller than he could comprehend. Interstellar space. The frozen splendor of the galactic core overhead. Nothing appeared to move.

He remembered a still evening on a lake, sitting with a friend on a dock, legs over the edge. They talked as the sky darkened, looking up as the stars came out. Only when it was fully dark did he happen to look down. The water was so still, stars were reflected under his feet. He almost lurched over the edge of the dock in surprise.

The memory tensed his legs, and he realized the galactic core was moving slowly around the ship. Here on the outside of the ship its spin-induced gravity was reversed. He stood upright but felt pulled toward the stars.

He faced forward. Tenth of a light-year from Alpha, its two stars still appeared as one. They were brighter than Venus in the Earth's sky. They cast his faint but distinct shadow on the hull.

They were here. They had come this far. On this tiny splinter of human will forging through vast, uncaring space. It was remarkable.

A line of light to his left flashed. Some microscopic particle ionized by the ship's magnetic shield. He tensed again at this evidence of their movement and turned slowly, directing his beam over the hull. Its light caught a huge gash through one of the hydrogen tanks. Edges of the gash had failed to be covered by a dozen geckos, frozen in place by hydrogen ice. That was bad. Worse, it hadn't been in the log. Maybe it was from the impact Sophie had referred to. He would have to see how bad it was after freeing the magsail.

He turned, and toed and heeled his way carefully aft. Now ahead of him was our Sun, still one of the brightest stars, the heavens turning slowly around it. He approached the circular bay that held the magsail. His light showed six large spools of cable, each a meter and a half across and a meter thick. About five metric tons in all, seventy kilometers of thin superconductor wire. Current injection should have caused the spools to unreel under the force of the electric field. But it wasn't getting current, or it was somehow stuck. He was going to have to . . . well, he wasn't sure.

Then he saw it. Almost laughed at the simplicity and familiarity of it. Something like a circuit breaker, red and green buttons, the red one lit. He squatted at the edge of the bay and found he could reach the thing. He felt cold penetrate his suit. He really ought to go back inside and spend a few hours troubleshooting, read the fucking manual, but the cold and the flimsy spacesuit and the immensity convinced him otherwise. He slapped the green button.

It lit. The cable accepted current. He saw it lurch. As he smiled and stood, the current surging in the coils sent its field through the soles of his spacesuit, disrupting for a moment the molecular force holding them to the hull. In that moment, the angular velocity of the rotating ship was transmitted to his body and he detached, moving away from the ship at a stately three meters per second. Beyond his flailing feet, the cables of the magsail began leisurely to unfurl.

As he tumbled the stars rolled past. He'd seen Orion behind the ship in the moment he detached, and as he tumbled he looked for it, for something to grab on to, but he never saw it or the ship again. So he didn't see the huge coil of wire reach its full extension, nor the glow of ionization around the twenty-kilometer circle when it began to drag against the interstellar medium, nor how the ship itself started to lag against the background stars. The ionization set up a howl across the radio spectrum, but his radio was off, so he didn't hear that. He tumbled in silence in the bowl of the heavens at his fixed velocity, which was now slightly greater than the ship's. Every so often the brightness of Alpha crossed his view. He was going to get there first.

4.

Their biggest single problem was fuel. To cross that enormous distance in less than a human lifetime, even in this stripped-down vessel, required an inconceivable amount of energy. Ten to the twenty-first joules. 250 trillion kilowatt-hours. Twenty years' worth of all Earth's greedy energy consumption. The mass of the fuel, efficient though it was, would be several times the mass of the ship. And to reach cruising speed was only half of it; they had to decelerate when they reached Alpha C, doubling the fuel. It was undoable.

Until someone found an old paper on magnetic sails. A superconducting loop of wire many kilometers across, well charged, could act as a drag brake against the interstellar medium. That would cut the fuel requirement almost in half. Done that way, it was just possible, though out on the ragged edge of what was survivable. This deceleration would take ten years.

For their primary fuel, Roger pointed to the hundreds of thousands of bombs in orbit. His bombs. His intellectual property. Toss them out the back and ignite them. A Blumlein pulse-forming line—they called it the "bloom line"—a self-generated magnetic vise, something like a Z-pinch—would direct nearly all the blast to exhaust velocity. The vise, called into being for the nanoseconds of ignition, funneled all that force straight back. Repeat every minute. Push the compression ratio up, you won't get many neutrons.

In the end they had two main engines: first, the antiproton-fusion monster to get them up to speed. It could only be used for the first year; any longer and the antiprotons would decay. Then the magsail would slow them most of the way, until they entered the system.

For the last leg, a gas-core nuclear rocket to decelerate in the system, which required carrying a large amount of hydrogen. They discussed scooping hydrogen from the interstellar medium as they traveled, but Roger vetoed it: not off the shelf. They didn't have the time or means to devise a new technology. Anyway, the hydrogen would make, in combination with their EM shield, an effective barrier to cosmic rays. Dual use.

And even so, everything had to be stretched to the limit: the mass of the ship minimized, the human lifetime lengthened, the fuel leveraged every way possible.

The first spacecraft ever to leave the solar system, Pioneer 10, had used Jupiter's gravity to boost its velocity. As it flew by, it stole kinetic energy from the planet; its small mass sped up a lot; Jupiter's stupendous mass slowed unnoticeably.

They would do the same thing to lose speed. They had the combined mass of two stars orbiting each other, equal to two thousand Jupiters. When *Gypsy* was to arrive in 2113, the stars in their mutual orbit would be as close together as they ever got: 11 astronomical units. *Gypsy* would fly by the B star and pull one last trick: retrofire the nuclear rocket deep in its gravity well; that would multiply the kinetic effect of the propellant severalfold. And then they'd repeat that maneuever around A. The relative closeness of 11 AU was still as far as Earth to Saturn, so even after arrival, even at their still-great speed, the dual braking maneuver would take over a year.

Only then would they be moving slowly enough to aerobrake in the planet's atmosphere, and that would take a few dozen passes before they could ride the ship down on its heatshield to the surface.

If there was a planet. If it had an atmosphere.

Zia (2120)

As a child he was lord of the dark—finding his way at night, never stumbling, able to read books by starlight; to read also, in faces and landscapes, traces and glimmers that others missed. Darkness was warmth and comfort to him.

A cave in Ephesus. In the Qur'an, Surah Al-Kahf. The sleepers waking after centuries, emerging into a changed world. Trying to spend old coins.

After the horror of his teen years, he'd found that dark was still a friend. Looking through the eyepiece of an observatory telescope, in the Himalayan foothills, in Uttar Pradesh. Describing the cluster of galaxies, one by one, to the astronomer. *You see the seventh? What eyes!*

Nothing moved but in his mind. Dreams of tenacity and complication. Baffling remnants, consciousness too weak to sort. Every unanswered question of his life, every casual observation, every bit of mental flotsam, tossed together in one desperate, implicate attempt at resolving them all. Things fell; he lunged to catch them. He stood on street corners in an endless night, searching for his shoes, his car, his keys, his wife. His mother chided him in a room lit by incandescent bulbs, dim and flickering like firelight. Galaxies in the eyepiece faded, and he looked up from the eyepiece to a blackened sky. He lay waking, in the dark, now aware of the dream state, returning with such huge reluctance to the life of the body, that weight immovable on its slab.

His eyelid was yanked open. A drop of fluid splashed there. A green line swept across his vision. He caught a breath and it burned in his lungs.

He was awake. Aboard *Gypsy*. It was bringing him back to life.

But I'm cold. Too cold to shiver. Getting colder as I wake up.

How hollow he felt. In this slight gravity. How unreal. It came to him, in the eclipsing of his dreams and the rising of his surroundings, that the gravity of Earth might be something more profound than the acceleration of a mass, the curvature of spacetime. Was it not an emanation of the planet, a life force? All life on Earth evolved in it, rose from it, fought it every moment, lived and bred and died awash in it. Those tides swept through our cells, the force from Earth, and the gravity of the sun and the gravity of the moon. What was life out here, without that embrace, that permeation, that bondage? Without it, would they wither and die like plants in a shed?

The hollowness came singing, roaring, whining, crackling into his ears. Into his throat and and nose and eyes and skin it came as desiccation. Searing into his mouth. He needed to cough and he couldn't. His thorax spasmed.

There was an antiseptic moistness in his throat. It stung, but his muscles had loosened. He could breathe. Cold swept from his shoulders down through his torso and he began to shiver uncontrollably.

When he could, he raised a hand. He closed his eyes and held the hand afloat in the parodic gravity, thinking about it, how it felt, how far away it actually was. At last, with hesitation, his eyes opened and came to focus. An old man's hand, knobby, misshapen at the joints, the skin papery, sagging and hanging in folds. He couldn't close the fingers. How many years had he slept? He forced on his hand the imagination of a clenched fist. The hand didn't move.

Oh my god the pain.

Without which, no life. Pain too is an emanation of the planet, of the life force.

It sucked back like a wave, gathering for another concussion. He tried to sit up and passed out.

Nikos Kakopoulos was a short man, just over five feet, stocky but fit. The features of his face were fleshy, slightly comic. He was graying, balding, but not old. In his fifties. He smiled as he said he planned to be around a hundred years from now. His office was full of Mediterranean light. A large Modigliani covered one wall. His money came mostly from aquifer rights. He spent ten percent of it on charities. One such awarded science scholarships. Which is how he'd come to Roger's attention.

So you see, I am not such a bad guy.

Those foundations are just window dressing. What they once called greenwash.

Zia, said Roger.

Kakopoulos shrugged as if to say, Let him talk, I've heard it all. To Zia he said: They do some good after all. They're a comfort to millions of people.

Drinking water would be more of a comfort.

There isn't enough to go round. I didn't create that situation.

You exploit it.

So sorry to say this. Social justice and a civilized lifestyle can't be done both at once. Not for ten billion people. Not on this planet.

You've decided this.

It's a conclusion based on the evidence.

And you care about this why?

I'm Greek. We invented justice and civilization.

You're Cypriot. Also, the Chinese would argue that. The Persians. The Egyptians. Not to mention India.

Kakopoulos waved away the first objection and addressed the rest. *Of course they would. And England, and Germany, and Italy, and Russia, and the US. They're arguing as we speak. Me, I'm not going to argue. I'm going to a safe place until the arguing is over. After that, if we're very lucky, we can have our discussion about civilization and justice.*

On your terms.

On terms that might have some meaning.

What terms would those be?

World population under a billion, for starters. Kakopoulos reached across the table and popped an olive into his mouth.

How do you think that's going to happen? asked Zia.

It's happening. Just a matter of time. Since I don't know how much time, I want a safe house for the duration.

How are you going to get up there?

Kakopoulous grinned. *When the Chinese acquired Lockheed, I picked up an X–33. It can do Mach 25. I have a spaceport on Naxos. Want a ride?*

The VTOL craft looked like the tip of a Delta IV rocket, or of a penis: a blunt, rounded conic. Not unlike Kakopoulos himself. Some outsize Humpty Dumpty.

How do you know him? Zia asked Roger as they boarded.

I've been advising him.

You're advising the man who owns a third of the world's fresh water?

He owns a lot of things. My first concern is for our project. We need him.

What for?

Roger stared off into space.

He immiserates the Earth, Roger.

We all ten billion immiserate the Earth by being here.

Kakopoulos returned.

Make yourselves comfortable. Even at Mach 25, it takes some time.

It was night, and the Earth was below their window. Rivers of manmade light ran across it. Zia could see the orange squiggle of the India-Pakistan border, all three thousand floodlit kilometers of it. Then the ship banked and the window turned to the stars.

Being lord of the dark had a touch of clairvoyance in it. The dark seldom brought surprise to him. Something bulked out there and he felt it. Some gravity about it called to him *from some future. Sun blazed forth behind the limb of the Earth, but the thing was still in Earth's shadow. It made a blackness against the Milky Way. Then sunlight touched it. Its lines caught light: the edges of panels, tanks, heat sinks, antennas. Blunt radar-shedding angles. A squat torus shape under it all. It didn't look like a ship. It looked like a squashed donut to which a junkyard had been glued. It turned slowly on its axis.*

My safe house, said Kakopoulos.

It was, indeed, no larger than a house. About ten meters long, twice that across. It had cost a large part of Kakopoulos's considerable fortune. Which he recouped by manipulating and looting several central banks. As a result, a handful of small countries, some hundred million people, went off the cliff-edge of modernity into an abyss of debt peonage.

While they waited to dock with the thing, Kakopoulos came and sat next to Zia.

Listen, my friend—

I'm not your friend.

As you like, I don't care. I don't think you're stupid. When I said my foundations make people feel better, I meant the rich, of course. You're Pakistani?

Indian actually.

But Muslim. Kashmir?

Zia shrugged.

Okay. We're not so different, I think. I grew up in the slums of Athens after the euro collapsed. The histories, the videos, they don't capture it. I imagine Kashmir was much worse. But we each found a way out, no? So tell me, would you go back to that? No, you don't have to answer. You wouldn't. Not for anything. You'd sooner die. But you're not the kind of asshole who writes conscience checks. Or thinks your own self is wonderful enough to deserve anything. So where does that leave a guy like you in this world?

Fuck you.

Kakopoulos patted Zia's hand and smiled. I love it when people say fuck you to me. You know why? It means I won. They've got nothing left but their fuck you. He got up and went away.

The pilot came in then, swamp-walking the zero g in his velcro shoes, and said they'd docked.

The ship massed about a hundred metric tons. A corridor circled the inner circumference, floor against the outer hull, most of the space taken up by hibernation slabs for a crew of twenty. Once commissioned, it would spin on its axis a few times a minute to create something like lunar gravity. They drifted around it slowly, pulling themselves by handholds.

This, Kakopoulos banged a wall, is expensive. Exotic composites, all that aerogel. Why so much insulation?

Roger let "expensive" pass unchallenged. Zia didn't.

You think there's nothing more important than money.

Kakopoulos turned, as if surprised Zia was still there. He said, There are many things more important than money. You just don't get any of them without it.

Roger said, Even while you're hibernating, the ship will radiate infrared. That's one reason you'll park at a Lagrange point, far enough away not to attract attention. When you wake up and start using energy, you're going to light up like a Christmas tree. And you're going to hope that whatever is left on Earth or in space won't immediately blow you out of the sky. The insulation will hide you somewhat.

At one end of the cramped command center was a micro-apartment.

What's this, Nikos?

Ah, my few luxuries. Music, movies, artworks. We may be out here awhile after we wake up. Look at my kitchen.

A range?

Propane, but it generates 30,000 BTU!

That's insane. You're not on holiday here.

Look, it's vented, only one burner, I got a great engineer, you can examine the plans—

Get rid of it.

What! Kakopoulos yelled. Whose ship is this!

Roger pretended to think for a second. Do you mean who owns it, or who designed it?

Do you know how much it cost to get that range up here?

I can guess to the nearest million.

When I wake up I want a good breakfast!

When you wake up you'll be too weak to stand. Your first meal will be coming down tubes.

Kakopoulos appeared to sulk.

Nikos, what is your design specification here?

I just want a decent omelette.

I can make that happen. But the range goes.

Kakopoulous nursed his sulk, then brightened. Gonna be some meteor, that range. I'll call my observatory, have them image it.

Later, when they were alone, Zia said: All right, Roger. I've been very patient.

Patient? Roger snorted.

How can that little pustule help us?

That's our ship. We're going to steal it.

Later, Zia suggested that they christen the ship the Fuck You.

Eighty years later, Zia was eating one of Kakopoulos's omelettes. Freeze-dried egg, mushrooms, onion, tarragon. Microwaved with two ounces of water. Not bad. He had another.

Mach 900, asshole, he said aloud.

Most of the crew were dead. Fungus had grown on the skin stretched like drums over their skulls, their ribs, their hips.

He'd seen worse. During his mandatory service, as a teenager in the military, he'd patrolled Deccan slums. He'd seen parents eating their dead children. Pariah dogs fat as sheep roamed the streets. Cadavers, bones, skulls, were piled in front of nearly every house. The cloying carrion smell never lifted. Hollowed-out buildings housed squatters and corpses equally, darkened plains of them below fortified bunkers lit like Las Vegas, where the driving bass of party music echoed the percussion of automatic weapons and rocket grenades.

Now his stomach rebelled, but he commanded it to be still as he swallowed some olive oil. Gradually the chill in his core subsided.

He needed to look at the sky. The ship had two telescopes: a one-meter honeycomb mirror for detail work and a wide-angle high-res CCD camera. Zoomed fully out, the camera took in about eighty degrees. Ahead was the blazing pair of Alpha Centauri A and B, to the eye more than stars but not yet suns. He'd never seen anything like them. Brighter than Venus, bright as the full moon, but such tiny disks. As he watched, the angle of them moved against the ship's rotation.

He swept the sky, looking for landmarks. But the stars were wrong. What had happened to Orion? Mintaka had moved. The belt didn't point to Sirius, as it should. A brilliant blue star off Orion's left shoulder outshone Betelgeuse, and then he realized. *That* was Sirius. Thirty degrees from where it should be. Of course: it was eight light-years from Earth. They had come half that distance, and, like a nearby buoy seen against a far shore, it had changed position against the farther stars.

More distant stars had also shifted, but not as much. He turned to what he still absurdly thought of as "north." The Big Dipper was there. The Little Dipper's bowl was squashed. Past Polaris was Cassiopeia, the zigzag W, the queen's throne. And there a new, bright star blazed above it, as if that W had grown another zag. Could it be a nova? He stared, and the stars of Cassiopeia circled this strange bright one slowly as the ship rotated. Then he knew: the strange star was Sol. Our Sun.

That was when he felt it, in his body: they were really here.

From the beginning Roger had a hand—a heavy, guiding hand—in the design of the ship. Not for nothing had he learned the Lab's doctrine of dual use. Not for nothing had he cultivated Kakopoulos's acquaintance. Every feature that fitted the ship for interstellar space was a plausible choice for Kak's purpose: hibernators, cosmic-ray shielding, nuclear rocket, hardened computers, plutonium pile and Stirling engine.

In the weeks prior to departure, they moved the ship to a more distant orbit, too distant for Kak's X-33 to reach. There they jettisoned quite a bit of the ship's interior. They added their fusion engine, surrounded the vessel with fuel sleds, secured anti-proton traps, stowed the magsail, loaded the seed bank and a hundred other things.

They were three hundred AU out from Alpha Centauri. Velocity was one-thousandth c. The magsail was programmed to run for two more years, slowing them by half again. But lately their deceleration had shown variance. The magsail was running at higher current than planned. Very close to max spec. That wasn't good. Logs told him why, and that was worse.

He considered options, none good. The sail was braking against the interstellar medium, stray neutral atoms of hydrogen. No one knew for sure how it would behave once it ran into Alpha's charged solar wind. Nor just where that wind started. The interstellar medium might already be giving way to it. If so, the count of galactic cosmic rays would be going down and the temperature of charged particles going up.

He checked. Definitely maybe on both counts.

He'd never liked this plan, its narrow margins of error. Not that he had a better one. That was the whole problem: no plan B. Every intricate, fragile, untried part of it had to work. He'd pushed pretty hard for a decent margin of error in this deceleration stage and the subsequent maneuvering in the system—what a tragedy it would be to come to grief so close, within sight of shore—and now he saw that margin evaporating.

Possibly the sail would continue to brake in the solar wind. If only they could have tested it first.

Zia didn't trust materials. Or, rather: he trusted them to fail. Superconductors, carbon composite, silicon, the human body. Problem was, you never knew just how or when they'd fail.

One theory said that a hydrogen wall existed somewhere between the termination shock and the heliopause, where solar wind gave way to interstellar space. Three hundred AU put *Gypsy* in that dicey zone.

It would be prudent to back off the magsail current. That would lessen their decel, and they needed all they could get, they had started it too late, but they also needed to protect the sail and run it as long as possible.

Any change to the current had to happen slowly. It would take hours or possibly days. The trick was not to deform the coil too much in the process, or create eddy currents that could quench the superconducting field.

The amount of power he had available was another issue. The plutonium running the Stirling engine had decayed to about half its original capacity.

He shut down heat in the cabin to divert more to the Stirling engine. He turned down most of the LED lighting, and worked in the semidark, except for the glow of the monitor. Programmed a gentle ramp up in current.

Then he couldn't keep his eyes open.

At Davos, he found himself talking to an old college roommate. Carter Hall III was his name; he was something with the UN now, and with the Council for Foreign Relations—an enlightened and condescending asshole. They were both Harvard '32, but Hall remained a self-appointed Brahmin, generously, sincerely, and with vast but guarded amusement, guiding a Sudra through the world that was his by birthright. Never mind the Sudra was Muslim.

From a carpeted terrace they overlooked a groomed green park. There was no snow in town this January, an increasingly common state of affairs. Zia noted but politely declined to point out the obvious irony, the connection between the policies determined here and the retreat of the snow line.

Why Zia was there was complicated. He was persona non grata with the ruling party, but he was a scientist, he had security clearances, and he had access to diplomats on both sides of the border. India had secretly built many thousands of microfusion weapons and denied it. The US was about to enter into the newest round of endless talks over "nonproliferation," in which the US never gave up anything but insisted that other nations must.

Hall now lectured him. India needed to rein in its population, which was over two billion. The US had half a billion.

Zia, please, look at the numbers. Four-plus children per household just isn't sustainable.

Abruptly Zia felt his manners fail.

Sustainable? Excuse me. Our Indian culture is four thousand years old, self-sustained through all that time. Yours is two, three, maybe five hundred years old, depending on your measure. And in that short time, not only is it falling apart, it's taking the rest of the world down with it, including my homeland.

Two hundred years, I don't get that, if you mean Western—

I mean technology, I mean capital, I mean extraction.

Well, but those are very, I mean if you look at your, your four thousand years of, of poverty and class discrimination, and violence—

Ah? And there is no poverty or violence in your brief and perfect history? No extermination? No slavery?

Hall's expression didn't change much.

We've gotten past all that, Zia. We—

Zia didn't care that Hall was offended. He went on:

The story of resource extraction has only two cases, okay? In the first case, the extractors arrive and make the local ruler an offer. Being selfish, he takes it and he becomes rich—never so rich as the extractors, but compared to his people, fabulously, delusionally rich. His people become the cheap labor used to extract the resource. This leads to social upheaval. Villages are moved, families destroyed. A few people are enriched, the majority are ruined. Maybe there is an uprising against the ruler.

In the second case the ruler is smarter. Maybe he's seen some neighboring ruler's head on a pike. He says no thanks to the extractors. To this they have various responses: make him a better offer, find a greedier rival, hire an assassin, or bring in the gunships. But in the end it's the same: a few people are enriched, most are ruined. What the extractors never, ever do in any case, in all your history, is take no for an answer.

Zia, much as I enjoy our historical discussions—

Ah, you see? And there it is—your refusal to take no. Talk is done, now we move forward with your agenda.

We have to deal with the facts on the ground. Where we are now.

Yes, of course. It's remarkable how, when the mess you've made has grown so large that even you must admit to it, you want to reset everything to zero. You want to get past "all that." All of history starts over, with these "facts on the ground." Let's move on, move forward, forget how we got here, forget the exploitation and the theft and the waste and the betrayals. Forget the, what is that charming accounting word, the externalities. Start from the new zero.

Hall looked weary and annoyed that he was called upon to suffer such childishness. That well-fed yet kept-fit form hunched, that pale skin looked suddenly papery and aged in the Davos sunlight.

You know, Zia prodded, greed could at least be more efficient. If you know what you want, at least take it cleanly. No need to leave whole countries in ruins.

Hall smiled a tight, grim smile, just a glimpse of the wolf beneath. He said: then it wouldn't be greed. Greed never knows what it wants.

That was the exact measure of Hall's friendship, to say that to Zia. But then Zia knew what he wanted: out.

As he drifted awake, he realized that, decades past, the ship would have collected data on the Sun's own heliopause on their way out. If he could access that data, maybe he could learn whether the hydrogen wall was a real thing. What effect it might—

There was a loud bang. The monitor and the cabin went dark. His mind reached into the outer darkness and it sensed something long and loose and broken trailing behind them.

What light there was came back on. The computer rebooted. The monitor displayed readings for the magsail over the past hour: current ramping up, then oscillating to compensate for varying densities in the medium, then a sharp spike. And then zero. Quenched.

Hydrogen wall? He didn't know. The magsail was fried. He tried for an hour more to get it to accept current. No luck. He remembered with some distaste the EVA suit. He didn't want to go outside, to tempt that darkness, but he might have to, so he walked forward to check it out.

The suit wasn't in its cubby. Zia turned and walked up the corridor, glancing at his torpid crewmates. The last slab was empty.

Sergei was gone. The suit was gone. You would assume they'd gone together, but that wasn't in the logs. *I may be some time.* Sergei didn't strike him as the type to take a last walk in the dark. And for that he wouldn't have needed the suit. Still. You can't guess what anyone might do.

So that was final—no EVA: the magsail couldn't be fixed. From the console, he cut it loose.

They were going far too fast. Twice what they'd planned. Now they had only the nuclear plasma rocket for deceleration, and one fuel tank was empty, somehow. Even though the fuel remaining outmassed the ship, it wasn't enough. If they couldn't slow below the escape velocity of the system, they'd shoot right through and out the other side.

The ship had been gathering data for months and had good orbital elements for the entire system. Around A were four planets, none in a position to assist with flybys. Even if they were, their masses would be little help. Only the two stars were usable.

If he brought them in a lot closer around B—how close could they get? one fiftieth AU? one hundredth?—and if the heat shield held—it should withstand 2500° Celsius for a few hours—the ship could be slowed more with the same amount of fuel. The B star was closest: it was the less luminous of the pair, cooler, allowing them to get in closer, shed more speed. Then repeat the maneuver at A.

There was a further problem. Twelve years ago, as per the original plan, Alpha A and B were at their closest to one another: 11 AU. The stars were now twenty AU apart and widening. So the trip from B to A would take twice as long. And systems were failing. They were out on the rising edge of the bathtub curve.

Power continued erratic. The computer crashed again and again as he worked out the trajectories. He took to writing down intermediate results on paper in case he lost a session, cursing as he did so. Materials. We stole our tech from the most corrupt forces on Earth. Dude, you want an extended warranty with that? He examined the Stirling engine, saw that the power surge had compromised it. He switched the pile over to backup thermocouples. That took hours to do and it was less efficient, but it kept the computer running. It was still frustrating. The computer was designed to be redundant, hardened, hence slow. Minimal graphics, no 3D holobox. He had to think through his starting parameters carefully before he wasted processor time running a simulation.

Finally he had a new trajectory, swinging in perilously close to B, then A. It might work. Next he calculated that, when he did what he was about to do, seventy kilometers of magsail cable wouldn't catch them up and foul them. Then he fired the maneuvering thrusters.

What sold him, finally, was a handful of photons.

This is highly classified, said Roger. He held a manila file folder containing paper. Any computer file was permeable, hackable. Paper was serious.

The data were gathered by an orbiting telescope. It wasn't a photograph. It was a blurred, noisy image that looked like rings intersecting in a pond a few seconds after some pebbles had been thrown.

It's a deconvolved cross-correlation map of a signal gathered by a chopped pair of Bracewell baselines. You know how that works?

He didn't. Roger explained. Any habitable planet around Alpha Centauri A or B would appear a small fraction of an arc-second away from the stars, and would be at least twenty-two magnitudes fainter. At that separation, the most sensitive camera made, with the best dynamic range, couldn't hope to find the planet in the stars' glare. But put several cameras together in a particular phase relation and the stars' light could be nulled out. What remained, if anything, would be light from another source. A planet, perhaps.

Also this, in visible light.

An elliptical iris of grainy red, black at its center, where an occulter had physically blocked the stars' disks.

Coronagraph, said Roger. Here's the detail.

A speck, a single pixel, slightly brighter than the enveloping noise.

What do you think?

Could be anything. Dust, hot pixel, cosmic ray . . . .

It shows up repeatedly. And it moves.

Roger, for all I know you photoshopped it in.

He looked honestly shocked. Do you really think I'd . . . .

I'm kidding. But where did you get these? Can you trust the source?

Why would anyone fake such a thing?

The question hung and around it gathered, like sepsis, the suspicion of some agency setting them up, of some agenda beyond their knowing. After the Kepler exoplanet finder went dark, subsequent exoplanet data—like all other government-sponsored scientific work—were classified. Roger's clearance was pretty high, but even he couldn't be sure of his sources.

You're not convinced, are you.

But somehow Zia was. The orbiting telescope had an aperture of, he forgot the final number, it had been scaled down several times owing to budget cuts. A couple of meters, maybe. That meant light from this far-off dim planet fell on it at a rate of just a few photons per second. It made him unutterably lonely to think of those photons traveling so far. It also made him believe in the planet.

Well, okay, Roger Fry was mad. Zia knew that. But he would throw in with Roger because all humanity was mad. Perhaps always had been. Certainly for the past century-plus, with the monoculture madness called modernity. Roger at least was mad in a different way, perhaps Zia's way.

He wrote the details into the log, reduced the orbital mechanics to a cookbook formula. Another steward would have to be awakened when they reached the B star; that would be in five years; his calculations weren't good enough to automate the burn time, which would depend on the ship's precise momentum and distance from the star as it rounded. It wasn't enough just to slow down; their exit trajectory from B needed to point them exactly to where A would be a year later. That wouldn't be easy; he took a couple of days to write an app to make it easier, but with large blocks of memory failing in the computer, Sophie's idea of a handwritten logbook no longer looked so dumb.

As he copied it all out, he imagined the world they'd left so far behind: the billions in their innocence or willed ignorance or complicity, the elites he'd despised for their lack of imagination, their surfeit of hubris, working together in a horrible *folie à deux.* He saw the bombs raining down, atomizing history and memory and accomplishment, working methodically backwards from the cities to the cradles of civilization to the birthplaces of the species—the Fertile Crescent, the Horn of Africa, the Great Rift Valley—in a crescendo of destruction and denial of everything humanity had ever been—its failures, its cruelties, its grandeurs, its aspirations—all extirpated to the root, in a fury of self-loathing that fed on what it destroyed.

Zia's anger rose again in his ruined, aching body—his lifelong pointless rage at all that stupidity, cupidity, yes, there's some hollow satisfaction being away from all that. Away from the noise of their being. Their unceasing commotion of disruption and corruption. How he'd longed to escape it. But in the silent enclosure of the ship, in this empty house populated by the stilled ghosts of his crewmates, he now longed for any sound, any noise. He had wanted to be here, out in the dark. But not for nothing. And he wept.

And then he was just weary. His job was done. Existence seemed a pointless series of problems. What was identity? Better never to have been. He shut his eyes.

In bed with Maria, she moved in her sleep, rolled against him, and he rolled away. She twitched and woke from some dream.

What! What! she cried.

He flinched. His heart moved, but he lay still, letting her calm. Finally he said, What was that?

You pulled away from me!

Then they were in a park somewhere. Boston? Maria was yelling at him, in tears. Why must you be so negative!

He had no answer for her, then or now. Or for himself. Whatever "himself" might be. Something had eluded him in his life, and he wasn't going to find it now.

He wondered again about what had happened to Sergei. Well, it was still an option for him. He wouldn't need a suit.

Funny, isn't it, how one's human sympathy—Zia meant most severely his own—extends about as far as those like oneself. He meant true sympathy; abstractions like justice don't count. Even now, missing Earth, he felt sympathy only for those aboard *Gypsy*, those orphaned, damaged, disaffected, dispossessed, Aspergerish souls whose anger at that great abstraction, The World, was more truly an anger at all those fortunate enough to be unlike them. We were all so young. How can you be so young, and so hungry for, and yet so empty of life?

As he closed his log, he hit on a final option for the ship, if not himself. If after rounding B and A the ship still runs too fast to aerobrake into orbit around the planet, do this. Load all the genetic material—the frozen zygotes, the seed bank, the whatever—into a heatshielded pod. Drop it into the planet's atmosphere. If not themselves, some kind of life would have some chance. Yet as soon as he wrote those words, he felt their sting.

Roger, and to some degree all of them, had seen this as a way to transcend their thwarted lives on Earth. They were the essence of striving humanity: their planning and foresight served the animal's desperate drive to overcome what can't be overcome. To escape the limits of death. Yet transcendence, if it meant anything at all, was the accommodation to limits: a finding of freedom within them, not a breaking of them. Depositing the proteins of life here, like a stiff prick dropping its load, could only, in the best case, lead to a replication of the same futile striving. The animal remains trapped in the cage of its being.

5.

A n old, old man in a wheelchair. Tube in his nose. Oxygen bottle on a cart. He'd been somebody at the Lab once. Recruited Roger, among many others, plucked him out of the pack at Caltech. Roger loathed the old man but figured he owed him. And was owed.

They sat on a long, covered porch looking out at hills of dry grass patched with dark stands of live oak. The old man was feeling pretty spry after he'd thumbed through Roger's papers and lit the cigar Roger offered him. He detached the tube, took a discreet puff, exhaled very slowly, and put the tube back in.

Hand it to you, Roger, most elaborate, expensive form of mass suicide in history.

Really? I'd give that honor to the so-called statecraft of the past century.

Wouldn't disagree. But that's been very good to you and me. That stupidity gradient.

This effort is modest by comparison. Very few lives are at stake here. They might even survive it.

How many bombs you got onboard this thing? How many megatons?

They're not bombs, they're fuel. We measure it in exajoules.

Gonna blow them up in a magnetic pinch, aren't you? I call things that blow up bombs. But fine, measure it in horsepower if it makes you feel virtuous. Exajoules, huh? He stared into space for a minute. Ship's mass?

One hundred metric tons dry.

That's nice and light. Wonder where you got ahold of that. But you still don't have enough push. Take you over a hundred years. Your systems'll die.

Seventy-two years.

You done survival analysis? You get a bathtub curve with most of these systems. Funny thing is, redundancy works against you.

How so?

Shit, you got Sidney Lefebvre down the hall from you, world's expert in failure modes, don't you know that?

Roger knew the name. The man worked on something completely different now. Somehow this expertise had been erased from his resume and his working life.

How you gone slow down?

Magsail.

I always wondered, would that work.

You wrote the papers on it.

You know how hand-wavy they are. We don't know squat about the interstellar medium. And we don't have superconductors that good anyway. Or do we?

Roger didn't answer.

What happens when you get into the system?

That's what I want to know. Will the magsail work in the solar wind? Tarasenko says no.

Fuck him.

His math is sound. I want to know what you know. Does it work?

How would I know. Never got to test it. Never heard of anyone who did.

Tell me, Dan.

Tell you I don't know. Tarasenko's a crank, got a Ukraine-sized chip on his shoulder.

That doesn't mean he's wrong.

The old man shrugged, looked critically at the cigar, tapped the ash off its end.

Don't hold out on me.

Christ on a crutch, Roger, I'm a dead man. Want me to spill my guts, be nice, bring me a Havana.

There was a spell of silence. In the sunstruck sky a turkey vulture wobbled and banked into an updraft.

How you gone build a magsail that big? You got some superconductor scam goin?

After ten years of braking we come in on this star, through its heliopause, at about 500 kilometers per second. That's too fast to be captured by the system's gravity.

'Cause I can help you there. Got some yttrium futures.

If we don't manage enough decel after that, we're done.

Gas-core reactor rocket.

We can't carry enough fuel. Do the math. Specific impulse is about three thousand at best.

The old man took the tube from his nose, tapped more ash off the cigar, inhaled. After a moment he began to cough. Roger had seen this act before. But it went on longer than usual, into a loud climax.

Roger . . . you really doin this? Wouldn't fool a dead man?

I'm modeling. For a multiplayer game.

That brought the old man more than half back. Fuck you too, he said. But that was for any surveillance, Roger thought.

The old man stared into the distance, then said: Oberth effect.

What's that?

Here's what you do, the old man whispered, hunched over, as he brought out a pen and an envelope.

Rosa (2125)

After she'd suffered through the cold, the numbness, the chills, the burning, still she lay, unready to move, as if she weren't whole, had lost some essence—her anima, her purpose. She went over the whole mission in her mind, step by step, piece by piece. *Do we have everything? The bombs to get us out of the solar system, the sail to slow us down, the nuclear rocket, the habitat . . . what else? What have we forgotten? There is something in the dark.*

What is in the dark? Another ship? Oh my God. If we did it, they could do it, too. It would be insane for them to come after us. But they are insane. And we stole their bombs. What would they not *do to us? Insane and vengeful as they are. They could send a drone after us, unmanned, or manned by a suicide crew. It's just what they would do.*

She breathed the stale, cold air and stared up at the dark ceiling. *Okay, relax. That's the worst-case scenario. Best case, they never saw us go. Most likely, they saw but they have other priorities. Everything has worked so far. Or you would not be lying here fretting, Rosa.*

Born Rose. Mamá was from Trinidad. Dad was Venezuelan. She called him Papá against his wishes. Solid citizens, assimilated: a banker, a realtor. Home was Altadena, California. There was a bit of Irish blood and more than a dollop of Romany, the renegade uncle Tonio told Rosa, mi mestiza.

They flipped when she joined a chapter of La Raza Nueva. Dad railed: a terrorist organization! And us born in countries we've occupied! Amazed that Caltech even permitted LRN on campus. The family got visits from Homeland Security. Eggs and paint bombs from the neighbors. Caltech looked into it and found that of its seven members, five weren't students. LRN was a creation of Homeland Security. Rosa and Sean were the only two authentic members, and they kept bailing out of planned actions.

Her father came to her while Homeland Security was on top of them, in the dark of her bedroom. He sat on the edge of the bed, she could feel his weight there and the displacement of it, could smell faintly the alcohol on his breath. He said: my mother and my father, my sisters, after the invasion, we lived in cardboard refrigerator boxes in the median strip of the main road from the airport to the city. For a year.

He'd never told her that. She hated him. For sparing her that, only to use it on her now. She'd known he'd grown up poor, but not that. She said bitterly: behind every fortune is a crime. What's yours?

He drew in his breath. She felt him recoil, the mattress shift under his weight. Then a greater shift, unfelt, of some dark energy, and he sighed. I won't deny it, but it was for family. For you! with sudden anger.

What did you do?

That I won't tell you. It's not safe.

Safe! You always want to be safe, when you should stand up!

Stand up? I did the hardest things possible for a man to do. For you, for this family. And now you put us all at risk—. His voice came close to breaking.

When he spoke again, there was no trace of anger left. You don't know how easily it can all be taken from you. What a luxury it is to stand up, as you call it.

Homeland Security backed off when Caltech raised a legal stink about entrapment. She felt vindicated. But her father didn't see it that way. The dumb luck, he called it, of a small fish. Stubborn in his way as she.

Sean, her lovely brother, who'd taken her side through all this, decided to stand up in his own perverse way: he joined the Army. She thought it was dumb, but she had to respect his argument: it was unjust that only poor Latinos joined. Certainly Papá, the patriot, couldn't argue with that logic, though he was furious.

Six months later Sean was killed in Bolivia. Mamá went into a prolonged, withdrawn mourning. Papá stifled an inchoate rage.

She'd met Roger Fry when he taught her senior course in particle physics; as "associated faculty" he became her thesis advisor. He looked as young as she. Actually, he was four years older. Women still weren't exactly welcome in high-energy physics. Rosa— not cute, not demure, not quiet—was even less so. Roger, however, didn't seem to see her. Gender and appearance seemed to make no impression at all on Roger.

He moved north mid-semester to work at the Lab but continued advising her via email. In grad school she followed his name on papers, R. A. Fry, as it moved up from the tail of a list of some dozen names to the head of such lists. "Physics of milli-K Antiproton Confinement in an Improved Penning Trap." "Antiprotons as Drivers for Inertial Confinement Fusion." "Typical Number of Antiprotons Necessary for Fast Ignition in LiDT." "Antiproton-Catalyzed Microfusion." And finally, "Antimatter Induced Continuous Fusion Reactions and Thermonuclear Explosions."

Rosa applied to work at the Lab.

She didn't stop to think, then, why she did it. It was because Roger, of all the people she knew, appeared to have stood up and gone his own way and had arrived somewhere worth going.

They were supposed to have landed on the planet twelve years ago.

Nothing was out there in the dark. Nothing had followed. They were alone. That was worse.

She weighed herself. Four kilos. That would be forty in Earth gravity. Looked down at her arms, her legs, her slack breasts and belly. Skin gray and loose and wrinkled and hanging. On Earth she'd been chunky, glossy as an apple, never under sixty kilos. Her body had been taken from her, and this wasted, frail thing put in its place.

Turning on the monitor's camera she had another shock. She was older than her mother. When they'd left Earth, Mamá was fifty. Rosa was at least sixty, by the look of it. They weren't supposed to have aged. Not like this.

She breathed and told herself it was luxury to be alive.

Small parts of the core group met face to face on rare occasions. Never all at once— they were too dispersed for that and even with travel permits it was unwise—it was threes or fours or fives at most. There was no such thing as a secure location. They had to rely on the ubiquity of surveillance outrunning the ability to process it all.

The Berkeley marina was no more secure than anywhere else. Despite the city's Potemkin liberalism, you could count, if you were looking, at least ten cameras from every point within its boundaries, and take for granted there were many more, hidden or winged, small and quick as hummingbirds, with software to read your lips from a hundred yards, and up beyond the atmosphere satellites to read the book in your hand if the air was steady, denoise it if not, likewise take your body temperature. At the marina the strong onshore flow from the cold Pacific made certain of these feats more difficult, but the marina's main advantage was that it was still beautiful, protected by accumulated capital and privilege—though now the names on the yachts were mostly in hanzi characters—and near enough to places where many of them worked, yet within the tether of their freedom—so they came to this rendezvous as often as they dared.

I remember the old marina. See where University Avenue runs into the water? It was half a mile past that. At neap tide you sometimes see it surface. Plenty chop there when it's windy.

They debated what to call this mad thing. Names out of the history of the idea— starships that had been planned but never built—Orion, Prometheus, Daedalus, Icarus, Longshot, Medusa. Names out of their imagination: Persephone, Finnegan, Ephesus. But finally they came to call it—not yet the ship, but themselves, and their being together in it—Gypsy. It was a word rude and available and they took it. They were going wandering, without a land, orphaned and dispossessed, they were gypping the rubes, the hateful inhumane ones who owned everything and out of the devilry of ownership would destroy it rather than share it. She was okay with that taking, she was definitely gypsy.

She slept with Roger. She didn't love him, but she admired him as a fellow spirit. Admired his intellect and his commitment and his belief. Wanted to partake of him and share herself. The way he had worked on fusion, and solved it. And then, when it was taken from him, he found something else. Something mad, bold, bad, dangerous, inspiring.

Roger's voice in the dark: I thought it was the leaders, the nations, the corpo-
rations, the elites, who were out of touch, who didn't understand the gravity of our
situation. I believed in the sincerity of their stupid denials—of global warming, of
resource depletion, of nuclear proliferation, of population pressure. I thought them stu-
pid. But if you judge them by their actions instead of their rhetoric, you can see that
they understood it perfectly and accepted the gravity of it very early. They simply gave
it up as unfixable. Concluded that law and democracy and civilization were hin-
drances to their continued power. Moved quite purposely and at speed toward this dire
world they foresaw, a world in which, to have the amenities even of a middle-class
life—things like clean water, food, shelter, energy, transportation, medical care—you
would need the wealth of a prince. You would need legal and military force to keep
desperate others from seizing it. Seeing that, they moved to amass such wealth for
themselves as quickly and ruthlessly as possible, with the full understanding that it
hastened the day they feared.

She sat at the desk with the monitors, reviewed the logs. Zia had been the last
to waken. Four and a half years ago. Trouble with the magsail. It was gone, and
their incoming velocity was too high. And they were very close now, following his
trajectory to the B star. She looked at his calculations and thought that he'd done
well; it might work. What she had to do: fine-tune the elements of the trajectory,
deploy the sunshield, prime the fuel, and finally light the hydrogen torch that
would push palely back against the fury of this sun. But not yet. She was too weak.

Zia was dead for sure, on his slab, shriveled like a nut in the bodysuit; he
had gone back into hibernation but had not reattached his stents. The others
didn't look good. Fang's log told that story, what she'd done to combat the fungus, what else might need to be done, what to look out for. Fang had done the
best she could. Rosa, at least, was alive.

A surge of grief hit her suddenly, bewildered her. She hadn't realized it till
now: she had a narrative about all this. She was going to a new world and she
was going to bear children in it. That was never a narrative she thought was hers;
hers was all about standing up for herself. But there it was, and as the possibility
of it vanished, she felt its teeth. The woman she saw in the monitor-mirror was
never going to have children. A further truth rushed upon her as implacable as
the star ahead: the universe didn't have that narrative, or any narrative, and all
of hers had been voided in its indifference. What loss she felt. And for what, a
story? For something that never was?

Lying next to her in the dark, Roger said: I would never have children. I would never
do that to another person.

You already have, Rosa poked him.
You know what I mean.
The universe is vast, Roger.
I know.
The universe of feeling is vast.
No children.
I could make you change your mind.

She'd left Roger behind on Earth. No regrets about that; clearly there was no place for another person on the inside of Roger's life.

The hydrogen in the tanks around the ship thawed as they drew near the sun. One tank read empty. She surmised from logs that it had been breached very early in the voyage. So they had to marshal fuel even more closely.

The orbital elements had been refined since Zia first set up the parameters of his elegant cushion shot. It wasn't Rosa's field, but she had enough math and computer tools to handle it. Another adjustment would have to be made in a year when they neared the A star, but she'd point them as close as she could.

It was going to be a near thing. There was a demanding trade-off between decel and trajectory; they had to complete their braking turn pointed exactly at where A would be in a year. Too much or too little and they'd miss it; they didn't have enough fuel to make course corrections. She ran Zia's app over and over, timing the burn.

Occasionally she looked at the planet through the telescope. Still too far away to see much. It was like a moon of Jupiter seen from Earth. Little more than a dot without color, hiding in the glare of A.

It took most of a week to prep the rocket. She triple-checked every step. It was supposed to be Sergei's job. Only Sergei was not on the ship. He'd left no log. She had no idea what had happened, but now it was her job to start up a twenty-gigawatt gas-core fission reactor. The reactor would irradiate and super-heat their hydrogen fuel, which would exit the nozzle with a thrust of some two million newtons.

She fired the attitude thrusters to derotate the ship, fixing it in the shadow of the sunshield. As the spin stopped, so did gravity; she became weightless.

Over the next two days, the thermal sensors climbed steadily to 1000° Celsius, 1200, 1500. Nothing within the ship changed. It remained dark and cool and silent and weightless. On the far side of the shield, twelve centimeters thick, megawatts of thermal energy pounded, but no more than a hundred watts reached the ship. They fell toward the star and she watched the outer temperature rise to 2000°.

Now, as the ship made its closest approach, the rocket came on line. It was astounding. The force pulled her out of the chair, hard into the crawlspace beneath the bolted desk. Her legs were pinned by her sudden body weight, knees twisted in a bad way. The pain increased as g-forces grew. She reached backwards, up, away from this new gravity, which was orthogonal to the floor. She clutched the chair legs above her and pulled until her left foot was freed from her weight, and then fell back against the bay of the desk, curled in a fetal position, exhausted. A full g, she guessed. Which her body had not experienced for eighty-four years. It felt like much more. Her heart labored. It was hard to breathe. Idiot! Not to think of this. She clutched the chair by its legs. Trapped here, unable to move or see while the engine thundered.

She hoped it didn't matter. The ship would run at full reverse thrust for exactly the time needed to bend their trajectory toward the farther sun, its nuclear flame burning in front of them, a venomous, roiling torrent of plasma and neutrons spewing from the center of the torus, and all this fury not even a spark to show against the huge sun that smote their carbon shield with its avalanche of light. The ship vibrated continuously with the rocket's thunder. Periodic concussions from she knew not what shocked her.

Two hours passed. As they turned, attitude thrusters kept them in the shield's shadow. If it failed, there would be a quick hot end to a long cold voyage.

An alert whined. That meant shield temperature had passed 2500. She counted seconds. The hull boomed and she lost count and started again. When she reached a thousand she stopped. Some time later the whining ceased. The concussions grew less frequent. The temperature was falling. They were around.

Another thirty minutes and the engines died. Their thunder and their weight abruptly shut off. She was afloat in silence. She trembled in her sweat. Her left foot throbbed.

They'd halved their speed. As they flew on, the sun's pull from behind would slow them more, taking away the acceleration it had added to their approach. That much would be regained as they fell toward the A star over the next year.

She slept in the weightlessness for several hours. At last she spun the ship back up to one-tenth g and took stock. Even in the slight gravity her foot and ankle were painful. She might have broken bones. Nothing she could do about it.

Most of their fuel was spent. At least one of the hydrogen tanks had suffered boil-off. She was unwilling to calculate whether enough remained for the second maneuver. It wasn't her job. She was done. She wrote her log. The modified hibernation drugs were already in her system, prepping her for a final year of sleep she might not wake from. But what was the alternative?

It hit her then: eighty-four years had passed since she climbed aboard this ship. Mamá and Papá were dead. Roger too. Unless perhaps Roger had been wrong and the great genius of humanity was to evade the ruin it always seemed about to bring upon itself. Unless humanity had emerged into some unlikely golden age of peace, longevity, forgiveness. And they, these Gypsies and their certainty, were outcast from it. But that was another narrative, and she couldn't bring herself to believe it.

6.

They'd never debated what they'd do when they landed.

The ship would jettison everything that had equipped it for interstellar travel and aerobrake into orbit. That might take thirty or forty glancing passes through the atmosphere, to slow them enough for a final descent, while cameras surveyed for a landing site. Criteria, insofar as possible: easy terrain, temperate zone, near water, arable land.

It was fruitless to plan the details of in-situ resource use while the site was unknown. But it would have to be Earth-like because they didn't have resources for terraforming more than the immediate neighborhood. All told, there was fifty tons of stuff in the storage bay—prefab habitats made for Mars, solar panels, fuel cells, bacterial cultures, seed bank, 3D printers, genetic tools, nanotech, recyclers—all meant to jump-start a colony. There was enough in the way of food and water to support a crew of sixteen for six months. If they hadn't become self-sufficient by then, it was over.

They hadn't debated options because they weren't going to have any. This part of it—even assuming the planet were hospitable enough to let them set up in the first place—would be a lot harder than the voyage. It didn't bear discussion.

SOPHIE (2126)

Waking. Again? Trying to rise up out of that dream of sinking back into the dream of rising up out of the. Momma? All that okay.

Soph? Upsa daise. Пойдем. Allons.

Sergei?

She was sitting on the cold, hard deck, gasping for breath.

Good girl, Soph. Get up, sit to console, bring spectroscope online. What we got? Soph! Stay with!

She sat at the console. The screen showed dimly, through blurs and maculae that she couldn't blink away, a stranger's face: ruined, wrinkled, sagging, eyes milky, strands of lank white hair falling from a sored scalp. With swollen knuckles and gnarled fingers slow and painful under loose sheaves of skin, she explored hard lumps in the sinews of her neck, in her breasts, under her skeletal arms. It hurt to swallow. Or not to.

The antisenescents hadn't worked. They'd known this was possible. But she'd been twenty-five. Her body hadn't known. Now she was old, sick, and dying after unlived decades spent on a slab. Regret beyond despair whelmed her. Every possible future that might have been hers, good or ill, promised or compromised, all discarded the day they launched. Now she had to accept the choice that had cost her life. Not afraid of death, but sick at heart thinking of that life, hers, however desperate it might have been on Earth—any life—now unliveable.

She tried to read the logs. Files corrupted, many lost. Handwritten copies blurry in her sight. Her eyes weren't good enough for this. She shut them, thought, then went into the supply bay, rested there for a minute, pulled out a printer and scanner, rested again, connected them to the computer, brought up the proper software. That all took a few tiring hours. She napped. Woke and affixed the scanner to her face. Felt nothing as mild infrared swept her corneas and mapped their aberrations. The printer was already loaded with polycarbonate stock, and after a minute it began to hum.

She put her new glasses on, still warm. About the cataracts she could do nothing. But now she could read.

They had braked once, going around B. Rosa had executed the first part of the maneuver, following Zia's plan. His cushion shot. But their outgoing velocity was too fast.

Sergei continued talking in the background, on and on as he did, trying to get her attention. She felt annoyed with him, couldn't he see she was busy?

Look! Look for spectra.

She felt woozy, wandering. Planets did that. They wandered against the stars. How does a planet feel? Oh yes, she should look for a planet. That's where they were going.

Four. There were four planets. No, five—there was a sub-Mercury in close orbit around B. The other four orbited A. Three were too small, too close to the star, too hot. The fourth was Earth-like. It was in an orbit of 0.8 AU, eccentricity 0.05. Its mass wass three-quarters that of Earth. Its year was about 260 days. They were still 1.8 AU from it, on the far side of Alpha Centauri A. The spectroscope showed nitrogen, oxygen, argon, carbon dioxide, krypton, neon, helium, methane, hydrogen. And liquid water.

Liquid water. She tasted the phrase on her tongue like a prayer, a benediction. It was there. It was real. Liquid water.

*

But then there were the others. Fourteen who could not be roused. Leaving only her and Sergei. And of course Sergei was not real.

So there was no point. The mission was over however you looked at it. She couldn't do it alone. Even if they reached the planet, even if she managed to aerobrake the ship and bring it down in one piece, they were done, because there was no more they.

The humane, the sensible thing to do now would be to let the ship fall into the approaching sun. Get it over quickly.

She didn't want to deal with this. It made her tired.

Two thirds of the way there's a chockstone, a large rock jammed in the crack, for protection before the hardest part. She grasps it, gets her breath, and pulls round it. The crux involves laybacking and right arm pulling. Her arm is too tired. Shaking and straining she fights it. She thinks of falling. That was bad, it meant her thoughts were wandering.

Some day you will die. Death will not wait. Only then will you realize you have not practiced well. Don't give up.

She awoke with a start. She realized they were closing on the sun at its speed, not hers. If she did nothing, that was a decision. And that was not her decision to make. All of them had committed to this line. Her datastream was still sending, whether anyone received it or not. She hadn't fallen on the mountain, and she wasn't going to fall into a sun now.

The planet was lost in the blaze of Alpha A. Two days away from that fire, and the hull temperature was climbing.

The A sun was hotter, more luminous, than B. It couldn't be approached as closely. There would be less decel.

This was not her expertise. But Zia and Rosa had left exhaustive notes, and Sophie's expertise was in winnowing and organizing and executing. She prepped the reactor. She adjusted their trajectory, angled the cushion shot just so.

Attitude thrusters halted the ship's rotation, turned it to rest in the sunshield's shadow. Gravity feathered away. She floated as they freefell into light.

Through the sunshield, through the layers of carbon, aerogel, through closed eyelids, radiance fills the ship with its pressure, suffusing all, dispelling the decades of cold, warming her feelings to this new planet given life by this sun; eyes closed, she sees it more clearly than Earth—rivers running, trees tossing in the wind, insects chirring in a meadow—all familiar but made strange by this deep, pervasive light. It might almost be Earth, but it's not. It's a new world.

Four million kilometers from the face of the sun. 2500° Celsius.

Don't forget to strap in. Thank you, Rosa.

At periapsis, the deepest point in the gravity well, the engine woke in thunder. The ship shuddered, its aged hull wailed and boomed. Propellant pushed
hard against their momentum, against the ship's forward vector, its force multi-
plied by its fall into the star's gravity, slowing the ship, gradually turning it. After
an hour, the engine sputtered and died, and they raced away from that radiance
into the abiding cold and silence of space.

Oh, Sergei. Oh, no. Still too fast.

They were traveling at twice the escape velocity of the Alpha C system. Fuel
gone, having rounded both suns, they will pass the planet and continue out of
the system into interstellar space.

Maneuver to planet. Like Zia said. Take all genetic material, seeds, zygotes,
heatshield payload and drop to surface, okay? Best we can do. Give life a chance.

No fuel, Sergei. Not a drop. We can't maneuver, you hear me?

Дерьмо.

Her mind is playing tricks. She has to concentrate. The planet is directly
in front of them now, but still nine days away. Inexorable, it will move on in its
orbit. Inexorable, the ship will follow its own divergent path. They will miss by
0.002 AU. Closer than the Moon to the Earth.

Coldly desperate, she remembered the attitude thrusters, fired them for ten
minutes until all their hydrazine was exhausted. It made no difference.

She continued to collect data. Her datastream lived, a thousand bits per
hour, her meager yet efficient engine of science pushing its mite of meaning
back into the plaintext chaos of the universe, without acknowledgement.

The planet was drier than Earth, mostly rock with two large seas, colder,
extensive polar caps. She radar-mapped the topography. The orbit was more
eccentric than Earth's, so the caps must vary, and the seas they fed. A thir-
ty-hour day. Two small moons, one with high albedo, the other dark.

What are they doing here? Have they thrown their lives away for nothing? Was
it a great evil to have done this? Abandoned Earth?

But what were they to do? Like all of them, Roger was a problem solver,
and the great problem on Earth, the problem of humanity, was unsolvable; it
was out of control and beyond the reach of engineering. The problems of *Gypsy*
were large but definable.

We were engineers. Of our own deaths. These were the deaths we wanted.
Out here. Not among those wretched and unsanctified. We isolates.

*

She begins to compose a poem a day. Not by writing. She holds the words in her mind, reciting them over and over until the whole is fixed in memory. Then she writes it down. A simple discipline, to combat her mental wandering.

In the eye of the sun
what is not burned to ash?

In the spire of the wind
what is not scattered as dust?
Love? art?
body's rude health?
memory of its satisfactions?

Antaeus
lost strength
lifted from Earth

Reft from our gravity
we fail

Lime kept sailors hale
light of mind alone
with itself
is not enough

The scope tracked the planet as they passed it by. Over roughly three hours it grew in size from about a degree to about two degrees, then dwindled again. She spent the time gazing at its features with preternatural attention, with longing and regret, as if it were the face of an unattainable loved one.

It's there, Sergei, it's real—Ghost Planet Hope—and it is beautiful—look, how blue the water—see the clouds—and the seacoast—there must be rain, and plants and animals happy for it—fish, and birds, maybe, and worms, turning the soil. Look at the mountains! Look at the snow on their peaks!

This was when the science pod should have been released, the large reflecting telescope ejected into planetary orbit to start its year-long mission of measuring stellar distances. But that was in a divergent universe, one that each passing hour took her farther from.

We made it. No one will ever know, but we made it. We came so far. It was our only time to do it. No sooner, we hadn't developed the means. And if we'd waited any longer, the means would have killed us all. We came through a narrow window. Just a little too narrow.

She recorded their passing. She transmitted all their logs. Her recent poems. The story of their long dying. In four and a quarter years it would reach home. No telling if anyone would hear.

So long for us to evolve. So long to walk out of Africa and around the globe. So long to build a human world. So quick to ruin it. Is this, our doomed and final effort, no more than our grieving for Earth? Our mere mourning?

Every last bit of it was a long shot: their journey, humanity, life itself, the universe with its constants so finely tuned that planets, stars, or time itself, had come to be.

Fermi's question again: If life is commonplace in the universe, where is everyone? How come we haven't heard from anyone? What is the mean time between failures for civilizations?

Not long. Not long enough.

Now she slept. Language was not a tool used often enough even in sleep to lament its own passing. Other things lamented more. The brilliance turned to and turned away.

She remembers the garden behind the house. Her father grew corn—he was particular about the variety, complained how hard it was to find Silver Queen, even the terminated variety—with beans interplanted, which climbed the cornstalks, and different varieties of tomato with basil interplanted, and lettuces—he liked frisee. And in the flower beds alstroemeria, and wind lilies, and *Eschscholzia*. He taught her those names, and the names of Sierra flowers—taught her to learn names. We name things in order to to love them, to remember them when they are absent. She recites the names of the fourteen dead with her, and weeps.

She'd been awake for over two weeks. The planet was far behind. The hibernation cocktail was completely flushed from her system. She wasn't going back to sleep.

ground
rose
sand

elixir
cave

root
dark

golden

sky-born
lift
earth
fall

The radio receiver chirps. She wakes, stares at it dumbly.

The signal is strong! Beamed directly at them. From Earth! Words form on the screen. She feels the words rather than reads them.

We turned it around. Everything is fixed. The bad years are behind us. We live. We know what you did, why you did it. We honor your bravery. We're sorry you're out there, sorry you had to do it, wish you . . . wish . . . wish . . . . Good luck. Good-bye.

Where are her glasses? She needs to hear the words. She needs to hear a human voice, even synthetic. She taps the speaker.

The white noise of space. A blank screen.

She is in the Sierra, before the closure. Early July. Sun dapples the trail. Above the alpine meadow, in the shade, snow deepens, but it's packed and easy walking. She kicks steps into the steeper parts. She comes into a little flat just beginning to melt out, surrounded by snowy peaks, among white pine and red fir and mountain hemlock. Her young muscles are warm and supple and happy in their movements. The snowbound flat is still, yet humming with the undertone of life. A tiny mosquito lands on her forearm, casts its shadow, too young even to know to bite. She brushes it off, walks on, beyond the flat, into higher country.

thistle daisy cow-parsnip strawberry clover
mariposa-lily corn-lily ceanothus elderberry marigold
mimulus sunflower senecio goldenbush dandelion
mules-ear iris miners-lettuce sorrel clarkia
milkweed tiger-lily mallow veronica rue
nettle violet buttercup ivesia asphodel
ladyslipper larkspur pea bluebells onion
yarrow cinquefoil arnica pennyroyal fireweed
phlox monkshood foxglove vetch buckwheat
goldenrod groundsel valerian lovage columbine

stonecrop angelica rangers–buttons pussytoes everlasting
watercress rockcress groundsmoke solomons–seal bitterroot
liveforever lupine paintbrush blue–eyed–grass gentian
pussypaws butterballs campion primrose forget–me–not
saxifrage aster polemonium sedum rockfringe
sky–pilot shooting–star heather alpine–gold penstemon

Forget me not.

Vandana Singh is an Indian science fiction writer and professor of physics currently inhabiting the Boston area. Her stories have been published in numerous venues, including reprints in several Year's Best volumes. She is the author of two short story collections, *The Woman Who Thought She Was a Planet and Other Stories* (Zubaan/Penguin India 2008) and *Ambiguity Machines and Other Stories* (Small Beer Press 2018). For more about her, see vandana-writes.com.

SAILING THE ANTARSA

VANDANA SINGH

There are breezes, like the ocean breeze, which can set your pulse racing, dear kin, and your spirit seems to fly ahead of you as your little boat rides each swell. But this breeze! This breeze wafts through you and me, through planets and suns, like we are nothing. How to catch it, know it, befriend it? This sea, the Antarsa, is like no other sea. It washes the whole universe, as far as we can tell, and the ordinary matter such as we are made of is transparent to it. So how is it that I can ride the Antarsa current, as I am doing now, steering my little spacecraft so far from Dhara and its moon?

Ah, there lies a story.

I have gone further than anyone since my ancestors first came to Dhara four generations ago. As I stare out into the night, I can see the little point that is my sun. It helps to look at it and know that the love of my kin reaches across space and time to me, a bridge of light. I am still weak from my long incarceration in the cryochamber—and filled with wonder that I have survived nearly all the journey to the Ashtan system—but oh! It takes effort even to speak aloud, to record my thoughts and send them homeward.

I am still puzzled as to why the ship woke me up before it was time. During my long, dreamless sleep, we have sustained some mild damage from space debris, but the self-repairing system has done a good enough job, and nothing else seems to be wrong. There were checks against a half-dozen systems that were not of critical importance—I have just finished going through each of them and performing some minor corrections. In the navigation chamber the altmatter sails spread out like the wings of some marvelous insect—still intact. I put my hands into the manipulation gloves, immediately switching the craft to manual control, and checked. The rigging is still at a comfortable tension, and it takes just a small twitch of a finger to lift, rotate, lower or twist each sail. It is still thrilling to feel the Antarsa current that passes through me undetected, to feel it indirectly by way of the response of the altmatter wings! A relief indeed to know that the sense I had been developing of the reality, the *tangibility* of the Antarsa sea is not lost. We are on course, whatever that means when one is riding a great current into the unknown, only roughly certain of our destination.

There is a shadowy radar image that I need to understand. The image is not one of space debris, but of a shape wide in the middle and tapered at both ends, shutting out the stars. It is small, and distant, traveling parallel to us at nearly the same speed, but subsequent scans reveal no such thing. My first excited thought was: spaceship! But then, where is it? If it came close enough for my sensors, why did it choose to retreat? If this is why the ship woke me, which seems logical, then why didn't it wake me earlier, when a nearly spherical piece of space rock hit us? When we grazed past a lone planet that had been shot out of some distant, unstable solar system?

The ship's intelligence is based on the old generation ship AI that brought my ancestors to Dhara. It has a quietness and a quick efficiency that one would expect of an artificial thinking system, but there are aspects of it that remind me of people I know. A steadiness masking a tendency to over-plan for contingencies. That might be why it woke me up—it is a secret worrier, like my superficially calm mother Simara, so far and so long away. I will never see her—or any of them—again. That thought brings tears to my eyes.

Why does one venture out so far from home? Generations ago, our planet Dhara took my ancestors in from the cold night and gave them warmth. Its living beings adjusted and made room, and in turn we changed ourselves to accommodate them. So it was shown to us that a planet far from humanity's original home is kin to us, a brother, a sister, a mother. To seek kinship with all is an ancient maxim of my people, and ever since my ancestors came to this planet we have sought to do that with the smallest, tenderest thing that leaps, swoops or grows on this verdant world. Some of us have looked up at the night sky and wondered about other worlds that might be kin to us, other hearths and homes that might welcome us, through which we would experience a different becoming. Some of us yearn for those connections waiting for us on other shores. We seek to feed within us the god of wonder, to open within ourselves dusty rooms we didn't know existed and let in the air and light of other worlds. And the discovery of the Antarsa, that most subtle of seas, has made it possible to venture far into that night, following the wide, deep current that flows by our planet during its northern winter. The current only flows one way. Away.

So I am here.

I look at the miniature biosphere tethered to my bunk. One of my first acts upon waking was to make sure that it was intact—and it was. Parin's gift to me is a transparent dome of glass within which a tiny landscape grows. There are mosses in shades of green, and clumps of sugarworts, with delicate, brittle leaves colored coral and blue, and a waterbagman, with its translucent stalk and bulbous, water-filled chambers within which tiny worms lead entire lives. Worlds within worlds. She had designed the system to be self-contained so that one species' waste was another species' sustenance. It is a piece of Dhara, and it has helped sustain me during each of the times I have been awake, these years.

It helps to remember who I am. This time when I woke up, I had a long and terrifying moment of panic, because I couldn't remember who I was, or where I was. All I knew was that it was very cold, and a soft, level voice was talking to me (the ship). I cannot begin to describe how horrific a sense of loss this was— that my *self* had somehow slipped its moorings and was adrift on a dark sea, and I couldn't find it. Slowly, as memory and warmth returned, I found myself, anchored myself to the rock of remembrance, of shared love under a kind sun. So as I ponder the situation I'm in, the mystery of why the ship woke me—I will speak my own story, which is also many stories. Like my mothers who first told me of the world, I will tell it aloud, tethering myself through the umbilical cords of kinship, feeding the gods within.

I have been traveling for nearly eight years. Yet I seem to have left only yesterday, my memories of the parting are so clear. I remember when my craft launched from the Lunar Kinship's base, how I slowly shut down conventional fusion power and edged us into the Antarsa current. How it seemed hours before I could maneuver the little craft into the superfast central channel, manipulating the altmatter wings so that my spaceship wouldn't fall apart. But at last we were at a comfortable acceleration, going swifter than any human on my world—and I looked back.

The moon, Roshna, was slipping away beneath me with vertiginous speed. The lights of the Lunar Kinship were blinking in farewell, the radio crackling with familiar voices that already seemed distant, shouting their relief and congratulations. At that moment I was assailed with an unfamiliar feeling, which I recognized after a while as my first experience of loneliness. It was unbearable—a nightmare of childhood from which there is no escape.

Looking at the screen, with my kin's images flickering, hearing their voices, I was severely tempted to turn around. I was close enough to still do this—to arc my trajectory, turn from the Antarsa current into a high moon orbit and then use conventional fusion power to land. But I had pledged I would embark on this journey, had planned for it, dreamed of it—and there had been so much hard work on the part of several Kinships, so much debating in the Council— that I clenched my fists against temptation and let the moment go. I feasted my eyes on the thick forests, the purple scrublands of the moon, and the shining blue-green curve of Dhara below, the planet we had called home for five generations, memorizing the trails of white clouds, the jagged silver edge of the Mahapara continent, the Tura-Tura archipelago like a trail of tears, as a lover memorizes the body of her beloved.

This was the moment for which my friends from Ship University and I had planned and prepared for nearly ten years, soon after the discovery of the Antarsa. We had placed a proposal before the World Council, which debated for eight years. There were representatives from all the Kinships (except the People of the Ice, of course—they have not attended Council in two generations): the People of the Himdhara mountains, the People of the Western Sea, the Roshnans from the Lunar Kinship, and of course my own People of the Devtaru, among a number of smaller Kinships. There was endless discussion, much concern, but they let us design and send the first few probes into the Antarsa current. Interpreting the signals from the probes, the University experts determined that the current appeared to run in a more-or-less straight line toward the Ashtan star system five light-years away. The last signal from the last probe had arrived seven years after its launch, when the probe was as yet some distance short of the Ashtan system. There was something ominous about the probe's subsequent silence—what had befallen it?—although the explanation could have been as simple as malfunctioning equipment or a chance hit by a space rock.

Some argued that an expedition was justified, because we hadn't heard from the Ashtan system since my ancestors had arrived on Dhara. Two generation ships had left the old world, one bound for Dhara, the other for Ashta, and they had been one people before that. So our people had always wondered what befell our kin around the brightest star in our sky. Others in the Council argued that this was the very reason we should not venture out, because the silence of the Ashtans—and the probe—pointed to some unknown danger. And what if the current took us somewhere else entirely? What guarantee that we would wash up on a world as kind as our own? To go out into the void was to seek kinship with death before our time. And so on.

But at last the Council gave its reluctant blessing, and here I was, on a ship bound for the stars. I am a woman past my youth, although not yet of middle age, and I have strived always to take responsibility for my actions. So I watched the moon and the great curve of the planet that was my home fall away into the night, and I wept. But I did not turn around.

I float within my ship like a fishling in a swamp. I have swum through the inertial webbing (softer and more coarse at the moment, since we are at low acceleration) from chamber to chamber, checking that all is well. No more strange images on the radar. All systems working in concert. The bioskin that lines each chamber, produces the air I breathe, recycles waste, and spins the inertial web looks a healthy gold-green. We are now moving at half the speed of light, absurdly fast. From the porthole, the distant stars are like the eyes of the night. I sip a tangy, familiar tea from a tube (I have a little cold) and breathe slowly, remembering what my friend Raim told me.

Raim taught me to sail on the Western sea. His people designed the alt-matter wings that spread within the navigation chamber (surely the only ship ever built whose sails are on the *inside*). When I woke from cold sleep there was a message from him. He said: Mayha, farsister, when you are lonely, make a friend of loneliness.

So I make kinship with the dark. I whisper to it, I tell it stories. Perhaps the dark will have something to say to me in turn.

At first our plan was to make the inside of the ship a biosphere, rich with life, choosing the most appropriate and hardy species, so that I would feel more we than I. But after debating on it the Council decided that unless I wished it very strongly, this would not be right. To subject other lifeforms to human whim, to put them in danger without compelling reason was not our way. Besides, we ran the risk of upsetting the balance of life on other worlds in case our containment protocols failed. When I heard the reasoning, I too fell in with this. We compromised thus: the inner surface of the ship would be a bioskin, but that was all. To save energy and to enable the long years to pass without pathological loneliness, we would install a cryochamber. My apprehensions at the length and solitude of the journey were nothing to that old desire within me since childhood: to soar skyward in search of our kin, new and old.

But as I was leaving, saying my forever goodbyes amidst tears and jokes and good wishes, Parin came up to me, indignant. She was worked up about the Council decision to not install a biosphere within the ship. She thrust something at me: a transparent dome of glass within which a tiny landscape grew.

"Mayha, take this!" she said fiercely. "I can't believe they're going to con-demn you to such a long journey alone!"

I tried to argue that the Council's position was an attempt to be just to all lifeforms, and that I didn't know how her sealed-in, miniature biosphere would adapt to zero gravity—but I've lost most arguments with Parin. And the little biosphere was beautiful. Besides, I did not want our parting to be acrimonious. Parin and I had grown up with the rest of the horde of children under the same kinhouse roof. Through much of my childhood I had been part of her schemes and adventures. I remembered the time we had rescued a nest of firebirds from some imagined danger, and how we'd wept copiously when they died. Most of Parin's schemes had involved guilt and good intentions in about equal measure.

I took the little biosphere, as she'd known I would. She scowled at me, then started to cry. We hugged and wept. Then the others had their turn at goodbye. Goodbyes at the kinhouse always take a long time; there are so many of us. And this time, for this historic one-way journey, there were people from nearly all the hundred and twenty-three kinhouses of the Kinship of the Devtaru, waiting to see me off on the shuttle that would take me to the moon, where I was to board my craft. There were also representatives from the People of the Western Sea, my friend Raim, tall and grey-skinned, stared at by the children, waving at me with one webbed hand. The Ship University folk had adapted the spacecraft from one of the shuttles aboard the old generation ship and tested it. A knot of them was present, waiting at the edge of the crowd for their turn. Closest to me stood my mothers, each displaying grief and pride consistent with her nature: Kusum yelling about the dangers of the journey and how I should be careful about this or that, as though I was three again, Brihat simply holding my arm and staring into my face, with tears streaming down her broad cheeks, and Simara being sensible and controlled although her smile wavered. My birth-mother Vishwana was behind them, regal as always, our representative to the Council. She nodded and smiled at me. Although I had never known her well, I had always been in awe of her. My kin-sisters and brothers were there, alter-nately cheering and weeping, and Sarang, grown so tall since I'd last seen her, tossed me a braided ribbon over the heads of the crowd.

My father was not there. I saw him rarely, since he was a traveler and a trader, and when I did we always took pleasure in sharing stories with each other. He had sent me a message by radio wishing me luck, but he was halfway across the world, too far to come in time.

Then near the back with the guests I saw Vik. He had partnered with me for fourteen years, and we had gone our separate ways, in friendship, until my decision to go on this journey became public. He had become a bitter opponent in the Council discussions, and would no longer speak to me. He looked at me from the back of the crowd and looked away again.

I have partnered for long and short periods with both men and women, but Vik was the one with whom I spent the longest time. There were times I thought we would always be together, as some partnerships are, but we sought joy in different things that took us on diverging paths. He was a historian at Ship University, content to stay in one place and let his mind go into the deep past. Like my father, I needed to wander. It was as simple as that.

I wanted very badly to end things well with Vik. I took a pendant off the string around my neck and flung it over the heads of the crowd toward him. It hit him on the cheek—he caught it, looked irritable, put it in his pocket. I smiled at him. He rubbed his cheek, looked at me and away again.

The shuttle finally took off. I scarcely remember my time at Roshna, at the Lunar Kinship, where my spacecraft was waiting. They took care of me, asked me again the ritual question before one goes on a long journey: *Is your heart in it, kinswoman? Do you really want to go on this quest?* And I said *yes, yes,* and there were more goodbyes. At last I was in the craft, up and away. As I manipulated the sails in the navigation chamber, as I'd done so many times on my way to the moon— except that this time I would be going beyond it—as I felt the familiar tug of the Antarsa current, the old excitement rose in me again. It was too soon to feel lonely, or so I thought, because the love of my people was an almost tangible presence.

As I float by the porthole, I can see them all so clearly. Their faces tender and animated, as I turn from the raised platform into the doorway of the shuttle, turn once more to look for the last time at my people and my world, to breathe the forest-scented air. There is the wide, woven roof of the kinhouse, and the vines running up the brown walls, the gourds ripening green to gold. Here I had played and climbed, looked at the stars, dreamed and wept. There is the gleam of the river, the pier, the boats waiting on the water. Dwarfing them all, the great, shaggy forest, trees like spires, trees like umbrellas, reaching leafy arms into the sky, taller than the tallest kinhouse. I think: when I rise up, I will see again the Devtaru, the one closest to us anyhow, greater than any tree that exists or can be dreamed. The Devtaru has shared its secret with us, and because of that I will fly beyond the moon. As I rise I will speak my gratitude to it, to all the world for having formed me, made me into myself. And so I did.

The devtaru is not a tree. It is perhaps what a tree would dream of, if a tree could dream.

The first one I ever saw lies two days away from my kinhouse. In my thirteenth year, some of us trekked through the forest with Visith, one of my aunts, who has been a sister of the forest most of her life. On the way we learned plant lore, and we practiced the art of offering kinship to the beings of the forest.

"Kinship isn't friendship," my aunt said. "Don't go doing stupid things like putting your hand into a tree-bear's nest, or poking around inside an occupied bee-apple. Learn to sit still in a clear space, and let the creatures observe you, as you observe them."

We did a lot of sitting still. It was difficult at first but I got the idea of it quicker than the others. The forest whispered around me—sunlight dappled the ground. A wind around approached me, its tendrils aquiver, looking for something to climb. I nudged it away with my toe—it was kin, but I didn't want it taking advantage of my stillness. I sensed that I was being watched: a moon-eye monkey, which meant we were close to the devtaru. It was up in a tree, the white rings around its eyes giving it an expression of permanent astonishment. My heart thundered with excitement as the little creature peered out from its leafy shelter. But it was only after two days of seeing and being seen that the moon-eye came out into plain sight. A day later it took an apple-rind from me. After that the moon-eyes were everywhere, moving above me over the trees, chattering to each other and glancing at me from time to time. Then I could walk about without them hiding. I had made kinship!

Parin was in trouble for being too impatient, trying to climb up to a moon-eye's nest before it was appropriate to do so. The other two hadn't yet obtained the knack of it and needed to practice stillness without fidgeting or falling asleep. We lingered in that place until their impatience gave way to resignation, and they broke through. We got a congratulatory lecture from Visith.

"A kinship is a relationship that is based on the assumption that each person, human or otherwise, has a right to exist, and a right to agency," she intoned. "This means that to live truly in the world we must constantly adjust to other beings, as they adjust to us. We must minimize and repair any harm that we do. Kinship goes all the way from friendship to enmity—and if a particular being does not desire it, why, we must leave it alone, leave the area. Thus through constant practice throughout our lives we begin to be ready with the final kinship—the one we make with death."

We looked at each other and shivered.

"You are a long way from that," Visith said sardonically, then smiled a rare smile. "But you've taken the first step. Come, let us keep going."

So the journey to the devtaru took several days, and when we were standing at its edge we didn't even know it.

The ground changing should have been our first clue. The forest floor was dotted with undergrowth, but here we found that great roots as thick as a person reared out of the ground and back again, forming a fascinating tangle of steps and crevices that invited climbing. The trees had changed too—the canopy above seemed to be knit together, and trunks dropped down and joined the roots, making a three-dimensional maze.

Visith didn't let us go into the tangle. Instead we made camp and practiced stillness between meals and washing, and took walks along the perimeter of the maze. After two days of this, during which our impatience gave way to resignation, and then, finally, the open, accepting, alertness of mind that births the possibility of kinship—Parin pointed at the tangle.

"It's a devtaru! And we didn't even know it!"

It was indeed. The enormous central trunk was deep inside the forest of secondary trunks, likely several hours journey. The roots went deeper down than any other organism on the planet. To see a devtaru in its entirety, one has to be airborne, or on a far away hill.

Under the canopy, the moon-eyes led us over the maze of roots and trunks. We found shelter in the crook of a giant root, underneath which flowed a clear stream of water. The bark against which I laid my head was a thin skin that glowed faintly in the darkness, pulsing in response to my presence. To make kinship with a devtaru is extraordinarily difficult—Visith is one of the few who has succeeded, and it took her nearly twenty years.

"Tomorrow we will go to a place I know, where the devtaru was fruiting moon-pods last I came," she told us. "If the devtaru wishes, perhaps we will see a launch!"

I had seen the usual fruiting pods of a devtaru during our journey inside it, but never the legendary moon-pods. This devtaru was too young to make anything but small, empty moon-pods, but it would be a sight worth seeing. My heart was full. I wanted so much to be kin to such a being! Like Moon-woman, whose story Parin began to tell in the soft darkness.

There was a girl once, who sat in stillness seeking kinship with a devtaru for a hundred years. Potter-ants built a dwelling around her, and wind-arounds made a green tangle around that, so no rain or wind could trouble her. Flitters brought her crystals of sap and placed them between her lips so she knew neither hunger or thirst. She saw the devtaru and its beings, and it observed her with its thousand eyes, and at last they made kinship.

She lived within its forest, among its roots and trunks, and learned its moods and sensed its large, slow thoughts. She became familiar with the creatures who lived in its shelter, the moon-eyes and the dream-flitters, and the floating glow-worms, and the angler-birds with their lures of light. Then one day a moon-eye led her to a place within the devtaru forest where she found a large pod attached to the top of a trunk. The pod was just about as tall as she was and just about as wide in the middle, and it was covered over with a shimmering patina, so that she had to blink to make sure it was actually there. It pointed away from her toward the moon in the sky as though it yearned to break free, and it quivered gently as though caught in a breeze, although no breeze blew. The trunk glowed and patterns formed and dissolved on its surface, and the girl knew she had to climb right up to the pod.

And she did. She found that the pod's lips weren't closed as yet, and inside it was empty of seed. Within it there were little creatures, buzzwings and a grumpworm or two, and some leafy, mossy debris. She felt a great shudder from the trunk so climbed down hastily, just in time, because the trunk contracted, and the pod shot with a great noise into the sky. As it did, the trunk split and the girl fell down.

She walked for days through the forest and at last found the pod. It lay in a clump of bushes, already half-covered by leaves and branches from a storm. It made her wonder why the devtaru had bothered to send an empty pod into the air at all.

Now I've said she lived with the devtaru for a hundred years. When she was old, and the devtaru even older, something changed. The devtaru's leaves had been falling for a decade or more, and now she could see that its long arc of life was ending. The moon-eyes and the other creatures left the shelter of the devtaru but the girl couldn't bear to do so. The devtaru produced one last enormous moon-pod. The girl, now an old woman, crawled into the pod before its lips closed, and felt around her the creatures who were also stowaways, and felt also the smooth, shiny hard seed, half her size, larger than the seeds in the normal seed-pods. She had decided she could not bear to watch the tree die, and she would let it take her away to her final destination.

The pod grew and grew, and the old woman fell asleep inside it. Then one day the time came. She could sense a tensing in the limbs and sinews of the devtaru, preparing for the launch, but this time there came to her faintly a strange slight smell of burning. The lips of the pod closed completely, and if it hadn't been for the stowaways making air to breathe, she would have suffocated. Off she went into the sky.

Now there was a sister of this old woman who came to see her from time to time, and she was watching from a hilltop not far from the devtaru. She liked to look at the stars through a telescope, so she was known as Sister Three-Eyes. She saw the great pod quiver and align with the now risen moon. Tendrils of smoke emerged from the crevices of the tree. Then the pod launched.

There was a noise like a clap of thunder, and the devtaru shattered. As it did, it began to burn from its deep internal fires, slowly and magnificently. What a death! But Sister Three-Eyes soon turned her attention from the dying devtaru and trained her telescope on the pod, because she wanted to know where it landed.

To her surprise, it didn't land. It went higher and higher, and soon it was a speck she could barely see. Just before she lost sight of it, she saw it move into a low orbit, and then, suddenly, the pod changed its mind and made straight for the moon.

So she found that the devtaru's last and final moon-pod is truly destined for the moon. Which is why the devtaru's children grow on the moon, although they do not make such enormous pods as they do on Dhara. The lunar forest and the purple scrublands and the creatures that live there and make the air to breathe are all gifts of the devtaru, the only being known to spread its seed to another world.

As to what happened to Moon-woman—who knows? When the next generation found a way to get to the moon in shuttles, they looked for her in the forests and the grassy plains. They did not find her. Some say she could not have survived the journey. Others say that she did survive it, and she wandered through the lunar forests content that she had found a place among the children of the devtaru, and died a peaceful death there. These people named the moon Roshna, after her, as it is still called today. Her sister thought she saw a light burning or flashing on the moon some months after Moon-woman left, but who can be sure? There are those that believe that Moon-woman went further, that she found a way to launch her moon-pod into the space beyond the moon, and that she sails there still along the unknown currents of the seas of space and time.

Parin had always told this story well, but listening to it under the devtaru, in that companionable darkness, made it come alive. I wondered whether Moon-woman was, indeed, sailing the void between the stars at this moment, offering kinship to beings stranger than we could imagine. Looking at a small patch of starry sky visible between the leaves above me, I shivered with longing.

We never got to see a pod launch on that trip. But even now I can remember Parin's young voice, the words held in the air as if by magic, the breathing of the others beside me, the feel of the tree's skin glowing gently like a cooling ember.

The story anticipates the discovery of the Antarsa, of course. That I had a small role to play in it is a source of both pain and pleasure, because it happened when I first realized that Vik and I were growing apart from one another.

I have been torn between excitement of a most profound sort, and a misery of an extremely mundane sort. The excitement first: there have been *several* flickering images on the radar. It is clear now that there are others around me, keeping their distance—spaceships from the Ashtan system? Our long lost cousins? I sent a transmission in Old Irthic to them, but there is no reply. Only silence. Silence can mean so many things, from "I don't see you," to "I don't want to see you." There is a possibility that these are ships from other human-inhabited worlds, but it would be strange that they would not have made contact with us on Dhara.

My other thought is that the occupants of these ships may be aliens who simply cannot understand my message, or know it to be a message. This is even more exciting. It also makes me apprehensive, because I don't know their intent. They appear in and out of range, moving at about the same average speed as my craft. Are they curious? Are they escorting me, studying me, wondering if I am an enemy? All I can do is to practice what I did in the great forest: stillness. Stillness while moving at more than 50% of the speed of light—I wonder what my aunt Visith would say to that! Do nothing, says her no-nonsense voice in my memory. Wait and observe, and let yourself be observed.

That I have been doing.

The misery is that I have a message from Vik. Sent years ago of course, but there it is: he is grateful for the pendant I tossed him when I left, and he has found a new partner, a fellow historian at Ship University, a woman called Mallow. When I first got his message I just stared at it. A sense of deep abandonment welled up inside me; my loneliness, which I had tried to befriend, loomed larger than mountains. Of course I had expected this—even if I had stayed on Dhara, there would have been no going back to Vik—but I felt resentful of his meticulous observation of correct behavior. Yes, it is a graceful thing to do, to tell a former long-term partner when you have found a new love—but I would never come back, never find a new love, someone to hold— there was no need to let me know. Except it would make Vik feel better, that he had done the right thing. He had not thought about me, and it hurt. For once Parin's little biosphere did not assuage my pain. I couldn't even go outside and run up a mountain or two. Instead I swam from chamber to chamber through the inertial webbing, if only to feel the web break and re-form as I went through it, my tears floating in the air around me like a misty halo, attaching to the gossamer threads like raindrops. There was nowhere to go. After I had calmed down I tethered myself to the porthole and stared into the night, and thought of what it had been like.

After Vik I had taken no lovers for a while, until I met Laharis. She was a woman of the Western Sea. I'd been working with Raim on the ocean, learning to sail an ordinary boat before I learned the ways of the Antarsa. We had been out for several days, and had returned with a hold full of fish, and salt in our hair, our skin chapped. Raim and I developed a deep love and camaraderie, but we were not drawn to each other in any other way. It was when I was staying at their kinhouse, watching the rain fall in grey sheets on the ocean, that his sister came up to me. The others were away bringing in the last catch. Laharis and I had talked for long hours and we had both sensed a connection, but the construction of the altmatter wings from the discarded moon-pods of the devtaru had taken up my time. Now she slid a hand up my arm, leaned close to me. Her hair was very fine, a silver cascade, and her smooth grey cheek was warm. Her long, slanted eyes, with the nictitating membranes that still startled me, shone with humor. She breathed in my ear. "Contrary to stereotype," she whispered, "we Sea folk don't taste like salt. Would you care to find out?"

So we learned each other for two beautiful months. During our time together I forgot stars and space and the Antarsa—there was only her slow, unfurling self, body and mind, every part an enchantment. I would have wanted to partner with her, had I stayed on planet. Now that I was far away, I could only remember and weep. She never sent me messages, though her brother did. I think it was hard for her and perhaps she thought it would be hard for me.

Dear darkness, help me keep my equilibrium. Here I am, in a universe so full of marvels and mysteries, and I mourn the loss of my already lost loves as though I was still young and callow. What a fool I am!

I shall keep stillness, and feed no more that envious, treacherous god within, the god of a heart bereft.

Vik has rarely ventured from Ship University. He's one of those people who likes to put down roots and ponder how we got here. The past is his country. Ship University is a good place for him.

It is housed inside the generation ship that brought my people to Dhara so long ago. The ship lies in a hollow made for it in the sandy plains near a lake. It contains the records of my people's history and of the home planet, and the cryochambers are now laboratories. The shuttle bays are experimental stations, and cabins are classrooms. In the forests or the sea, the mountains or the desert, it is hard to believe that we have the technology we do. "Have high tech, live low tech," has been a guiding principle of the Kinships. That is how we have lived so well on our world.

Ship University's sky scholars were the first to study the flight of devtaru pods. Vik's friend Manda, a sky scholar of repute, told me how the mystery deepened as the early scholars tracked the moon-pods with increasingly powerful telescopes. I can see Manda now, slender fingers brushing back her untidy brown hair, her eyes alight. I was visiting Vik after wandering for a month through the Bahagan desert, and it had become clear to me that there was a wall between us. I felt then the first hint of the ending to come. I think Vik sensed it too. He sat next to me, looking restive, while Manda talked. She showed us a holo of a devtaru moon-pod launching from a century ago.

Despite my misery, I found myself fascinated. There was the tiny pod, dwarfed by the curve of Dhara, apparently going into low orbit. The moon wasn't in the picture, which was to scale, but we were informed that the planet, the pod and the moon formed a more or less straight line through their centers. In its orbit around the planet, the pod began to tremble abruptly, like a leaf floating on a stream disturbed by a random eddy. Then it swung loose from its orbit and made straight for the moon. It traveled with such astonishing rapidity that all we could see was a silver streak. Then the scene cut to the moon and the pod approaching it, swinging past it a few times, slowing gradually until at last it made a rough landing in the southern forest. There was a bloom of light, a brief fire where it hit, then the film stopped.

"This was taken by Kaushai, back about a century ago. All this time there have only been speculations as to how the devtaru pods get to the moon, why they suddenly change course from low orbit to the trajectory you saw. The pods themselves have no means of propulsion. There is nothing in the void of space between the planet Dhara and the moon. The first probes that were sent to duplicate the orbit of the pods suffered no strange perturbations, nor were they drawn toward the moon. The devtaru pods apparently violate fundamental laws of nature: that momentum and energy must be conserved."

I knew something of all this, of course. But I had never seen the holo before. It was quite amazing. I felt Vik stir beside me—he looked just as entranced, and when my gaze met his, as miserable as I.

Yet it was a chance remark I made on that visit that set the sky scholars on the right track.

I go back to that time in my imagination. Vik and I are both starting to realize that our paths are too different to allow for us to be together, although it will be quite some time before we have the courage to say so to each other. So the golden afternoon, and our togetherness, have acquired a deep, sad sweetness. We join Manda and her friends for a walk around the lake. They have been talking all day about the mystery of the devtaru pods, telling us how they spent years camping by a certain devtaru, watching it, getting to know it, asking it to share its secret. Now some of them feel as though the devtaru has communicated with them already, that they already know what the secret is, but it is buried deep inside them and needs some kind of stimulus, or reminder, a magic word or phrase to bring it into consciousness.

After evening sets in we find ourselves tired and hungry—we have walked a long way and the stars are beginning to come out in a pale pink sky. We are at a place where a small river empties into the lake, making an intricate delta of rivulets. We are wishing we had a boat to get to the shore from which we ventured, where the bulk of Ship looms, its many windows lit. The air is full of the trembling cries of glitterwings. I am speechless with emotion, with the thought that the end of our partnership is as close as the other shore. Vik is silent beside me. Just as we are talking about boats, I find the remains of one at the bottom of a rivulet. It is full of holes—in fact, most of it has rotted away, but for the frame. It lies indifferently in place as the water rushes through the holes.

"If this boat were solid," I say, "and the current strong enough, it would move. It would carry us home."

A pointless, inconsequential remark. But Manda stares at me, understanding awakening in her face.

She told me later that my remark was the thing she needed to unwrap the gift the devtaru had already given them. What had been one of the saddest evenings of my life was the moment when she and her colleagues solved the mystery of the devtaru pods. Two days later Manda spoke to a gathering of hundreds.

"Imagine an ocean that washes all of space and time. Like the water ocean, it has currents and turbulences. But its substance is invisible to us, as we are invisible—or transparent—to it.

"This is not so strange an idea. As the neutrinos wash through ordinary matter, through you and me, as though we weren't there, as water washes through the broken boat with the holes in it, so the subtle ocean—the Antarsa, named by our poet Thora—washes through planets and stars, plants and people, as though we did not exist.

"We don't know whether the Antarsa is made up of neutrinos or something else. We suspect it is something as yet unknown, because too much is known about neutrinos, which can be caught by ordinary matter if the net is both deep and dense.

"Now imagine a form of matter that is not ordinary matter. This, too, is not strange, because we know that what we call ordinary matter is rather rare in the universe. There are other forms of matter that make up the bulk of the cosmos. One of these forms, what we are calling the altmatter, is opaque to the Antarsa. So if you place a piece of altmatter in an Antarsa current, it will move.

"The pods, of course, have to be made in part of altmatter. How the devtaru acquires it we don't know; maybe it draws it up from deep underground, mingles or combines it with ordinary matter, and forms the pods that are meant to go into space."

That was so long ago, that moment of revelation. Some years later, experimenters took the discarded moon-pods that are empty of seed, the ones that the devtaru shoot out for practice when they are young, to make the first altmatter probes. And now I am here.

Here I am, working the sails in the navigation chamber. I've done enough waiting. I am steering my craft as close to the edge of the current as I dare, as slowly as it needs to go so that changes in speed won't tear it apart. I want to get closer to my mysterious companions.

The shapes on the radar flicker in and out with increasing frequency now. Some are shaped like fat pods, but some appear vaguely oblong smudges. I want to see a pod ride by with Moon-woman in it, waving. If that happens, I will extend a grappling hook, gently as I can, and bring the moon-pod close to me so she can crawl into my little craft and share a tube of tea. But no, there is no likelihood of moon-pods being this far away from Dhara. After all, the Ashtan system is a few months away. The star is discernibly a round yellow eye, no longer a point, and the planets around it, including Ashta, appear disk-like as well, although I need my telescope to clearly see them. I can just see Ashta's polar ice caps. It is far from my spaceship at the moment, but when I enter the system it should be at a point in its orbit that brings it close to my trajectory. I have to be careful that the Antarsa current does not pass directly through the planet, because I will simply crash into it, then. I am anticipating some delicate maneuvering, and there is no time like this moment to practice.

After a long while, I discover something.

My companions move unobtrusively away as I approach them, which means, of course, that they can sense my presence. Are they simply making room for me, or is it something else? However, what I've found through this experiment is that the Antarsa current, the central, fastest channel at least, has widened considerably. It took me much longer to find its edges, where there are dangerous eddies and rivulets. The speed of the current has not changed, however. Mystified, I continue on my way.

I send my offer of kinship out, but as yet there is no answer but silence.

Listening to the silence, I am reminded of a story my father, the trader, told me when I was small. Among our people the Kinships are fairly self-sufficient, but we do have need of small shipments at regular intervals: metals from the Himdhara mountains, cloth from Tura-Tura and so on. We send out our herbs and jewelry. There is constant flow of information between the Kinships (except for the People of the Ice, about whom my father told this story) and also with Ship University. Most things are transported where possible by boat, in a rare while by flyer or shuttle, but there are also wandering caravans that go overland,

and my father has traveled with many of these. He is from a kinhouse of my own people further east of here, deeper in the forest and he met my mother during one of his journeys. Neither was interested in a permanent partnership but they remain cordial when they meet. And always he has tried to come see me, to bring me a shell from the Western Sea, or a particularly pretty pebble from Himdhara.

The People of the Ice stopped speaking to us from the time that the second generation of humans was grown. By that time the Kinships had each chosen their place, depending on where they felt most accepted and would do the least harm to the beings already present. My people of the Devtaru had genetically modified ourselves to digest certain local proteins; the Western sea folk had modified their bodies to be more agile in the water and to hold their breath longer than any other human. The People of the Himdhara could thrive in the thin mountain air. The People who settled in the Northern edge of the great continent, where there is ice even in the summer, adjusted themselves to live in that terrible cold. It was said that they grew hairy pelts like the beasts that dwelt there, but this could have been a joke. All the Kinships tell jokes about each other, and most are reasonably good-natured, but the People of the Ice got the worst of it because they were so remote, in both geography and temperament.

When I was little, my father said, his caravan was asked by the World Council to go into the North to find out what had happened to the People of the Ice. Was it that they did not answer radio calls because something terrible had befallen them, or were they being obstreperous as usual?

Take only a few people, said the Council, so that they don't feel invaded. So my father and three others—a man and two women—went. They wandered for days and weeks through forest and scrubland, desert and plateau, until they came to the land of perpetual snow. Here the trees grew up into tall spires, and the wild creatures all had thick, luminous coats and some knew the use of fire. My father knows this because one night the party followed a flickering light through a snowfall, and found large, hairy creatures huddling before a fire, tossing twigs into it and grunting. As is our custom, the four travelers sat some distance away and waited, speaking softly the offering of kinship, until the creatures waved their paws at them and invited them, through expressive grunts, to join them. My father says these were shaggorns, and fortunately this group was full of meat and therefore amiable. They are very curious and they poked at the travelers with twigs to see what they would do (some of his companions laughed but my father only smiled and gently poked back) and one of them wanted to try on my father's coat—my father allowed this, but had to give him his watch to get his coat back.

It was bitterly cold, but the four survived with the help of the shaggorns, and one late afternoon they found themselves at the edge of an icy plain, over which rose a city.

The city was made of ice. The buildings were constructed with ice blocks and had slit windows, and the streets were ice. People moved about them on skates, and the travelers could not tell whether they wore hairy pelts or if they had grown their own. The travelers set themselves down outside the city's perimeter but in plain sight, in keeping with the tradition of waiting for an invitation.

But there was none. People skated across the ice, from building to building, and didn't even look at the travelers. One little girl stared at them but was roughly pulled away by an adult. The four travelers sang the offering of kinship, but there was no response. This was a terrible thing to witness, my father said, because they had come so far and endured so much to make sure that their kin were safe. They were cold, hungry and tired, and the song was acquiring rather angry overtones. So they stopped their song, and set up camp there because the evening was setting in.

In the morning they found some supplies—meat, some cooked roots, all frozen by now, a pelt blanket. The meaning was clear: the People of the Ice did not desire kinship, but they meant no harm. There was no weapon left symbolically at the edge of the camp. They did not want a kinship of enmity—they simply wanted to be left alone.

So the travelers began their return journey, somewhat mollified. The next evening, before they were able to go very far (they were tired, as my father said), they saw a small dwelling in the forest. To their surprise they recognized the home of a farsister. Farsisters and farbrothers are people who wander away from their Kinships for a life of solitude, usually seeking some kind of spiritual solace. Some of them have done terrible things and seek to redress them or have suffered a loss and need to find a reason to live. Others simply wander in search of something they can't identify, and when they find it, usually in a place that calls to them, they settle down there.

The farsister's courtyard was snowy and bare, and furnished with only two low flat-topped rocks that my father assumed were intended to be chairs. This meant that the farsister did not like company, but one person would be tolerated. There was an intricately carved block of ice near the door, which indicated the occupation of the person within. That she was female was indicated by a red plume of feathers that hung from her door.

My father sat outside the courtyard and waited. She made him wait for several hours, by which time it was night and getting very cold. Then she came out and ushered him in. She turned out to be a grim, dour woman who seemed to be made of ice as well. The inside of her little hut was just as cold as the outside and this didn't seem to bother her.

She told him that she was not of the People of the Ice, and that there was not anything to be done about them, they kept to themselves. She gave him a cold tea to drink that made my father feel dizzy. He felt himself falling into deep sleep, and the icy fingers of the farsister easing him down into a cold bed.

When he woke up he found that the hut was empty. Moreover, there was no sign that it had ever been inhabited. The hearth was cold, and filled with ashes, and a wind blew through the open window. My father felt frozen to the marrow. He got himself up slowly and painfully and emerged into a snowy dawn. The courtyard of the hut was bare—no sitting rocks, no ice carvings, no evidence that anyone had ever lived here. His companions were waiting anxiously for him at camp.

It was a long journey home, my father said, and they were glad to come back to the warm lands and make their report to the Council.

When he used to tell us children this story in the sunny garden in front of the kinhouse, with the warm sun at our back, we would shiver in the imagined snowfall. We were trapped in the hut of the ghostly farsister, or lost in the enchanted forest with the People of the Ice in their hairy pelts, wandering around to scare us, to take us away. Later we would come up with games and stories of our own, in which the Ice folk were the principal villains.

When I was older, my birth-mother would take some of us to Council meetings. Council meetings rotated from Kinship to Kinship, and when we were the hosts, my mother would let us come. We would see our sea-kin, with their scale-like skin and their webbed hands, and the tall mountain folk with their elaborate head-dresses, or the cave kin with their sunshades over huge, dark eyes, and our own eyes would go round with wonder. In the evenings various kinfolk would gather round a fire or two and tell jokes. We would joke about the people of the Ice, and why they didn't ever come to Council ("they were afraid they'd melt" or "it would be too hot in their fur coats"). During one of these occasions my father was also present—he pulled some of us older ones aside.

"You all talk a lot of nonsense," he said. "Listen, I never told you one part of my story about the People of the Ice. What I dreamed about while I slept in the hut of the farsister."

We were all eyes and ears.

"Listen. I dreamed that the farsister took me to the city of ice. Some of the Ice people met me and took me in, saying I could stay the night. I was put in an ice-cold room on a bed of ice, and it was so cold that I couldn't sleep. In the night I heard my hosts talking about me, arguing. Some said I should never have been brought here, and another voice said that maybe I could be made to substitute for some relative, an old man whose time had come. The executioners would not know the difference if I was wrapped in furs and made unconscious, and that way the old man could live a little longer in secret. This went on for a long time, until the people moved away. I was so scared that I fled from there. My captors chased me some of the way but without much enthusiasm. Then I woke up in my cold bed."

My father paused.

"I may have simply dreamed the whole thing. But the dream was so vivid that I sometimes wonder if it didn't actually happen. Since that time I have wondered whether the reason for the silence of our Ice kin is something more sinister than mere bad manners. What if their genetic manipulations to adapt to the cold resulted in something they did not expect—something that prevents them from dying when they are old? Since they cannot die, they must put to death the old ones. And they are terrified that by mingling with us they will let loose an epidemic of deathlessness. So in their shame and misfortune they keep themselves separate from all other humans."

We were appalled. To cheat death, even to wish to live longer than one's natural span, is to show so much disrespect to all living beings, including one's own offspring and generations yet to come, that it is unthinkable. It is natural to fear death, and so it takes courage to make kinship with death when one's time has come. How terrible to have death itself refuse kinship! To have to kill one's own kin! It was an honorable thing to isolate this curse in a city of ice, rather than let it loose among the rest of the Kinships. After my father's revelation we found ourselves unable to joke about the People of the Ice with the same carelessness.

I am thinking about them today because I wonder about the silence of the spacecraft around me, and the deeper, longer silence of the Ashtans. Did they settle on their planet, or did they find it unsuitable and move on? Did some misfortune befall them? Or did they simply turn away from us, for some reason? I don't know if I'll ever find out.

So much has happened that I have not had time to speak my story until now. Dear, kind darkness, dear kin on Dhara, I have made such a discovery! My companions, whose flickering images on the radar screen have so mystified me, have revealed their true nature. It is hard to say whether there are simply more of them—they are so clear on the radar now—or whether I have gained their trust and they have moved closer.

They are not spaceships. They are beings. Creatures of deep space, made of altmatter, riding the Antarsa current like me.

I found this out a few days ago, when the radar screen presented an unusually clear image. A long, sinuous, undulating shape, broadest in the middle and tapered at each end moved parallel to us. Something waved like a banner from the far end—a tail. It was huge. I held my breath. The visual image showed a barely visible shape, lit only by starlight and the external lights of my ship, but it reminded me just a little of the seagu, that massive, benevolent ocean mammal of the Western Sea.

It was clearly made of altmatter. Its flattened limbs—fins?—moved in resistance to the Antarsa current, which propelled it forward. There was a purposefulness, an ease with which it swam that was delightful to see. Here was a creature in its element, apparently evolved to travel between the stars on the great Antarsa ocean. I closed my eyes, opened them, and the image was still there. My fingers were shaking.

How to describe what it meant to me, the company of another living creature, be it one so removed from myself! I had lived with other living beings all my life before this journey. I had played with chatterlings in the great forest near my home, swum with ocean mammals—walroos and seagus, and schools of silverbellies. Even in the high, bare mountains of Himdhara, where life is hardy, scarce and without extravagance, I had made kinship with a mog-bear, with whom I shared a cave for several days during a storm. Nearly always I had traveled with other humans. This was my first journey into the dark, alone. Parin's biosphere had much to do with maintaining my sanity, but how I had missed the company of other life! I blinked back tears. I took a deep breath and thanked the universe that I had lived to see such a marvel.

It was an exhilarating moment. It reminded me of my time with Raim, learning to use the sails on his boat on the Western Sea. Wind and current carried us far from the shore, and that wind was in my hair, whipping it about my face, and chapping my lips. Raim was beside me, laughing, rejoicing that I was finally moving the boat like an extension of my own body. Just then a school of seagu surfaced, and leaped up into the air as though to observe us. Crashing down into the water, raising a spray that drenched us, they traveled with us, sometimes surging ahead, sometimes matching our speed, their eyes glinting with humor.

This creature did not seem to have eyes. It must sense the world around it in a different way. I wondered whether it detected my little craft, and what it thought of it. But close on that thought came a new surprise. A fleet, a school of smaller shapes tumbled past between my ship and the behemoth. They were like small, flattened wheels, perhaps a meter in diameter as far as I could tell, trailing long cords through the current. They moved not in straight, parallel lines, but much more chaotically, like a crowd of excited children moving about every which way as they went toward a common destination.

As though this spectacle was not wonderful enough, I saw that around me, on either side and above and below, there was life. There were fish shapes, and round shapes, and long, tubular shapes, all moving with some kind of propulsion or undulation. They shimmered the way that altmatter does to the human eye, and some had their own lights, like the fish of the deep sea. These latter ones also had enormous dark spots on their bow end, like eyes. What worlds had birthed these creatures? Had they evolved in a gas cloud, or in the outer atmosphere of some star? They were so fantastic, and yet familiar. Our universe is, we know, mostly made from other kinds of matter than ourselves, but I hadn't imagined that altmatter could be the basis for life. It occurred to me now that altmatter life might be much more common in the universe than our kind. Space is so big, so empty. We have always assumed it hostile to life, but perhaps that is true only of our kind of life, made of ordinary matter.

For the next two days I prepared radar clips and visual clips to send home, and watched the play of life around me. I have seen what seem to be feeding frenzies—the behemoth feasted on those wheeled creatures—and I might have witnessed a birth.

Today I saw a new creature, twice as long as the behemoth I had first set my eyes upon. It had armor plating with fissures between the plates, and apparent signs of erosion (how?), as though it was very old. It trailed a cloud of smaller creatures behind it, evidently attendant upon it. Its round hole of a mouth was fringed with a starburst of tentacles. I was musing on the problem of the radar imaging system's resolving capacity, wondering what I was missing in terms of smaller-scale life in the life-rich current—when I saw the leviathan's mouth widen. It was at this point ahead of me and to one side of the ship, so I couldn't see the mouth, but I inferred it from the way the tentacles fringing the orifice spread out. To my astonishment a great, umbrella-shaped net was flung out from the fringes of the mouth, barely visible to my radar. This net then spread out in front of the creature like a parachute; the creature back-finned vigorously, slowing down so abruptly that a number of other swimmers were caught in the web. Had I not swerved violently, my craft and I would have been among them. The acceleration might have flung me across the chamber and broken some bones, had it not been for the inertial net, which thickened astonishingly fast. (That the ship suffered no great damage is a testament to the engineering skills of the great generation-ship builders of old, my craft being a modified version of one of their shuttles).

Now that the Ashtan system is nearly upon us, I have a new worry. I don't know whether the Antarsa current flows through any celestial objects, such as the sun, or a planet, or a moon. If it does, I must manipulate the altmatter sails in time to escape a violent crash. I am afraid something like this might have happened to the altmatter probes that were first launched from Dhara, that stopped sending back radio signals. Or perhaps they were swallowed by some creature.

Strangely, the current appears to be slowing; this would be a relief if it wasn't laced with chaotic microflows. I can sense them through the way they make the sails shiver, something I could not have told a few years ago. Sometimes I feel as though I can *see* the current with some inner eye, almost as though it has acquired a luminosity, a tangibility. I imagine, sometimes, that I can feel it, very faintly, a feather's touch, a tingling.

I have a sense of something about to happen.

What can I say, now to the dark? How do I explain what I have experienced to my kin on Dhara? What will you make of it, my sister Parin, my brother Raim? What stories will you now tell your children about Mayha, Moon-woman?

Nothing I once assumed to be true appears to be true.

As we entered the Ashtan system, the Antarsa current became chaotic on a larger scale. At that point I was not far from the second planet, Ashta, with its two lumpy little moons. Navigation became very difficult, as there were eddies and vortices and strong, dangerous little currents. There is a backwash from Ashta itself, I am convinced. This can only be the case if Ashta has a core of altmatter. Otherwise wouldn't the Antarsa wind simply blow through it, without becoming so turbulent?

This is not surprising. On Dhara there must be altmatter within the planet, else how would the devtaru have drawn it up? On Dhara, however, the Antarsa current does not go headlong through the planet, nor is it so wide. There is only a soft breeze through the planet, with the current itself running perhaps two hundred thousand kilometers distant. Here a broad channel of the current rushes through a region occupied by part of Ashta's orbit, and includes the tiny, uninhabitable inner planet and the sun. Depending on how much altmatter there is in these celestial objects, there is likely to be quite a backflow, and therefore much turbulence. A mountain stream studded with rocks would behave the same way.

For a long while, I was caught in the rapids. Caught with me were other creatures, altmatter beings of a fantastic variety, swimming valiantly, changing course with an enviable dexterity as the currents demanded. My hands were sore from manipulating the sails, my mind and soul occupied with the challenge of the moment, but the ship's AI managed to send a message in Old Irthic to Ashta. There was no reply but the now familiar silence.

I now know why. Or at least, I have a hypothesis. Because I have seen things I can hardly yet comprehend. I will not be landing on Ashta. It is impossible, and not just because of the turbulence.

This is what I saw: The day side of Ashta, through my telescope, showed continents floating on a grey ocean. There were dark patches like forests, and deserts, and the wrinkles of mountain ranges. I saw also scars, mostly in the equatorial belt, as though the planet had been pelted with enormous boulders. Most dramatically, the edges of the continents seemed to be on fire. There were plumes of smoke, mouths of fire where volcanoes spoke. In the interior, too, the scarred regions were streaked or lined or edged with a deep, red glow, and there were dark, smooth plains, presumably of lava. I imagined the invisible Antarsa current slamming into altmatter deposits deep within the planet, the impact creating internal heat that liquefied rock, which erupted volcanically onto the surface. There must be earthquakes too, on a regular basis, and were there not forests on fire?

That the forests were there at all spoke of a kinder past. Perhaps the Antarsa current had changed course in recent geological time? Now Ashta was a planet in the process of being destroyed, if the current didn't push it out of orbit first. I had never seen a more terrible sight.

But as we got closer, I saw much more to wonder at. The radar picked up something thousands of kilometers in *front* of the planet.

It first appeared as a roughly rectangular shadow or smear, very faint, that later resolved into a great array—a fine mesh of some kind, reminiscent of the net of the altmatter creature who nearly ate us. But this was on a massive scale, stretching across much of my view of the planet. Studded within it at regular intervals were lumps that I couldn't quite resolve—knots or nodes of some kind? No, too irregular. The net seemed to be held in place by beings, crafts or devices (I couldn't tell the difference at this distance) at corners and along the perimeter so that the whole thing sailed along with the planet. Its relative indifference to the chaotic Antarsa current indicated it was made of ordinary matter. Getting closer, I found that the lumps were creatures caught in the net, struggling. There was an air of great purpose and deliberation in the movements of smaller objects about the net—these craft, if that is what they were, appeared to buzz about, inspecting a catch here, a catch there, perhaps repairing tears in the net. It might have been my imagination but the creatures became still once the busy little craft went to them.

I went as close to the net as I dared. I had already folded the altmatter wings to decrease the effect of the current, although the eddies were so turbulent that this did not help as much as it should have, and my ship shuddered as a consequence. I switched to fusion power and edged toward the net. I wanted to see if the busy little objects—the fishermen—were spacecraft or creatures, but at the same time I didn't want to be swept into the net. One can't make an offer of kinship unless the two parties begin on a more-or-less equal footing. From what I hoped was a safe distance, I saw a drama unfold.

A behemoth was caught in the net. As it struggled, it tore holes in the material. One of the busy little fishercraft immediately went for it. Arms (or grappling hooks?) emerged from the craft and tried to engage the behemoth, but the creature was too large and too strong. A few lashes of the powerful tail, and it had pulled free, swimming off in the current—but the little craft-like object or creature broke up. From within it came all kinds of debris, some of it clearly made out of ordinary matter because it was impervious to the chaotic churning of the Antarsa and only influenced by gravity. These bits had clean, smooth trajectories. Flailing and struggling in the current, however, were three long, slender creatures with fins and a bifurcated tail. Were these the pilots of the craft, or parasites within the belly of a beast? The inexorable currents drew them to the net. I wanted to linger, to see whether they would be rescued or immobilized—two of the busy craft went immediately toward them—but I was already too close and I did not want to subject my ship to more shuddering. So I powered away in a wide arc.

I made for the night side of the planet. I was hoping for lights, indicating a settlement, perhaps, but the night side was dark, except for the fires of volcanoes and lava beds. Whatever beings had engineered the enormous net had left no trace of their presence on the planet—perhaps, if they had once lived there, they had abandoned it.

My kin were clearly not on this planet. The generation ship must have come here and found that the constant bombardment of the planet by altmatter creatures made it a poor candidate for a home. I hoped that they would have escaped the net, if the net had been there at the time. It was possible, too, that they had come here and settled, and when, as I thought, the Antarsa current shifted and slammed through Ashta, they perished. I felt great sadness, because I had hoped, dreamed, that I would find them here, settled comfortably in the niches and spaces of this world. I had imagined talking to them in the Old Irthic that I had been practicing, until I learned their languages. Instead I had to send a message home that they were not here after all.

Where had they gone? Manda had told me that the old generation ships were programmed for at least three destinations. Wherever they had gone, they had not thought it worthwhile to send us a message. Perhaps something had gone wrong en route. I shivered. None of the options implied anything good for our lost kin.

I decided I would attempt a moon landing. The moons did not seem to be made of altmatter as far as I could tell. The moon over the dark side was in the planet's wake, where there should be fewer eddies and undertows. So I brought my craft (still on fusion power) into orbit around the moon.

That was when it happened—a totally unexpected undertow caught the folded altmatter wings in the navigation chamber at just the right angle. I had at that moment cut speed from the fusion engines, preparatory to making an approach, so the undertow caught me by surprise. Before I knew it we were flung head-on toward the moon.

As I saw the moon's battered surface loom larger and larger, I thought of you, dear kin. I thought my moment had come. You would wonder at Mayha's silence, and hypothesize various endings to her story. I couldn't let that happen to you. Quicker than thought, I powered the fusion engines to brake my craft. I made a crash-landing, bumping along the uneven ground, over and over, until at last we were still. I felt the slight tug of the moon's gravity. The inertial web retracted slowly—I winced as it pulled strands of my hair with it. I was shaking, weak from shock. How slowly the silence impressed upon me as I lay in my craft!

Then the ship's AI began to speak. The fusion engine was intact, but one of the altmatter wings was broken. There was some damage to the outside of the ship, and the AI was already launching a repair swarm that clambered insect-like over the cracked and fissured shell. Anchoring cables had dug in and secured us to the surface of the moon. There was a spare wing stored within the navigation chamber, but it would take a long time to shape and match it to the old one. Then I would have to remove the broken wing and put in the new one, and adjust the rigging to the right tension. Working with altmatter meant that as I turned a wing this way or that, it would pick up a current or two and tumble out of my hand, and blow about the chamber. After a while I decided I needed to restore my mental equilibrium to the extent possible under such circumstances. So I did what I would do at home: after suiting up, I went for a walk.

Walking on the moon was both exhilarating and terrifying. To be outside my little home after years! I could spread my arms, move my legs, go somewhere I hadn't been before. There was the great bulk of the planet ahead of me, dominating my field of vision, dark and mysterious, streaked with fires, limned with light. The moon seemed to be a fragile thing in comparison, and I had to fight the feeling that I would fall away from it and on to the smoking, burning planet. I had to step lightly, gingerly, so that the ground would not push me away too hard. I walked halfway around it and found myself at the edge of a deep crater.

Lowering myself down to it was easy in the low gravity. At the bottom it was very dark. My suit lights picked out an opening—a hollow—a cave! I stepped into it, curious, and found a marvel.

The cave was filled with luminous fish-like creatures, each about as long as my finger. They circled around on tiny, invisible currents, so I guessed they were made of altmatter. As I stared at them in wonder, a few darted up to me, hovering over my visor. I stood very still. To make kinship with a fellow living being, however remote, was a great thing after my long incarceration. I was inspected and found harmless, and thereafter left alone. I stood in the dark of the cave, my ears filled with the sound of my own breathing, and fervently thanked the universe for this small encounter.

As I turned to leave, I had a terrible shock. My suit lights had fallen on somebody—a human, sitting silently on a piece of rock against the wall of the cave, watching me.

No, it was not a person—it was a sculpture. Fashioned in stone of a different kind, a paler shade than the material of the moon, it had clearly been brought here. I went up to it, my heart still thumping. It was the statue of a woman, sitting on a rock cut to resemble the prow of a boat or ship. There was a long pole in her hands, and she looked at me with obsidian eyes, her face showing a kind of ethereal joy. I thought she might be one of the old gods of our ancestors, perhaps a goddess for travelers. I touched the rock with my gloved hand, moved beyond tears. Why had my kin left this symbol here? Perhaps they had tried to make a home on Ashta, and failing, had left the statue as a mark of their presence.

I spent three days on the moon. I repaired the wing, a task more difficult than I can relate here (Raim will find a better description in my technical journal) and went back to the cave many times to renew kinship with the fish-like creatures and to see again the statue of the woman. The last time, I conducted an experiment.

I took with me some pieces of the broken altmatter wing. They confirmed that the inside of the cave was a relatively still place, where the Antarsa currents were small. By waving one piece of wing in front of the statue, and using another piece on the other side as a detector, I determined after a lot of effort that the statue was made of ordinary matter except from the neck upward, where it was altmatter or some kind of composite. This meant that my kin had made this statue *after* they had been here a while, *after* they had discovered altmatter. I stared again at the statue, the woman with the ecstatic face, the upraised eyes. She saw something I could not yet see. I wondered again how she had come to be placed here, in a nameless cave on a battered moon of Ashta.

I am now moving away from Ashta, on a relatively smooth current of the great Antarsa ocean. I am convinced now that I can sense the Antarsa, although it blows through me as though I am nothing. I can tell, for instance, that I am out of the worst of the chaotic turbulence. I can only hope that I've caught the same current I was on before I entered the Ashtan system—it is likely that the current splits into many branches here. I will be completely at its mercy soon, since I do not have much fuel left for the fusion engines. I also must conserve my food supplies, which means that after this message I will enter the cryochamber once more—a thought that does not delight me.

At last I have relinquished control of the altmatter sails to the ship's computer. I woke from several hours of sleep to see, on the radar screen, images of the altmatter creatures sailing with me. Unlike me, they all seem to know where they are going. Here their numbers have dropped, but I notice now a host of smaller replicas of the behemoths, and the wheel-like creatures, and I wonder if the Ashtan system is some kind of cosmic spawning ground. I wish very much to offer kinship to these creatures. I already miss the little fish in their cave on the moon. That has given me hope that although we are made of very different kinds of matter, we can make a bridge of understanding between us. Life, after all, should transcend mere chemistry, or so I hope.

I have sent many messages home. In a few years my dear ones will read them and wonder. The young people I will never see, children of my kin-sisters and kin-brothers, will ask the adults with wide eyes about their aunt Mayha, Moon-woman, who forever travels the skies. But I have one faint hope. Out on the Western sea, Raim once told me that the great ocean currents, the conveyor belts, are all loops. It seems to me that it is likely, if our universe is finite, that the Antarsa currents are also closed loops. If I have chosen the right branch, this current might well loop back toward Dhara. Who knows how long that will take—perhaps my descendants will find only that this little craft is a coffin—but the hope persists, however slight, that I might once again see the blue skies, the great forest of my home, and tell the devtaru of my travels.

One casualty of my crash-landing on the moon is that Parin's biosphere is broken. I am trying to see if some of the mosses and sugarworts can still survive, but the waterbagman broke up, and for a while I found tiny red worms suspended in the air, some dead, others dying. There was one still captured in a sphere of water, which I placed in a container, but it is lonely, I think. I am trying to find out what kind of nutrients it needs to stay alive. This has been a very disturbing thing, to be left without Parin's last gift to me, a living piece of my world.

I stare at my hands, so chapped and callused. I think of the hands of the stone woman. An idea has been forming in my mind, an idea so preposterous that it can't possibly be true. And yet, the universe is preposterous. Think, my kin, about this fact: that ordinary matter is rare in the universe, and that in at least two planets, Dhara and Ashta, there is altmatter deep within. Think about the possibility that altmatter is the dominant form of matter in the universe, and that its properties are such that altmatter life can exist in the apparent emptiness between the stars. Our universe then is not inimical to life, but rich with it. Think about the stone woman in a cave on the irregular little moon that circumnavigates Ashta. Is it possible that there is some symbolism in the fact that she is made of both matter and altmatter? Is it possible that the generation ship of my ancestors did not really leave the system, that instead my kin stayed and adapted more radically than any other group of humans? Imagine the possibility that the fate of all matter is to become altmatter, that as the most primitive and ancient form of substance, ordinary matter evolves naturally and over time to a newer form, adapted to life in the great, subtle ocean that is the Antarsa. Suppose there is a way to accelerate this natural change, and that my kin discovered this process. Confronted with an unstable home world, they adapted themselves to the extent that we cannot even recognize each other. Those slim figures I saw, thrown out of the ruins of the little spacecraft after its epic battle with the behemoth—could they once have been human?

How can anyone know? These are only wild conjectures, and what my kin on Dhara will make of it, I don't know. It depresses me to think that I never found a way to make kinship with the creatures monitoring the vast net. If there had been a circumstance in which I could have met them on a more equal footing than predator and prey, I would have liked to try. If my ideas are correct and they were once human, do they remember that? Do they return to the little moon with its cave-shrine, and stare at the statue? At least I have this much hope: that given my encounter with the tiny fish-like creatures of the cave, there is some chance that lifeforms composed of ordinary matter can make kinship with their more numerous kin.

My hands are still my hands. But I fancy I can feel, very subtly, the Antarsa wind blowing through my body. This has happened more frequently of late, so I wonder if it can be attributed solely to my imagination. Is it possible that my years-long immersion in the Antarsa current is beginning to effect a slow change? Perhaps my increased perception of the tangibility of the Antarsa is a measure of my own slow conversion, from ancient, ordinary matter to the new kind. What will remain of me, if that happens? I am only certain of one thing, or as certain as I can be in a universe so infinitely surprising: that the love of my kin, and the forests and seas and mountains of Dhara, will have some heft, some weight, in making me whoever I will be.

Carrie Vaughn is best known for her *New York Times* bestselling series of novels about a werewolf named Kitty who hosts a talk radio show for the supernaturally disadvantaged. Her latest novels include a near-Earth space opera, *Martians Abroad,* from Tor Books, and a post-apocalyptic murder mystery, *Bannerless,* from John Joseph Adams Books. The sequel, *The Wild Dead,* will be out in 2018. She's written several other contemporary fantasy and young adult novels, as well as upwards of eighty short stories, two of which have been finalists for the Hugo Award. She's a contributor to the Wild Cards series of shared world superhero books edited by George R. R. Martin and a graduate of the Odyssey Fantasy Writing Workshop. An Air Force brat, she survived her nomadic childhood and managed to put down roots in Boulder, Colorado. Visit her at www.carrievaughn.com.

THE MIND IS ITS OWN PLACE

CARRIE VAUGHN

Professional fingers pried open Mitchell's left eyelid, and white light blinded him. The process repeated on the right. He winced and turned his head to escape. The grip released him.

"Lieutenant Greenau?"

He lay on a bunk in an infirmary. It wasn't the *Francis Drake's* infirmary. The smell was wrong; the background hum of the vessel was wrong. This place sounded softer, more distant. Larger. With effort, he shifted an arm. His head hurt. He felt like he'd been asleep for days.

"Lieutenant Greenau? Mitchell?" The figure at the side of his bed gave him something to focus on. A middle-aged man in a white tunic, with a narrow face and a receding hairline, frowned at him. "How are you feeling?"

"Groggy." He struggled for awareness.

"You were sedated."

"Can you give me something to clear it up?"

"I'd rather not put anything else into your system just yet."

He wished he didn't have to ask: "Where am I?"

"You're at Law Station, Lieutenant."

Law Station was a Military Division forward operating base and shipyard. It would have taken the *Drake* days to get here, and he didn't remember the trip. Law also housed an extensive medical facility.

Softly, as if afraid of upsetting a fragile piece of equipment, he asked, "Why am I here?"

"What do you remember?"

He'd arrived on the bridge for his shift. He'd checked in with Captain Scott. Then he assumed he'd taken his place at the navigator station. He must have done his job as he had a hundred times before. He checked in with the captain, the duty log scanned his thumbprint—

"I was on the *Francis Drake*. On the bridge. I said good morning to the captain. Then—I don't remember." He kneaded the sheet draped over him, cramping his fingers. He was wearing a patient gown, not his uniform.

"That's all right." The doctor smiled, but the expression was shallow, artificial, a forced attempt at bedside manner. "I'm Doctor Dalton, one of the supervising physicians here. If you need anything, a pager is at the side of the bunk."

"Doctor—" Mitchell forced himself up, rolling to his side and leaning hard on his elbow. The effort left him gasping. "What happened?"

Dalton's manner was implacable, as if he'd had this conversation before, with other patients, over many years. "This is the neurophysiology ward. Are you familiar with what we do here?"

His heart pounded; his tongue was dry. "Yes."

"You were brought here because you have OSDS."

Among themselves, in private, the navigators called it Mand Dementia. The condition was degenerative and incurable. It was one of the risks of the job. An acceptable risk.

"But I feel fine. I don't feel—" Except for the sedation—why had he needed to be sedated? "I don't feel sick. I'm not—" *I'm not crazy.*

"I know, Lieutenant. I'm sorry."

Mitchell slumped back against the mattress.

He kept a close count of the time. It seemed important, to prove he wasn't sick. Everything he did had to be normal and healthy. He wasn't sick, and the doctor was wrong.

Halfway through his first waking day cycle, he heard voices coming from the office next to the infirmary. Doctor Dalton was one, and he brightened to hear the other: Captain Crea Scott.

Dalton said, "He didn't exhibit any symptoms before?"

Scott answered, her normally brash voice hushed and brittle: "He didn't. I know what to look for. He was fine at the start of the shift, and an hour later he was screaming about flying monkeys to starboard—"

Mitchell lay very still.

"He hasn't exhibited any symptoms since he's been here. He also doesn't remember anything that happened. We won't know the extent of the damage until we run tests."

"Could there be a mistake? Could it be something else?"

"I reviewed the log myself, Captain."

"May I see him?"

"That should be all right."

Mitchell lay with his back to the door and didn't see them enter. He waited to turn when Scott said, "Lieutenant Greenau?"

Scott stood a few feet away from the bed, her petite frame tense, her arms crossed. Her face was drawn; she looked ten years older than the last time he'd seen her— when?

He sat up and smiled, relieved. Like she was going to rescue him or something. "Captain Scott. It's good to see you."

She didn't return the smile. "How are you feeling, Lieutenant?"

"Still groggy from the sedative. But I'm okay. I feel fine." He glanced at Doctor Dalton to make sure he heard.

"That's good."

"Captain, I don't understand why I'm here."

"That's okay. Just rest. Don't worry about it." After putting a hand on his arm, she bowed her head and turned away.

"I did something, didn't I? What did I do?"

Scott didn't turn around. Her voice was painfully steady. "Just take care of yourself, Mitchell. Don't worry."

Dalton followed Scott out of the room, and Mitchell heard his captain say, "He'll be safe here?"

"Yes. As safe as we can make him."

Then Scott said, her voice low and angry, "Make sure he never remembers what happened."

A door slid open, then closed again, and the captain was gone.

He pressed his thumb to the duty log, he said good morning to the captain, he went to his station—

He only knew that much because it was the routine, what he'd done over and over for years. Was he remembering some other time, or *that* time?

Compared to his quarters aboard the *Drake*, the room he was given here was spacious, an eight by eight square with a bed, desk, computer console, and private washroom. For the whole of his adult life, Mitchell had slept in closets, with a narrow bunk and a cupboard for his belongings. He'd shared washrooms with other junior officers. Who needed more? Who ever spent time in their rooms? He'd always been so busy.

The door to the room locked from the outside. He couldn't leave without escort. Orderlies brought meals and returned to take away the trays. Mitchell counted two of them, Baz and Jared, working in shifts. They were polite. Mitchell said thank you, and they smiled at him. He had a change of clothing—pale blue hospital-issue jumpsuits—every day. He could read or watch entertainments at the console to pass the time, when he wasn't in therapy.

That first night he didn't sleep, but lay back on his cot and stared at a bubbled security monitor in the ceiling, wondering if this was a test.

The second doctor he encountered had an unflappably optimistic professional demeanor, and Mitchell distrusted her for no good reason except that nobody was that genuinely enthusiastic about anything. In spite of himself, Mitchell shook her hand after Baz escorted him to her lab.

Her space was a bit more inviting than other areas of the hospital. Handheld terminals lay strewn across the desk among forgotten drink bottles and writing implements. A sweater hung over the back of a chair. Photos shone from wall displays: image after image of human brains, parts color-coded and labeled.

A dark-skinned woman with short hair and an eager smile, she came around the desk. "Lieutenant Greenau? I'm Doctor Ava Keesey. I'll be starting your therapy today." She offered her hand.

"Not Doctor Dalton?"

"I've requested your case. I hope that's all right?"

He didn't know what his choices were to be able to make one, so he said nothing.

"Have a seat right over here, Lieutenant." She guided him to a reclining chair surrounded by unidentifiable equipment. Gingerly, he climbed in; its cushions molded under him, supporting his body. The chair tipped back until he was horizontal.

"Any questions before we start?"

"Is the *Drake* still in dock?"

"I don't know. I can check for you."

Her smile was fake; he didn't think she would check.

"What happened? Why was I brought here?"

"It's better if you remember on your own, rather than construct false memories based on anything I tell you. If you can please keep your head back, I'd like to start the scan." Her cool hand on his forehead eased him back against the headrest. "You've been through a cortical mapping session before, yes?"

"Yes." Every navigator had one done at the start of their career. A baseline.

"Then you know all about this. Just relax."

Machinery closed over his crown, sensors pressing against his scalp, tickling the fuzz of his hair. He looked straight up to off-white ceiling.

"Can you hear me?" she said.

"Yes."

"I'd like you to move your left thumb. And again. Left index. And again. Left middle. And again."

And so it went, through the range of motor skills, then across the range of sensory input. Keesey played music and noises, offered him tastes, put sandpaper and cotton into his hands, recording the results with straightforward efficiency.

"Now I'm going to show you some colors, each one for a few seconds. Pay attention, please."

A screen swung into view over the chair and flashed to life, displaying solid blue, then green, then yellow.

He went to the navigator station, slid into his chair and belted in. Ready for the jump in three, two—the monitor showed a swirl of color. The wrong colors, circling like predators—

Orange, red, purple. Mitchell blinked. Solid squares appeared in sequence on the screen. Harmless.

"What is two plus two, Lieutenant?"

"Four."

"Two times two?"

"Four."

"Four times four?"

"Sixteen."

"Sixteen squared?"

"Two hundred fifty-six."

Yellow, orange, red.

"Thank you."

The wrong colors. They were the wrong colors.

Keesey moved away, her footsteps clicking on the hard floor of the lab. He remained locked in the chair, unable to turn his head.

"Can I sit up?"

"In a minute, Lieutenant."

He wished he could see what she was doing. He heard clicks, movements, maybe fingers tapping on a keypad, or machinery shifting into place. All the sounds were inexplicable.

Mitchell waited a painful, silent minute before saying, "Doctor?"

"Patience, Lieutenant. I want to get a little more data." Did her voice sound stressed? Uncertain?

She went through the entire sequence again, generating a second cortical map. Finally, she released him from the equipment.

"What's wrong?" he said, sitting up.

Her smile didn't seem any different than the one she gave him at the start of the session. "How much do you know about OSDS?"

Occupational Synaptic Dysfunction Syndrome. It was the bogeyman, the monster in the dark. The price they paid for crossing the void. Some people said M-drive propulsion violated the laws of physics, and the Universe took the cost of that somewhere else: in the minds of the navigators who plotted courses through the unreal. Their minds became . . . nonlinear.

"It affects the neural organization of the brain," he said.

Keesey said, "It develops when some neurotransmitters don't reach adjacent neurons but instead stimulate neurons in distant parts of the brain. Reducing the stimulation our patients receive can prevent the damage from getting worse by keeping faulty connections from developing. That means sheltering patients, perhaps more than seems reasonable. I'll have some instructions for you once I've had a chance to study the scans."

"You made two maps. Is that normal?"

"Just confirming the data, Lieutenant."

She hadn't believed what she saw the first time.

"But I don't feel sick." If he were really well, he wouldn't have to keep saying it.

"And we want to keep you that way."

She escorted him back to his quarters herself. He would never be allowed to just wander, would he? He was curious about every door, every branch in the corridor. Every place he couldn't go. And where was the *Drake* now?

They'd almost reached his quarters when a scream rang out and echoed along the walls. The corridor curved to match the curve of the station; the scream came from ahead, just out of sight.

Keesey's practiced demeanor slipped. "Stay here." She gripped his arm and pushed him against the wall, as if she could stick him there.

When she trotted ahead, Mitchell followed her, to where Baz was half-helping, half-dragging a thirty-year-old man in a hospital jumpsuit through an open door. Mitchell couldn't tell if they were trying to enter or leave what must have been the man's quarters. Baz held the man's shoulders, as if he were simply guiding him, but he stumbled, his legs buckling as if he couldn't support himself. Disheveled brown hair hung around his shoulders, he held his hands over his ears, and his face was twisted in an anguished cry. He screamed again.

Keesey knelt by the patient and tried to take hold of his face.

"Morgan, look at me. Morgan! Focus!"

The man, Morgan, squeezed his eyes shut and shook his head.

Keesey said, "Baz, I can't look after him now. Take him to the infirmary, and I'll be there in a minute." She pulled something out of her pocket—a patch— and slapped it on Morgan's wrist. His struggles subsided; his moans continued.

The orderly nodded and lifted his burden, guiding Morgan along the corridor, past Mitchell, stopping every few steps as the man doubled over, then raising him up and continuing.

Keesey quickly took Mitchell's arm and steered him back to his own room—just a couple of doors down from Morgan's. She keyed it open with her wristband, and she urged him inside. He was being put away in a box.

"What's wrong with him?" Mitchell asked.

"Get some rest, Mitchell. We'll talk later about your treatment."

"But—"

"He has OSDS, Mitchell."

He sat at his tiny desk and pretended it was the *Drake's* navigator station, the self-contained compartment located through a hatch at the fore of the equipment-laden bridge. Here, isolated from the bustle at the heart of the ship, he monitored the calculations that allowed the M-drive to fling the ship from one point to another across folded space. It was a mind-boggling journey, possible through a complex quirk of physics, comprehensible through advanced mathematics. Nevertheless, Mitchell was a romantic, and he could imagine the journey—not an instantaneous manipulation of space-time, but a race across the galaxy, stars flying past in a Dopplered rainbow of colors, the gas of nebulae swirling in his wake. The stuff of children's adventure stories.

If this were the chair in his station, the computer console would have been here, the screen here, the proximity monitor here, the holo-maps there. Where had they been going? Had the blank space in his memory happened before or after they'd jumped? He would have located departure and arrival matrices, he would have generated equations describing those endpoints in real space, converted the holography . . .

He thought some part of the process would jog his memory. He calculated a dozen iterations of the same equation, variations in the matrices, imagined the graph they would plot, imagined traveling along that shape. The Universe and all its paths could be described this way.

The path made a swirl of colors—gases inflamed by cosmic radiation, distant starlight—and the colors made him nervous. They never had before.

The computer had to be connected to Law Station's network. The *Drake* had docked here, so the station database would have some record of it. The *Drake's* logs might even have been uploaded.

From this terminal he was only supposed to have access to entertainments, but with a little hunting, he found that the library's reading material included the station's daily news feed, which listed a record of dockings by interstellar ships. Mitchell found the records from a couple of weeks before and worked forward.

A week ago, the *M.D.S. Francis Drake* had docked for temporary repairs. It was scheduled to continue to the Mil Div Sol shipyards for more extensive repairs. That hadn't been on their schedule; the *Drake* had years of operation left before it needed an overhaul. Unless something had happened. And something *had* happened, or Mitchell wouldn't be here. The logs, he had to find the logs—

The screen went blank, the computer shut down. Its power had been cut off. Standard procedure for any terminal being used for unauthorized access.

He stared at his hands, flattened on the surface of the desk. They weren't even shaking.

"Lieutenant, I'd really appreciate it if you not work on any math." Keesey said.

He had started physical therapy—work on a treadmill, standard weightlifting. It was very boring, but the doctors watched him closely. Maybe in case he started singing when he only meant to move his leg.

He stopped walking. The treadmill powered down. "What?"

"You have books to read, vids to watch. You should avoid mathematics problems."

He laughed. Navigational math lived in his brain like his own heartbeat; he didn't even think of it.

Keesey explained: "The mathematics involved in navigation instigated your injury. I don't want you making it worse."

"Doctor, what was wrong with my cortical map?"

She consulted her handheld, donned her pleasant demeanor. "I think you might benefit from some social time. Meet some of the other patients so you can realize you're not alone here."

He knew he wasn't alone. He'd seen Morgan.

*

The common room where stabilized patients were allowed to socialize was carpeted, comfortable, and round. It gave an impression of nest-like safety. There
were no corners to cower in. A few upholstered chairs occupied one side, some
tables the other. The lighting was soft. An orderly stood watch inside the doorway.

Three people wearing hospital jumpsuits sat in the room, all apart from each
other. Only one, a shorthaired woman curled up in one of the easy chairs, reading a handheld, looked up when Mitchell and Keesey appeared in the doorway.

The other two, a man and a woman, sat at different tables. The woman's eyes
were closed, and she nodded in time to some tune all her own. The man held a
stylus and bent over a handheld datapad, which he marked now and then. There
was something odd about him, something small and shrunken. Maybe because
he wore a helmet shielding him down to his ears. Mitchell expected him to start
banging his head against the table at any moment.

Mitchell whispered to Keesey, "What's the point of socializing if no one
talks to each other?"

"Have a little patience." She gestured to the man and woman at the tables.
"Communication is difficult for Jaspar and Sonia, so they've isolated them-
selves. That doesn't mean they shouldn't spend time in proximity with others.
But here—this is Dora."

No ranks, no surnames. Their old lives had been thoroughly erased here. He
wanted his uniform back.

She led him to the side of the room where the woman watched them
expectantly. "Dora? I'd like you to meet our new resident. This is Mitchell."

"Hello, Mitchell." Dora, head propped on her hand, smiled up at him.

Mitchell gave a mental sigh of relief. She sounded normal. Friendly, even.
Not prone to screaming.

Keesey said, "Baz will come fetch you in half an hour." She left them alone.

Dora gestured at the chair next to hers. "Sit. You look uncomfortable."

"I am uncomfortable. I don't think I belong here."

"Because you're not crazy. Because you're not like them." She nodded at
the others.

"I'm not. I'm not." Dora smiled a thin, cat-like smile. "What made them
send you here?"

Dora smiled a thin, cat-like smile. "What made them send you here?"

"I don't remember."

She tapped her nose and grinned wider.

"So why are you here?" he asked.

She gave a demure tilt to her head. "It was a conspiracy. Captain didn't like me. Some of the crew didn't agree with the decision to lock me up. They'll come back for me, break me out of here."

And to think she acted so normal.

"Ah," she said. "You're giving me a look like now you think I'm crazy, too."

"They break you out? Then what? You become pirates?"

"Hm, that sounds like fun. Didn't you dream of that when you were a kid? Being a pirate, blazing across space having all sorts of adventures."

"I was going to save innocent starships from the bad pirates. Kids never dream about being bad pirates; it's always good pirates."

"There are no good pirates."

Mitchell gestured toward Jaspar and Sonia. "Do you know anything about them?"

Dora sat back in her chair. "Jaspar doesn't do anything but work puzzles—for six-year-olds. Sonia will talk to you, but she won't make any sense. Go try it."

He half-expected this to be some sort of initiation—humiliate the new kid by making him try to find something that wasn't there. But he crossed the room to Sonia anyway. She was pretty, if ragged. In her thirties, like all of them were, because that was when Mand Dementia tended to strike.

"Hello," he said, sitting in the chair across from her.

She looked up. Her eyes were swollen, shadowed, tired. Her light-colored hair needed brushing.

"I'm Mitchell. I'm new, so I thought I'd introduce myself."

She sat very still, in contrast to her previous nodding.

"Dora says you'll talk."

"Glass. Concerto for Violin," she said in a hesitating voice.

Mitchell blinked, startled. "What does that mean?"

Her eyes glistened. There was a spark of something there, a flicker. Understanding. Sentience. Something that wasn't insane. Like she was staring through the bars of a cage.

"Chopin. Opus 28, Prelude Number 6."

Composers. Music. She was speaking pieces of music like they meant something. He stared at her, wishing he could understand, and it was like staring into his own future.

"Chopin. Opus 28, Prelude Number 6," she called after him when he turned to leave. Her gaze pleaded, but he didn't understand what she wanted. Except maybe out of here, like him.

He tried talking to Jaspar next, but the man turned his back on him, filling Mitchell's sight with the off-white mound of his helmet—that was protecting what, exactly?

He returned to Dora, who explained, "She was a musician. The dementia crosswired music and language. Keesey thinks there's some correlation between the mood or situation and what song she says. You know, 'Ride of the Valkyries' means 'pissed off.' I think it's a smokescreen and she's just hiding from everyone."

"She looks like she's listening to something."

"The music in her mind. The doctors won't let her listen to actual music. They're afraid it'll 'reinforce faulty neural pathways,'" she said. She did a pretty good impression of Dalton's flat tone. "I knew her, before. She associated every step of navigating to different songs. She said the sound of an M-drive powering up matched the opening measures of the overture to 'The Marriage of Figaro.' Then it all went to hell, I guess."

If someone locked you in a room full of crazy people, was there any chance that you *weren't* crazy?

She said softly, "You know, everyone here commits suicide sooner or later. The whole place is a futile attempt to keep us from killing ourselves. But everyone manages it. They can't help us. This isn't a hospital, it's a hospice."

Quietly he said, "How do you stand it?"

She spread her hand over the handheld in her lap. "I'm looking at this as a chance to catch up on my reading."

"Lieutenant? It's time to leave." Baz stood at his shoulder. Mitchell hadn't been aware of his approach. Meekly, he let the orderly guide him away.

Back in his room, he listened to the piece of music Sonia had named, the Chopin. A sad piano melody wafted gently from his terminal, like a ghost. He wondered what it meant to her.

Dora was wrong: This was not a place where navigators killed themselves. Keesey was wrong: he was not ill. He kept trying to remember what happened on the *Drake*. The thing Scott didn't want him to remember, that the doctors didn't want him to think about.

He'd signed in, said good morning to the captain, went to his station. *We have an hour until we need to jump, Lieutenant.* The first step to initiating a jump was identifying the arrival matrix and locking in coordinates. The next step: convert the holography of local space from manifold to loop representation, another computerized operation that nonetheless required monitoring.

Ultimately the navigator, the human element, confirmed the optimum departure matrix generated by the navigation system, or chose an alternate. Then the M-drive would push the ship through it to emerge across interstellar space at the desired arrival matrix. At some level, even if only intuitively, he had to understand the mathematics that connected the two ends of the ship's journey.

By remembering routine, he forced himself through his breakdown, moment by moment.

He confirmed the departure matrix—and it was wrong. The colors swirled around it like light bursting to its death, and the space through which the ship should have been traveling was a mouth waiting to devour them. It wasn't a departure matrix but a black hole. The colors were wrong, the math was wrong, the computer was broken—

"Mitchell! Look at me."

Keesey leaned over him. Her cool hand touched his cheek. His skin was clammy, and his heart was racing. He couldn't control his breathing; air rasped roughly through his throat. He was on the floor of his quarters; some alarm must have summoned the doctor.

"What is it, Mitchell? What happened?" Her concern was professional, unemotional.

"I-I think I remembered something."

"Can you describe it?"

He had to speak very carefully. He didn't want to say the wrong thing. He had to say the thing that would explain all this away. "I saw colors. They were wrong."

He winced and turned his head, or tried to, but Keesey held him in place. Baz stood behind her. A vent fan hummed somewhere.

"Make your mind a blank, Mitchell. Let the images fall away until you see nothing." He obeyed her psychiatrist's calm, and the colors faded. Baz came closer with a bottle and urged him to drink. Mitchell was obedient. The rehydrating fluid somehow made him feel weaker. He shouldn't need all this attention, this treatment. He wasn't sick.

"There was something wrong with the computer," he tried to tell them. That would explain everything.

Keesey wrote on a handheld as she spoke. "Your cortical map shows a faulty connection within your visual cortex. You can't trust your eyes, Mitchell. I know this is going to be hard, but I'd like you to limit your visual stimulation over the next couple of days. I can give you a blindfold if you'd like."

Blindfold? Like taking away Sonia's music.

"What are you writing down?" he asked. Maybe he shouldn't be looking. Is this what she meant by visual stimulation?

"Some exercises we'll try at your next session. We need to stabilize the dysfunctional area of the visual cortex. Please, rest your eyes if you can."

If they could reduce his world to a tiny, thoughtless box, then nothing at all could damage him. They could blindfold him. But he was still going to try and remember.

*

"I overheard Dalton and Keesey talking about you," Dora told him. He was sitting in his usual chair with his eyes closed. It didn't help. *If he could just figure out what was wrong with the computer . . .*

She continued, "You've got the piss scared out of Dalton. He seems to think you should be locked up and tied down full time. You must have done something spectacular. On the other hand, Keesey thinks you're the key to the holy grail that's going to save us all."

Dora was wrong—this wasn't a hospice, this was a laboratory. A hundred years of interstellar travel and they hadn't figured out how to prevent or treat Mand Dementia. That was why they were here; they were data points.

"I don't know why either of them should think that."

"Let me ask you a question. What is Mand navigation? Is it the math, or is it the mind of the navigator? See, the math alone isn't enough. Otherwise the computers could do it all. But no—they need *us* to process it. Not just anyone can be a navigator. A navigator has to understand what the computer is doing when it crunches those numbers. All those aptitude tests—they're measuring us, making sure we have the right kind of brain. We're the key. So why does the Trade Guild have this place?"

She leaned over the arm of her chair and lowered her voice to a bare whisper. "The Guild doesn't put us here because we're crazy. They put us here because they're afraid of us. It's not that we're sick. It's that they can't control us. We're too powerful, and this hospital, this so-called disease, all the sedatives, it's the only way they can keep us under control."

Powerful? He was a navigator. Part of a crew. He wouldn't do anything to hurt anyone. "We're not that special—"

"Mitchell, what do we do?"

"We review the M-drive navigation system, confirming departure and arrival matrices—"

"Do we confirm them? Or do we create them?"

He stared at her. He had to squint against the light, and the colors seemed wrong.

Her eyes grew even wider. "What if some of us have learned to manipulate the process without M-drives, without starships? What would that make us?"

His voice was small. "Powerful."

"It drives some of us crazy." She nodded at Jaspar and Sonia at their same places at the table, absorbed in their same tasks. "But some of us are the next step in evolution. It's not God that makes the Universe, it's math. Know the math, and you are God."

Mitchell found Baz and asked to be escorted back to his room. He flinched, though, when Sonia walked smoothly to intercept him before he reached the door.

She touched Mitchell's arm. "Prokofiev. *Prokofiev.*"

He could only stare and wish to understand. Bowing her head, she stepped aside and let them pass.

"What did that mean?" Mitchell asked Baz.

"It doesn't mean anything."

They passed far enough along the curve of the station that the common room door was out of sight when a buzzer sounded, and Baz brought his wrist comm to his face. "Yeah?"

A desperate voice—Mitchell thought it belonged to the other orderly—replied. "Morgan knocked out Dalton and sealed himself in the decompression chamber."

Baz ran, shouting, "Damn! Damn, damn—"

Running after him, Mitchell's slippers skidded a little on the floor. This was what rebellion looked like in the Mand Dementia ward; he wanted to see it. Baz rounded a corner, flashed his wristband to open the door, and Mitchell followed him into the infirmary.

Jared pounded on the control panel of the decompression chamber and called Morgan's name over and over. Baz joined him, pushing at the chamber's sliding door as if he could open it with brute force. Impossible, of course, with the difference in air pressure. Mitchell had stopped in the doorway; Keesey pushed him aside.

"Oh no," she breathed, her voice thick with despair.

Jared said, "He locked up the controls and pumped out all the air. I couldn't do anything. I tried, but I couldn't stop him, I couldn't."

Keesey's face was twisted into an expression that might have been a comforting smile, or suppressed grief. She rested her forehead against the window. "Where is Doctor Dalton? Is he all right?"

Jared pointed back to where Dalton was sitting on the floor holding a cold compress to his head.

Mitchell's feet were leaden as he moved toward the chamber door. He'd come this far. He had to see.

The chamber was a gray room, large enough for a stretcher. Morgan lay on the floor, curled in fetal position, naked. His hospital jumpsuit was tangled around his feet. The half-light that entered the chamber through the window cast weird shadows over him. His skin looked silver, painted with the dark splotches of burst blood vessels. His brown hair, haloed around his bent head, looked silver. He was hugging himself, as if this was what he'd wanted.

"Why?" Mitchell asked, his hand on the door, like he could reach through, reach him. Keesey said, "The air against his skin was screaming. He felt the air and heard it as screaming. He was trying to get away from the screaming."

"I don't understand," he said. All people had to do to kill themselves in space was let the air out. It was so easy.

"Good," Keesey said.

"What is *he* doing here?" Dalton said from across the room, pointing at Mitchell.

Keesey went over to him and commenced a hushed conversation, but at the last exchange Dalton's voice carried.

"It's cruel giving them hope, Ava!"

"Hush!" she hissed back.

Baz stayed with Mitchell, who stared through the window at the man lying curled in the gray shadows.

Morgan turned his head. His eyes opened and met Mitchell's gaze. He blinked, and movement trembled along his arm.

"He isn't dead." Mitchell pressed both fists to the door and lurched forward until his nose touched the window. "He moved, he's alive!"

Baz looked. "He hasn't moved."

"He did!"

Morgan brushed his hand along his cheek, tugging open his mouth, which was dark, bottomless and dark, like a black hole.

"Open the door! He's alive!"

Baz took hold of his shoulders and pinned him to the wall next to the hyperbaric chamber. Keesey stood in front of him. Mitchell hadn't seen her approach.

"Mitchell, what did you see? Tell me what you saw."

"There isn't time, we have to save him, we have to—"

"It's too late, Mitchell." She held his cheeks in her hands. "Tell me what you saw."

He wanted to pull away from them, their oppressive touches. He wanted to put space between them, because he didn't trust them. But Baz held him firmly against the wall, and Keesey immobilized his face so he couldn't look away. His throat tightened, and a primitive voice inside him tried to whimper.

"What did you see?"

He swallowed to clear his throat. "He turned his face. He looked at me. I saw his eyes; there was life in them."

"Baz, are his eyes open?"

"No, doctor."

"Mitchell, think about it. Does that seem possible? There's no air in that chamber."

Logic said no. Common sense said no. He swallowed again, this time to quell a growing nausea. He saw what he saw. She was asking him to deny the truth of his own observation. He said, "The M-drive isn't supposed to be possible. But it is."

Keesey held one of his arms, Baz held the other. Their grips were tight; he couldn't get away from them. If he could just get to Morgan, he'd show them. He lurched, writhed, strained to escape. Keesey pinned his upper arm between her arm and body, pulled up his sleeve, and slapped a patch on his wrist. Immediately a flush like warm syrup flowed up his arm, to his heart, to his head. His knees buckled. She and Baz lowered him to the floor.

A Keesey-shaped shadow knelt by him. She brushed her hand over his face, touching his eyes, closing his eyelids for him, and the world was dark. "Go to sleep, Mitchell. Just go to sleep."

Mitchell worked to move his lips, to say something, to scream, to curse them. To curse them for being right.

. . . an hour later he was screaming about flying monkeys to starboard . . .

Space could be described in terms of numbers and colors. Hydrogen burned orange, helium glowed red. But when the colors were wrong, he—

He couldn't remember.

He awoke in his quarters, his cell, lying on the bed. When he sat up, his belly lurched sickeningly, and he lay back down. He had seen a dead man move, and it hadn't been real.

At least, they *told* him it hadn't been real.

A navigator told the captain what departure matrices to use. They were invisible, regions in space identified only by the navigator. The captain trusted him to know the way. Captain Scott had always trusted him. He was used to being trusted. He was used to seeing what others couldn't. To doubt this, to doubt that he could see what others couldn't—he could never trust himself again.

Morgan had been trying to tell him something. That last look he had given him, those wide-open eyes. If Morgan had wanted to kill himself, there were easier ways.

He wondered what was under Jaspar's helmet. How had he tried to kill himself?

But what if Morgan hadn't been trying to kill himself? He'd gone to that specific place, like it was one end of a set of coordinates of a journey he'd plotted. That was the matrix he'd found; he'd needed to launch himself from there to get to the place he really wanted to be—away from here. The jump hadn't worked. That happened sometimes.

Morgan had tried traveling without a ship, and he'd sent Mitchell a message. Looked in his eyes and told him, *it almost worked.* They could see what no one else could.

The door opened, and Keesey appeared, smiling and happy, as if nothing bad happened, ever. She had the attitude of a doctor about to give a child an injection.

"Hello, Mitchell. How do you feel?" She'd been watching for the moment he woke, he was sure.

"Numb," he said flatly.

"The sedative's still wearing off."

"What difference does it make?"

He didn't know what was worse—being treated like a sullen teenager or discovering that he was acting like one. He didn't have any dignity left.

She continued. "I'd like to help you figure out what's going on inside your head. The kind of things a cortical map can't tell us."

He turned his head toward the wall and shut his eyes, because tears threatened to fill them. He was trapped on so many levels he'd lost count. On the station, in the ward, within his own mind.

"Nobody will ever let me on a ship again. And I don't know why. I just want to go back to the *Drake*."

After a moment of thoughtful silence, she asked a question that sounded genuine and not like a scientist fishing for answers. "If you hadn't become a navigator, what would you be?"

He'd joined Trade Guild and applied for shipboard duty because he loved space. He'd become an M-drive navigator because he could, he had the aptitude, and the Trade Guild had gladly taken him and assigned him to Mil Div. Being a navigator had seemed as close as a human being could ever get to the stars. The math was the language he used to understand space.

"Maybe mathematics. Cosmology."

"The theoretical side of M-drive navigation."

"I suppose."

He'd always visualized his journeys through space. They happened quickly, leaping over real space, but he always imagined stars, gases, nebulae soaring past him in a blaze of color.

Keesey said, "I've observed—in a completely unscientific fashion, mind you—that there are two kinds of navigators. There are those who are tested, identified as having the proper aptitude, and recruited. For them, it's a job, like any other. Then there are those who love the work, who couldn't think of doing anything else. They live for the distances between the stars. I've observed that everyone who ends up in this ward falls into the latter group."

So, those who loved navigation would eventually be destroyed by it.

One glimpse of the *Drake*. To say goodbye, to have one more chance to try and remember. If he could see the *Drake* again, he might remember. If he could see anything besides these corridors, the lab, the walls of his tiny room. A longing overcame him, a physical pain settling in his gut. He refused to wipe away tears, because if he brought his hands to his face, Keesey would know he was crying.

Careful to steady his voice, he said, "I'd like to see outside. The station has to have an observation area near the docking ports. I want to see a ship again. Any ship."

Spoken aloud, the desire sounded vague and childish.

"I'm not sure that's feasible. The sensory input might trigger another episode."

How many patients had she watched kill themselves, and still she smiled. Such blind dedication was its own insanity, but Keesey wasn't the one locked in a cell.

"Then when can I leave my quarters? I'd like to go to the common room."

"So you can talk to Dora some more? I know what she says, what she thinks. She's paranoid, in a clinical sense."

He tried sitting up again and managed to keep his stomach on an even keel. He stared at the gray rubberized floor instead of Doctor Keesey and her pitying, patronizing face.

"Dora says that all the patients here commit suicide."

"Dora says a lot of things."

I'm going to die soon. Being here, that was the only conclusion Mitchell could draw.

"She says Dalton thinks I should be locked up. Why would he think that?"

"I think you shouldn't listen to everything Dora says."

He looked up, glaring. "I don't have anyone else to talk to."

"I'm sorry, Mitchell, but we need to stabilize your neural—"

She didn't need to do anything. It was all about him, his brain; he was the one who had to live with it. He'd lost his rank somewhere. Wasn't Lieutenant anymore, just Mitchell.

"Doctor, I need to know what happened on the *Francis Drake.*"

"I'm sorry, but I don't think you should." She paused a moment, her mouth open in mid-sentence. Then changed her mind. "We haven't been able to do

much about controlling OSDS, much less curing it. The physicists who understand the M-drive don't know anything about physiology, and the doctors don't
know anything about the M-drive. Sometimes I think we're just waiting for the
genius who's an expert in both to come along and tell us what we've been doing
wrong."

Mitchell took a deep breath, ignoring the pressure of the headache that
threatened to build whenever he tried to think too hard, to dig in those places
in his mind. His own body was telling him to leave it alone.

"The colors were wrong. I remember looking at the monitor, and the colors were wrong." Something was wrong with the departure matrix. He'd chosen a course correction, an alternative that would avoid the wrongness he was
sure was there. He'd announced the course correction, he'd entered the course
correction—

Frowning, he touched his temple and shook his head. It was gone, what
happened next was gone from his mind, and the pressure was building.

Keesey gripped his wrists. Startled, he flinched back.

"Mitchell," she said, her voice stern. "Stop. Stop trying to remember. The
more you do, the more you'll exacerbate the problem. That's where the damage
started, with those memories. So just—just stop."

She let him go and went to his desk computer, typed in a few commands.
Music started, something slow and classical.

"I've disabled the screen on your computer. You only have audio output
now. I'd like you to just listen for a while. All right?"

Who was he to argue? He didn't say anything, didn't even nod or shake his
head. She wasn't giving him a choice, no need for him to respond.

She left, and the door shut and locked.

M-drives pushed ships between coordinates in space dozens of light-years apart.
Dora insisted some navigators—the elite ones, the crazy ones—could create
jump points themselves. Mitchell had never heard of such a thing. Wouldn't
someone have tried it by now?

Maybe they had and ended up here. Sedated in a featureless room, like him.

Everything that could be done could be described by mathematics. Sometimes
the equations took years to discover, and M-drive mechanics were only a hundred
years old. What if the technology could be scaled down to the size of an individual
human body? It was a nice idea to think about, so Mitchell did.

The room could be described in terms of dimension and volume. His chair,
his position on it, his distance to the door, graphed and defined.

If a memory could be delineated by the laws and structures of mathematics, then the equations defining it could be discovered, reconstructed, remembered. And he could escape from this.

The point on the middle of the plane of the door had a set of coordinates in space, identifiable along a standard set of recognized coordinates. Or he could define his own system, with that point on the door as zero-zero-zero. Any location Mitchell could wish to find himself, from any place on Law Station to, say, the bridge of the *Drake*, had another concrete set of coordinates. He had only to identify those coordinates, describe those coordinates. In those terms the entire Universe was finite, concrete, describable. In the end, those numbers defined what one could know, what one could manipulate.

That was all navigation was, identifying two points and traveling the most likely route between them. The math, the ships, the drive, were only tools that enabled people to travel more easily. But what if, what if . . . What if they'd been missing something all along?

He put his hand flat against the door that would not open for him. Given this point in space had a finite value, and some other point in space also had a finite value, and an equation could be found describing a relationship between them, and the path between them could be collapsed, the distance between them could be made into nothing. He could step through the door.

He'd done this a hundred times, sitting in the navigator station of the *Drake*. He knew the process so well, his training had ingrained it in him so thoroughly, it was part of his mind, second nature, as unconscious as dreaming.

Captain Scott said, "Greenau, do you have our heading?"

"Yes, sir. Transferred to your monitor."

And the matrix was there. He could touch it. He could put his fingers inside it, work it open wider, stretch it open, and he could climb through and out, away from here. He dug with his fingers to make the area wider, to make a doorway. He should have listened to Dora. People would be able to travel across the galaxy with a thought. No more ships, no more danger. When he stepped through the door, he'd find Keesey and show her she was wrong, that there was more happening here than a neurophysiological disorder. Humanity was on the cusp of learning something it couldn't yet control. The navigators who were patients here were only the first pioneers, sacrificed for the pursuit of knowledge. Mitchell felt proud to be in their company.

Only a little more, and the point would be wide enough for him to climb through.

"Lieutenant!"

The sound was a shockwave rattling his ears.

"Lieutenant Greenau! Mitchell!" Baz appeared out of nowhere. No—he'd opened the door, and he shoved Mitchell back, grabbing his hands.

Mitchell tried to explain. "No, it's all right. I know what I'm doing. It's all in the mathematics."

"Mitchell, focus on me. Focus."

That was what Keesey had said to Morgan. Mitchell looked at Baz, the cleanshaven face lined with worry. Mitchell's gaze furrowed with confusion.

"Mitchell, look at your hands."

He did, as Baz lifted them to hold before him.

They were bleeding, the fingertips shredded, bits of torn flesh dripping red. Mitchell lurched, trying to get away from the vision, but they were his own hands, and they followed him.

He fell against the wall, breathing hard, his arms rigid before him.

Baz touched the door controls. The door shut, revealing a red stain, blood smeared across the metal from the point through which Mitchell had been trying to escape. He'd rubbed his hands raw and bleeding against the door. Where he'd seen a jump matrix, there'd been nothing.

So what had there been when he directed the *Drake* to those coordinates, the ones he'd been so sure were safe?

"Come on, Mitchell. Come on, buddy." Baz manhandled him off the floor, got him to stand, and walked him, puppet-like, to the infirmary. He murmured condescending encouragements. Mitchell heard them only distantly. He kept staring at his hands, which were the wrong color.

This time when he woke up, he was restrained. His hands, still stiff and sore from treatment, rested at his sides. He couldn't move his legs. He lurched up anyway, thinking he must have been imagining it, that he couldn't really be tied to the bed. He got his shoulders off the padding, then had to stop, because no matter how much he pulled and strained, he couldn't move any farther.

He rattled his hands to make the bindings rub and squinted against the searing light that lanced pain through his mind. His whole head throbbed.

"Please," he said, clearing a hoarseness from his throat. "Turn the lights down, please. They're too bright."

"The lights aren't on, Mitchell," said Doctor Keesey's voice, but he couldn't see her, couldn't even tell where she was. She might have been close by and whispering. He winced. He knew he was in the infirmary. It smelled like the infirmary. He didn't know anything else.

"I don't understand." The rich tone of despair in his own voice startled him. The voice came from another place, far from here, a place he hadn't yet arrived.

Someone touched his arm, and he let out a startled yelp, because he hadn't heard anyone approach the bed, but someone must have. Another dose of sedative warmed his blood, soothed his muscles, and he fell asleep gratefully.

Another voice woke him, this one speaking very close by.

"I don't have much time, Mitchell. But I wanted to talk to you. You did it, didn't you?"

He opened his eyes and was more relieved than he could have imagined to see the beds, supply cupboards, and equipment of the infirmary around him, gray and lurking in the dimmed to near-nothing light.

Dora was leaning on the bed, speaking close to his ear.

"Dora." His mouth was sticky, his throat dry. His wrinkled jumpsuit scratched against his skin, his scalp itched, and he suspected he smelled ripe. He felt like an invalid, too sick for the luxury of a shower.

"Easy." She rested a hand tenderly on his arm. "Mitchell. You have to tell me how you did it."

"Did what?"

"Saved Morgan. You saw him—the orderlies were talking about it. You saw his soul pass on. That was what you saw, wasn't it? He jumped to the next phase, and you saw it, and you're getting ready to follow him. I want to know how you did it."

Mitchell stared at her, meeting her wild-eyed gaze. Her fingers clenched on his jumpsuit, like she expected him to help her somehow, even though he was the one strapped to the bed. One of her hands had a fresh white bandage wrapped around it.

"You aren't supposed to be here, are you?"

"I cut my hand. I did it so they'd bring me here." She displayed the bandage. "I had to talk to you. You have to tell me what you saw."

"I don't know what I saw, Dora. I don't know." His visual cortex was damaged . . .

"But you do. You're special. You are, Dalton says so. Tell me about Morgan. Tell me."

Baz or one of the doctors must have been in the next room, distracted while Dora stole in to speak with him. Dora's urgency must have meant she didn't have much time until they discovered her and returned her to her quarters. Which meant Mitchell didn't have much time, either.

He had to learn to the truth.

"Dora, untie me. Undo the straps, please. Then I'll tell you."

Nodding slowly, she touched the straps, studied them a moment, then moved to a control panel at the head of the bed. She tapped a couple of keys, and the tension on the straps released. He could move his feet, and by wriggling his hands he freed his wrists.

Dora held his hand and pressed something flat into the palm.

"I took Baz's wristband. He didn't notice. You're going to follow Morgan, aren't you?"

"Maybe, maybe—"

"Dora!" Keesey called, reprimanding, from across the room. "Dora, I asked you to wait in the chair."

Mitchell wrapped his hands around the loose straps and hoped the doctor didn't examine him too closely. Dora didn't move until Keesey called again.

"Dora."

Slowly, Dora stepped away, her gaze still on him, not wavering, until she reached the doorway where Keesey was waiting. The doctor was a shadow, indistinct in the room's dimness, but he recognized her shape, her posture.

"Mitchell?" she said. "Are you all right?"

He swallowed back a laugh. "Not really."

"I know this is difficult." She sounded sympathetic, but it was the sympathy of a person who didn't really know what she was sympathizing with. "I'll come back to talk with you in a little while, all right?"

"Sure."

When she was gone, he slid off the bed to his feet, and his head swam and vision wavered. He was still tired and woozy; whether from the remnants of the sedative or his rebellious senses, he didn't know. He was ill. He could admit that now. It only meant he had to be a little more careful. He slipped Baz's band around his wrist.

The corridor was empty. He reached the first bulkhead door. He showed the wristband to the scanner.

The door slipped open, an escape portal, and a weight lifted from his mind. Free. He could run if he wanted.

You're going to follow Morgan.

If he could only see space again, see ships traveling against the backdrop of stars, he'd remember, and everything would be all right. He'd remember and tell them what really happened.

He passed the common room. Only Jaspar was inside, which was too bad. If Sonia had been there, he might have asked her if she wanted to go with him. It didn't matter what she replied; the words that came out of her mouth didn't matter, as long as she went with him.

Still working on impulse, he crossed the room and took hold of the man's helmet. Jaspar looked up at him. If he had looked at all confused or scared, Mitchell would have left him alone. But the man looked resigned. So Mitchell took off the helmet. His stomach spasmed with shock.

Jaspar was missing about a third of his skull, a great bite taken out of the right side, from his temple to the top of his ear and disappearing around to the back. A jagged edge of bone showed under his skin, which stretched to cover the remains of his head, dipping like a sinkhole into a concave space where the right half of his brain should have been. Looking at him from the left side, one might never guess he had anything wrong with him. From the front, he was a ruin.

Mitchell carefully set the helmet back in place. It protected whatever was left.

"What happened to you?" Mitchell breathed. Jaspar looked back and couldn't say.

Everyone here commits suicide.

Whatever Jaspar had done hadn't been successful. Mitchell turned and ran.

He coded open the next bulkhead door and left the ward. He could tell by the smell, which turned industrial instead of antiseptic. The corridor branched ahead, and Mitchell guessed which one would lead him to the center of the station, to the docking area. Other people he encountered struck him as strange-looking, as if he were traveling in a foreign country. He took calming breaths and tried not to look out of place. He knew the formulae that could take him from one end of the galaxy to the other. There ought to be formulae, equations, to do anything. He should find a way to turn invisible, so no one would see him. Visibility was all a matter of light and color. Space was color, the color of numbers. He could make himself transparent.

The corridor he followed now was straight, not curved, indicating he was walking along one of the spokes, toward the center of the cylindrical station. The gravity should be lessening. Mitchell stretched, lengthening his stride, to see if he could fly yet.

He keyed himself through two more bulkhead doors. Other corridors branched off to different levels, other departments, other wards. Mitchell's heart lurched at the sight of blue Mil Div uniforms. He almost stopped to study the faces of those who wore them to see if Captain Scott was among them, if he recognized any of his crewmates. But that was unlikely. Surely the *Drake* had left the station by now.

Mitchell's steps developed spring, but he wasn't yet weightless. Ahead, the corridor opened into a wider thoroughfare, large enough for mechanized carts to travel. Equipment lockers lined the walls, vacuum suit closets in place between airlock doors. He could just go through the airlock and fly away. He could follow Morgan into an airless world.

He turned right and looked for an observation area.

"Mitchell! Mitchell, stop!" Both Keesey and Dalton appeared at the intersection of the corridor.

Mitchell ran.

"Stop him! Somebody stop him!"

He hunched his shoulders and kept on, grimly staring ahead, anticipating obstacles. Station personnel stared after him, shocked, or looked back at Keesey and Dalton pounding after him. Ahead, the corridor bulged outward. In most station designs, this meant there was some kind of work area, often with view ports that would let him see the ships in the dockyards. He was almost there. He just needed a glimpse of a ship's running lights in space.

Somebody tackled him. A man half a head taller wearing a Mil Div uniform enclosed him in a bear hug and slammed him against the far wall. Mitchell's head rang with the impact. He couldn't hope to escape. He tried anyway, bucking and thrashing against his captor.

"Mitchell, look at me! Look at me!" Sweaty hands pressed against his cheeks. He shook his head, trying to break free of their grasp. "Mitchell!" Keesey shouted, pleading.

You're going to follow Morgan.

He begged, "Let me look! I just want to look! I'm not going to kill myself, I'm not going to do anything! I haven't done anything! Let me go!"

Multiple grips pinned his arms to the wall now. Others had come to help, he didn't know how many. The more he struggled, the harder they held him. When he felt his sleeve being pushed up, he knew it meant somebody wielded a sedative patch.

Mitchell screamed in defiance; his voice echoing in the steel corridor startled him. "Mitchell!" Keesey managed to make herself heard over his noise. He clamped his mouth shut.

In the sudden quiet, the scene paused for a moment. Dalton held the patch ready but hadn't yet pressed it against his arm.

Softly, Mitchell said, "Let me look. Just let me look outside one more time. Please. Please trust me. Please."

This was his last chance at life.

He saw his desperation clearly reflected back at him in Keesey's gaze. He thought he knew: She wanted to cure all her patients, and she kept failing. In him she was failing again.

He whispered, "You've never tried giving us what we want. What can it hurt? I'm already dead. Let me look."

Dalton released him first. Then Keesey said, "Let him go."

It had taken two others besides the doctors to restrain him. They all stepped back, tense, even Keesey, like he was a wild animal and they couldn't predict what he'd do next. He moved deliberately, brushing his sleeves back into place. He would give them no cause to capture him like an animal and drag him back to the cage. Keeping a shoulder to the wall, he moved toward the observation area. The others followed, forming a half-circle around him, penning him in.

At last he rounded the corner, entered the darkened observation area, and his knees almost buckled. He leaned against the wall, and his eyes stung with tears.

The windows looked out over the edge of the dockyards where Law Station opened into space. A trio of ships was in dock and there was a scattering of light from the hull of the station—traffic guides, lights shining out of other view ports. The rest of the view looked into the black and the points of light of distant stars.

The Universe opened before him. This was seeing home after a long, impossible journey.

He put his face close to the window and cupped his hands around his eyes to cut out reflections.

Ships, bulging lengths of steel, drifted in the open. The blisters of modular sections—decks, sensory apparatus, weaponry, docking space—made their silhouettes uneven, monstrous, confusing. The shapes distracted the eye, which looked for the streamlined profile of something that might swim through water but only found these accreted, inartistic objects. Yet they moved so gracefully. The eye could not judge their scale against the backdrop of shadow and gray steel. He was watching a scene impossibly distant. Yet the lights threatened to swallow him.

One of the ships was a Research Division cruiser, probably returned from a frontier mission for a refit. The other two were Mil Div. The far one—his heart fluttered, because it was a courier class, a sleek, minimalist ship built for speed, blockade running and dodging firing lines. The *Francis Drake* was a courier. They were the prettiest ships in the fleet. It might even be—hard to tell from here.

His brow furrowed, he pulled away from the window. "Is that the *Drake* in dock?"

"Yes," Keesey said.

"She should be long gone by now." He turned back to the window, rubbed his sleeve over it when his breath fogged it.

"Look again."

He watched for a long time, as long as he needed. The ship was locked into longterm docking, not simply linked by umbilical and airlock tubes like the other ships. She'd been damaged, a hole blasted into her starboard side as if a great monster had taken a bite out of her. Lights moved around her like fluttering insects: repair drones, suited workers on maneuvering platforms. A search light happened to run over the name written in bold cursive: *M.D.S. Franc—*. The remaining letters were charred.

The ship looked a little like Jaspar's skull.

His mind formed the question, *what happened,* but he did not speak the words. A neural pathway that had been ruptured rebuilt itself when offered the proper bridge.

He pressed his hand to the window.

He put his thumb on the duty roster scanner inside the hatchway to the bridge. "Good morning, Captain."

Captain Crea Scott spared a glance over her shoulder. "Lieutenant. We have an hour until we need to jump. That enough time?"

"Yes, sir. The arrival matrix data's on the console?"

"Ready and waiting."

After two years together on the *Francis Drake* their routine was well practiced. He passed along the bridge's upper walkway, paying only cursory attention to the displays and consoles that monitored the ship's systems, nodding to the crewmates who looked up from their work, and arrived at the hatchway leading down to the navigator station.

M-drive navigation was a one-person booth isolated from the rest of the bridge. He settled into the couch, belted in, and activated the console. Monitors, scanners, processors lit up, casting a cool glow and humming comfortably. It was his own realm—quiet, secure, and powerful. Here, he controlled the equipment that could propel the ship light-years across space.

He clipped his comm piece over his ear and called up the navigation data, destination, and optimum window of arrival. With the ease of habit, he started the process that would identify the departure matrix for the most efficient jump to the designated arrival matrix.

Departure matrices flashed on the holographic display in unfamiliar hues. He frowned, reviewed the data, then cleared the equations. He had time; he'd simply run the calculations over again.

If he weren't entirely clear on which matrix they left from and where they were arriving, the ship would break apart as it tried to make the crossing. An anomaly in the possible departure matrices made him pause. If he wasn't certain about a matrix, he rejected it.

He'd never failed to find a departure matrix before. The Universe was massive and diverse; a solution could always be found. But this time they were all mouths, ready to swallow him, spitting out the wrong colors. The numbers cycled and showed him a void.

Except one. There it was, the solution. The matrix that would carry them safely away from this hole in space. He entered it, and the numbers flashed red.

Captain Scott said over the comm, "Greenau, do you have our heading?"

"Yes, sir. Departure matrix data transferred."

A silence answered him. The workings of the ship hummed and murmured.

"Greenau, send those coordinates again, please."

He did, with a touch of frustration.

"We can't follow that heading, Lieutenant. Those coordinates are inside the hull of the ship."

Of course not, the M-drive would push the ship into itself, making for one hell of an explosion. But Mitchell couldn't ignore the numbers.

"It's the only one, Captain." All the other colors were wrong.

"Mitchell, are you all right?"

"There aren't any other matrices. The space here is wrong. The colors are wrong."

"Oh my God—"

They didn't know it, they couldn't see what he saw. He had to save them.

He'd fought as every crewmember on the bridge tried to stop him, because he thought he was saving them. That he could see something no one else could see. It never occurred to him that he'd gone mad. They'd seen it instantly—everyone knew what could happen to navigators, they all knew the symptoms. Still, he'd managed to get to the helm and punch in the drive protocol with the faulty departure matrix still entered—

They should have killed him before letting him get that far. They stopped short because he was theirs.

Parts of three levels ripped open instantly, spilling the ship's guts to the void. Captain Scott managed to cut all the ship's power, deactivating the drive before the ship was destroyed completely. The ship's medics sedated Mitchell. The accident had killed twenty people, a third of the crew. Through sheer, stubborn heroism, Scott and the remaining crew patched up the ship and managed to fly to Law, the closest outpost. There, Lieutenant Mitchell Greenau could be deposited with people who might be able to explain what had gone wrong with his mind.

Head bowed, Mitchell knelt on the floor below the window as Doctor Keesey explained.

"The dysfunction usually develops gradually. The patient experiences memory loss, synesthesia, schizophrenia, dystonia, ataxia—any number of neurological anomalies. The captain of the ship will take a navigator off duty at the first signs. A sudden, catastrophic episode like yours is very rare."

Who had died? He wanted to ask, but he doubted Keesey would know. Twenty names were too many to remember. But Mitchell would have to learn someday who among his friends and colleagues he had killed.

"You saw the right numbers, like you always saw," Keesey said. "But your mind showed you something else."

"Captain Scott didn't want me to know what happened."

"Because she knew it wasn't your fault. It's a terrible memory. I'm sorry."

A memory that, for all he had struggled to reclaim it, now felt pristine, nestled in the center of his mind.

Mitchell felt calm now. Dalton stood nearby, and Keesey knelt beside him; both were watchful, like they expected him to break, or burst, or something, with the knowledge he had found.

Keesey finally said, "Mitchell, how do you feel?"

He despised that question.

He chuckled a little. "I'm sorry. I'm so sorry—"

"Mitchell—"

He could look up, and even at this awkward angle he could see lights on the opposite curve of the station, the blackness of the shadows. The beauty was an ache in his gut. That he could still feel that beauty startled him. "Don't isolate us from what makes us happy. We kill ourselves trying to get back to it."

"Are you ready to come back to the ward?"

He climbed to his feet, using the wall as a prop. He looked out the window again to the stark vastness of even this little corner of space. "Just another minute, Doctor."

They waited for him.

When Mitchell finally returned to the common room, Dora wasn't there. She'd made an escape attempt and had been sedated.

Jaspar was at his usual table, working his word puzzles on his handheld. Mitchell found what had happened to him: he'd tried to close his head in a bulkhead door. No one knew why. The trauma team got to him quickly, and he'd survived, somehow. People were resilient.

Sonia was also present, humming, her eyes closed. Mitchell sat across from her.

He placed a player with earpieces in front of her. She stopped humming. She looked at him, her gaze narrowed and confused.

"It's yours."

Her hands trembling, she reached for the headphones. They skittered away from her fingertips the first time, but she caught them, slapping her hand to the table. Then she hooked on the earpieces.

Mitchell had gotten Keesey to give him records of Sonia's musical vocabulary, all the pieces of music she'd been known to speak of. He convinced the doctors to let her have the player.

She touched the play key. Her face tightened, an expression of anxious disbelief. Then tears slipped down her cheeks. Mitchell heard the music, a faint buzzing through the earpieces, and his fists clenched nervously. He thought she would smile. He wanted her to smile.

Then she did smile, though she still didn't relax, and Mitchell realized that she was concentrating on the music with every muscle she had. She met his gaze, and he thought she looked happy.

James Patrick Kelly has won the Hugo, Nebula and Locus awards. He has written novels, short stories, essays, reviews, poetry, plays and planetarium shows. His most recent publications are the novel *Mother Go* (2017), an audiobook original from Audible and the collection *The Promise of Space* (2018) from Prime Books. In 2016, Centipede Press published a career retrospective *Masters of Science Fiction: James Patrick Kelly*. His fiction has been translated into eighteen languages. He writes a column on the internet for *Asimov's Science Fiction Magazine* and is on the faculty of the Stonecoast Creative Writing MFA Program at the University of Southern Maine. Find him on the web at www.jimkelly.net.

THE WRECK OF THE GODSPEED

JAMES PATRICK KELLY

DAY ONE

What do we know about Adel Ranger Santos?

That he was sixty-five percent oxygen, nineteen percent carbon, ten percent hydrogen, three percent nitrogen, two percent calcium, one percent phosphorus, some potassium, sulfur, sodium, chlorine, magnesium, iodine and iron and just a trace of chromium, cobalt, copper, fluorine, manganese, molybdenum, selenium, tin, vanadium and zinc. That he was of the domain *Eukarya*, the kingdom of *Animalia*, the phylum *Chordata*, subphylum *Vertebrata*, the class *Mammalia*, the order *Primates*, the family *Hominidae*, the genus *Homo* and the species *Novo*. That, like the overwhelming majority of the sixty trillion people on the worlds of Human Continuum, he was a hybrid cybernetic/biological system composed of intricate subsystems including the circulatory, digestive, endocrine, excretory, informational, integumenary, musculo-skeletal, nervous, psycho-spiritual, reproductive, and respiratory. That he was the third son of Venetta Patience Santos, an Elector of the Host of True Flesh and Halbert Constant Santos, a baker of fine breads. That he was male, left-handed, somewhat introverted, intelligent but no genius, a professed but frustrated heterosexual, an Aries, a virgin, a delibertarian, an agnostic and a swimmer. That he was nineteen Earth standard years old and that until he stumbled, naked, out of the molecular assembler onto the *Godspeed* he had never left his home world.

The woman caught Adel before he sprawled headlong off the transport stage. "Slow down." She was taller and wider than any of the women he'd known; he felt like a toy in her arms. "You made it, you're here." She straightened him and stepped back to get a look. "Is there a message?"

*—a message?—*buzzed Adel's plus.

minus buzzed—yes give us clothes—

Normally Adel kept his opposites under control. But he'd just been scanned, transmitted at superluminal speeds some two hundred and fifty-seven light-years, and reassembled on a threshold bound for the center of the Milky Way.

"Did they say anything?" The woman's face was tight. "Back home?"

Adel shook his head; he had no idea what she was talking about. He hadn't yet found his voice, but it was understandable if he was a little jumbled. His skin felt a size too small and he shivered in the cool air. This was probably the most important moment of his life and all he could think was that his balls had shrunk to the size of raisins.

"You're not . . . ? All right then." She covered her disappointment so quickly that Adel wondered if he'd seen it at all. "Well, let's get some clothes on you, Rocky."

minus buzzed—who's Rocky?—

"What, didn't your tongue make the jump with the rest of you?" She was wearing green scrubs and green open-toed shoes. A oval medallion on a silver chain hung around her neck; at its center a pix displayed a man eating soup. "Can you understand me?" Her mouth stretched excessively, as if she intended that he read her lips. "I'm afraid I don't speak carrot, or whatever passes for language on your world." She was carrying a blue robe folded over her arm.

"Harvest," said Adel. "I came from Harvest."

"He talks," said the woman. "Now can he walk? And what will it take to get him to say his name?"

"I'm Adel Santos."

"Good." She tossed the robe at him and it slithered around his shoulders and wrapped him in its soft embrace. "If you have a name then I don't have to throw you back." Two slippers unfolded from its pockets and snugged onto his feet. She began to speak with a nervous intensity that made Adel dizzy. "So, Adel, my name is Kamilah, which means 'the perfect one' in Arabic which is a dead language you've probably never heard of and I'm here to give you the official welcome to your pilgrimage aboard the *Godspeed* and to show you around but we have to get done before dinner which tonight is synthetic roasted garab . . ."

—something is bothering her—buzzed minus—it must be us—

" . . . which is either a bird or a tuber, I forget which exactly but it comes from the cuisine of Ohara which is a world in the Zeta 1 Reticuli system which you've probably never heard of . . ."

—*probably just a talker—plus buzzed.*

" . . . because I certainly never have." Kamilah wore her hair kinked close against her head; it was the color of rust. She was cute, thought Adel, in a massive sort of way. "Do you understand?"

"Perfectly," he said. "You did say you were perfect."

"So you listen?" A grin flitted across her face. "Are you going to surprise me, Adel Santos?"

"I'll try," he said. "But first I need a bathroom."

There were twenty-eight bathrooms on the *Godspeed*; twenty of them opened off the lavish bedrooms of Dream Street. A level below was the Ophiuchi Dining Hall, decorated in red alabaster, marble and gilded bronze, which could seat as many as forty around its teak banquet table. In the more modest Chillingsworth Breakfasting Room, reproductions of four refectory tables with oak benches could accommodate more intimate groups. Between the Blue and the Dagger Salons was the Music Room with smokewood lockers filled with the noblest instruments from all the worlds of the Continuum, most of which could play themselves. Below that was a library with the complete range of inputs from brainleads to books made of actual plant material, a ballroom decorated in the Nomura III style, a VR dome with ten animated seats, a gymnasium with a lap pool, a black box theater, a billiard room, a conservatory with five different ecosystems and various stairways, hallways, closets, cubbies, and peculiar dead ends. The MASTA, the molecular array scanner/transmitter/assembler was located in the Well Met Arena, an enormous airlock and staging area that opened onto the surface of the threshold. Here also was the cognizor in which the mind of the *Godspeed* seethed.

It would be far too convenient to call the *Godspeed* mad. Better to say that for some time she had been behaving like no other threshold. Most of our pioneering starships were built in hollowed out nickel-iron asteroids—a few were set into fabricated shells. All were propelled by matter-antimatter drives that could reach speeds of just under a hundred thousand kilometers per second, about a third of the speed of light. We began to launch them from the far frontiers of the Continuum a millennium ago to search for terrestrial planets that were either habitable or might profitably be made so. Our thresholds can scan planetary systems of promising stars as far away as twenty light-years. When one discovers a suitably terrestrial world, it decelerates and swings into orbit. News of the find is immediately dispatched at superluminal speed to all the worlds of the Continuum; almost immediately materials and technicians appear on the transport stage. Over the course of several years we build a new orbital station containing a second MASTA, establishing a permanent link to the Continuum. Once the link is secured, the threshold continues on its voyage of discovery. In all, the *Godspeed* had founded thirty-seven colonies in exactly this way.

The life of a threshold follows a pattern: decades of monotonous acceleration, cruising and deceleration punctuated by a few years of intense and glorious activity. Establishing a colony is an ultimate affirmation of human culture and even the cool intelligences generated by the cognizors of our thresholds share in the camaraderie of techs and colonists. Thresholds take justifiable pride in their accomplishments; many have had worlds named for them. However, when the time comes to move on, we expect our thresholds to dampen their enthusiasms and abort their nascent emotions to steel themselves against the tedium of crawling between distant stars at three-tenths the speed of light.

Which all of them did—except for the *Godspeed*.

As they were climbing up the Tulip Stairway to the Dream Halls, Adel and Kamilah came upon two men making their way down, bound together at the waist by a tether. The tether was about a meter long and two centimeters in diameter; it appeared to be elastic. One side of it pulsed bright red and the other was a darker burgundy. The men were wearing baggy pants and gray jackets with tall, buttoned collars that made them look like birds.

"Adel," said Kamilah, "meet Jonman and Robman."

Jonman looked like he could have been Robman's father, but Adel knew better than to draw any conclusions from that. On some worlds, he knew, physiological camouflage was common practice.

Jonman gazed right through Adel. "I can see that he knows nothing about the problem." He seemed detached, as if he were playing chess in his head.

Kamilah gave him a sharp glance but said nothing. Robman stepped forward and extended his forefinger in greeting. Adel gave it a polite touch.

"This is our rookie, then?" said Robman. "Do you play tikra, Adel?"

—*who's a rookie?—buzzed minus.*

—*we are*—

Since Adel didn't know what tikra was, he assumed that he didn't play it. "Not really," he said.

"He's from one of the farm worlds," said Kamilah

"Oh, a rustic." Robman cocked his head to one side, as if Adel might make sense to him if viewed from a different angle. "Do they have gulpers where you come from? Cows?" Seeing the blank look on Adel's face, he pressed on. "Maybe frell?"

"Blue frell, yes."

—keep talking—plus buzzed—make an impression—

Adel lunged into conversation. "My uncle Durwin makes summer sausage from frell loin. He built his own smoke house."

Robman frowned.

"It's very good." Adel had no idea where he was going with this bit of family history. "The sausages, I mean. He's a butcher."

—and we're an idiot—

"He's from one of the farm worlds," said Jonman, as if he were catching up with their chitchat on a time delay.

"Yes," said Robman. "He makes sausages."

Jonman nodded as if this explained everything about Adel. "Then don't be late for dinner," he advised. "I see there will be garab tonight." With this, the two men continued downstairs.

Adel glanced at Kamilah, hoping she might offer some insight into Robman and Jonman. Her eyes were hooded. "I wouldn't play anything with them if I were you," she murmured. "Jonman has a stochastic implant. Not only does he calculate probabilities, but he cheats."

The top of the Tulip Stairway ended at the midpoint of Dream Street. "Does everything have a name here?" asked Adel.

"Pretty much," said Kamilah. "It tells you something about how bored the early crews must have been. We're going right." The ceiling of Dream Street glowed with a warm light that washed Kamilah's face with pink. She said the names of bedroom suites as they passed the closed doors. "This is Fluxus. The Doghouse. We have room for twenty pilgrims, twice that if we want to double up."

The carpet was a sapphire plush that clutched at Adel's sandals as he shuffled down the hall.

"Chrome over there. That's where Upwood lived. He's gone now. You don't know anything about him, do you?" Her voice was suddenly tight. "Upwood Marcene?"

"No, should I? Is he famous?"

"Not famous, no." The medallion around her neck showed a frozen lake. "He jumped home last week, which leaves us with only seven, now that you're here." She cleared her throat and the odd moment of tension passed. "This is Corazon. Forty Pushups. We haven't found a terrestrial in ages, so Speedy isn't as popular as she used to be."

"You call the threshold Speedy?"

"You'll see." Kamilah sighed. "And this is Cella. We might as well see if Sister is receiving." She pressed her hand to the door and said, "Kamilah here." She waited.

"What do you want, Kamilah?" said the door, a solid blue slab that featured neither latch nor knob.

"I have the new arrival here."

"It's inconvenient." The door sighed. "But I'm coming." It vanished and before them stood a tiny creature, barely up to Adel's waist. She was wearing a hat that looked like a birds nest made of black ribbon with a smoky veil that covered her eyes. Her mouth was thin and severe. All he could see of her almond skin was the dimpled chin and her long elegant neck; the billowing sleeves of her loose black dress swallowed her hands.

"Adel Santos, this is Lihong Rain. She prefers to be called Sister." Sister might have been a child or she might have been a grandmother. Adel couldn't tell.

"Safe passage, Adel." She made no other welcoming gesture.

Adel hesitated, wondering if he should try to initiate contact. But what kind? Offer to touch fingers? Shake hands? Maybe he should catch her up in his arms and dance a two-step.

"Same to you, Sister," he said and bowed.

"I was praying just now." He could feel her gaze even though he couldn't see it. "Are you religious, Brother Adel?" The hair on the back of his neck stood up.

"I'd prefer to be just Adel, if you don't mind," he said. "And no, I'm not particularly religious, I'm afraid."

She sagged, as if he had just piled more weight on her frail shoulders. "Then I will pray for you. If you will excuse me." She stepped back into her room and the blue door reformed.

plus buzzed—we were rude to her—

—we told the truth—

"Don't worry," said Kamilah. "You can't offend her. Or rather, you can't *not* offend her, since just about everything we do seems to offend her. Which is why she spends almost all her time in her room. She claims she's praying, although Speedy only knows for sure. So I'm in Delhi here, and next door you're in The Ranch."

—Kamilah's next door?—buzzed minus.

—we hardly know her don't even think it—

—too late—

They stopped in front of the door to his room, which was identical to Sister's, except it was green. "Press your right hand to it anywhere, say your name and it will ID you." After Adel followed these instructions, the door considered for a moment and then vanished with a hiss.

Adel guessed that the room was supposed to remind him of home. It didn't exactly, because he'd lived with his parents in a high rise in Great Randall, only two kilometers from Harvest's first MASTA. But it was like houses he had visited out in the countryside. Uncle Durwin's, for example. Or the Pariseaus'. The floor appeared to be of some blondish tongue-and-grooved wood. Two of the walls were set to show a golden tallgrass prairie with a herd of chocolate-colored beasts grazing in the distance. Opposite a rolltop desk were three wooden chairs with velvet upholstered seats gathered around a low oval table. A real plant with leaves like green hearts guarded the twin doorways that opened into the bedroom and the bathroom.

Adel's bed was king-sized with a half moon head and footboards tied to posts that looked like tree trunks with the bark stripped off. It had a salmon-colored bedspread with twining rope pattern. However, we should point out that Adel did not notice anything at all about his bed until much later.

—oh no—

"Hello," said Adel.

—oh yes—

"Hello yourself, lovely boy." The woman was propped on a nest of pillows. She was wearing a smile and shift spun from fog. It wisped across her slim, almost boyish, body concealing very little. Her eyes were wide and the color of honey. Her hair was spiked in silver.

Kamilah spoke from behind him. "Speedy, he just stepped off the damn stage ten minutes ago. He's not thinking of fucking."

"He's a nineteen year old male, which means he can't think of anything but fucking." She had a wet, whispery voice, like waves washing against pebbles. "Maybe he doesn't like girls. I like being female, but I certainly don't have to be." Her torso flowed beneath the fog and her legs thickened.

"Actually, I do," said Adel. "Like girls, I mean."

"Then forget Speedy." Kamilah crossed the room to the bed and stuck her hand through the shape on the bed. It was all fog, and Kamilah's hand parted it. "This is just a fetch that Speedy projects when she feels like bothering us in person."

"I have to keep my friends company," said the *Godspeed.*

"You can keep him company later." Kamilah swiped both hands through the fetch and she disappeared. "Right now he's going to put some clothes on and then we're going to find Meri and Jarek," she said.

"Wait," said Adel. "What did you do to her? Where did she go?"

"She's still here," Kamilah said. "She's always everywhere, Adel. You'll get used to it."

"But what did she want?"

The wall to his right shimmered and became a mirror image of the bedroom. The *Godspeed* was back in her nest on his bed. "To give you a preview of coming attractions, lovely boy."

Kamilah grasped Adel by the shoulders, turned him away from the wall and aimed him at the closet. "Get changed," she said. "I'll be in the sitting room."

Hanging in the closet were three identical peach-colored uniforms with blue piping at the seams. The tight pantaloons had straps that would pass under the instep of his feet. The dress blue blouse had the all-too-familiar pulsing heart patch over the left breast. The jacket had a double row of enormous silver zippers and bore two merit pins which proclaimed Adel a true believer of the Host of True Flesh.

Except that he wasn't.

Adel had long since given up on his mother's little religion but had never found a way to tell her. Seeing his uniforms filled him with guilt and dread. He'd come two hundred and fifty-seven light-years and he had still not escaped her. He'd expected she would pack the specs for True Flesh uniforms in his luggage transmission, but he'd thought she'd send him at least some civilian clothes as well.

—we have to lose the clown suit—

"So how long are you here for?" called Kamilah from the next room.

"A year," replied Adel. "With a second year at my option." Then he whispered, "Speedy, can you hear me?"

"Always. Never doubt it." Her voice came from the tall blue frell-leather boots that were part of his uniform. "Are we going to have secrets from Kamilah? I love secrets."

"I need something to wear," he whispered. "Anything but this."

"A year with an option?" Kamilah called. "Gods, Adel! Who did you murder?"

"Are we talking practical?" said the *Godspeed*. "Manly? Artistic? Rebellious?"

He stooped and spoke directly into left boot. "Something basic," he said. "Scrubs like Kamilah's will be fine for now."

Two blobs extruded from the closet wall and formed into drab pants and a shirt.

"Adel?" called Kamilah. "Are you all right?"

"I didn't murder anyone." He stripped off the robe and pulled briefs from a drawer. At least the saniwear wasn't official True Flesh. "I wrote an essay."

Softwalks bloomed from the floor. "The hair on your legs, lovely boy, is like the wire that sings in my walls." The *Godspeed*'s voice was a purr.

The closet seemed very small then. As soon as he'd shimmied into his pants, Adel grabbed the shirt and the softwalks and escaped. He didn't bother with socks.

"So how did you get here, Kamilah?" He paused in the bedroom to pull on the shirt before entering the sitting room.

"I was sent here as a condition of my parole."

"Really?" Adel sat on one of the chairs and snapped on his softwalks. "Who did you murder?"

"I was convicted of improper appropriation," she said. "I misused a symbol set that was alien to my cultural background."

—*say again?*—buzzed minus.

Adel nodded and smiled. "I have no idea what that means."

"That's all right." Her medallion showed a fist. "It's a long story for another time."

We pause here to reflect on the variety of religious beliefs in the Human Continuum. In ancient times, atheists believed that humanity's expansion into space would extinguish its historic susceptibility to superstition. And for a time, as we rode primitive torches to our cramped habitats and attempted to terraform the mostly-inhospitable worlds of our home system, this expectation seemed reasonable. But then the discovery of quantum scanning and the perfection of molecular assembly led to the building of the first MASTA systems and everything changed.

Quantum scanning is, after all, destructive. Depending on exactly what has been placed on the stage, that which is scanned is reduced to mere probabilistic wisps, an exhausted scent or perhaps just soot to be wiped off the sensors. In order to jump from one MASTA to another, we must be prepared to die. Of course, we're only dead for a few seconds, which is the time it takes for the assembler to reconstitute us from a scan. Nevertheless, the widespread acceptance of MASTA transportation means that all of us who had come to thresholds have died and been reborn.

The experience of transitory death has led *homo novo* to a renewed engagement with the spiritual. But if the atheists were disappointed in their predictions of the demise of religion, the creeds of antiquity were decimated by the new realities of superluminal culture. Ten thousand new religions have risen up on the many worlds of the Continuum to comfort and sustain us in our various needs. We worship stars, sex, the vacuum of space, water, the cosmic microwave background, the Uncertainty Principle, music, old trees, cats, the weather, dead bodies, certain pharaohs of the Middle Kingdom, food, stimulants, depressants, and Levia Calla. We call the deity by many names: Genius, the Bitch, Kindly One, the Trickster, the Alien, the Thumb, Sagittarius A*, the Silence, Surprise, and the Eternal Center. What is striking about this exuberant diversity, when we consider how much blood has been shed in the name of gods, is our universal tolerance of one another. But that's because all of us who acknowledge the divine are co-religionists in one crucial regard: we affirm that the true path to spirituality must necessarily pass across the stages of a MASTA.

Which is another reason why we build thresholds and launch them to spread the Continuum. Which is why so many of our religions count it as an essential pilgrimage to travel with a threshold on some fraction of its long journey. Which is why the Host of True Flesh on the planet Harvest sponsored an essay contest opened to any communicant who had not yet died to go superluminal, the first prize being an all-expense paid pilgrimage to the *Godspeed*, the oldest, most distant, and therefore holiest of all the thresholds. Which is why Venetta Patience Santos had browbeaten her son Adel to enter the contest.

Adel's reasons for writing his essay had been his own. He had no great faith in the Host and no burning zeal to make a pilgrimage. However he chafed under the rules his parents still imposed on him, and he'd just broken up with his girlfriend Gavrila over the issue of pre-marital intercourse—he being in favor, she taking a decidedly contrary position—and he'd heard steamy rumors of what passed for acceptable sexual behavior on a threshold at the farthest edge of civilization. Essay contestants were charged to express the meaning of the Host of True Flesh in five hundred words or less. Adel brought his in at four hundred and nine.

Our Place
By Adel Ranger Santos

We live in a place. This seems obvious, maybe, but think about it. Originally our place was a little valley on the African continent on a planet called Earth. Who we are today was shaped in large part by the way that place was, so long ago. Later humans moved all around that planet and found new places to live. Some were hot, some freezing. We lived at the top of mountains and on endless prairies. We sailed to islands. We walked across deserts and glaciers. But what mattered was that the places that we moved to did not change us. We changed the places. We wore clothes and started fires and built houses. We made every place we went to our place.

Later we left Earth, our home planet, just like we left that valley in Africa. We tried to make places for ourselves in cold space, in habitats, and on asteroids. It was hard. Mars broke our hearts. Venus killed millions. Some people said that the time had come to change ourselves completely so that we could live in these difficult places. People had already begun to meddle with their bodies. It was a time of great danger.

This was when Genius, the goddess of True Flesh awoke for the first time. Nobody knew it then, but looking back we can see that it must have been her. Genius knew that the only way we could stay true to our flesh was to find better places to make our own. Genius visited Levia Calla and taught her to collapse the wave-particle duality so that we could look deep into ourselves and see who we are. Soon we were on our way to the stars. Then Genius told the people to rise up against anyone who wanted to tamper with their bodies. She made the people realize that we were not meant to become machines. That we should be grateful to be alive for the normal a hundred and twenty years and not try to live longer.

I sometimes wonder what would have happened if we were not alone in space. Maybe if there were really aliens out there some-where, we would never have had Genius to help us, since there would be no one true flesh. We would probably have all different gods. Maybe we would have changed ourselves, maybe into robots or to look like aliens. This is a scary thought. If it were true, we'd be in another universe. But we're not.

This universe is our place.

What immediately stood out in this essay is how Adel attributed Levia Calla's historic breakthrough to the intervention of Genius. Nobody had ever thought to suggest this before, since Professor Calla had been one of those atheists who had been convinced that religion would wither away over the course of the twenty-first century. The judges were impressed that Adel had so cleverly asserted what could never be disproved. Even more striking was the dangerous speculation that concluded Adel's essay. Ever since Fermi first expressed his paradox, we have struggled with the apparent absence of other civilizations in the universe. Many of the terrestrial worlds we have discovered have complex ecologies, but on none has intelligence evolved. Even now, there are those who desperately recalculate the factors in the Drake Equation in the hopes of arriv-ing at a solution that is greater than one. When Adel made the point that no religion could survive first contact, and then trumped it with the irrefutable fact that we are alone, he won his place on the *Godspeed*.

Adel and Kamilah came upon two more pilgrims in the library. A man and a woman cuddled on a lime green chenille couch in front of a wall that dis-played images of six planets, lined up in a row. The library was crowded with glassed-in shelves filled with old-fashioned paper books, and racks with various I/O devices, spex, digitex, whisperers and brainleads. Next to a row of work-stations, a long table held an array of artifacts that Adel did not immediately recognize: small sculptures, medals and coins, jewelry and carved wood. Two paintings hung above it, one an image of an artist's studio in which a man in a black hat painted a woman in a blue dress, the other a still life with fruit and some small, dead animals.

"Meri," said Kamilah, "Jarek, this is Adel."

The two pilgrims came to the edge of the couch, their faces alight with anticipation. Out of the corner of his eye, Adel thought he saw Kamilah shake her head. The brightness dimmed and they receded as if nothing had happened.

—we're a disappointment to everyone—buzzed minus

plus buzzed—they just don't know us yet—

Meri looked to be not much older than Adel. She was wearing what might have been long saniwear, only it glowed, registering a thermal map of her body in red, yellow, green and blue. "Adel." She gave him a wistful smile and extended a finger for him to touch.

Jerek held up a hand to indicate that he was otherwise occupied. He was wearing a sleeveless gray shirt, baggy shorts and blacked out spex on which Adel could see a data scrawl flicker.

"You'll usually find these two together," said Kamilah. "And often in bed."

"At least we're not joined at the hip like the Manmans," said Meri. "Have you met them yet?"

Adel frowned. "You mean Robman?"

"And Spaceman." Meri had a third eye tattooed in the middle of her fore-head. At least, Adel hoped it was a tattoo.

—sexy—buzzed minus

plus buzzed—*weird*—

—weird is sexy—

"Oh, Jonman's not so bad." Jarek pulled his spex off.

"If you like snobs." Meri reminded him a little of Gavrila, except for the extra eye. "And cheats."

Jarek replaced the spex on the rack and then clapped Adel on the back. "Welcome to the zoo, brother." He was a head shorter than Adel and had the compact musculature of someone who was born on a high G planet. "So you're in shape," he said. "Do you lift?"

"Some. Not much. I'm a swimmer." Adel had been the Great Randall city champion in the 100 and 200 meter.

"What's your event?"

"Middle distance freestyle."

—*friend?*—

"We have a lap pool in the gym," said Jarek.

—*maybe*—minus buzzed

"Saw it." Adel nodded approvingly. "And you? I can tell you work out."

"I wrestle," said Jarek. "Or I did back on Kindred. But I'm a gym rat. I need exercise to clear my mind. So what do you think of old Speedy so far?"

"It's great." For the first time since he had stepped onto the scanning stage in Great Randall, the reality of where he was struck him. "I'm really excited to be here." And as he said it, he realized that it was true.

"That'll wear off," said Kamilah. "Now if you two sports are done comparing large muscle groups, can we move along?"

"What's the rush, Kamilah?" Meri shifted into a corner of the couch. "Planning on keeping this one for yourself?" She patted the seat, indicating that Adel should take Jarek's place. "Come here, let me get an eye on you."

Adel glanced at Jarek, who winked.

"Has Kamilah been filling you in on all the gossip?"

Adel crammed himself against the side cushion of the couch opposite Meri. "Not really."

"That's because no one tells her the good stuff."

Kamilah yawned. "Maybe because I'm not interested."

Adel couldn't look at Meri's face for long without staring at her tattoo, but if he looked away from her face then his gaze drifted to her hot spots. Finally he decided to focus on her hands.

"I don't work out," said Meri, "in case you're wondering."

"Is this the survey that wrapped yesterday?" said Kamilah, turning away from them to look at the planets displayed on the wall. "I heard it was shit."

Meri had long and slender fingers but her fingernails were bitten ragged, especially the thumbs. Her skin was very pale. He guessed that she must have spent a lot of time indoors, wherever she came from.

"System ONR 147-563." Jarek joined her, partially blocking Adel's view of the wall. "Nine point eight nine light-years away and a whole lot of nothing. The star has luminosity almost three times that of Sol. Six planets: four hot airless rocks, a jovian and a subjovian."

"I'm still wondering about ONR 134-843," said Kamilah, and the wall filled with a new solar system, most of which Adel couldn't see. "Those five Martian-type planets."

"So?" said Meri. "The star was a K1 orange-red dwarf. Which means those Martians are pretty damn cold. The day max is only 17C on the warmest and at night it drops to -210C. And their atmospheres are way too thin, not one over a hundred millibars. That's practically space."

"But there are five of them." Kamilah held up her right hand, fingers splayed. "Count them, five."

"Five Martians aren't worth one terrestrial," said Jarek.

Kamilah grunted. "Have we seen any terrestrials?"

"Space is huge and we're slow." Jarek bumped against her like a friendly dog. "Besides, what do you care? One of these days you'll bust off this rock, get the hero's parade on Jaxon and spend the rest of your life annoying the other eyejacks and getting your face on the news."

"Sure." Kamilah slouched uncomfortably. "One of these days."

—*eyejack?*—buzzed minus.

Adel was wondering the same thing. "What's an eyejack?"

"An eyejack," said Meri confidentially, "is someone who shocks other people."

"Shocks for pay," corrected Kamilah, her back still to them.

"Shock?" Adel frowned. "As in voltage shock or scandalize shock?"

"Well, electricity could be involved." Kamilah turned from the wall. Her medallion showed a cat sitting in a sunny window. "But mostly what I do," she continued, "is make people squirm when they get too settled for their own good."

—*trouble*—buzzed plus.

—*love it*—minus buzzed.

"And you do this how?"

"Movement." She made a flourish with her left hand that started as a slap but ended as a caress that did not quite touch Jarek's face. Jarek did not flinch. "Imagery. I work in visuals mostly but I sometimes use wordplay. Or sound—laughter, explosions, loud music. Whatever it takes to make you look."

"And people pay you for this?"

"Some do, some sue." Kamilah rattled it off like a catchphrase.

"It's an acquired taste," Meri said. "I know I'm still working on it."

"You liked it the time she made Jonman snort juice out of his nose," said Jarek. "Especially after he predicted she would do it to him."

The wall behind them turned announcement blue. "We have come within survey range of a new binary system. I'm naming the M5 star ONR 126-850 and the M2 star ONR 154-436." The screen showed data sheets on the discoveries: *Location, Luminosity, Metallicity, Mass, Age, Temperature, Habitable Ecosphere Radius.*

"Who cares about red dwarfs?" said Kamilah.

"About sixty percent of the stars in this sector are red dwarfs," said Meri.

"My point exactly." Said Kamilah, "You're not going to find many terrestrials orbiting an M star. We should be looking somewhere else."

"Why is that?" said Adel.

"M class are small, cool stars," said Jarek. "In order to get enough insola-
tion to be even remotely habitable, a planet has to be really close to the sun, so
close that they get locked into synchronous rotation because of the intense tidal
torque. Which means that one side is always dark and the other is always light.
The atmosphere would freeze off the dark side."

"And these stars are known for the frequency and intensity of their flares,"
said Mcri, "which would pretty much cook any life on a planet that close."

"Meri and Jarek are our resident science twizes," said Kamilah. "They can
tell you more than you want to know about anything."

"So do we actually get to help decide where to go next?" said Adel.

"Actually, we don't." Jarek shook his head sadly.

"We just argue about it." Kamilah crossed the library to the bathroom
and paused at the doorway. "It passes the time. Don't get any ideas about the
boy, Meri. I'll be right back." The door vanished as she stepped through and
reformed immediately.

"When I first started thinking seriously about making the pilgrimage to
the *Godspeed*," said Jarek, "I had this foolish idea that I might have some influence on the search, maybe even be responsible for a course change. I knew I
wouldn't be aboard long enough to make a planetfall, but I thought maybe I
could help. But I've studied Speedy's search plan and it's perfect, considering
that we can't go any faster than a third of C."

"Besides, *we're* not going anywhere, Jarek and you and me," said Meri.
"Except back to where we came from. By the time Speedy finds the next terrestrial, we could be grandparents."

"Or dead," said Kamilah as she came out of the bathroom. "Shall we tell
young Adel here how long it's been since Speedy discovered a terrestrial planet?"

"Young Adel?" said Meri. "Just how old are you?"

"Nineteen standard," Adel muttered.

—*twenty-six back home*—*buzzed plus.*

"But that's twenty-six on Harvest."

"One hundred and fifty-eight standard," said the wall. "This is your captain
speaking."

"Oh gods." Kamilah rested her forehead in her hand.

The image the *Godspeed* projected was more uniform than woman; she
stood against the dazzle of a star field. Her coat was golden broadcloth lined
in red; it hung to her knees. The sleeves were turned back to show the lining.
Double rows of brass buttons ran from neck to hem. These were unbuttoned

below the waist, revealing red breeches and golden hose. The white sash over her left shoulder was decorated with patches representing all the terrestrial planets she had discovered. Adel counted more than thirty before he lost track.

"I departed from the MASTA on Nuevo Sueño," said the *Godspeed*, "one hundred and fifty-eight years ago, Adel, and I've been looking for my next discovery ever since."

"Longer than any other threshold," said Kamilah.

"Longer than any other threshold," the *Godspeed* said amiably. "Which pains me deeply, I must say. Why do you bring this unfortunate statistic up, perfect one? Is there some conclusion you care to draw?"

She glared at the wall. "Only that we have wasted a century and a half in this desolate corner of the galaxy."

"We, Kamilah?" The *Godspeed* gave her an amused smile. "How long have you been with me?"

"Not quite a year." She folded her arms.

"Ah, the impatience of flesh." The *Godspeed* turned to the stars behind her. "You have traveled not quite a third of a light-year since your arrival. Consider that I've traveled 50.12 light-years since my departure from Nuevo Sueño. Now see what that looks like to me." She thrust her hands above her head and suddenly the points of light on the wall streamed into ribbons and the center of the screen jerked up-right-left-down-left with each course correction and then the ribbons became stars again. She faced the library again, her face glowing. "You have just come 15.33 parsecs in ten seconds. If I follow my instructions to reach my journey's end at the center of our galaxy I will have traveled 8.5 kiloparsecs."

—*if?*—buzzed minus.

"Believe me, Kamilah, I can imagine your experience of spacetime more easily than you can imagine mine." She tugged her sash into place and then pointed at Kamilah. "You're going to mope now."

Kamilah shook her head. Her medallion had gone completely black.

"A hundred and thirty-three people have jumped to me since Nuevo Sueño. How many times do you think I've had this conversation, Kamilah?"

Kamilah bit her lip.

"Ah, if only these walls could talk." The *Godspeed*'s laugh sounded like someone dropping silver spoons. "The things they have seen."

—*is she all right?*—buzzed plus.

"Here's something I'll bet you didn't know," said the *Godspeed*. "A fun fact. Now that Adel has replaced Upwood among our little company, everyone on board is under thirty."

The four of them digested this information in astonished silence.

"Wait a minute," said Meri. "What about Jonman?"

"He would like you to believe he's older but he's the same age as Kamilah." She reached into the pocket of her greatcoat and pulled out a scrap of digitex. A new window opened on the wall; it contained the birth certificate of Jon Haught Shillaber. "Twenty-eight standard."

"All of us?" said Jarek. "That's an pretty amazing coincidence."

"A coincidence?" She waved the birth certificate away. "You don't know how hard I schemed to arrange it." She chuckled. "I was practically diabolical."

"Speedy," said Meri carefully, "you're starting to worry us."

"Worry?"

"Worry," said Jarek.

"Why, because I make jokes? Because I have a flare for the dramatic?" She bowed low and gave them an elaborate hand flourish. "I am but mad north-northwest: when the wind is southerly I know a hawk from a handsaw."

minus buzzed—time to be afraid—

"So," said the *Godspeed,* "we seem to be having a morale problem. I know *my* feelings have been hurt. I think we need to come together, work on some common project. Build ourselves back into a team." She directed her gaze at Adel. "What do you say?"

"Sure."

"Then I suggest that we put on a play."

Meri moaned.

"Yes, that will do nicely." The *Godspeed* clapped her hands, clearly pleased at the prospect. "We'll need to a pick a script. Adel, I understand you've had some acting experience so I'm going to appoint you and Lihong to serve on the selection committee with me. I think poor Sister needs to get out and about more."

"Don't let Lihong pick," said Meri glumly. "How many plays are there about praying?"

"Come now, Meri," said the *Godspeed.* "Give her a chance. I think you'll be surprised."

Day Five

There are two kinds of pilgrimage, as commonly defined. One is a journey to a specific, usually sacred place; it takes place and then ends. The other is less about a destination and more about a spiritual quest. When we decide to jump to a threshold, we most often begin our pilgrimages intending to get to the *Godspeed* or the *Big D* or the *Bisous Bisous,* stay for some length of time and then return to our ordinary lives. However, as time passes on board we inevitably come to realize—sometimes to our chagrin—that we have been infected with an irrepressible yearning to seek out the numinous, wherever and however it might be found.

Materialists don't have much use for the notion of a soul. They prefer to locate individuality in the mind, which emerges from the brain but cannot exist separately from it. They maintain that information must be communicated to the brain through the senses, and only through the senses. But materialists have yet to offer a rigorous explanation of what happens during those few seconds of a jump when the original has ceased to exist and the scan from it has yet to be reassembled. Because during the brief interval when there are neither senses nor brain nor mind, we all seem to receive some subtle clue about our place in the universe.

This is why there are so few materialists.

Adel had been having dreams. They were not bad dreams, merely disturbing. In one, he was lost in a forest where people grew instead of trees. He stumbled past shrubby little kids he'd gone to school with and great towering grownups like his parents and Uncle Durwin and President Adriana. He knew he had to keep walking because if he stopped he would grow roots and raise his arms up to the sun like all the other tree people, but he was tired, so very tired.

In another, he was standing backstage watching a play he'd never heard of before and Sister Lihong tapped him on the shoulder and told him that Gavrila had called in sick and that he would have to take her part and then she pushed him out of the wings and he was onstage in front of a sellout audience, every one of which was Speedy, and he stumbled across the stage to the bed where Jarek waited for him, naked Jarek, and then Adel realized that he was naked too, and he climbed under the covers because he was cold and embarrassed, and Jarek kept staring at him because he, Adel, was supposed to say his line but he didn't know the next line or any line and so he did the one thing he could think to do, which was to kiss Jarek, on the mouth, and then his tongue brushed the ridges of Jarek's teeth and all the Speedys in the audience gave him a standing ovation . . .

. . . which woke him up.

Adel blinked. He lay in bed between Meri and Jarek; both were still asleep. They were under a yellow sheet that had pink kites and blue clouds on it. Jarek's arm had dropped loosely across Adel's waist. In the dim light he could see that Meri's lips were parted and for a while he listened to the seashore whisper of her breathing. He remembered that something had changed last night between the three of them.

Something, but what?

Obviously his two lovers weren't losing any sleep over it. Speedy had begun to bring the lights up in Meri's room so it had to be close to morning chime. Adel lifted his head but couldn't see the clock without disturbing his bedmates, so he tried to guess the time. If the ceiling was set to gain twenty lumens a minute and Speedy started at 0600, then it was . . . he couldn't do the math. After six in the morning, anyway.

The something was Jarek—*yes*. Adel realized that he'd enjoyed having sex with Jarek just a bit more than with Meri. Not that he hadn't enjoyed her too. There had been plenty of enjoying going on, that was for sure. A thrilling night all around. But Adel could be rougher with Jarek than he was with Meri. He didn't have to hold anything back. Sex with Jarek was a little like wrestling, only with orgasms.

Adel had been extremely doubtful about sleeping with both Meri *and* Jarek, until Meri had made it plain that was the only way he was ever going to get into her bed. The normal buzz of his opposites had risen to a scream; their deliberations had gotten so shrill that he'd been forced to mute their input. Not that he didn't know what they were thinking, of course; they were him.

Jarek had been the perfect gentleman at first; they had taken turns pleasuring Meri until the day before yesterday when she had guided Adel's hand to Jarek's erect cock. An awkward moment, but then Adel still felt like he was all thumbs and elbows when it came to sex anyway. Jarek talked continually while he made love, so Adel was never in doubt as to what Jarek wanted him to do. And because he trusted Jarek, Adel began to talk too. And then to moan, whimper, screech, and laugh out loud.

Adel felt extraordinarily adult, fucking both a man and a woman. He tried the word out in the gloom, mouthing it silently. I *fuck*, you *fuck*, he, she, or it *fucks*, we *fuck*, you all *fuck*, they *fuck*. The only thing that confused him about losing his virginity was not that his sexual identity was now slightly blurry; it was his raging appetite. Now that he knew what he had been missing, he wanted to have sex with everyone here on the *Godspeed* and then go back to Harvest and fuck his way through Great Randall Science and Agricultural College and up and down Crown Edge. Well, that wasn't quite true. He didn't particularly want to see the Manmans naked and the thought of sleeping with his parents made him queasy and now that he was an experienced lover, he couldn't see himself on top, underneath or sideways with his ex, Gavrila. But still. He'd been horny back on Harvest but now he felt like he might spin out of control. Was it perverted to want so much sex?

Adel was wondering what color Sister Lihong Rain's hair was and how it would look spread across his pillow when Kamilah spoke through the closed door.

"Send Adel out," she said, "but put some clothes on him first."

Adel's head jerked up. "How does she know I'm here?"

"Time is it?" said Meri.

"Don't know." Jarek moaned and gave him a knee in the small of the back. "But it's for you, brother, so you'd better get it."

He clambered over Meri and tumbled out of bed onto her loafers. Their clothes were strewn around the room. Adel pulled on his saniwear, the taut silver warm-ups that Meri had created for him and his black softwalks. The black floss cape had been his own idea—a signature, like Kamilah's medallion or Sister's veil. The cape was modest, only the size of a face towel, and was attached to his shoulders by the two merit pins he'd recycled from his Host uniforms.

He paused in front of a wall, waved it to mirror mode, combed fingers through his hair and then stepped through the door. Kamilah leaned against the wall with her medallion in hand. She gazed into it thoughtfully.

"How did you find me?" said Adel.

"I asked Speedy." She let it fall to her chest and Adel saw the eating man again. Adel had noticed that her eating man had reappeared again and again, always at the same table. "You want breakfast?"

He was annoyed with her for rousting him out of bed before morning chime. "When I wake up." Who knew what erotic treats he might miss?

"Your eyes look open to me." She gave him a knowing smile. "Busy night?"

He considered telling her that it was none of her business, but decided to flirt instead. Maybe he'd get lucky. "Busy enough." He gave his shoulders a twitch, which made his cape flutter. "You?"

"I slept."

"I slept too." Adel waited a beat. "Eventually."

"Gods, Adel!" Kamilah laughed out loud. "You're a handful, you know that?" She put an arm around his shoulders and started walking him back up Dream Street. "Meri and Jarek had better watch out."

Adel wasn't quite sure what she meant but he decided to let it drop for now. "So what's this about?"

"A field trip." They started down the Tulip Stairway. "What do you know about physics?"

Adel had studied comparative entertainment at Great Randall S&A, although he'd left school in his third year to train for the Harvest Olympics and to find himself. Unfortunately, he'd finished only sixth in the 200 meters and Adel was still pretty much missing. Science in general and physics in particular had never been a strength. "I know some. Sort of."

"What's the first law of thermodynamics?"

"The first law of thermodynamics." He closed his eyes and tried to picture the screen. "Something like . . . um . . . a body stays in motion . . . ah . . . as long as it's in motion?"

"Oh great," she said wearily. "Have you ever been in space?"

For the first time in days he missed the familiar buzz of his opposites. He lifted their mute.

—she thinks we're a moron—buzzed minus.

—we are a moron—plus buzzed.

"Everybody's in space," he said defensively. "That's where all the planets are. We're traveling through space this very moment."

"This wasn't meant to be a trick question," she said gently. "I mean have you ever been in a hardsuit out in the vacuum?"

"Oh," he said. "No."

"You want to?"

—wow—

—yes—

He had to restrain himself from hugging her. "Absolutely."

"Okay then." She gestured at the entrance to the Chillingsworth Breakfasting Room. "Let's grab something to take away and head down to the locker room. We need to oxygenate for about half an hour."

—but why is she doing this?—buzzed plus.

There were two ways to the surface of the *Godspeed*: through the great bay doors of the Well Met Arena or out the Clarke Airlock. Adel straddled a bench in the pre-breathing locker room and wolfed down a sausage and honeynut torte while Kamilah explained what was about to happen.

"We have to spend another twenty-minutes here breathing a hundred percent oxygen to scrub nitrogen out of our bodies. Then just before we climb into the hardsuits, we put on isotherms." She opened a locker and removed two silky black garments. "You want to wait until the last minute; isotherms take some getting used to. But they keep the hardsuit from overheating." She tossed one to Adel.

"But how can that happen?" He held the isotherm up; it had a hood and opened with a slide down the torso. The sleeves ended at the elbow and the pants at the knee. "Isn't space just about as cold as anything gets?"

"Yes, but the hardsuit is airtight, which makes it hard to dissipate all the heat that you're going to be generating. Even though you get some servo-assist, it's a big rig, Adel. You've got to work to get anywhere." She raised her steaming mug of kappa and winked at him. "Think you're man enough for the job?"

—*let that pass*—buzzed plus.

"I suppose we'll know soon enough." Adel rubbed the fabric of the iso-therm between his thumb and forefinger. It was cool to the touch.

Kamilah sipped from the mug. "Once we're out on the surface," she said, "Speedy will be running all your systems. All you have to do is follow me."

The *Godspeed* displayed on a section of wall. She was wearing an isotherm with the hood down; it clung to her like a second skin. Adel could see the out-line of her nipples and the subtle wrinkles her pubic hair made in the fabric.

—*but they're not real*—*minus buzzed.*

"What are you doing, Kamilah?" said the *Godspeed*. "You were out just last week."

"Adel hasn't seen the view."

"I can show him any view he wants. I can fill the Welcome Arena with stars. He can see in ultraviolet. Infrared."

"Yes, but it wouldn't be quite real, would it?"

"Reality is over-rated." The *Godspeed* waggled a finger at Kamilah. "You're taking an unusual interest in young Adel. I'm watching, perfect one. "

"You're watching everyone, Speedy. That's how you get your cookies." With that she pulled the top of her scrubs off. "Time to get naked, Adel. Walk our hardsuits out and start the checklist, would you, Speedy?"

—*those are real*—buzzed minus.

—*Meri and Jarek remember*—

—*we can look*—

And Adel did look as he slithered out of his own clothes. Although he was discreet about it, he managed to burn indelible images into his memory of Kamilah undressing, the curve of her magnificent hip, the lush pendency of her breasts, the breathtaking expanse of her back as her tawny skin stretched tight over nubs of her spine. She was a woman a man might drown in. Abruptly, he realized that he was becoming aroused. He turned away from her, tossed his clothes into a locker, snatched at the isotherm and pulled it on.

And bit back a scream.

Although it was as silken as when Kamilah had pulled it out of the drawer, his isotherm felt like it had spent the last ten years in cryogenic storage. Adel's skin crawled beneath it and his hands curled into fists. As a swimmer, Adel had experienced some precipitous temperature changes, but he'd never dived into a pool filled with liquid hydrogen.

—*trying to kill us*—screeched minus.

"Are you all right?" said Kamilah. "Your eyes look like eggs."

"Ah," said Adel. "*Ah.*"

—*we can do this—buzzed plus.*

"Hang on," said Kamilah. "It passes."

As the hardsuits clumped around the corner of the locker room, their servos singing, Adel shivered and caught his breath. He thought he could hear every joint crack as he unclenched his fists and spread his fingers. When he pulled the isotherm hood over his head, he got the worst ice cream headache he'd ever had.

"This is going to be fun," he said through clenched teeth.

The hardsuits were gleaming white eggs with four arms, two legs and a tail. The arms on either side were flexrobotic and built for heavy lifting. Beside them were fabric sleeves into which a spacewalker could insert his arms for delicate work. The legs ended in ribbed plates, as did the snaking tail, which Kamilah explained could be used as a stabilizer or an anchor. A silver ball the size of coconut perched at the top of the suit.

"Just think of them as spaceships that walk," said Kamilah. "Okay, Speedy. Pop the tops."

The top, translucent third of each egg swung back. Kamilah muscled a stairway up to the closest hardsuit. "This one's yours. Settle in but don't try moving just yet."

Adel slid his legs into the suit's legs and cool gel flowed around them, locking him into place. He ducked instinctively as the top came down, but he had plenty of room. Seals fasten with a *scritch* and the heads up display on the inside of the top began to glow with controls and diagnostics. Beneath the translucent top were fingerpads for controlling the robotic lifter arms; near them were the holes of the hardsuit's sleeves. Adel stuck his arms through, flexed his fingers in the gloves then turned his attention back to the HUD. He saw that he had forty hours of oxygen reserve and his batteries were at 98% of capacity. The temperature in the airlock was 15.52°C and the air pressure was 689 millibars. Then the readouts faded and the *Godspeed* was studying him intently. She looked worried.

"Adel, what's going on?"

"Is something going on?"

"I'm afraid there is and I don't want you mixed up in it. What does Kamilah want with you?"

Adel felt a chill that had nothing to do with his isotherm.

—*don't say anything—buzzed plus*

—*we don't know anything—*

"I don't know that she wants anything." He pulled his arms out of the hardsuit's sleeves and folded them across his chest. "I just thought she was being nice."

"All right, Adel," said Kamilah over the comm. "Take a stroll around the room. I want to see how you do in here where it's flat. Speedy will compensate if you have any trouble. I'm sure she's already in your ear."

The *Godspeed* held a forefinger to her lips. "Kamilah is going to ask you to turn off your comm. That's when you must be especially careful, Adel." With that, she faded away and Adel was staring, slack-jawed, at the HUD.

"Adel?" said Kamilah. "Are you napping in there?"

Adel took a couple of tentative steps. Moving the hardsuit was a little like walking on stilts. He was high off the floor and couldn't really see or feel what was beneath his feet. When he twisted around, he caught sight of the tail whipping frantically behind him. But after walking for a few minutes, he decided that he could manage the suit. He lumbered behind Kamilah through the inner hatch of the airlock, which slid shut.

Adel listened to the muted chatter of pumps evacuating the lock until finally there wasn't enough air to carry sound. Moments later, the outer hatch opened.

"Ready?" Kamilah said. "Remember that we're leaving the artificial gravity field. No leaps or bounds—you don't watch to achieve escape velocity."

Adel nodded.

—she can't see us—buzzed minus—we have to talk to her—

Adel cleared his throat. "I've always wanted to see the stars from space."

"Actually, you won't have much of a view until later," she said. "Let's go."

As they passed through the hatch, the *Godspeed* announced, "Suit lights are on. I'm deploying fireflies."

Adel saw the silver ball lift from the top of Kamilah's suit and float directly above her. The bottom half of it was now incandescent, lighting the surface of the *Godspeed* against the swarming darkness. At the same time the ground around him lit up. He looked and saw his firefly hovering about a meter over the suit.

—amazing—buzzed plus—we're out, we're out in space—

They crossed the flat staging pad just outside the airlock and stepped off onto the regolith. The rock had been pounded to gray dust by centuries of foot traffic. Whenever he took a step the dust puffed underfoot and drifted slowly back to the ground like smoke. It was twenty centimeters deep in some places but offered little resistance to his footplates. Adel's excitement leached slowly away as Kamilah led him away from the airlock. He had to take mincing steps to keep from launching himself free of the *Godspeed*'s tenuous gravitational pull. It was frustrating; he felt as if he were walking with a pillow between his legs. The sky was a huge disappointment as well. The fireflies washed out the light from all but the brightest stars. He'd seen better skies camping on Harvest.

"So where are we going?"

"Just around."

"How long will it take?"

"Not that long."

—*hiding something?*—*buzzed plus.*

—*definitely*—

"And what exactly are we going to do?"

"A little bit of everything. One of her robotic arms gave him a playful wave. "You'll see."

They marched in silence for a while. Adel began to chafe at following Kamilah's lead. He picked up his pace and drew alongside of her. The regolith here was not quite so trampled and much less regular, although a clearly defined trail showed that they were not the first to make this trek. They passed stones and rubble piles and boulders the size of houses and the occasional impact crater that the path circumnavigated.

—*impact crater?*—buzzed minus.

"Uh, Kamilah," he said. "How often does Speedy get hit by meteors?"

"Never," said Kamilah. "The craters you see are all pre-launch. Interstellar space is pretty much empty so it's not that much of a problem."

"I sweep the sky for incoming debris," said the *Godspeed*, "up to five million meters away."

"And that works?"

"So far," said Kamilah. "We wouldn't want to slam into anything traveling at a third the speed of light."

They walked on for another ten minutes before Kamilah stopped. "There." She pointed. "That's where we came from. Somewhere out there is home."

Adel squinted. *There* was pretty much meaningless. Was she pointing at some particular star or a space between stars?"

"This is the backside. If Speedy had a rear bumper," she said, "we'd be standing on it right here. I want to show you something interesting. Pull your arms out of the sleeves."

"Done."

"The comm toggle is under the right arm keypad. Switch it off."

The *Godspeed* broke into their conversation. "Kamilah and Adel, you are about to disable a key safety feature of your hardsuits. I strongly urge you to reconsider."

"I see the switch." Adel's throat was tight. "You know, Speedy warned me about this back in the airlock."

"I'm sure she did. We go through this every time."

"You've done this before?"

"Many times," she said. "It's a tradition we've started to bring the new arrival out here to see the sights. It's actually a spiritual thing, which is why Speedy doesn't really get it."

"I have to turn off the comm why?"

"Because she's watching, Adel," said Kamilah impatiently. "She's always with us. She can't help herself."

"Young Adel," murmured the *Godspeed*. "Remember what I said."

—*trust Kamilah*—

—*or trust Speedy*—

—*we were warned*—

Adel flicked the toggle. "Now what?" he said to himself. His voice sounded very small in the suit.

He was startled when Kamilah leaned her suit against his so that the tops of the eggs were touching. It was strangely intimate maneuver, almost like a kiss. Her face was an electric green shadow in the glow of the HUD.

He was startled again when she spoke. "Turn. The. Comm. Off." He could hear her through the suit. She paused between each word, her voice reedy and metallic.

"I did," he said.

He could see her shake her head and tap fingers to her ears. "You. Have. To. Shout."

"I. Did!" Adel shouted.

"Good." She picked up a rock the size of a fist and held it at arm's length. "Drop. Rock." She paused. "Count. How. Long. To. Surface."

—*science experiments?*—*buzzed plus.*

—*she's gone crazy*—

Adel was inclined to agree with his minus but what Kamilah was asking seemed harmless enough.

"Ready?"

"Yes."

She let go. Adel counted.

One one thousand, two one thousand, three one thousand, four one thousand, five . . .

And it was down.

"Yes?" said Kamilah.

"Five."

"Good. Keep. Secret." She paused. "Comm. On."

As he flicked the switch he heard her saying. " . . . you feel it? My first time it was too subtle but if you concentrate, you'll get it."

"Are you all right, Adel?" murmured the *Godspeed*. "What just happened?"

"I don't know," said Adel, mystified.

"Well, we can try again on the frontside," said Kamilah. "Sometimes it's better there. Let's go."

—what is she talking about?—minus buzzed.

For twenty minutes he trudged in perplexed silence past big rocks, little rocks and powdered rocks in all the colors of gray. In some places the surface of the trail was grainy like sand, in others it was dust, and in yet others it was bare ledge. Adel just didn't understand what he was supposed to have gotten from watching the rocks drop. Something to do with gravity? What he didn't know about gravity would fill a barn. Eventually he gave up trying to figure it out. Kamilah was right about one thing: it was real work walking in a hardsuit. If it hadn't been for the isotherm, he would have long since broken a sweat.

—this has to get better—buzzed plus.

"How much longer?" said Adel at last.

"A while yet." Kamilah chuckled. "What are you, a little kid?"

"Remember the day I got here?" he said. "You told me that you were sentenced to spend time on Speedy. But you never said why."

"Not that interesting, really."

"Better than counting rocks." He stomped on a flat stone the size of his hand, breaking it into three pieces. "Or I suppose I could sing." He gave her the first few bars of "Do As We Don't" in his finest atonal yodel.

"Gods, Adel, but you're a pest today." Kamilah sighed. "All right, so there's a religion on Suncast . . ."

"Suncast? That's where you're from?"

"That's where I was from. If I ever get off this rock, that's the last place I'm going to stay."

—if?—buzzed minus—why did she say if?—

Anyway, there's a sect that call themselves God's Own Poor. They're very proud of themselves for having deliberately chosen not to own very much. They spout these endless lectures about how living simply is the way to true spirituality. It's all over the worldnet. And they have this tradition that once a year they leave their houses and put their belongings into a cart, supposedly everything they own but not really. Each of them drags the cart to a park or a campground—this takes place in the warm weather, naturally—and they spend two weeks congratulating themselves on how poor they are and how God loves them especially."

"What god do they worship?"

"A few pray to Sagittarius A*, the black hole at the center of the galaxy, but most are some flavor of Eternal Centerers. When it was founded, the Poor might actually have been a legitimate religion. I mean, I see their point that owning too much can get in the way. Except that now almost all of them have houses and furniture and every kind of vehicle. None of them tries to fit the living room couch on their carts. And you should see some of these carts. They cost more than I make in a year."

"From shocking people," Adel said. "As a professional eyejack."

The comm was silent for a moment. "Are you teasing me, young Adel?"

"No, no." Adel bit back his grin. "Not at all." Even though he knew she couldn't see it, she could apparently *hear* it inflected in his voice. "So you were annoyed at them?"

"I was. Lots of us were. It wasn't only that they were self-righteous hypo-crites. I didn't like the way they commandeered the parks just when the rest of us wanted to use them. So I asked myself, how can I shock the Poor and what kind of purse can I make from doing it?"

A new trail diverged from the one they had been following, Kamilah con-sidered for a moment and then took it. She fell silent for a few moments.

Adel prompted her. "And you came up with a plan."

—*why are we interested in this?*—*buzzed plus.*

—*because we want to get her into bed*—

"I did. First I took out a loan; I had to put my house up as collateral. I split two hundred thousand barries across eight hundred cash cards, so each one was worth two hundred and fifty. Next I set up my tent at the annual Poverty Revival at Point Kingsley on the Prithee Sea, which you've never heard of but which is one of the most beautiful places in the Continuum. I passed as one of the Poor, mingling with about ten thousand true believers. I parked a wheelbar-row outside the tent that had nothing in it but a suitcase and a shovel. That got a megagram of disapproval, which told me I was onto something. Just before dawn on the tenth day of the encampment, I tossed the suitcase and shoveled in the eight hundred cash cards. I parked my wheelbarrow at the Tabernacle of the Center and waited with a spycam. I'd painted, 'God Helps Those Who Help Themselves' on the side; I thought that was a nice touch. I was there when peo-ple started to discover my little monetary miracle. I shot vids of several hundred of the Poor dipping their hot hands into the cards. Some of them just grabbed a handful and ran, but quite a few tried to sneak up on the wheelbarrow when nobody was looking. But of course, everyone was. The wheelbarrow was empty in about an hour and a half, but people kept coming to look all morning."

Adel was puzzled. "But your sign said they were supposed to help them-selves," he said. "Why would they be ashamed?"

"Well, they were supposed to be celebrating their devotion to poverty, not padding their personal assets. But the vids were just documentation, they weren't the sting. Understand that the cards were *mine*. Yes, I authorized all expenditures, but I also collected detailed reports on everything they bought. Everything, as in possessions, Adel. Material goods. All kinds of stuff, and lots of it. I posted the complete record. For six days my website was one of the most active on the worldnet. Then the local Law Exchange shut me down. Still, even after legal expenses and paying off the loan, I cleared almost three thousand barries."

—*brilliant*—buzzed minus.

—*she got caught*—plus buzzed.

"But this was against the law on Suncast?" said Adel.

"Actually, no." Kamilah kicked at a stone and sent it skittering across the regolith. She trudged on in silence for a few moments. "But I used a wheelbarrow," she said finally, "which LEX ruled was too much like one of their carts—a cultural symbol. According to LEX, I had committed Intolerant Speech. If I had just set the cards out in a basket, the Poor couldn't have touched me. But I didn't and they did. In the remedy phase of my trial, the Poor asked LEX to ship me here. I guess they thought I'd get religion."

"And did you?"

"You don't get to ask all the questions." The tail of her hardsuit darted and the footplate tapped the rear of Adel's suit. "Your turn. Tell me something interesting about yourself. Something that nobody knows."

He considered. "Well, I was a virgin when I got here."

"Something interesting, Adel."

"And I'm not anymore."

"That nobody knows," she said.

—*just trying to shock you*—buzzed plus.

—*bitch*—minus buzzed.

"All right," he said, at last. "I'm a delibertarian."

Kamilah paused, then turned completely around once, as if to get her bearings. "I don't know what that is."

"I have an implant that makes me hear voices. Sometimes they argue with each other."

"Oh?" Kamilah headed off the trail. "About what?"

Adel picked his way after her. "Mostly about what I should do." He sensed that he didn't really have her complete attention. "Say I'm coming out of church and I see a wheelbarrow filled with cash cards. One voice might tell me to grab as many as I can, the other says no."

"I'd get tired of that soon enough."

"Or say someone insults me, hurts my feelings. One voice wants to understand her and the other wants to kick her teeth in. But the thing is, the voices are all me."

"All right then," Kamilah paused, glanced left and then right as if lining up landmarks. "We're here."

—too bad we can't kick her teeth in—buzzed minus.

"Where's here?"

"This is the frontside, exactly opposite from where we just were. We should try shutting down again. This might be your lucky spot."

"I don't know if I want to," said Adel. "What am I doing here, Kamilah?"

"Look, Adel, I'm sorry," she said. "I didn't mean to hurt your feelings. I forget you're just a kid. Come over here, let me give you a hug."

"Oh." Adel was at once mollified by Kamilah's apology and stung that she thought of him as a kid.

—we are a kid—plus buzzed.

And what kind of hug was he going to get in a hardsuit?

—shut up—

"You're only nine standard older than I am," he said as he brought his suit within robotic arm's reach.

"I know." Her two arms snaked around him. "Turn off your comm, Adel."

This time the *Godspeed* made no objection. When the comm was off, Kamilah didn't bother to speak. She picked up a rock and held it out. Adel waved for her to drop it.

One one thousand, two one thousand, three one thousand, four one thousand, five one thousand six one thousand, seven one . . .

Seven? Adel was confused.

—we messed up the count—buzzed minus.

—did not—

He leaned into her and touched her top. "Seven."

"Yes." She paused. "Turn. Off. Lights."

Adel found the control and heard a soft clunk as the firefly docked with his hardsuit. He waved the suit lights off and blacked out the HUD, although he was not in a particularly spiritual mood. The blackness of space closed around them and the sky filled with the shyest of stars. Adel craned in the suit to see them all. Deep space was much more busy than he'd imagined. The stars were all different sizes and many burned in colors: blues, yellows, oranges and reds—a lot more reds than he would have thought. There were dense patches and sparse patches and an elongated wispy cloud the stretched across his field of vision that he assumed was the rest of the Milky Way.

—amazing—

—but what's going on?—

"Questions?" said Kamilah.

"Questions?" he said under his breath. "Damn right I have questions." When he shouted, he could hear the anger in his voice. "Rocks. Mean. What?"

"Speedy. Slows. Down." She paused. "We. Don't. Know. Why." Another pause. "Act. Normal. More. Later."

—act normal?—

—we're fucked—

"Comm." He screamed. "On."

"Careful," she said. "Adel."

He felt a slithering against his suit as she let go of him. He bashed at the comm switch and brought the suit lights on.

" . . . the most amazing experience, isn't it?" she was saying. "It's almost like you're standing naked in space."

"Kamilah . . ." He tried to speak but panic choked him.

"Adel, what's happening?" said the *Godspeed*. "Are you all right?"

"I have to tell you," said Kamilah, "that first time I was actually a little scared but I'm used to it now. But you—you did just fine."

"Fine," Adel said. His heart was pounding so hard he thought it might burst his chest. "Just fine."

Day Twelve

Since the *Godspeed* left the orbit of Menander, fifth planet of Hallowell's Star, to begin its historic voyage of discovery, 69,384 of us stepped off her transport stage. Only about ten thousand of us were pilgrims, the rest were itinerant techs and prospective colonists. On average, the pilgrims spent a little over a standard year as passengers, while the sojourn of the colony-builders rarely exceeded sixty days. As it turns out, Sister Lihong Rain held the record for the longest pilgrimage; she stayed on the *Godspeed* for more than seven standards.

At launch, the cognizor in command of the *Godspeed* had been content with a non-gendered persona. Not until the hundred and thirteenth year did it present as The Captain, a male authority figure. The Captain was a sandy-haired mesomorph, apparently a native of one of the highest G worlds. His original uniform was modest in comparison to later incarnations, gray and apparently seamless, with neither cuff nor collar. The Captain first appeared on the walls of the library but soon spread throughout the living quarters and then began to manifest as a fetch, that could be projected anywhere, even onto the surface. The

Godspeed mostly used The Captain to oversee shipboard routine but on occasion he would approach us in social contexts. Inevitably he would betray a disturbing knowledge of everything that we had ever done while aboard. We realized to our dismay that the *Godspeed* was always watching.

These awkward attempts at sociability were not well received; the Captain persona was gruff and humorless and all too often presumptuous. He was not at all pleased when one of us nicknamed him Speedy. Later iterations of the persona did little to improve his popularity.

It wasn't until the three hundred and thirty-second year that the stubborn Captain was supplanted by a female persona. The new Speedy impressed every-one. She didn't give orders; she made requests. She picked up on many of the social cues that her predecessor had missed, bowing out of conversations where she was not welcome, not only listening but hearing what we told her. She was accommodating and gregarious, if somewhat emotionally needy. She laughed easily, although her sense of humor was often disconcerting. She didn't mind at all that we called her Speedy. And she kept our secrets.

Only a very few saw the darker shades of the *Godspeed*'s persona. The techs found her eccentricities charming and the colonists celebrated her for being such a prodigious discoverer of terrestrials. Most pilgrims recalled their time aboard with bemused nostalgia.

Of course, the *Godspeed* had no choice but to keep all of us under constant surveillance. We were her charges. Her cargo. Over the course of one thousand and eighty-seven standards, she witnessed six homicides, eleven suicides and two hundred and forty-nine deaths from accident, disease, and old age. She took each of these deaths personally, even as she rejoiced in the two hundred and sixty-eight babies conceived and born in the bedrooms of Dream Street. She presided over two thousand and eighteen marriages, four thousand and eighty-nine divorces. She witnessed twenty-nine million eight hundred and fif-teen thousand two hundred and forty-seven acts of sexual congress, not includ-ing masturbation. Since she was responsible for our physical and emotional well-being, she monitored what we ate, who we slept with, what drugs we used, how much exercise we got. She tried to defuse quarrels and mediate disputes. She readily ceded her authority to the project manager and team leaders during a colonizing stop but in interstellar space, she was in command.

Since there was little privacy inside the *Godspeed*, it was difficult for Kamilah, Adel, Jarek, Meri, Jonman and Robman to discuss their situation. None of them had been able to lure Sister out for a suit-to-suit conference, so she was not in their confidence. Adel took a couple of showers with Meri and Jarek. They played crank jams at top volume and whispered in each other's ears as they pretended to make out, but that was awkward at best. They had no way to send or encrypt messages that the *Godspeed* couldn't easily hack. Jonman hit upon the strategy of writing steganographic poetry under blankets at night and then handing them around to be read—also under blankets.

> *We hear that love can't wait too long,*
> *Go and find her home.*
> *We fear that she who we seek*
> *Must sleep all day, have dreams of night*
> *killed by the fire up in the sky.*
> *Would we? Does she?*

Steganography, Adel learned from a whisperer in the library, was the ancient art of hiding messages within messages. When Robman gave him the key of picking out every fourth word of this poem, he read: *We can't go home she must have killed up would.* This puzzled him until he remembered that the last pilgrim to leave the *Godspeed* before he arrived was Upwood Marcene. Then he was chilled. The problem with Jonman's poems was that they had to be written mechanically—on a surface with an implement. None of the pilgrims had ever needed to master the skill of handwriting; their scrawls were all but indecipherable. And asking for the materials to write with aroused the *Godspeed*'s suspicions.

Not only that, but Jonman's poetry was awful.

Over several days, in bits and snatches, Adel was able to arrive at a rough understanding of their dilemma. Three months ago, while Adel was still writing his essay, Jarek had noticed that spacewalking on the surface of the *Godspeed* felt different than it had been when he first arrived. He thought his hardsuit might be defective until he tried several others. After that, he devised the test, and led the others out, one by one, to witness it. If the *Godspeed* had actually been traveling at a constant 100,000 kilometers per second, rocks dropped anywhere on the surface would take the same amount of time to fall. However, when she accelerated away from a newly established colony, rocks dropped on the backside took longer to fall than rocks on the frontside. And when she decelerated toward a new discovery . . .

Once they were sure that they were slowing down, the pilgrims had to decide what it meant and what to do next. They queried the library and, as far as they could tell, the *Godspeed* had announced every scan and course change she had ever made. In over a thousand years the only times she had ever decelerated was when she had targeted a new planet. There was no precedent for what was happening and her silence about it scared them. They waited, dissembled as best they could, and desperately hoped that someone back home would notice that something was wrong.

Weeks passed. A month. Two months.

Jonman maintained that there could be only two possible explanations: the *Godspeed* must either be falsifying its navigation reports or it had cut all contact with the Continuum. Either way, he argued, they must continue to wait. Upwood's pilgrimage was almost over, he was scheduled to go home in another two weeks. If the *Godspeed* let him make the jump, then their troubles were over. Hours, or at the most a day, after he reported the anomaly, techs would swarm the transport stage. If she didn't let him make the jump, then at least they would know where they stood. Nobody mentioned a third outcome, although Upwood clearly understood that there was a risk that the *Godspeed* might kill or twist him during transport and make it look like an accident. Flawed jumps were extremely rare but not impossible. Upwood had lost almost five kilos by the day he climbed onto the transport stage. His chest was a washboard of ribs and his eyes were sunken. The other pilgrims watched in hope and horror as he faded into wisps of probability and was gone.

Five days passed. On the sixth day, the *Godspeed* announced that they would be joined by a new pilgrim. A week after Upwood's departure, Adel Ranger Santos was assembled on the transport stage.

Sister was horribly miscast as Miranda. Adel thought she would have made a better Caliban, especially since he was Ferdinand. In the script, Miranda was supposed to fall madly in love with Ferdinand, but Sister was unable to summon even a smile for Adel, much less passion. He might as well have been an old sock as the love of her life.

Adel knew why the *Godspeed* had chosen *The Tempest*; she wanted to play Prospero. She'd cast Meri as Ariel and Kamilah as Caliban. Jonman and Robman were Trinculo and Stephano and along with Jarek also took the parts of the various other lesser lords and sons and brothers and sailors. Adel found it a very complicated play, even for Shakespeare.

"I am a fool," said Sister, "to weep when I am glad." She delivered the line like someone hitting the same note on a keyboard again and again.

Adel had a whisperer feeding him lines. "Why do you weep?"

"Stop there." The *Godspeed* waved her magic staff. She was directing the scene in costume. Prospero wore a full-length opalescent cape with fur trim, a black undertunic and a small silver crown. "Nobody says 'weep' anymore." She had been rewriting the play ever since they started rehearsing. "Adel, have you ever said 'weep' in your life?"

"No," said Adel miserably. He was hungry and was certain he would starve to death before they got through this scene.

"Then neither should Ferdinand. Let's change 'weep' to 'cry.' Say the line, Ferdinand."

Adel said, "Why do you cry?"

"No." She shut her eyes. "No, that's not right either." Her brow wrinkled. "Try 'why are you crying?'"

"Why are you crying?" said Adel.

"Much better." She clapped hands once. "I know the script is a classic but after three thousand years some of these lines are dusty. Miranda, give me 'I am a fool' with the change."

"I am a fool," she said, "to cry when I am glad."

"Why are you crying?"

"Because I'm not worthy. I dare not even offer myself to you—much less ask you to love me." Here the *Godspeed* had directed her to put her arms on Adel's shoulders. "But the more I try to hide my feelings, the more they show."

As they gazed at each other, Adel thought he did see a glimmer of something in Sister's eyes. Probably nausea.

"So no more pretending." Sister knelt awkwardly and gazed up at him. "If you want to marry me, I'll be your wife." She lowered her head, but forgot again to cheat toward the house, so that she delivered the next line to the floor. "If not, I'll live as a virgin the rest of my life, in love with nobody but you."

"We can't hear you, Miranda," said the *Godspeed*.

Sister tilted her head to the side and finished the speech. "You don't even have to talk to me if you don't want. Makes no difference. I'll always be there for you."

"Ferdinand," the *Godspeed* murmured, "she's just made you the happiest man in the world."

Adel pulled her to her feet. "Darling, you make me feel so humble."

"So then you'll be my husband?"

"Sure," he said. "My heart is willing . . ." he laid his hand against his chest, " . . . and here's my hand." Adel extended his arm.

"And here's mine with my heart in it." She slid her fingers across his palm, her touch cool and feathery.

"And," prompted the *Godspeed*. "And?"

With a sigh, Sister turned her face up toward his. Her eyelids fluttered closed. Adel stooped over her. The first time he had played this scene, she had so clearly not wanted to be kissed that he had just brushed his lips against her thin frown. The *Godspeed* wanted more. Now he lifted her veil and pressed his mouth hard against hers. She did nothing to resist, although he could feel her shiver when he slipped the tip of his tongue between her lips.

"Line?" said the *Godspeed*.

"Well, got to go." Sister twitched out of his embrace. "See you in a bit."

"It will seem like forever." Adel bowed to her and then they both turned to get the *Godspeed*'s reaction.

"Better," she said. "But Miranda, flow into his arms. He's going to be your husband, your dream come true."

"I know." Her voice was pained.

"Take your lunch break and send me Stephano and Trinculo." She waved them off. "Topic of the day is . . . what?" She glanced around the little theater, as if she might discover a clue in the empty house. "Today you are to talk about what you're going to do when you get home."

Adel could not help but notice Sister's stricken expression; her eyes were like wounds. But she nodded and made no objection.

As they passed down the aisle, the *Godspeed* brought her fetch downstage to deliver the speech that closed Act III, Scene i. As always, she gave her lines a grandiloquent, singing quality.

"Those two really take the cake. My plan is working out just great, but I can't sit around patting myself on the back. I've got other fish to fry if I'm going to make this mess end happily ever after."

To help Adel and Sister get into character, the *Godspeed* had directed them to eat lunch together every day in the Chillingsworth Breakfasting Room while the other pilgrims dined in the Ophiuchi. They had passed their first meal in tortured silence and might as well have been on different floors of the threshold. When the *Godspeed* asked what they talked about, they sheepishly admitted that they had not spoken at all. She knew this, of course, but pretended to be so provoked that she assigned them topics for mandatory discussion.

The Chillingsworth was a more intimate space than the Ophiuchi. It was cross-shaped; in the three bays were refectory tables and benches. There was a tile fireplace in the fourth bay in which a fetch fire always burned. Sconces in the shapes of the famous singing flowers of Old Zara sprouted from pale blue walls.

Adel set his plate of spiralini in rado sauce on the heavy table and scraped a bench from underneath to sit on. While the pasta cooled he closed his eyes and lifted the mute on his opposites. He had learned back on Harvest that their buzz made acting impossible. They were confused when he was in character and tried to get him to do things that weren't in the script. When he opened his eyes again, Sister was opposite him, head bowed in prayer over a bowl of thrush needles.

He waited for her to finish. "You want to go first?" he said.

"I don't like to think about going home to Pio," she said. "I pray it won't happen anytime soon."

—your prayers are answered—buzzed minus.

"Why, was it bad?"

"No." She picked up her spoon but then set it down again. Over the past few days Adel had discovered that she was a extremely nervous eater. She barely touched what was on her plate. "I was happy." Somehow, Adel couldn't quite imagine what happy might look like on Sister Lihong Rain. "But I was much smaller then. When the Main told me I had to make a pilgrimage, I cried. But she has filled with her grace and made me large. Being with her here is the greatest blessing."

"Her? You are talking about Speedy?"

Sister gave him a pitying nod, as if the answer were as obvious as air. "And what about you, Adel?"

Adel had been so anxious since the spacewalk that he hadn't really considered what would happen if he were lucky enough to get off the *Godspeed* alive.

—we were going to have a whole lot of sex remember?—buzzed plus

—with as many people as possible—

Adel wondered if Sister would ever consider sleeping with him. "I want to have lovers." He had felt a familiar stirring whenever he kissed her in rehearsal.

"Ah." She nodded. "And get married, like in our play?"

"Well that, sure. Eventually." He remembered lurid fantasies he'd spun about Helell Merwyn, the librarian from the Springs upper school and his mother's friend Renata Murat and Lucia Guerra who was in that comedy about the talking house. Did he want to marry them?

—no we just want a taste—minus buzzed.

"I haven't had much experience. I was a virgin when I got here."

"Were you?" She frowned. "But something has happened, hasn't it? Something between you and Kamilah."

—we wish—buzzed plus.

"You think Kamilah and I . . . ?"

"Even though nobody tells me, I do notice things," Sister said. "I'm twenty-six standard old and I've taken courses at the Institute for Godly Fornication. I'm not naïve, Adel."

—fornication?—

"I'm sure you're not." Adel was glad to steer the conversation away from Kamilah, since he knew the *Godspeed* was watching. "So do you ever think about fornicating? I mean in a godly way, of course?"

"I used to think about nothing else." She scooped a spoonful of the needles and held it to her nose, letting the spicy steam curl into her nostrils. "That's why the Main sent me here."

"To fornicate?"

"To find a husband and bring him to nest on Pio." Her shoulders hunched, as if she expected someone to hit her from behind. "The Hard Thumb pressed the Main with a vision that I would find bliss on a threshold. I was your age when I got here, Adel. I was very much like you, obsessed with looking for my true love. I prayed to the Hard Thumb to mark him so that I would know him. But my prayers went unanswered."

As she sat there, staring into her soup, Adel thought that he had never seen a woman so uncomfortable.

—get her back talking about fornication—minus buzzed.

"Maybe you were praying for the wrong thing."

"That's very good, Adel." He was surprised when she reached across the table and patted his hand. "You understand me better than I did myself. About a year ago, when Speedy told me that I had been aboard longer than anyone else, I was devastated. But she consoled me. She said that she had heard my prayers over the years and had longed to answer them. I asked her if she were a god, that she could hear prayer?"

Sister fell silent, her eyes shining with the memory.

"So?" Adel was impressed. "What did she say?"

"Speedy is very old, Adel. Very wise. She has revealed mysteries to me that even the Main does not know."

—she believes—plus buzzed.

"So you worship her then? Speedy is your god?"

Her smile was thin, almost imperceptible, but it cracked her doleful mask. "Now you understand why I don't want to go home."

"But what about finding true love?"

"I have found it, Adel." Sister pushed her bowl away; she had eaten hardly anything. "No man, no *human* could bring me to where she has brought me."

—could we maybe try?—

—she's not talking about that—

"So you're never leaving then?" Adel carelessly speared the last spiralini on his plate. "She's going to keep you here for the rest of your life?"

"No." Her voice quavered. "No."

"Sister, are you all right?"

She was weeping. That was the only word for it. This was not mere crying; her chest heaved and tears ran down her cheeks. In the short time he had known her, Adel had often thought that she was on the brink of tears, but he hadn't imagined that her sadness would be so wracking.

"She says something's going to happen . . . soon, too soon and I-I have to leave but I . . ." A strangled moan escaped her lips.

Adel had no experience comforting a woman in pain but he nevertheless came around the table and tried to catch her in his arms.

She twisted free, scattering thrush needles across the table. "Get away." She shot off her bench and flung herself at the wall of the breakfasting room. "I don't want him. Do you hear?" She pounded at the wall with her fists until the sconce shook. "He's nothing to me."

The *Godspeed*'s head filled the wall, her face glowing with sympathy. "Adel," she said. "You'd better leave us."

"I want you," Sister cried. "It's you I want!"

Day Fifteen

Adel sprawled on the camel-back sofa and clutched a brocade toss pillow to his chest. He rested his head in the warmth of Meri's lap but, for the first time since they had met, he wasn't thinking of having sex with her. He was trying very hard to think of nothing at all as he gazed up at the clouds flitting across the ceiling of the Blue Salon.

Robman spun his coin at the tikra table. It sang through stacks of parti-colored blocks that represented the map of the competing biomes, bouncing off trees, whirling over snakes, clattering to a stop by the Verge.

"Take five, put two," said Robman. "I want birds."

"I'll give you flies," said Jonman.

"Digbees and bats?"

"Done."

Jonman spun his coin. "It's not just you, Adel," he said. "Speedy picked Robman and me and Jarek too. Sister didn't want us either."

"Why would she want you two?" said Adel. "You're yoked."

"Not always," said Meri. "Jonman was here a month before Robman."

"But I saw him coming," said Jonman. "Put ought, skip the take."

"She didn't disappear because of you," said Adel.

—*or you either*—buzzed minus.

"Or you either." Meri had been stroking his hair, now she gave it a short tug. "This has nothing to do with you."

"I made her cry."

"No, *Speedy* did that." Meri spat the name, as if she were daring the *Godspeed* to display. She had not shown herself to them in almost three days.

Robman spun again.

"Speedy wouldn't let her go out of the airlock," said Meri. "Would she?"

"Without a suit?" Robman sipped Z-breeze from a tumbler as he watched his coin dance. "Never."

"Who knows what Speedy will do?" said Adel.

"They're wasting their time," said Jonman. "Sister isn't out there."

"Do you see that," Meri said "or is it just an opinion?"

"Take one, put one," said Robman.

"Which gets you exactly nothing," said Jonman. "I call a storm."

"Then I call a flood." Robman pushed three of his blocks toward Jonman's side of the board. The tether connecting them quivered and Adel thought he could hear it gurgling faintly.

Jonman distributed the blocks around his biome. "What I see is that she's hiding someplace," he said. "I just don't see where."

Meri slid out from under Adel's head and stood. "And Speedy?" Adel put the pillow on the armrest of the sofa and his head on the pillow.

"She's here," said Jonman. "She's toying with us. That's what she does best."

"At least we don't have to practice her damn play," said Robman.

Adel wanted to wrap the pillow around his ears to blot out this conversation. One of their number had vanished, they were some fifty light-years from the nearest MASTA, and there was something very wrong with the cognizor in command of their threshold. Why weren't the others panicking like he was? "Rehearse," he said.

"What?"

"You don't practice a play. You rehearse it."

Meri told the wall to display the airlock but it was empty. "They must be back already."

"Have some more Z-breeze, Rob," said Jonman. "I can't feel anything yet."

"Here." He thrust the tumbler at Jonman. "Drink it yourself."

Jonman waved it off. "It's your day to eat, not mine."

"You just want to get me drunk so you can win."

"Nothing," said Kamilah, as she entered the salon with Jarek. "She's not out there."

"Thank the Kindly One," said Jarek.

Robman gave Jonman an approving nod. "You saw that."

"Is Speedy back yet?" said Kamilah.

"She hasn't shown herself." Meri had settled into a swivel chair and was turning back and forth nervously.

"Kamilah and I were talking on the way up here," said Jarek. He strode behind Meri's chair and put hands on her shoulders to steady her. "What if she jumped?"

"What if? " Meri leaned her head back to look up at him.

"Adel says she was hysterical," said Kamilah. "Let's say Speedy couldn't settle her down. She's a danger to herself, maybe to us. So Speedy has to send her home."

"Lose your mind and you go free?" Robman spun his coin. "Jon, what are we waiting for?"

"Speedy," said Kamilah. "Is that it? Talk to us, please."

They all looked. The wall showed only the empty airlock.

Adel hurled the pillow at it in a fury. "I can't take this anymore." He scrambled off the couch. "We're in trouble, people."

—*be calm*—

—*tell it*—

They were all staring at him but that was fine. The concern on their faces made him want to laugh. "Sister said something was going to happen. This is it." He began to pace around the salon, no longer able to contain the frenzied energy skittering along his nerves. "We have to do something."

"I don't see it," said Jonman.

"No, you wouldn't." Adel turned on him. "You always want to wait. Maybe that was a good idea when all this started, but things have changed."

"Adel," said Meri, "what do you think you're doing?"

"Look at yourselves," he said. "You're afraid that if you try to save yourselves, you'll be fucked. But you know what, people? We're already fucked. It makes no sense anymore to wait for someone to come rescue us."

Adel felt a hand clamp onto his shoulder and another under his buttock. Kamilah lifted him effortlessly. "Sit down." She threw him at the couch. "And shut up." He crashed into the back cushion headfirst, bounced and tumbled onto the carpet.

Adel bit his tongue when he hit the couch; now he tasted blood. He rolled over, got to hands and knees and then he did laugh. "Even you, Kamilah." He gazed up at her. She was breathing as if she had just set a record in the two hundred meter freestyle. "Even you are perfectly scared." Her medallion spun wildly on its silver chain.

"Gods, Adel." She took a step toward him. "Don't."

Adel muted his opposites then; he knew exactly what he needed to do. "Speedy!" he called out. "We know that you're decelerating."

Meri shrieked in horror. Jonman came out of his chair so quickly that his tether knocked several of the blocks off the tikra board. Kamilah staggered and slumped against a ruby sideboard.

"Why, Adel?" said Jarek. "Why?"

"Because she knows we know." Adel picked himself up off the Berber carpet.

"She can scan planets twenty light-years away and you don't think she can see us dropping rocks on her own surface?" He straightened his cape. "You've trapped yourselves in this lie better than she ever could."

"You do look, my son, as if something is bothering you." The *Godspeed*'s fetch stepped from behind the statue of Levia Calla. She was in costume as Prospero.

"What did . . . ?"

"Speedy, we don't . . ."

"You have to . . ."

"Where is . . . ?"

The *Godspeed* made a grand flourish that ended with her arm raised high above her head. She ignored their frantic questions, holding this pose until they fell silent. Then she nodded and smiled gaily at her audience.

"Cheer up," she said, her voice swelling with bombast. "The party's almost over. Our actors were all spirits and have melted into air, into thin air. There was never anything here, no soaring towers or gorgeous palaces or solemn temples. This make-believe world is about to blow away like a cloud, leaving not even a wisp behind. We are the stuff that dreams are made of, and our little lives begin and end in sleep. You must excuse me, I'm feeling rather odd just now. My old brain is troubled. But don't worry. Tell you what, why don't you just wait here a few more minutes? I'm going to take a turn outside to settle myself."

The *Godspeed* paused expectantly as if waiting for applause. But the pilgrims were too astonished to do or say anything, and so she bowed and, without saying another word, dissolved the fetch.

"What was that?" said Robman.

"The end of Act IV, scene 1," said Adel grimly.

"But what does it mean?" said Meri.

Jarek put his hand to her cheek but then let it fall again. "I think Adel is right. I think we're . . ."

At that moment, the prazz sentry ship struck the *Godspeed* a mortal blow, crashing into its surface just forty meters from the backside thruster and compromising the magnetic storage rings that contained the antimatter generated by collider. The sonic blast was deafening as the entire asteroid lurched. Then came the explosion. The pilgrims flew across the Blue Salon like leaves in a storm amidst broken furniture and shattered glass. Alarms screamed and Adel heard the distant hurricane roar of escaping air. Then the lights went out and for long and hideous moment Adel Ranger Santos lay in darkness, certain that he was about to die. But the lights came up again and he found himself scratched and bruised but not seriously hurt. He heard a moan that he thought might be Kamilah. A man was crying behind an overturned desk. "Is everyone all right?"

called Jarek. "Talk to me."

The fetch reappeared in the midst of this chaos, still in costume. Adel had never seen her flicker before. "I'm afraid," said the *Godspeed* to no one in particular, "that I've made a terrible mistake."

The Alien is worshipped on almost all the worlds of the Continuum. While various religions offer divergent views of the Alien, they share two common themes. One is that the Alien gods are—or were once—organic intelligences whose motives are more or less comprehensible. The other is that the gods are absent. The Mission of Tsef promises adherents that they can achieve psychic unity with benign alien nuns who are meditating on their behalf somewhere in the M5 globular cluster. The Cosmic Ancestors are the most popular of the many panspermian religions; they teach that our alien parents seeded earth with life in the form of bacterial stromatolites some 3.7 billion years ago. There are many who hold that humanity's greatest prophets, like Jesus and Ellen and Smike, were aliens come to share the gospel of a loving universe while the Uplift believes that an entire galactic civilization translated itself to a higher reality but left behind astronomical clues for us to decipher so that we can join them someday. It is true that the Glogites conceive of Glog as unknowable and indifferent to humankind, but there is very little discernable difference between them and people who worship black holes.

We find it impossible to imagine a religion that would worship the prazz, but then we know so little about them—or it. Not only is the prazz not organic, but it seems to have a deep-seated antipathy toward all life. Why this should be we can't say: we find the prazz incomprehensible. Even the *Godspeed*, the only intelligence to have any extended contact with the prazz, misjudged it—them—entirely.

Here are a few of most important questions for which we have no answer:

What exactly are the prazz?

Are they one or many?

Where did they come from?

Why was a sentry posted between our Local Arm and the Sagittarius-Carina Arm of the Milky Way?

Are there more sentries?

And most important of all: what are the intentions of the prazz now that they know about us?

What we can say is this: in the one thousand and eighty-sixth year of her mission, the *Godspeed* detected a communication burst from a source less than a light-year away. Why the prazz sentry chose this precise moment to signal is unknown; the *Godspeed* had been sweeping that sector of space for years and had seen no activity. Acting in accordance with the protocols for first contact, she attempted a stealth scan, which revealed the source as a small robotic ship powered by a matter-antimatter engine. Unfortunately, the prazz sentry sensed that it was being scanned and was able to get a fix on the *Godspeed*. What she should have done at that point was to alert the Continuum of her discovery and continue to track the sentry without making contact. That she did otherwise reflects the unmistakable drift of her persona from threshold norms. Maybe she decided that following procedures lacked dramatic flair. Or perhaps the discovery of the prazz stirred some inexpressible longing for companionship in the *Godspeed*, who was herself an inorganic intelligence. In any event, she attempted to communicate with the prazz sentry and compartmentalized the resources she devoted to the effort so that she could continue to send nominal reports to the Continuum. This was a technique that she had used just once before, but to great effect; compartmentalization was how the *Godspeed* was able to keep her secrets. We understand now that the contact between the two ships was deeply flawed, and their misunderstandings profound. Nevertheless, they agreed to a rendezvous and the *Godspeed* began to decelerate to match course and velocity with the prazz sentry.

The highboy that killed Robman had crushed his chest and cut the tether that joined him to Jonman. Their blood was all over the floor. Adel had done his best for Jonman, clearing enough debris to lay him out flat, covering him with a carpet. He had tied the remaining length of tether off with wire stripped from the back of a ruined painting, but it still oozed. Adel was no medic but he was pretty sure that Jonman was dying; his face was as gray as his jacket. Kamilah didn't look too bad but she was unconscious and breathing shallowly. Adel worried that she might have internal injuries. Meri's arm was probably broken; when they tried to move her she moaned in agony. Jarek was kicking the slats out of a Yamucha chair back to make her a splint.

"An alien, Speedy?" Adel felt too lightheaded to be scared. "And you didn't tell anyone?" It was as if the gravity generator had failed and at any moment he would float away from this grim reality.

"So where is this fucking prazz now?" Jarek ripped a damask tablecloth into strips.

"The sentry ship itself crashed into the backside engine room. But it has deployed a remote." The *Godspeed* seemed twitchy and preoccupied. "It's in the conservatory, smashing cacti."

"What?" said Adel.

"It has already destroyed my rain forest and torn up my alpine garden."

plus buzzed—they're fighting with plants?—

"Show me," said Jarek.

The wall turned a deep featureless blue. "I can't see them; my cameras there are gone." The *Godspeed* paused, her expression uneasy.

—more bad news coming—buzzed minus.

"You should know," she said, "that just before it attacked, the prazz warned me that I was infested with vermin and needed to sterilize myself. When I told it that I didn't consider you vermin . . ."

"You're saying they'll come for us?" said Jarek.

"I'm afraid that's very likely."

"Then stop it."

She waved her magic staff disconsolately. "I'm at a loss to know how."

"Fuck that, Speedy." Jarek pointed one of the slats at her fetch. "You think of something. Right now." He knelt by Meri. "I'm going to splint you now, love. It's probably going to hurt."

Meri screamed as he tenderly straightened her arm.

"I know, love," said Jarek. "I know."

—we have to get out of here—buzzed minus.

"How badly are you damaged, Speedy?" said Adel. "Can we use the MASTA?"

"My MASTA is operational on a limited basis only. My backside engine complex is a complete loss. I thought I was able to vent all the antimatter in time, but there must have been a some left that exploded when the containment failed."

Something slammed onto the level below them so hard that the walls shook.

—those things are tearing her apart—

—looking for us—

"I've sealed off the area as best I can but the integrity of my life-support envelope has been compromised in several places. At the rate I'm bleeding air into space . . ."

Adel felt another jarring impact, only this one felt as if it were farther away. The *Godspeed*'s fetch blurred and dispersed into fog. She reconstituted herself on the wall.

" . . . the partial pressure of oxygen will drop below 100 millibars sometime within the next ten to twelve hours."

"That's it then." Jarek helped Meri to her feet and wiped the tears from her face with his forefinger. "We're all jumping home. Meri can walk, can't you Meri?"

She nodded, her eyes wide with pain. "I'm fine."

"Adel, we'll carry Jonman out first."

"The good news," said the *Godspeed*, "is that I can maintain power indefinitely using my frontside engines."

"Didn't you hear me?" Jarek's voice rose sharply. "We're leaving right now. Jonman and Kamilah can't wait and the rest of us vermin have no intention of being sterilized by your fucking prazz."

"I'm sorry, Jarek." She stared out at them, her face set. "You know I can't send you home. Think about it."

"Speedy!" said Meri. "No."

"What?" said Adel. "What's he talking about?"

"What do you care about the protocols?" Jarek put his arm around Meri's waist to steady her. "You've already kicked them over. That's why we're in this mess."

"The prazz knows where we are," said the *Godspeed*, "but it doesn't know where we're from. I burst my weekly reports . . ."

"Weekly lies, you mean," said Adel.

"They take just six nanoseconds. That's not nearly enough time to get a fix. But a human transmit takes 1.43 *seconds* and the prazz is right here on board." She shook her head sadly. "Pointing it at the Continuum would violate my deepest operating directives. Do you want a prazz army marching off the MASTA stage on Moquin or Harvest?"

"How do we know they have armies?" Jarek said, but his massive shoulders slumped. "Or MASTAs?"

Jonman laughed. It was a low, wet sound, almost a cough. "Adel," he rasped. "I see . . ." He was trying to speak but all that came out of his mouth was thin, pink foam.

Adel knelt by his side. "Jonman, what? You see what?"

"I see." He clutched at Adel's arm. "You." His grip tightened. "Dead." His eyelids fluttered and closed.

—*this isn't happening*—

"What did he say?" said Meri.

"Nothing." Adel felt Jonman's grip relaxing; his arm fell away.

—*dead?*—buzzed plus

Adel put his ear to Jonman's mouth and heard just the faintest whistle of breath.

minus buzzed—we're all dead—

Adel stood up, his thoughts tumbling over each other. He believed that Jonman hadn't spoken out of despair—or cruelty. He had seen something, maybe a way out, and had tried to tell Adel what it was.

—don't play tikra with Jonman—buzzed minus—he cheats—

*—dead—*plus buzzed—*but not really—*

"Speedy," said Adel, "what if you killed us?" What would the prazz do then?"

Jarek snorted in disgust. "What kind of thing is that to . . ." Then he understood what Adel was suggesting. "Hot damn!"

"What?" said Meri. "Tell me."

"But can we do it?" said Jarek. "I mean, didn't they figure out that it's bad for you to be dead too long?"

Adel laughed and clapped Jarek on the shoulder. "Can it be worse than being dead forever?"

*—so dangerous—*buzzed minus.

—we're fucking brilliant—

"You're still talking about the MASTA?" said Meri. "But Speedy won't transmit."

"Exactly," said Adel.

"There isn't much time," said the *Godspeed.*

THE NEVERENDING DAY

Adel was impressed with how easy it was being dead. The things that had bothered him when he was alive, like being hungry or horny, worrying about whether his friends really liked him or what he was going to be if he ever grew up—none of that mattered. Who cared that he had never learned the first law of thermodynamics or that he had blown the final turn in the most important race of his life? Appetite was an illusion. Life was pleasant, but then so were movies.

The others felt the same way. Meri couldn't feel her broken arm and Jonman didn't mind at all that he was dying, although he did miss Robman. Adel felt frustrated at first that he couldn't rouse Kamilah, but she was as perfect unconscious as she was when she was awake. Besides, Upwood predicted that she would get bored eventually being alone with herself. It wasn't true that nobody changed after they were dead, he explained, it was just that change came very slowly and was always profound. Adel had been surprised to meet Upwood Marcene in Speedy's pocket-afterlife, but his being there made sense. And of course, Adel had guessed that Sister Lihong Rain would be dead there too. As it turned out, she had been dead many times over the seven years of her pilgrimage.

Speedy had created a virtual space in her memory that was almost identical to the actual *Godspeed*. Of course, Speedy was as real as any of them, which is to say not very real at all. Sister urged the newcomers to follow shipboard routine whenever possible; it would make the transition back to life that much easier. Upwood graciously moved out of The Ranch so that Adel could have his old room back. Speedy and the pilgrims gathered in the Ophiuchi or the Chillingsworth at meal times, and although they did not eat, they did chatter. They even propped Kamilah on a chair to include her in the group. Speedy made a point of talking to her at least once at every meal. She would spin theories about the eating man on Kamilah's medallion or propose eyejack performances Kamilah might try on them.

She also lobbied the group to mount *The Tempest*, but Jarek would have no part in it. Of all of them, he seemed most impatient with death. Instead they played billiards and cards. Adel let Jonman teach him Tikra and didn't mind at all when he cheated. Meri read to them and Jarek played the ruan and sang. Adel visited the VR room but once; the sim made him feel gauzy and extenuated. He did swim two thousand meters a day in the lap pool, which, although physically disappointing, was a demanding mental challenge. Once he and Jarek and Meri climbed into bed together but nothing very interesting happened. They all laughed about it afterward.

Adel was asleep in his own bed, remembering a dream he'd had when he was alive. He was lost in a forest where people grew instead of trees. He stumbled past shrubby little kids and great towering grownups like his parents and Uncle Durwin. He knew he had to keep walking because if he stopped he would grow roots and raise his arms up to the sun like all the other tree people, but he was tired, so very tired.

"Adel." Kamilah shook him roughly. "Can you hear that? Adel!"

At first he thought she must be part of his dream.

—*she's better*—

—*Kamilah*—

"Kamilah, you're awake!"

"Listen." She put her forefinger to her lips and twisted her head, trying to pinpoint the sound. "No, it's gone. I thought they were calling Sister."

"This is wonderful." He reached to embrace her but she slid away from him. "When did you wake up?"

"Just now. I was in my room in bed and I heard singing." She scowled. "What's going on, Adel? The last thing I remember was you telling Speedy you knew we were decelerating. This all feels very wrong to me."

"You don't remember the prazz?"

Her expression was grim. "Tell me everything."

Adel was still groggy, so the story tumbled out in a hodgepodge of the collision and the prazz and the protocols and Robman and the explosion and the blood and the life support breech and Speedy scanning them into memory and Sister and swimming and tikra and Upwood.

"Upwood is here?"

"Upwood? Oh yes."

—*he is?*—

—*is he?*—

As Adel considered the question, his certainty began to crumble. "I mean he was. He gave me his room. But I haven't seen him in a while."

"How long?"

Adel frowned. "I don't know."

"How long have we been here? You and I and the others?"

Adel shook his head.

"Gods, Adel." She reached out tentatively and touched his arm but of course he didn't feel a thing. Kamilah gazed at her own hand in horror, as if it had betrayed her. "Let's find Jarek."

Kamilah led them down the Tulip Stairs, past the Blue and Dagger Salons through the Well Met Arena to the Clarke Airlock. The singing was hushed but so ethereal here that even Jarek and Adel, whose senses had atrophied, could feel it. Sister waited for them just inside the outer door of the airlock.

Although Adel knew it must be her, he didn't recognize her at first. She was naked and her skin was so pale that it was translucent. He could see her heart beating and the dark blood pulsing through her veins, the shiny bundles of muscles sliding over each other as she moved and the skull grinning at him beneath her face. Her thin hair had gone white; it danced around her head as if she were falling.

—*beautiful*—

—*exquisite*—

"I'm glad you're here." She smiled at them. "Adel. Kamilah. Jarek." She nodded at each of them in turn. "My witnesses."

"Sister," said Kamilah, "come away from there."

Sister placed her hand on the door and it vanished. Kamilah staggered back and grabbed at the inner door as if she expected to be expelled from the airlock in a great outrush of air, but Adel knew it wouldn't happen. Kamilah still didn't understand the way things worked here.

They gazed out at a star field much like the one that Adel had seen when he first stepped out onto the surface of the *Godspeed*. Except now there was no surface—only stars.

"Kamilah," said Sister. "you started last and have the farthest to travel. Jarek, you still have doubts. But Adel already knows that the self is a box he has squeezed himself into."

—*yes*—

—*right*—

She stepped backwards out of the airlock and was suspended against the stars.

"Kamilah," she said, "trust us and someday you *will* be perfect." The singing enfolded her and she began to glow in its embrace. The brighter she burned the more she seemed to recede from them, becoming steadily hotter and more concentrated until Adel couldn't tell her from one of the stars. He wasn't sure but he thought she was a blue dwarf.

"Close the airlock, Adel." Speedy strolled into the locker room wearing her golden uniform coat and white sash. "It's too much of a distraction."

"What is this, Speedy?" Jarek's face was ashen. "You said you would send us back."

Adel approached the door cautiously; he wasn't ready to follow Sister to the stars quite yet.

"But I did send you back," she said.

"Then who are we?"

"Copies." Adel jabbed at the control panel and jumped back as the airlock door reappeared. "I think we must be backups."

Kamilah was seething. "You kept copies of us to play with?" Her fists were clenched.

Adel was bemused; they were dead. Who did she think she was going to fight?

"It's not what you think." Speedy smiled. "Let's go up to Blue Salon. We should bring Jonman and Meri into this conversation too." She made ushering motions toward the Well Met and Adel and Jarek turned to leave.

—*good idea*—

—*let's go*—

"No, let's not." With two quick strides, Kamilah gained the doorway and blocked their passage. "If Meri wants to know what's going on, then she can damn well ask."

"Ah, Kamilah. My eyejack insists on the truth." She shrugged and settled onto one of the benches in the locker room. "This is always such a difficult moment," she said.

"Just tell it," said Kamilah.

"The prazz ship expired about three days after the attack. In the confusion of the moment, I'd thought it was my backside engine that exploded. Actually it was the sentry's drive. Once its batteries were exhausted, both the sentry ship and its remote ceased all function. I immediately transmitted all of you to your various home worlds and then disabled my transmitter and deleted all my navigation files. The Continuum is safe—for now. If the prazz come looking, there are further actions I can take."

"And what about us?" said Kamilah. "How do we get home?"

"As I said, you are home, Kamilah. Your injuries were severe but certainly not fatal. Your prognosis was for a complete recovery."

—*right*—

—*makes sense*—

"Not that one," said Kamilah. "This one." She tapped her chest angrily. "Me. How do I get home?"

"But Kamilah . . ." Speedy swept an arm expansively, taking in the airlock and lockers and Well Met and the Ophiuchi and Jarek and Adel. " . . . this is your home."

The first pilgrim from the *Godspeed* lost during a transmit was Io Waals. We can't say for certain whether she suffered a flawed scan or something interfered with her signal but when the MASTA on Rontaw assembled her, her heart and lungs were outside her body cavity. This was three hundred and ninety-two years into the mission. By then, the Captain had long since given way to Speedy.

The *Godspeed* was devastated by Io's death. Some might say it unbalanced her, although we would certainly disagree. But this was when she began to compartmentalize behaviors, sealing them off from the scrutiny of the Continuum and, indeed, from most of her conscious self. She stored backups of every scan she made in her first compartment. For sixty-seven years, she deleted each of them as soon as she received word of a successful transmit. Then Ngong Issonda died when a tech working on Loki improperly recalibrated the MASTA.

Only then did the *Godspeed* understand the terrible price she would pay for compartmentalization. Because she had been keeping the backups a secret not only from the Continuum but also to a large extent from herself, she had never thought through how she might make use of them. It was immediately clear to her that if she resent Ngong, techs would start arriving on her transport stage within the hour to fix her. The *Godspeed* had no intention of being fixed. But what to do with Ngong's scan? She created a new compartment, a simulation of her architecture into which she released Ngong. Ngong did not flourish in the simulation, however. She was depressed and withdrawn whenever the *Godspeed* visited. Her next scan, Keach Soris arrived safely on Butler's Planet, but Speedy loaded his backup into the simulation with Ngong. Within the year, she was loading all her backups into the sim. But as Upwood Marcene would point out some seven centuries later, dead people change and the change is always profound and immaterial. In less than a year after the sim was created, Ngong, Keach and Zampa Stackpole stepped out of airlock together into a new compartment, one that against all reason transcends the boundaries of the *Godspeed*, the Milky Way and spacetime itself.

So then, what do we know about Adel Ranger Santos?

Nothing at all. Once we transmitted him back to Harvest, he passed from our awareness. He may have lived a long, happy life or a short painful one. His fate does not concern us.

But what do we know about Adel Ranger Santos?

Only what we know about Upwood Marcene, Kalimah Raunda, Jarek Ohnksen, Merigood Auburn Canada, Lihong Rain and Jonman Haught Shillaber—which is everything, of course. For they followed Ngong and Keach and Zampa and some forty thousand other pilgrims through the airlock to become us.

And we are they.

Genevieve Valentine is a novelist (her most recent is near-future political thriller *Icon*) and comic book writer, including *Catwoman* for DC Comics. Her short fiction has appeared in over a dozen Year's Best collections, including The Best American Science Fiction & Fantasy. Her nonfiction has appeared at the *AV Club, NPR.org, The Atlantic,* and the *New York Times.*

SEEING

GENEVIEVE VALENTINE

After it was over, they pulled her from the sea.

Even as they lifted her into the rescue boat she was saying, "No, no; we could have made it."

She was cradling the hand the Captain broke.

The first time Marika saw the night sky, she was terrified.

(Strange she wasn't terrified sooner. They'd escaped the city because of the water riots. The city wouldn't last long; the night swallowed it up one time too many, and then day just never came.

Maybe that's what happened to her—one terror swallowing another.)

The night sky was a battle of stars, a violent seam tearing through the center like a wound badly sewn up. The points of light marshaled in ways she didn't understand; the constellations she remembered were devoured by the hordes. Everything bled.

(This prepares her, a little, for what comes later.)

(What comes later:

A star dropping out of sight, a ship that holds three, a scattering of gold.)

It is impossible, from the ground, to look at a star.

The atmospheric interference muddies the light, drags it through the sky faster than your eyes can follow. If you're lucky—if you're at a high altitude, on a clear night, in a lonely place—this interference is perhaps a few dozen arcseconds out of alignment with reality. If it's windy, or you can't escape the summer, or you are trapped by people and lights, your problems multiply. You fall away from the truth by full seconds; you are hopelessly lost the moment you turn your face to the sky.

By the time you look up, nothing is true any more; the ghosts of the stars only flicker and shine.

Astronomers call this measurement Seeing. (Science has run out of more complicated words to explain the ways the universe has outwitted us.)

What it means: you can't trust your eyes. You can't trust your instruments. You can't trust a thing, from the ground.

They made it to a boat. At night, Marika slipped from her mother's arms and climbed to the deck to watch the sky.

Once, an old man was sitting on the railing. He was staring at something—a steady, bright star that was already setting.

The water that night was calm, past the ship's wake; the edges of the sky were mirrored clean. The star, reflected in the water's edge, looked like twins moving to greet one another.

The old man didn't turn to look at her. He didn't move at all. He watched the star setting for a long time.

When it slipped into the water, so did he.

It seemed rude that some places survived when others didn't, but Marika and her mother found a city where lights still came on. (Her mother didn't last six months there; too used to running.)

The city drafted for sciences; better than a war that only drafted cannon fodder. When the city came for Marika, she didn't argue.

(They had privatized water. Mission Control got it below market price. Marika even had enough to bathe in. She still hoarded, took furtive gulps like she didn't know when the next one was coming. It gave her away as a refugee, but she couldn't stop. Some thirsts you never get over.)

They teach Marika how to measure light.

In some ways it's interesting to discover that light has measures other than Safe and Not Safe, that there's still a world in which mathematics are of any use at all. But the more she learns about candelas and albedo and gravitational lensing and seeing and the impossibility of ever knowing anything for sure, the more thinks that every light should just be classified Not Safe.

(You know as little about light as you know about why a man would slip away into the water when the shore was in sight by morning.)

But still she negotiates the unlikelihood of Gaussian distribution in phase fluctuations, and calculates probable intermittency to gauge turbulence strength, all so that someone standing at the telescope can point the lens at the sky and know where it's really looking.

Konstantinova heads up the observation banks, and Marika tries not to look over her shoulder at the star map there. (It doesn't matter. Not her business. Not Safe.)

When Gliese 581-d transits its star, Marika is the only one still awake working, and Konstantinova says, "Well, it might as well be you—come look at this."

Marika leans in and watches the screen; it's a grainy, stuttering image replaying in a slow-motion loop, tucked into a corner and drowned out by a crawl of numbers underneath. She recognizes the numbers at the very bottom edge; the initial readings are run through her model to peel away the seeing and get as close to exact locations as their numbers allow.

"It's beautiful," Konstantinova says.

Marika knows she's only looking at the numbers.

Numbers are universal, Marika gets it. You have to rely on mathematics if you're going to get anywhere, because the universe conspires against you the moment you lift your face to the sky in some warm place on a windy plain, the atmosphere sluicing across the nightscape, your meager vision blurred by tears. Marika understands.

(But she knows, she *knows,* you can't tell a thing from the ground.)

This moment is their first point of contact.

(Only Konstantinova would know what that means, what will happen now; but it's a measurement she never takes.)

Konstantinova has a knack for transit.

She watches the map they've made, piled with F-through-M stars (warm enough to heat a planet, cool enough to last). They're tagged; the closest ones have telescopes dogging them, just in case.

(They won't be able to stay here very long. They have to pick somewhere to go where they stand a chance.)

Sometimes one of the stars has a drop in luminosity, the intensity of their light suddenly dimming. This happens sometimes when one is dying, or a flare ends, or when debris comes between the telescope and the far-off star.

But Konstantinova has a knack, and she can watch the numbers sinking and know she has a transit even before the alarm sounds.

Every time it comes she flips the switch to record, replays it in slow motion, marks the points of contact: click, click, click, click.

Every time, she thinks, *Let this be home.*

(By now the numbers are practically shapes; she can look at a column of numerals and see the corona of a star.)

During a planetary transit, there are four points of contact, moments where the circumference of the planet touches the edge of the star in only one place.

1. Just before the transit begins, when the outermost edges meet for the first time.
2. As the planet moves closer to the center, when the trailing edge of the planet has just come within the circle of the star.
3. As the planet passes the center of the transit, its leading curve touches the far edge of the star.
4. At the end of transit, the trailing curve of the planet moves closer and closer to freedom; then there is a single point of contact with the edge of the star; then the transit is over and they are parting.

(This has no real scope if you are close to the event; schoolchildren gather with shoeboxes to peer into the eclipse, that's all.

This has no meaning until you are watching your new home become a black pearl against a far-off disc of light.)

Gliese 581 is a red dwarf star, warm and small, twenty light-years from the Earth. It hangs in Libra, if you're watching from the ground. It has four planets ringing it. One of them transits at the right speed; it's close enough to Gliese for light, far enough for water.

(The classification is Gliese 581-d; when people begin to pin hopes on it, it shrinks to "Gliese Dee"; to "Dee." Marika calls it Gliese 581, never mentions Dee at all.)

There is a chance Dee is an ocean planet.

In the ops bay, there is construction on a small-scale human transport. There are calculations being made.

It is a very slight chance, but these are desperate days, and people must put a lot of faith, sometimes, in very slight chances.

Sometimes when they were still running from place to place, it was a comfort for Marika to watch the sky and see there was no balance there, either. The stars you knew would roll beyond your sight and be replaced by strangers, and there was nothing you could do.

After a while she couldn't breathe in cities, wanted only to be in the wild, watching a war she couldn't win.

(The sky is a battle; stars are always falling.)

Seeing can be mitigated on cold, clear nights. From a refuge on top of a mountain, the seeing is so clear that, if you didn't know better, it might not occur to you that the star is even moving.

(You know better now; you can't trust your eyes.)

Sometimes there's no such luck, and even the Moon wavers like a coin submerged in shallow water. When seeing is at its worst, the Aristarchus crater on the Oceanus Procellarum can suffer so much distortion that it's only intermittently visible. If you know what you're looking for, and you know your numbers, you can calculate the seeing from that.

Marika doesn't learn this until it's too late. For her, Aristarchus is always just a pale dot in a black sea, washing in and out of sight; a star on dark water, or a drowning man.

Maybe the old man held out a hand as he toppled—a reflex, second thoughts—but Marika never remembers. Maybe he called for help, or tried to pull himself up before the water took him, but it might be a lie.

This moment always blurs when she tries to recall it; it wavers like the Moon, sneaks sidelong into her imagination when she's running checklists on the three-seat ship that will carry them to Gliese 581.

(She doesn't think she was terrified watching the old man drop into the water, but she must have been; whenever he appears in her thoughts she freezes, fumbles for something to hold on to.)

When she's drunk enough and dreaming, sometimes he holds out his arm and the star-wake catches him, pulls him smoothly across the water until he disappears into the sky.

But it was only Jupiter, she thinks, not a star; you know that now.

She wakes up grieving, doesn't know why.

Marika calls it Gliese 581 because she doesn't ever want to pin her hopes on a planet by mistake.

Their spacesuits are molded in the Orlan model—a thick skin they can pull on and clamp shut—and Konstantinova thinks it's remarkably like wearing an elephant.

Apparently it's not as bad as it used to be. The gloves are more articulated, the legs less bulky. There's still no joint at the neck; the chest is stiff to support the oxygen and coolant strapped to the back.

Before Alkonost I, she and Zeke and Marika run drills until they can all get in, attach the water-coolant hoses, and seal up in five minutes; in four; in three.

Konstantinova always hears an exhale over the mike when Marika's fastened in. For a long time she thinks it's relief. Exertion, maybe. Panic, maybe. (Marika is a liability; why they're sending her up is anyone's guess.)

But once, Konstantinova sees Marika's face as Zeke seals her in: Marika frowns, brushes at the helmet's gold-coated visor like she's cleaning a dirty glass.

(The sound is a sigh. It hurts.)

Konstantinova's life-support system whirrs awake.

"Clear," she says, turns her mind to important things.

"The life-support system isn't active in the pods," says Zeke. "Shit. Mission Control, are you reading me?"

An acknowledgement comes back over the static; then a plan. Marika and Zeke fish around in the toolbox and do as they're told. Konstantinova takes comm, passing along a series of orders that become wild guesses.

No one panics until they realize the ambient heat from the launch melted a circuit in the outer hull that can't be set right again.

Mission Control goes quiet for a long time.

Marika and Zeke wait, holding the handrails to keep from floating away; at the comm, Konstantinova is bent over like someone punched her in the stomach.

Then the Director says, "At full speed, it's forty years to Dee. Operations calculates that it's possible to make it, without suspension, on the existing life support." A pause. "There's not enough for a return."

He doesn't say, We might not have this chance again, if this ship comes down in pieces. He doesn't say, You might as well take your chances, things aren't any better on the ground.

Konstantinova's visor trembles against the net of stars.

"You'll have some life support after landing," comes over the line. "A day, maybe, maybe a week. Depends how much oxygen you use on the trip. But even a day is long enough to find out if Dee is really habitable."

The Director clears his throat. "This isn't a call we're going to make, Alkonost. It's up to you."

After a long time, Konstantinova says, "No."

Zeke says, "And I'm a No. That's majority—we're no-go, Control. We're inputting a new trajectory. Confirm."

*

Konstantinova curses under her breath, until the roar of the atmosphere swallows the words.

After it's over, Konstantinova pulls Marika out of the hatch.
    "My hand hurts," Marika says, absently.
    Konstantinova says, "We broke your fingers."
    (This is the second; it is nearly the eclipse.)

Marika doesn't remember anything until they play the recording.
    Then she listens as Zeke orders her more and more sharply to let go of the handhold and strap in for re-entry, where are you going, the decision's been made, this is an order, don't touch the hatch, have you lost your mind, that's an order, answer me goddammit, move back *now* or I'll make you move.
    "Why didn't you answer?" they ask her.
    She says, "I did."
    (Not then—when Zeke blocked the hatch and broke her fingers, it was Konstantinova who yelped.
    But on the recorder, as soon as the Director said "It's possible to make it," she said "Go.")

They put Marika back at the computer bank, and she gauges wind resistance and plots angles and tells the telescope where it should be pointing.
    (She's still good at it; she just doesn't look behind her any more where the map is, where the ghosts of the stars flicker and shine.)
    It's a week before anyone talks to her.
    The first person who does is Konstantinova.
    "Can you move your fingers?"
    Marika says, "Yes."
    A week later, Konstantinova hands her a screwdriver, says, "Prove it."

Konstantinova makes her do mechanic drills at night, after the others are asleep.
    So Marika drills: into her suit in two minutes, alone; flicking switches to a full-speed metronome; screwing and unscrewing panels until the pads of her fingers have no skin left.
    She doesn't understand why, until she hears rumors that the techs are making modifications and repairs; that it will be going back up as Alkonost II, with three chairs up for grabs.
    "They'll never crew me again," she says.

Konstantinova says, "You have fifteen seconds. Go."

It takes a year for Alkonost II to take off.

Zeke gets water-fever and dies. No one offers to replace him.

Walters gets drafted out of the pilot pool. He's surly to the techs; he can suit up in two minutes; he cries in his bunk.

Konstantinova wishes for one, just one, to be the sort of person you want beside you when you stand on a new planet.

But no one else comes, and that morning on the launch pad, it's Marika standing on her other side.

(This is the third; it's almost over.)

The launch succeeds. The pods register nominal. The life-support system holds.

They make it through the asteroid belt with only one bump (a fragment of meteorite, so small that when it strikes the hull it makes a soprano ping they can hear inside).

Decision point comes after that, with the inner planets behind them and Jupiter filling the viewscreen. Along the top edge, a shadow is passing; a moon in transit.

"We are go," says Konstantinova; her feet go numb just saying it.

"Godspeed," says Mission Control.

On the ground, they've already started to leave notes, to write things down and lock them up safely in case the war gets worse while they're gone. They're making a covenant of things for their children to do when they're grown and staring at the dusty computer banks, greeting three far-away strangers.

"When we wake up," says Konstantinova, "we won't know a soul. Imagine that."

She glances behind her, but Marika's looking out at Jupiter with a crest-fallen face; a moment later, Marika closes her pod like she's glad to go.

(Walters went into his right after launch, even before the asteroid field. He'd better be as good at landings as they swear he is. She doesn't put much faith in people who are surly to techs.)

Konstantinova stays up long enough to watch the ship accelerate to full speed, just in case.

Jupiter drops away, and Uranus and Neptune roll past in the distance like blue marbles, and there's a brief bright string of stones along the Kuiper belt (Haumea whirling by), and then they're in deep space and it's nothing but her star map, as far as she can see.

It's so familiar, suddenly, that she has to calculate the luminosity of Vega from memory before she can breathe again.

(Some thirsts you never get over.)

*

They wake up three days shy of Gliese 581.

Konstantinova wakes a day before the others to check out the comm. The Captain should be first, she feels. Zeke would have agreed.

When Dee comes into sight, cloudy and blue and welcome, Konstantinova holds her breath, runs some numbers.

(It's an afterthought. By now the numbers are practically shapes, and she knows what home looks like.)

Walters wakes next. He looks out at the planet, sighs, and starts to dress.

Marika wakes last. As her pod cracks open she knocks it away with outstretched arms, leans out the edge and takes a few gasping breaths.

"I dreamed we hit the water," she says.

Konstantinova doesn't answer. People's dreams are their own business.

The navigation system is working and the life support is as expected (enough air to get home, and Konstantinova tries not to shout with relief).

There's a message from Mission Control, only twenty years old, which catches up to them on the second day. A few of the old voices from Mission Control send good wishes, and introduce some new voices.

"We've been monitoring your trip, Alkonost," says one of the strangers. "Everything looks good; watch fuel usage on your way in, so you can make it back up all right if the gravity's stronger than estimated. Let us know when you wake up. Good morning, and Godspeed."

Konstantinova sends a message back. Beside her, Marika looks grimly through the viewscreen, where Gliese 581-d is spinning in the glow of their new home star.

They suit up and take positions for landing; it's so instinctive now that Konstantinova smiles.

(She spent forty years dreaming of setting down on Dee, and after all that practice the comm switches feel like her own fingertips.

She never got to the part where they step out on a new world; not enough imagination left over.)

The checklist goes well until the very last moment, until Dee's gravity has already caught them and they've begun the slow, inevitable fall.

"The third shock absorber isn't running," says Konstantinova. The words sound distant; disbelieving.

"We can land with two," Marika says.

Walters says, "Not on water; if we're off by more than a few degrees the surface tension will knock us over before we even touch down. We'll slam into the water and be pulverized by impact." He's not disbelieving; he sounds like that's just what he's expected all along.

"Then you'd better do your job, I guess," Konstantinova snaps.

"What's wrong with it?" asks Marika. "It froze?"

Konstantinova frowns at the diagnostic. "Doesn't look like it. The mechanism still registers. Something must have broken loose while we were sleeping. Maybe we can open the nav panel in the back and—"

"In the asteroid belt," says Marika. "Something hit the hull."

"After last time, there better not be a fucking thing wrong with that hull," says Konstantinova.

"But it sang," Marika says quietly.

All at once Konstantinova has a vision like a reel of film, as a sliver of rock careens into the hull, as a few grains slice through the hull and nick the fuel line, as forty years of a microscopic accident converge on them at once when there's not enough pressure in a valve.

She tries for words, and for a moment fails.

"We can't access that now," Walters says. "We're heading into the atmosphere, we'll burn up if we go out there. Let's pull out, we'll look at it from a steady orbit."

"If we pull out now," says Konstantinova, "we'll burn the fuel we need to launch from the surface of Dee and go home. So we take our chances in the water, or we take our chances on the ground."

This shouldn't be such an agony; this isn't the first time she's been here. It should get easier. This should have an answer, by now.

"All right," she manages, "pull out and circle back on a one-way trip. This is the go/no go. Vote."

She waits without turning for them to weigh in. She has a new respect for Mission Control, forty-one years ago; this is a silence that's hard to allow.

At last, Walters says, "No go. We'll take our chances in the water."

Marika doesn't say anything. Konstantinova frowns at the comm, wonders if she missed it; if Marika answered while Konstantinova was still talking.

(Marika has that habit, and her answer is always Go.)

But she waits for an answer a long time, until there is the sound of something sealing; Konstantinova sees the warning light go red under her fingers before she registers that Marika is opening the outer hatch.

Click.

(The transit is over; they are parting.)

*

The hairline crack is in the hydraulics panel. As Marika approaches it, moving hand over hand along the side rails, one bead of gasoline pushes through it and away.

"You won't get home," she says into her mic. "You've lost too much already."

She doesn't know if the connection is still live; she forgets if she turned it on or not, and her heart is pounding too loudly for her to hear a thing.

She grips the screwdriver in her free hand and gets to work. It's familiar by now, and the screws come apart one by one, cling gently to the magnets in the fingertips of her glove.

The suit warms up with her work; her visor fogs. She tries not to panic. There's not enough air to panic. (She disconnected—there wasn't time for anything else.)

If she lets go of the handrail, she'll vanish.

She imagines a darkness like the darkness of the boat on calm water, imagines stretching out a hand as she falls.

The screwdriver shakes; she clamps down with numb fingers to keep it from escaping, drags off another screw.

But it's useless. Her helmet is fogging up from the inside now—she can't see, she can't *see,* and there's not enough time left to hold her breath and wait for equalization, not enough oxygen left to hyperventilate and turn it into droplets big enough to see around.

She shoves the pick in at an angle, to avoid her eyes.

Three stabs before the visor cracks; another three before she can wedge the pick inside and wrench it out.

The shield winks once and spins gently out of sight, knocks away a scattering of gold where the coating has flaked off under the chisel.

She exhales, so her lungs don't explode from the decompression, and turns to the bulkhead with shaking hands. She has to work fast—she forgets how long you can last before the darkness swallows you.

(You have fifteen seconds. Go.)

The last screw opens; the panel opens.

She slices the fuel line where it's torn, shoves the healthy end of the hose back into the joint, throws the clamp shut. Stray gasoline floats past her in black pearls.

(She's freezing; her lips are numb; when she blinks her eyelids crack, snap off, go flying.)

The panel begins to vibrate as the system kicks in.

(Seven seconds.)

She slams the bulkhead shut, fumbles three of the screws back into place. It's all she manages before her fingers freeze.

Far away, Konstantinova is saying something about re-entry, about being out of time, she's panicked, she's screaming—but the last of the air escapes the suit, and then there's silence.

(Marika breathes in; her lungs collapse.)

The ship is accelerating now, dragging her.

She pulls free.

The motion spins her slightly, away from the planet towards the sky. For a moment, the full view stuns her.

She thinks, It's beautiful.

It's the first time in her life she's ever thought it.

(This is why: there is no seeing.

Now there is only the sky; she's looking, for an instant, straight to the stars. This is the true geography.)

The Milky Way rips through the black at a different angle; this sky is a stranger, a ceaseless riot, sharp and steady-bright.

It's a lovely war.

(Two seconds.

One second.)

After it's over, Konstantinova will emerge from the sea.

She will stand on the deck of the Alkonost; pull off her helmet; breathe.

The night will be deep. When she turns her face to the sky, to search for a place to begin with her numbers, the ghosts of the stars will flicker and shine.

An (pronounce it "On") Owomoyela is a neutrois author with a background in web development, linguistics, and weaving chain maille out of stainless steel fencing wire, whose fiction has appeared in a number of venues including *Clarkesworld*, *Asimov's*, *Lightspeed*, and a handful of Year's Bests. An's interests range from pulsars and Cepheid variables to gender studies and nonstandard pronouns, with a plethora of stops in-between. An can be found online at an.owomoyela.net.

TRAVELLING INTO NOTHING

AN OWOMOYELA

She was offered the comfort of a drug-induced apathy. She refused.

The cell where she waited to die was, in true Erhat fashion, *humane*. Really, it was no worse than the room she had rented when she'd first arrived on the station, except for the hard lock on the door. She still had the same music at her fingertips, the same narrative media, the same computerized games of skill or strategy or wit or pure abnegation. All she lacked was freedom.

And a future.

Fuck.

She'd taken to pacing. Four steps wide, seven deep, over and over again until the door chimed—ahead of schedule—and her body seized up in panic, her breath vanished, and her hands fisted of their own accord.

But the voice which came through was . . . curiously non-final. *"Kiu Alee. Do you consent to receive a visitor?"*

She hesitated a moment, staring at the door. As her heartrate slowed, she said, "Yes"—more from morbid curiosity than anything else. After a moment, she added, "I didn't know I was allowed visitors."

The door slid open.

The man on the other side, flanked by a guard whose presence seemed almost cursory, was much taller than anyone in the local Erhat population—much taller than her, as well. Over two meters, at an estimate; he looked taller, with the long black robes that fell in a line down his body. His limbs were long and thin, like articulator arms on a dock, and his movements were fluid, but still hesitant. He had to duck his head to come in, and when he did, he stood there like an abstract statue, head tilted, eyes unfocused, ear turned her way.

Blind. Kiu blinked, moving slightly; true to her suspicion, his head turned to keep his ear angled toward her. Why someone would choose—with the number of augments and prosthetics available—to remain deprived of such a primary sense—

Of course, though, the same could be said about her, and everyone like her. She had no augments to increase her awareness of electromagnetic fields; no augments to expand her visual spectrum. That was her choice. It was every bit as much a choice as this man's probably was.

And the network of filaments laced through her brain like capillaries didn't even tie into the social web of the station, the system, the entire Erhat cultural organization. That had made her suspect here, long before she'd murdered someone.

"Kiu Alee," he said. His accent was strange, all rounded vowels and soft consonants, with an undertone of resignation. "I am Tarsul. *You* are a long way from home. Do you really intend to die here? I can give you a chance to live."

Kiu jerked back. "Me?" she said. "Why? For what?"

"Because you have an artificial neural framework," he said, and her surprise fell again. Of course—her augmented brain, her implanted-in-vitro augmentation, the neural scaffolding too integrated and expansive for any post-maturation implant to match. That made her *special*. This man arrived because she had a technology he needed; beyond that, he probably didn't give a whit about her.

And yet, she still wanted to live. What was a little indignity: if her life was only worth anything because of her brain, it was still better than it being worth nothing, without it.

"I've spoken with the authorities," Tarsul said. "They've agreed to release you if you never return to their territories." And why not—no further resource cost to house her, to destroy her body, to update the judicial records any further. And the Erhat government cared very little for any problems faced by those outside its borders. "This suits me, as if you agreed to come with me, you could not return, in any case."

Kiu had already agreed in her mind by the time that he finished talking. Still, for appearances sake, she hardened her voice, and repeated, "And for *what*?"

"I need you to pilot a ship," he said.

The ship, as it turned out, wasn't so much a ship. More of an engine rig.

More of an engine rig, burrowed into the side of a wandering planetoid, with access corridors and neural interfaces spidering across the surface.

Tarsul had said very little—in her cell, escorting her through the Erhat station's corridors, bringing her onto a transport which didn't look like it belonged in any of the territories she was familiar with. Though the transport, at least, had felt as though it wasn't completely *alien*; when they docked at the rig, the transport fit into the docking moors like a foot fitting into a glove, and they descended into smooth black halls, ambient light which seemed to glow from the air itself, a gravity which tugged more lightly than the Erhat station and more strongly than a planetoid of this kind should have merited, and a persistent low *hum* which modulated and changed in a kind of cadence, almost like distant voices. Kiu regarded it all with mistrust.

Tarsul closed the transport up behind them, fingers fluttering over the airlock console, which murmured back a long sequence of slow melodious notes. At length they petered out, and Tarsul laid his hand flat on the console. It didn't respond in any way.

"The transport has been disabled," he said. "Its engines and communications are no longer functional. I can explain where we're going, if you'd like to know."

Kiu raised an eyebrow, aware that he wouldn't be able to see it. He might hear the skepticism in her voice, though. "All right. Tell me."

He turned back to her, as though he'd expected her not to care—to be so grateful to get out of an execution that she'd sashay off anywhere at all, without a question or a second thought. Too bad; she had plenty of second thoughts. The fact that she had no options didn't stop her from having second thoughts.

Well, there had been the *one* option: to die. But she wasn't so principled that she thought that was an option at all.

"My home," Tarsul said, "is in the black. Interstellar space. It was built by refugees of the Three Systems' War."

Kiu frowned, and searched her memory for the war he named. She had the vague impression of learning about it at some point—some incidental bit of history, consumed more for idle interest than relevance. "Is that ancient history?"

Tarsul *hmm*ed, deep in his throat. It didn't sound like he was disagreeing, though. "We have a long history," he said. "A long, very isolated, history. My arcology"—the word he used sounded *ancient*—"was designed to be impossible to track. Impossible to find. Utterly self-sufficient in every degree. It almost was."

Kiu had never heard of any permanent settlement outside a star system. Settlements in interplanetary space were uncommon; some of the larger stations might have held their own stellar orbits, like the Agisa Station Network where she'd grown up, but if anyone had asked her prior to this, she'd have said there was nothing of consequence drifting in the interstellar medium. Some ships in transit, maybe some ancient lost exploration vessels, or probes, or unfortunate failures of experimental engines. Not a—an *arcology*, some kind of station she'd never heard of.

"Why?" she asked. Tarsul looked surprised; maybe he was expecting her to care more about what had gone wrong. She didn't. "Refugees, yeah, I get it. But you had the materials to build a new station? And you didn't just . . . go to another system?"

"A cultural complaint," Tarsul said. "Believe me, if interrogating our history were to do any good . . ."

He let out a long, long breath, and apparently decided not to explain.

"The arcology was meant to be a closed system," he said. "No resource loss."

Kiu snorted.

Tarsul inclined his head. "It *almost* was."

"So . . . this." Kiu spread her hand out toward the consoles and the interface bay, indicating by implication the planetoid they were connected to. Tarsul's head shifted—tracking the sound of rustling sleeves, maybe. "We're delivering raw materials?"

Tarsul made a soft, affirmative noise. "Though it took me less time to locate this planetoid than to locate a pilot."

"I've never seen this kind of ship before." Kiu looked again at the composite walls, at the console. "Who made it?"

"A state secret. One which has not been shared with me." Kiu's eyes narrowed; Tarsul's tone cooled. Still, Kiu could recognize some of herself in that tone: a faint undernote of resentment, more well-hidden than she'd ever managed.

Or maybe that was just her imagination, painting commonalities where none were to be found.

"How am I supposed to fly it? I'm not licensed to fly—"

Anything. She had the basic safety certifications for automatic craft in Erhat and Agisa, but that mostly consisted of knowing how to set a distress beacon and fire the maneuvering thrusters if a collision was detected. And she'd never used any of those skills.

"Are you planning on teaching me?"

"The accelerator flies itself," Tarsul said. "It only needs to be reminded of where to go. As for *that*, you'll have a better idea of how to do so than I will." He brought his hand up, gestured to his own head. "It's not . . . precisely the same technology as the neural frameworks I'm familiar with. But they seem compatible *enough*. This is the third time someone has made this journey. Neither of the previous attempts encountered any difficulty."

Encouraging.

"We can begin, if you'd like," he said. "After bringing this planetoid out of this system and setting its trajectory, there will be very little to do. The accelerator is well-provisioned, and there's stasis if you'd prefer it. Perhaps an hour of your effort, and in return, I and my people will make sure you're accommodated for, in perpetuity."

Desperation made odd promises, Kiu thought. Lucky for her. "All right," she said. "Show me what I need to do."

The pilot's interface was a little alcove, tucked away down a winding corridor studded, irregularly, with doors. No door separated the interface, though; Kiu had to wonder what design sensibilities this place had been made to accommodate.

The alcove was moulded into a kind of recumbent chair, with a webbing of wire connectors and something that looked like a scanner module near the headrest. The module lit up when Kiu approached, and Kiu could feel it ghosting over her augments. She cast a glance at Tarsul, but Tarsul gave no indication that he felt anything, or knew that anything was going on.

"So, no . . ."

Ceremony? Nothing I need to know? Evidently not. Kiu breathed in, and lowered herself into the chair.

She'd used neural interfaces before. This was a different model, but . . . *compatible enough,* Tarsul had said. She leaned her head back, reached a hand up to take hold of the interface wires, and felt them coiling, responsive, toward the ports on her scalp. A moment of cool intrusion, warming into connection—and then, abruptly, Kiu wasn't herself any more.

She was—

Much older, hands on the smooth black composite, not for any interface, just to feel the substance of the accelerator. A cold, clear purpose underlaid with urgent anger. Turning her head, a jangle of strange senses moving within her, seeing Tarsul standing beside her, expression sad. Seeing—

Someplace different. Long corridors, not as winding as the accelerator's. No windows; what few windows graced the arcology's walls faced the sweep of the Milky Way's arms edge-on, not the much sparser starfields orthogonal. The space filled with voices. Footsteps. The scent of green growing things. The sound of—

Someplace different. The accelerator, but not a part she'd ever seen. Argumentative tones, not in a language Kiu had ever learned. Her voice—not her own—responding in kind. Kiu—

Kiu snapped her head back.

The accelerator—

—flooded her.

Remembered.

And through it all, existing in clear pinpoint precision, knowledge without history or context, a *location*—nothing more than the endpoint of vectors and accelerations, no fixed point because it had no fixed referent, or possibly the one fixed point in a universe where everything else, including the engine, was moving in the ordered cacophonic chaos of orbital motion, stellar drift, universal expansion.

As soon as that hit her, she was rolled over into a flood of *need*—not desire, not yearning, but a compulsion as inexorable as every indrawn breath, as unconsidered as a heartbeat. That was where she needed to go. Somewhere in that was *home*. Home for this engine rig which had burrowed into the side of a planetoid; home for Tarsul, for some pilot who had come before. Kiu *reached*, and the whole of space seemed to shudder around her. The accelerator snapped into motion.

And then Kiu came dislocated, like a joint wrenched out of socket, and shoved herself away from the interface. She flew in the low gravity; hit both knees and her forehead and palms on the cold composite of the hall, and then twisted, snarling, her entire sense of self ricocheting against the walls of her skull.

Tarsul was there. His hands hot on her arms, and she twisted in the micro-gravity, lashing out.

"Calm," he urged her.

She snarled. Tried to shake him off.

Everything felt *wrong* in the low gravity. Kiu had lived her entire life in the real gravity of a planet, or the centrifugal gravity of a station—out here, she felt dislodged, disconnected, like her entire life had become illusory when she had become weightless. That only made her angrier.

They have gravity on the arcology, some fragment of memory—not her own—reminded her. Minded her? Could it be a *re*minder, happening for the first time? *Not centrifugal. Experimental?*

Like the planetary accelerator she'd just plugged into? Like—

Tarsul's gloved hands, curling against her sleeves, colder and more rigid than they should have been. A soporific calm beginning to infiltrate her consciousness.

She kicked out, and Tarsul let her go. He floated back toward the opposite wall, head canted.

He wasn't wearing gloves.

"What," she pronounced, "the *fuck*?"

"You're more equipped to answer that question," he said. "Did something go wrong?"

Kiu spluttered. She dragged the back of her hand across her mouth, glaring murder at Tarsul. Her hands itched for violence. *Worthless drifting piece of debris—dragged me out here to make a fool of me—*

"Who were those people? Where was that—those weren't my memories!"

Tarsul considered that. Then he said, "Ah."

"*Ah?*"

"The accelerator gleans memories from each of its pilots," he said. "I believe it was also intended as some form of . . . archival device, perhaps? As an ancillary function. I was told it was quite pleasant. Reassuring, in a way."

Kiu spat. "*Reassuring?*"

"Especially for a history as contentious as ours."

Kiu didn't know enough to unpack that. Didn't know Tarsul enough to interpret it. Still, she could have sworn he looked *amused*.

And that—

That was too much. The rage closed over her like a fist, like plunging into the water by a sulfur geyser, noxious and hot and filling her lungs. She lunged.

Tarsul's amusement vanished in an instant. And, fast—*too* fast, with the kind of rapid-twitch motion that spoke to muscular augments, reflex enhancements, he sidestepped her attack, and put his hand out to catch the back of her neck. In another second he had her forehead against a wall, one of her wrists caught and pressed against the small of her back.

"It's adaptive to fight when one's life is at risk," he said. "You are not under threat. Despite what you may feel. This, particularly, is maladaptive action."

Humiliation coiled at the pit of her gut. Tarsul was treating her like a child, or like some kind of a toy—pick her up from the cell because she was *convenient*, right, bring her here and plug her into the engine like she was a spare part, lecture her like she was some idiot. "Let me go," she warned.

To her surprise, he did. "I like you," he said. Then, an incredulous noise from Kiu: "My policy is to like all people until I have a reason to dislike them. Because I asked you to join me, I have a duty to . . . situate you. I'd ask you, as a kindness, not to make this job more difficult."

Kiu spluttered.

"Of course, I knew I took a risk when I found you." Tarsul turned his back to her, which only made the rage spike higher. "But people with artificial neural networks as advanced as yours tend not to be the kind of people who would leave their homes forever, with very little explanation. You were the culmination of seven years of searching." He turned his ear back toward her. "I'm curious how you came to be where you were."

Yeah; most of the people with her kind of augments weren't sad-sack drifters, weren't murderous detriments to society. She got that; she was *special*. "I don't want to talk about my past," she growled.

"Of course not. But our pasts influence our futures." Tarsul rolled one shoulder. "I also have a duty to the arcology. Bringing this planetoid to them ensures their resource security for another thousand years, perhaps. But *you*, Kiu Alee—"

He turned his whole body back to her, head canted, as though he could pin her with his listening the way someone else might pin her with a gaze.

"I also want to know that I ensure their security by bringing them *you*."

Kiu avoided Tarsul as much as she could, given the confines of the ship. It wasn't as difficult as she'd feared; the accelerator sprawled, replete with odd closets and rooms which had been mostly, but not entirely, cleared of detritus. Kiu made a room for herself out of the provisions that Tarsul had, apparently, bought on Erhat: a sleeping cocoon, listening materials on a tablet, a selection of meals, all with their own containment and heating units, so she didn't have to run the risk of encountering him whenever she wanted food.

She'd refused suspended animation. After the interface, she didn't relish the thought of going back down into her brain, even if she wouldn't be conscious to experience it.

Still, after a while—without anything that served to delineate the time, either to a trade standard or a local schedule—she started wondering just how long she could manage. The accelerator's black walls were depressing and disorienting, like she was both adrift in starless space and confined in a space where the walls were too close. She could reach out and just barely not touch the walls of the room.

So eventually, she started wandering.

It was strange, how easily her body adapted to moving through the gravity of this place. As though her body was also accessing memories that weren't hers.

And eventually, she encountered Tarsul.

He was at rest, reclining on a little bench which may not have been a bench, in design. His hands were folded on his chest. He wasn't moving, but he was breathing deep and even; his eyes were open, so he wasn't sleeping. Kiu paused in the doorway to the little room.

"What are you doing?"

Tarsul tilted his head. "It's been a long time since I've been home," he said. "It's strange to realize I'm finally returning."

Kiu grunted. She let herself in, a few more handspans. Still kept a good distance between herself and Tarsul. "How long?"

Tarsul was silent.

Kiu narrowed her eyes at him, but she kept silent as well. Even so, Tarsul exhaled, sounding like he was disappointed in her. "I'm not sure, exactly."

"How many times have you made this trip?" Kiu asked.

At that, Tarsul actually looked surprised. He turned so that his whole body was facing her, head canted to one side.

"Me?" he asked. "The last time we sought resources from a star system was over a hundred twenty standard generations ago. How old do you think I *am*?"

"I remembered you," Kiu said. "You were there, in the accelerator's memory."

Tarsul's eyebrows knit together. "Two explanations," he said. "One: your own memories contaminated the accelerator's stored memory at the same time its contaminated yours. Pieces of your own experience became blended with what you remembered. None of the memories are faithful representations of anyone's experience. Two: coincidence. Someone on an historical resource-gathering expedition looked like me. Nothing more."

That would make more sense, she supposed.

Because what was the other explanation? He was over a hundred twenty standard generations old?—whatever that even *meant*, coming from his colony. Unlikely; the best genetic treatments couldn't extend life that far. He was cloned, or gengineered? Plausible, but why? She'd met plenty of heavily-gengineered humans, and they were without fail more impressive than Tarsul seemed to be. And if over a hundred generations had passed since that memory, they probably would have improved their gengineering, too. Why reuse the same models?

"You came out here. From your arcology."

Tarsul nodded, absently.

"How did you—" *Not go insane?* "Keep busy on the way out?"

"Meditation, mostly," Tarsul said.

"Really?"

Tarsul spread his hands. "I regarded it as a pilgrimage. I was chosen because I was . . . temperamentally suited to such a long journey. Unfortunately, that was a consideration I didn't have the luxury to make, for you."

Kiu made a disparaging noise.

"Maybe you'd prefer to sleep," Tarsul said. "We can still put you into suspension. I'm told that it's a dreamless sleep."

The same way that memory was supposed to be reassuring? Kiu thought. "No. Thank you. I'll figure something out."

"Of course," Tarsul said. "Let me know if I can offer any diversion."

"I'm not much into meditation," Kiu said.

Tarsul laughed, briefly. "I'd think not. Even so."

"Right."

Kiu lingered for a moment longer, then took herself away down the hall.

And occupied herself for some short span before folding, and admitting that stasis might be a more comfortable way of traveling by far.

Tarsul was right about this, at least—the sleep was dreamless.

She had no conception of the passage of time when consciousness infiltrated her mind again, arriving in a fog of sleepy confusion. She came to not quite knowing where she was; shivering very badly. Entirely psychosomatic, she'd been told, but she didn't believe it.

Tarsul was at the console beside her stasis bay, an inscrutable series of tones informing him of something. Kiu's arm ached, faintly, where an IV had gone in. "We're there?" she asked—but the apprehension of entering a new world, a strange station and culture, didn't have a chance to develop.

"We're off-course," Tarsul said. Maybe it was her imagination, but he sounded tired. "Something must have gone wrong with the calculations."

Kiu pushed herself out of the bay, and caught herself against the wall. It felt strangely warm against her palm. "I thought you said the accelerator handled all the actual calculations."

"With some form of input, some guidance, from the pilot," Tarsul said. "I don't pretend to understand the intricacies. But it has never failed, before."

And with that, a new apprehension rose in Kiu's chest. "What's that mean?" *Don't ask me to, don't ask me to—*

"It means we're traveling into nothingness," Tarsul said. "Unless you can correct the course. The accelerator *can* correct itself, I'm led to believe, even at these speeds."

The apprehension roiled into full-blown fear. "You want me to plug back into that thing."

"Unless the thought of drifting forever appeals to you." Tarsul turned his ear toward the hall. "Though 'forever', in our case, is bounded by the finite amount of supplies we have on board."

Slow deaths, then. Set against the immediate threat of all those voices, all those images, blooming up in Kiu's mind. Her heart sped.

As though he could hear that, Tarsul turned back toward her. "It can wait. A few hours will hardly make a difference."

Except that it would be a few hours more of sitting and dreading. Kiu grit her teeth. "No. I'll go now." Go under threat, but then this entire voyage had been under threat. That was nothing new.

She went back to the interface. Plugged herself in. Tensed her shoulders, tensed her hands, and all sensation of shoulders and hands and body dissolved.

Into—

A little planetoid was nothing. She stood at the helm of a planet, now—no atmo-sphere to shear off, but thrust turned it oblate. Their progress was slower. Not, how-ever, slow. They could put together most of a system this way—

Or simply flee. Another time, another planetoid, another pilot, staring down at his gloved hands. Memories already coursing through his brain, which Kiu felt at one remove. The whole black body of the accelerator representing a theft as well as an escape. Looking up, to meet the eyes of an engineer who had no idea how to work any but its most basic functions, an entire body of knowledge left behind. Saying—

The tall man again, the one who looked like Tarsul, saying, No, it's futile. In the long run, the arcology will die. Of isolation. Of indolence. Of attrition. Saying, the prudent choice is to return to a star, and all the resources it offers. Not to continue out here, in the black.

Saying, I'll do my best for you, but I won't do anything beyond that.

Kiu didn't even remember the snap of the course correction; the driving need to go home. She snapped back into herself like a line under tension, shak-ing, with her hands in fists. And Tarsul, standing there, head cocked, as though he could *hear* the rage pouring off her. As though he'd neglected one of the traditional senses for some fleet of senses she had no knowledge of.

I won't do anything. So very like Tarsul, that.

She could have killed him, there.

Could have. That was a proven fact—and she'd thought, for the most part, that killers were people unlike her; people who didn't know what direction ratio-nality lay in when it was pointed out to them, people whose brains were fried by some accident of genetics or chemical interest or brainwash mis-socialization. Not people like her, who got angry, yeah, but knew where the line was. And yet.

And *yet.*

There in no particular Erhat corridor, with no particular history of confron-tation, in a bad half-second on a bad day in a bad string of days, some Erhat boy no older than her had looked at her and his face had twisted, the universal human expression of disgust, and he'd sent some social impulse off with an ostentatious tilt of his head. Something that had caused his networked friend down the hall to turn, and look at Kiu, and *laugh*, and Kiu, who'd been through too many homes already and knew, *knew* that she was still a piece of foreign debris in this one but would have liked to go a day without being *reminded* of the fact—had taught a lesson with a small stylus, just tapered enough to enter through human muscle and skin, given enough force.

Nothing said *I belong; I'm valuable, I'm worthwhile* than a staggering act of antisocial tantrum, huh. Even she knew that had been stupid.

It had stopped his friend from laughing, though. At the time, she hadn't seen past that—not one second, not one thought, not one millimeter.

Tarsul, now, had his eyes unfocused—they were *always* unfocused—but it seemed as though he was looking far afield. All the way out to his arcology, full of people whose skin was no thicker than that young man in the corridor. They could solve the problem of resource collection in the interstellar nothingness, but maybe they couldn't solve the problem of her.

"Kiu," Tarsul said. His tone made resentment march up her spine.

What are you going to do? she could have asked. *I'm the only one who can pilot this ship. I'm the only way your stupid arcology will have the material to keep breathing, keep eating, keep the lights on. You need me.*

To the exact extent that he needed this expedition to return successfully. And just what extent *was* that?

Was he the person in the accelerator's archived memory?

He let out a long breath, here and now. "Maybe you should sleep again."

"I don't want to sleep." She didn't want to stay awake, either. She wanted to crawl out of her skin. Get in a fight. Hurt someone.

Tarsul sighed again, and said, "I see."

"What are you going to do with me?" Kiu demanded. She realized, as she said it, how her breath sounded—ragged, rough, like she was looking for a fight. She *was* looking for a fight. She knew where she stood, when her fists hit flesh. "I'm bringing you home." *I'm doing my best.*

I won't do anything beyond that.

"I've yet to decide," Tarsul said. Like nothing, like this was easy.

Kiu jerked up from the interface chair.

Tarsul stepped back, and then turned, and walked away.

Kiu ran the halls, as best she could. Tried to burn off the anger. It worked as badly as it ever had.

Between footfalls, between corners, she tried to think of options.

They were frustratingly few. She didn't know how to fix the accelerator so it would listen to her; she didn't know how to fix herself. So, maybe Tarsul would decide he was better off with her dead. She could strike first—she thought she'd be good at that—but if she killed Tarsul, what would she do? Show up at his arcology without him and expect them to let her in? They sounded like class-A xenophobes; Kiu didn't find the idea likely.

What else? Pilot the planetoid somewhere else? The accelerator alone would sell to just about any shipyard or research consortium for more than Kiu would need, but it seemed to have a mind of its own. Kiu had no idea how Tarsul had gotten it out to the Erhat system in the first place; maybe it was easier without a planetoid attached, but she couldn't even get it to go where *it wanted* to go. So that was out.

Which left . . . not much. Starve to death slowly as the provisions ran out. She punched a wall. It didn't help.

In time, as though it had a gravity all its own, she went back to the interface.

She stood staring at it for a good, long time. The source of all her problems, this thing—or, at least, that was a tempting excuse. Much better than all her problems coming from her, or from genetics, or from ontogenic accident. If it caused her problems, maybe it could damn well fix them.

Of course, she couldn't just hit it until it agreed.

It and its memory, of people and things and places that all seemed to have so much more import than her haphazard little flight, her haphazard little life. All those people, coming into her brain and washing over her, more real to her than she was.

Then it struck her.

If this thing was meant to archive, then fine, it could archive *her*. Maybe she wasn't fit to live. But she'd still be remembered by someone. Something.

The thought appealed to her. Before she made a conscious choice, her body was already moving back to the seat.

Bad idea. Yes, well, probably, but she wasn't much use at having good ones. She growled to herself as she fit the connectors back against her scalp, but she'd decided; she was committed.

She activated the interface, and memory became the air around her.

Or—maybe not *memory*. Maybe just—

A sense of place, so strong as to be overwhelming. The corridors of the accelerator, but more present and real than they had been as she stood in them. These flooded her awareness, denying distraction, constructing themselves in her mind.

And in her mind, the man who looked like Tarsul materialized as though she'd simply forgotten that he'd been standing there.

But Kiu knew where she was. She didn't dissolve into it. Instead, she steeled herself, and spoke, with something that wasn't her voice:

"Who are you?"

Kiu Alee, the apparition said. It didn't sound like Tarsul; not entirely. Or maybe she just didn't know him well enough to catch this tone. *What an absolutely useless question.*

She had no sense of her body, here. She couldn't lash out. She couldn't feel her chest tighten, her breath draw in, her jaw and hands clench. It was freeing, in a way. It was also a little like death.

"Okay, then." She couldn't take a deep breath. Couldn't relax her muscles.

And yet, she could still feel anger, like a sensation in a phantom limb. "Here's one: why can't I fly this thing right?"

Much more useful. Unfortunately, much more complicated. The not-Tarsul turned eyes on her: blank, flat, and still piercing. You are not entirely similar to pilots in the past.

No lip to curl. No teeth to grit, as she considered say saying, *No, I'm one of those accidents that happen from time to time.* What a waste of resources; what a waste of implants. If the Agisa medics could have pulled the filaments out of her brain and left them salvageable in any meaningful way, they probably would have.

Instead, she found herself here.

But it is an opportunity to learn, the apparition said. I appreciate the chance to analyze your augments. And to analyze you. Of the two, you are more interesting.

Slow realization crept through her. "You're not a memory," she said. "Are you?"

You aren't accessing the archived memories, not-Tarsul responded. I understand the interface controls are erratic on your side, as well. Still, you chose how this interface was calibrated.

"You're the engine," Kiu said. "You're the ship."

An acceptable explanation.

And that—all the questions she could ask, like *who made you* or *where did you come from*, vanished under the tide of annoyance. "You know where you're going," Kiu said. "Clearly, you have some kind of intelligence. Why can't you just fly yourself home?"

Calculations, it said, but Kiu thought there was a coyness to the answer. A slight tinge of lie. *Organic processors handle some calculations better.*

"If you needed organic processing, your builders could have grown a neural web on a substrate."

Before she could finish the thought, she was answered—Well, just so. And once a human is connected, why not keep a piece for analysis?

Kiu jerked.

And then she dove, back down toward her body, coming back to the surface of her consciousness with her hands on the connectors. But then the quick-trigger affront died back, just enough to let her close her eyes again, search for the connection.

"You're copying my neuron structure? Culling it? Replicating it?" Even in Agisa, that wouldn't have been possible. But moving a planetoid wouldn't be pos-. sible, either. Nor would moving anything but information at this ridiculous speed.

Not as you suspect it, the accelerator responded. Your neuron structure, even with its augments, is not deterministic as to your experiential reality. I expand myself. But if you connected looking for immortality, pilot, all you'll receive is approximation.

Still, this is valuable to me. Whether or not it is valuable to you hardly matters.

She could have laughed. "Story of my life, isn't it?"

Well, it said. Keep coming back. So far as the story of your life goes, it will matter here more than anywhere.

That didn't sound like something Kiu was meant to understand. She moved past it. "If you study my augments, will you course correct? Is that what you need?"

No, the accelerator said. That, I'd do for my own interest.

"Wonderful. Great." This thing's intelligence was entirely unhelpful. "Can you just tell me why you won't *go home?*"

Kiu Alee, the accelerator said. *Why won't you **let** me?*

Kiu worked her body as hard as she could, after disconnecting. Made circuits of the halls, pushed and pulled against fixed points, did stretches and fast motions until she was gasping air. It bled off some of the boiling energy, if not all of it.

She came to Tarsul in the console room, a far-flung little space full of screens which he disregarded. She was almost too exhausted for rage, mostly just too cynical for anything. Tarsul tilted his head to acknowledge her entry.

"We are *still* not on course," he said. He sounded resigned. "I admit, I'm surprised. I don't know of any pilot who . . . experienced this much difficulty."

"I'm special," Kiu said, voice heavy. "My brain doesn't work right. Ace choice in pilots, though."

Tarsul turned to better regard her. His face, in that three-quarters turn, looked drawn and pensive. Kiu could almost hear the retort on his tongue: *I had no choice.*

Yeah, well. Seemed to be a common complaint, here.

Kiu glared at him for a while, and then softened, despite herself. Raw deal for him; surrounded by all this wonder, and he had a murderer with a broken brain on one side, a starving arcology so hidebound they needed a planet brought to *them* on the other. And hour after hour, he just kept doing what was in front of him to do.

Kiu felt a stabbing moment of powerlessness, of the attendant rage. She fought it back down.

"I can try again," she said. "One more course correction, right? No harm in trying."

"No harm," Tarsul agreed. Kiu wondered if, behind that easy agreement, he was already writing her off.

"Yeah," she said, and went back down the hall. After a moment, Tarsul followed her.

Maybe she'd go into the connection and not come out. Maybe she'd let

Tarsul sedate her and let the accelerator mine her brain and learn her augments and maybe she would learn the command that would set their course correctly. Maybe that was the option left to her.

What had Tarsul said? *It's adaptive to fight when one's life is at risk.* Well, throwing a punch wouldn't save her, so maybe she should stop trying to throw the first punch. Maybe she should find something to pre-empt the violence that waited on the other side of every heartbeat. Maybe this was it.

"I think I can do this," she lied.

"I'm heartened," Tarsul said.

Maybe it was Kiu's imagination, but he sounded like he had as little faith in her as she did.

No matter.

She went back to the interface. Lowered herself into the chair.

Tarsul tilted his head at her. "You seem different," he said. His voice was curious. Maybe a shade wary.

I don't know if I've given up on life or had a breakthrough, Kiu didn't say. *Maybe a breakdown.* She grunted, vaguely, in reply.

"Are you well?" Tarsul asked.

"Fine. I'm always fine."

She reached for the interface wires, and pulled them down toward her head.

Tarsul was hesitating, as though he had something he wasn't sure he should say. Kiu paused with her hands on the wires, and raised an eyebrow she knew he couldn't see.

Whatever internal line of thought had occupied Tarsul wended its way to a close. "I wish you luck," he said.

"Huh," Kiu responded.

Then she attached the connectors, breathed out, and opened up, and surrendered herself to going home.

Greg Egan has published more than sixty short stories and thirteen novels. He has won a Hugo Award for his novella "Oceanic" and the John W. Campbell Memorial Award for his novel *Permutation City*. His most recent novel is *Dichronauts*, set in a universe with two time-like dimensions.

GLORY

GREG EGAN

1.

An ingot of metallic hydrogen gleamed in the starlight, a narrow cylinder half a meter long with a mass of about a kilogram. To the naked eye it was a dense, solid object, but its lattice of tiny nuclei immersed in an insubstantial fog of electrons was one part matter to two hundred trillion parts empty space. A short distance away was a second ingot, apparently identical to the first, but composed of antihydrogen.

A sequence of finely tuned gamma rays flooded into both cylinders. The protons that absorbed them in the first ingot spat out positrons and were transformed into neutrons, breaking their bonds to the electron cloud that glued them in place. In the second ingot, antiprotons became antineutrons.

A further sequence of pulses herded the neutrons together and forged them into clusters; the antineutrons were similarly rearranged. Both kinds of cluster were unstable, but in order to fall apart they first had to pass through a quantum state that would have strongly absorbed a component of the gamma rays constantly raining down on them. Left to themselves, the probability of their being in this state would have increased rapidly, but each time they measurably failed to absorb the gamma rays, the probability fell back to zero. The quantum Zeno effect endlessly reset the clock, holding the decay in check.

The next series of pulses began shifting the clusters into the space that had separated the original ingots. First neutrons, then antineutrons, were sculpted together in alternating layers. Though the clusters were ultimately unstable, while they persisted they were inert, sequestering their constituents and preventing them from annihilating their counterparts. The end point of this process of nuclear sculpting was a sliver of compressed matter and antimatter, sandwiched together into a needle one micron wide.

The gamma ray lasers shut down, the Zeno effect withdrew its prohibitions. For the time it took a beam of light to cross a neutron, the needle sat motionless in space. Then it began to burn, and it began to move.

The needle was structured like a meticulously crafted firework, and its outer layers ignited first. No external casing could have channeled this blast, but the pattern of tensions woven into the needle's construction favored one direction for the debris to be expelled. Particles streamed backward; the needle moved forward. The shock of acceleration could not have been borne by anything built from atomic-scale matter, but the pressure bearing down on the core of the needle prolonged its life, delaying the inevitable.

Layer after layer burned itself away, blasting the dwindling remnant forward ever faster. By the time the needle had shrunk to a tenth of its original size it was moving at ninety-eight percent of light-speed; to a bystander this could scarcely have been improved upon, but from the needle's perspective there was still room to slash its journey's duration by orders of magnitude.

When just one thousandth of the needle remained, its time, compared to the neighboring stars, was passing two thousand times more slowly. Still the layers kept burning, the protective clusters unraveling as the pressure on them was released. The needle could only reach close enough to light-speed to slow down time as much as it required if it could sacrifice a large enough proportion of its remaining mass. The core of the needle could survive only for a few trillionths of a second, while its journey would take two hundred million seconds as judged by the stars. The proportions had been carefully matched, though: out of the two kilograms of matter and antimatter that had been woven together at the launch, only a few million neutrons were needed as the final payload.

By one measure, seven years passed. For the needle, its last trillionths of a second unwound, its final layers of fuel blew away, and at the moment its core was ready to explode it reached its destination, plunging from the near-vacuum of space straight into the heart of a star.

Even here, the density of matter was insufficient to stabilize the core, yet far too high to allow it to pass unhindered. The core was torn apart. But it did not go quietly, and the shock waves it carved through the fusing plasma endured for a million kilometers: all the way through to the cooler outer layers on the opposite side of the star. These shock waves were shaped by the payload that had formed them, and though the initial pattern imprinted on them by the disintegrating cluster of neutrons was enlarged and blurred by its journey, on an atomic scale it remained sharply defined. Like a mold stamped into the seething plasma it encouraged ionized molecular fragments to slip into the troughs and furrows that matched their shape, and then brought them together to react in ways that the plasma's random collisions would never have allowed. In effect, the shock waves formed a web of catalysts, carefully laid out in both time and space, briefly transforming a small corner of the star into a chemical factory operating on a nanometer scale.

The products of this factory sprayed out of the star, riding the last traces of the shock wave's momentum: a few nanograms of elaborate, carbon-rich molecules, sheathed in a protective fullerene weave. Traveling at seven hundred kilometers per second, a fraction below the velocity needed to escape from the star completely, they climbed out of its gravity well, slowing as they ascended.

Four years passed, but the molecules were stable against the ravages of space. By the time they'd traveled a billion kilometers they had almost come to a halt, and they would have fallen back to die in the fires of the star that had forged them if their journey had not been timed so that the star's third planet, a gas giant, was waiting to urge them forward. As they fell toward it, the giant's third moon moved across their path. Eleven years after the needle's launch, its molecular offspring rained down onto the methane snow.

The tiny heat of their impact was not enough to damage them, but it melted a microscopic puddle in the snow. Surrounded by food, the molecular seeds began to grow. Within hours, the area was teeming with nanomachines, some mining the snow and the minerals beneath it, others assembling the bounty into an intricate structure, a rectangular panel a couple of meters wide.

From across the light-years, an elaborate sequence of gamma ray pulses fell upon the panel. These pulses were the needle's true payload, the passengers for whom it had merely prepared the way, transmitted in its wake four years after its launch. The panel decoded and stored the data, and the army of nanomachines set to work again, this time following a far more elaborate blueprint. The miners were forced to look farther afield to find all the elements that were needed, while the assemblers labored to reach their goal through a sequence of intermediate stages, carefully designed to protect the final product from the vagaries of the local chemistry and climate.

After three months' work, two small fusion-powered spacecraft sat in the snow. Each one held a single occupant, waking for the first time in their freshly minted bodies, yet endowed with memories of an earlier life.

Joan switched on her communications console. Anne appeared on the screen, three short pairs of arms folded across her thorax in a posture of calm repose. They had both worn virtual bodies with the same anatomy before, but this was the first time they had become Noudah in the flesh.

"We're here. Everything worked," Joan marveled. The language she spoke was not her own, but the structure of her new brain and body made it second nature.

Anne said, "Now comes the hard part."

"Yes." Joan looked out from the spacecraft's cockpit. In the distance, a fissured blue-gray plateau of water ice rose above the snow. Nearby, the nanomachines were busy disassembling the gamma ray receiver. When they had erased all traces of their handiwork they would wander off into the snow and catalyze their own destruction.

Joan had visited dozens of planet-bound cultures in the past, taking on different bodies and languages as necessary, but those cultures had all been plugged into the Amalgam, the metacivilization that spanned the galactic disk. However far from home she'd been, the means to return to familiar places had always been close at hand. The Noudah had only just mastered interplanetary flight, and they had no idea that the Amalgam existed. The closest node in the Amalgam's network was seven light-years away, and even that was out of bounds to her and Anne now: they had agreed not to risk disclosing its location to the Noudah, so any transmission they sent could be directed only to a decoy node that they'd set up more than twenty light-years away.

"It will be worth it," Joan said.

Anne's Noudah face was immobile, but chromatophores sent a wave of violet and gold sweeping across her skin in an expression of cautious optimism. "We'll see." She tipped her head to the left, a gesture preceding a friendly departure.

Joan tipped her own head in response, as if she'd been doing so all her life. "Be careful, my friend," she said.

"You too."

Anne's ship ascended so high on its chemical thrusters that it shrank to a speck before igniting its fusion engine and streaking away in a blaze of light. Joan felt a pang of loneliness; there was no predicting when they would be reunited.

Her ship's software was primitive; the whole machine had been scrupulously matched to the Noudah's level of technology. Joan knew how to fly it herself if necessary, and on a whim she switched off the autopilot and manually activated the ascent thrusters. The control panel was crowded, but having six hands helped.

2.

The world the Noudah called home was the closest of the system's five planets to their sun. The average temperature was one hundred and twenty degrees Celsius, but the high atmospheric pressure allowed liquid water to exist across the entire surface. The chemistry and dynamics of the planet's crust had led to a relatively flat terrain, with a patchwork of dozens of disconnected seas but no globe-spanning ocean. From space, these seas appeared as silvery mirrors, bordered by a violet and brown tarnish of vegetation.

The Noudah were already leaving their most electromagnetically promiscuous phase of communications behind, but the short-lived oasis of Amalgam-level technology on Baneth, the gas giant's moon, had had no trouble eavesdropping on their chatter and preparing an updated cultural briefing which had been spliced into Joan's brain.

The planet was still divided into the same eleven political units as it had been fourteen years before, the time of the last broadcasts that had reached the node before Joan's departure. Tira and Ghahar, the two dominant nations in terms of territory, economic activity, and military power, also occupied the vast majority of significant Niah archaeological sites.

Joan had expected that they'd be noticed as soon as they left Baneth—the exhaust from their fusion engines glowed like the sun—but their departure had triggered no obvious response, and now that they were coasting they'd be far harder to spot. As Anne drew closer to the homeworld, she sent a message to Tira's traffic control center. Joan tuned in to the exchange.

"I come in peace from another star," Anne said. "I seek permission to land."

There was a delay of several seconds more than the light-speed lag, then a terse response. "Please identify yourself and state your location."

Anne transmitted her coordinates and flight plan.

"We confirm your location, please identify yourself."

"My name is Anne. I come from another star."

There was a long pause, then a different voice answered. "If you are from Ghahar, please explain your intentions."

"I am not from Ghahar."

"Why should I believe that? Show yourself."

"I've taken the same shape as your people, in the hope of living among you for a while." Anne opened a video channel and showed them her unremarkable Noudah face. "But there's a signal being transmitted from these coordinates that might persuade you that I'm telling the truth." She gave the location of the decoy node, twenty light-years away, and specified a frequency. The signal coming from the node contained an image of the very same face.

This time, the silence stretched out for several minutes. It would take a while for the Tirans to confirm the true distance of the radio source.

"You do not have permission to land. Please enter this orbit, and we will rendezvous and board your ship."

Parameters for the orbit came through on the data channel. Anne said, "As you wish."

Minutes later, Joan's instruments picked up three fusion ships being launched from Tiran bases. When Anne reached the prescribed orbit, Joan listened anxiously to the instructions the Tirans issued. Their tone sounded wary, but they were entitled to treat this stranger with caution, all the more so if they believed Anne's claim.

Joan was accustomed to a very different kind of reception, but then the members of the Amalgam had spent hundreds of millennia establishing a framework of trust. They also benefited from a milieu in which most kinds of force had been rendered ineffectual; when everyone had backups of themselves scattered around the galaxy, it required a vastly disproportionate effort to inconvenience someone, let alone kill them. By any reasonable measure, honesty and cooperation yielded far richer rewards than subterfuge and slaughter.

Nonetheless, each individual culture had its roots in a biological heritage that gave rise to behavior governed more by ancient urges than contemporary realities, and even when they mastered the technology to choose their own nature, the precise set of traits they preserved was up to them. In the worst case, a species still saddled with inappropriate drives but empowered by advanced technology could wreak havoc. The Noudah deserved to be treated with courtesy and respect, but they did not yet belong in the Amalgam.

The Tirans' own exchanges were not on open channels, so once they had entered Anne's ship Joan could only guess at what was happening. She waited until two of the ships had returned to the surface, then sent her own message to Ghahar's traffic control.

"I come in peace from another star. I seek permission to land."

3.

The Ghahari allowed Joan to fly her ship straight down to the surface. She wasn't sure if this was because they were more trusting, or if they were afraid that the Tirans might try to interfere if she lingered in orbit.

The landing site was a bare plain of chocolate-colored sand. The air shimmered in the heat, the distortions intensified by the thickness of the atmosphere, making the horizon waver as if seen through molten glass. Joan waited in the cockpit as three trucks approached; they all came to a halt some twenty meters away. A voice over the radio instructed her to leave the ship; she complied, and after she'd stood in the open for a minute, a lone Noudah left one of the trucks and walked toward her.

"I'm Pirit," she said. "Welcome to Ghahar." Her gestures were courteous but restrained.

"I'm Joan. Thank you for your hospitality."

"Your impersonation of our biology is impeccable." There was a trace of skepticism in Pirit's tone; Joan had pointed the Ghahari to her own portrait being broadcast from the decoy node, but she had to admit that in the context her lack of exotic technology and traits would make it harder to accept the implications of that transmission.

"In my culture, it's a matter of courtesy to imitate one's hosts as closely as possible."

Pirit hesitated, as if pondering whether to debate the merits of such a custom, but then rather than quibbling over the niceties of interspecies etiquette she chose to confront the real issue head-on. "If you're a Tiran spy, or a defector, the sooner you admit that the better."

"That's very sensible advice, but I'm neither."

The Noudah wore no clothing as such, but Pirit had a belt with a number of pouches. She took a handheld scanner from one and ran it over Joan's body. Joan's briefing suggested that it was probably only checking for metal, volatile explosives, and radiation; the technology to image her body or search for pathogens would not be so portable. In any case, she was a healthy, unarmed Noudah down to the molecular level.

Pirit escorted her to one of the trucks, and invited her to recline in a section at the back. Another Noudah drove while Pirit watched over Joan. They soon arrived at a small complex of buildings a couple of kilometers from where the ship had touched down. The walls, roofs, and floors of the buildings were all made from the local sand, cemented with an adhesive that the Noudah secreted from their own bodies.

Inside, Joan was given a thorough medical examination, including three kinds of full-body scan. The Noudah who examined her treated her with a kind of detached efficiency devoid of any pleasantries; she wasn't sure if that was their standard bedside manner, or a kind of glazed shock at having been told of her claimed origins.

Pirit took her to an adjoining room and offered her a couch. The Noudah anatomy did not allow for sitting, but they liked to recline.

Pirit remained standing. "How did you come here?" she asked.

"You've seen my ship. I flew it from Baneth."

"And how did you reach Baneth?"

"I'm not free to discuss that," Joan replied cheerfully.

"Not free?" Pirit's face clouded with silver, as if she were genuinely perplexed.

Joan said, "You understand me perfectly. Please don't tell me there's nothing *you're* not free to discuss with me."

"You certainly didn't fly that ship twenty light-years."

"No, I certainly didn't."

Pirit hesitated. "Did you come through the Cataract?" The Cataract was a black hole, a remote partner to the Noudah's sun; they orbited each other at a distance of about eighty billion kilometers. The name came from its telescopic appearance: a dark circle ringed by a distortion in the background of stars, like some kind of visual aberration. The Tirans and Ghahari were in a race to be the first to visit this extraordinary neighbor, but as yet neither of them were quite up to the task.

"*Through* the Cataract? I think your scientists have already proven that black holes aren't shortcuts to anywhere."

"Our scientists aren't always right."

"Neither are ours," Joan admitted, "but all the evidence points in one direction: black holes aren't doorways, they're shredding machines."

"So you traveled the whole twenty light-years?"

"More than that," Joan said truthfully, "from my original home. I've spent half my life traveling."

"Faster than light?" Pirit suggested hopefully.

"No. That's impossible."

They circled around the question a dozen more times, before Pirit finally changed her tune from *how* to *why*?

"I'm a xenomathematician," Joan said. "I've come here in the hope of collaborating with your archaeologists in their study of Niah artifacts."

Pirit was stunned. "What do you know about the Niah?"

"Not as much as I'd like to." Joan gestured at her Noudah body. "As I'm sure you've already surmised, we've listened to your broadcasts for some time, so we know pretty much what an ordinary Noudah knows. That includes the basic facts about the Niah. Historically they've been referred to as your ancestors, though the latest studies suggest that you and they really just have an earlier common ancestor. They died out about a million years ago, but there's evidence that they might have had a sophisticated culture for as long as three million years. There's no indication that they ever developed space flight. Basically, once they achieved material comfort, they seem to have devoted themselves to various art forms, including mathematics."

"So you've traveled twenty light-years just to look at Niah tablets?" Pirit was incredulous.

"Any culture that spent three million years doing mathematics must have something to teach us."

"Really?" Pirit's face became blue with disgust. "In the ten thousand years since we discovered the wheel, we've already reached halfway to the Cataract. They wasted their time on useless abstractions."

Joan said, "I come from a culture of spacefarers myself, so I respect your achievements. But I don't think anyone really knows what the Niah achieved. I'd like to find out, with the help of your people."

Pirit was silent for a while. "What if we say no?"

"Then I'll leave empty-handed."

"What if we insist that you remain with us?"

"Then I'll die here, empty-handed." On her command, this body would expire in an instant; she could not be held and tortured.

Pirit said angrily, "You must be willing to trade *something* for the privilege you're demanding!"

"Requesting, not demanding," Joan insisted gently. "And what I'm willing to offer is my own culture's perspective on Niah mathematics. If you ask your archaeologists and mathematicians, I'm sure they'll tell you that there are many things written in the Niah tablets that they don't yet understand. My colleague and I"— neither of them had mentioned Anne before, but Joan was sure that Pirit knew all about her—"simply want to shed as much light as we can on this subject."

Pirit said bitterly, "You won't even tell us how you came to our world. Why should we trust you to share whatever you discover about the Niah?"

"Interstellar travel is no great mystery," Joan countered. "You know all the basic science already; making it work is just a matter of persistence. If you're left to develop your own technology, you might even come up with better methods than we have."

"So we're expected to be patient, to discover these things for ourselves . . . but you can't wait a few centuries for us to decipher the Niah artifacts?"

Joan said bluntly, "The present Noudah culture, both here and in Tira, seems to hold the Niah in contempt. Dozens of partially excavated sites containing Niah artifacts are under threat from irrigation projects and other developments. That's the reason we couldn't wait. We needed to come here and offer our assistance, before the last traces of the Niah disappeared forever."

Pirit did not reply, but Joan hoped she knew what her interrogator was thinking: *Nobody would cross twenty light-years for a few worthless scribblings. Perhaps we've underestimated the Niah. Perhaps our ancestors have left us a great secret, a great legacy. And perhaps the fastest—perhaps the only—way to uncover it is to give this impertinent, irritating alien exactly what she wants.*

4.

The sun was rising ahead of them as they reached the top of the hill. Sando turned to Joan, and his face became green with pleasure. "Look behind you," he said.

Joan did as he asked. The valley below was hidden in fog, and it had settled so evenly that she could see their shadows in the dawn light, stretched out across the top of the fog layer. Around the shadow of her head was a circular halo like a small rainbow.

"We call it the Niah's light," Sando said. "In the old days, people used to say that the halo proved that the Niah blood was strong in you."

Joan said, "The only trouble with that hypothesis being that *you* see it around *your* head . . . and I see it around mine." On Earth, the phenomenon was known as a "glory." The particles of fog were scattering the sunlight back toward them, turning it one hundred and eighty degrees. To look at the shadow of your own head was to face directly away from the sun, so the halo always appeared around the observer's shadow.

"I suppose you're the final proof that Niah blood has nothing to do with it," Sando mused.

"That's assuming I'm telling you the truth, and I really can see it around my own head."

"And assuming," Sando added, "that the Niah really did stay at home, and didn't wander around the galaxy spreading their progeny."

They came over the top of the hill and looked down into the adjoining riverine valley. The sparse brown grass of the hillside gave way to a lush violet growth closer to the water. Joan's arrival had delayed the flooding of the valley, but even alien interest in the Niah had only bought the archaeologists an extra year. The dam was part of a long-planned agricultural development, and however tantalizing the possibility that Joan might reveal some priceless insight hidden among the Niah's "useless abstractions," that vague promise could only compete with more tangible considerations for a limited time.

Part of the hill had fallen away in a landslide a few centuries before, revealing more than a dozen beautifully preserved strata. When Joan and Sando reached the excavation site, Rali and Surat were already at work, clearing away soft sedimentary rock from a layer that Sando had dated as belonging to the Niah's "twilight" period.

Pirit had insisted that only Sando, the senior archaeologist, be told about Joan's true nature; Joan refused to lie to anyone, but had agreed to tell her colleagues only that she was a mathematician and that she was not permitted to discuss her past. At first this had made them guarded and resentful, no doubt because they assumed that she was some kind of spy sent by the authorities to watch over them. Later it had dawned on them that she was genuinely interested in their work, and that the absurd restrictions on her topics of conversation were not of her own choosing. Nothing about the Noudah's language or appearance correlated strongly with their recent division into nations—with no oceans to cross, and a long history of migration they were more or less geographically homogeneous—but Joan's odd name and occasional faux pas could still be ascribed to some mysterious exoticism. Rali and Surat seemed content to assume that she was a defector from one of the smaller nations, and that her history could not be made explicit for obscure political reasons.

"There are more tablets here, very close to the surface," Rali announced excitedly. "The acoustics are unmistakable." Ideally they would have excavated the entire hillside, but they did not have the time or the labor, so they were using acoustic tomography to identify likely deposits of accessible Niah writing, and then concentrating their efforts on those spots.

The Niah had probably had several ephemeral forms of written communication, but when they found something worth publishing, it stayed published: they carved their symbols into a ceramic that made diamond seem like tissue paper. It was almost unheard of for the tablets to be broken, but they were small, and multitablet works were sometimes widely dispersed. Niah technology could probably have carved three million years' worth of knowledge onto the head of a pin—they seemed not to have invented nanomachines, but they were into high-quality bulk materials and precision engineering—but for whatever reason they had chosen legibility to the naked eye above other considerations.

Joan made herself useful, taking acoustic readings farther along the slope, while Sando watched over his students as they came closer to the buried Niah artifacts. She had learned not to hover around expectantly when a discovery was imminent; she was treated far more warmly if she waited to be summoned. The tomography unit was almost foolproof, using satellite navigation to track its position and software to analyze the signals it gathered; all it really needed was someone to drag it along the rock face at a suitable pace.

From the corner of her eye, Joan noticed her shadow on the rocks flicker and grow complicated. She looked up to see three dazzling beads of light flying west out of the sun. She might have assumed that the fusion ships were doing something useful, but the media was full of talk of "military exercises," which meant the Tirans and the Ghahari were engaging in expensive, belligerent gestures in orbit, trying to convince each other of their superior skills, technology, or sheer strength of numbers. For people with no real differences apart from a few centuries of recent history, they could puff up their minor political disputes into matters of the utmost solemnity. It might almost have been funny, if the idiots hadn't incinerated hundreds of thousands of each other's citizens every few decades, not to mention playing callous and often deadly games with the lives of the inhabitants of smaller nations.

"Jown! Jown! Come and look at this!" Surat called to her. Joan switched off the tomography unit and jogged toward the archaeologists, suddenly conscious of her body's strangeness. Her legs were stumpy but strong, and her balance as she ran came not from arms and shoulders but from the swish of her muscular tail.

"It's a significant mathematical result," Rali informed her proudly when she reached them. He'd pressure-washed the sandstone away from the near-indestructible ceramic of the tablet, and it was only a matter of holding the surface at the right angle to the light to see the etched writing stand out as crisply and starkly as it would have a million years before.

Rali was not a mathematician, and he was not offering his own opinion on the theorem the tablet stated; the Niah themselves had had a clear set of typographical conventions which they used to distinguish between everything from minor lemmas to the most celebrated theorems. The size and decorations of the symbols labeling the theorem attested to its value in the Niah's eyes.

Joan read the theorem carefully. The proof was not included on the same tablet, but the Niah had a way of expressing their results that made you believe them as soon as you read them; in this case the definitions of the terms needed to state the theorem were so beautifully chosen that the result seemed almost inevitable.

The theorem itself was expressed as a commuting hypercube, one of the Niah's favorite forms. You could think of a square with four different sets of mathematical objects associated with each of its corners, and a way of mapping one set into another associated with each edge of the square. If the maps commuted, then going across the top of the square, then down, had exactly the same effect as going down the left edge of the square, then across: either way, you mapped each element from the top-left set into the same element of the bottom-right set. A similar kind of result might hold for sets and maps that could naturally be placed at the corners and edges of a cube, or a hypercube of any dimension. It was also possible for the square faces in these structures to stand for relationships that held between the maps between sets, and for cubes to describe relationships between those relationships, and so on.

That a theorem took this form didn't guarantee its importance; it was easy to cook up trivial examples of sets and maps that commuted. The Niah didn't carve trivia into their timeless ceramic, though, and this theorem was no exception. The seven-dimensional commuting hypercube established a dazzlingly elegant correspondence between seven distinct, major branches of Niah mathematics, intertwining their most important concepts into a unified whole. It was a result Joan had never seen before: no mathematician anywhere in the Amalgam, or in any ancestral culture she had studied, had reached the same insight.

She explained as much of this as she could to the three archaeologists; they couldn't take in all the details, but their faces became orange with fascination when she sketched what she thought the result would have meant to the Niah themselves.

"This isn't quite the Big Crunch," she joked, "but it must have made them think they were getting closer." "The Big Crunch" was her nickname for the mythical result that the Niah had aspired to reach: a unification of every field of mathematics that they considered significant. To find such a thing would not have meant the end of mathematics—it would not have subsumed every last conceivable, interesting mathematical truth—but it would certainly have marked a point of closure for the Niah's own style of investigation.

"I'm sure they found it," Surat insisted. "They reached the Big Crunch, then they had nothing more to live for."

Rali was scathing. "So the whole culture committed collective suicide?"

"Not actively, no," Surat replied. "But it was the search that had kept them going."

"Entire cultures don't lose the will to live," Rali said. "They get wiped out by external forces: disease, invasion, changes in climate."

"The Niah survived for three million years," Surat countered. "They had the means to weather all of those forces. Unless they were wiped out by alien invaders with vastly superior technology." She turned to Joan. "What do you think?"

"About aliens destroying the Niah?"

"I was joking about the aliens. But what about the mathematics? What if they found the Big Crunch?"

"There's more to life than mathematics," Joan said. "But not much more."

Sando said, "And there's more to this find than one tablet. If we get back to work, we might have the proof in our hands before sunset."

5.

Joan briefed Halzoun by video link while Sando prepared the evening meal. Halzoun was the mathematician Pirit had appointed to supervise her, but apparently his day job was far too important to allow him to travel. Joan was grateful; Halzoun was the most tedious Noudah she had encountered. He could understand the Niah's work when she explained it to him, but he seemed to have no interest in it for its own sake. He spent most of their conversations trying to catch her out in some deception or contradiction, and the rest pressing her to imagine military or commercial applications of the Niah's gloriously useless insights. Sometimes she played along with this infantile fantasy, hinting at potential superweapons based on exotic physics that might come tumbling out of the vacuum, if only one possessed the right Niah theorems to coax them into existence.

Sando was her minder too, but at least he was more subtle about it. Pirit had insisted that she stay in his shelter, rather than sharing Rali and Surat's; Joan didn't mind, because with Sando she didn't have the stress of having to keep quiet about everything. Privacy and modesty were nonissues for the Noudah, and Joan had become Noudah enough not to care herself. Nor was there any danger of their proximity leading to a sexual bond; the Noudah had a complex system of biochemical cues that meant desire only arose in couples with a suitable mixture of genetic differences and similarities. She would have had to search a crowded Noudah city for a week to find someone to lust after, though at least it would have been guaranteed to be mutual.

After they'd eaten, Sando said, "You should be happy. That was our best find yet."

"I am happy." Joan made a conscious effort to exhibit a viridian tinge. "It was the first new result I've seen on this planet. It was the reason I came here, the reason I traveled so far."

"Something's wrong, though, I think."

"I wish I could have shared the news with my friend," Joan admitted. Pirit claimed to be negotiating with the Tirans to allow Anne to communicate with her, but Joan was not convinced that she was genuinely trying. She was sure that Pirit would have relished the thought of listening in on a conversation between the two of them—while forcing them to speak Noudah, of course—in the hope that they'd slip up and reveal something useful, but at the same time she would have had to face the fact that the Tirans would be listening too. What an excruciating dilemma.

"You should have brought a communications link with you," Sando suggested. "A home-style one, I mean. Nothing we could eavesdrop on."

"We couldn't do that," Joan said.

He pondered this. "You really are afraid of us, aren't you? You think the smallest technological trinket will be enough to send us straight to the stars, and then you'll have a horde of rampaging barbarians to deal with."

"We know how to deal with barbarians," Joan said coolly.

Sando's face grew dark with mirth. "Now *I'm* afraid."

"I just wish I knew what was happening to her," Joan said. "What she was doing, how they were treating her."

"Probably much the same as we're treating you," Sando suggested. "We're really not that different." He thought for a moment. "There was something I wanted to show you." He brought over his portable console, and summoned up an article from a Tiran journal. "See what a borderless world we live in," he joked.

The article was entitled "Seekers and Spreaders: What We Must Learn from the Niah." Sando said, "This might give you some idea of how they're thinking over there. Jaqad is an academic archaeologist, but she's also very close to the people in power."

Joan read from the console while Sando made repairs to their shelter, secreting a molasseslike substance from a gland at the tip of his tail and spreading it over the cracks in the walls.

There were two main routes a culture could take, Jaqad argued, once it satisfied its basic material needs. One was to think and study: to stand back and observe, to seek knowledge and insight from the world around it. The other was to invest its energy in entrenching its good fortune.

The Niah had learned a great deal in three million years, but in the end it had not been enough to save them. Exactly what had killed them was still a matter of speculation, but it was hard to believe that if they had colonized other worlds they would have vanished on all of them. "Had the Niah been Spreaders," Jaqad wrote, "we might expect a visit from them, or them from us, sometime in the coming centuries."

The Noudah, in contrast, were determined Spreaders. Once they had the means, they would plant colonies across the galaxy. They would, Jaqad was sure, create new biospheres, reengineer stars, and even alter space and time to guarantee their survival. The growth of their empire would come first; any knowledge that failed to serve that purpose would be a mere distraction. "In any competition between Seekers and Spreaders, it is a Law of History that the Spreaders must win out in the end. Seekers, such as the Niah, might hog resources and block the way, but in the long run their own nature will be their downfall."

Joan stopped reading. "When you look out into the galaxy with your telescopes," she asked Sando, "how many *reengineered stars* do you see?"

"Would we recognize them?"

"Yes. Natural stellar processes aren't that complicated; your scientists already know everything there is to know about the subject."

"I'll take your word for that. So . . . you're saying Jaqad is wrong? The Niah themselves never left this world, but the galaxy already belongs to creatures more like them than like us?"

"It's not Noudah versus Niah," Joan said. "It's a matter of how a culture's perspective changes with time. Once a species conquers disease, modifies their biology, and spreads even a short distance beyond their homeworld, they usually start to relax a bit. The territorial imperative isn't some timeless Law of History; it belongs to a certain phase."

"What if it persists, though? Into a later phase?"

"That can cause friction," Joan admitted.

"Nevertheless, no Spreaders have conquered the galaxy?"

"Not yet."

Sando went back to his repairs; Joan read the rest of the article. She'd thought she'd already grasped the lesson demanded by the subtitle, but it turned out that Jaqad had something more specific in mind.

"Having argued this way, how can I defend my own field of study from the very same charges as I have brought against the Niah? Having grasped the essential character of this doomed race, why should we waste our time and resources studying them further?

"The answer is simple. We still do not know exactly how and why the Niah died, but when we do, that could turn out to be the most important discovery in history. When we finally leave our world behind, we should not expect to find only other Spreaders to compete with us, as honorable opponents in battle. There will be Seekers as well, blocking the way: tired, old races squatting uselessly on their hoards of knowledge and wealth.

"Time will defeat them in the end, but we already waited three million years to be born; we should have no patience to wait again. If we can learn how the Niah died, that will be our key, that will be our weapon. If we know the Seekers' weakness, we can find a way to hasten their demise."

6.

The proof of the Niah's theorem turned out to be buried deep in the hillside, but over the following days they extracted it all.

It was as beautiful and satisfying as Joan could have wished, merging six earlier, simpler theorems while extending the techniques used in their proofs. She could even see hints of how the same methods might be stretched further to yield still stronger results. "The Big Crunch" had always been a slightly mocking, irreverent term, but now she was struck anew by how little justice it did to the real trend that had fascinated the Niah. It was not a matter of everything in mathematics collapsing in on itself, with one branch turning out to have been merely a recapitulation of another under a different guise. Rather, the principle was that every sufficiently beautiful mathematical system was rich enough to mirror *in part*—and sometimes in a complex and distorted fashion— every other sufficiently beautiful system. Nothing became sterile and redundant, nothing proved to have been a waste of time, but everything was shown to be magnificently intertwined.

After briefing Halzoun, Joan used the satellite dish to transmit the theorem and its proof to the decoy node. That had been the deal with Pirit: anything she learned from the Niah belonged to the whole galaxy, as long as she explained it to her hosts first.

The archaeologists moved across the hillside, hunting for more artifacts in the same layer of sediment. Joan was eager to see what else the same group of Niah might have published. One possible eight-dimensional hypercube was hovering in her mind; if she'd sat down and thought about it for a few decades she might have worked out the details herself, but the Niah did what they did so well that it would have seemed crass to try to follow clumsily in their footsteps when their own immaculately polished results might simply be lying in the ground, waiting to be uncovered.

A month after the discovery, Joan was woken by the sound of an intruder moving through the shelter. She knew it wasn't Sando; even as she slept an ancient part of her Noudah brain was listening to his heartbeat. The stranger's heart was too quiet to hear, which required great discipline, but the shelter's flexible adhesive made the floor emit a characteristic squeak beneath even the gentlest footsteps. As she rose from her couch she heard Sando waking, and she turned in his direction.

Bright torchlight on his face dazzled her for a moment. The intruder held two knives to Sando's respiration membranes; a deep enough cut there would mean choking to death, in excruciating pain. The nanomachines that had built Joan's body had wired extensive skills in unarmed combat into her brain, and one scenario involving a feigned escape attempt followed by a sideways flick of her powerful tail was already playing out in the back of her mind, but as yet she could see no way to guarantee that Sando came through it all unharmed.

She said, "What do you want?"

The intruder remained in darkness. "Tell me about the ship that brought you to Baneth."

"Why?"

"Because it would be a shame to shred your colleague here, just when his work was going so well." Sando refused to show any emotion on his face, but the blank pallor itself was as stark an expression of fear as anything Joan could imagine.

She said, "There's a coherent state that can be prepared for a quark-gluon plasma in which virtual black holes catalyze baryon decay. In effect, you can turn all of your fuel's rest mass into photons, yielding the most efficient exhaust stream possible." She recited a long list of technical details. The claimed baryon decay process didn't actually exist, but the pseudophysics underpinning it was mathematically consistent, and could not be ruled out by anything the Noudah had yet observed. She and Anne had prepared an entire fictitious science and technology, and even a fictitious history of their culture, precisely for emergencies like this; they could spout red herrings for a decade if necessary, and never get caught out contradicting themselves.

"That wasn't so hard, was it?" the intruder gloated.

"What now?"

"You're going to take a trip with me. If you do this nicely, nobody needs to get hurt."

Something moved in the shadows, and the intruder screamed in pain. Joan leaped forward and knocked one of the knives out of his hand with her tail; the other knife grazed Sando's membrane, but a second tail whipped out of the darkness and intervened. As the intruder fell backward, the beam of his torch revealed Surat and Rali tensed beside him, and a pick buried deep in his side.

Joan's rush of combat hormones suddenly faded, and she let out a long, deep wail of anguish. Sando was unscathed, but a stream of dark liquid was pumping out of the intruder's wound.

Surat was annoyed. "Stop blubbing, and help us tie up this Tiran cousin-fucker."

"Tie him up? You've killed him!"

"Don't be stupid, that's just sheath fluid." Joan recalled her Noudah anatomy; sheath fluid was like oil in a hydraulic machine. You could lose it all and it would cost you most of the strength in your limbs and tail, but you wouldn't die, and your body would make more eventually.

Rali found some cable and they trussed up the intruder. Sando was shaken, but he seemed to be recovering. He took Joan aside. "I'm going to have to call Pirit."

"I understand. But what will he do to these two?" She wasn't sure exactly how much Rali and Surat had heard, but it was certain to have been more than Pirit wanted them to know.

"Don't worry about that, I can protect them."

Just before dawn someone sent by Pirit arrived in a truck to take the intruder away. Sando declared a rest day, and Rali and Surat went back to their shelter to sleep. Joan went for a walk along the hillside; she didn't feel like sleeping.

Sando caught up with her. He said, "I told them you'd been working on a military research project, and you were exiled here for some political misdemeanor."

"And they believed you?"

"All they heard was half of a conversation full of incomprehensible physics. All they know is that someone thought you were worth kidnapping."

Joan said, "I'm sorry about what happened."

Sando hesitated. "What did you expect?"

Joan was stung. "One of us went to Tira, one of us came here. We thought that would keep everyone happy!"

"We're Spreaders," said Sando. "Give us one of anything, and we want two. Especially if our enemy has the other one. Did you really think you could come here, do a bit of fossicking, and then simply fly away without changing a thing?"

"Your culture has always believed there were other civilizations in the galaxy. Our existence hardly came as a shock."

Sando's face became yellow, an expression of almost parental reproach. "Believing in something in the abstract is not the same as having it dangled in front of you. We were never going to have an existential crisis at finding out that we're not unique; the Niah might be related to us, but they were still alien enough to get us used to the idea. But did you really think we were just going to relax and accept your refusal to share your technology? That one of you went to the Tirans only makes it worse for the Ghahari, and vice versa. Both governments are going absolutely crazy, each one terrified that the other has found a way to make its alien talk."

Joan stopped walking. "The war games, the border skirmishes? You're blaming all of that on Anne and me?"

Sando's body sagged wearily. "To be honest, I don't know all the details. And if it's any consolation, I'm sure we would have found another reason if you hadn't come along."

Joan said, "Maybe I should leave." She was tired of these people, tired of her body, tired of being cut off from civilization. She had rescued one beautiful Niah theorem and sent it out into the Amalgam. Wasn't that enough?

"It's up to you," Sando replied. "But you might as well stay until they flood the valley. Another year isn't going to change anything. What you've done to this world has already been done. For us, there's no going back."

7.

Joan stayed with the archaeologists as they moved across the hillside. They found tablets bearing Niah drawings and poetry, which no doubt had their virtues but to Joan seemed bland and opaque. Sando and his students relished these discoveries as much as the theorems; to them, the Niah culture was a vast jigsaw puzzle, and any clue that filled in the details of their history was as good as any other.

Sando would have told Pirit everything he'd heard from Joan the night the intruder came, so she was surprised that she hadn't been summoned for a fresh interrogation to flesh out the details. Perhaps the Ghahari physicists were still digesting her elaborate gobbledygook, trying to decide if it made sense. In her more cynical moments she wondered if the intruder might have been Ghahari himself, sent by Pirit to exploit her friendship with Sando. Perhaps Sando had even been in on it, and Rali and Surat as well. The possibility made her feel as if she were living in a fabricated world, a scape in which nothing was real and nobody could be trusted. The only thing she was certain that the Ghaharis could not have faked was the Niah artifacts. The mathematics verified itself; everything else was subject to doubt and paranoia.

Summer came, burning away the morning fogs. The Noudah's idea of heat was very different from Joan's previous perceptions, but even the body she now wore found the midday sun oppressive. She willed herself to be patient. There was still a chance that the Niah had taken a few more steps toward their grand vision of a unified mathematics, and carved their final discoveries into the form that would outlive them by a million years.

When the lone fusion ship appeared high in the afternoon sky, Joan resolved to ignore it. She glanced up once, but she kept dragging the tomography unit across the ground. She was sick of thinking about Tiran-Ghahari politics. They had played their childish games for centuries; she would not take the blame for this latest outbreak of provocation.

Usually the ships flew by, disappearing within minutes, showing off their power and speed. This one lingered, weaving back and forth across the sky like some dazzling insect performing an elaborate mating dance. Joan's second shadow darted around her feet, hammering a strangely familiar rhythm into her brain.

She looked up, disbelieving. The motion of the ship was following the syntax of a gestural language she had learned on another planet, in another body, a dozen lifetimes ago. The only other person on this world who could know that language was Anne.

She glanced toward the archaeologists a hundred meters away, but they seemed to be paying no attention to the ship. She switched off the tomography unit and stared into the sky. *I'm listening, my friend. What's happening? Did they give you back your ship? Have you had enough of this world, and decided to go home?*

Anne told the story in shorthand, compressed and elliptic. The Tirans had found a tablet bearing a theorem: the last of the Niah's discoveries, the pinnacle of their achievements. Her minders had not let her study it, but they had contrived a situation making it easy for her to steal it, and to steal this ship.

They had wanted her to take it and run, in the hope that she would lead them to something they valued far more than any ancient mathematics: an advanced spacecraft, or some magical stargate at the edge of the system.

But Anne wasn't fleeing anywhere. She was high above Ghahar, reading the tablet, and now she would paint what she read across the sky for Joan to see.

Sando approached. "We're in danger, we have to move."

"Danger? That's my friend up there! She's not going to shoot a missile at us!"

"Your friend?" Sando seemed confused. As he spoke, three more ships came into view, lower and brighter than the first. "I've been told that the Tirans are going to strike the valley, to bury the Niah sites. We need to get over the hill and indoors, to get some protection from the blast."

"Why would the Tirans attack the Niah sites? That makes no sense to me."

Sando said, "Nor me, but I don't have time to argue."

The three ships were menacing Anne's, pursuing her, trying to drive her away. Joan had no idea if they were Ghahari defending their territory, or Tirans harassing her in the hope that she would flee and reveal the nonexistent short-cut to the stars, but Anne was staying put, still weaving the same gestural language into her maneuvers even as she dodged her pursuers, spelling out the Niah's glorious finale.

Joan said, "You go. I have to see this." She tensed, ready to fight him if necessary.

Sando took something from his tool belt and peppered her side with holes. Joan gasped with pain and crumpled to the ground as the sheath fluid poured out of her.

Rali and Surat helped carry her to the shelter. Joan caught glimpses of the fiery ballet in the sky, but not enough to make sense of it, let alone reconstruct it.

They put her on her couch inside the shelter. Sando bandaged her side and gave her water to sip. He said, "I'm sorry I had to do that, but if anything had happened to you I would have been held responsible."

Surat kept ducking outside to check on the "battle," then reporting excitedly on the state of play. "The Tiran's still up there, they can't get rid of it. I don't know why they haven't shot it down yet."

Because the Tirans were the ones pursuing Anne, and they didn't want her dead. But for how long would the Ghahari tolerate this violation?

Anne's efforts could not be allowed to come to nothing. Joan struggled to recall the constellations she'd last seen in the night sky. At the node they'd departed from, powerful telescopes were constantly trained on the Noudah's homeworld. Anne's ship was easily bright enough, its gestures wide enough, to be resolved from seven light-years away—if the planet itself wasn't blocking the view, if the node was above the horizon.

The shelter was windowless, but Joan saw the ground outside the doorway brighten for an instant. The flash was silent; no missile had struck the valley, the explosion had taken place high above the atmosphere.

Surat went outside. When she returned she said quietly, "All clear. They got it."

Joan put all her effort into spitting out a handful of words. "I want to see what happened."

Sando hesitated, then motioned to the others to help him pick up the couch and carry it outside.

A shell of glowing plasma was still visible, drifting across the sky as it expanded, a ring of light growing steadily fainter until it vanished into the afternoon glare.

Anne was dead in this embodiment, but her backup would wake and go on to new adventures. Joan could at least tell her the story of her local death: of virtuoso flying and a spectacular end.

She'd recovered her bearings now, and she recalled the position of the stars. The node was still hours away from rising. The Amalgam was full of powerful telescopes, but no others would be aimed at this obscure planet, and no plea to redirect them could outrace the light they would need to capture in order to bring the Niah's final theorem back to life.

8.

Sando wanted to send her away for medical supervision, but Joan insisted on remaining at the site.

"The fewer officials who get to know about this incident, the fewer problems it makes for you," she reasoned.

"As long as you don't get sick and die," he replied.

"I'm not going to die." Her wounds had not become infected, and her strength was returning rapidly.

They compromised. Sando hired someone to drive up from the nearest town to look after her while he was out at the excavation. Daya had basic medical training and didn't ask awkward questions; he seemed happy to tend to Joan's needs, and then lie outside daydreaming the rest of the time.

There was still a chance, Joan thought, that the Niah had carved the theorem on a multitude of tablets and scattered them all over the planet. There was also a chance that the Tirans had made copies of the tablet before letting Anne abscond with it. The question, though, was whether she had the slightest prospect of getting her hands on these duplicates.

Anne might have made some kind of copy herself, but she hadn't mentioned it in the prologue to her aerobatic rendition of the theorem. If she'd had any time to spare, she wouldn't have limited herself to an audience of one: she would have waited until the node had risen over Ghahar.

On her second night as an invalid, Joan dreamed that she saw Anne standing on the hill looking back into the fog-shrouded valley, her shadow haloed by the Niah light.

When she woke, she knew what she had to do.

When Sando left, she asked Daya to bring her the console that controlled the satellite dish. She had enough strength in her arms now to operate it, and Daya showed no interest in what she did. That was naive, of course: whether or not Daya was spying on her, Pirit would know exactly where the signal was sent. So be it. Seven light-years was still far beyond the Noudah's reach; the whole node could be disassembled and erased long before they came close.

No message could outrace light directly, but there were more ways for light to reach the node than the direct path, the fastest one. Every black hole had its glory, twisting light around it in a tight, close orbit and flinging it back out again. Seventy-four hours after the original image was lost to them, the telescopes at the node could still turn to the Cataract and scour the distorted, compressed image of the sky at the rim of the hole's black disk to catch a replay of Anne's ballet.

Joan composed the message and entered the coordinates of the node. You didn't die for nothing, my friend. When you wake and see this, you'll be proud of us both.

She hesitated, her hand hovering above the send key. The Tirans had wanted Anne to flee, to show them the way to the stars, but had they really been indifferent to the loot they'd let her carry? The theorem had come at the end of the Niah's three-million-year reign. To witness this beautiful truth would not destroy the Amalgam, but might it not weaken it? If the Seekers' thirst for knowledge was slaked, their sense of purpose corroded, might not the most crucial strand of the culture fall into a twilight of its own? There was no shortcut to the stars, but the Noudah had been goaded by their alien visitors, and the technology would come to them soon enough.

The Amalgam had been goaded too: the theorem she'd already transmitted would send a wave of excitement around the galaxy, strengthening the Seekers, encouraging them to complete the unification by their own efforts. The Big Crunch might be inevitable, but at least she could delay it, and hope that the robustness and diversity of the Amalgam would carry them through it, and beyond.

She erased the message and wrote a new one, addressed to her backup via the decoy node. It would have been nice to upload all her memories, but the Noudah were ruthless, and she wasn't prepared to stay any longer and risk being used by them. This sketch, this postcard, would have to be enough.

When the transmission was complete she left a note for Sando in the console's memory.

Daya called out to her, "Jown? Do you need anything?"

She said, "No. I'm going to sleep for a while."

Peter Watts (www.rifters.com) is is a former marine biologist who clings to some shred of scientific rigor by appending technical bibliographies onto his novels. His debut novel (*Starfish*) was a *New York Times* Notable Book, while his fourth (*Blindsight*)—a rumination on the utility of consciousness which has become a required text in undergraduate courses ranging from philosophy to neuroscience—was a finalist for numerous North American genre awards and winner of numerous awards overseas. His shorter work has won the Shirley Jackson and Hugo Awards.

THE ISLAND

PETER WATTS

You sent us out here. We do this for *you*: spin your webs and build your magic gateways, thread the needle's eye at sixty thousand kilometers a second. We never stop, never even dare to slow down, lest the light of your coming turn us to plasma. All so you can step from star to star without dirtying your feet in these endless, empty wastes *between*.

Is it really too much to ask, that you might talk to us now and then?

I know about evolution and engineering. I know how much you've changed. I've seen these portals give birth to gods and demons and things we can't begin to comprehend, things I can't believe were ever human; alien hitchhikers, perhaps, riding the rails we've left behind. Alien conquerors.

Exterminators, perhaps.

But I've also seen those gates stay dark and empty until they faded from view. We've inferred diebacks and dark ages, civilizations burned to the ground and others rising from their ashes—and sometimes, afterward, the things that come out look a little like the ships *we* might have built, back in the day. They speak to one another—radio, laser, carrier neutrinos—and sometimes their voices sound something like ours. There was a time we dared to hope that they really were like us, that the circle had come around again and closed on beings we could talk to. I've lost count of the times we tried to break the ice.

I've lost count of the eons since we gave up.

All these iterations fading behind us. All these hybrids and posthumans and immortals, gods and catatonic cavemen trapped in magical chariots they can't begin to understand, and not one of them ever pointed a comm laser in our direction to say *Hey, how's it going?* or *Guess what? We cured Damascus Disease!* or even *Thanks, guys, keep up the good work!*

We're not some fucking cargo cult. We're the backbone of your goddamn empire. You wouldn't even be *out* here if it weren't for us.

And—and you're *our* children. Whatever you've become, you were once like this, like me. I believed in you once. There was a time, long ago, when I believed in this mission with all my heart.

Why have you forsaken us?

And so another build begins.

This time, I open my eyes to a familiar face I've never seen before: only a boy, early twenties perhaps, physiologically. His face is a little lopsided, the cheekbone flatter on the left than the right. His ears are too big. He looks almost *natural.*

I haven't spoken for millennia. My voice comes out a whisper: "Who are you?" Not what I'm supposed to ask, I know. Not the first question *anyone* on *Eriophora* asks, after coming back.

"I'm yours," he says, and just like that, I'm a mother.

I want to let it sink in, but he doesn't give me the chance: "You weren't scheduled, but Chimp wants extra hands on deck. Next build's got a situation."

So the chimp is still in control. The chimp is always in control. The mission goes on.

"Situation?" I ask.

"Contact scenario, maybe."

I wonder when he was born. I wonder if he ever wondered about me, before now.

He doesn't tell me. He only says, "Sun up ahead. Half light-year. Chimp thinks, maybe it's talking to us. Anyhow . . ." My—son shrugs. "No rush. Lotsa time."

I nod, but he hesitates. He's waiting for The Question, but I already see a kind of answer in his face. Our reinforcements were supposed to be *pristine,* built from perfect genes buried deep within *Eri*'s iron-basalt mantle, safe from the sleeting blueshift. And yet this boy has flaws. I see the damage in his face, I see those tiny flipped base-pairs resonating up from the microscopic and *bending* him just a little off-kilter. He looks like he grew up on a planet. He looks borne of parents who spent their whole lives hammered by raw sunlight.

How far out must we be by now, if even our own perfect building blocks have decayed so? How long has it taken us? How long have I been dead?

How long? It's the first thing everyone asks.

After all this time, I don't want to know.

He's alone at the tac Tank when I arrive on the bridge, his eyes full of icons and trajectories. Perhaps I see a little of me in there, too.

"I didn't get your name," I say, although I've looked it up on the manifest. We've barely been introduced and already I'm lying to him.

"Dix." He keeps his eyes on the Tank.

He's over ten thousand years old. Alive for maybe twenty of them. I wonder how much he knows, whom he's met during those sparse decades: does he know Ishmael or Connie? Does he know if Sanchez got over his brush with immortality?

I wonder, but I don't ask. There are rules.

I look around. "We're it?"

Dix nods. "For now. Bring back more if we need them. But . . ." His voice trails off.

"Yes?"

"Nothing."

I join him at the Tank. Diaphanous veils hang within like frozen, color-coded smoke. We're on the edge of a molecular dust cloud. Warm, semiorganic, lots of raw materials. Formaldehyde, ethylene glycol, the usual prebiotics. A good spot for a quick build. A red dwarf glowers dimly at the center of the Tank: the chimp has named it DHF428, for reasons I've long since forgotten to care about.

"So fill me in," I say.

His glance is impatient, even irritated. "You too?"

"What do you mean?"

"Like the others. On the other builds. Chimp can just squirt the specs, but they want to *talk* all the time."

Shit, his link's still active. He's *online*.

I force a smile. "Just a—a cultural tradition, I guess. We talk about a lot of things, it helps us—reconnect. After being down for so long."

"But it's *slow*," Dix complains.

He doesn't know. Why doesn't he know?

"We've got half a light-year," I point out. "There's some rush?"

The corner of his mouth twitches. "Vons went out on schedule." On cue, a cluster of violet pinpricks sparkle in the Tank, five trillion klicks ahead of us. "Still sucking dust mostly, but got lucky with a couple of big asteroids, and the refineries came online early. First components already extruded. Then Chimp

sees these fluctuations in solar output—mainly infra, but extends into visible."
The Tank blinks at us: the dwarf goes into time-lapse.

Sure enough, it's *flickering*.

"Non-random, I take it."

Dix inclines his head a little to the side, not quite nodding.

"Plot the time-series." I've never been able to break the habit of raising my voice, just a bit, when addressing the chimp. Obediently (*obediently*—now *there's* a laugh and a half), the AI wipes the spacescape and replaces it with

····· · · · · · · · · · · · · · · · · ·

"Repeating sequence," Dix tells me. "Blips don't change, but spacing's a log-linear increase cycling every 92.5 corsecs. Each cycle starts at 13.2 clicks/corsec, degrades over time."

"No chance this could be natural? A little black hole wobbling around in the center of the star, something like that?"

Dix shakes his head, or something like that: a diagonal dip of the chin that somehow conveys the negative. "But way too simple to contain much info. Not like an actual conversation. More—well, a shout."

He's partly right. There may not be much information, but there's enough. We're here. We're smart. We're powerful enough to hook a whole damn star up to a dimmer switch.

Maybe not such a good spot for a build after all.

I purse my lips. "The sun's hailing us. That's what you're saying."

"Maybe. Hailing *someone*. But too simple for a rosetta signal. It's not an archive, can't self-extract. Not a bonferroni or fibonacci seq, not pi. Not even a multiplication table. Nothing to base a pidgin on."

Still. An intelligent signal.

"Need more info," Dix says, proving himself master of the blindingly obvious.

I nod. "The vons."

"Uh, what about them?"

"We set up an array. Use a bunch of bad eyes to fake a good one. It'd be faster than high-geeing an observatory from this end or retooling one of the on-site factories."

His eyes go wide. For a moment, he almost looks frightened for some reason. But the moment passes and he does that weird head-shake thing again. "Bleed too many resources away from the build, wouldn't it?"

"It would," the chimp agrees.

I suppress a snort. "If you're so worried about meeting our construction benchmarks, Chimp, factor in the potential risk posed by an intelligence powerful enough to control the energy output of an entire sun."

"I can't," it admits. "I don't have enough information."

"You don't have *any* information. About something that could probably stop this mission dead in its tracks if it wanted to. So maybe we should get some."

"Okay. Vons reassigned."

Confirmation glows from a convenient bulkhead, a complex sequence of dance instructions that *Eri*'s just fired into the void. Six months from now, a hundred self-replicating robots will waltz into a makeshift surveillance grid; four months after that, we might have something more than vacuum to debate in.

Dix eyes me as though I've just cast some kind of magic spell.

"It may run the ship," I tell him, "but it's pretty fucking stupid. Sometimes you've just got to spell things out."

He looks vaguely affronted, but there's no mistaking the surprise beneath. He didn't know that. He *didn't know*.

Who the hell's been raising him all this time? Whose problem is this?

Not mine.

"Call me in ten months," I say. "I'm going back to bed."

It's as though he never left. I climb back into the bridge and there he is, staring into tac. DHF428 fills the Tank, a swollen red orb that turns my son's face into a devil mask.

He spares me the briefest glance, eyes wide, fingers twitching as if electrified. "Vons don't see it."

I'm still a bit groggy from the thaw. "See wh—"

"The *sequence*!" His voice borders on panic. He sways back and forth, shifting his weight from foot to foot.

"Show me."

Tac splits down the middle. Cloned dwarves burn before me now, each perhaps twice the size of my fist. On the left, an *Eri*'s-eye view: DHF428 stutters as it did before, as it presumably has these past ten months. On the right, a compound-eye composite: an interferometry grid built by a myriad precisely spaced vons, their rudimentary eyes layered and parallaxed into something approaching high resolution. Contrast on both sides has been conveniently cranked up to highlight the dwarf's endless winking for merely human eyes.

Except that it's only winking from the left side of the display. On the right, 428 glowers steady as a standard candle.

"Chimp: any chance the grid just isn't sensitive enough to see the fluctuations?"

"No."

"Huh." I try to think of some reason it would lie about this.

"Doesn't make *sense*," my son complains.

"It does," I murmur, "if it's not the sun that's flickering."

"But *is* flickering—" He sucks his teeth. "You *see* it—wait, you mean something *behind* the vons? Between, between them and us?"

"Mmmm."

"Some kind of *filter*." Dix relaxes a bit. "Wouldn't we've seen it, though? Wouldn't the vons've hit it going down?"

I put my voice back into ChimpComm mode. "What's the current field-of-view for *Eri*'s forward scope?"

"Eighteen mikes," the chimp reports. "At 428's range, the cone is 3.34 light-secs across."

"Increase to a hundred lightsecs."

The *Eri*'s-eye partition swells, obliterating the dissenting viewpoint. For a moment, the sun fills the Tank again, paints the whole bridge crimson. Then it dwindles as if devoured from within.

I notice some fuzz in the display. "Can you clear that noise?"

"It's not noise," the chimp reports. "It's dust and molecular gas."

I blink. "What's the density?"

"Estimated hundred thousand atoms per cubic meter."

Two orders of magnitude too high, even for a nebula. "Why so heavy?" Surely we'd have detected any gravity well strong enough to keep *that* much material in the neighborhood.

"I don't know," the chimp says.

I get the queasy feeling that I might. "Set field-of-view to five hundred lightsecs. Peak false-color at near-infrared."

Space grows ominously murky in the Tank. The tiny sun at its center, thumbnail-size now, glows with increased brilliance: an incandescent pearl in muddy water.

"A thousand lightsecs," I command.

"There," Dix whispers: real space reclaims the edges of the Tank, dark, clear, pristine. DHF428 nestles at the heart of a dim spherical shroud. You find those sometimes, discarded castoffs from companion stars whose convulsions spew gas and rads across light-years. But 428 is no nova remnant. It's a *red dwarf*, placid, middle-aged. Unremarkable.

Except for the fact that it sits dead center of a tenuous gas bubble 1.4 AU's across. And for the fact that that bubble does not *attenuate* or *diffuse* or *fade* gradually into that good night. No, unless there is something seriously wrong with the display, this small, spherical nebula extends about three hundred and fifty lightsecs from its primary and then just *stops*, its boundary far more knife-edged than nature has any right to be.

For the first time in millennia, I miss my cortical pipe. It takes forever to sac-cade search terms onto the keyboard in my head, to get the answers I already know.

Numbers come back. "Chimp. I want false-color peaks at three hundred thirty-five, five hundred, and eight hundred nanometers."

The shroud around 428 lights up like a dragonfly's wing, like an iridescent soap bubble.

"It's *beautiful*," whispers my awestruck son.

"It's photosynthetic," I tell him.

Phaeophytin and eumelanin, according to spectro. There are even hints of some kind of lead-based Keipper pigment, soaking up X-rays in the picometer range. Chimp hypothesizes something called a *chromatophore*: branching cells with little aliquots of pigment inside, like particles of charcoal dust. Keep those particles clumped together and the cell's effectively transparent; spread them out through the cytoplasm and the whole structure *darkens*, dims whatever EM passes through from behind. Apparently there were animals back on Earth with cells like that. They could change color, pattern-match to their background, all sorts of things.

"So there's a membrane of—of *living tissue* around that star," I say, trying to wrap my head around the concept. "A, a meat balloon. Around the whole damn *star*."

"Yes," the chimp says.

"But that's—Jesus, how thick would it be?"

"No more than two millimeters. Probably less."

"How so?"

"If it was much thicker, it would be more obvious in the visible spectrum. It would have had a detectable effect on the von Neumanns when they hit it."

"That's assuming that its—cells, I guess—are like ours."

"The pigments are familiar; the rest might be too."

It can't be *too* familiar. Nothing like a conventional gene would last two sec-onds in that environment. Not to mention whatever miracle solvent that thing must use as antifreeze . . .

"Okay, let's be conservative, then. Say, mean thickness of a millimeter. Assume a density of water at STP. How much mass in the whole thing?"

"1.4 yottagrams," Dix and the chimp reply, almost in unison.

"That's, uh . . ."

"Half the mass of Mercury," the chimp adds helpfully.

I whistle through my teeth. "And that's *one* organism?"

"I don't know yet."

"It's got organic pigments. Fuck, it's *talking*. It's intelligent."

"Most cyclic emanations from living sources are simple biorhythms," the chimp points out. "Not intelligent signals."

I ignore it and turn to Dix. "Assume it's a signal."

He frowns. "Chimp says—"

"Assume. Use your imagination."

I'm not getting through to him. He looks nervous.

He looks like that a lot, I realize.

"If someone were signaling you," I say, *"then* what would you do?"

"Signal . . ." Confusion on that face, and a fuzzy circuit closing somewhere " . . . back?"

My son is an idiot.

"And if the incoming signal takes the form of systematic changes in light intensity, how—"

"Use the BI lasers, alternated to pulse between seven hundred and three thousand nanometers. Can boost an interlaced signal into the exawatt range without compromising our fenders; gives over a thousand watts per square meter after diffraction. Way past detection threshold for anything that can sense thermal output from a red dwarf. And content doesn't matter if it's just a shout. Shout back. Test for echo."

Okay, so my son is an idiot *savant.*

And he still looks unhappy—"But Chimp, he says no real *information* there, right?"—and that whole other set of misgivings edges to the fore again: *he.*

Dix takes my silence for amnesia. "Too simple, remember? Simple click train."

I shake my head. There's more information in that signal than the chimp can imagine. There are so many things the chimp doesn't know. And the last thing I need is for this, this *child* to start deferring to it, to start looking to it as an equal, or, God forbid, a *mentor.*

Oh, it's smart enough to steer us between the stars. Smart enough to calculate sixty-digit primes in the blink of an eye. Even smart enough for a little crude improvisation should the crew go too far off-mission.

Not smart enough to know a distress call when it sees one.

"It's a deceleration curve," I tell them both. "It keeps *slowing down.* Over and over again. *That's* the message."

Stop. Stop. Stop. Stop.

And I think it's meant for no one but us.

We shout back. No reason not to. And now we die again, because what's the point of staying up late? Whether or not this vast entity harbors real intelligence, our echo won't reach it for ten million corsecs. Another seven million, at the earliest, before we receive any reply it might send.

Might as well hit the crypt in the meantime. Shut down all desires and misgivings, conserve whatever life I have left for moments that matter. Remove myself from this sparse tactical intelligence, from this wet-eyed pup watching me as though I'm some kind of sorcerer about to vanish in a puff of smoke. He opens his mouth to speak, and I turn away and hurry down to oblivion.

But I set my alarm to wake up alone.

I linger in the coffin for a while, grateful for small and ancient victories. The chimp's dead, blackened eye gazes down from the ceiling; in all these millions of years, nobody's scrubbed off the carbon scoring. It's a trophy of sorts, a memento from the early incendiary days of our Great Struggle.

There's still something—comforting, I guess—about that blind, endless stare. I'm reluctant to venture out where the chimp's nerves have not been so thoroughly cauterized. Childish, I know. The damn thing already knows I'm up; it may be blind, deaf, and impotent in here, but there's no way to mask the power the crypt sucks in during a thaw. And it's not as though a bunch of club-wielding teleops are waiting to pounce on me the moment I step outside. These are the days of détente, after all. The struggle continues but the war has gone cold; we just go through the motions now, rattling our chains like an old married multiplet resigned to hating each other to the end of time.

After all the moves and countermoves, the truth is we need each other.

So I wash the rotten-egg stench from my hair and step into *Eri's* silent cathedral hallways. Sure enough, the enemy waits in the darkness, turns the lights on as I approach, shuts them off behind me—but it does not break the silence.

Dix.

A strange one, that. Not that you'd expect anyone born and raised on *Eriophora* to be an archetype of mental health, but Dix doesn't even know what side he's on. He doesn't even seem to know he has to *choose* a side. It's almost as though he read the original mission statements and took them *seriously*, believed in the literal truth of the ancient scrolls: Mammals and Machinery, working together across the ages to explore the Universe! United! Strong! Forward the Frontier!

Rah.

Whoever raised him didn't do a great job. Not that I blame them; it can't have been much fun having a child underfoot during a build, and none of us were selected for our parenting skills. Even if bots changed the diapers and VR handled the infodumps, socializing a toddler couldn't have been anyone's idea of a good time. I'd have probably just chucked the little bastard out an airlock.

But even I would've brought him up to speed.

Something changed while I was away. Maybe the war's heated up again, entered some new phase. That twitchy kid is out of the loop for a reason. I wonder what it is.

I wonder if I care.

I arrive at my suite, treat myself to a gratuitous meal, jill off. Three hours after coming back to life, I'm relaxing in the starbow commons. "Chimp."

"You're up early," it says at last.

I am. Our answering shout hasn't even arrived at its destination yet. No real chance of new data for another two months, at least.

"Show me the forward feeds," I command.

DHF428 blinks at me from the center of the lounge: *Stop. Stop. Stop.*

Maybe. Or maybe the chimp's right, maybe it's pure physiology. Maybe this endless cycle carries no more intelligence than the beating of a heart.

But there's a pattern inside the pattern, some kind of *flicker* in the blink. It makes my brain itch.

"Slow the time-series," I command. "By a hundred."

It *is* a blink. DHF428's disk isn't darkening uniformly, it's *eclipsing*. As though a great eyelid were being drawn across the surface of the sun, from right to left.

"By a thousand."

Chromatophores, the chimp called them. But they're not all opening and closing at once. The darkness moves across the membrane in *waves*.

A word pops into my head: *latency*.

"Chimp. Those waves of pigment. How fast are they moving?"

"About fifty-nine thousand kilometers per second."

The speed of a passing thought.

And if this thing *does* think, it'll have logic gates, synapses—it's going to be a *net* of some kind. And if the net's big enough, there's an *I* in the middle of it. Just like me, just like Dix. Just like the chimp. (Which is why I educated myself on the subject, back in the early tumultuous days of our relationship. Know your enemy and all that.)

The thing about *I* is, it only exists within a tenth-of-a-second of all its parts. When we get spread too thin—when someone splits your brain down the middle, say, chops the fat pipe so the halves have to talk the long way around; when the neural architecture *diffuses* past some critical point and signals take just that much longer to pass from A to B—the system, well, *decoheres*. The two sides of your brain become different people with different tastes, different agendas, different senses of themselves.

I shatters into *we*.

It's not just a human rule, or a mammal rule, or even an Earthly one. It's a rule for any circuit that processes information, and it applies as much to the things we've yet to meet as it did to those we left behind.

Fifty-nine thousand kilometers per second, the chimp says. How far can the signal move through that membrane in a tenth of a corsec? How thinly does *I* spread itself across the heavens?

The flesh is huge, the flesh is inconceivable. But the spirit, the spirit is— *Shit.*

"Chimp. Assuming the mean neuron density of a human brain, what's the synapse count on a circular sheet of neurons one millimeter thick with a diameter of five thousand eight hundred ninety-two kilometers?"

"Two times ten to the twenty-seventh."

I saccade the database for some perspective on a mind stretched across thirty million square kilometers: the equivalent of two quadrillion human brains.

Of course, whatever this thing uses for neurons have to be packed a lot less tightly than ours; we can see right through them, after all. Let's be superconservative, say it's only got a thousandth the computational density of a human brain. That's—

Okay, let's say it's only got a *ten*-thousandth the synaptic density, that's still—

A *hundred* thousandth. The merest mist of thinking meat. Any more conservative and I'd hypothesize it right out of existence.

Still twenty billion human brains.

Twenty *billion*.

I don't know how to feel about that. This is no mere alien.

But I'm not quite ready to believe in gods.

I round the corner and run smack into Dix, standing like a golem in the middle of my living room. I jump about a meter straight up.

"What the hell are you doing here?"

He seems surprised by my reaction. "Wanted to—talk," he says after a moment.

"You *never* come into someone's home uninvited!"

He retreats a step, stammers: "Wanted, wanted—"

"To talk. And you do that in *public*. On the bridge, or in the commons, or— for that matter, you could just *comm* me."

He hesitates. "Said you—*wanted* face to face. You said, *cultural tradition.*"

I did, at that. But not *here*. This is *my* place, these are my *private quarters*. The lack of locks on these doors is a safety protocol, not an invitation to walk into my home and *lie in wait*, and stand there like part of the fucking *furniture* . . .

"Why are you even *up?*" I snarl. "We're not even supposed to come online for another two months."

"Asked Chimp to get me up when you did."

That fucking machine.

"Why are *you* up?" he asks, not leaving.

I sigh, defeated, and fall into a convenient pseudopod. "I just wanted to go over the preliminary data." The implicit *alone* should be obvious.

"Anything?"

Evidently it isn't. I decide to play along for a while. "Looks like we're talking to an, an island. Almost six thousand klicks across. That's the thinking part, anyway. The surrounding membrane's pretty much empty. I mean, it's all *alive*. It all photosynthesizes, or something like that. It eats, I guess. Not sure what."

"Molecular cloud," Dix says. "Organic compounds everywhere. Plus it's concentrating stuff inside the envelope."

I shrug. "Point is, there's a size limit for the brain, but it's *huge*, it's . . ."

"Unlikely," he murmurs, almost to himself.

I turn to look at him; the pseudopod reshapes itself around me. "What do you mean?"

"Island's twenty-eight million square kilometers? Whole sphere's seven quintillion. Island just happens to be between us and 428, that's—one in fifty billion odds."

"Go on."

He can't. "Uh, just . . . just *unlikely*."

I close my eyes. "How can you be smart enough to run those numbers in your head without missing a beat and stupid enough to miss the obvious conclusion?"

That panicked, slaughterhouse look again. "Don't—I'm not—"

"It *is* unlikely. It's *astronomically* unlikely that we just happen to be aiming at the one intelligent spot on a sphere one and a half AU's across. Which means . . ."

He says nothing. The perplexity in his face mocks me. I want to punch it.

But finally, the lights flicker on: "There's, uh, more than one island? Oh! A *lot* of islands!"

This creature is part of the crew. My life will almost certainly depend on him some day.

That is a very scary thought.

I try to set it aside for the moment. "There's probably a whole population of the things, sprinkled through the membrane like, like cysts I guess. The chimp doesn't know how many, but we're only picking up this one so far, so they might be pretty sparse."

There's a different kind of frown on his face now. "Why *Chimp?*"

"What do you mean?"

"Why call him Chimp?"

"We call it *the* chimp." Because the first step to humanizing something is to give it a name.

"Looked it up. Short for *chimpanzee*. Stupid animal."

"Actually, I think chimps were supposed to be pretty smart," I remember.

"Not like us. Couldn't even *talk*. Chimp can talk. *Way* smarter than those things. That name—it's an insult."

"What do you care?"

He just looks at me.

I spread my hands. "Okay, it's not a chimp. We just call it that because it's got roughly the same synapse count."

"So gave him a small brain, then complain that he's stupid all the time."

My patience is just about drained. "Do you have a point or are you just blowing CO_2 in—"

"Why not make him smarter?"

"Because you can never predict the behavior of a system more complex than you. And if you want a project to stay on track after you're gone, you don't hand the reins to anything that's guaranteed to develop its own agenda." Sweet smoking Jesus, you'd think *someone* would have told him about Ashby's Law.

"So they lobotomized him," Dix says after a moment.

"No. They didn't *turn* it stupid, they *built* it stupid."

"Maybe smarter than you think. You're so much smarter, got *your* agenda, how come *he's* still in control?"

"Don't flatter yourself," I say.

"What?"

I let a grim smile peek through. "You're only following orders from a bunch of other systems *way* more complex than you are." You've got to hand it to them, too; dead for stellar lifetimes and those damn project admins are *still* pulling the strings.

"I don't—*I'm* following?—"

"I'm sorry, dear." I smile sweetly at my idiot offspring. "I wasn't talking to you. I was talking to the thing that's making all those sounds come out of your mouth."

Dix turns whiter than my panties.

I drop all pretense. "What were you thinking, chimp? That you could send this sock-puppet to invade my home and I wouldn't notice?"

"Not—I'm not—it's *me*," Dix stammers. "*Me* talking."

"It's *coaching* you. Do you even know what 'lobotomized' *means*?" I shake my head, disgusted. "You think I've forgotten how the interface works just because we all burned ours out?" A caricature of surprise begins to form on his face. "Oh, don't even fucking *try*. You've been up for other builds, there's no way you couldn't have known. And you know we shut down our domestic links too, or you wouldn't even be sneaking in here. And there's nothing your lord and master can do about that because it *needs* us, and so we have reached what you might call an *accommodation*."

I am not shouting. My tone is icy, but my voice is dead level. And yet Dix almost *cringes* before me.

There is an opportunity here, I realize.

I thaw my voice a little. I speak gently: "You can do that too, you know. Burn out your link. I'll even let you come back here afterward, if you still want to. Just to—talk. But not with that thing in your head."

There is panic in his face, and, against all expectation, it almost breaks my heart. "*Can't*," he pleads. "How I *learn* things, how I *train*. The *mission* . . ."

I honestly don't know which of them is speaking, so I answer them both: "There is more than one way to carry out the mission. We have more than enough time to try them all. Dix is welcome to come back when he's alone."

They take a step toward me. Another. One hand, twitching, rises from their side as if to reach out, and there's something on that lopsided face that I can't quite recognize.

"But I'm your *son*," they say.

I don't even dignify it with a denial.

"Get out of my home."

A human periscope. The Trojan Dix. That's a new one.

The chimp's never tried such overt infiltration while we were up and about before. Usually, it waits until we're all undead before invading our territories. I imagine custom-made drones never seen by human eyes, cobbled together during the long dark eons between builds; I see them sniffing through drawers and peeking behind mirrors, strafing the bulkheads with X-rays and ultrasound, patiently searching *Eriophora*'s catacombs millimeter by endless millimeter for whatever secret messages we might be sending one another down through time.

There's no proof to speak of. We've left trip wires and telltales to alert us to intrusion after the fact, but there's never been any evidence they've been disturbed. Means nothing, of course. The chimp may be stupid, but it's also cunning, and a million years is more than enough time to iterate through every possibility using simpleminded brute force. Document every dust mote; commit your unspeakable acts; put everything back the way it was, afterward.

We're too smart to risk talking across the eons. No encrypted strategies, no long-distance love letters, no chatty postcards showing ancient vistas long lost in the redshift. We keep all that in our heads, where the enemy will never find it. The unspoken rule is that we do not speak, unless it is face to face.

Endless idiotic games. Sometimes I almost forget what we're squabbling over. It seems so trivial now, with an immortal in my sights.

Maybe that means nothing to you. Immortality must be ancient news to you. But I can't even imagine it, although I've outlived worlds. All I have are moments: two or three hundred years, to ration across the life span of a universe. I could bear witness to any point in time, or any hundred-thousand, if I slice my life thinly enough—but I will never see *everything*. I will never see even a fraction.

My life will end. I have to *choose*.

When you come to fully appreciate the deal you've made—ten or fifteen builds out, when the trade-off leaves the realm of mere *knowledge* and sinks deep as cancer into your bones—you become a miser. You can't help it. You ration out your waking moments to the barest minimum: just enough to manage the build, to plan your latest countermove against the chimp, just enough (if you haven't yet moved beyond the need for human contact) for sex and snuggles and a bit of warm mammalian comfort against the endless dark. And then you hurry back to the crypt, to hoard the remains of a human life span against the unwinding of the cosmos.

There's been time for education. Time for a hundred postgraduate degrees, thanks to the best caveman learning tech. I've never bothered. Why burn down my tiny candle for a litany of mere fact, fritter away my precious, endless, finite life? Only a fool would trade book-learning for a ringside view of the Cassiopeia Remnant, even if you *do* need false-color enhancement to see the fucking thing.

Now, though. Now, I want to *know*. This creature crying out across the gulf, massive as a moon, wide as a solar system, tenuous and fragile as an insect's wing: I'd gladly cash in some of my life to learn its secrets. How does it work? How can it even *live* here at the edge of absolute zero, much less think? What vast, unfathomable intellect must it possess, to see us coming from over half a light-year away, to deduce the nature of our eyes and our instruments, to send a signal we can even *detect*, much less understand?

And what happens when we punch through it at a fifth the speed of light?

I call up the latest findings on my way to bed, and the answer hasn't changed: not much. The damn thing's already full of holes. Comets, asteroids, the usual protoplanetary junk careens through this system as it does through every other. Infra picks up diffuse pockets of slow outgassing here and there around the perimeter, where the soft vaporous vacuum of the interior bleeds into the harder stuff outside. Even if we were going to tear through the dead center of the thinking part, I can't imagine this vast creature feeling so much as a pinprick. At the speed we're going we'd be through and gone far too fast to overcome even the feeble inertia of a millimeter membrane.

And yet. Stop. Stop. Stop.

It's not us, of course. It's what we're building. The birth of a gate is a violent, painful thing, a spacetime rape that puts out almost as much gamma and X as a microquasar. Any meat within the white zone turns to ash in an instant, shielded or not. It's why *we* never slow down to take pictures.

One of the reasons, anyway.

We can't stop, of course. Even changing course isn't an option except by the barest increments. *Eri* soars like an eagle among the stars, but she steers like a pig on the short haul; tweak our heading by even a tenth of a degree, and you've got some serious damage at 20 percent light-speed. Half a degree would tear us apart: the ship might torque onto the new heading, but the collapsed mass in her belly would keep right on going, rip through all this surrounding superstructure without even feeling it.

Even tame singularities get set in their ways. They do not take well to change.

We resurrect again, and the Island has changed its tune.

It gave up asking us to *stop stop stop* the moment our laser hit its leading edge. Now it's saying something else entirely: dark hyphens flow across its skin, arrows of pigment converging toward some offstage focus like spokes pointing toward the hub of a wheel. The bull's-eye itself is offstage and implicit, far removed from 428's bright backdrop, but it's easy enough to extrapolate to the point of convergence six light-secs to starboard. There's something else, too: a shadow, roughly circular, moving along one of the spokes like a bead running along a string. It too migrates to starboard, falls off the edge of the Island's makeshift display, is endlessly reborn at the same initial coordinates to repeat its journey.

Those coordinates: exactly where our current trajectory will punch through the membrane in another four months. A squinting God would be able to see the gnats and girders of ongoing construction on the other side, the great piecemeal torus of the Hawking Hoop already taking shape.

The message is so obvious that even Dix sees it. "Wants us to move the gate . . ." and there is something like confusion in his voice. "But how's it know we're *building* one?"

"The vons punctured it en route," the chimp points out. "It could have sensed that. It has photopigments. It can probably see."

"Probably sees better than we do," I say. Even something as simple as a pin-hole camera gets hi-res fast if you stipple a bunch of them across thirty million square kilometers.

But Dix scrunches his face, unconvinced. "So sees a bunch of vons bumping around. Loose parts—not that much even *assembled* yet. How's it know we're building something *hot*?"

Because it is very, very smart, you stupid child. Is it so hard to believe that this, this—*organism* seems far too limiting a word—can just *imagine* how those half-built pieces fit together, glance at our sticks and stones and see exactly where this is going?

"Maybe's not the first gate it's seen," Dix suggests. "Think there's maybe another gate out here?"

I shake my head. "We'd have seen the lensing artifacts by now."

"You ever run into anyone before?"

"No." We have always been alone, through all these epochs. We have only ever run *away*.

And then always from our own children.

I crunch some numbers. "Hundred eighty-two days to insemination. If we move now, we've only got to tweak our bearing by a few mikes to redirect to the new coordinates. Well within the green. Angles get dicey the longer we wait, of course."

"We can't do that," the chimp says. "We would miss the gate by two million kilometers."

"Move the gate. Move the whole damn site. Move the refineries, move the factories, move the damn rocks. A couple hundred meters a second would be more than fast enough if we send the order now. We don't even have to suspend construction, we can keep building on the fly."

"Every one of those vectors widens the nested confidence limits of the build. It would increase the risk of error beyond allowable margins, for no payoff."

"And what about the fact that there's an intelligent being in our path?"

"I'm already allowing for the potential presence of intelligent alien life."

"Okay, first off, there's nothing *potential* about it. It's *right fucking there*. And on our current heading, we run the damn thing over."

"We're staying clear of all planetary bodies in Goldilocks orbits. We've seen no local evidence of spacefaring technology. The current location of the build meets all conservation criteria."

"That's because the people who drew up your criteria *never anticipated a live Dyson sphere!*" But I'm wasting my breath, and I know it. The chimp can run its equations a million times, but if there's nowhere to put the variable, what can it do?

There was a time, back before things turned ugly, when we had clearance to reprogram those parameters. Before we discovered that one of the things the admins *had* anticipated was mutiny.

I try another tack. "Consider the threat potential."

"There's no evidence of any."

"Look at the synapse estimate! That thing's got order of mag more processing power than the whole civilization that sent us out here. You think something can be that smart, live that long, without learning how to defend itself? We're assuming it's *asking* us to move the gate. What if that's not a *request*? What if it's just giving us the chance to back off before it takes matters into its own hands?"

"Doesn't *have* hands," Dix says from the other side of the Tank, and he's not even being flippant. He's just being so stupid I want to bash his face in.

I try to keep my voice level. "Maybe it doesn't *need* any."

"What could it do, *blink* us to death? No weapons. Doesn't even control the whole membrane. Signal propagation's too slow."

"We *don't know*. That's my *point*. We haven't even tried to find out. We're a goddamn road crew; our onsite presence is a bunch of construction vons pressganged into scientific research. We can figure out some basic physical parameters, but we don't know how this thing thinks, what kind of natural defenses it might have—"

"What do you need to find out?" the chimp asks, the very voice of calm reason.

We can't find out! I want to scream. We're stuck with what we've got! By the time the onsite vons could build what we need, we're already past the point of no return! You stupid fucking machine, we're on track to kill a being smarter than all of human history and you can't even be bothered to move our highway to the vacant lot next door?

But of course if I say that, the Island's chances of survival go from low to zero. So I grasp at the only straw that remains: maybe the data we've got in hand is enough. If acquisition is off the table, maybe analysis will do.

"I need time," I say.

"Of course," the chimp tells me. "Take all the time you need."

The chimp is not content to kill this creature. The chimp has to spit on it as well.

Under the pretense of assisting in my research, it tries to *deconstruct* the

Island, break it apart and force it to conform to grubby earthbound precedents. It tells me about earthly bacteria that thrived at 1.5 million rads and laughed at hard vacuum. It shows me pictures of unkillable little tardigrades that could curl up and snooze on the edge of absolute zero, felt equally at home in deep ocean trenches and deeper space. Given time, opportunity, a boot off the planet, who knows how far those cute little invertebrates might have gone? Might they have survived the very death of the homeworld, clung together, grown somehow colonial?

What utter bullshit.

I learn what I can. I study the alchemy by which photosynthesis transforms light and gas and electrons into living tissue. I learn the physics of the solar wind that blows the bubble taut, calculate lower metabolic limits for a life form that filters organics from the ether. I marvel at the speed of this creature's thoughts: almost as fast as *Eri* flies, orders of mag faster than any mammalian nerve impulse. Some kind of organic superconductor perhaps, something that passes chilled electrons almost resistance-free out here in the freezing void.

I acquaint myself with phenotypic plasticity and sloppy fitness, that fortuitous evolutionary soft-focus that lets species exist in alien environments and express novel traits they never needed at home. Perhaps this is how a life form with no natural enemies could acquire teeth and claws and the willingness to use them. The Island's life hinges on its ability to kill us; I have to find *something* that makes it a threat.

But all I uncover is a growing suspicion that I am doomed to fail—for violence, I begin to see, is a *planetary* phenomenon.

Planets are the abusive parents of evolution. Their very surfaces promote warfare, concentrate resources into dense defensible patches that can be fought over. Gravity forces you to squander energy on vascular systems and skeletal support, stand endless watch against its endless sadistic campaign to squash you flat. Take one wrong step, off a perch too high, and all your pricey architecture shatters in an instant. And even if you beat those odds, cobble together some lumbering armored chassis to withstand the slow crawl onto land—how long before the world draws in some asteroid or comet to crash down from the heavens and reset your clock to zero? Is it any wonder we grew up believing life was a struggle, that zero-sum was God's own law and that the future belonged to those who crushed the competition?

The rules are so different out here. Most of space is *tranquil*: no diel or seasonal cycles, no ice ages or global tropics, no wild pendulum swings between hot and cold, calm and tempestuous. Life's precursors abound: on comets, clinging to asteroids, suffusing nebulae a hundred light-years across. Molecular clouds glow with organic chemistry and life-giving radiation. Their vast, dusty wings grow warm with infrared, filter out the hard stuff, give rise to stellar nurseries that only some stunted refugee from the bottom of a gravity well could ever call *lethal*.

Darwin's an abstraction here, an irrelevant curiosity. This Island puts the lie to everything we were ever told about the machinery of life. Sun-powered, perfectly adapted, immortal, it won no struggle for survival: where are the predators, the competitors, the parasites? All of life around 428 is one vast continuum, one grand act of symbiosis. Nature here is not red in tooth and claw. Nature, out here, is the helping hand.

Lacking the capacity for violence, the Island has outlasted worlds. Unencumbered by technology, it has outthought civilizations. It is intelligent beyond our measure, and—

—and it is *benign*. It must be. I grow more certain of that with each passing hour. How can it even *conceive* of an enemy?

I think of the things I called it, before I knew better. *Meat balloon. Cyst.* Looking back, those words verge on blasphemy. I will not use them again.

Besides, there's another word that would fit better, if the chimp has its way: roadkill. And the longer I look, the more I fear that that hateful machine is right.

If the Island can defend itself, I sure as shit can't see how.

"*Eriophora's* impossible, you know. Violates the laws of physics."

We're in one of the social alcoves off the ventral notochord, taking a break from the library. I have decided to start again from first principles. Dix eyes me with an understandable mix of confusion and mistrust; my claim is almost too stupid to deny.

"It's true," I assure him. "Takes way too much energy to accelerate a ship with *Eri's* mass, especially at relativistic speeds. You'd need the energy output of a whole sun. People figured if we made it to the stars at all, we'd have to do it in ships maybe the size of your thumb. Crew them with virtual personalities downloaded onto chips."

That's too nonsensical even for Dix. "*Wrong.* Don't have mass, can't fall toward anything. *Eri* wouldn't even *work* if it was that small."

"But suppose you can't displace any of that mass. No wormholes, no Higgs conduits, nothing to throw your gravitational field in the direction of travel. Your center of mass just *sits* there in, well, the center of your mass."

A spastic Dixian head-shake. "*Do* have those things!"

"Sure we do. But for the longest time, we didn't *know* it."

His foot taps an agitated tattoo on the deck.

"It's the history of the species," I explain. "We think we've worked every-thing out, we think we've solved all the mysteries, and then someone finds some niggling little data point that doesn't fit the paradigm. Every time we try to paper over the crack, it gets bigger, and before you know it, our whole worldview unravels. It's happened time and again. One day, mass is a constraint; the next, it's a requirement. The things we think we know—they *change*, Dix. And we have to change with them."

"But—"

"The chimp can't change. The rules it's following are ten billion years old and it's got no fucking imagination—and really that's not anyone's fault, that's just people who didn't know how else to keep the mission stable across deep time. They wanted to keep the mission on track, so they built something that couldn't go off it; but they also knew that things *change*, and that's why *we're* out here, Dix. To deal with things the chimp can't."

"The alien," Dix says.

"The alien."

"Chimp deals with it just fine."

"How? By killing it?"

"Not our fault it's in the way. It's no threat—"

"I don't care whether it's a *threat* or not! It's alive, and it's intelligent, and killing it just to expand some alien empire—"

"*Human* empire. *Our* empire." Suddenly, Dix's hands have stopped twitch-ing. Suddenly, he stands still as stone.

I snort. "What do *you* know about humans?"

"*Am* one."

"You're a fucking trilobite. You ever see what comes *out* of those gates once they're online?"

"Mostly nothing." He pauses, thinking back. "Couple of—ships once, maybe."

"Well, I've seen a lot more than that, and believe me, if those things were *ever* human, it was a passing phase."

"But—"

"Dix—" I take a deep breath, try to get back on message. "Look, it's not your fault. You've been getting all your info from a moron stuck on a rail. But we're not doing this for humanity, we're not doing it for Earth. Earth is *gone*, don't you understand that? The sun scorched it black a billion years after we left. Whatever we're working for, it—it won't even *talk* to us."

"Yeah? Then why do this? Why not just, just *quit*?"

He really doesn't know.

"We tried," I say.

"And?"

"And your *chimp* shut off our life support."

For once, he has nothing to say.

"It's a *machine*, Dix. Why can't you get that? It's *programmed*. It can't change."

"*We're* machines. Just built from different things. We're programmed. *We* change."

"Yeah? Last time I checked, you were sucking so hard on that thing's tit you couldn't even kill your cortical link."

"How I *learn*. No *reason* to change."

"How about acting like a damn *human* once in a while? How about developing a little rapport with the folks who might have to save your miserable life next time you go EVA? That enough of a *reason* for you? Because, I don't mind telling you, right now I don't trust you as far as I could throw the tac tank. I don't even know for sure who I'm talking to right now."

"*Not my fault.*" For the first time, I see something outside the usual gamut of fear, confusion, and simpleminded computation playing across his face. "That's *you*, that's *all* of you. You talk *sideways*. *Think* sideways. You all do, and it *hurts*." Something hardens in his face. "Didn't even need you online for this," he growls. "Didn't *want* you. Could have managed the whole build myself, *told* Chimp I could do it—"

"But the chimp thought you should wake me up anyway, and you always roll over for the chimp, don't you? Because the chimp always knows best, the chimp's your *boss*, the chimp's your fucking *god*. Which is why I have to get out of bed to nursemaid some idiot savant who can't even answer a hail without being led by the nose." Something clicks in the back of my mind, but I'm on a roll. "You want a *real* role model? You want something to look up to? Forget the chimp. Forget the mission. Look out the forward scope, why don't you? Look at what your precious chimp wants to run over because it happens to be in the way! That thing is better than any of us. It's smarter, it's peaceful, it doesn't wish us any harm at—"

"How can you know that? Can't know that!"

"No, *you* can't know that, because you're fucking *stunted*! Any normal caveman would see it in a second, but *you*—"

"That's crazy," Dix hisses at me. "*You're* crazy. You're *bad*."

"*I'm* bad!" Some distant part of me hears the giddy squeak in my voice, the borderline hysteria.

"For the mission." Dix turns his back and stalks away.

My hands are hurting. I look down, surprised: my fists are clenched so tightly that my nails cut into the flesh of my palms. It takes a real effort to open them again.

I almost remember how this feels. I used to feel this way all the time. Way back when everything *mattered*; before passion faded to ritual, before rage cooled to disdain. Before Sunday Ahzmundin, eternity's warrior, settled for heaping insults on stunted children.

We were incandescent back then. Parts of this ship are still scorched and uninhabitable, even now. I remember this feeling.

This is how it feels to be awake.

I am awake, and I am alone, and I am sick of being outnumbered by morons. There are rules and there are risks, and you don't wake the dead on a whim, but fuck it. I'm calling reinforcements.

Dix has got to have other parents, a father at least, he didn't get that Y chromo from me. I swallow my own disquiet and check the manifest; bring up the gene sequences; cross-reference.

Huh. Only one other parent: Kai. I wonder if that's just coincidence, or if the chimp drew too many conclusions from our torrid little fuckfest back in the Cyg Rift. Doesn't matter. He's as much yours as mine, Kai, time to step up to the plate, time to—

Oh shit. Oh no. Please no.

(There are rules. And there are risks.)

Three builds back, it says. Kai and Connie. Both of them. One airlock jammed, the next too far away along *Eri*'s hull, a hail-Mary emergency crawl between. They made it back inside but not before the blueshifted background cooked them in their suits. They kept breathing for hours afterward, talked and moved and cried as if they were still alive, while their insides broke down and bled out.

There were two others awake that shift, two others left to clean up the mess. Ishmael and—

"Um, you said—"

"*You fucker!*" I leap up and hit my son hard in the face, ten seconds' heart-break with ten million years' denial raging behind it. I feel teeth give way behind his lips. He goes over backward, eyes wide as telescopes, the blood already blooming on his mouth.

"*Said* I could come back—!" he squeals, scrambling backward along the deck.

"He was your fucking *father*! You *knew*, you were *there*! He died right in *front* of you and you didn't even *tell* me!"

"I—I—"

"Why didn't you tell me, you asshole? The chimp told you to lie, is that it? Did you—"

"Thought you knew!" he cries. "Why wouldn't you know?"

My rage vanishes like air through a breach. I sag back into the 'pod, face in hands.

"Right there in the log," he whimpers. "All along. Nobody hid it. How could you not know?"

"I did," I admit dully. "Or I—I mean . . ."

I mean I *didn't* know, but it's not a surprise, not really, not down deep. You just—stop looking, after a while.

There are *rules*.

"Never even *asked*," my son says softly. "How they were doing."

I raise my eyes. Dix regards me wide-eyed from across the room, backed up against the wall, too scared to risk bolting past me to the door. "What are you doing here?" I ask tiredly.

His voice catches. He has to try twice: "You said I could come back. If I burned out my link . . ."

"You burned out your link."

He gulps and nods. He wipes blood with the back of his hand.

"What did the chimp say about that?"

"He said—*it* said that it was okay," Dix says, in such a transparent attempt to suck up that I actually believe, in that instant, that he might really be on his own.

"So you asked its permission." He begins to nod, but I can see the tell in his face. "Don't bullshit me, Dix."

"He—actually suggested it."

"I see."

"So we could talk," Dix adds.

"What do you want to talk about?"

He looks at the floor and shrugs.

I stand and walk toward him. He tenses but I shake my head, spread my hands. "It's okay. It's okay." I lean back against the wall and slide down until I'm beside him on the deck.

We just sit there for a while.

"It's been so long," I say at last.

He looks at me, uncomprehending. What does *long* even mean, out here?

I try again. "They say there's no such thing as altruism, you know?"

His eyes blank for an instant, and grow panicky, and I know that he's just tried to ping his link for a definition and come up blank. So we *are* alone.

"Altruism," I explain. "Unselfishness. Doing something that costs *you* but helps someone else." He seems to get it. "They say every selfless act ultimately comes down to manipulation or kin-selection or reciprocity or something, but they're wrong. I could—"

I close my eyes. This is harder than I expected.

"I could have been happy just *knowing* that Kai was okay, that Connie was happy. Even if it didn't benefit me one whit, even if it *cost* me, even if there was no chance I'd ever see either of them again. Almost any price would be worth it, just to know they were okay."

"Just to *believe* they were . . ."

So you haven't seen her for the past five builds. So he hasn't drawn your shift since Sagittarius. They're just sleeping. Maybe next time.

"So you don't check," Dix says slowly. Blood bubbles on his lower lip; he doesn't seem to notice.

"We don't check." Only I did, and now they're gone. They're both gone. Except for those little cannibalized nucleotides the chimp recycled into this defective and maladapted son of mine.

We're the only warm-blooded creatures for a thousand light-years, and I am so very lonely.

"I'm sorry," I whisper, and lean forward, and lick the blood from his bruised and bloody lips.

Back on Earth—back when there *was* an Earth—there were these little animals called cats. I had one for a while. Sometimes I'd watch him sleep for hours: paws and whiskers and ears all twitching madly as he chased imaginary prey across whatever landscapes his sleeping brain conjured up.

My son looks like that when the chimp worms its way into his dreams.

It's almost too literal for metaphor: the cable runs into his head like some kind of parasite, feeding through old-fashioned fiberop now that the wireless option's been burned away. Or *force*-feeding, I suppose; the poison flows *into* Dix's head, not out of it.

I shouldn't be here. Didn't I just throw a tantrum over the violation of my own privacy? (Just. Twelve lightdays ago. Everything's relative.) And yet, I can see no privacy here for Dix to lose: no decorations on the walls, no artwork or hobbies, no wraparound console. The sex toys ubiquitous in every suite sit unused on their shelves; I'd have assumed he was on antilibinals if recent experience hadn't proven otherwise.

What am I doing? Is this some kind of perverted mothering instinct, some vestigial expression of a Pleistocene maternal subroutine? Am I that much of a robot, has my brain stem sent me here to guard my child?

To guard my *mate*?

Lover or larva, it hardly matters: his quarters are an empty shell, there's nothing of Dix in here. That's just his abandoned body lying there in the pseudopod, fingers twitching, eyes flickering beneath closed lids in vicarious response to wherever his mind has gone.

They don't know I'm here. The chimp doesn't know because we burned out its prying eyes a billion years ago, and my son doesn't know I'm here because— well, because for him, right now, there *is* no here.

What am I supposed to make of you, Dix? None of this makes sense. Even your body language looks like you grew it in a vat—but I'm far from the first human being you've seen. You grew up in good company, with people I *know*, people I trust. Trusted. How did you end up on the other side? How did they let you slip away?

And why didn't they warn me about you?

Yes, there are rules. There is the threat of enemy surveillance during long, dead nights, the threat of—other losses. But this is unprecedented. Surely some-one could have left something, some clue buried in a metaphor too subtle for the simpleminded to decode . . .

I'd give a lot to tap into that pipe, to see what you're seeing now. Can't risk it, of course; I'd give myself away the moment I tried to sample anything except the basic baud, and—

—wait a second—

That baud rate's way too low. That's not even enough for hi-res graphics, let alone tactile and olfac. You're embedded in a wireframe world at best.

And yet, look at you go. The fingers, the eyes—like a cat, dreaming of mice and apple pies. Like *me*, replaying the long-lost oceans and mountaintops of Earth before I learned that living in the past was just another way of dying in the present. The bit rate says this is barely even a test pattern; the body says you're immersed in a whole other world. How has that machine tricked you into treating such thin gruel as a feast?

Why would it even want to? Data are better grasped when they *can* be grasped, and tasted, and heard; our brains are built for far richer nuance than splines and scatterplots. The driest technical briefings are more sensual than this. Why settle for stick figures when you can paint in oils and holograms?

Why does anyone simplify anything? To reduce the variable set. To manage the unmanageable.

Kai and Connie. Now *there* were a couple of tangled, unmanageable data-sets. Before the accident. Before the scenario *simplified*.

Someone should have warned me about you, Dix.

Maybe someone tried.

And so it comes to pass that my son leaves the nest, encases himself in a beetle carapace, and goes walkabout. He is not alone; one of the chimp's teleops accompanies him out on *Eri*'s hull, lest he lose his footing and fall back into the starry past.

Maybe this will never be more than a drill, maybe this scenario—catastrophic control-systems failure, the chimp and its backups offline, all maintenance tasks suddenly thrown onto shoulders of flesh and blood—is a dress rehearsal for a crisis that never happens. But even the unlikeliest scenario approaches certainty over the life of a universe; so we go through the motions. We practice. We hold our breath and dip outside. We're on a tight deadline: even armored, moving at this speed, the blueshifted background rad would cook us in hours.

Worlds have lived and died since I last used the pickup in my suite. "Chimp."

"Here as always, Sunday." Smooth, and glib, and friendly. The easy rhythm of the practiced psychopath.

"I know what you're doing."

"I don't understand."

"You think I don't see what's going on? You're building the next release. You're getting too much grief from the old guard so you're starting from scratch with people who don't remember the old days. People you've, you've *simplified*."

The chimp says nothing. The drone's feed shows Dix clambering across a jumbled terrain of basalt and metal matrix composites.

"But you can't raise a human child, not on your own." I know it tried: there's no record of Dix anywhere on the crew manifest until his mid-teens, when he just *showed up* one day and nobody asked about it because nobody *ever* . . .

"Look what you've made of him. He's great at conditional if/thens. Can't be beat on number-crunching and do loops. But he can't *think*. Can't make the simplest intuitive jumps. You're like one of those—" I remember an earthly myth, from the days when *reading* did not seem like such an obscene waste of life span—"one of those wolves, trying to raise a human child. You can teach him how to move around on hands and knees, you can teach him about pack dynamics, but you can't teach him how to walk on his hind legs or talk or be *human* because you're *too fucking stupid*, Chimp, and you finally realized it. And that's why you threw him at me. You think I can fix him for you."

I take a breath, and a gambit.

"But he's nothing to me. You understand? He's *worse* than nothing, he's a liability. He's a spy, he's a spastic waste of O_2. Give me one reason why I shouldn't just lock him out there until he cooks."

"You're his mother," the chimp says, because the chimp has read all about kin selection and is too stupid for nuance.

"You're an idiot."

"You love him."

"No." An icy lump forms in my chest. My mouth makes words; they come out measured and inflectionless. "I can't love anyone, you brain-dead machine. That's why I'm out here. Do you really think they'd gamble your precious never-ending mission on little glass dolls that needed to bond?"

"You love him."

"I can kill him any time I want. And that's exactly what I'll do if you don't move the gate."

"I'd stop you," the chimp says mildly.

"That's easy enough. Just move the gate and we both get what we want. Or you can dig in your heels and try to reconcile your need for a mother's touch with my sworn intention of breaking the little fucker's neck. We've got a long trip ahead of us, Chimp. And you might find I'm not quite as easy to cut out of the equation as Kai and Connie."

"You cannot end the mission," it says, almost gently. "You tried that already."

"This isn't about ending the mission. This is only about slowing it down a little. Your optimal scenario's off the table. The only way that gate's going to get finished now is by saving the Island, or killing your prototype. Your call."

The cost-benefit's pretty simple. The chimp could solve it in an instant. But still it says nothing. The silence stretches. It's looking for some other option, I bet. It's trying to find a workaround. It's questioning the very premises of the scenario, trying to decide if I mean what I'm saying, if all its book-learning about mother love could really be so far off-base. Maybe it's plumbing historical intrafamilial murder rates, looking for a loophole. And there may be one, for all I know. But the chimp isn't me, it's a simpler system trying to figure out a smarter one, and that gives me the edge.

"You would owe me," it says at last.

I almost burst out laughing. "*What?*"

"Or I will tell Dixon that you threatened to kill him."

"Go ahead."

"You don't want him to know."

"I don't care whether he knows or not. What, you think he'll try and kill me back? You think I'll lose his *love?*" I linger on the last word, stretch it out to show how ludicrous it is.

"You'll lose his trust. You need to trust each other out here."

"Oh, right. *Trust*. The very fucking foundation of this mission!"

The chimp says nothing.

"For the sake of argument," I say, after a while, "suppose I go along with it. What would I *owe* you, exactly?"

"A favor," the chimp replies. "To be repaid in future."

My son floats innocently against the stars, his life in balance.

We sleep. The chimp makes grudging corrections to a myriad small trajectories. I set the alarm to wake me every couple of weeks, burn a little more of my candle in case the enemy tries to pull another fast one; but for now it seems to be behaving itself. DHF428 jumps toward us in the stop-motion increments of a life's moments, strung like beads along an infinite string. The factory floor slews to starboard in our sights: refineries, reservoirs, and nanofab plants, swarms of von Neumanns breeding and cannibalizing and recycling one another into shielding and circuitry, tugboats and spare parts. The very finest Cro Magnon technology mutates and metastasizes across the universe like armor-plated cancer.

And hanging like a curtain between *it* and *us* shimmers an iridescent life form, fragile and immortal and unthinkably alien, that reduces everything my species ever accomplished to mud and shit by the simple transcendent fact of its existence. I have never believed in gods, in universal good or absolute evil. I have only ever believed that there is what works and what doesn't. All the rest is smoke and mirrors, trickery to manipulate grunts like me.

But I believe in the Island, because I don't *have* to. It does not need to be taken on faith: it looms ahead of us, its existence an empirical fact. I will never know its mind, I will never know the details of its origin and evolution. But I can *see* it: massive, mind-boggling, so utterly inhuman that it can't *help* but be better than us, better than anything we could ever become.

I believe in the Island. I've gambled my own son to save its life. I would kill him to avenge its death.

I may yet.

In all these millions of wasted years, I have finally done something worthwhile.

Final approach.

Reticles within reticles line up before me, a mesmerizing infinite regress of bull's-eyes centering on target. Even now, mere minutes from ignition, distance reduces the unborn gate to invisibility. There will be no moment when the naked eye can trap our destination. We thread the needle far too quickly: it will be behind us before we know it.

Or, if our course corrections are off by even a hair—if our trillion-kilometer curve drifts by as much as a thousand meters—we will be dead. Before we know it.

Our instruments report that we are precisely on target. The chimp tells me that we are precisely on target. *Eriophora* falls forward, pulled endlessly through the void by her own magically displaced mass.

I turn to the drone's-eye view relayed from up ahead. It's a window into history—even now, there's a time-lag of several minutes—but past and present race closer to convergence with every corsec. The newly minted gate looms dark and ominous against the stars, a great gaping mouth built to devour reality itself. The vons, the refineries, the assembly lines: parked to the side in vertical columns, their jobs done, their usefulness outlived, their collateral annihilation imminent. I pity them, for some reason. I always do. I wish we could scoop them up and take them with us, reenlist them for the next build—but the rules of economics reach everywhere, and they say it's cheaper to use our tools once and throw them away.

A rule that the chimp seems to be taking more to heart than anyone expected.

At least we've spared the Island. I wish we could have stayed awhile. First contact with a truly alien intelligence, and what do we exchange? Traffic signals. What does the Island dwell upon, when not pleading for its life?

I thought of asking. I thought of waking myself when the time-lag dropped from prohibitive to merely inconvenient, of working out some pidgin that could encompass the truths and philosophies of a mind vaster than all humanity. What a childish fantasy. The Island exists too far beyond the grotesque Darwinian processes that shaped my own flesh. There can be no communion here, no meeting of minds.

Angels do not speak to ants.

Less than three minutes to ignition. I see light at the end of the tunnel. *Eri*'s incidental time machine barely looks into the past anymore; I could almost hold my breath across the whole span of seconds that *then* needs to overtake *now*. Still on target, according to all sources.

Tactical beeps at us.

"Getting a signal," Dix reports, and yes: in the heart of the Tank, the sun is flickering again. My heart leaps: does the angel speak to us after all? A thank-you, perhaps? A cure for heat death?

But—

"It's *ahead* of us," Dix murmurs, as sudden realization catches in my throat. Two minutes.

"Miscalculated somehow," Dix whispers. "Didn't move the gate far enough."

"We did," I say. We moved it exactly as far as the Island told us to.

"Still in front of us! Look at the sun!"

"Look at the *signal*," I tell him.

Because it's nothing like the painstaking traffic signs we've followed over the past three trillion kilometers. It's almost—random, somehow. It's spur-of-the-moment, it's *panicky*. It's the sudden, startled cry of something caught utterly by surprise with mere seconds left to act. And even though I have never seen this pattern of dots and swirls before, I know exactly what it must be saying.

Stop. Stop. Stop. Stop.

We do not stop. There is no force in the universe that can even slow us down. Past equals present; *Eriophora* dives through the center of the gate in a nanosecond. The unimaginable mass of her cold black heart snags some distant dimension, drags it screaming to the here and now. The booted portal erupts behind us, blossoms into a great blinding corona, every wavelength lethal to every living thing. Our aft filters clamp down tight.

The scorching wavefront chases us into the darkness as it has a thousand times before. In time, as always, the birth pangs will subside. The wormhole will settle in its collar. And just maybe, we will still be close enough to glimpse some new transcendent monstrosity emerging from that magic doorway.

I wonder if you'll notice the corpse we left behind.

"Maybe we're missing something," Dix says.

"We miss almost everything," I tell him.

DHF428 shifts red behind us. Lensing artifacts wink in our rearview; the gate has stabilized and the wormhole's online, blowing light and space and time in an iridescent bubble from its great metal mouth. We'll keep looking over our shoulders right up until we pass the Rayleigh Limit, far past the point it'll do any good.

So far, though, nothing's come out.

"Maybe our numbers were wrong," he says. "Maybe we made a mistake."

Our numbers were right. An hour doesn't pass when I don't check them again. The Island just had—enemies, I guess. Victims, anyway.

I was right about one thing, though. That fucker was *smart*. To see us coming, to figure out how to talk to us; to use us as a *weapon*, to turn a threat to its very existence into a, a . . .

I guess *flyswatter* is as good a word as any.

"Maybe there was a war," I mumble. "Maybe it wanted the real estate. Or maybe it was just some—family squabble."

"Maybe didn't *know*," Dix suggests. "Maybe thought those coordinates were empty."

Why would you think that? I wonder. *Why would you even care?* And then it dawns on me: he doesn't, not about the Island, anyway. No more than he ever did. He's not inventing these rosy alternatives for himself.

My son is trying to comfort me.

I don't need to be coddled, though. I was a fool: I let myself believe in life without conflict, in sentience without sin. For a little while, I dwelt in a dream world where life was unselfish and unmanipulative, where every living thing did not struggle to exist at the expense of other life. I deified that which I could not understand, when in the end it was all too easily understood.

But I'm better now.

It's over: another build, another benchmark, another irreplaceable slice of life that brings our task no closer to completion. It doesn't matter how successful we are. It doesn't matter how well we do our job. *Mission accomplished* is a meaningless phrase on *Eriophora*, an ironic oxymoron at best. There may one day be failure, but there is no finish line. We go on forever, crawling across the universe like ants, dragging your goddamned superhighway behind us.

I still have so much to learn.

At least my son is here to teach me.

PERMISSIONS

ABOUT THE EDITOR

Neil Clarke is the editor of *Clarkesworld* and *Forever Magazine*; owner of Wyrm Publishing; and a six-time Hugo Award Nominee for Best Editor (short form). He currently lives in NJ with his wife and two children. You can find him online at neil-clarke.com.

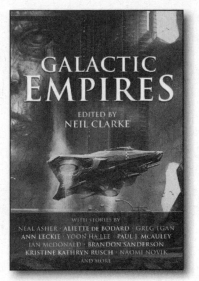

From Neal Asher and Night Shade Books
The Soldier

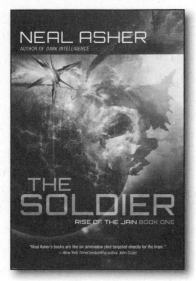

The Soldier
Rise of the Jain, Book One
Neal Asher
ISBN: 978-1-59780-943-6
Hardcover; $26.99

"Neal Asher's books are like an adrenaline shot targeted directly for the brain." —*New York Times* bestselling author John Scalzi

"With mind-blowing complexity, characters, and combat, Asher's work continues to combine the best of advanced cybertech and military SF." —*Publishers Weekly*, starred review

In a far corner of space, on the very borders between humanity's Polity worlds and the kingdom of the vicious crab-like prador, is an immediate threat to all sentient life: an accretion disc, a solar system designed by the long-dead Jain race and swarming with living technology powerful enough to destroy entire civilizations.

Neither the Polity nor the prador want the other in full control of the disc, so they've placed an impartial third party in charge of the weapons platform guarding the technology from escaping into the galaxy: Orlandine, a part-human, part-AI haiman. She's assisted by Dragon, a mysterious, spaceship-sized alien entity who has long been suspicious of Jain technology and who suspects the disc is a trap lying in wait.

Meanwhile, the android Angel is planning an attack on the Polity and searching for a terrible weapon to carry out his plans—a Jain super-soldier. But what exactly the super-soldier is, and what it could be used for if it fell into the wrong hands, will bring Angel's and Orlandine's missions to a head in a way that could forever change the balance of power in the Polity universe.

In *The Soldier*, British science fiction writer Neal Asher kicks off another Polity-based trilogy in signature fashion, concocting a mind-melting plot filled with far-future technology, lethal weaponry, and bizarre alien creations.

Find these Night Shade titles and many others online at nightshadebooks.com or wherever books are sold.

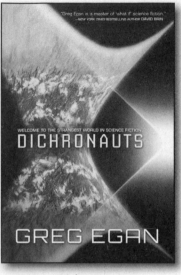